Onetho
1001 dark nights. Bundle
five / six novellas

$22.99
ocn953440230

T5-ADA-195

# 1001 Dark Nights
Bundle Five

1001 Dark Nights Bundle 5
ISBN: 978-1-682305-74-4

Caress of Pleasure by Julie Kenner
Copyright 2015 Julie Kenner

Adored by Lexi Blake
Copyright 2015 DLZ Entertainment, LLC

Hades by Larissa Ione
Copyright 2015 Larissa Ione

Ravaged by Elisabeth Naughton
Copyright 2015 Elisabeth Naughton

Naughty Little Gift by Angle Payne
Copyright 2016 Angel Payne

The Sentinel by Michelle St. James
Copyright 2016 by Michelle St. James aka Michelle Zink

Foreword: Copyright 2014 M. J. Rose

Published by Evil Eye Concepts, Incorporated

All rights reserved. No part of this book may be reproduced, scanned, or distributed in any printed or electronic form without permission. Please do not participate in or encourage piracy of copyrighted materials in violation of the author's rights.

This is a work of fiction. Names, places, characters and incidents are the product of the author's imagination and are fictitious. Any resemblance to actual persons, living or dead, events or establishments is solely coincidental.

# 1001 Dark Nights Bundle Five

Six Novellas
By

Julie Kenner
Lexi Blake
Larissa Ione
Elisabeth Naughton

and Introducing
Angel Payne
and
Michelle St. James

1001 Dark Nights

EVIL EYE
CONCEPTS

Sign up for the 1001 Dark Nights Newsletter
and be entered to win a Tiffany Key necklace.

There's a contest every month!

Go to www.1001DarkNights.com to subscribe.

As a bonus, all subscribers will receive a free
1001 Dark Nights story
The First Night
by Lexi Blake & M.J. Rose

# Table of Contents

| | |
|---|---|
| Foreword | 10 |
| Caress of Pleasure by Julie Kenner | 13 |
| Adored by Lexi Blake | 95 |
| Hades by Larissa Ione | 269 |
| Ravaged by Elisabeth Naughton | 411 |
| Naughty Little Gift by Angel Payne | 543 |
| The Sentinel by Michelle St. James | 713 |
| Discover 1001 Dark Nights Collection One | 826 |
| Discover 1001 Dark Nights Collection Two | 827 |
| Discover 1001 Dark Nights Collection Three | 828 |
| Special Thanks | 831 |

# One Thousand and One Dark Nights

*Once upon a time, in the future...*

*I was a student fascinated with stories and learning. I studied philosophy, poetry, history, the occult, and the art and science of love and magic. I had a vast library at my father's home and collected thousands of volumes of fantastic tales.*

*I learned all about ancient races and bygone times. About myths and legends and dreams of all people through the millennium. And the more I read the stronger my imagination grew until I discovered that I was able to travel into the stories... to actually become part of them.*

*I wish I could say that I listened to my teacher and respected my gift, as I ought to have. If I had, I would not be telling you this tale now. But I was foolhardy and confused, showing off with bravery.*

*One afternoon, curious about the myth of the Arabian Nights, I traveled back to ancient Persia to see for myself if it was true that every day Shahryar (Persian: رايرهش, "king") married a new virgin, and then sent yesterday's wife to be beheaded. It was written and I had read, that by the time he met Scheherazade, the vizier's daughter, he'd killed one thousand women.*

*Something went wrong with my efforts. I arrived in the midst of the story and somehow exchanged places with Scheherazade – a phenomena that had never occurred before and that still to this day, I cannot explain.*

*Now I am trapped in that ancient past. I have taken on Scheherazade's life and the only way I can protect myself and stay alive is to do what she did to protect herself and stay alive.*

*Every night the King calls for me and listens as I spin tales. And when the evening ends and dawn breaks, I stop at a point that leaves him breathless and yearning for more. And so the King spares my life for one more day, so that he might hear the rest of my dark tale.*

*As soon as I finish a story... I begin a new one... like the one that you, dear reader, have before you now.*

# Caress of Pleasure
A Dark Pleasures Novella
By Julie Kenner

# Chapter One

Dante strode through the members' area of Dark Pleasures, ignoring the coy looks from two women, both of whom he'd fucked within the last six months. He wasn't interested in them. Hell, he wasn't even interested in the exceptionally nubile young actress who'd spent the last two nights in his bed. Or in the curvy detective who'd warmed his sheets for three days before that.

His fling with that leggy gallery owner had lasted almost two weeks, but he'd known it was doomed from the beginning. There was never a real spark, and when he'd caught his mind wandering while she was sucking his cock, he knew that it was time to move on.

He was drowning in a sea of women, and he'd never been more lonely.

Damn, but he was fucked up.

With a sigh, he paused in front of the long mahogany bar. He turned, leaning back against it and letting the soft strains of music from the five-piece orchestra in the corner drift over him. After a moment, Gregory, the club's newly hired bartender, approached from behind. "Anything for you, sir?"

Dante shook his head. "I'm not staying. Not tonight." He turned to face the younger man. Twenty-six, an aspiring actor. He was a recent hire and had the bearing and respectful attitude that did the members-only club credit.

As one of the owners, Dante spent a great deal of time in this room, chatting up members at the bar, discussing literature in the corners while smoking a fine cigar and sipping scotch. Flirting with the women in the shadows, and then inviting a select few back to his brownstone next door.

It had become a routine, sometimes a pleasure. Always a

distraction.

Tonight, he wanted none of it.

Although, actually, he did want a drink. Five or six, even. Just not here.

One of the women—Lisa? Liesl?—tried to catch his attention as he pushed away from the bar, but he passed her without comment as he moved with purpose to the far side of the room, then punched his code into the keypad to enter the private VIP area, exclusive only to Dark Pleasures' owners and their special guests.

He stepped inside, relieved to be away from the crowd, to not have to be on his best behavior. And to not have to watch every tiny word he said, lest he give some inadvertent hint that Dark Pleasures—and the men who owned it—weren't exactly as they seemed.

The decor in the VIP lounge was similar to that in the main area—stunning paintings, comfortable furniture, leather and wood, and the kind of dim lighting that gave the place a smoky feel appropriate for an establishment that focused on fine liquor and even finer cigars.

But unlike the members' area, the lounge had an additional quality of casual camaraderie. Of coming home. Because to the men and women of the Phoenix Brotherhood, this place really was a second home. Certainly, it was where they gathered to be with family.

Here, no bartender was needed, and Dante headed straight to the bar, grabbed one of the whiskey glasses, and poured himself two fingers of Glenmorangie.

He kept his back to the room, letting the voices of his friends in the brotherhood drift over him. Liam, Mal, Raine. And the women, Jessica and Callie and Christina. He hadn't seen Dagny when he entered, and he didn't hear her now.

He wasn't surprised. She'd been spending time with a mortal—Christina's old roommate and best friend. And while Dagny swore it wasn't serious, Dante could see that hungry look in her eyes—and oh, dear Christ, he pitied her. He'd fallen for a mortal, after all. And after thirteen years, the memory of Brenna Hart still had the power to wreck him.

Hell, it was wrecking him right now.

*Fuck.*

He pushed through the melancholy, forcing it out of his mind by checking out and just letting the sounds and scents flow through him some more. The drift of conversation. The clink of ice in glasses. That uniquely sweet scent of scotch mixed with the pungent tang of fine cigars. Even in his current mood, it was soothing.

Hell, it was home.

Of course, not everyone was around. Asher and Trace were both out of the country this week, and Pieter, who had spent the last twenty years heading up the Bangkok office, was busy moving into the guest apartment until he decided where he wanted to settle in Manhattan.

Slowly, Dante rolled his neck, working out the kinks. Then he tossed back the scotch and poured himself another.

A moment later, Raine edged up beside him, grabbed the bottle, and poured a glass of his own. Dante glanced at his friend from the corner of his eye.

Raine ran a hand over his close-shaved head, sighed, and then took a long swallow before shifting his stance to prop his elbow on the bar and focus that razor-sharp attention on Dante.

For centuries, Raine had walked with a shadow. Hell, he'd seemed dead, which was damned ironic considering he was immortal. But that shadow had dissipated months ago. Now, Raine practically burst with life. And Dante knew the reason—Callie. Raine had been reunited with his mate, and while Dante was happy as shit for his friend, he was also so goddamn fucking jealous he was making himself crazy.

*Shit.*

He poured again. He drank again.

And then he refilled his glass one more time.

Beside him, Raine eyed him impassively. "Bad day?"

"Bad century," Dante said, then corrected himself. "No, bad thirteen years. Fuck." He tossed back the last of his drink, then grabbed the bottle.

"Dante..."

Raine's voice held an edge of understanding, and Dante cringed. Truth was, if anyone understood it would be Raine. For thousands of years Raine had been alone, believing his love was lost forever. So, yeah, maybe he got it.

But right now, Dante didn't care about understanding. He didn't care about pity. He wanted only one thing, and that was something he couldn't have.

He'd tossed Brenna away with both hands thirteen years ago because it was impossible, and though he knew he'd done the right thing, every few years the weight of the loss seemed to add up until it finally pushed him down and he had to just give in and wallow.

Tomorrow, he'd find another woman to take the edge off. Tonight, he'd lie in bed, drink, and remember.

"Come on, man," Raine said. "Mal's got a call with London so he's not up for a game of chess, but I could use one."

"I'm not good company tonight."

"Planning a bender?"

"Gonna do my best." Considering his—and all the brotherhood's—remarkable ability to heal, getting drunk really wasn't in the cards. But if he tossed back shot after shot, maybe he could at least get a little buzz on. Right now, the prospect was pretty damned appealing.

"You wanna talk about it?"

Dante actually chuckled. Raine was a damn good friend, but touchy-feely he wasn't. If he was offering Dante the chance to spill his emotional debris all over the polished wooden floor, then Dante must look more wrecked than he'd thought.

He glanced across the room and saw Callie, Raine's mate. His wife. The woman he'd been bound to thousands of years ago—and at the same time the woman he'd known for only a few months. And there was Mal, sitting on the leather sofa talking into his phone while Christina curled up beside him, her feet on his lap as she read a book. They'd been reunited after thousands of years apart. Mated. Bound.

Fated.

And as for Liam and Jessica, they'd been side-by-side for three thousand years, and now she was whispering something in his ear and he had his arm around her waist, and it was all just so goddamn fucking perfect that Dante—

"No," he said firmly. "I don't want to talk about it."

No way was he shitting all over his friends' happiness.

Better to try and drown his troubles. Or at least take a long nap. He lifted the bottle as if in salute. "I'll be back to myself tomorrow. Tonight, I'm just a little fucked up. You'll excuse me. I need to go valiantly try to drink myself into oblivion. I'll fail, but I'm up for the challenge."

* * * *

"Dante, hold up a second!"

Mal's voice rang out from across the room, and Dante swallowed a curse before he turned around to face his friend, who also happened to be the co-leader of the brotherhood along with Liam. But leader or not, Dante was going to tell Mal that whatever it was could wait until morning.

Or he was going to say that until he saw the look on Mal's face. Shock and grief and the gray sheen of past pain. And underneath that, Dante saw just the slightest hint of hope.

Just like that, he tossed away his plan to spend a long evening with a bottle and his memories. And he headed across the room toward his friend.

Malcolm Greer was a man good at hiding his emotions—god knows he'd had enough years of practice.

Tonight, he wasn't even trying. Christina had sat up and was leaning against him, and Mal was holding her close as if she was a lifeline, his gray eyes full of storm clouds.

"Talk to me," Dante said even as Raine and Liam joined them.

"What's going—"

But Raine's question was cut off by Liam's gruff, "So it's true."

Mal nodded, just one quick affirmative motion.

"Dammit, Mal," Dante said. "What's true?"

"Merrick," Mal said. "He's alive."

It was the last thing that Dante had expected to hear, and he reached blindly for the armrest of the chair behind him. He sank into it, barely even noticing the motion, as he glanced over at Raine, who appeared about as shell-shocked as Dante felt.

"Merrick?" Dante repeated, just in case he was having a sudden attack of insanity. "You're talking about our Merrick?"

Merrick had been one of their team when the brotherhood had crash-landed in this dimension and on this planet so many millennia ago. He'd been one of their strongest warriors, but the battle with the fuerie—the enemy they'd been chasing across dimensions—had been brutal, and he'd been thrust back into the void, his essence dispersed. *Dead.* Or at least as dead as a creature made of pure energy could be.

"Apparently he didn't go into the void." Mal's voice was flat. Harsh. "He was captured. And all this time we didn't have a fucking clue."

"Captured?" Raine repeated. "But—how? Where? It's been three thousand years, how could they—?"

"A gemstone," Liam said softly, and Dante nodded in understanding. Gemstones held and channeled energy—that was one reason they were often used by mortals to heal—and because of that energy, they could also be used to bind creatures like the fuerie and those in the brotherhood.

"A few weeks ago, Christina noticed something odd during her morning scan," Mal said, picking up the thread of conversation. "A blip—something off in the energy pattern that she was seeing in the London area." He glanced at Christina for confirmation.

"I wasn't sure what I was seeing," she said. "And then it was gone. And I didn't see it again for a few more days."

Everyone in the brotherhood had unique skills, but Christina's were especially honed, the remnant of having suffered her own torment at the hand of the fuerie. Now, she had the ability to see a map of the world in her mind. And that map showed her not only the fuerie's energy, but the energy from certain gemstones, and also the energy of the brothers' themselves. She'd discovered the latter after a few months of practicing her skill, and it had proved handy for keeping tabs on members of the brotherhood who were out on missions.

"You saw Merrick's energy," Raine said.

"Yes and no. It was strange. Like the energy of a gemstone, but with a hint of the brotherhood, too. I didn't understand it, and at first neither did Mal."

"It took us a while to figure out what she was seeing, but we have confirmation now—Merrick didn't go into the void. He's trapped in a gemstone and has been for millennia. And now it's our job to get him out."

"Holy fuck," Dante said. "You're certain?"

Liam nodded. "We are. Merrick and Livia were the only two who went unwitnessed into the void. We assumed. We were wrong." He looked at Raine as he spoke. Livia had been his mate and for millennia, he'd believed he had lost her, only to learn that she had escaped the void by merging her essence with a human's. And that human turned out to be one of Callie's ancestors.

"I won't go into everything we've done since Christina first saw the hint of his essence," Mal put in. "The bottom line is that he was trapped inside a gemstone—presumably by the fuerie. That stone ended up in a gem-encrusted brooch owned by various royal families."

"The brooch is in the shape of a phoenix." Liam's mouth curved into an ironic smile. The brotherhood had come to call themselves the Phoenix Brotherhood specifically because of the unique manifestation of their mortality. They could be killed, yes, but they were born again in fire.

"Coincidence?" Raine asked.

Christina shook her head. "I don't think so. As far as we know, the fuerie don't know how to shield a gemstone's energy. But this stone seems to be shielded. When we were tracing the provenance, we saw that the brooch came into existence in the fourteenth century. Before that, the stone was in an ancient Egyptian ornament. But during the Renaissance, an artisan worked it into the brooch. And that artisan had a reputation as a sorcerer."

"Of the fuerie?" Dante asked

"More likely one of the rare humans who understands energy the way we do," Mal said. "Perhaps he discovered a way. Perhaps the fuerie hired him to make the brooch—and to shield it."

"We may never know for certain," Christina said. "But the bottom line is that it disappears from the map periodically, but then pops up again. The shield is wearing off. And that means we can find it. We can acquire it."

"Where is it?" Dante asked.

"It went recently into the private market and Michael Folsom hired an intermediary to acquire it on his behalf," Liam said, referring to a local Manhattan billionaire who had a penchant for collecting unusual things.

"Are the fuerie after it?"

"I don't know," Christina said. "They may have lost interest centuries ago. It's floated around museums and private collections. It's in the city now, but I haven't detected the fuerie in this area in weeks." She looked at Dante. "Have you?"

He shook his head. His power was nowhere near as strong as Christina's, but he was constantly reaching out, searching his surroundings for the slightest hint that the fuerie were nearby.

"And we're certain that it's Merrick in this gemstone?"

Liam and Mal exchanged glances. "As confident as we can be until we free him," Mal said. "But we're also confident that time is short. His essence is escaping—and we've confirmed that the stone has acquired a flaw, and I think his essence is being pulled out. He's fighting to remain, but if he's drawn fully out into the ether..."

"Then his essence will be dissipated throughout the universe, and we'll lose the consciousness that we know as Merrick forever." Dante sighed. "Well, fuck."

"How much time?" Raine asked.

Christina lifted a shoulder. "We're not sure. Days. I doubt we even have a week."

"So we get him back. Hell, we go in today. We'll extract him from the damaged stone and tuck him safely away in another until we can find a host for him."

"Who will be the host?" Christina asked.

Liam shook his head. "I don't know. It would take an extraordinary human to be willing to merge with him. We were fortunate when we arrived in this dimension that the priest's visions had told him of our coming and he had found men and women willing to take on the burden."

"We'll find someone in this century," Dante said. "It may take a while, but he's been trapped for thousands of years. A few more will be only a blip."

Mal nodded agreement. "We will. If we have to scour the earth to do it. So that's essentially the plan. We'll touch base with the intermediary to negotiate acquisition of the brooch at any price before it's delivered to Folsom. If that doesn't pan out, we'll fall back on surveillance, pinpoint the location, and acquire it by less legitimate means."

Dante grinned. "You mean steal it."

"Of course."

Liam shifted so that he faced Dante more directly. "You're on point. We've learned that the intermediary is staying at the Algonquin Hotel."

"Fine," Dante said. What the hell. A new mission would keep his mind occupied. God knew he needed an escape from his memories and regrets. "What's his name? Have we got a dossier?"

"Her," Mal corrected with a quick glance toward Liam. "And we do."

Liam handed Dante a thin folder. He opened it—and found himself staring into the eyes of Brenna Hart.

The only women he'd ever loved.

The woman he could not have.

The woman who, he was certain, absolutely hated his guts.

# Chapter Two

"Brenna! Oh my god, oh my god! Look at you!"

I bite back a grin that is equal parts amusement and embarrassment. Despite having just turned thirty-five, Whitney Green is bouncing like a teenager in the lobby of the famous Algonquin Hotel.

"Stand up! Stand up!"

Since there's really no battling Whitney when she is determined, I comply. She takes a step back and looks me up and down, her eyes narrowed in professional appraisal. "Brenna Hart, you are amazing. I swear you look just like you did at twenty-three."

I laugh. "You know I love you, Whitney, but you are such a liar."

"Don't even. You're gorgeous and you know it."

I don't, actually. Pretty, yes. Gorgeous, no. But I'm fine with that. In my work it pays to be able to blend. Glam it up if I need to mix with celebrities or politicians. Dress it down for the working-class folk. Minimal makeup and gray suits if I'm doing the corporate thing. I'm a human chameleon, and that works for me.

Today, I'm somewhere between glam and corporate. I've got that day-at-the-salon glow coupled with the tiger-in-the-boardroom mentality. I discovered long ago that it pays to know what my clients find both attractive and trustworthy. For Michael Folsom, that's competence coupled with a moneyed privilege.

No problem there; I can pull that off in spades.

In Folsom's case, it doesn't hurt that he wants to get me in bed. And I wasn't averse to using that knowledge to drive up my price. After all, any type of risk increases my fee; that's the nature of the business.

In his case, the job itself was reasonably easy—convince the daughter of an elderly earl to sell me a lovely Renaissance brooch rather than donating it to the British Museum. Honestly, she practically tripped over herself to accept my first offer on Michael's behalf.

But the fact that Michael very obviously wanted to celebrate after I pulled off the deal? Well, anything that tilts toward intimacy, my emotions, or starts to smell like sex is going to have me ratcheting those fees up.

I played fast and loose with my emotions once before and I'd lost big time. Now I keep my heart locked up tighter than most of the museums I work with. That's not to say I'm not open to sex—frankly, it's a sport I enjoy, and at thirty-six, I think I've developed a nice little toolbox of skills. But if I even smell a relationship, I take the next train to singles-ville with no regrets and no looking back.

Not that I explained any of that to Michael. I just caught the scent of interest and upped the price. No harm no foul, and the worst that could happen was that he walked. The best, my already happy bank account got another dose of glee.

In Michael's case, it was the latter. And, frankly, he wanted that brooch so much he would have paid a whole lot more.

As my mind has been wandering, Whitney has been chattering and leading us through the lobby toward the Blue Bar, the cozy watering hole inside the hotel. The space itself is narrow, with dim lighting highlighted by glowing blue fixtures scattered about and walls of drawings by Al Hirschfeld featuring all sorts of Broadway shows.

I especially love the whimsy of the sparkling lights set into the bar itself, and the Sinatra tunes that are pumped out through the sound system never fail to make me smile.

We take seats at the bar, order dirty martinis, and settle in to drink and catch up. We met in London when I was doing an internship at one of the premiere auction houses and she was trying to make it as a model. Now she lives in New York and owns a salon that is constantly booked solid with celebrities and socialites. I still live in London and work as a private acquisitions consultant. In other words, people hire me to get things for them.

It's an excellent, lucrative job with all sorts of benefits, not the least of which is traveling. And it's all the more fabulous because I invented the job myself, which means that I call all the shots, make all the decisions, take all the risks, and reap all the rewards.

My life more or less fell apart when I was twenty-three, and from my heartache spouted an epiphany. Now I rely only on myself, and I expect nothing from anyone else.

It makes for much less disappointment, that's for damn sure.

"—total brats," Whitney is saying, as we move along our conversational map. "He refused to discipline them. Just refused. And conversation? Good god, the man thought that talking about the television lineup was scintillating. I don't know how he earned the fortune he did."

"You told him to take a hike," I say.

"Eventually." She flashes the crooked smile I remember from our wild London days. "First I used him shamelessly. His cock was the best thing going for him."

I have just taken a sip of my martini, and it's all I can do not to spit it out when I laugh.

"You seeing anyone serious?" she asks me.

"Not even remotely."

She leans forward, her breath evidencing the three martinis we have each now had. "Speaking of you and your love life, do you remember the guy you dated when we lived in London?"

My heart does an unpleasant skittering thing. "You're kidding, right?" I dated only one man in London, and it was the most emotional, sensual, mind-blowing relationship of my life. It was also the relationship that ripped my heart out, stomped on it, kicked it to the curb, and had me swearing off men for over a year. Which on the whole was a good thing. After all, battery-powered boyfriends don't tell you they love you and then walk off into the sunset on the arm of another woman.

Now, of course, I have my new and improved fuck 'em and leave 'em approach to dating. But I still keep the vibrator in the top drawer of my bedside table.

Whitney has the decency to wince a bit, even as her cheeks turn pink. "Sorry. That was stupid. I mean, you don't forget the biggest asshole to ever warm your bed, right?"

I press my hand over hers and look her deep in the eyes. "Whitney, I love you. But you get no more martinis. I mean, why are we even talking about this?"

"What was his name?"

I really don't want to talk about this, but like the Energizer Bunny, Whitney will just keep going and going.

Besides, I can say his name without it hurting. It's been thirteen years. My wounds have healed and my scars have faded. And, frankly, he did me a favor. If not for him, I wouldn't have my job, my approach to life, any of it.

"Dante," I say. "Why?"

"Because I think he's behind you. Sitting at that table near the door."

Suddenly, it is very, very cold in here. And at the same time, it's very, very warm. Beads of sweat pop up at the base of my neck, and my underarms feel suddenly damp. Honestly, I'm having a little trouble breathing.

*Not possible. Absolutely not possible.*

I reach for my martini and take a long swallow. And then I take another.

"No way," I say, as the warm flush of alcohol hits my veins. "Why on earth would he be in New York?"

"You're in New York. I'm in New York."

"Yes, but—" Okay, actually, she has a point.

"Aren't you going to turn around?"

I remain perfectly still.

"Well?" Whitney demands.

"Give me a second. I'm thinking." Honestly, I know I shouldn't look. Dante Storm had swept into my life just as his name suggested. I'd been twenty-three at the time, awed and amazed that a man fifteen years older than me would be even remotely interested in a somewhat introverted girl who couldn't even make up her mind what canapé to choose, much less what to do with herself for the rest of her life.

We'd met at a party thrown by the owner of Dashiell's, an

auction house on par with Christie's or Sotheby's. I was spending a year abroad, interning there while I tried to decide if I wanted to simply jump headfirst into life or go back to the States and finish my dissertation.

I suppose I was primed for a distraction, and Dante was a distraction times ten. Even now, I can feel the way my chest tightened and my pulse kicked up when he walked through the wide double doors, the black dinner jacket and slacks making him look like a man from another era. A man with dark blond hair swept back from his face in a way that highlighted his hypnotic, golden eyes. His wide shoulders looked as though they could bear the weight of the world, and something about his regal posture suggested that they did.

I'd never seen him before, and I knew he wasn't a regular at Dashiell's. Even so, he strode into the room like he owned it—and drew the attention of every person at the event, male and female, as he did.

How is it possible that I can barely remember the name of the guy I slept with last week, and yet I can recall everything about Dante. His scent, all spice and musk with just a hint of cinnamon. His touch, so deceptively gentle that when it turned rough it was all the more exciting. The scar that sliced from his shoulder down to his hipbone. A reminder, he'd called it. But I'd dubbed it a map and let my kisses follow it home.

And his tattoos. Five amazing, brilliantly colored birds in a cluster on his back. Phoenixes, he'd said.

He'd had a way of making me feel alive. Beautiful. Vibrant.

With Dante, I felt as though I was lit from the inside. At least until he'd snuffed that light out for good.

He'd hurt me, more than I'd ever been hurt before or since. And I absolutely, one-hundred percent have no interest in seeing him now.

Really.

*Oh, hell.*

I turn.

And the moment I do, I'm certain I've just made the biggest mistake of my life.

He hasn't changed. Not one iota. And I know that I must be

seeing him through the eyes of my youth because he is fifteen years older than me, and fifty-one-year-old men do not look that hot. Even celebrities can't hold back Mother Nature the way that Dante can.

Except, dear god, he has. He is still perfection. Frankly, from my new thirty-something perspective, he's even more perfect than he was before. I'd been intrigued by his older-man persona, but now I'm simply drawn to his masculinity. He's a man, not a boy. And so help me, my pulse is pounding, my skin tingling in anticipation of his touch. And despite thirteen long years, it feels as though not a moment has passed, and the wild burn of our connection still courses through me.

A connection I crave but can no longer trust.

I swallow, realizing that those wild, golden eyes have been taking me in, and I know the man well enough to know that he has seen my reaction. My weakness.

I turn back to Whitney, certain that I am flushed.

More than that, certain that I am wet.

*Fuck.*

I close my hand over the clutch-style purse I'd put next to me on the bar. "I should run," I say. "I have a meeting in the morning. Sign it to my room, okay? And I'll call the spa tomorrow. We can plan on lunch before I go back."

"Oh, hell," she says. "I should have kept my mouth shut."

"No, really. It's okay. I just need to—" I cut myself off because I'm doing a terrible job of lying, but I really want to get out of here. I start to slide off the stool, but when I see Whitney's face—her tiny little wince—I know that I am completely and royally screwed.

Honestly, I don't know that I even needed to see her face. Because the moment I stop moving, I can feel him behind me. The heat of him. The way he upsets the fabric of the universe, so that the air around him seems to thrum, making my body suddenly hyperaware all over again.

*Double fuck.*

I draw a deep breath, then plaster on my corporate smile. I turn in the chair, planning to say something witty, though I haven't worked out exactly what that might be yet.

Or perhaps I'll just meet his eyes then walk away, letting him know in no uncertain terms that he is part of my past and needs to stay there.

In the end, I do none of those things.

I turn.

I see him.

And before I can stop myself, I pick up my martini and throw it in his face.

# Chapter Three

I push past him, keeping my head down because looking at this man would be a very bad idea, and I don't stop until I reach the elevator bank.

Unfortunately for me, there are no elevators waiting, and my fantasy that I will be magically whisked away from him is only that—a fantasy.

In reality, he's walking straight toward me, his long strides eating up the ground between us. He is looking right at me, and he is moving with such bearing and confidence that for a moment I have to wonder if I imagined tossing a drink all over him.

But no, as he gets closer I see that his shirt is damp and his hair is slicked back, as if he's used the vodka as hair tonic.

"Not the greeting I'd hoped for," he says as he approaches. "But probably one I should have expected."

"You walked out on me, you bastard." I snap the words out, surprising myself. First I toss alcohol, then I verbally pounce. For a woman who prides herself on being icy calm in high-level negotiations, I am running seriously hot.

Apparently, that's what three dirty martinis in under an hour will do to a girl.

"Yes," he says. "I did."

His easy acknowledgment doesn't smooth my ruffled feathers in the least. "Not only that, but you walked away from me on the arm of another woman."

At that, I think I see something like pain flash in his eyes. But he offers no rebuttal or explanation. He simply says, "It's been a long time, Brenna. And I didn't come to talk about the past."

*I didn't come.*

Well, that answers the question I'd been too ruffled to even raise in my own mind: This wasn't a chance encounter, this was a full-blown surprise attack.

"You prick," I say. "You had to know how seeing you would upset me. You couldn't have called me? Called the hotel? Had the bellboy deliver a message while you waited in the lobby."

"I'm sorry I hurt you. Truly. I can't even begin to tell you how sorry I am. But I have a job for you, and time is of the essence, and—"

"You know what, Dante? Just shut the fuck up."

His eyes actually widen and I silently applaud myself. I have balls of steel in business, but I've never put up much of a fight where my personal life is concerned. I tell myself that I have the alcohol to thank, but a tiny, secret part of me knows that's not the truth—the truth is that I haven't much cared about my personal life for the last thirteen years.

I rush on before my nerve or my buzz fades. "I thought we had something real. *Six months.* Christ, Dante, I was ready to marry you and have your babies. I loved you so much it fucking terrified me. And now all you say is that you're sorry you hurt me? Well, guess what, Dante. I am over you. I am so over you it isn't even funny. And you know what else? Fuck you."

I spit the last two words at him, and while I should storm off, the elevator has come and gone during my tirade and there is no place to which I can storm.

Not only that, those last two words are hanging between us in giant cartoon letters in pulsating purple neon. And as I watch him watching me, a single, horrible, wonderful thought rises within me, and as much as I want to tamp it back, I can't seem to make it go away.

*Fuck you.*

*Fuck you, Dante.*

*Fuck. Me.*

Oh, dear god, I must be going insane, but in that moment, I want him in my bed. I want to fuck him out of my system. I want to prove to myself that the fact that I haven't been able to get him out of my head for thirteen freaking years is because I was young and relatively inexperienced. But I'm not anymore, and one more go between the sheets will prove that he's nothing special. And maybe—*maybe*—I can move on instead of feeling the way I feel now.

Which is that I want him to touch me.

Which is pathetic after so damn long. But, dammit, I can't seem to erase the thought from my head.

Dante, thank goodness, doesn't seem to be able to read my mind. "I can say I'm sorry as many times as you want me to," he says, "but when I'm done I'll still need your help." He takes a step toward me, and once again I can feel the universe shift and bubble. The air is thick and I'm having a little trouble breathing. I try to stand perfectly still because I don't want him to see the effect he is having on me. For that matter, I don't want to be affected.

So much for wishes and wants...

"This is hard for me, too, Brenna," and there is such heated longing in his voice that I almost believe him. But I know damn well that he doesn't want me anymore. He's the one who walked away. I frown and rub my temples, sure that I am hearing an emotion that really isn't there.

"But this is important," he continues. "You acquired a piece recently for a client. I need to acquire it from you."

I know what piece he's talking about, of course. I charge a significant amount for my services, which means that I have the luxury of taking off between jobs. Since I've had only one job in the last four months, I know that he is talking about Folsom's brooch.

"I'm afraid that's not possible. Even if I were inclined to screw over my client and sell it to you instead of him, I don't have it. I delivered the brooch about two hours ago. Right in that bar."

If the news fazes Dante, he doesn't show it. I remember that he'd worked in private security and that his emotions had always been hard to read. He was skilled at hiding them—except when we were alone and he was unguarded.

Or, at least, I'd always believed in the honesty of those unguarded moments in bed. But knowing what I know now—that he'd dumped me at the drop of a hat and left the country with another woman with no warning whatsoever—I have to wonder if those moments weren't an act. Some sort of fantasy designed to make me believe he loved me.

But why?

What the hell was the point, other than to torture me?

For a long moment he stays silent. Then he says, "You misunderstand. We want to hire you to acquire it. Or, at least, to smooth the way for us to arrange our own acquisition."

I cross my arms over my chest. "I see." I speak slowly, figuring I need time to gather my courage. But I've drunk three glasses of liquid courage already and have bolstered that with thirteen years' worth of anger. So there's not much gathering to do. On the contrary, I'm more like a roller coaster, making the slow climb to a dropping off point, and when I go over, there'll be no stopping me.

I step toward him, and as I do I feel that frisson of desire, that slice of need. I remember the touch of his hands upon my breasts, the feel of his lips upon my skin. I hear the sweet words he whispered. Promises of eternity, of forever, of a love that would last through time.

And that is the final push—I go over and down, hurtling toward a solution that will either kill me or save me, but at this point there is no getting off the ride.

"I don't want your money, Dante. I want you in my bed. I've had you in my head for thirteen years, and I just want to move on. One last fuck, Dante, and then it's over. Give me that, and I'll see if I can't reacquire that damn brooch for you."

I keep business cards in the front pocket of my purse, and I tuck one now into the breast pocket of his tailored suit. "My cell number's on the card," I say. "Let me know what you decide."

Then—because finally the fates are in my favor—the elevator doors slide open and I slip inside.

But as the doors are closing, Dante thrusts his hand in, triggering the safety mechanism. The doors slide open again and he bursts inside, his eyes flaring with a violent heat. He's in front of me in an instant, his arms caging me, and my back is pressed against the wall so that the handrail digs painfully into my lower back. I welcome it, though, because—*oh, god, yes*—this is the kind of primal heat I am craving. The wild, violent claiming that will melt away all the hard edges I've built up over the years.

This is what I want. What I need.

This is what will destroy me, but as his mouth crushes against mine, I really don't care. In fact, I can manage only one coherent

thought.
*Surrender.*
And so I do.

* * * *

*Dear god, he'd missed this.*
The touch of her. The feel of her. That fiery temper and her no-nonsense approach to life.

Being with her when she was twenty-three had been like embracing a lightning bolt, wild and vibrant, but just a little bit unfocused. Now, though, she was like the phoenix fire. Brilliant and bold and full of a magical heat that had the power to both reduce him to ashes and bring him back to life.

And oh, Christ but she was responsive. She'd been stiff at first, her body frozen with surprise by his unexpected assault. But she had soon melted under his touch, her mouth opening to him. Letting him tease and taste even as she did the same, her tongue working a kind of magic that was spreading through him, making his skin heat and his cock grow so goddamn hard that all he could think about was her words, her offer. *One last fuck.*

*No.* Dammit, he knew better. He couldn't go there. No matter how much he might still crave her, the idea of sinking his cock into her sweet, wet heat belonged safely in the realm of fantasy.

It had killed him once to let her go.

He wouldn't survive doing it twice.

*Except this wasn't about him. This was about Merrick. Trapped. Dying. This was about how far he would go to save a friend.*

And, yes, this was about wanting her touch, even at the cost of his sanity.

Right now, that sanity was hanging by a thread. She was pressed against him, her breasts just as firm as he remembered, her nipples so tight he could feel the nubs through the thin material of her shirt and bra. One of her hands was on his shoulder, giving her leverage to rise up on her toes and kiss him, and oh, god, oh damn, all he wanted to do was yank up her skirt and fuck her hard, right here, right now, to hell with the security cameras and all the rest of that bullshit.

He pushed away, breaking the kiss roughly, a bit unsettled by the potency of his need.

She was breathing hard, her pale skin flushed. She reached up and dragged her fingers through her shoulder-length brown hair. It hung in waves to her shoulders, shorter than it had been in London, but the look was flattering. It accentuated those sharp cheekbones and drew the focus to her gunmetal gray eyes.

"Is that a yes?" Her voice was breathy, and he knew if he agreed they'd go to her room right now and not come out until morning.

*That was just too goddamned tempting.*

"I want to," he admitted, as her eyes dipped toward his crotch where his erection was even now tenting the slacks he'd worn.

When she looked up, he met her eyes unapologetically. "I want to very much."

She licked her lips, then nodded, as if conceding some unspoken contest.

"But only on the terms you set," he continued. He drew in a breath because this was the part he didn't want to say, but knew that he had to. "Because I will walk away again. So think long and hard about what you want. I hurt you once. I don't relish the idea of doing it again."

"I told you what I want." Her voice was cold now, without a trace of the heat he'd just felt in her touch. "You don't have to worry about me. I'm not going to get a taste of your magical cock and then fall head over heels for you again. I'm not twenty-three anymore, and I no longer believe in fairy tales. At least not the kind that come with happy endings."

Her words twisted inside him because he knew damn well he was the one who stole that from her. But before he could think what to say, she continued.

"I told you the truth, Dante. All I want is a fuck." She met his eyes, hers as hard as steel. "I don't want you."

He didn't flinch, even though her words cut him more than he had anticipated. "All right," he said. "But I want you to think about it, anyway. You can have your fee—whatever amount you want—or you can have me. Tell me tomorrow morning. Money or me." He drew out a business card of his own, this one with his home address. "I'll expect you by eight. Time is of the essence, baby."

"Maybe I don't want the job at all," she said.

"You want it," he said. And when the elevator doors opened again on her floor, he slipped out. Then he walked down the hall to the stairwell, not bothering to look back. He didn't need to; he knew that she was watching him go.

* * * *

*Are you still in the bar?*

My room in the Algonquin is small, and it takes little time for me to pace the length of it and back again. I've done three laps before Whitney answers my text.

*I am. After that show, I had to have another drink. So? Tell????*

I start to give her my room number and tell her to come on up, but honestly, I need another drink, too. I may have been humming on three martinis, but Dante burned them right out of my system.

*Order me a dirty martini. I'll be down in five.*

I arrive right as the martini does, and I take a long swallow even before climbing onto the barstool. Then I take another five minutes to explain what he needs and what I offered.

Then I have to wait three more minutes for her to quit laughing and high-fiving me. Apparently, I have just become a role model to women everywhere.

Except I don't much feel like a role model. Now that the alcohol has mostly faded from my veins, I feel just the opposite, actually. I feel a bit like an idiot.

"This is stupid," I say. "I say over and over that he won't break my heart, but that's a lie. Or maybe it's not. Because how do you break something that's already shattered?"

I put my elbows on the bar and bury my head in my hands. "I'm pathetic, you know. Thirteen years, and he can still wound me."

"Which begs the question of why you propositioned the guy," Whitney says, then cringes when I lift my head and scowl at her. "Okay, the reason he can still hurt you is because you loved him. You thought you were going to ride off into the sunset together." She shrugs. "Simple as that."

Which, of course, isn't simple at all.

"It scared me," I admit. "What he and I had. Did I tell you that back then? That it really, really terrified me."

She shakes her head. "No, but I get that. He was older and settled in a career and you were just starting out."

"True, but it was more than that. I felt—I don't know, I guess I felt so alive, so *right* that I didn't trust it. I mean, I was just this normal girl from a normal life. How could I suddenly be in the middle of this epic love? I was afraid it was all going to be ripped away."

She rolled her eyes. "You always did over-analyze everything. You should have told me. I would have smacked some sense into you."

"Except I was right," I say, and she makes a face.

"Not because you were normal. It didn't work because he was an asshole. Not because you didn't deserve him."

But I'm not really listening anymore. "I tested it on my own." I half-smile, remembering my own stupidity. "Remember Rob? The guy who worked at that museum in Prague? He took me out to dinner one night, and I could tell he was interested, and I just wanted to know—"

"You slept with him? Oh my god, Brenna!"

"No! I just—I just let him kiss me. I guess I wanted to see if it would sweep me away the way Dante's kisses did."

"Did it?"

I shake my head. "Not at all. And afterward, all I could think of was how horrible I was because Dante was my everything."

I stifle a shudder as I remember the rest. Because less than a week later, Dante walked away. And even though it's foolish, ever since, I've felt like I broke a spell that day. Or that I brought on a curse.

Either way, somehow I screwed up my happily ever after.

And that's the real reason I don't believe in fairy tales anymore. They're too damn fragile.

# Chapter Four

*He really was a goddamn fool.*

Dante paced the length of his first floor den, from fireplace to wet bar and then back again as the morning sun streamed in through the front windows. He'd bought the brownstone almost two centuries ago when it had come on the market, sold by an industrialist who'd climbed too high, too fast and had spent his great fortune on wine, women, and food, apparently thinking that those sweet perks of the nascent modern age would never fade.

They had faded, though, at least for him. And Dante had stepped in to pick up the pieces.

He loved the building—five stories, each carefully decorated over the years with pieces that he had painstakingly sought to acquire. When one lived forever, there was no need to hurry, and Dante had taken his time making this home.

The only thing it lacked was a companion.

*Fuck.*

He paused in front of the wet bar and talked himself out of pouring a drink. It was still a quarter to eight in the morning, and he ought to observe at least one or two proprieties.

But damned if he didn't want the buzz. Because Brenna would be here soon, and goddamn him all to hell, he really didn't know what he wanted her answer to be.

He wanted her. Dear god, he wanted her. Had been wanting her—missing her for thirteen long years.

But to have her now would only bring heartache to both of them because it couldn't last. All that the future could hold for them was for her to grow old in his arms. For her to suffer as her body shifted and changed and finally failed, while he stayed young and strong. Constant. Unchanging. Except for the added pain in his heart as he went through the rest of eternity knowing that he had held perfection only to watch it fade in the blink of an eye.

There was no escaping that inevitability. As much as he might wish it otherwise, he could not shed his immortality as a snake sheds its skin.

During his darkest times, he craved the abyss of death. He was so lonely. But that was a relatively new sensation—one that he had not experienced before he met Brenna.

Before her, he had been content to live out his days in the company of as many women as were willing to share his bed. He told himself he enjoyed the variety of which his brothers who were mated could no longer partake. For thousands of years, he had lived that way and had told himself he was living the good life.

Then he'd met her—a dark-haired girl with a quick wit and a lithe body. A girl with gunmetal gray eyes that seemed to see right through him—and that silently called him a liar.

Because he was, dammit. It wasn't variety he wanted, it was her. Miraculously, she had wanted him, too.

They had fallen headfirst together into love, their days filled with laughter, their nights with passion. She had told him her dreams, her ambitions. He had shared his work, his passions, his stories.

He had longed for the day when it would feel right to also share his secrets, but he hadn't rushed. He had believed in his heart that such a day was coming, and that his astounding revelation would not shake her to the core.

Like a fool, he had believed that she was his one, his mate, his true match. That he could keep her by his side for all eternity.

He had believed that the depth of her feelings matched the depth of his own.

But then he had seen her in the arms of another man, and he was struck hard by the painful realization that what he had believed she felt was only an illusion. He did not doubt that she cared for him, but he knew that she could not be truly his. And no matter how much he had hoped and believed otherwise, she could not share eternity with him.

She was mortal—and he could not make it otherwise. Because the phoenix fire could only bring immortality to a true mate, a timeless passion. Anything less, and the fire would do what fire does best—it would burn, but not restore.

Dante knew of only eight women who braved the phoenix fire over the millennia. Each had professed a heart overflowing with love and passion. With a pure, timeless longing.

Seven had been reduced to dust, their deaths breaking the hearts of the brothers who had loved them dearly.

Only one woman had stepped from the flame unscathed, a fresh tattoo of a phoenix marking her shoulder as a sign of both immortality and the challenge that she had faced and won.

Once, Dante had believed that Brenna could survive the flame, though he was never certain if he could actually ask her to risk it. Because if he was wrong, he did not think he could stand the horror of knowing the woman he loved had burned because of him.

But after he saw her in the arms of another man, that hesitation became moot. She was not his mate, and he would not stay.

Now, seeing her again, it had brought back both the passion and the pain.

He wanted her in his arms again. Wanted to taste her. Wanted to bend her to his will and make her groan. He wanted to take her to the heights of passion—to punish her with pleasure. To let her know just how much she had given up by not loving him the way he loved her.

Was he really that much of an asshole?

*Yeah*, he thought. *He was.*

Frustrated, he ran his fingers through his hair. He should never have taunted her. He should have simply said no. That he'd write her a check, but he wouldn't trade sex for commerce.

What would be even smarter would be to walk away from her permanently and get the brooch some other way. But he'd texted Liam and Mal after leaving the Algonquin last night, and Mal had one of the brothers in the Parisian office contact Folsom directly and offer to buy the brooch.

Folsom had turned him down flat, despite a truly obscene offer. "I have more money than I know what to do with," Folsom had said. "Now I indulge my passions."

A little more digging had turned up the unsurprising fact that Brenna was one of his passions. He'd taken her to dinner twice over the last month, and according to his personal assistant—who needed extra cash to help out her drug-addicted sister—he had made a number of calls to her on the pretense of discussing the acquisition, but which had really seemed designed for no purpose other than to hear her voice.

Dante could hardly fault the man for that.

Dante also knew that Brenna had turned down Folsom's efforts to get her into his bed, presumably because that would strain their professional relationship. What he didn't know was if she would slide between the sheets now that their business arrangement had come to a close.

The thought roiled in his stomach, and the taste of jealousy sat bitter on his tongue.

He was about to rethink his decision not to have a shot of scotch this early when his door chimed.

For a moment, he just stood there. Then he shook himself, feeling like an ass. No, more like a thirteen-year-old boy. Not that he had ever actually been a thirteen-year-old boy...

Frustrated with himself, he went to the door and pulled it open. She stood there, her loose hair framing her lovely face, and all he wanted to do was take her into his arms and hold her.

*Get a fucking grip.*

He ordered himself to step back, to hold the door open for her. Each step thought out and executed, just as if she was a mission.

Because he damn sure couldn't treat her like most of the women who crossed his threshold.

Women he took. Women he claimed.

Women who melted with pleasure at his touch, and then went on their way when the next day's sun rose in the east.

He might want her in his arms, but hadn't he already lectured himself that it would be a bad idea? Because if he had her again, he knew damn well that he wouldn't want her to leave in the morning.

*Cash.* She needed to choose cash. It was the best way to keep her from getting hurt again.

As for him?

Nothing was going to heal his hurt. Nothing but time. And god knew he had an eternity of that.

He realized she was still standing in the doorway, eyeing him with curiosity. "You can come on in," he said, gesturing to the living area that opened off the foyer.

She shoved her hands into the pockets of her sundress. The action tugged the material down, making it pull taut against her breasts. He could see the outline of her nipples, and he felt his cock twitch.

Christ, he was a mess. He'd spent three millennia walking this earth. He'd fought in wars. He'd dined with kings. He'd hobnobbed with men and women whose names now filled history books.

How was it that this one woman shattered his senses?

Since he needed to move, he turned away from her as if to lead the way, but the brush of her fingers on his sleeve had him turning back. Had him swallowing a groan simply from the reaction that innocent touch had elicited.

"Wait." Her voice was soft, and he saw that she was biting her lower lip. "I—I should apologize for yesterday. My—ah, the price I quoted was unprofessional. I was a little drunk and a lot pissed. Or maybe vice-versa. At any rate, I was being foolish." She drew in a breath, then managed a smile. "I'll take the job. I'll take it for cash."

He told himself it was relief that had him reeling. Too bad he knew that was a lie.

She dragged her fingers through her hair, mussing it and making him remember how she looked in bed after a long night of making love.

He forced himself to look down.

"You messed me up a long time ago, Dante." Her voice was soft but firm. "But I'm a grown woman now, and although I am quite certain that having you back in my bed would be exciting and wonderful, it was stupid of me to suggest it. Stupid and vindictive and—" She halted, and something about the way her breath hitched had him looking up. "—and dangerous," she finished.

"Dangerous?"

She shrugged, her eyes aimed somewhere over his left shoulder.

"Look at me." He kept his voice low. Commanding.

She looked, and he saw a desire reflected back at him that equaled his own.

"Tell me what you mean." He knew he should drop it. This is what he wanted—cold, hard cash, and nothing personal between them. Didn't matter. He took a step toward her anyway, and as he did, the heat between them built. A heat sufficient to burn away all his good sense. "Tell me why it would be dangerous."

"Don't." The word was strained. Full of a plea. Full of pain.

And he cursed himself silently for being an ass. For being confused. For wanting her. For knowing he couldn't have her. And for letting his cock do the thinking instead of his head.

"Sorry. Right. Cash it is." He took a step back in order to allow more oxygen to his brain. "My office is next door. Come on. We'll go cut you a check."

"I prefer a wire transfer," she said, but she fell in step beside him. He was reaching for the doorknob when he realized that she'd stopped. He turned, then cringed when he saw her looking at the original Monet hanging by his front door.

"I acquired that painting. It was one of my first jobs when I went out on my own."

He knew that, of course. Hadn't he watched her career for five solid years? He'd probably still be watching it if Liam and Mal hadn't convinced him that he was sinking into a dangerous quicksand, and just might be crossing the line into stalker-ville, too.

"I wanted the Monet," he said, struggling to reveal nothing in his voice. The painting revealed enough. "You had the ability to acquire it."

"Why didn't you tell me that you're PB Enterprises?"

*Because PB Enterprises doesn't exist. Because I only acquired the painting because we'd seen it together one afternoon at the British Museum. Because I felt like a fool wanting you so desperately and knowing that you didn't want me. Not fully. Not completely.*

*Not enough to last through eternity.*

He said none of that. Instead, he said flatly, "It didn't seem important."

"Oh." She swallowed. "No, why would it be?" The smile that touched her lips seemed fake. "We should probably get to your office."

She started toward the door, and he knew that the moment she went through it, his opportunity would be lost. It would be a cash-only transaction. Hands off. Purely business.

Just as it should be.

*Oh, fuck it.*

He grabbed her, then pulled her toward him with such a wild, violent motion that she stumbled against him and had to cling to his shoulders to steady herself, breathing hard.

"Why?" he growled.

"Why what?"

"You don't need the money. Why take cash? Why not take me?"

Her breath shuddered, and he caught the minty scent of toothpaste. He didn't just want the scent—he wanted the taste.

"I told you. I was being stupid. Angry. Unprofessional."

"That's not it."

She struggled in his arms; he tightened them.

"Dammit, Dante, let me go."

"Tell me the truth."

Her gray eyes flashed. "Maybe I just don't want you."

"The hell you don't. You're wet right now, and we both know it. You're as wet as I am hard. And baby, I'm very, very hard."

He could feel her pulse kick up. He saw her pupils dilate and her skin flush. Her lips parted.

Every inch of her body screamed the truth of his words. But with her mouth, she said only, "Bullshit."

He stroked his hand slowly up her back as his other hand cupped her ass. He couldn't be sure, but he thought she was biting the inside of her cheek. "Fair enough," he said. "Maybe you're just scared."

"Very little scares me," she retorted. "Least of all you."

"Really? Well, that makes only one of us. Because baby, you scare me to death. One look and you can melt me. One kiss and you could destroy me."

"Then why not just let me go?" She asked the question plaintively, but the breathiness of her voice told a different story. And so did her body. She'd moved closer. Just barely, but he could tell. Her chest was crushed against his, and he could feel her pebble-hard nipples brush against him.

"Just give me the money." Now he heard the plea. "Walk away and be done with me just like you did before."

"I should," he admitted. His throat was raw. "I really should. But I'm just so goddamned hungry."

# Chapter Five

"Hungry?"

I ask the question as if I don't understand what he means. But I do. Oh, dear god, I do. Being in his arms feels like coming home, and though I know that I am making a mistake, I cannot help myself. Hell, I don't want to help myself.

I surrender to him.

But at the same time, I claim him, too. His mouth. His body. My fingers twine in his hair, remembering the sensual feel of those silky strands. My tongue wars with his, demanding and taking. And when he slides one hand up between our bodies to cup my breast, I moan against his mouth, then grind my pelvis against him.

"Harder," I demand when he teases my nipple between his fingers.

He pulls back, his eyes searching mine.

"You know what I like," I whisper. "I know you remember."

"I remember everything about you," he agrees. "The way you tremble when I stroke my tongue along the curve of your ear. The way your breath shudders when I kiss my way down your belly. The way you cry out when you come." He nips my lower lip, making me squirm. "And I remember that you rarely asked for what you wanted."

"I was young and naïve. I'm a woman now, Dante. A lot of things have changed." I meet his eyes, and I know that mine must be a bit hesitant. Because there's no denying that my body has changed. That when he peels off this dress he will not see the tight, taut body of a girl in her early twenties with a Pilates addiction. Instead, he'll see the body of a thirty-six-year-old woman. Still in good shape, yes, thanks to those same Pilates and a personal trainer with a scary disposition. But nature is a bitch and you can only fight her so hard.

Then again, Dante seems to have figured out how to do that. My hands are all over him, and he is as tight and firm as I remember. There are no new lines on his face, no signs that life has treated him badly, or even that it has treated him at all. It is as if he is living on another plane, and those of us who are mere mortals are passing by beneath, moving down the conveyor of aging while he moves on the slower track ten stories above.

I won't deny that the hard perfection of his body is a delicious turn-on, but at the same time it makes me even more self-conscious.

I realize that I have looked away, lost in my thoughts and maybe even lost in a bit of self-pity. I am still in his arms, but the wildness has faded. Instead, he is looking at me so tenderly it makes me want to cry.

"I never thought you could be more beautiful," he says. "I was wrong. You're exceptional, Brenna. Your confidence. Your poise. Your fire. It shines in you. You have a strength now that you didn't have before, and baby, it's sexy as hell."

I manage a crooked smile. "You always did know how to say the right things."

"I like that you know how to say what you want."

"Do you?" I hear the challenge in his words.

"Tell me what you want, Brenna. Tell me every little thing."

My breath is coming hard, my nipples so tight it is painful. This is not a game I usually play. It's one thing to tell a man to touch you harder or faster. It's another thing entirely to direct the action. Especially when all I want to do is submit.

"I want you to touch me, Dante." I meet his eyes, my breath coming hard. "I want you to take me. Hard. Fast. I don't want to think. I just want to feel."

I watch the effect of my words play across his face. Confusion at first, and then a growing desire. And then—oh, god, and then—

He grabs my shoulders, then slams me back against the door. His mouth covers mine, hard and hot. Not a kiss so much as a sex, his tongue demanding entrance, warring with mine, taking and claiming and making me so goddamn wet that my panties are soaked and I can feel the slickness on my thighs.

I'm wearing a summer sundress, and as his tongue fucks my mouth, his hand fondles my breast, hard the way I like it, with his fingers teasing my nipple. I groan, then gasp when I realize that his other hand is sliding up my bare thigh to thrust inside my now soaked panties.

"Christ," he says, as he thrusts his fingers inside me. "You're so fucking wet."

I cry out in pleasure at the invasion, but he swallows the sound then breaks the kiss, his eyes studying my face as he fingerfucks me hard against the door.

"Is this what you wanted?" he asks, his voice a low growl of pleasure and demand.

"Yes." I can barely make the sound. I am too lost in pleasure. Too lost in the feel of him.

"No," he says. "More."

And before I can even process what he means, he has flipped me around so that I'm facing the wall, and he has thrust my dress up so that it's bundled around my waist.

"I'm going to fuck you, baby. I don't have a condom, but I'm clean. I have to have you—Christ, I think I'll die if I don't get inside you soon—but if you want me to stop, now's the time."

I say nothing. I just spread my legs and lean forward. I want this. Right now, I can think of nothing else I want more. Not even to breathe.

With one hand, he clutches my breast, holding me in place even as he ratchets up my arousal with the thumb that flicks roughly over my nipple. With his other, he yanks down my panties until they are stretched tight across my thighs, then even tighter when he orders me to spread my legs. I do, and his hand strokes me, his fingers teasing my core, thrusting inside me, taking what he wants and making me tremble with longing in the process.

He makes a sound that is somewhere between a sigh and a groan, and then I hear the wonderful, delicious, dangerous sound of his zipper easing down. I feel the head of his cock against my ass, and then the hard press of it against my core. He starts slow, easing inside me, and it is as if he is deliberately teasing me. Because I want it hard. Dammit, I want to be fucked.

I realize that he wants me to say it. To demand it. And I want it bad enough that I am not going to be shy—not now. Not with him.

"Harder," I beg. "Please, Dante, please, fuck me harder."

"Baby—" The endearment is ripped from him, and he slams into me, his body thrusting against mine, skin on skin, slick and intimate and wonderful.

He takes his hand off my breast so that he can hold me steady around my waist. Then with his other hand he reaches around to stroke my clit until I am little more than a mass of pleasure, so sweet and intense and wild and wonderful that it's a miracle I can even hold onto consciousness.

He bends forward, his body covering mine, his lips brushing the back of my neck, the curve of my ear, and that is when I lose it. Electric tremors shoot through me like lighting bolts converging at my cunt, and my muscles squeeze him, convulsions of pleasure that milk him until he cries out, the sound raw against my ear, and his arms tighten around me, pulling me close to him before we both sink to the ground.

"Holy crap," I say. I'm curled against him, my back against his chest, my dress still bunched around my waist.

He brushes my shoulder with a kiss and holds me close for a few moments before getting up. "Stay," he says softly, then returns a moment later with a warm, damp cloth.

He tugs my panties off, then gently cleans me. I meet his eyes, a little undone by the tenderness of this moment.

When he holds out a hand to help me up, I take it. "I need my panties," I say, holding out my hand.

He shakes his head. "I don't think so," he says. He tucks them in his pocket. I smirk as I adjust my dress.

I look at him. Just look at him. At the warmth in his eyes. The lines of his face. The strength in his body.

And the tenderness at the core of him.

I fell in love with him once—and I'm honestly not sure that I ever fell out of love.

But I do know one thing for sure—Dante Storm is dangerous to my heart. And whatever we started just now is something that we can't finish.

I meet his eyes and am about to say just that when he shakes his head. "No. Don't say it. You don't need to say it."

"What?"

"That we can't do it again."

"We can't."

"I know."

I stand in silence. I know why I can't; it's because he will break my heart.

But I don't know why he doesn't want me. I only know that he doesn't. I only know that he walked away once, and that he has already told me he will walk away again.

That should be enough, but then I have to go and open my mouth. I have to ask— "Why? Why did you leave?"

For a minute, I don't think that he's going to answer. But he surprises me by saying, "Because I was looking at forever."

"And you don't think I was, too?" I'm baffled. With Dante, forever was my mantra.

He looks at me, his eyes so sad I want to cry. "No," he says, "I know you weren't."

I start to protest, but he just shakes his head, like a dog shaking off water. "Let's go transfer your money."

"No," I say, standing firm.

He cocks his head, then winces. "We shouldn't have done this. It won't happen again. But please don't back out. I really need your help. I can't tell you how urgent this is."

"I'll help," I say. "But I don't want your money. And I don't want sex." That's not entirely true. I want it; I don't think I can handle it.

"Then why?"

"I don't know," I say. "Maybe because I loved you once upon a time."

*Maybe because I still do.*

\* \* \* \*

Dante leads me through the first floor of his brownstone to a sunroom that opens up onto a courtyard. That courtyard connects to another brownstone, and it is into that building that we enter. "The front is a private club—scotch and cigars, jazz and conversation," he says. "Dark Pleasures."

"I've heard of it," I admit. "It has a reputation for being both excellent and exclusive. You're a member?"

"One of the owners," he says. He looks at me. "I have been for a very long time."

"Even when you lived in London?"

"Even then."

I nod, taking in the simple fact that I don't know this man as well as I had thought. I think that is what he is trying to show me in his not so subtle way. But it doesn't matter. I know the core of him. I've known that since the first moment I looked into his eyes when he brought me a glass of wine and told me I looked like sunshine. I've known it since our first meal when he brushed a dab of ketchup from the corner of my mouth and I shivered all the way down to my toes. I think I've known it since our first touch, our first kiss.

I exhale, forcing myself to shake off my melancholy as I follow him to an old-fashioned elevator with a cage-style door. We step in, then rise to the third floor, the gears creaking as we move. "The club takes up the first and second floors," he says. But the third is office space, for both the club and Phoenix Security."

I nod. *That* job I remember. "You're still with the company?"

His grin is almost a smirk. "I think it's fair to say that I'm a lifer."

I cock my head. "You own that company as well?"

"A piece of it, anyway."

He points to the floors above us as the elevator slows to a stop. "Four is reserved for guests. Five is my friend Raine's private apartment. Odds are good he'll be at the meeting."

I nod, trying to remember it all. I'm not sure why it matters, though. He's sharing life trivia when he has already made it clear he has no interest in sharing a life.

I follow him down a balcony-style hallway that overlooks what obviously used to be the grand ballroom in this converted brownstone. The last door is polished oak, and it has a brass placard identifying it as the office of Phoenix Security.

We enter and step into a classy, polished reception area. A dark-haired man with a lean, bad-boy appearance, who looks like he could be Hollywood's new hot thing, steps in from a door on the far side. He's wearing jeans and a black T-shirt with a white phoenix embroidered on the breast pocket. "You must be Brenna. I'm Malcolm Greer." He steps forward and I shake his hand. "Glad you're helping us out."

"Happy to," I say, glancing sideways at Dante.

"Mal is one of the company presidents," Dante says. "With Liam," he adds, pointing to a linebacker-sized man with a wide smile and serious eyes. "And Raine's just along for the ride." The third man has close-cropped hair and sleeves of tats that disappear under a T-shirt similar to the black one worn by his friends.

Dante formally introduces me, we do the meet and greet thing, and I follow the men into a conference room. Honestly, it's like being in a pressure cooker of hotness laced with a helping of testosterone.

"Dante explained what we need?" Mal asks.

"The brooch," I say. "Though I have no idea why there's so much urgency."

"I'm afraid that's harder to explain," Liam says. "And you'll forgive me if I don't try. It's not actually necessary for what we're hiring you to do."

I lean back in my chair, not bothering to correct him. I'm not really being hired. I was well-fucked, and this is now a freebie. Frankly, that's not something I feel the need to share. "Why me? Why don't one of you call him? Make him an offer he can't refuse."

"We tried that already, Ms. Hart," Raine says. "Got shot down."

"Really?" I frown. My experience with Michael is that he's very interested in his bottom line. "Did he say why?"

"He said that he's a collector of cursed artifacts," Liam said, "and that this isn't about the money."

Beside me, Dante shifts. "When did he say that? The report I read simply indicated that he wasn't interested in parting with the piece."

"You read the e-mail report. The secure communication came about half an hour later. Cursed," Liam repeats as if that word holds special import. And from the way Dante leans forward, his forehead creased into a frown, I guess that it does.

"I do a lot of research on every item I try to acquire," I say. "I assure you, this one has no history of a curse." I glance at each of them in turn. "So what is that code for?"

Mal glances at Dante and smiles. I have the oddest feeling that it's a smile of approval.

"We need you to gain access to Mr. Folsom's house. We need you to talk with him. We need you to learn the location of the brooch—presumably it's in a safe, and presumably Folsom has several safes on site. And that, Ms. Hart, is all that we need. We'll wire you so that we can see what you see. It will help us to map the location after the fact."

I look at all of them in turn. "You're going to *steal* it?"

"Yeah," Dante says. "We're going to steal it."

"But—"

He closes his hand over mine, and when he looks in my eyes I feel that delicious little quiver. "Just temporarily. We'll return it almost immediately. Intact."

I lift a brow, but nothing I can think of to say seems quite sarcastic or cutting enough.

"Please, Brenna," he says. "I need you to trust me."

And—against all reason and better judgment—I do.

# Chapter Six

I am thinking that perhaps I should have paid more attention to my reason and better judgment as I stride over the threshold and into Michael Folsom's swank penthouse apartment. It takes up the top three stories of the Xavier Building, one of the city's most sought after addresses on Fifth Avenue. Folsom no longer owns the building, but he used to. When he sold it, he retained ownership of the top three floors and had them converted into one residence.

Rumor has it that he spent more on the conversion and remodel than he received for the sale of the entire remaining building. Until now, I thought that was a ridiculous urban legend. But looking around at this incredible interior with its elegant finish, attention to detail, and high-quality furnishings, I think the story might actually be true.

"I'm so glad you called," he says, taking my hand and pressing a gentlemanly kiss to my fingertips. "I was beginning to feel snubbed."

I laugh lightly. "You've retained me enough times to know that I don't mix business with pleasure."

"You're not currently working for me." The heat in his voice is obvious. So is the invitation.

On any normal day, I would shut this down right now.

But this is not a normal day.

I lick my lips, conjure a smile, and wonder what Dante is thinking at this very moment. Because he is seeing and hearing everything.

And for some reason, that makes me want to kick the show up

into high gear.

I take a single step toward Folsom. "No," I say huskily. "I'm not."

I see the reflection of my reply on his face immediately. A man who not only wants a woman, but expects to get her.

The truth is, under other circumstances I might actually be interested. Michael Folsom isn't my type, but there's no denying that he's attractive. He has soft, almost boyish features. A sort of Leonardo DiCaprio vibe that doesn't usually do it for me, but I've seen plenty of evidence of other women's interest. And the fact is, just a man's interest can be a turn-on, and Folsom has never made his a secret.

If he weren't my client and if I weren't with Dante...well, he might be the perfect companion for blowing off a little steam.

But he is my client and while I can't say that I'm *with* Dante, I can say that I want to be.

Me, the woman who avoids relationships.

But that's not entirely true, either. I don't really avoid relationships. I've just spent over a decade avoiding them with men other than Dante.

"Brenna?"

Michael is looking at me, his arm outstretched to lead me further into his home.

"Sorry. Long, weird day. My mind was wandering."

"Let me take you to dinner. A drink. A bite. Enchanting conversation."

I conjure a provocative smile. "I'd like that. But I think I'd prefer to stay in. Maybe we could just settle for the drink and the conversation. And who knows what else?"

I watch him swallow, and my confidence ratchets up. "Yes," he says. "I think that sounds just fine."

He leads me into a well-lit room that opens onto a terrace. The door is open, letting in a summer breeze. I take a seat on the couch, then put my purse on the coffee table, trying to position it so that the fisheye lens that is camouflaged by the clasp can get the widest view. The purse is only a camera. The audio is coming through the diamond-studded watch that I am wearing today. And there is another camera hidden in the cameo necklace that hangs around my neck.

Michael has gone to the bar and is opening a bottle of wine. "You like Cabernet, I recall?"

"Very much."

I take the glass he offers me, then slip off my shoe and tuck one leg under me so that I am seated almost sideways on the couch. I smile at him as if this is the perfect position, though I know that he would prefer to scoot closer so that his leg could brush my thigh or his arm could go around my shoulder.

"We so rarely get a chance to talk."

"What would you like to talk about?"

"You, of course," I say, but I punctuate the words with a laugh. "Seriously, I've gotten so many pieces for you over the years. Six, isn't it?" I glance around the room. "And I know you're not monogamous." I pause so he can chuckle at the manner in which I've referred to the other people like me he has hired to find various pieces. "I was expecting to walk into a house that felt like a museum. But you have nothing out. Where is it all?"

He grins, just like a little boy. "Would you really like to see?"

"Of course."

He reaches for a television remote on the table, only it turns out not to be for the television. Instead, the push of a button closes the patio doors, then closes the blinds, dropping the room into darkness.

"Michael?"

"Hold on."

A moment later, hidden panels in the wall begin to open to reveal backlit glass cases. I gasp, genuinely surprised, and stand up. "This is incredible," I say as I walk to one of the walls of cases. So many artifacts are hidden within. From ancient coins to statues to jewelry. Some items appear medieval and look as though they were put to good use during the Inquisition. Others appear innocent, but the neatly printed cards beside them have clues as to their nature—*poison, revenge, deceit.*

I glance up at Michael. "There's a theme, isn't there?" I remember what Dante and his partners had said about cursed artifacts.

"I have a passion for acquiring articles with a story. With a curse."

I laugh. "Do you believe in that?"

"Good god, no. But it makes for a fabulous conversation starter."

At that, my laugh is real.

"All right," I say. "Show me the brooch. What's its horrible backstory?"

He leads me to the opposite wall, and there is the brooch, still in the Lucite box that I had put it in for safe travel. I fiddle with my necklace, trying to ensure that the men back on East 63rd Street have a clear view.

"Why is it still packaged?" I ask.

"I'm selling it," he says.

I turn to him with a frown. "You are?" Had the men from Phoenix made another offer? Hadn't he just turned them down cold?

"The buyer's representative is arriving in three days to acquire the piece," he says, confusing me even more.

"Who's the buyer?"

"A group. Also collectors."

I shake my head with a teasing smile, hoping he can't spot my confusion. "Well, I'm surprised you want to part with it. It's so unusual, and you were so dead set on acquiring it." I actually pull off a small pout. "Should my feelings be hurt?"

He steps closer, moving into my personal space. I force myself not to back up.

"This group has access to a number of items I've been trying to acquire for years. Items that are at the heart of some very interesting lore regarding curses and black magic." He eases behind me, his hands on my shoulders. "You see? It's not about money, but about what they can offer me."

He bends so that his breath tickles my neck and ear. "There are more displays in the bedroom," he says gruffly. "Would you like to see?"

I close my eyes as if in satisfaction and desire. "That sounds wonderful," I murmur. "Why don't you lead the way?"

## Chapter Seven

"Lead the way?" Dante's stomach twisted as her words—her tone—played again in his head, as if on an endless loop. He was jealous. He knew it.

Honestly, he didn't much care.

He leaned in closer and actually smacked the side of the second monitor, as if that would stop her. "She needs to be getting the hell out of there, not playing footsies with loverboy."

"She's playing the role," Raine said, and Dante heard the amusement in his friend's voice. "Ditch too soon and it will look suspicious."

"Fuck that," Dante said. "We need to pull her right now. Three days? That means we need to get in tomorrow morning, extract Merrick, and get the brooch returned by the day after at the latest."

"Agreed."

"We don't have time for her to play games with him." He shot another glance at the bank of monitors. The purse was still aimed at the display case, but the camera around her neck showed that they were approaching a bedroom. He could see the king-sized bed through the open door. And goddamn fucking hell if there weren't lit candles.

The prick had intended to get her back there all the time.

Not that this was any great revelation. But the knowledge that Folsom might touch her—that she might let him, even as part of the scheme—curled unpleasantly in his gut.

No way. They had what they needed. He was shutting this puppy down.

He grabbed his phone and sent a text—*9-1-1*.

Over the speakers, he heard the *ding-dong* of her text message alert. On screen, he saw the perspective shift as she turned back toward the living room.

"Just a second," she said to Folsom. "My assistant's been having some issues with a client. I should make sure there's no crisis."

*Smart girl.*

She headed back, the purse becoming larger in the first monitor. Then she reached down and withdrew the phone. She was standing in front of the purse cam now, blocking the view of the display cases. But he could see her face, and the relief he saw when she glanced at the message filled him. *She didn't want Folsom. Thank god for that.*

She snatched up the purse, then licked her lips and made a show of furrowing her brow, all the while with her back to Folsom. Dante couldn't stop his grin. Apparently, she was getting into character.

"Michael," she said. "I'm so sorry. It is a crisis." She approached him—hell, she actually pressed a hand against his cheek. "Rain check?"

For a moment, it looked like Folsom was going to argue. Then he just looked sad.

"Sure," he said. "That would be wonderful."

And as Brenna headed for his front door, Dante couldn't help but feel a little bit sorry for the guy.

Not *that* sorry, of course. But a little.

* * * *

The moment I get out of the taxi, the front door to Dante's condo opens, and he steps outside. I hurry toward him, feeling the rush of adrenaline from having accomplished my super-secret spy mission.

"Did you watch?" I ask as I follow him into the brownstone. "It was as easy as pie."

He nods. His expression is tight. Presumably he is still coming off a flood of worry. He'd been concerned that I couldn't pull it off—hell, I'd been a little concerned, too—but the mission had gone seamlessly.

I'm not sure what I had expected. Perhaps that Michael would tell me he didn't share his collections. Or that he would only reveal them for a trade—I strip, he shows me the brooch, which is something that I really wouldn't have liked. Except for the fact that Dante would be watching through the camera. *That* might make it interesting.

I shake my head, feeling a little silly and a lot giddy. "So what now?"

"Raine and Jessica and Pieter are putting together a counterfeit brooch. It won't stand up to scrutiny, but with any luck it will only need to be in that case for a few hours. We'll go in tomorrow morning when he goes for his morning jog. He's religious about that. And then we'll return the brooch in the evening. We've confirmed that he's planning to see a show tomorrow night."

He speaks firmly. Matter-of-factly.

And honestly, I just don't get it. I want someone to share my victory. I'd expected it to be Dante, and I'm not at all sure what his problem is.

I force my thoughts away from him and back to his words, then frown. "You're just going to walk into his apartment? Did you see the security? There's more electronic locks and gadgets than on the space shuttle."

"We've got it under control." Again, his answer is clipped. Curt. Frankly, it's starting to piss me off.

"Fine," I say. "Good for you. But why the hell do you only need it for a few hours?"

"We have our reasons."

"You know what, Dante? Just screw it. I'm going back to my hotel." I turn to head toward the door, but he grabs my arm and pulls me back.

I stand ramrod straight in front of him, practically vibrating with anger.

"It has a microdot," he says. "We need to retrieve it. That's all."

"That is *so* not all." I grind the words out, and they are harsh. They are an accusation.

For a moment, he says nothing. Just meets my eyes. Just

breathes.

Then he seems to sag.

Nothing changes. Not his expression, not his posture. But I know this man, and I see the change in him. And when he looks in my eyes, I see the sadness, too. "I didn't like it." His words are flat. Almost cold.

"Like what?"

"You," he says. "With Folsom. I didn't like the way he looked at you. I didn't like the way he touched you. I didn't like the way you flirted with him. And I damn sure didn't like what he intended to do with you in that bed."

"You didn't?" I can't help myself—I'm smiling.

He notices, and the corner of his lip curves up, too. "No. No, I didn't."

He takes a step toward me. "But it doesn't matter what I like, what I didn't like."

I feel my pulse kick up in tempo. "Why not?"

"Because we said we were done." He reaches out, then gently brushes his fingers down my arm. "No more touching." He takes another step toward me, so that there is barely any distance between us at all, and I forget the muscle contractions required to breathe. "No more fucking," he adds.

"That's what we agreed." It takes all of my willpower to form words, and then even more to take a single step toward him. "Those are the rules."

Now there are only inches between us, and I catch the scent of him—soap and aftershave and, oh god yes, the musky scent of arousal.

I glance down and see his cock, hard now inside his jeans. Straining. My cunt is wet and throbbing, and I cannot help myself. I have to relieve some of the pressure.

I drag my teeth over my lower lip, and as I do, I slide my hand down, then cup myself between my legs over the thin material of my skirt.

Inches from me, Dante groans—and that sound of pure, male arousal fuels me. I use my fingers to ease up my skirt. I'm exposing my thigh—a little bit, then a little bit more. And then the edge of my panties. And then all of them.

The pale blue silk is soaked through, so wet that the material clings to my bare pubis, sticking to my vulva, dipping into my folds. I slide my hand slowly up my thigh and then ease my flat palm under the material.

My skin is so hot, my cunt so wet. And right then, all I want to do is fuck myself with him watching. All I want to do is make him crazy—make him come.

I skim my fingers over myself, and the pressure on my clit makes me shiver. I keep going, my fingers gliding over my slick heat, and then I thrust one, two fingers inside. I swallow a moan, my head thrown back, my eyes closed, as I gyrate my hips, pumping my own hand and imagining that it is Dante.

"Oh, baby," he says. "Fuck the rules."

He drops to his knees and one hand goes to my hip, his thumb hooking in the band of my panties. He tugs them down, then uses his other hand to get them all of the way off.

Then he takes my hand, ignoring my groan of both protest and excitement as cool air brushes over me, as arousing as a lover's touch.

Slowly, he sucks on each of my drenched fingers, and the sensation is so intensely erotic that my knees go weak and I have to cling to his shoulder so as not to fall over.

But when he leans forward and laves me with his tongue, I know that I am going to explode. "No," I protest, taking a step back. "Not yet. I want you inside me when I come. Please, Dante. Please, fuck me."

He looks up at me, and I think that he is going to lay me flat right there and thrust his cock hard inside me. And, oh dear god, I hope he does.

Instead he stands, his golden eyes lit like flames. "Upstairs," he says. "I want you in my bed. Naked and spread-eagled, your pale skin against my black sheets. Your hands fisted in the material as I take you. And I want to hear the echo of your scream when you come."

I can't even manage a response. His words have turned my body to liquid lust, and it is all I can do to nod in blissful, eager agreement.

He has an elevator in his brownstone similar to the one next door, and he leads me up to a masculine room with rich leather and dark wood. A huge bed dominates the space, and yes, the bed is made up with black linens.

Beside it a window is open to the courtyard below. Pale yellow light filters up from a lamp below to cast the room in what looks like candlelight.

"Take off your dress," he says. "I want to see you naked."

"Take off your pants," I counter. "I want to see your cock."

He laughs, and the sound washes over me. "Dear god, Brenna, I lo—I love that mouth of yours."

I draw in a ragged breath because we both know what he intended to say. And it's true for me, too. I still love him. Wildly. Passionately.

I just don't know what that means.

At the moment, I'm not inclined to analyze. I simply want his hands on me, his cock inside me. And as he follows orders and strips, I do the same, grinning at him as we both move fast, as if in silent competition.

He finishes first, and for a moment, I can only stare at him. At the hard perfection of his body.

A little too perfect, actually, because the scar I remember—that I loved tracing—is gone. And I'm not entirely sure how that can be. It is as if he has a fresh coat of skin, and the old, scarred skin was shed and left behind.

That, of course, makes no sense.

Or it makes as much sense as Dante not aging.

He is looking at me warily, as if he knows what I am thinking. I frown, then make a circular motion with my finger. Slowly, he shows me his back. Where there had been five luscious birds inked on his back, now there are six.

"You got another. Why?"

"A reminder," he says.

"Of what?"

"That I shouldn't lose fights."

He turns back around, and now his face is hard, as if he is afraid that I am getting close to some dark secret. Honestly, I think that I am.

I reach out and touch his chest, then run my finger along the long path of the now-missing scar that once ended just above his pubic bone. He shivers in response to my touch, his already hard cock growing harder.

"I don't understand," I say. "How—"

He takes my hand and cups my fingers around his cock. "Is that really what you want to talk about right now?"

Part of me wants to scream *yes, yes*, because something inside me knows that this is so very important. That this is the key.

But the other part of me—the part now holding velvet steel in my hand, the part that is wet and throbbing with desire—can think about nothing but his hands, his lips, his cock.

Slowly, I shake my head. "No. That's not what I want to talk about."

"Then get on the bed."

I slowly draw my hand over his cock, making him moan before stepping back and releasing him. Then I do as he asks. I get on the bed. I spread my arms. And, yes, I spread my legs.

He is looking right at me, and rather than embarrass me, the sight of his eyes trained right at my core only arouses me more, and I give in to my body's urge to move. To wriggle. To let my hips dance and sway in a futile attempt to find satisfaction.

He takes pity on me and moves to the bed. And though I had told him I couldn't wait to have his cock inside me, I cannot deny that the stroke of his hands upon my bare skin coupled with the kisses he now trails up my leg have me writhing with a building, agonizing pleasure.

He laves my clit, then thrusts his tongue inside me with such wild ferocity it makes me buck. He lifts his head and smiles at me, and though I want more, he continues up my body until his mouth closes over my breast and his teeth bite down on my nipple, softly at first, and then hard enough to make me cry out—even as that pain ricochets down my body from breast to cunt.

"Now," he says, and in one swift and confident movement, he has rolled onto his back and is turning me with him. I end up straddling him, my legs on either side of his waist, his cock standing at attention behind me and teasing my ass in a way that is undeniably enticing.

"Fuck me," he says. "As hard as you want. As deep as you

want. And keep your eyes open. I want to watch your face as you come."

I whimper a bit, but I don't protest. Instead I rise up, then scoot back so that I am over his cock, the head placed right at my core. I ease down slowly, then harder. Until finally I can't take the tease and I slam my body down hard before rising up on my knees and repeating the process.

It feels incredible. Like fireworks in my womb spreading out to my fingers and toes.

I feel alive and in love, and even in the midst of this wild passion, I know that is a very dangerous way to feel.

At the moment, I don't much care.

I ride him hard, fondling my breasts when he tells me to, playing with my clit when he tells me to do that.

And when he tells me to come, I do that as well, my body primed to his demands and desires. So yes, I explode on top of him, my body drawing him in, milking him, taking him all the way to his own, violent, explosion.

After, I collapse forward on him and breathe deep, recovering from the power of what just crashed through me. It was more than sex, more than an orgasm. It was a communion, and I am not sure that I can ever be the same.

His arms are around me, holding me close, and we lay like that for a long, long time.

But once the tremors of the orgasm have faded, I slide out of his embrace and pad naked to the window. I hug myself and look down at the courtyard we'd passed through yesterday to get to his office. He's told me that there is another courtyard on the other side of Number 36 and another brownstone, and that one is owned by Mal.

I can't help but wonder about the amount of money these men and Phoenix Security command, or about what they do. In truth, I know very little about them. But I know my heart. And I know what—and who—I want.

I also know what I fear, because I will not survive being tossed away again.

"Brenna?"

I turn to see Dante propped up in bed.

"Are you okay?"

I shake my head. "I should probably go."

He stands up and comes to me. "Talk to me."

I raise a brow. "Talk to you? What is there to talk about? You almost said you loved me—no, don't try to deny it. But, dammit Dante, you've also told me you're going to walk away. You told me that day at the Algonquin, and nothing has changed. And I don't want to lose you again. *Dammit.*"

I didn't mean to spill all of that, much less these damned tears. But it's the truth, and I have no interest in skirting around my feelings. Not now. Not when I have him back in my life.

"I know," he says. "But it can't work," he says, and the pain I hear in his voice is so sharp it feels like a knife that is cutting me to ribbons.

"Why?" I demand. "How the hell do you know if we don't try?"

"Try?" He slides out of bed and comes to stand beside me. He clutches tight to my arms. Almost too tight. "Try?" he repeats. "There's no room for risk in this game, Brenna."

I shake my head, not understanding.

"Dammit, don't you get it?" He is still clutching my arms, so tight I anticipate bruises. "I want you, Brenna. I've wanted you from the moment I met you, and I still want you. I want you, and I don't ever want to let you go."

"Don't do this to me again," I say, tears flooding my eyes. "You told me that in London. You said we had an eternal love. A love that spanned time and distance, and all sorts of pretty words. But then you left. You just left."

"Because it can't work," he repeats. His words are so harsh it sounds as though he is spitting them. "It can't fucking work."

"Why not?" I demand. "I love you, Dante. I wish I didn't. The last thirteen years would have been one hell of a lot less lonely if I could have forgotten about you. But I love you, and every moment that I don't have you is like a knife through my heart. You're the one who left—*you*. So dammit, Dante, I want an explanation. You say it won't work? Then you need to tell me why!"

I am screaming, my voice rising with each word. I can't remember ever being so angry. So hurt. "Tell me," I demand. "Tell me right now."

"You want to know? Fine. *This* is the goddamn reason."

As he speaks, he races toward the window and bursts through the glass. And as my scream fills the room, he falls five stories, then lands in a broken heap in the courtyard below.

## Chapter Eight

My scream still hangs in the air as I toss my dress over my head and race out of the room and down the stairs.

*Oh god oh god oh god...*

Another flight, then another.

*Oh Christ oh shit...*

And again and again until finally I reach the door to the courtyard and I burst through just as Raine and a tall woman with long dark hair race out of the door of Number 36 across from me.

I stare at the woman. I'd seen her only once from a distance, but her image is burned into my mind.

"You?"

She is the woman Dante left me for. And like Dante, she has not aged a day.

"I'm Jessica," she says. "And no. I'm not with Dante. I never was. Trust me, Liam would be pissed."

"Liam?" I think about the huge, gorgeous man with the kind eyes.

"My mate—my husband."

"But—but, Dante said—"

She nods pointedly at his broken body that lies still on the concrete. "He'll explain."

It is those nonsensical words that break the spell. *Shock, I must be in shock.*

"*Explain?*" The word is ripped out of me. "But he's—Oh, god. He needs an ambulance," I cry. "Please, he's—"

"An ambulance won't do him any good. He's dead," Jessica says. "But it will be all right. Trust me. I'm a doctor."

I'm not sure if I should be terrified of this truly crazy woman or feel sorry for her. But I take the chance of turning my back on her and hurry toward Dante. Raine is crouching beside him, but now he stands up and steps away from Dante and toward me, his hand held out as if to stop me.

"You shouldn't go closer," he says.

"The hell I won't." I know he's dead—I can look at him and see that—but I can't make myself believe it. I can't lose him again. Not when I was so close to getting him back. And somehow I know that if I can just hold him then it will turn out that this is all a dream, and—

I try to rush past Raine, but he jerks me to a halt. "Brenna, no. You'll get hurt."

*Hurt?*

And then, before I have time to ask the question, a wall of flames seems to encircle Dante, the fire moving in to lick at his naked body. Burning away his skin. His beautiful tattoos.

Destroying all that is left of the man I love.

I look at Raine. At Jessica. They are doing nothing about this. If anything, they seem pleased, and all that I can think is that this is crazy. Completely crazy.

I start to scream. To cry. To fall into full-blown, horrible, hysterical grief.

"Brenna, it'll be okay." Jessica's voice is soft beside me, but it is not soothing. I want to hate this woman. This kind woman who presses a hand to my shoulder and says, very gently, "It will be better when you wake. Sleep now, sweetie. Go ahead, just sleep."

I don't want to—I really don't. But my body is so heavy and I start to slip toward the ground.

The last thing I see is Dante's ashes dancing in a circle of fire.

And the last thing I feel is Raine's strong arms going around me and keeping me from collapsing in a heap on the ground.

\* \* \* \*

I wake, groggy and disoriented, in Dante's bed, the man himself sitting beside me, studying my face with concern. And with something else that looks like hope.

"Hey," I say as scrub sleep out of my eyes. "I had the most bizarre dream." But even as I say the words, the freakish, impossible truth is settling over me.

*It wasn't a dream.*

He is wearing pajama bottoms and no shirt. And there is a vibrant phoenix now tattooed on his chest, just over his heart.

I shake my head because none of this makes sense. "Just spit it out," I say. "Please—whatever this is, whatever is going on—it will be easier if you just tell me in one quick burst."

His eyes study mine, and then he nods. "All right," he says. His voice is soft and soothing. "I don't know where to start."

"Anywhere." The word is ripped from me. "I just need words. Please, just start talking because I need your words to ground me."

He seems to understand that because he takes my hand, and I cling tight to it, as if I'm afraid that his words are going to rip him from me.

"I love you," he says, and the words curl around me, warm and comforting. "I should start with that. But it can't—it can't work because I'm immortal. That's what I was trying to tell you. What I had to show you."

I start to say something, but really, there just aren't words. So I close my mouth, and I keep listening.

"I'm not from here—this dimension, this world. None of us are. Me, Raine, Liam, Mal. Jessica. The others—you'll meet them. We came on a mission from our world, chasing a horrible enemy. We call it the fuerie, and in the chase we were thrown off course. We—and the fuerie—crashed in this dimension."

"When?" It is the only word I can manage.

"About three thousand years ago."

"Oh." I try to process that, but it's too big. So I just nod and latch onto the important part. *Immortal.* Or at least pretty damn close.

"Yes," he agrees when I say as much. "I'm getting there. You see, we are not originally creatures of matter. We're energy. Pure, sentient energy. But we can't exist without form in this dimension. Our essence has to be bound or else it dissipates and we lose our identity. So after we crashed here, we had to find a form."

"So you what? Possessed humans?"

"The fuerie did, yes. They steal bodies. They burn through them. They move through this world spreading evil." He draws a breath. "But that isn't our way. We were met by a group of men and women sent by an Egyptian prince who had visions. He understood what we needed, and we merged with volunteers. Our essence merging with theirs. We became human—and yet not. And, yes, we are immortal. Our bodies do not age. They do not change. And unless we are killed, we go on forever as we are."

"But you just said you're immortal. What do you mean, unless you're killed?"

"You saw it yourself. If we are mortally wounded, we seem to die, but then we are reborn again in the phoenix fire." He points to the seventh tattoo that has appeared on his chest. "With each death, we get a new mark."

I nod slowly. "All right," I finally say.

He looks at me, apparently baffled. "All right?"

"Well, yes." I frown, not sure what he expects.

"You believe me?"

I laugh. "Well, I'd be hard pressed to argue." He's still looking at me as if he is completely gobsmacked. I take his hand. "It's weird, I'll give you that. But it also makes a lot of sense. And—okay, this is going to sound really crazy—but it almost feels like something I knew. But just never realized I knew."

He's still looking at me strangely. Now he shakes his head. "I didn't expect that."

"Why not? Do I seem that close-minded? Like I just toss away evidence that's right in front of my nose?"

"No, no. It's just that such easy acceptance..." He stands and goes to look through the broken window. "We've just always believed it was a sign of—"

I sit up straighter. "Of what?"

He shakes his head. "It doesn't matter." I watch as his shoulders rise and fall, then he turns to face me. "This is why we have to end this. Between us, I mean."

"Oh, I know what you mean. And no."

His brow rises. "No? I don't have a say?"

"Not if I can help it." I slide out of bed and move into his arms. "You're being an ass."

"An ass?" I can't tell if he's amused or annoyed. "I'm trying to protect you. There's no future here. No matter what else might happen, you will grow old, Brenna. You will die. We can't—" His breath hitches. "We can't be together. Not forever."

"Then let's be together for now." My voice is so soft I can barely hear it. "Is that why you pretended with Jessica? To push me away? Because eventually it would end?"

He hesitates, then nods.

"Idiot. Ass. Dumbfuck."

He narrows his eyes at me.

"I mean it. I mean, come on, Dante. I've got at least a few more decades left in me." I frown, struck by the fact that I am in a conversation discussing my own mortality. Not exactly happy fun times.

"You should spend your years with someone you can grow old with."

"Oh, so you'd just toss me aside at the first sign of wrinkles for some tight young thing?" I'm teasing, but the pain in his voice when he answers is real.

"God, no. But—"

I feel the tears burn in my eyes, and I press my palm to his cheek. "Then stop it. Because I want to spend my years with you. So stop worrying about the future. Let's just take the now. We can figure out the rest later." The tears stream freely down my face. "I've missed you so much. You shouldn't have left me. Not because of this."

"It can't last forever," he says. "I thought—" He shakes his head. "God, never mind what I thought. You're here now." He takes my hand and leads me back to the bed.

"Make love to me," I whisper. "We still have a few hours until morning. Make love to me slowly and sweetly. Please," I beg. "Dante, I need you."

His eyes meet mine. "Oh, baby, I need you, too."

# Chapter Nine

I am still glowing from Dante's touch the next morning as I sip coffee in the VIP lounge of Dark Pleasures.

I've never been here before, but it feels like home. Welcoming, with rich leather and wood and the scent of alcohol and cigars.

Dante brought me with him to his operational meeting with Raine and Mal and Liam.

"I'll run the operation from here," Liam had said. "The three of you will get in and get out fast."

Jessica and Callie and Christina were also there, and Dagny joined us halfway through the meeting.

"Why you three?" I'd asked Dante once the meeting wrapped.

"I'm going because I can detect the fuerie," he said.

"Your enemy? Why would they—"

He cut me off. "We're trying to rescue a brother they trapped. It's reasonable to assume they'll want to stop us. Don't worry," he'd said, seeing my face. "We fight the fuerie all the time—it's what we do. And right now, there aren't any nearby anyway. Besides," he added with a cocky grin, "immortal. Remember?"

I pointed to Mal and Raine. "And those two? They feel the fuerie as well?"

"Mal can manipulate memory. He'll clean up for us afterward with the security staff, doorman, anyone else we come across. And Raine can talk to electronics. He'll get us into the apartment and then into that display case."

My head was spinning. "Seriously?"

"We're creatures of energy," he said. "That gives us a unique knowledge of how to manipulate that energy. Don't worry," he added before kissing me hard. "The mission will go just fine."

Now, sitting with the women while Liam has gone off to the

Phoenix Security office to monitor the action, I can only hope that he was right about the mission going well.

"Relax," Jessica says kindly. "This is what we do, and the coast is clear. No fuerie nearby and Folsom is out for his jog. This mission will be a walk in the park."

I nod, then sit back, holding my coffee tight in both hands because I want the warmth for comfort. I'm trying not to worry—truly—but it's hard.

"So what happens to the man you're trying to rescue?" Maybe if I keep talking, I won't imagine everything that can possibly go wrong.

"If his essence escapes from that gemstone without being bound in another or in a human, then Merrick is essentially dead. So we're going to form an energy field around him. All of the brotherhood gather our energy, then we direct it to pull his essence from the flawed gem and into a pure one."

"So then he just lives in a new gem forever?"

Jessica frowns. "Unfortunately, until we find a human willing to merge with him, that's true. He could take over a human's body, but that's not the way we operate. But this way he will still be alive, and I promise you that time doesn't mean the same thing to him as it does to you."

I nod, but I realize I'm hugging myself. All of this is a lot to take in. I let my gaze wander around the room, giving me a little time to think. Across from the chair I'm curled up in, Christina sits cross-legged on a sofa, her eyes closed, her wrists resting on her knees.

I lean toward Jessica, who I've come to consider my personal instructor. "What's she doing?"

"She can see the fuerie. But it's different than Dante. She has to call up a map in her mind. Great for intelligence. Less practical in the midst of a mission."

I watch, and Jessica is right. It looks like Christina is watching a movie in her mind.

After a moment, she opens her eyes. "All clear," she says and sets a timer on her phone for thirty minutes. "No fuerie on Manhattan, and none for miles."

"So how does it work for Dante?" I ask.

"He can just reach out with his mind. He doesn't have to call up a map. So it's much faster. But he can only feel the fuerie if they are nearby. Christina sees a map of the entire world."

"Wow."

"Pretty much," Jessica agrees.

"He'll look, right?" I ask. "During the mission, I mean. He'll keep reaching out?" I can't shake the feeling that something bad is going to happen.

"Of course." Jessica's voice is soft. Tender. "That's his job. He'll be fine." She takes my hand. "I'm glad you two are back together. In London, he was so gone over for you. I don't think I'd ever seen him so happy, and I've known Dante for a very long time."

"Then why did he leave? Why did you two pretend to be a couple?"

"It's hard," Jessica says. "Everybody wants a forever kind of love, us most of all, because to us, forever is so very real. And when he got through his head that he couldn't have that with you, he tossed away happiness in the now because he couldn't have it in the forever."

"But I love him," I say. "And he loves me. Why wouldn't he just be grateful for the time we could have?"

She lifts a shoulder. "I think he was a little hurt. He'd thought you were truly his—that you really could be his forever. But that's so rare that he shouldn't have even let the possibility enter his mind."

"It's hard not to," Dagny puts in, even as I'm trying to figure out what exactly we're talking about. "I mean, I felt that punch when I met Braydon, and for a while I fantasized that he might really be my mate. But it was just that sexual attraction. Awesome and wonderful and I love him to death, but he's not my forever guy."

"I wish he was," Christina says. "He's my best friend, and I hate the thought that I'm going to live forever and I won't have him to talk to even in just a hundred short years."

My head is spinning. "Wait. Wait, you guys are saying that sometimes mortals really can stay with you forever?"

The three glance at each other, then at me. It's Jessica who speaks. "I thought Dante explained everything to you last night."

"He explained a lot," I say. "This, not so much."

"Shit."

"Tell me," I demand. "What are you talking about?"

Jessica meets Dagny's eyes, and the other girl nods. For a moment, I think that Jessica is going to ignore this tacit permission, but then Jessica draws in a breath. "In our world, finding your mate is a permanent thing. It's more than a bond. It's like a merging. So it's very rare for someone from our dimension to truly mate with a human. But sometimes—very rarely—a true mate is found. It's like what you call soul mates, only more so."

"Okay," I say, certain that Dante is absolutely my soul mate. "But how does a human soul mate live forever?"

"If a human goes into the phoenix fire," Dagny says, "she'll die. Burn up. End of story. But if that human enters her true mate's phoenix fire, she'll be transformed. She'll become immortal. She'll be bound with him and will become one of us."

I'm trying to process all of that. "Wait. Are you saying that if I'd gone into that fire last night, I could be immortal now? That I could be with Dante forever? Why the hell did you stop me?"

"Because you're not his true mate," Jessica says flatly, her words sitting like rocks in my stomach. "You're not truly his."

"The hell I'm not." A slow burn of fury is rising in me. Not only did they not tell me about the fire that could have brought Dante and I together forever, now they're telling me that we're not really meant to be. "Are you saying he doesn't love me enough?"

Surely not. I've seen the passion in his eyes. Felt it in his touch. But if that's true—oh, god, please let it not be true—then I need to know. Because what I feel with him is so over the top and out of control that I cannot even imagine a world in which he doesn't love me just as deeply.

"He's head over heels for you," Jessica says. "But there's no shame in your not feeling the same way. You can be feel all that and still not be someone's true mate. I mean, seven times before a woman has believed she loved one of the brothers that completely, but she ended up perishing in the flame, anyway."

Christina's timer starts to beep, as if underscoring these awful words.

Dagny shivers. "It was horrible. Only one has ever been a true mate and became immortal. There may have been others, but none willing to risk the fire." She shrugs. "But if they don't want the risk, maybe it's not true."

I'm not interested in these horror stories. They don't apply to me; I'm certain of it. "What makes you think I don't love him enough? That we're not connected enough?"

Dagny and Jessica exchange looks. "He saw you, Brenna. He saw you kissing another man."

It takes me a second, and then I realize what she is talking about. I shake my head, horrified. "What, Rob? He's nothing. No one. He had a crush on me, and I was so scared about the magnitude of what I was feeling for Dante that I let him kiss me. But it meant nothing. I felt nothing."

I drag my fingers through my hair. "Why didn't he say something back then? Hell, why didn't he ask me about it now?"

Jessica sighs. "Oh, sweetie, do you think he could stand knowing he'd lose you? You had doubts. Even if you swear that you didn't—and even if you mean it—your uncertainty must have been there, buried deep. Better to end it fast and hard and walk away than to suffer and then lose each other."

I shake my head vehemently. "No. No doubts. I love Dante," I say. "I always have."

"I believe you believe that. But love doesn't necessarily mean— and what we're talking about—the depth of emotion—it's so big. And if you were scared, having doubts..."

She trails off, looking as miserable as I feel.

"I would survive the fire," I say. "I'm sure of it."

Dagny and Jessica exchange another glance. "I'm sorry," Jessica finally says. "But I'm not sure at all."

A few feet from us, Christina's eyes fly open and she jerks, as if thrown out of a trance. *"The fuerie,"* she says. "I have no idea how they got to the city so quickly. But they're here—and it looks like they're heading to Folsom's house."

# Chapter Ten

"*Fuerie*," Dante cried. "They're converging. Finish it up and lets get the hell out of here."

"Got it." Raine said, sliding the gemstone into the bag he wore around his waist. "We're good to go."

"How long?" Mal asked.

"They're moving fast," Dante said. "A car. Motorcycles. Not sure. But there's no reason to think they know about us. They're coming to do the same thing—steal the gem with Merrick from Folsom."

"His buyer who could supply cursed artifacts," Raine said with a snort. "Fuck that. Poor guy doesn't even know the scum he's dealing with."

They hurried out, with Mal doing whatever memory manipulation he had to in order to clean up the trail they were blazing.

The Phoenix Security SUV was right outside the building, and Dennis, their driver, had the engine revving. Raine climbed in first, then Mal.

Dante was about to do the same when Jessica's Ferrari skidded to a stop across Fifth Avenue, to the consternation of nearby cars and taxis.

"Brenna!" She called to Dante from across the street. "Christina told us about the fuerie, and she took off running. This way. To find you."

*Fuck.*

"Go," he shouted to Dennis, then slammed the door to the SUV. Not one to question authority, Dennis peeled away from the curb and disappeared back toward Number 36.

"I'll help you find her," Jessica said as she abandoned the car and raced across the street toward him.

"No. Merrick's too far gone. Get to Number 36. Do the ritual without me. Do it now, Jessica, before we lose him. Get Merrick safe. I'll take care of Brenna."

She hesitated, then nodded. "Be careful," she said. "There are fuerie around."

"I know the danger." And he did. Even though the brothers' bodies couldn't die, after enough deaths, their souls were burned out of them, rendering them hollow. Empty. Mad.

The fuerie knew that, too. And took great pleasure in seeking the death of the brothers.

But that wasn't even Dante's first concern. Because the fuerie were like feral beasts, and they would smell the scent of a brother on her. And if they did, they would kill her simply because she belonged to him.

*Brenna.*

Oh, god, Brenna.

\* \* \* \*

I do not know why I am running, I only know that I have to. That it seems foolish, but it is not.

Because I know by some sixth sense I trust that this is my chance to have him. To save him. To save us.

And so I race down Fifth Avenue, silently thanking my Pilates instructor because at least I'm not completely winded, though I do have one hell of a stitch in my side.

But I can't stop. I have to find him. Have to hold him. Have to look him in the eye and tell him that he is a huge asshole. A prick. A complete and total dumbfuck.

Because how the hell could he not know the depth of my feelings?

Then again, I didn't understand my feelings either, which was why I let Rob kiss me.

So clearly I'm just as much of a dumbfuck.

Apparently, we really are meant for each other. A perfect pair.

The thought makes me giddy and I run faster—then quicken my pace even more when I hear my name and see him in the distance.

He's running toward me from the opposite direction, and for one brief, surreal moment it feels like we are living in a movie. A sappy romance, and soon he will grab me around the waist and swing me around and the soundtrack will swell.

Except, of course, this is not a movie. Or if it is, it's not a romance. Because just as he is about to cross the street to reach my block, someone tall and muscular tackles me from the side, and we go down hard.

"Bitch!"

I kick, getting the bastard in the face, and then race down the street toward Dante, screaming his name.

He runs to me and grabs my hand. "Fuerie," he says, then makes a sharp right turn into an alley between two residential buildings.

The man—the fuerie—comes along, too. And apparently they travel in pairs because another one is right there behind him.

I scream because this alley is a dead end and I'm really not sure what else to do.

But then they are attacking, wild and crazy, with swords that seem more like whips but slice through everything. One catches the edge of my ankle and I scream, the pain almost more than I can bear.

He grins, as if the sound makes him happy, and starts to advance toward me.

Beside me, Dante is fighting the other one, who has a whip of his own, but at my cry, he kicks it into high gear. He has a weapon—like a sword of vibrant light. And he is slashing and hacking. I have never seen him fight, and he moves with grace and power, and in no time at all, the fuerie is headless. He stabs the sword through the fuerie's heart, and the dead creature combusts, leaving only a pile of ash.

The other one lets out a wild cry and rushes me. I scream as it raises its whip hand, and Dante leaps in front of me, taking the brunt of the blow, the whip slicing hard across his neck and ripping open his chest.

He falls, his blood staining the asphalt.

I stand in shock. The fuerie is right there, sneering at me.

Coming at me.

I grab Dante's sword and I lunge, terror taking the place of skill. And though I do not know how I do it, somehow I manage to take the fuerie down. And then, with a burst of satisfaction, I drive Dante's sword through the creature's heart.

"Baby." Dante's voice is weak, and I kneel beside him.

"You fool," I say, as tears stream down my face. "How could you not believe? How could you not know? Of course I love you. Of course I'm yours. I always have been. And I always will be."

He shakes his head. "No, too risky. Doubt. That man. Don't do it." His eyes meet mine. "Don't do it."

But I know that I will. I know that I have to.

More than that, I cannot wait.

I take his sword, and I look my love in the eyes. And then I stand over his fallen body, one leg on either side of his waist. "I love you," I say as I thrust the sword down and through his heart. "And now I'm going to prove it."

\* \* \* \*

*Pain.*

And the sickening smell of burning flesh.

I am standing in a firestorm. The world and my body alight.

And with every tiny ounce of sanity within me I want to leap out of this circle. I want to run to the hospital and let them treat my burns.

I am immolating myself, and the pain—oh, the pain rips through me like talons, tearing my insides out, melting me, destroying me.

I try to gasp. To breathe, but the fire burns my throat. I am dying, I am living.

I am life and death all twisted around into one thing. One horrible, painful, writhing thing.

And then I am going. Death taking. The world darkening.

Fear wells in me, and I try to reach out. Try to call his name.

Because I am afraid that I am leaving now. That it is over.

That I have made a mistake.

And that I will never see Dante again.

# Chapter Eleven

*I'm alive.*

I'm breathing, and I'm alive, and I'm his.

Joy sweeps through me, and I open my eyes to see Dante smiling over me. "You stupid woman," he says, and I hear the fear in his voice. "You stupid, stupid woman." He pulls me to him, hugging me tight even as I hug him right back. "You could have burned to death."

"No," I say. I pull back so that I can see his eyes, then I slowly tug down the neck of the nightgown that someone has dressed me in to reveal the new small phoenix now inked on my shoulder. "See? I couldn't have."

His laugh sounds a lot like a muffled cry.

And then he kisses me, hard and hungry, and it feels as though he has never kissed me before. And honestly, I suppose he really hasn't. We're bound now, truly together, in a way that we have never been before.

I'm his, and he is mine. *Forever.*

It sounds so long.

Hell, it sounds so wonderful.

I break the kiss, then press my palms flat against his shirt before looking up to meet his eyes. "Touch me," I say. "Take me."

His slow smile is all the answer I need, and I shift as he pulls the sheet back, then lift my hips so that he can peel the nightgown off me. I'm wearing nothing underneath, my clothes having burned away in the phoenix flame.

He bends to me, then presses his lips to the phoenix that now marks my shoulder. The sensation of his lips on my skin seems to cut through me, sweet and wondrous. As if it is a map of circuits and he has suddenly lit me up.

But he is not satisfied with that.

Slowly, and so deliciously sweetly, he starts to trail kisses all over my body, his ministrations setting me on fire. Again, I think, and then I laugh.

He looks up. "What?"

"You're setting me on fire," I say, and his laugh joins with mine.

"I'll do more than that."

He turns back to his task with focused determination. His hands hold my legs apart, and he very thoroughly kisses his way up my legs, then slowly—so painfully slowly—teases my sex with his tongue.

"Please," I beg. "Please, I need you inside me. I need to feel you."

"I know, baby. Me, too." He straddles me, then slowly enters me, stretching and filling me until I can't tell where he ends and I begin. We rock together, and it's not frantic or wild, but gentle and sweet and wonderful. So many ways to touch him, to know him. And we have barely even scratched the surface.

"I can't hold back," he says. "I have to feel you."

"Never hold back," I say. "Not with me."

His response is a low groan, and he thrusts hard into me, then faster and faster until the pressure builds between us and we explode together, our bodies and our souls twined as one.

I make a soft noise of satisfaction and go completely limp. "Mmm." That is about the only sound I can manage.

He chuckles and pulls me close, and we stay like that for a moment, simply feeling. Simply enjoying.

"They were able to save Merrick?" I ask after a few moments, my eyes heavy.

"They were."

"Who will he merge with?"

"I don't know," Dante says. "Someone extraordinary. But he's safe now. He's safe because of you."

I roll over so that I am straddling him, then use my finger to trace the outline of another newly inked phoenix on his breast. "We wasted so much time. Thirteen years lost because I was a fool, too scared to believe that I'd really found true love."

"Don't look at it that way," he says. "Think of what could have happened if you'd walked away from me that first night in London. Or if you'd refused to help me when I found you in the Algonquin. So many things tried to drive us apart, Brenna. But it was love that pulled us back together. Don't mourn those thirteen years," he says, brushing his thumb gently under my eye to wipe away an errant tear.

"They're just a blip," he says. "And baby, we have all the time in the world waiting for us."

# A note from JK

I hope you enjoyed *Caress of Pleasure!*

Be sure not to miss any of the stories in the Dark Pleasures series:

*Caress of Darkness* (Callie and Raine's story)
*Find Me in Darkness* (Mal and Christina, part 1)
*Find Me in Pleasure* (Mal and Christina, part 2)
*Find Me in Passion* (Mal and Christina, part 3)
*Caress of Pleasure* (Dante and Brenna's story)

Learn more at my website, http://www.juliekenner.com

And be sure to subscribe to my newsletter so you don't miss a thing: http://bit.ly/JK_newsletter

# About Julie Kenner

J. Kenner (aka Julie Kenner) is the *New York Times*, *USA Today*, *Publishers Weekly*, *Wall Street Journal* and #1 International bestselling author of over seventy novels, novellas and short stories in a variety of genres.

Though known primarily for her award-winning and international bestselling erotic romances (including the Stark and Most Wanted series) that have reached as high as #2 on the *New York Times* bestseller list, JK has been writing full time for over a decade in a variety of genres including paranormal and contemporary romance, "chicklit" suspense, urban fantasy, and paranormal mommy lit.

Her foray into the latter, *Carpe Demon: Adventures of a Demon-Hunting Soccer Mom* by Julie Kenner, has been consistently in development in Hollywood since prior to publication. Most recently, it has been optioned by Warner Brothers Television for development as series on the CW Network with Alloy Entertainment producing.

JK has been praised by *Publishers Weekly* as an author with a "flair for dialogue and eccentric characterizations" and by *RT Bookclub* for having "cornered the market on sinfully attractive, dominant antiheroes and the women who swoon for them." A four time finalist for Romance Writers of America's prestigious RITA award, JK took home the first RITA trophy awarded in the category of erotic romance in 2014 for her novel, *Claim Me* (book 2 of her Stark Trilogy).

Her books have sold well over a million copies and are published in over over twenty countries.

In her previous career as an attorney, JK worked as a clerk on the Fifth Circuit Court of Appeals, and practiced primarily civil, entertainment and First Amendment litigation in Los Angeles and Irvine, California, as well as in Austin, Texas. She currently lives in Central Texas, with her husband, two daughters, and two rather spastic cats.

# Also From JK

*Erotic romance*

*As Julie Kenner*
*Caress of Darkness*
*Find Me in Darkness*
*Find Me in Pleasure*
*Find Me in Passion*
*Caress of Pleasure*

*As J. Kenner*
*Stark Series novels*
*Release Me (a New York Times and USA Today bestseller)*
*Claim Me (a #2 New York Times bestseller!)*
*Complete Me (a #2 New York Times bestseller!)*

*Stark Ever After novellas*
*Take Me*
*Have Me*
*Play My Game*

*Stark International novels*
*Say My Name*
*On My Knees*
*Under My Skin*

*Stark International novellas*
*Tame Me*

*The Most Wanted series*
*Wanted*
*Heated*
*Ignited*

*Other Genres*

*Kate Connor Demon-Hunting Soccer Mom Series (suburban fantasy/paranormal)*
*Carpe Demon*
*California Demon*

*Demons Are Forever*
*The Demon You Know*
*Deja Demon*
*Demon Ex Machina*
*Pax Demonica*

*The Protector (Superhero) Series (paranormal romance)*
*The Cat's Fancy (prequel)*
*Aphrodite's Kiss*
*Aphrodite's Passion*
*Aphrodite's Secret*
*Aphrodite's Flame*
*Aphrodite's Embrace*
*Aphrodite's Delight*
*Aphrodite's Charms (boxed set)*
*Dead Friends and Other Dating Dilemmas*

*Blood Lily Chronicles (urban fantasy romance)*
*Tainted*
*Torn*
*Turned*
*The Blood Lily Chronicles (boxed set)*

*Devil May Care Series (paranormal romance)*
*Raising Hell*
*Sure As Hell*

*By J. Kenner as J.K. Beck:*
*Shadow Keepers Series (dark paranormal romance)*
*When Blood Calls*
*When Pleasure Rules*
*When Wicked Craves*
*Shadow Keepers: Midnight (e-novella)*
*When Passion Lies*
*When Darkness Hungers*
*When Temptation Burns*

# Say My Name

Don't miss *Say My Name*, the first book in the new Stark International trilogy by J. Kenner!

*I never let anyone get too close—but he's the only man who's ever made me feel alive.*

Meeting Jackson Steele was a shock to my senses. Confident and commanding, he could take charge of any room . . . or any woman. And Jackson wanted me. The mere sight of him took my breath away, and his touch made me break all my rules.

Our bond was immediate, our passion untamed. I wanted to surrender completely to his kiss, but I couldn't risk his knowing the truth about my past. Yet Jackson carried secrets too, and in our desire we found our escape, pushing our boundaries as far as they could go.

Learning to trust is never easy. In my mind, I knew I should run. But in my heart, I never felt a fire this strong—and it could either save me or scorch me forever.

\* \* \* \*

"I want to know why you ended it."

My chest tightens and I have to resist the urge to hug myself. I can feel the anxiety reaching for me even now, along with the nightmares and twisted memories that slink along, too. Slithering out of the night to fill my days. I shake my head, determined to keep it all banished, far and away. "It doesn't matter."

He turns from the window, his face a wild mixture of anger and hurt. "The hell it doesn't."

"My reasons are my own, Jackson." I can hear the panic creeping into my voice, and I fear that he can as well. Deliberately, I take slow, even breaths. I want to calm myself. And, damn me, I want to soothe him.

I want to ease the hurt that I caused, but that's impossible, because I can't answer his question.

"Why?" he asks again, only now there's a gentleness in his voice that unnerves me.

I stiffen in automatic defense, afraid I'll melt in the face of any tenderness from this man. "You didn't want to end it," Jackson continues. "Even now, you want it."

"You have no idea what I want," I say sharply, though that is a lie as well.

"Don't I?" There is anger in his voice. Hurt, too. "I know you want the resort."

I've been looking at the tabletop, and now I lift my head. "Yes." The word is simple. It may be the first completely true thing I've said to him since Atlanta. "Will you take it? You and I both know it's the opportunity of a lifetime. Are you really going to let our past stand in the way of what can be a truly magnificent achievement?"

I watch his shoulders rise and fall as he takes a breath. Then he turns away from me to look out the window once again. "I want the project, Sylvia."

Relief sweeps over me, and I have to physically press my hands to the table to forestall the urge to leap to my feet and embrace him.

"But I want you, too." He turns as he speaks, and when he faces me straight on, there is no denying the truth—or the longing—in his eyes.

I swallow as what feels like a swarm of electric butterflies dances over my skin, making the tiny hairs stand up. And making me aware of everything from the solidity of the floor beneath my feet to the breath of air from a vent across the room.

I force myself to remain seated. Because damn me, my instinct is to go to him and slide into his arms. "I—I don't understand." The lie lingers in the air, and I am proud of the way I kept my voice from shaking.

"Then let me be perfectly clear." He closes the distance between us, then uses his forefinger to tilt my head up so that he is looking deep into my eyes. I shift, not only because the contact sends a jolt of electricity right through me, but because I'm afraid that if he looks too deeply into my eyes, he will see a truth I want to keep hidden.

"No," he says. "Look at me, Sylvia. Because I'm not going to say this again. I told you once that I'm a man who goes after what he wants, and I want you in my bed. I want to feel you naked and hot beneath me. I want to hear you cry out when you come, and I want to know that I am the man who took you there."

# Adored
A Masters and Mercenaries Novella
By Lexi Blake

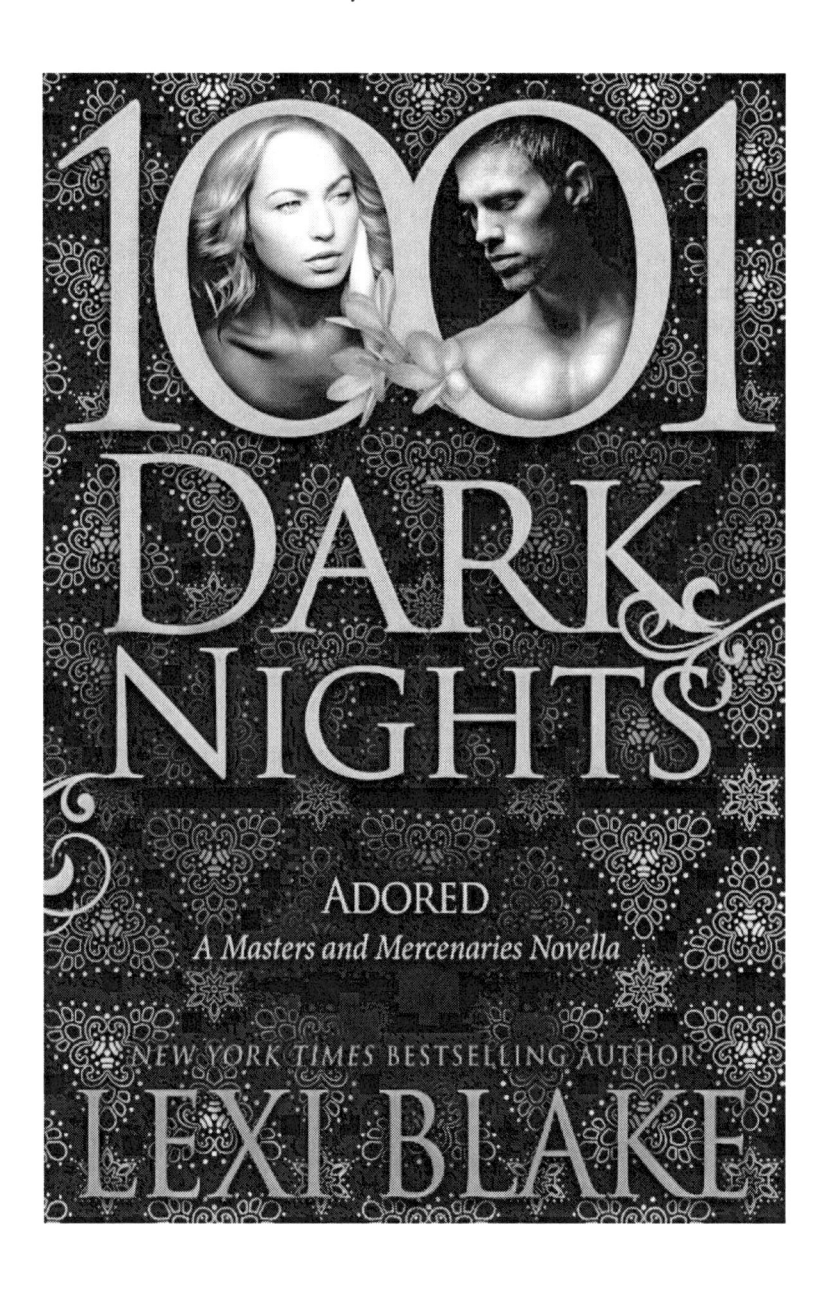

# Author Acknowledgments

Thanks to Liz, MJ, Jillian, Pam and the whole crew at Evil Eye. It's always a pleasure to work with truly creative people. As always thanks to my own crew – Chloe, Riane, Stormy, my husband and my son who will likely yell at me because of all the italics in this book. And to the amazing Steve Berry who I owe for the inspiration to make Mitch a lawyer. I also owe him five dollars.

This book is dedicated to the parents out there. No matter how it happens children change our lives, our marriages, and our souls for the better.

# Chapter One

Mitchell Bradford stared down at the phone and wondered if he could somehow manage to reach through it and strangle the man on the other end of the line. His office was cool, but he could feel the temperature rising with each word he heard. He was certain Kai Ferguson would tell him he had anger issues and should come in for a session. Then Mitch could kill the fucker in person. "What do you mean you paired Laurel with the new Master? Which Laurel would that be because you couldn't possibly be talking about Laurel Daley, my paralegal. I believe I told Big Tag that she was to be refused admission to Sanctum."

Kai chuckled over the line. "Oh, you know, Big Tag has a soft spot for a well-meaning sub."

He took his cell off speaker and pressed it to his ear, as though bringing it closer would make his point more clear. "The only thing Laurel means by joining Sanctum is to push me into a jealous rage. She's manipulating me. That means she's manipulating Tag, too. Deny her application, Kai."

Laurel Daley was rapidly becoming a pain in his…damn it. Thinking about the gorgeous, not even thirty-year-old brunette made his cock hard. She was stunning. Smart and capable, he'd thought about firing her more than once because his brain shut off the minute she walked in a room. He'd hired her sight unseen because she was his best friend's sister. She'd needed a job and he'd needed help.

His best friend. There had been times Will Daley had been his only friend. Will had picked him up and dusted him off and made sure he didn't kill himself with booze. How did he tell his best friend in the world that he wanted to fuck his sister so badly he dreamed about it every night?

He might have been able to deal with the entire situation if Laurel hadn't lost her damn mind and decided she wanted him, too.

One of them had to be sensible.

"I can't deny her application. She's perfectly sane." Kai was his other friend. He and Will and Kai had taken to hanging out together. Unfortunately Kai was also the gateway to Sanctum. He was the club's resident shrink, with the power to approve or disapprove membership applications.

"You wouldn't think that if you saw how pissed off she gets at fictional characters. The woman yells at her e-reader. She threw it across the room the other day and her only explanation was that someone named Joshua Lake was being a butthead." He'd narrowly missed having his head taken off with the damn thing. Luckily, the e-reader seemed pretty tough. The thing hadn't had a scratch on it and she was right back to reading after she'd finished the first draft of the contract she was working on.

Kai chuckled over the line. "Those women are serious about their book boyfriends. If that was a sign of insanity, I would have to get rid of most of the submissives at Sanctum. Face it, Mitch. You're going to have to deal with her."

Laurel would soon be running around Sanctum, likely wearing very little.

Sanctum was his sanctuary. It was a BDSM club, a very exclusive one. He'd had to pay through the nose and give Ian Taggart, the owner, a massive discount on legal services in order to get in. Apparently all his paralegal had to do was bat her eyelashes. His stomach turned and he wondered if he had any antacids. He wasn't exactly sure what he would do if he couldn't spend his nights at Sanctum. His friends were there. It was how he blew off steam.

*So take her and train her. She wants to learn about D/s and you want to find out how tight her pussy is and how she'll whimper when you fuck her hard. You can have her sign a contract. This is actually perfect, dude. Stop thinking so much and let me take over. Have I ever steered you wrong, buddy?*

"Mitch, is your penis talking to you again?"

He should never have admitted that to a shrink. He tried to

move the conversation back to the point. "Why did you pick Master T? He's obviously wrong for her."

He wasn't going into the fact that his libido was sometimes a voice inside his head. And fuck you very much, penis, but yes, his dick had led him astray on numerous occasions leading to two disastrous marriages. Twice he'd been forced to start his life over again with nothing. He'd had to build not one, not two, but three businesses from scratch, and he wasn't doing that again. No matter how well intentioned he would be going into a casual relationship with Laurel Daley, he knew how it would end up. It would start with amazing sex and end in divorce because the only thing stupider than his dick was his heart.

"Master T has become quite proficient at all aspects of D/s. I think he's a good match for training Laurel," Kai explained in a very logical voice.

Master T. They were all using the alias, but Mitch happened to know that Master T was actually Tennessee Smith, disavowed CIA agent in deep cover. He didn't have all the specifics of Ten's new mission. He only knew that the handsome agent was dangerous and that meant Laurel should stay away from him. Ian was planning to use Sanctum to run some kind of operation in the next couple of months, and Mitch didn't want Laurel anywhere near Smith when he got to work. Hell, he didn't want her anywhere near the handsome ex-agent for any reason.

"What about the married Masters?" It was how things were done at Sanctum. The married Masters tended to be the most experienced. They and their submissives often trained both Doms and subs for several months.

There was a pause on the line. "She's worked with Ian and Liam for six weeks. They think she's ready to move on and so do I."

He stopped, the phone heavy in his hand. "She's been going to Sanctum?"

"She comes in on Thursday nights for training and works the nursery on Saturday nights."

Well, that explained it. He didn't go in on Thursdays and there was no reason for him to ever visit the nursery. "And no one thought to tell me my paralegal has joined the club I attend?"

Kai's voice went a bit hard. "I'm only telling you now out of courtesy because Master T prefers to train on Friday nights. The confidentiality of our club members is very important, as you would know."

"But she's Laurel. You know what she means to me," he rasped into the phone. Laurel was all he could think about half the time.

"Then you should have claimed her, Mitchell. She's done waiting for you and I think it's the healthiest choice she's made in the time I've known her. I applaud her for taking control of her life and deciding what she wants. She wants to explore D/s. You won't train her."

"You know why I won't train her." He'd already fucked up his life beyond repair. Twice. He wasn't about to screw up hers, too. He was too old for her. He was too rough and hard for her. She was a kid starting out and he'd run through all his chances.

"Yes, I fully understand all of your psychological reasons for pushing her aside. That is your choice. This is hers."

"She's trying to manipulate me. She thinks if I have to see her with another man, I'll come around."

A long sigh came over the line and Mitch could practically feel the weight of Kai's disappointment. "Then this is your chance to prove her wrong, Mitch. You should thank me. Master T will be taking responsibility for her. I believe they're signing a month-long contract. If it doesn't work out, I've got a couple of Doms looking for permanent partners. You don't have to worry anymore. She'll be taken care of. She won't bother you once she's found a proper top."

She wouldn't bother him? Seeing Laurel was the best part of his day. He'd hired her six months before and every second of every day since had been about catching sight of her or arguing some point of law with her or trying to keep his hands off her. The idea of her with another man…

"Let me find her a Dom. It can't be Master T. He's too old for her. He's too cold."

"He's too much like you?" Kai's voice had softened, was almost sympathetic.

"She deserves better." He was ten years older than her and about a hundred years wiser, though much of his wisdom was made of things a sane person would avoid. "She's a bright light, Kai. She's one of those people you can't help but adore. She shouldn't be with a Master who will grind her under his boot. She needs someone young and positive."

"Does it help if I tell you her contract forbids sex for the first three weeks? They can decide afterward if they want to take the relationship further."

Did it help? Not really. "She needs more. Even during training. Have you thought about Theo Taggart? I know he's in the program. Or Michael Malone?"

He hated the idea of either man laying hands on her, but he had to stop being a selfish prick. She was lonely. He wanted her to be happy. Theo Taggart had a ready smile and a positive outlook on life and Malone came from a wealthy, loving, completely functional family. Neither man had been married before so they didn't have three tons of baggage they dragged through life.

"Mitch, will you listen to yourself? This is ridiculous. She wants you. She's made that plain."

"She's a little girl with daddy issues."

A sharp gasp had him turning around pronto. Shit. Why hadn't he closed the door? Laurel Daley stood there, a clipboard in her hand and her face about three shades paler than normal. "Kai, I'm going to have to call you back."

"She's listening, isn't she?" Kai sounded almost excited at the prospect. "I can be there in twenty minutes for a session if you like. I think if we all sit down, we can find a middle ground…"

He hung up. Kai could go on and on about therapy, and Mitch wasn't interested. He set the phone down. "You could knock, you know."

Yes, arrogance worked in situations like this. No wonder his wives always left him.

Laurel's jaw tightened. "Sharon was at lunch so I was watching the front desk. You have a walk-in. Do you want me to tell him to go away? He claims it's urgent."

Urgent was way better than dealing with her wounded eyes. "What's his name? Or rather company name?"

He was an expert at corporate law. He'd specialized this time around, taking on no partners who could potentially fuck his wife and then take his business over. He was a high-priced consultant. His only real courtroom work anymore was when his friends needed him. He'd recently dealt with a tenancy issue for Sean Taggart's restaurant, Top, and managed to get Case Taggart's speeding tickets taken care of. Dude needed less road rage. So he didn't get a whole ton of walk-in clients. It was usually Big Tag trying to get him to sue someone who had pissed him off. He only tried the lawsuits because his wife, Charlotte, had forbidden assassinations.

Yep, this was his world. He wasn't sure sweet Laurel Daley fit into it. No. That wasn't right. He didn't want Laurel in it. She should be married with a few babies, depending on a husband who loved her and only her and had never made the kinds of mistakes Mitch had made.

"He's with a firm called Dixon Technologies."

It didn't ring a bell, but he often dealt with tech firms. They constantly had intellectual property issues. "Send him in."

"All right. I'll try to put aside my daddy issues long enough to go out there and give him directions to your office."

When she turned that smart mouth on him his cock pulsed, but then it pretty much did that whenever she walked into a room. He was thirty-eight. She wasn't even thirty. Why couldn't his dick pick a more appropriate focus?

*Because I want that one. God, just fucking look at her, man. Look at those breasts. Firm. Round. So sweet. And that bratty mouth. Come on, hands. Aren't you itching to smack that pretty ass?*

"Laurel." He put a little bite to his tone.

She turned immediately and her eyes slid to the floor before coming back up. She steeled herself as though she needed to remember not to defer to him. Yeah, his dick liked that, too. He'd realized his mistake about five minutes after she walked through his door. Laurel was a natural submissive. She deferred to those around her, sometimes to the point of burying her own needs. It was exactly the kind of thing a well-meaning Dominant partner could help her with. A Dom with good intentions, who loved and cared for her, would protect her and teach her how valuable she was.

"What?" Her chin came up and a stubborn glint hit her eyes.

He knew her well enough at this point to know this was Laurel trying to shove her emotions deep. He'd said something that hurt her. He should gather her up and put her in his lap and stroke her hair while he apologized. Unfortunately, that would lead to fucking her on his desk, so he settled for words. "I don't suppose you heard the part of the conversation where I talked about how I wanted you to be happy?"

She was obviously unmoved. "Nope and I know you have a very creative mind so I'll suspend my disbelief." She stopped and her mouth softened slightly. "I take it you found out about me joining the trainee program at Sanctum."

"I don't think it's a good idea. I don't think it's professional for the two of us to be at the same club together. I count on that club, Laurel. The few friends I have in life are there."

"All right. I'll let them know I won't be coming anymore." She took a deep breath and there was a hollowness to her expression he despised. It was only there for a moment and then her face was a polite blank. "Do you need anything? Coffee? You skipped lunch. I could get you a sandwich."

"Just like that? You'll leave it like that? I expected more of a fight out of you."

She shook her head. "I didn't join to cause you harm or to take something away from you. I joined because I wanted to explore that side of myself. Since you've made it plain that my presence takes away from your enjoyment of something you need, I'll leave."

How did she do this to him? She'd had him in knots since the moment he'd met her. "Could you give me a couple of minutes to catch up? I didn't even know you were interested in the lifestyle."

Now her inner brat made an appearance, those pretty blue eyes rolling. "Of course you did, Mitchell. That's a complete cop out and unworthy of you, counselor. If you're going to defend yourself at least do it properly. You've known I was interested in D/s since the moment you hired me."

He had. He'd found books by Sanctum's resident authors, Amber Rose and Dakota Cheyenne. Silly pen names for Serena Dean-Miles and Laurel's sister-in-law, Bridget Daley. Bridget was the one who had sparked Laurel's interest, though he'd rather thought it had all been a means to an end. "I thought it was really me you were interested in."

She stepped back in his office. The whole place had been redecorated. It had been a dull beige with brown carpets and fixtures from the seventies when he'd bought it and he'd done nothing to update until Laurel had taken the project over. Now the whole office was modernized, with the exception of his desk. Laurel had tried to get rid of it, but he'd put his foot down. His crappy old chair had been replaced with something ergonomic. A week in he'd noticed his shoulder didn't hurt anymore after a long day. He'd also noticed how the brighter colors had livened up the place, given it an elegance and grace that matched the woman who had overseen its design.

"You've made it very clear that you're not interested in pursuing a relationship with me, Mitch. You made it clear that night. I've stayed away since then."

The night he'd gotten slightly drunk in Hawaii and kissed her. It had been her brother's impromptu wedding that had done it. He'd been Will Daley's best man and watched as his friend married the woman of his dreams. Sure Will had some surly, mouthy and bratty dreams, but Bridget was also creative and funny and kind.

A lot like Laurel.

Watching Will get married made him wonder what it would have been like if he'd met Laurel before. Before his divorces. Before life had ground him down. When she'd joined him on the beach, he hadn't been able to resist pulling her into his arms and finally tasting her mouth. He could still feel how soft she was, how her body had fit perfectly against his. And he could still see how hurt she'd been when he'd pushed her away.

"That night was a mistake. I shouldn't have kissed you."

Her eyes slid away from his. "Yes, you've mentioned it a couple of times."

"So why join my club?"

"Because it's the only one I'm allowed to join. I tried to find another one. My brother took exception."

Mitch felt his stomach drop. "You went to another club?"

She shrugged. "I knew you wouldn't like me going to Sanctum. Honestly, I thought it was weird going to a club with my brother, too. So I found another one out in the suburbs. Horrible, actually. Anyway, I went twice and Will found out and he showed up and hauled me out. It was horrifically embarrassing. I spent some time on a website, but nothing panned out. Bridget invited me to Sanctum and then I think with all the babies they needed subs who were willing to work the daycare, so I signed on. I might still offer to work with the babies. I've grown quite fond of them."

He was stuck on the fact that not only had she gone to some club he knew nothing about, but she'd spent time on the Internet. "What did you do, Laurel? Did you upload a profile at FetLife? Maybe advertise on Craig's List for a Dom? Do you want someone to murder you? Because that's pretty much what you're asking for."

Her jaw firmed, eyes flashing, and he was pretty sure this was one of those times it would have been better to take a step back and measure his words. "I wanted to figure myself out, you giant ass. What right do you have to tell me what I can and…" Another deep breath. "It no longer matters. I'll let Mr. Dixon know you can see him now."

"Laurel, we're not done discussing this."

Her eyes narrowed and he was sure she was about to tell him where he could shove it when a thin man with wire-framed glasses stepped into the doorway.

"Mr. Bradford, thank god. It's imperative that I speak with you."

He wasn't done with Laurel. He needed to make her understand that the way she was going about this wasn't good.

And how should she go about it? He'd told her she couldn't go to the safest place. Then told her she couldn't go anywhere else either. She was trying to figure herself out. If she meant those words, how could he hold her back? Didn't she deserve the same chance he'd had?

*No. Laurel is supposed to be normal. Laurel is supposed to not need the rough stuff because she's a sweet princess. Wake up. This is what you do. You put a woman on a pedestal. You aren't sexually liberated. You're still the same pathetic boy who wanted his father to take two seconds with him.*

Now who had daddy issues?

"Mr. Bradford?" the man asked.

"Laurel," he said, more softly this time. "Can we please discuss this further?"

She shook her head. "There's no need. I'll keep my private life private from now on."

"Hey, I'm serious about needing to talk," the man said, his shoulders straightening.

"In a minute, buddy." He needed to talk to Laurel. He didn't like the look in her eyes. In that moment he realized the only thing worse than having Laurel around was not having her around. If she quit, he wouldn't be able to watch out for her. He wouldn't know where she was or what she was getting into—like offering herself up on the fucking Internet. "Laurel, let's talk."

"No. I need to talk, damn it." The thin man had turned a brilliant shade of red and sweat had broken out on his forehead. "You have to listen to me, Bradford. My brother is going to kill you. Harvey has sworn to not stop trying until you and everyone you love is dead."

The room seemed to chill.

"Okay, then. Why don't you sit down?" It looked like his talk with Laurel was going to have to wait.

\* \* \* \*

Thank god for crazy people and their death threats. Laurel Daley sat down and was very aware that most people wouldn't be happy that their boss had been threatened, but it was a well-timed announcement. She'd been about to cry and she'd promised herself she wouldn't do that over Mitchell Bradford anymore.

Besides, it certainly wouldn't be the first time someone had threatened to kill her cantankerous boss. Hell, she thought about doing the deed herself about ten times a day. She was thinking about doing it now.

What right did he have to tell her she couldn't go to Sanctum? Asshole. Selfish prick.

*She's a bright light, Kai. She's one of those people you can't help but adore.*

Selfish prick who said the sweetest things when he thought no one was listening. He was also a selfish prick with serious insecurities, with a truckload of baggage it looked like she wasn't going to be able to plow through.

"I understand your brother is angry with me," Mitch was

saying. He was back behind the massive desk he hadn't allowed her to get rid of. It was a refugee from the 1960's, when apparently men compensated with large oak desks instead of sports cars. At least she'd been able to get rid of his crappy chair and replace it with one that wouldn't mangle his spinal cord. "I'm a lawyer. A lot of people get angry with me."

"It's in his job description," she quipped.

His dark eyes moved her way, and it took all she had not to fall to the floor in a submissive pose. But she wasn't going to. Nope. Not for him.

"As I was saying, my line of work tends to bring out the worst in people, but I'll admit I don't remember your brother. You said his name was Harvey? Harvey Dixon?"

"We don't have a file on him, sir," Laurel said, knowing damn well that the "sir" would get his motor running, and that was why she merely meant it as a politeness. She wasn't even thinking of capitalizing the word the way she would with Master Ian or Master Liam. If Mitch wanted the relationship professional, then he better get used to a lowercase *s*.

He frowned at her, his handsome face going all gruff in a way that somehow managed to make him look more masculine. "How do you know? Do you have the files memorized now?"

She could have them memorized if she wanted to, but that would cut into her reading time. "Nope. I checked my tablet. I scanned in all the files and where they're stored about a month after you hired me. We're fully automated."

His brows formed that *V* he got whenever something confused and disturbed him. "No one told me. I don't think that's a very good idea."

He was often like the old guy on his lawn shaking his fist at those young people. For a superman of not even forty, he was very adverse to change. "And that's why I didn't tell you."

She often had to go around her gorgeous grump in order to get anything done. Mitch had a smoking body and the finest legal mind she'd ever met, but he also had a few quirks, and he could be a massive ass when he wanted to be.

"You can't go around destroying my files."

"Good god, Mitchell. I didn't destroy the files. I scanned them in. Please tell me you don't think that involves the computer eating the files or something."

"Of course not." The look in Mitch's eyes told her he would have a discussion with her after this was over. Which was good since she intended to have a discussion with him, too.

He turned back to their guest. "Why do you believe your brother intends to kill me?"

Patrick Dixon shifted in his chair, his hands nervously moving along the arms. "Well, my first indication was when he told me he was going to spend the rest of his life trying to rip your heart from your chest, eat it and then…well, the rest is all digestion but he used much more crude language."

"He wants to shit my heart out?" Mitch asked, his eyes rolling. "Like I never heard that one before. Is there a reason he wants me in his bowels?"

"He shouldn't given how much red meat you eat. It might be harder to pass than he thinks." She tried to force him to work a salad in every now and then.

Dixon ignored her. "My brother considers himself quite the inventor. Over the years he's been awarded twenty-two different patents. He's a brilliant engineer, but he prefers to work for himself, and the patents have never panned out, if you know what I mean."

"Just because you patent something doesn't mean you're going to make money from it," Mitch replied.

"Exactly." Patrick sighed as though this was something he'd thought about long and hard. "Some of his inventions didn't have much use or purpose in the real world. We managed to get a few of his ideas to market, but it wasn't enough for Harvey. He always thought about the ones that got away. A few of his more brilliant ideas were taken by large companies."

Mitch shook his head. "Was he working for them at the time? Are you trying to say they stole his patents?"

"No. While my brother is very smart, his processes can be a bit convoluted, difficult to understand."

"Ah," Mitch said with a nod. "So someone swoops in and refines the idea, changes the process so it's easier to produce the wanted effect."

"It's not fair," Patrick said, his hands forming fists.

Mitch shrugged. "A patent applies to a process for bringing about a result. It doesn't apply to the result itself. Otherwise, we'd have monopolies all over the place on manufacturing. If someone took your brother's ideas and made them simpler, easier to get to market, then they win the prize. It's Edison vs. Tesla."

This was why she'd hung around. Mitch was brilliant and all that law knowledge seemed to have taken up the majority of space in his brain. He didn't have a whole lot of tact. He obviously couldn't see that Dixon was on the edge of an emotional outburst.

Laurel leaned forward and patted the man's arm. "I'm so sorry to hear that. It must have been very frustrating for him."

Dixon immediately calmed, his eyes sad now but resolute. "It is, Miss Daley. It's hard to watch someone you care about struggle. I have to admit that my brother isn't the most stable of people. He's brilliant but not stable."

She couldn't say that about her boss. Yes, he was gruff and he obviously didn't put any stock in chemistry and wouldn't know the prefect sub if she bit him in the ass—actually she hadn't tried that—but Mitchell Bradford was stable. Since the day she'd met him, he'd been the man who walked her to her car every day, even if it was afternoon, even when he wasn't leaving himself. He was the one who wanted a text to make sure she'd made it home all right. Mitch was the one who flipped out when he realized her car had a warning light that had been blinking away for six weeks. He was also the one who took her car down himself because he didn't trust mechanics to not take advantage of her.

"None of this explains why I'm his target. Or why he has a target at all," Mitch said gruffly.

Dixon leaned forward. "You have to understand that Harvey has always had big dreams. He would make a little money and then spend it all on the next invention because he didn't want to simply be comfortable. He wanted to be rich, famous. He's had many offers over the years for stable employment but he turned them all down because his wealth was always right around the corner."

Laurel understood the type. "He was always swinging for the fences because getting on base wasn't enough, right?"

Dixon nodded. "Exactly. That seemed to work during his twenties, but he got involved with drugs at some point and it went downhill. He became paranoid. He worked less, but was angrier about the failures. Then two years ago he started working on a way to store solar power."

"The Bentley Industries project." Laurel immediately pulled up the file. As solar energy became an actual option for individual homes, the issue of storage had become a problem. Engineers had been trying to find a way to store up energy for longer periods of time so the houses with the capability could be more self-reliant rather than having to switch back to the electricity grid. So sunny summer days could be saved to power winter days. Bentley Industries had recently filed for a patent on a system that would allow for solar storage of up to a month and had confidence they could refine the process to go much longer.

Mitchell Bradford was their attorney and stood to gain a percentage of the profits. He'd also been the spokesman for the company when they'd done the talk show rounds.

"Yes," Patrick agreed. "I don't even think Harvey was close to anything, but he's decided this was his last shot. He's back on drugs and he believes that Mitch somehow stole his idea. I tried to go to the police, but they said there was no proof and when they talked to Harvey, he was in one of his lucid stages. He can be very convincing when he's like that. I've been his partner for twenty years and I've never seen him so angry."

"What makes you think this isn't just talk, Mr. Dixon?" Mitch asked. If it bugged him that someone wanted him dead, he didn't show it. His gorgeous face was as passive as it was when he talked about the weather.

But once it had been animated and fierce. She couldn't forget the possessive look that had lit those dark eyes as he'd lowered his lips to hers and devoured her like a starving man.

She shook her head because every time she thought about their one and only kiss, the room seemed to heat up. It had been months, but she could still feel the way his hands had tightened on her body as though he would never let her go.

He had, of course, and now he was quite good at evading her web of seduction. Or maybe she wasn't any good at the seduction part.

"It's a feeling," Patrick was saying. "I know that something is off with him. I truly believe he's going to make an attempt on your life. You have to be careful. I don't think I'll be able to stop him."

The poor man was shaking. Laurel leaned over and put a hand on his. "It's all right. We'll look into it. Thank you so much for telling us about the threat. I can't imagine what it cost you to come in this afternoon."

"He's my brother." Patrick sniffled slightly and that sent Laurel running for a tissue. Naturally Mitch didn't have any. He tried to pawn off anyone who looked like they would get even vaguely emotional on her, so she excused herself. She kept a box in her office.

That was when she saw the man in the lobby. A hoodie was pulled down over his face. He stood in the hallway outside their doors. The building housed several businesses. This particular floor was shared by their office, a dentist, and an accounting agency.

He was probably looking for the dentist. He was dressed too casually for business.

She grabbed the tissues off Sharon's desk and was about to turn when the man suddenly shifted toward her.

The hoodie covered his eyes, but she wasn't really looking at him anymore. Nope. She was standing stock-still at the sight of what was in his hands.

A gun.

She managed to scream right before he pulled the trigger.

# Chapter Two

"Derek, I want this asshole found. Do you understand?" Three hours later, Mitch could still feel his heart pounding.

Harvey Dixon had taken a shot at Laurel. He'd shot at her through the ceiling to floor glass windows the real estate agent who had sold him on this building had sworn gave the place a professional feel.

They gave the place a clear line of sight to shoot into it. He was done with that shit. Steel-enforced walls. He would have them put in as soon as possible. Surely Big Tag knew some crazy doomsday preppers who could outfit his office with everything one would need to keep out people who shot at his paralegal.

"He understands, Mitch. You've yelled at him for an hour," Laurel said with a sigh.

Derek Brighton, a lieutenant with the Dallas Police Department, merely shook his head. "He can yell all he likes. He's had a scare."

"I was the one who nearly got shot and no one even offered me a lollipop." Laurel looked sulky at the thought.

The EMT had offered her more than a lollipop, Mitch was sure. The kid couldn't have been much past twenty-five and he'd flirted like mad with Laurel before declaring her perfectly fine.

"And I want another EMT. She needs to go to the hospital." That was what people who got shot did. She'd almost been shot. Maybe the kid had spent so much time flirting with her that he'd missed a gunshot wound. It could happen. Adrenaline could make a person ignore pain.

He wanted to run his hands over her himself. It had been his first instinct. He'd needed to feel her skin under his palm, to make sure she was warm and alive. He'd pulled her up, but before he could get her in his arms, she'd stepped back, keeping a professional distance between them.

"I think I might send you to the hospital, buddy. You look like you might have a heart attack. Why don't you sit down, Mitch?" Derek was a friend from Sanctum. He'd shown up with the first responders, having recognized the address. "You're going to wear a hole in the carpet."

"I don't want to sit." He still might have a damn heart attack. Since that moment he'd heard the glass cracking and realized what that sound had really been, his heart had kicked into overdrive. He'd run out into reception only to find Laurel on the ground. It had taken him a moment to realize she wasn't hurt. Before she'd turned over and reached a hand up, he'd thought she was dead.

Hollow. The world for a moment had been so utterly hollow.

"All right, well, I think we have what we need. I hate to tell you this, but it wasn't Harvey Dixon. I just got a report that he's in a rehab facility and has been for the last two weeks. I informed his brother and he's already on his way over. Turns out he hadn't talked to him lately. He found some stuff Harvey had written in a journal a couple of months back. Besides, we've got this guy on camera. He's a good twenty years younger than Harvey Dixon. The dentist next door says he's had some trouble with break-ins. Kids come looking for drugs. He claims to have complained to the landlord but apparently the landlord is a difficult asshole. His words, not mine."

Mitch sighed. He was the freaking landlord. "Trust me. I'll have a new security system complete with those eye scan things. No one's getting in here again."

"That could be bad for business," Laurel said with a sigh.

"Yeah, well, I don't care about business anymore." Except he better because until his new ventures started coming in, he had one ex-wife who would haul him in front of a California judge if he missed her alimony check.

Derek held out a hand. "I'll get this kid. He was probably high. I already have some officers canvassing the area to see if he's local. I'll check with the other buildings. I saw some security cameras up and down the street. We might be able to get a better view of him. You want me to give Big Tag a call?"

Big Tag had recently had a set of twins. Another reason to never get a woman pregnant. Sometimes they gave birth to litters. "Nah. If Harvey Dixon is actually locked up in rehab, I suppose we're all right. Can someone inform me if he checks himself out?"

"I've already asked the facility to let me know. He's there on court-ordered rehab, so he can't leave unless he wants to spend his time in prison instead. I'll monitor the situation and let you know what I find out. I'll also check phone records and see if he's called anyone, but Dixon was fairly certain he was after you, so I don't see why he would take a shot at Laurel." Derek gave Laurel a smile. "I'm thrilled you weren't horribly murdered. If you're still up for it, Karina and I will be at your place at eight on Friday, okay?"

Laurel paled. "Oh, actually I'm not going to be able to go, but thanks. Please tell Karina hello for me."

Derek's eyes narrowed. "You all right?"

Laurel nodded. "Yes, something came up. I can't go on Friday."

"Okay, but if you change your mind or you want to go on Saturday, we'll be there. With Will and Bridget at that conference of hers, you call me if you need a ride." Derek nodded and strode out.

Everyone had known about Laurel's foray into submission with the exception of him.

Sharon walked in. His secretary was in her mid-fifties and was much more worried about her grandkids and their myriad of social activities than she was about working, but every time he tried to fire her Laurel intervened. She was his tenth secretary in the last four years and it looked like he needed a new one. "Okay, I called the glass company and they're sending someone out tonight to fix the glass. He can't be here until after six and I have to be at Afton's school play, so someone's going to have to stay to let them in."

The poorly named Afton was actually a boy, but that didn't matter to Mitch. "I didn't give you those orders, Sharon, and I don't want glass."

"No, I did and I've already approved the amount. We are not turning this office into a steel-reinforced bunker." For a woman who had recently been shot at, Laurel was surprisingly on top of things.

He should have known she would plot against him. This was what life with Laurel would be like. Every day was a minor war between the two of them. He wanted steak and potatoes for lunch and she ordered in some kind of salad. He wanted a filing system he understood and she computerized everything. He wanted her to not be shot and she made arrangements for windows and possibly hunting blinds throughout the office. He wouldn't put it past her. She would do it to challenge his authority. He was putting his foot down. "We're closing up the windows and that's that."

Sharon smiled and utterly ignored him. "Okay then, Laurel. I'll see y'all tomorrow. But not too early. I want to go with Denise and the baby to her doctor's appointment. I'm going to be a grandma again."

She walked out and he was left shaking his head. "How many does that make? Are her children rabbits?"

"Seven," Laurel shot back. "She has three kids and seven lovely grandchildren. They're all very sweet."

Another reason to step back from Laurel. She wanted babies. He didn't want babies. The last thing he was going to do with his life was ruin some kid's. His childhood had been a long series of short-term stays with his mother and her revolving door of boyfriends, and the occasional card from his father. No. He wasn't going to inflict that on anyone.

"I don't want windows. People can shoot at you through windows," he said. It looked like it would be a long night. He started after Sharon. The woman could move when she wanted to get out of work. She was down the stairs and out of the building before he knew it. "And that woman is fired."

Laurel followed him, her heels clacking on the stairs. "You can't fire her. Why would you even want to? Because she's not coming in until late? You don't have a single appointment tomorrow. You should be happy. You've scared everyone off."

He liked not having appointments. It made his day much nicer to not have to deal with people. "I'm firing her because she took too long for lunch. If she'd been at her desk, she could have handed you the tissue and then you wouldn't have spooked the crackhead. So she's fired." He swiftly locked the door and set the security alarm that was getting a serious upgrade in the morning.

When he turned, Laurel was standing on the bottom step. They were completely alone in the building he'd bought with pretty much everything he'd had left after the divorce from Joy, aspiring actress and expert at manipulating men. If she'd been half as good at auditions as she'd been in the courtroom, she wouldn't have needed half his assets and three grand a month in alimony.

"I should call your brother." Now that he was alone with her, his heart was still pounding but his dick was pulsing too. He couldn't forget how still she'd been, how there'd been blood on her arms from the glass cutting her. "I would feel better if he looked you over instead of that hormonal puppy who practically humped your leg instead of properly examining you."

"Mitchell, he was gay. We were talking about how much he liked my shoes."

He frowned. "Really?"

"No, not really. He asked me out, but the truth of the matter is it's none of your business and we're not calling my brother because he's with Bridget in Chicago. She's at book convention being worshipped for the goddess she is. I'm fine. You should head home. I'll handle the contractor. They're coming in with pre-cut glass so it shouldn't take them long at all."

"I'm not going anywhere and I'm serious about reinforcing our doors."

She turned and sighed. "We won't get any of the natural light from the skylight if you do that. You'll turn the entire reception area into a gloomy cave. It will utterly ruin everything the decorator did in the last six months."

That was where he had her. "Yeah, well it won't matter because I'm filling in the skylight, too." There was a massive glass structure on the roof that filtered light down through the building. The four-story building had a courtyard style setting in the middle and glass elevators that ran up the back. That glass over his head might be pretty, but now he was thinking of all the ways assassins could break through and enter, and his security system wouldn't protect anyone at all. "I'm calling Taggart in the morning and having him redo security for the whole building. I'm going to need you to make a couple of those lemon cakes he likes. Even with a discount the big bastard is ridiculously expensive."

She turned and her face was in a fierce frown. Her golden brown hair was slightly disheveled. Sex hair. It looked like she had sex hair instead of almost-got-murdered hair. "I am not going to help you do something like that. Do you know how hard I've worked to make this a nice place? Do you even care?" Tears shone in her eyes and she shook her head. "You don't. You couldn't care less that the office is beautiful now. Nothing I do matters. You know what? You can keep Sanctum. I'll find my own place and Will is going to have to be all right with it. Hell, maybe I'll talk to Master T and he'll train me privately."

She pivoted on her heels and started back up the stairs.

His gut rolled with anger. He was doing everything in order to keep her safe and she was treating him like this? "Laurel! Stop right where you are."

She kept moving. "I don't have to. You're not my Dom. You're not my boyfriend."

"I'm your boss."

"Not anymore. I quit. I'm not staying in a place where I work my ass off but my boss doesn't care. You don't want me but you won't let anyone else have me."

They were going to do this here? He started up after her, his blood pressure ticking up every second she didn't turn around and fight with him. He stepped up the pace because they weren't done. He knew even as he thought it that it was perverse. He knew he couldn't have her, knew he should be happy that she was leaving and taking temptation out of his path. But all he could think about was the fact that if she quit, he wouldn't have her in his life. He wouldn't be able to watch over her. Not again. She was trouble. A lot of trouble. She didn't search it out, but it seemed to follow her around.

He pounded up the stairs, disregarding all the alarms that were going off in his head. It was a mistake to follow her. His palm was itching, his cock threatening to take over. She was pushing all his buttons and she had been all damn day. He hadn't missed the way she'd called him sir. She knew exactly what she was doing.

And the entire idea of her being at Sanctum both disturbed and titillated him. What if they could compartmentalize their relationship? What if they could make it work? If he put her under a contract, he could control how much influence she had on his life.

"Laurel!"

She stomped her way back to the office she'd spent six months turning into something warm and inviting. It wasn't that he didn't understand the work she'd put into it. It was just that now all he would be able to see was her on that floor. He'd only be able to see how many different ways someone could get to her.

She held a hand up. That wouldn't have been so bad if she hadn't only had a single finger sticking up. Yes. She was giving him the finger.

He had a couple of things to give to her. His blood started to thrum through his system and his good sense was beginning to seem like a far-off thing. Up ahead he could see the way her hips swayed and how perfectly she walked in those four-inch heels. It made him wonder what else she could do.

She'd almost died. Some asswipe had leveled a gun at her and pulled the trigger and only her quick movements had saved her life. She could be dead. She could be gone, her unique kindness and beauty stopped by a single bullet.

He should have been questioning himself, but it no longer mattered. She'd pushed him past thought and into action. He hadn't had the chance to save her before. She'd been on her own in a place that should have been safe for her. But he could take action now.

She turned at the door and there was a sudden flare of fear in her eyes that sent a thrill through his system. She was finally aware of him. She wasn't looking at him like some sad sack she could push around, but like the predator he'd always hidden from her.

He had to give her one more way out. His cock was threatening to pound out of his slacks, but he still had enough willpower and common sense to give her a shot at coming out of this whole. "If you very politely apologize, I'll walk you to you car and you can leave, Laurel. We can talk about this in the morning like sane adults."

"And if I don't?"

"Don't push me again, Laurel. I've had enough. You push me one more time and you're going to see a side of me you don't want to see." For the second time that day, adrenaline pounded through his system.

*Come on, baby. Push me again. Let me take over.*

His dick was so close to getting what it wanted. All these months and it had been ruthlessly controlled, tamped down and put on a leash. Hell, since he'd met Laurel he hadn't taken a lover, not even for a night. He didn't want anyone else. He wanted her and if she pushed him one more time, he could chuck his morality for the night and have her. He'd given her every out. She was a smart girl and he'd given her control. All she had to do was make the sensible choice for both of them.

"Fuck you, Mitch."

Decision made. He fell on her like a hungry lion.

* * * *

Laurel's whole body came alive when Mitch's muscular body pressed her against the door. She could feel the wood at her back, but there was more at her front. He was hard, his cock already thick, and he didn't hold it back. It was pressed against her belly, insistently telling her that no matter what happened, nothing was going to be the same after tonight.

"I fucking warned you. I won't stop this time. I won't play the gentleman again," he whispered before his mouth descended on hers.

Thank god. Six months. They'd passed and every night she dreamed about what they could have had if he hadn't played the damn gentleman that night in Hawaii. They'd wasted six months. Six months when she could have felt him against her, when she could have had the heat of his body to warm her own. They could have been sleeping together, sharing a life beyond the confines of this office.

His lips found hers and he was ravenous. He slanted over her mouth again and again, dominating and taking what he wanted. His tongue surged in and she could feel that slow slide in her womb.

Just like that she was wet and ready. Her body felt malleable, as though it knew this man was the one who could mold her and bring her to fruition. Every inch of her body felt primed. Her nipples rasped against the fabric of her bra, her breasts heavy and wanting.

Her clothes were suddenly too tight and she wanted nothing more than to throw them off. She didn't need clothes around him.

A sudden vision of what it would be like now that Mitch was finally claiming her stamped itself in her brain. She could hear him commanding her to be naked when they were alone. She would curl up at his feet as they relaxed. It would be the two of them and they wouldn't have to argue. They would be together.

His hands found her backside, squeezing. A low groan ground out of his mouth as he explored her. She could feel herself softening, offering herself up for his slow exploration. This was the man who would finally teach her what all the fuss was about.

Mitch pushed her to be better than she was, to think more clearly about points of law and to challenge herself to greater heights. She'd always known it would be the same in the bedroom. She'd had lovers before, but sex had been something to do, a way to show affection. Sex with Mitch was a force of freaking nature.

He pressed her against the door. His mouth was a marauder, plunging in and taking what he wanted. His hands gripped her hips and suddenly she felt her feet leave the ground. Mitch had a good half a foot on her, but it didn't seem to matter. He simply lifted her to where he wanted her to be.

"Feel that. That's what you fucking do to me," he growled against her mouth.

His cock. His very large cock, from the feel of it, was pressed right against her pussy. She had to gasp when he ground that big erection against her clit.

She intended to give as good as she got. "You can't tell what you do to me because there are way too many clothes between us."

"Tell me, Laurel. Tell me how wet your pussy is." His voice had gone deep, smooth and richer than normal. This was his Dom voice and it made her obey with ease.

"So wet. My pussy is already soft and wet for you, Sir."

"Do you want my cock?"

"I want everything," she answered honestly. She wanted him to take her in every way a man could take a woman. She wanted long nights where they simply explored their boundaries. She'd been fooling herself. Sanctum wouldn't mean anything without Mitchell as her Master. She only wanted to submit to him and only in the bedroom. She wanted to be his partner out of it. He needed her. He needed her to push him past his shell and she needed him for so many things. She needed the safety she'd found with him. No one had ever taken care of her the way he did.

His hips kept moving as he kissed his way across her face. He licked the lobe of her ear. Damn but that felt good. He nipped her before lifting her easily. "Put your legs around me. I don't want to wait. I can't. I need to be inside you. I've waited too fucking long."

She did as he asked because she'd waited too long, too. Months of yearning made her reckless. She wrapped her legs around his waist, forcing her skirt up around her upper thighs. She could already feel the way her panties were damp and clinging. She was going to make a mess of his slacks, but it didn't matter. Her brain couldn't wrap itself around anything but how good he felt as he held her up and opened the door.

He strode through the office she'd worked so hard to turn into something comfortable for him, past her own office where she kept the set of legal books Mitch had bought for her when she'd finished her paralegal certification classes. He'd said anyone who could put up with him while she attended school deserved something. Most women would see them as a simple tool, but the law was the only thing Mitch truly loved, and sharing it with her had been an act of affection on his part.

She could see through him, see to the softer side of the man. Why had it taken him this long to acknowledge that they were good together?

He strode into his office, her weight not holding him back at all. She'd watched him as he played basketball with her brother and their friends, so she knew the strength that lay under his white dress shirts. Always white with black slacks. He had what must be fifteen pairs. The only things that changed were his ties.

He kissed her as he moved toward his desk. Their tongues melded and there was nothing awkward. She'd always found kissing awkward, a little messy. She was never sure what to do with her hands or how to move. She didn't have to with Mitchell. He took over. He moved and she followed as though they'd done this a thousand times before.

Heat flashed through her system. She'd never been so aroused in her life. It was like all the tension of the day, of the last six months, was being crushed under a tidal wave of desire. Her blood thrummed through her system, waking up parts of her body she'd never thought of as sexual. When he touched her back, she shivered all along her spine.

She heard a crash and realized Mitch had shoved everything off the top of his big desk. He set her there, one arm around her at all times. Even in his passion, he was gentle with her, making sure she was safe. Now she could see the advantages to the massive thing as he settled her on it. He didn't stop kissing her for a second. Their mouths moved together, tongues sliding and playing.

His big body was in between her legs, forcing them apart as his hand moved under her skirt. She felt his palm on her thigh, moving up and up to where she needed him to be. Her head fell back as his fingers moved under the waistband of her undies and started to slide over her labia.

"You're so wet," he groaned against her neck.

"I told you, Sir. I've never been this wet before." Only for him. He invaded her every thought, all her dreams. She had no idea why this surly, gloriously masculine misanthrope did it for her, but he did. Chemistry. They had it in spades. Mitch walking into a room could make her temperature spike.

He moved back and she watched as he pulled his soaked fingers from her core and brought them up to his nose. He breathed her in deep. "God, you smell like fucking sunshine, Laurel." He sucked them inside his mouth, licking her essence off. "And you taste even better. I knew you would. I knew you would be the sweetest thing I'd ever tasted."

"Please, Mitch." She knew she was begging, but she couldn't do the whole foreplay thing. She needed him. They'd waited far too long to take their time.

His face turned savage. "Yes, I think it's about fucking time I pleased Mitch."

His hand went to the buckle of his belt and he shoved his slacks and boxers down with a single thrust, his cock jutting out. She caught a brief glimpse of the gorgeous monster before he was kissing her again. His fingers were back on her pussy, but he seemed to be pushing her undies aside…and then he was there.

Oh, she had to force herself to breathe as she felt the broad head of his cock start to push its way inside.

Alarms bells started to go off in her head, but they were a distant thing. She clutched at his arms, feeling the muscles of his big biceps through the fabric. She loved how his daily wardrobe hid the gloriously masculine body underneath. It made her want to unwrap him, to slowly rid him of the garments until he was naked in front of her and there was nothing else between them.

She longed to throw off her clothes, but the moment was coming too fast. It was like life had sped up the minute she'd started to climb those stairs. Anger had fueled her and she'd wanted nothing more in that moment but to piss him off. He pushed her buttons, too. Sometimes she thought they were gasoline and fire. They could fight until they were blue in the face but neither one would leave.

But this, this was what it had all led up to.

"God, Laurel, you're so tight." He gripped her hips and pushed in.

She could barely breathe. "I'm perfectly normal. You're too big. God, don't stop, Mitch."

One of his hands found her hair, tangling in it and pulling her head back. There was the tiniest bite to his hold that had her scalp lighting up with sensation. "Even here you argue with me."

For a second she felt like he was disappointed, but the moment passed as he forced his cock in another inch. He kissed her again and she held on for dear life as he thrust in using small movements. In and out. Gaining ground with each pass. He was so big. She was stretched and super wet, but he still was almost too much for her.

"I'm not going to last. You're too tight. Too long." His breath sawed from his chest. "Gotta make it good for you."

She bit her lip as he held himself still. His hand made its way between their bodies and then she was the one who was whimpering. His finger slid against her clitoris. He rubbed the pearly button while their mouths played together. His tongue slid inside as though trying to make up for the fact that his cock was still. Over and over he rubbed and played and the pressure built inside Laurel until she came, her body bowing, nails digging into his arms as she rode out the pleasure.

He moved his hand to her thigh and drove his cock deep. It was like she'd let him off the leash and he pounded inside her. She looked up and his eyes were closed, his head thrown back as he shoved in one last time and she felt heat streaming from him to her.

She looked up, ready for another kiss, another caress from him. They had all night. It might take forever to get enough of this man.

Mitch stared down at her. Just for a moment, his eyes were soft, as though he was utterly satisfied. That look was quickly replaced with tension and dawning regret as he took a step back, pulling up his slacks. "I can't believe we just did that."

"Mitchell?" She'd felt so sexy a moment before, utterly lost in the moment. But apparently the moment had passed and the Dom had left the building because it was Mitch's frown on that handsome face.

She sat up, her undies shifting back though they were soaked beyond repair at this point.

Soaked because Mitch hadn't used a condom.

Oh, god. They hadn't used a condom.

"Laurel, this was a mistake." He scrubbed a hand through his hair and turned away from her as if he couldn't stand to look at her another moment. "God, what did I do?"

She got up on shaky legs. "You simply did what was inevitable, Mitch. We've been moving toward this for six months."

His hands were fists at his sides. "I've been fighting to avoid this for six months, Laurel. I didn't want this. I didn't want any of this. God, am I ever going to grow the fuck up?"

Tears pricked her eyes and she tried to smooth out her skirt. It was a mess. She was a mess. She could still feel him inside her. Her mind was complete chaos, but her heart was a nasty, aching mess. How could he not have felt what she felt?

"I'm going home."

He finally turned to her, but he wouldn't look her in the eyes. "Yes, I think that's a good idea. We can forget this ever happened. We can go back to the way it was."

Go back to the way it was? Hardly. But she'd learned where arguing with him got her. It got her screwed. What he didn't realize was that she argued and fought with him because she cared about him, wanted the best for him.

Now she wanted to curl into a ball and cry because she'd been wrong. She'd thought if she could get him to make love to her, everything would fall into place.

Stupid. She'd been so stupid.

And she might pay the price. She tried to remember when her last period was.

"Laurel?"

She couldn't look at him. They hadn't even taken off their clothes. She'd thought at the time it was because they'd been too much in the moment, but now she knew he'd never had plans to slow down. She'd been a quick lay for him, a way to burn off the tension of the day.

He'd warned her. He'd told her he wasn't good enough for her. She could see now all the times he'd practically begged her to leave well enough alone. He'd told her he was too old for her, too damaged, and she hadn't listened. Even tonight he'd given her shot after shot of leaving well enough alone, but she had to poke the beast.

She'd learned her lesson.

"I'm fine, Mitch. I just want to get home and take a shower." Her voice sounded hollow even to her own ears. Devoid of emotion, which was a complete joke because she was weeping inside.

*Please hold it together. Don't let him see you cry. Don't. Don't make a bigger fool of yourself than you already have.*

"Laurel, I didn't use anything."

She was not having this conversation with him. "It's fine. It's not a problem."

For the first time she heard some relief in his voice. "Good. That's good. The last thing we need…"

She was out the door before he could finish that sentence. Yes, she'd been an idiot. There wasn't some soft Mitchell Bradford waiting under the surface. All of that had been spent on his two ex-wives, and all that was left for Laurel was a man who meant it when he said he didn't want another commitment, didn't want to even try to love her.

Or maybe he simply couldn't. He sure as hell had never lied to her about wanting marriage and kids. He'd been plain about that.

He'd never lied.

She'd lied to herself.

She grabbed her purse and her computer bag. "I'm going to take tomorrow off."

He was standing in his doorway, his shirt untucked and his eyes grave. "All right."

"I'll call and cancel the glass on my way home."

"Why? I thought it would stop the natural light or something."

She shook her head. "It's your office. You're the boss. I'll cancel it and you do what you like."

"Laurel, why don't we have a drink? I've got some Scotch. We fucked up. We should talk about it. Please, I'll let you handle the glass and stuff. You're better at that than I am. Come and sit with me and we'll talk about it."

He sounded so lost, like a little boy who didn't know what he wanted but he knew he didn't want to be alone.

She forced herself to turn away. "No. I need to go."

He followed her out the door and down the stairs. She didn't argue. He'd always walked her to her car. He wasn't going to change. Mitchell Bradford didn't change and it would do her well to remember that one rule of the universe.

She waited for him to shut off the alarm and then stepped out and into the parking lot. Her Honda was sitting next to his massive SUV. Even his car could rip hers apart.

"Laurel?"

She unlocked her car and turned to see him standing in front of the building. "What do you want, Mitchell?"

It was the question she should have asked before. She'd gone into her whole relationship with him asking what she wanted and having one answer—him. She'd never asked him what he wanted for the simple fact that she knew. He didn't want her.

He stared at her. "I'm so sorry, Laurel."

She nodded and got into her car. When she looked in the rearview mirror, he was still standing there.

She drove off, determined to never make the same mistake again.

# Chapter Three

Two weeks later Mitch stared at her through the big bay windows of The Legal Defense Aid office. Laurel was talking to some kid, probably right out of law school. He was tall and lanky, with a handsome face and stylish clothes. He probably didn't wear the same white shirt and black slacks day in and day out. Laurel smiled at him, her face vibrant. And then she turned to her sisters, obviously introducing them to the man. Lisa smiled and gave Laurel a wink that let Mitch know she liked the new guy.

Laurel was good. She was happy.

"Mitch? Are you going to go in?"

He took a deep breath before turning and facing the one person he didn't want to face. He'd been ducking Will Daley's calls for ten days, ever since he'd gotten back from Chicago. The demise of his relationship with Laurel was almost certainly the end of his friendship with Will, and damn but he would miss the guy. He turned and shook his head. "No. I was just checking in. I won't bother her."

He'd tried to bother her. He'd called and sent her e-mails, and all he'd gotten back was one terse reply.

*Thank you for you concern, Mr. Bradford. I'm quite well, but under the circumstances, I think it would be best for both of us if I quit. I'm attaching the resumes of two paralegals who would do quite well in my place. Please know I don't blame you. You were never anything less than honest with me. I was only fooling myself. I beg your forgiveness for quitting in such a cowardly way, but find I can't meet with you again. Also, you don't have to worry about meeting up with me again in a social fashion. I've let Mr. Taggart know I'm no longer interested in his club.*

*Yours,*
*LD*

An e-mail. He'd gotten an e-mail from her. He had to guess that was better than the divorce papers he'd gotten from his last two women.

"I'm having lunch with my sisters, but I can call and tell them I'm running later than usual if you need to talk. I could buy you a drink." Will gestured to the bar across the street. It looked like exactly the type of seedy place that fit in this part of town. Legal Defense Aid wasn't exactly a money-making venture, so their building wasn't in an upscale neighborhood.

He didn't like to think about Laurel here at night, but he doubted she would care that he was worried. And Will didn't have to worry either. "No need, buddy. I should get back to the office. She looks like she's settling in nicely. Like I said, I won't bother her again."

He turned to go, but Will stuck to his side like glue. "Yes, you said that. Tell me something. Did she finally push you too far and you fired her? What did she do? Go behind your back and change your lunch order? Because she's so good at that."

He'd had two weeks of getting to eat whatever he wanted. Two weeks of no one bugging him about his cholesterol or working too long.

It kind of sucked.

"She quit. She decided I was too surly to deal with." He was surprised she hadn't told her brother, but now that he thought about it, maybe he shouldn't be. She wouldn't want him to know any more than Mitch did. He wasn't about to tell his best friend that Laurel had taken exception to his lack of romantic tendencies.

He definitely wasn't going to tell anyone that he'd shown up on Monday morning and placed a dozen red roses and a box of her favorite Danishes on her desk.

And then waited. And waited. And at ten o'clock, he finally found her letter of resignation in his inbox.

No. He'd go to the grave with that information.

"Did something happen between the two of you?" Will asked. His voice was deceptively soft.

Mitch knew him well enough though. "I told you I didn't think a relationship between Laurel and I would work. I think she finally understood that I was serious and she chose to cut her losses."

And he would go to his grave remembering the feel of her wrapped around him. He would remember that for a moment he'd been bigger than himself, larger than he'd been before he'd taken her. For that one moment he'd been a part of her, and it had been the single most intimate episode of his life.

It had terrified him.

Will put a hand on his back as they made it to Mitch's SUV. "I told you she could be tenacious but once she's done, she's done. So you shouldn't have to worry about her any more."

"I like your sister, Will. I'm going to miss her." He already did. He felt alone without her. He was a man who craved solitude, but over the months Laurel had taught him he wanted a partner in his self-imposed bubble. He wanted her.

He simply shouldn't.

"Laurel is amazing, but she's so young. She's just starting out. I think you made the right choice. Mitch, you've done so much for her. She never would have gone back to school if it hadn't been for you. She's found a real passion and it shows. I don't think she ever would have found out how much she loves legal work without you."

"She would be a good lawyer. Encourage her to give law school a try." He had his keys in hand, ready to make a swift getaway, but he couldn't seem to help himself. "Are they paying her at the new place?"

Will chuckled. "Not much, but she's one of the few paid positions. She's doing a ton of the up-front work so the lawyers who are working pro bono don't have to."

A good paralegal like Laurel could do a lot of legal work all on her own. "That's good. If she ever wants to move back into a more lucrative position I can ask around, maybe find her a job."

"I'll keep that in mind. So where have you been hiding? You going to Sanctum tonight? It's the last weekend before the big reveal. I don't know if you've been working on it lately, but Big Tag has got some crazy shit in the new Sanctum. Did you know he put in a human hamster wheel? I'm a little afraid that's not for subs. I heard him saying something about shoving Adam Miles in it when he pisses Big Tag off."

He was certain the new Sanctum was going to be a mind trip. "I'm actually taking some time off. I'm buried in work over this solar deal."

He was working on the sale of the company Harvey Dixon had taken such exception to. It was one good thing that had come from Laurel quitting. He no longer had to worry about her getting in his line of fire.

Dixon was still in rehab, but weird things had started happening. His tires had been slashed three nights before. He'd called Derek, but there wasn't much he could do. He'd checked in on Dixon and then explained that three other vehicles had been vandalized in the area that very night. Kids?

He was paranoid, but that didn't mean someone wasn't out to get him. At least he no longer had to worry about Laurel.

Except he did. Every single night.

"Is there something I'm not getting here, Mitch?" Will was staring at him suspiciously.

Mitch shook his head and put his best game face on. "Nope. This is a very complex contract and I stand to make an enormous amount of money off it. Once this deal goes through, I might think about retiring, maybe go down to the coast and do some fishing."

Will's eyes had gone wide. "You don't fish."

He shrugged. "Just because I haven't before doesn't mean I won't in the future. This deal should set me up for a good long while as long as I'm not stupid enough to get married again. Hence the fishing."

"I'll believe it when I see it," Will said with a smile. "I hope you'll change your mind. I haven't seen you in weeks. Kai says he hasn't either. At least come to poker night if you don't want to play. Though I have heard there are a couple of new sub trainees."

And that was something he took exception to. "Including your sisters."

Will had the good grace to blush. His face screwed up as he

winced. "That was so not my idea. Laurel and Lisa got interested because of Bridget. They have very romantic notions about D/s. I almost had a heart attack when I found out they'd tried another club. Despite the fact that it's weird to see my sisters there, I'm happier having them at Sanctum. Thank god, Lila has a boyfriend and neither of them seem to have any interest in kink at all. Although now it seems Laurel has lost interest, too. She turned down her further training but asked if she could keep working there. I guess she likes babies more than Doms."

But she wouldn't always. He intended to leave Dallas in a few months after this deal was done and then everything would be open to her. Her one night with him would be nothing but a much-regretted mistake that would fade away once she found her soul mate. "I think she'll want to try eventually, but don't let Taggart put her with someone cold like Smith. Talk to Kai. Get involved. She needs a softer hand. Try someone her age."

Will was back to looking suspicious. "For someone who's not interested in my sister, you seem to have thought this through."

He shrugged. There wasn't much else to do. "She was my employee for…well, for longer than most. I've got to get going. I've got a couple of interviews this afternoon."

"You having a hard time replacing her?" Will asked.

"I'll never replace her." That was a stupid thing to say. "You know. I'll never find anyone as willing to argue with me. See you around."

He didn't like the way Will stared at him as he drove away. As though he was a puzzle. Will liked to solve puzzles.

It didn't matter. He had things to do and plans to make. Plans that didn't involve her.

\* \* \* \*

"Will's late. It's the doctor thing," Lila said with a frown on her pretty face. "They think they're all gods and we mere mortals should wait at their leisure."

Laurel thought Lila had been a nurse for way too long. "Or he's stuck in traffic."

Laurel kind of wished her brother would get here. She thought she'd seen his car pull up a few minutes before, but he hadn't walked in yet. She'd skipped breakfast and now she was shaky. She was totally ready for her neurologist brother and trauma nurse sister to pay for lunch. Especially since she'd taken a pay cut in order to salvage her pride.

"Where are we going?" Lisa asked as she stepped up, settling her purse on her shoulder. Her little sister was a senior in college, and she'd done it the hard way. She'd been working part time and going to school full time for most of her adult life, and it was all going to pay off in a few months. Baby sis was graduating with an MBA, and she was already in talks with Bridget's sister, Amy, about going to work for Slaten Industries.

"Mexican, please," Laurel said. She was totally willing to beg. "I've been dreaming about enchiladas all day."

"Is that why you didn't eat breakfast this morning?" Lila asked with a judgmental eye.

Yeah, it was awesome to live in the same apartment complex with her two sisters. Lila would show up randomly to make sure she was eating right. They'd had to watch out for each other growing up due to their mom's preference for drugs over parenting, and it seemed her older sister hadn't gotten out of the habit.

"Are you on some weird diet again?" Lisa asked.

"You know how those diets go," Lila said with a sigh. "You starve yourself and then binge later. It's not good for you."

Said the two skinny chicks. She sometimes wondered who her father was. Not because she had a grand desire to meet the man so much as to punch him in the face for passing on his faulty metabolism. Lila and Lisa were graceful and willowy. Will was lean and athletic. Laurel got teased all through school for being on the chunky side.

Maybe that was why Mitch hadn't wanted her. Maybe he'd wanted a slender, graceful sub. She wondered what the two exes looked like. Probably movie stars.

"I'm not on a diet. I just was a little off this morning." A bit nauseous, but that could be anything.

*Or you could be pregnant. Because you had sex without a condom. You had crazy, wild, can't-forget-about-it sex without a condom and Mitchell Bradford's sperm are probably as masculine and arrogant and aggressive as the rest of him. Knocked up. You're all kinds of knocked up.*

She shoved that thinking to the side because she was an optimist. She wasn't late. Her period was coming sometime this week. She'd already felt crampy and had a nice ache in her back and her boobs were slightly tender. All signs that Mother Nature was sending her a monthly package and her egg had been wilier than that army of sperm Mitch had sent her way.

The nausea this morning could be explained away as nerves about starting a new job. She'd only been here for a week and she got a little nervous about handling cases without having Mitch on call to answer questions. That was all.

She wondered if Mitch had hired either of the paralegals she'd sent his way. Tom and Cindy were both exceptional. And Cindy was married, so Mitch wouldn't have to worry about another employee hitting on him and making things uncomfortable.

Now that she looked back at it, she'd been the one to behave badly and Mitch had to put up with it. Yes, they had chemistry, but he'd been clear about not wanting to act on it. She'd practically sexually harassed the man.

"Are you all right?" Lila asked. "You went pale. Give me your hand."

She didn't have to. Lila moved in, grasping her right hand and feeling for her pulse.

"What's going on?" Will asked, his eyes concerned as he strode in. Her brother was dressed in slacks and a snowy-white dress shirt. He'd likely left his white coat in the car. Sometimes she thought he should wear a Superman shirt under his clothes. Super Doc. That was her big bro.

"Her pulse rate is high," Lila said, her voice the same flat monotone she used in the ER.

"I'm fine." She pulled her arm out of Lila's hand, but then Will was checking her. She rolled her eyes and looked to her youngest sibling. "Have I thanked you for not going into the medical field?"

Lisa grinned. "They would have been bossy either way."

Will let go. "She's fine, though she is paler than normal."

"Complain to my northern European ancestors. Can we please get some food now? We're supposed to be celebrating Lisa passing her classes, not worrying about my health. Which is fine by the way.

I'm perfectly normal."

*Because it was normal to get pregnant when you have sex while you're ovulating and forget to wear protection of any kind.*

She was done. She was stopping by after work and getting a stupid pee on the stick pregnancy test and putting these thoughts out of her head. Worrying about being pregnant was making her insane. Of course, so was worrying about Mitch.

Had he fired Sharon? She should call and see. Had he managed to turn the office into a fortress yet? She would bet he'd blocked off all the natural light and now the only illumination was fluorescent. And he'd likely eaten like crap and stopped recycling.

None of that was her concern. She was off the Mitchell Bradford improvement committee.

"All right, you say you're fine, I'll believe you," Lila said with a nod. "I'm going to run to the bathroom and then I'll be ready to go."

"I'll go with you." Lisa followed their sister.

She was left alone with Will, who was staring at her the same way he had when she'd been fifteen and had snuck out of their trailer to make out with Jimmy Hodges.

"What happened with Mitch?"

She rolled her eyes. She'd been playing the brat with her brother since before she knew the word had more than one meaning. "He was difficult, to say the least. He was absolutely the most annoying boss I've ever worked for."

And weirdly the most thoughtful. He'd been the one to push her to become a paralegal. He'd supported her through all the training. Most bosses would have offered to hire her back when she was done with school, but Mitch had understood she needed the money. He'd let her work part time but never changed her salary and never complained when he had to do things she would have done as the office manager.

And he'd given her those law books for graduation and told her if she wanted to go further, he would support her through law school.

He'd actually been a great boss. He simply couldn't love her.

"I got sick of banging my head against the massive wall that is Mitchell Bradford. I need a job where I don't have to fight the boss every single time I need to change something. Back when I was only his office manager, I had the time to plot and plan my way around him. Now that I'm also his paralegal…was his paralegal, I don't have time to try to make the new copy machine look like the old copy machine because Mitch has issues with change. I had to kick the damn thing in exactly the right place to get it to work, but does the high-and-mighty Mitch see reason? Nope. He liked the copy machine. He brought the stupid copy machine with him from California. He claimed the copy machine had been more faithful than his last wife."

Will winced. "I told you not to get him started on his ex-wives. It's a sore spot for him."

It was more than a sore spot. The two ex-Mrs. Bradfords were very likely the reason Mitch had never been willing to give her a shot. He'd spent his love and affection on women who hadn't returned it and now he wouldn't try again. He would hold on to his bitterness the same way he'd attempted to hold on to that rattrap old copy machine. Of course, she'd managed to get around that. While Mitch had been playing poker with the Taggart brothers one Friday afternoon, she'd simply had a new one brought in and the old one scrapped.

And now he loved the new copy machine.

"Well, I don't have to worry about any of it now. I have a spiffy new job."

"That pays less than half of what your old job did."

She frowned. Where were Lila and Lisa? This was starting to seem very much like a classic Will interrogation. And how did Will know what she was making? "I'm going to get a lot of experience here."

"Will they let you go to law school and continue to pay you? Because I believe that was Mitch's offer. You're telling me he was so difficult that you would walk away from twice the pay and a boss who supports you financially through school for some experience that won't mean anything if you don't go to law school?"

Yep. This was an interrogation. "It wasn't working. It was too hard. Look, Will, you know I had feelings for him."

"Yes, which is exactly why I had to wonder if Mitch had done something he shouldn't."

She was getting weak in the knees. "No. He didn't do anything. I decided it was a good time to start over. I like it here so can we stop talking about this?"

He slanted a suspicious stare her way. "Fine. You don't want to work with Mitch any more. Is there a reason you no longer want your Sanctum membership? Because the last time we discussed it, you were quite adamant about getting training. You jumped through all the hoops, and you've even been spending your weekends watching kids to pay your way. But now, all of the sudden you quit without any better reason than you changed your mind."

"I did." She wasn't sure what else to say. Everyone had been right. She'd been interested in D/s because of Mitch. She didn't want anyone but Mitch. Hopefully in a few months she would be able to get the irritating man out of her head. "I changed my mind."

"Without even meeting the training Dom selected for you? I'm supposed to believe that? You fought me, tried to get around me, and all so you can quit before you start?"

Her head was now extremely light and it made her stomach churn. "I'm keeping my promises. I told Taggart I would continue to work in the nursery, and he's going to pay me now."

Will was frowning at her, but it seemed like that was all he'd done since he'd walked in the door. "Are you all right? Laurel, sit down. You're very pale."

But it was already too late. Her peripheral vision was fading. She heard Will shout as she started toward the floor.

Four hours later she was doing some frowning of her own. "I'm fine. I needed to get something to eat and now I've wasted an entire afternoon, and I don't even want to think about how much that ambulance trip is going to cost me. I could have solved the problem with a five-dollar sandwich but no, Dr. Daley has to subject me to a million and one medical tests."

Will sighed as he moved to her hospital bed. He glanced around the room where Lila and Lisa were sitting. "Has she been this surly the whole time?"

Lisa nodded. "Yep. And don't get her started on the food."

No one would let her have any food until all the vampires had done their worst. Finally, after they'd decided she wasn't dying, she got to have some pudding. Yippee.

"I'm ready to go home, Will. I'm fine. I feel great. I want to go home." She was sick of being bullied by Will and Lila, who were using the whole "we work at this hospital" thing to their advantage.

She was really glad there was that patient confidentiality law in place.

Will held his hands up. "All right. I'll push the nurse to get you out of here as soon as your blood work comes back."

The doctor chose that moment to enter. He was a kid, probably in his first year or two of residency. He had a clipboard in his hand and a big smile on his face. "Dr. Daley, your sister's blood work is all perfectly fine."

"Hey, what happened to confidentiality?" She sat up but took a deep breath. She was fine. Her blood work was fine.

She wasn't pregnant. That was good. That was amazing.

So why did she feel so…lost?

Will patted the ER doc on the back. "Thanks, Barry. I appreciate it. I know I've been a little paranoid, but she's my sister. I've been watching out for her for a very long time."

Barry practically beamed at Will. "Of course, sir. All her blood work is normal. I'm glad to be the bearer of good tidings and, on another note, I'm so excited to be on your service next week. I'm looking forward to a stint in neuro, and you're the best."

She was going to vomit for different reasons now.

Lila was on her feet. "I'd like to see her blood work, please. Something's off with her and it has been for a couple of weeks."

Now that she wasn't hiding anything, she didn't think twice about letting Lila take a look at her chart. She didn't care. She wasn't pregnant. She wasn't carrying Mitchell's baby and it was all over. That was a good thing.

Wasn't it?

Barry turned the chart over. "Of course. At this point, I'm sure she feels a little off. Remind her to eat and to get enough rest. She's healthy. The pregnancy is in its early stages, so she needs to eat and get enough water and rest and she'll be fine."

The room seemed to stop. Everything got very quiet, and slowly all three of her siblings turned her way.

Barry seemed to understand something had gone wrong. His eyes went wide. "Uhm, so no one knew she was pregnant?"

"I thought you said my blood work was normal." She was pregnant. Knocked up. Having his baby. Oh, god. She was having Mitch's baby.

He shrugged and stuttered as he started backing out of the room. "It's perfectly normal for a pregnant woman. I assumed since you're surrounded by medical people that someone would have figured out you're pregnant. I mean, I haven't examined you, but I thought you're probably just a couple of weeks into your first trimester. Right?"

Will's face had turned a nice shade of pink. "I don't have to examine her. I'm pretty sure she's two weeks pregnant. Is that about right, Laurel?"

Lila was combing through her chart. "How can you tell, Will?"

"Because that's when she quit working for Mitch," Will said, every word dropping like a lead pipe.

Lisa was the only one who didn't look grim. "Whoa. You quit working for Mitch because you finally went at it like a couple of rabbits, didn't you? This is some serious drama. We're going to need more pudding cups. Don't they keep popsicles somewhere?"

Will sent their youngest sister a stern glare.

Lisa simply shrugged. "Laurel isn't the only one who had to skip lunch. I might not be eating for two, but I'm still hungry."

"I'm going to get someone to run these results again." Lila shook her head at the chart. "Laurel isn't this foolish. There is no way she's pregnant. I'll call in Dr. Bates."

Will nodded. "She's who I would call. But you're wrong about Laurel. She is that foolish."

"No. She couldn't be." Lila squared off with Will.

Lisa hopped up on Laurel's bed. "I think we're about to get the mom lecture again."

"Laurel wouldn't be so completely irresponsible as to not use birth control. She saw what happened to our mother. She knows how terrible it can be for a child to not even know who her father is," Lila said passionately.

"Oh, I know who the father is," Will shot back. "Don't worry. He'll be in this kid's life. Well, unless I kill him first."

Tears streamed down her face. She had been irresponsible. So irresponsible. She was having a baby and the father didn't want a child. She'd grown up without a father, depending on Will to take care of her when she was younger, and now she was putting her own baby in the same position.

Unwanted. Unloved. A mistake.

Lisa's hand found hers. "Hey, it's going to be okay, Laurel. It's all right."

She shook her head. "No, it's not."

There was a brief knock on the door and Laurel was certain they were about to be asked to keep the noise down. They would have to move this party out of the ER.

She would try to sneak away, try to get back to her tiny apartment that would be terrible for raising a baby in. There was barely enough room for her. Babies required lots of stuff. Babies required love and affection and care, and how was she going to make it work?

The door opened and Mitch Bradford stood there looking like he'd run a couple of miles without bothering to change into sweats. He was still wearing his everyday armor, but his hair was windblown and he had a nice sheen of sweat on his brow. "Laurel, I just got the text from Will. Are you all right?"

Her brother had texted Mitch?

Before she could say a thing, her brother let his fist do the talking. Will reared back and Mitch went flying out of the room.

It looked like the worst day of her life wasn't over yet.

# Chapter Four

Mitch hit the nurse's station with a crash, his spine slamming into the edge. It took him a moment to truly register the fact that Will had gone completely insane and was attacking him.

"Someone call security." He heard the nurse's voice behind him.

"No need," Will said. "I can take out the trash myself."

Will came at him, throwing another punch, but this time Mitch was ready. He ducked, narrowly missing getting clocked right across the nose. Will was serious. He wasn't fucking around. He'd obviously found out what had happened with Laurel.

Had Laurel told her brother it was all his fault? He certainly hadn't expected that from her.

"Nothing happened?" Will asked the question in a mocking tone. "Earlier today you told me nothing happened. Want to amend that statement, Counselor?"

Mitch held his ground. If they were going to do this here, then he would take his punishment, but he wasn't going to go out quietly and he wasn't going to stand here and let Will beat the shit out of him. "What happened is between me and Laurel."

"Will, stop it. You are going to break a hand and then where will you be?" The three Daley sisters were standing right outside the door to Laurel's room. The oldest one, Lila, was staring at both of them with a ferocious frown on her face. "Also, none of this helps Laurel."

"I don't care right now," Will shot back and then returned his attention to Mitch. "You promised me she would be safe with you.

You promised you would take care of her."

Shit. This was about the incident? He hadn't mentioned that Laurel had been shot at because she'd begged him not to and there hadn't been anything Will could do. He'd been in Chicago at the time. No wonder the man was pissed. "I'm so sorry. I wasn't expecting it, obviously. It never occurred to me that she would be in that kind of danger. I swear if it had, I would have put a guard in front of that door."

Will stopped. "What are you talking about? She didn't need a guard. She needed a fucking condom, asshole."

"Oh, Mitch is talking about when Laurel got shot at two weeks ago," Lisa supplied helpfully.

"What?" Will turned again, this time sending that glare Laurel's way.

Condom? Why was Laurel in the hospital? "I'm perfectly clean. I had a damn checkup a few weeks ago. Call Sanctum. My blood tests are clean."

Laurel looked so young and vulnerable standing there in a hospital gown. It looked like she'd cried off her mascara. His gut clenched. She'd been crying. She clutched at the back of the gown to keep it together. Why was she here? What had happened? In that moment, he no longer cared what she'd said about him. He merely wanted to know she was all right.

"Laurel, I swear I don't have any kind of STD." He kept his distance because it looked like he was the bad guy in this scenario. "My blood tests are clean and I'll be honest, I haven't had sex with anyone in a good long while. Anyone else, obviously. Baby, if you're sick, something's gone wrong, but I swear it's not me. I would never put you at risk."

"You don't have the clap, asshole. You have working sperm," Will said between clenched teeth. "Hence the need for a condom."

The words didn't compute. He stood there like a complete idiot as everyone stared at him.

His best friend waved a hand in front of his face. Ex-best friend. It looked like that was done. He was good at collecting exes. Ex-wives, ex-friends, ex-lovers who promised there wasn't a problem…

"She's on the pill," he said. That's what they were talking

about, right? Sperm had been mentioned.

*Yes, I am fully functional, buddy, and guess what? We flooded her that night. Is it really any wonder we're here? And you can thank me later.*

His dick was still getting him in trouble. Had his dick gotten them all in trouble? Like serious trouble. Like lifetime of being bound together kind of trouble.

Like he couldn't give up Laurel because he'd gotten her pregnant kind of trouble?

All eyes swung Laurel's way and she flushed.

"Did you tell him you were on the pill?" Will asked. He had the pissed-off father-figure thing down.

Father. He was going to be a father. Was he going to be a father? It wasn't like Laurel didn't have a choice in the matter.

"I never said that," Laurel replied and Mitch watched as she steeled herself.

"I asked you about it and you said everything was fine." He'd gone over that night about three hundred times since then.

"It is fine. I'm fine. You don't have to worry." Her chin came up in what he liked to think of as her queenly pose. When she looked at him like that he knew he was in for stubbornness. "Thank you for worrying, but I'll be fine. I'm going to get dressed now. I would appreciate it if the two of you could stop making a scene."

She turned and walked back into her room. Lisa gave him a grin and a wink before turning and following her sister, but Lila remained even after the door had closed behind the other two.

"Well, this is a mess. Will, you're not making this better," Lila said.

"I'm sorry. I lost my head for a minute there," Will admitted.

"You knew she had a thing for him," Lila complained.

Will shrugged. "I did. At the time, I didn't think it would be so bad. I thought Mitch cared about her, too."

"I do. I care about her." Laurel was pregnant. She was carrying his very small, probably-no-more-than-a-couple-of-cells child inside her body right that very moment.

He didn't want kids. He'd never wanted them. It wasn't that he didn't like them. He liked his friends' kids fine, but he would be a shit dad. He hadn't been close to his own but his mother never let up that he was exactly like the bastard. Unreliable. Selfish.

Two failed marriages had proven her right.

"Then what are you going to do?" Lila asked, though a bit more softly now. "Mr. Bradford, I've only met you a couple of times, but I've seen the way you look at my sister. Let me see if I can figure out what happened. Laurel is a stubborn girl and she learned early to fight for what she wants. She decided she wanted you and she pushed you to the point that you gave in. You then did something stupid and caused her to run."

"What did you do that was stupid?" Will asked. "Wait. I want to get back to the shooting thing."

He was stunned. He was actually lucky his freaking knees were still working because the knowledge that Laurel was pregnant—with his baby—was…he wasn't even quite sure what it was. His mind was working overtime, but his mouth seemed to move on its own.

"Derek is sure that it was some kid trying to rob the dentist next door. Apparently he was high and he was looking to get higher. Laurel startled him and he shot at her through the glass in the reception area."

"Oh my god. Why wasn't I told?"

Lila chuckled. "Uhm, because you tend to lose your cool, big brother. Thank you, Randy. I think we've got everything under control. Dr. Daley was a bit upset, but he's calmed down now and he's not going to cause any more trouble with the lawyer who'll probably sue the hell out of him and the hospital we work at."

Mitch turned. Lila was talking to a security guard who looked deeply unhappy he'd been pulled from his nap or something.

"Mitch isn't going to sue us," Will replied.

"No, but if I ever get the chance to punch you, I'll take it."

"Was I right?" Lila asked.

Mitch was totally happy he'd drawn the middle Daley sister. Lisa was an imp who didn't seem to take anything seriously and Lila kind of scared him. And he didn't scare easy. Laurel was stubborn, but she didn't have Lila's grim determination. "About what happened? Yeah. She pushed the hell out of me and things exploded and I was a little freaked out afterward."

"You didn't think you two should talk about it beyond asking briefly if she was on birth control?" Will was right back to pissed off.

Maybe Randy the guard shouldn't have shuffled off so quickly. "She left me, Will. I wanted to talk, but she walked out and she didn't walk back in. I gave her space. Hell, I needed space. I called her on Saturday and again on Sunday. She didn't answer. I walked back in Monday morning like a fucking idiot with flowers and shit and she quit with an e-mail. An e-mail."

She'd decided he was a bad bet and he couldn't blame her.

Was she scared that she'd be stuck with him for the rest of her life?

And so much for going to his grave with the flowers secret. His mouth wouldn't stop.

"Good. Then you and Laurel can work this out." Lila gave him a nod. "I suggest you do that thing you two seem obsessed with doing or she'll walk all over you."

"What thing?" Mitch asked.

Lila gave him a mysterious smile and disappeared into the room.

"She's telling you to top Laurel." Will scrubbed a hand through his hair. "She's probably right. Laurel isn't reasonable when she feels like she's in a corner. You've convinced her you don't want her."

"I never said I don't want her. I simply want better for her." She deserved better than he could give her.

Will stepped in front of him. "You're all she's got now. So man up and be better for her because you've got one shot at this. I get that you've always thought we're so different. You come from money and I don't, but we both had shitty parents who did nothing to get us ready for kids of our own. I had to grow up a long time ago. It's your turn. It's your turn to shove all that shit aside and be more. She needs you to be more."

"I didn't mean to hurt her." And he hadn't really come from money. Sure his father had been wealthy and he'd been given a trust fund on his eighteenth birthday, but his mother had made her money the hard way—by marrying it over and over and over again.

"I know. Why did you lie to me? You said nothing happened."

"I was trying to protect us both, I guess." God, he was going to miss Will. "I didn't want to lose your friendship and I knew

Laurel wouldn't want you to know about it. She said everything was fine."

"Lesson number one. When she says she's fine, you're in trouble. There's no such thing as fine. It's like Southern chicks saying bless your heart. What they actually mean is you're an idiot. Fine means something like the same thing except it carries connotations that violence could happen if you don't figure out what's wrong. How bad was it?"

"The sex? It was fantastic." It had been the absolute best sex of his life.

Will groaned. "No, asshole. Never, ever tell me that. Ever. Again." He shuddered. "I was talking about whatever you did to make her run."

He needed to stop being so literal. "I said it was a mistake."

Will winced. "Okay, well, the flowers thing was a good idea. Maybe you can try that again. She also likes those cheese Danishes from the bakery down the street from her place."

"I tried that, too." At least he was on the right track. "Unfortunately, I brought them in with the flowers and…"

"She quit via e-mail. I'm sorry about that, man. It was a cowardly thing to do."

Or she'd stopped caring. This was kind of what he did. He was difficult and after a while, people stopped caring and they disappeared. "I know I let you down, Will. I'm sorry about that."

Will sighed. "You lost your head over a girl and now you're going to do the right thing. I knew you two were combustible the minute you got in the same room together. I thought she would be good for you and vice versa."

What had he been thinking? "How am I good for her?"

"You push her. Laurel sometimes accepts her place far too easily. Did you know she didn't even negotiate her salary at the new place? I have a friend who works there and I had him look into it. She simply accepted the offer and never thought about requesting more. Without you, she never would have gone back to school. She wouldn't have become a paralegal. She stays an office manager, and there's nothing wrong with that, but Laurel needs more."

"She's too smart to get stuck. She should go to law school. She would enjoy it. She needs a job where pay doesn't matter, so get off her back about this one. This type of work is exactly where she should be. Helping people. That's what makes Laurel tick."

"Yes, and you saw that and you made it possible for her to do that, and in a safe environment, and you made sure she didn't lack for money. So get over your damage, as Kai would say. You're good for her."

He leaned against the wall, studying Will. Maybe this wasn't as bad as he'd thought it would be. "Kai would never say that. He would sound like a massive intellectual douchebag. 'Mitchell, your problems stem from a childhood abandonment by your father and verbal abuse and neglect from your maternal influences.'"

Will made a vomiting sound. "I love the dude, but I want to strangle him when he gets going about childhood issues. Doesn't he know manly men don't talk about that shit? We beat each other up and then get a beer. You want a beer, man?"

At least he hadn't lost his best friend. "I would love one, but I think I need to talk to your sister."

"The good news is she came in an ambulance so she doesn't have a car. I'll do you a solid and refuse to give her a ride back. If she gives you any trouble, just pick her up and move her."

He went a little shaky at the thought. "I can't do that. She's pregnant."

Will shook his head. "No. Don't even think that way. She's here today because she didn't eat breakfast and got woozy. She's not a delicate flower. The baby is seriously tiny. So don't let her fool you into thinking she's fragile. Laurel's strong. She'll be fine and the two of you have a lot to talk about. Don't let her shut you out."

The door opened and Laurel emerged, followed by her sisters. She'd changed back into the same clothes she'd been wearing earlier, a sweet-looking floral print skirt, a pink blouse, and flats. Her hair was pulled back and she was looking more like her normal, competent self than before when she'd looked like she needed him.

She did need him. And Will was right. It was time to man up.

"Well, I think the two of you have a lot to talk about," Lila said. "Mitch, weren't you going to say something to Laurel?"

His heart was suddenly pounding because these were waters he'd promised he'd never, ever swim in again. He was about to dive into the deep end of the pool. "Yes. I do have something to say.

Laurel, I'll marry you."

Will groaned again. "Buddy, we're going to have to work on your delivery."

Laurel simply turned and walked away.

He went after her because this time, she wasn't getting away from him.

* * * *

I'll marry you.

Laurel walked toward the exit. It didn't matter that she didn't have a ride. She would catch a bus or walk to a train station. She was not going to stay there with Mitch "I'll marry you because I have to" Bradford. He'd said the words with all the enthusiasm of a man on his way to an execution.

Pregnant. She was pregnant and Mitch knew, and now he was ready to do right by the woman he'd apparently soiled. That's how her brother had reacted. For a moment, she'd been transported back in time to where Will was going to fight a duel over her lost honor.

She hadn't lost a damn thing. No. She'd gained a whole other human being and all because she hadn't been able to think straight when Mitch touched her.

That was absolutely no reason to marry the man.

"Laurel!"

She settled her purse on her shoulder and ignored him. There was a train station two blocks over. She knew exactly where it was because she'd come out to this hospital many times to see Will and Lila, though she never would again because neither of those ungrateful wretches had offered her a ride. They were cut off.

Actually, it served her right to have to hoof it. It proved that when a girl screwed up as totally as she had, she was on her own. Or she would be if Mitch would stop pursuing her.

"Laurel!"

She kept walking. Outside, it was a glorious day. It was spring and everything was in bloom. Even her damn womb.

Mitch caught up with her. "Laurel, sweetheart, I'm going to give you a chance to save this. Stop now and come with me. We'll get something to eat and talk about this."

She didn't look his way. "I think I'll take door number two."

"You won't like door number two," he warned.

She was far too stubborn to care.

"All right then. Door number two it is."

Laurel nearly screamed because one minute she'd been walking and the next she was up and in his arms, being cradled against that masculine chest of his. "Hey, you can't do that. Put me down."

"Nope. This is door number two and unfortunately, I'm parked on the other side of the lot." Mitch had turned and was walking right back toward where they'd just left. "What have you had to eat today?"

She was oddly comfortable in his arms. She couldn't remember the last time a man had picked her up and carried her around, her body protected by his. Probably not since she'd been a child and Will had carried her when she'd been hurt or sick. The sweetness of it pierced her. And then she remembered the only reason he was doing it was for the baby. "You should put me down. You're going to throw out your back."

He stopped and stared down at her. "What did you say?"

Oh, that was new. He was cold, arctic cold even as his arms tightened around her. "I said I'm too heavy and you should put me down."

"That's what I thought you said." He started moving again, his eyes back up. "All right. I'm going to give you that one because I've never set rules with you. Here's rule number one. I hear you insult yourself again and there will be punishment. How do you expect to raise a girl who gives a damn about herself if her mother doesn't? How do you expect to raise a boy who respects women if his mother doesn't care about herself? So expect the punishment for those infractions to be harsh."

What was happening? And when the hell did Mitch become the voice of reason? She couldn't come up with one logical argument. He was right. "What are you doing, Mitch?"

"Setting the rules. Now answer my question. When was the last time you ate?"

They were about to walk past the ER doors and toward the west lot. Naturally her siblings were now outside and they were all watching the show.

"She started a bowl of cereal this morning." Lisa had impeccable hearing. "But it was the diet kind and she didn't eat it because she had morning sickness. At the time I thought it might be a bug, but now we know it's y'all's illicit love child."

She had another shot at getting out of here. Lila would be the weak link. Lisa had obviously become a spy for Team Mitchell and Will was being a jerkface. "Lila, go and get security. Tell them I'm being kidnapped. Mitch, let me down now."

Lila smiled and gave her a friendly wave. "No, honey. I think he's being the sensible one."

"You take care of her." Will's words were for Mitch.

"I intend to. She might not like how I do it though. Can someone pack a bag for her? I'm afraid if I let her inside her apartment, she'll lock me out."

"Damn straight I will."

"I have a key," Lisa said. "I'll do it. Come on, Laurel. Don't look at me that way. He's doing the Dom thing. And isn't this kind of what you wanted? Mitch and a baby? Looks like you get both."

Mitch and a baby. Was that what she'd wanted?

Mitch thanked Lisa and then strode toward his massive, gas-guzzling SUV she'd thought at first was to make up for his penis, and then she'd seen his penis. His penis probably needed the roomy interior of the SUV to feel comfortable.

Mitch and a family were what she had wanted, but she'd been willing to settle for just Mitch. Now it was Mitch who would be settling.

"If I set you down are you going to run?"

And be less mature than she'd already been today? One thing was right. They needed to talk. "No."

He gently set her on her feet and opened the door. "Will you please eat something? I'll take you anywhere you want. We need to figure out how this is going to work."

She'd wanted enchiladas earlier in the day, but now all she could think about was pasta and she knew exactly where to get it. "Take me to Top."

Twenty minutes later, she sighed as Sean Taggart placed a plate of pasta carbonara in front of her. She'd already inhaled a Caesar salad. She might have been nauseous this morning, but she was ravenous now.

"Are you sure I can't get you a glass of wine? The sommelier has this paired with a Chablis that truly complements the creamy texture of the dish," Sean explained. He was dressed in his chef whites. She was much more used to calling him Master Sean and seeing him in leathers, but then Sean Taggart was a Master of more than one thing. He was definitely a master with pasta and sauces.

She was about to turn him down when Mitch decided to take over.

"She can't because she's pregnant."

Why did she suddenly feel like every eye in the place was on her? The crowd was light at this time of day, and it seemed like Mitch had shouted out into an almost silent room.

Sean held out a hand, a smile creasing his handsome face. "Really? That's exciting news. Congratulations, man. I didn't know you two were even seeing each other."

That was just like a man. "We're not seeing each other and how do you know the baby is his? Maybe it's someone else's. And I'm barely pregnant."

"The baby is absolutely, one hundred percent mine, and we're definitely seeing each other now. We're getting married," Mitch declared with ruthless determination.

Sean put a friendly hand on Mitch's shoulder. "Good to hear it, man. Let us know when the wedding is and we'll be happy to cater. Macon's been dying to do a wedding cake. He and Ally got married in Vegas so he didn't do his own. You two enjoy and let me know if I can get you anything else. The dessert this evening is a bread pudding, so you'll want to save room."

She was almost distracted by that. Almost.

"Why did you tell him that?" She leaned over so she could maybe minimize the damage. The servers were looking her way and whispering behind their hands. It wouldn't have been a big deal if it was Ally. She knew Ally, but there were two women she didn't know talking about her "engagement" that wasn't going to happen. "He didn't need to know that."

Mitch looked at her over his porterhouse with truffle mashed potatoes and shrugged. "Everyone's going to find out anyway. And there's no such thing as being barely pregnant. You're either pregnant or you're not."

"Well maybe I would like more than three minutes to process it before we tell the world that we screwed up."

"Did we?"

She sat back, regarding him. He looked tired. Like he wasn't sleeping or he was staying at the office. He did that at times. She would walk in and find him asleep on the couch in his office and she would close the shades and put a blanket over him and try to let him get an hour or two. "What is that supposed to mean, Mitch?"

This was the type of conversation that would typically upset her stomach. Not so now. She couldn't resist the siren call of that creamy sauce or the bacon and pancetta. Even the noodles were perfect.

"It means that I didn't use a condom and you didn't ask me to use one."

She leaned over. "I didn't think. I wasn't thinking, Mitchell."

He cut a piece of steak but didn't eat it. "Do you usually not think?"

"Of course not." How did she put this without sounding pathetic? "Not that there have been many times for me to not think."

"I never have sex without a condom, Laurel. I'll be honest, there hasn't been a lot lately, but that's simply not something I do. I'm always careful. The last thing I want is to get trapped again."

"Well, I guess I should thank you for at least being honest." Maybe she was going to lose her appetite.

He reached across the table and put a hand on hers. It was the first time he'd willingly touched her outside the kiss or that night they'd had sex or when he was trying to kidnap her. Tender. He was trying to be tender with her and it made Laurel stop.

"I wasn't saying you trapped me, Laurel. I was wondering if maybe deep down I wanted to be trapped with you. I was wondering if subconsciously maybe we knew what we were doing and we took the risk anyway because deep down we wondered if it wouldn't be so bad."

She'd wondered the same thing herself. "Maybe we did."

"How many boyfriends have you had?"

"How many girlfriends have you had?"

He shrugged. "Two. But if you're asking about women I've slept with, it's a lot more. I'd ballpark it at thirty."

That was a big number. And only two girlfriends? "You married both of your girlfriends?"

"No. Margot was my college girlfriend. We went to law school together and when we got out, I built my firm from the ground up. My father threw me a bone and got me hooked up with a man named Garrison Cage."

She knew his business story. She'd spent long nights looking him up on the Internet. "The tech guru. That's why they called you the Silicon Counselor."

He'd been a legal consultant to some of the biggest tech firms in the business. He'd made millions before it all fell apart.

"Yeah, I had a partner in the firm. Nolan Pence. We got close in law school. He was kind of my first friend, I guess. I moved around a lot as a kid. I never made close friends. Anyway, he decided he liked both the company and my wife. I'd been stupid because I'd made Margot a partner even though she wasn't practicing at the time. She was mostly fucking Nolan. They had the majority of the firm behind the two of them, so I was asked to leave."

Yes, she knew that part, too. "So who was the other girlfriend if it wasn't your second wife?"

She asked the question with a cautious tone because this was the first conversation they'd had about his personal life. They'd had long lunches talking about the law or sports or politics, but they'd never done this.

They'd had sex and made a baby and they'd never even gone on a date.

"I had a girlfriend when I was a teenager. My mom sent me to boarding school the last couple of years of high school. Best thing that ever happened to me. Her name was Natalie. She went to the girls' school. I guess I was wrong. I guess she was really my first friend. We were together for three years."

"Did you break up when you went to college?"

He shook his head. "She died. Car accident. She was coming home with some friends and a drunk driver killed them all. I found out from the news the next day because all the people who would have told me were dead." He took a quick drink of the Coke he'd ordered. "Those were my two girlfriends. I wouldn't call Joy so much a girlfriend as a hookup gone wrong. I left San Francisco and moved to LA, where I started a new firm, and I met Joy at a Hollywood party. I was drinking a lot back then. I woke up in Vegas married about two weeks later. The marriage lasted three years and then she divorced me and now she's living in our old Hollywood Hills house that I still pay the upkeep for. So that's how I have two girlfriends and two wives but not the same. Now, I've politely answered your question. Could you please answer mine?"

She felt a little battered. He'd spoken in a monotone, but how was she supposed to handle that? The girl he'd loved had died and he'd tried twice more and gotten screwed in every way a man could. And she expected him to try again? The enormity of his losses weighed on her, but she answered him anyway. "I've had three serious boyfriends and that's how many guys I've slept with, too. Well, four now."

Three boyfriends. Not a one of them had cheated on her. There was no grand trauma in her past concerning men. Her high school boyfriend had moved away for college and they'd drifted apart. The guy she'd dated through college had asked her to marry him, but she'd known they were far too similar and broken it off. And she'd split up with her recent boyfriend shortly after she'd met Mitchell Bradford and realized she couldn't feel for the man anything close to what she felt for Mitch.

And now she was wondering if it was all for nothing because Mitch had been through too much. Will had told her once that Mitch was broken. She'd thought she could fix him.

"That's all? That's not a lot, Laurel," he said, his face grim. "I was somewhat wild at certain points in my life."

"I never did anything wild in my life. Well, until that night." Until she'd thrown caution right out the door and made a baby with the man who had fascinated her from the moment she met him.

But now she had to wonder if that meant she loved him. She didn't even know him. Not the real Mitch. She wasn't sure he let anyone know the real him. He was a man who believed in contracts and exchanges.

Marriage was a contract, but not one he put a lot of faith in. But there was another type he did believe in.

"I think we should get married, Laurel."

What if she could get to know him? What if she could find some way inside the puzzle that was Mitch Bradford? It scared her, but her optimism was starting to return. Didn't she owe it to her child? She had to find out where his head really was on this subject.

"I don't have to have the baby, Mitch. There's a simple solution to all of this."

He went white. Like sheet white. "I don't want that. I can't stop you, but I don't want that. I know I've been a shit husband before and if I'd had my way, I wouldn't have had kids. But…Laurel, I don't want that. I don't want to get rid of anything that's a part of you."

And just like that she knew she was going to try and she knew she was going to give her all, and not only for the baby. She was going to try for her, too. She was going to try because the universe was giving her another shot and she was going to take it. "Good because I don't want that either. I'm pregnant and I think I should have the baby, but I don't think that's reason enough to get married."

"I think the baby…our baby might disagree. I grew up without a father."

"So did I. I'm not trying to cut you out, Mitch. If you want to be a part of this baby's life, I think that's great, but have you considered that you could be a part of his or her life and not be a part of mine? You were adamant about not having a relationship with me. I'm the one who pushed it."

"Laurel, I don't think I'm good for you. I'm too old and honestly, I'm tired of the whole marriage thing. I'm not any good at it. But I'm willing to try because I think if we're going to have a baby then we should try to be the best we can be. Can we try?"

Trying was what she'd always wanted to do, but she couldn't end up being another one of his ex-wives.

Maybe there was something else they could try. Something she'd always wanted to try.

"I don't like that look on your face, Laurel."

She smiled because he probably wasn't going to like her plan either.

But she'd definitely gotten her appetite back. She dug in and planned her next step.

# Chapter Five

Mitch looked down at the document he'd drafted. It was a contract. He drafted those every day. It was what he did. He wasn't usually the one who signed them though. And he'd never thought he'd be writing this one.

"Is it ready?" Laurel walked in carrying a mug.

"I don't think you're supposed to be drinking coffee. Are pregnant women supposed to drink coffee?" He'd read that somewhere.

Her eyes narrowed.

"Or you could drink whatever you want," he amended. Maybe he should have written a food and drink clause into the contract.

The D/s contract he wasn't completely sure he should sign with her.

Her lips curled up and she sank onto the couch in front of him. "Good. And because you asked, no, this isn't coffee. It's hot tea. I carry some bags in my purse. I have a couple of herbals that help with things like tension and anxiety."

She was anxious? "We don't have to do this tonight. We can go to bed and talk about it again in the morning."

"I'm not anxious about the contract. I'm just tense. It's been a rough day. I have a lot to think about, you know. I need to figure out what I'm going to do about my job. I talked to Lyle. He's the head of the paralegals. He gave me the afternoon off, but he's not going to be happy to find out that I'll need maternity leave so soon. Oh, and I also had to drink tea because you have nothing but sports drinks and beer. And there is nothing in your fridge. What do you eat?"

She always asked him multiple questions at a time. It threw him off. He'd thought on more than one occasion that was her intention.

"Tomorrow, we'll go buy groceries and I'll get rid of the beer."

"Why?"

"It doesn't seem fair that I can drink and you can't. Besides, I lean on it too often at times, and I won't do that when I have a submissive in my home. As for your job, you don't have to have one or you can come back and work for me. I never actually did the paperwork to let you go. Technically, you're still my employee."

"Why didn't you do the paperwork?"

Because he hadn't wanted to let her go. Because it had seemed so permanent. "I'm lazy and Sharon gets confused about using the computer for anything but sending her grandkids e-mails."

"Sharon is still there. I'm impressed."

"Don't be. I fired her twice. She keeps showing back up."

A wide smile crossed her face. "I told her working for you would require tenacity. It's good to know someone listens. I like my new job, Mitch. I like what we do. My only problem is my insurance doesn't kick in for another couple of weeks."

She would never have to worry about money. "We'll pay out of pocket until then."

"Okay." Once he agreed to sign a D/s contract with her, she'd become quite amenable. She hadn't fought him when he'd taken her to his home instead of her own. Lisa was dropping off a bag after she finished up her night class and tomorrow he'd take her to her place after work and figure out what she needed for a long-term stay. "So should we sign the contract? I filled out the list of places you can put stuff in."

Ah, the hard and soft limits questionnaire. "It's called my penis. Let's not call it stuff."

She shrugged. "I thought you played around with vibrators and those glass things. Why glass by the way?"

"Dildos, and the glass is for play. It can be heated up or chilled for the sensation. Don't forget butt plugs, sweetheart. If you sign this, you'll get familiar with those. I like anal sex. I'll want you to try it." It wasn't a hard limit for her. She'd put it down as something she was curious about. "And you're right, you have had a hard day. Take your time and read this contract. It's got everything we talked about in it."

She picked it up. "Anything new in there? You throwing me any curve balls, like I have to greet you at the door each night naked and kiss your feet?"

He liked the naked part. His feet were actually surprisingly sensitive. "No. I did write a specific clause that's catered to our unique position and that goes on past the terms of the original contract."

Her brows rose and she picked up the contract, flipping to the back. She knew him pretty well, it seemed. She knew exactly where he would put it.

"A pregnancy clause? Interesting. You know for a man who said he didn't want kids, you sure want to be there for everything." Her eyes moved over the words, taking them in before she set it back down. Her eyes were soft as she looked at him. "You know I would never lock you out. I agree to all the terms of the clause and I'll sign it, but I want you to know I wouldn't block you even if we didn't have a contract."

The clause stated plainly that he would accompany her to all prenatal visits, all parenting and childbirth classes, and be in the delivery room and welcome at the hospital. It also stated that both parties would work out a child custody agreement no later than a month before the anticipated birth of the Bradford-Daley child in the event the parties were no longer living together.

"Were you going to tell me?" He wondered. He believed her when she said the hospital was the first time she truly knew she was pregnant, but she had to have had a clue.

"Yes. I would have told you. I might have taken a day or two, but trust me, I would have shown up on your doorstep, Mitch. I'm not a 'suffer in silence' kind of girl." Her lips quirked up and so did his dick. She was here. She was sitting on his crappy couch with her shoes off, relaxed and accepting.

If she signed that contract tonight, he was going to have her. He was going to have her every fucking night he could until the day she woke up and realized it was all a mistake.

"Laurel, do you need time to read the rest of the contract? I'm a bit more hardcore than your brother. You should think about this. I need control outside of the bedroom. I'm not picking your clothes or telling you what to eat, but I'll want a nightly routine. I'll want you here with me at night. If you do go out with your girlfriends, I'll want to know where you're going and I'll likely want to drop you off and pick you up. I'll be obnoxious about your safety and god, Laurel, don't ignore phone calls because I will never ignore yours."

She started looking through the bulk of the contract. "And what happens if I'm working or can't answer at that particular time."

"I've set up protocols."

She nodded. "Yes, I can see that."

He was going to lose her. She was going to see all the crap he would put her through and walk away to find one of those "I only want control in the bedroom" Doms.

She picked up a pen and scratched through what seemed to be a paragraph. "I'm not doing that, Mitch. The no talking about our relationship thing is never going to happen, and anyone who tells you they'll honor it is lying. I've got two sisters. I'm going to talk to them."

"I simply think it's best that we keep our relationship private." Maybe he shouldn't have sent her for her paralegal certification. He doubted the sweet office manager would have boldly marked out his clauses.

"Babe, there's no such thing. Maybe if we were having an affair that we intended to keep brief and unemotional we could, but I'm going to give this thing a go. I want to see if we can make it work, and that means I'll talk to my sisters and my friends and you should definitely talk to yours. You don't have to be an island, Mitch."

It was one clause and they were negotiating. "All right. I'll agree to lose that requirement. Do you agree to the communication protocols?"

"Yes, I will text you if I'm going to be out of pocket for more than thirty minutes. I will make every attempt to return your call within an hour and will allow you to track my phone because you're a paranoid weirdo."

"That's five smacks. Did you not read the clause where you're forbidden from calling me a paranoid weirdo?"

She started combing through the contract. "No. I didn't see that."

He chuckled. "I was kidding, Laurel. I can joke, too. I need the comfort of routine, but I'm not so insecure I can't handle your smart mouth. All big decisions that concern both of us have to be discussed. I've got a schedule that we can also discuss and agree upon. If it helps, you can track my phone, too. I'll leave you a list of my passwords."

"I already have those. I was your office manager for six months. I take it when you say decisions that concern both of us, you're talking about me making changes to the house. Because I already want to do that."

She always wanted to change things. "No. I'm not moving on that. This is my house. Maybe if we get married we can discuss certain renovations to rooms that are yours, but I think it's best we have our own spaces."

"You don't want to sleep with me?"

That was not going to happen. "What? No. That's totally in there. We share a bedroom. We sleep together and you can't kick me out without good cause. I was talking about my office and my media room. I like them the way they are. You can have the living room and the kitchen and the guestroom. If we get married. I don't know. We'll have to negotiate again."

Laurel huffed, an irritated sound, and then signed the document. "Fine. Here is your contract. I can see we have a lot of negotiating to do. I want a pretty collar. One I can wear during the day. I'll wear a more pronounced one when we're at Sanctum, but I want pretty and delicate for daywear."

She placed the contract on the table between them. She was demanding a collar. Of course, he'd covered that in the contract. He'd actually stated that she was to wear any collar he deemed fit for her, but shouldn't she like it? He wanted to please her.

"I'll let you pick your day collar. I get to pick your club collar and all your clothes for Sanctum."

"Agreed."

Fuck, he was hard. The idea that she was going to be with him at Sanctum made his cock pulse against his slacks. She would wear his collar, live in his home, let him take care of her.

She would devastate him when she left.

He shoved that thought aside. The truth was he couldn't push her away. They were having a baby and that baby would be a more permanent tie than any contract. He wasn't going to walk out on his kid. He wasn't going to toss money the kid's way and hope Laurel took care of him.

"How much have you learned?" He had to get out of that dangerous headspace. Thoughts like that could send him into dark places, and he wasn't going there with her. She was his responsibility now and he had the paperwork to prove it. He had to be in the moment with her. That was what he would do. He would live in the here and now and not worry about the future or brood over the past. Now was truly all the time they had anyway.

"About D/s? I've been reading a lot. Mostly Bridget's and Serena's and Chris's books, but they're all in the lifestyle."

"Yes, but they write a highly romanticized version of the lifestyle. How much real training have you had?"

"I've been to the classes Eve and Grace teach to new submissives and I've done some work with the married Doms, but nothing serious since someone decided he didn't want me working with Master T."

What the hell had Tag been thinking? The idea of her working with that dangerous Southerner…no. He wasn't going there. He was being in the present. "So most of what you know is intellectual."

"Yes."

"Why don't you show me how the submissives in Bridget's books greet their Doms. I think it would be a nice ritual after being apart for long periods. Something for me to look forward to."

"You would, wouldn't you? You would look forward to me greeting you at the end of the day."

Maybe that made him a pervert, but it was true. It would be the best part of his day. "Yes."

She stood up, setting the contract down beside her mug. She moved from behind the coffee table and sank down to her knees, her head dropping forward. Her knees spread and she placed her palms flat on her thighs. "Welcome home, Sir."

That wouldn't do. "I hardly think that's how Bridget wrote it. I know Will allows her to run wild, but he has his rules, too, and he would never allow Bridget to greet him like that."

Her head came up. "This is exactly how…" She turned a sweet

shade of pink. "You're talking about the fact that I'm dressed. You want me to greet you naked. Mitch, you know that might not be possible with a kid."

"The kid is in utero. He doesn't care and can't be embarrassed at this point, so I'll have my naked time with his mom. He's just renting. According to that contract, I own." He owned her body. That gorgeous form was his to please, to hold, to lick and suck and fuck as he liked. He was plain about that in the contract.

He hadn't actually seen her naked. They'd made a baby, but he didn't know what her breasts looked like. It had been so quick, and now he wanted to take his time. They had months before they were going to become parents, before they had to figure everything out. He was going to use that time to memorize her body, to teach her to expect pleasure from him. He wanted her to associate him with long nights in bed spent worshipping her body.

She took a deep breath and seemed to come to some kind of decision.

Before she could rise, he held out a hand.

She looked up at him. "I thought you were a hardcore Dom. Shouldn't I rise gracefully at your command?"

"I'm the Dom who wants to make sure you're safe, Laurel. I'm the Dom who will never watch as you struggle without lending you a hand. I like ritual, but I like being there for you more, so when you get up, I will always be there to help you."

"You know sometimes you're really good at this." She placed her hand in his.

"Remember it because there will also be times I'm really bad at it. Laurel, I'm not very romantic. I forget things. I try to remember, but they slip away and I get caught up in work. I'm going to try to hold up my end of the bargain."

"Can you sum up your end of the bargain for me, counselor? In layman's terms, please."

"To make sure you're safe and happy and taken care of."

"That is a very good deal for me." There was a sheen of tears to her eyes, but he was pretty sure she wasn't sad because she moved toward him, placing her hands on his waist as she looked up at him. "And I'll do the same."

She went on her toes and lightly kissed his cheek before

stepping back. Her hands worked the back of her skirt.

He sat back down because this was his time. He was the Dom and his sub was undressing for him. She needed to understand that she had his complete and undivided attention.

Her skirt slipped to the floor and she started on the buttons of her blouse, undoing each with care and precision and possibly the knowledge that she was driving him insane. It was a good insane. Or maybe she was like him. Maybe she wanted to slow down this time and make it last in a way it hadn't before. This time they'd set down the ground rules.

This time it could work.

"Take off the bra," he commanded after she'd divested herself of the blouse and was standing there in her white cotton underwear. It wasn't plain though. She had something on her panties. "Are those flamingos?"

She winced. "I probably would have worn something pretty if I'd realized I was going to get hauled to the hospital and then undress for my Dom. You should know that most of my underwear has cute stuff on it."

Then he would be buying her a whole lot of new underwear. He wasn't a Dom who wanted her to toss out the underwear completely. He liked unwrapping his present, but he wanted her in something that fit her beauty. She should be in silk and satin and lace. He was pretty sure the flamingos were wearing party hats. "Take those off, too. They're distracting."

He hadn't even looked at her breasts. He was too horrified by the underwear.

She stepped out of the offensive panties and he got his first look at Laurel in her glory. He had to catch his breath because she was even more beautiful than he'd imagined her. She was a fucking fertility goddess with her curvy hips and full breasts. There was a slight curve to her belly that made him wonder what she was going to look like when she was full and ripe with child. His child. "Come here, Laurel."

Her golden brown hair was loose around her shoulders, her eyes slightly suspicious. Did she think he was about to reject her? Was she worried she wasn't pretty enough? Because he thought he'd already shown her how much he wanted her.

"Grip your wrists behind your back," he ordered when she moved close enough.

She took a deep breath and complied, the position causing her breasts to thrust out.

Fuck those were gorgeous. She had full breasts, likely a large C cup, maybe even a D, with big pink and brown nipples he could suck on for days. "How sensitive are they?"

"They're sensitive, but they don't hurt."

He reached out and let his fingers trace a line from her collarbone to her right nipple. The minute he brushed the top of her breast, the skin underneath flushed, the nipple hardened. Like a flower blooming to his touch.

Because he was sitting down, those pretty nipples were almost at the level of his mouth. He leaned over and placed a very chaste kiss on one and then the other. "Do you know what I'm going to do to you tonight?"

"I'm kinda hoping you're planning on fooling around."

He traced the areole of her nipple with his fingertip, utterly fascinated with her beauty. "Don't be ridiculous. Fooling around is for high school kids. I'm going to make love to you. Properly this time, and with complete control. I acted like an idiot that night."

"You were passionate."

"Passion tends to get us into trouble. I'm going to be thoughtful this time. I'm going to make you scream for me. I'm going to teach you what it means to be my sub. Tell me something and be honest with me. I'll know if you're not honest. I might not be in the courtroom a lot, but I can tell when a witness is lying."

"You're quite good at it," she agreed in a breathless voice.

"Why did you join Sanctum?"

She hesitated and he worried that she wouldn't answer. He filled in the time by moving his hands down to her hips and kissing his way to her belly. He breathed in the sweet scent of her arousal.

Finally, she replied. "To try to get close to you."

"So you were hoping to make me jealous." Her pussy was perfect, but he couldn't truly see it. "Sit down on the coffee table and spread your legs for me."

"Mitch, I don't think that's a good idea."

"I'm going to be patient with you because you're new and

we're learning together, so let me make this plain. You have ten seconds to sit on the coffee table, spread your legs, and show me your pussy, or I'll put you over my lap and we'll start with a count of fifteen." He reached around her and grabbed her mug and the contract. Now the coffee table was perfectly clutter free and ready for her. He held a hand out to help her sit down.

Her lips had firmed, her jawline becoming harder than normal. Ah, she was chafing at the confines. He intended to push her a bit harder.

"I wasn't trying to make you jealous." Even as she was arguing, she let him help her down. She placed herself on the coffee table he'd bought because it had a sturdy feel to it. He'd bought nothing for simple beauty, preferring function over form.

Now he had to think that having a naked Laurel totally brought the décor up. He sat back down and couldn't help the smile that threatened. "I was jealous, Laurel. I was blindingly jealous. God, you're lovely. Lean back a little. I want to look at your pussy."

"Mitch, this is bordering on the weird," she began, but did as he asked. "I'm sorry I made you jealous. I won't do it again. I suppose if I'm honest, I was willing to do just about anything to have you see me. Though I wasn't thinking of a gynecological exam at the time."

He waved her off and got down on his knees. He let his hands find the skin at her ankles and started to work his way up those sweet legs that would eventually get propped on his shoulders while he fucked her hard and long. "If your gynecologist does what I'm about to do, let me know because we're going to sue the motherfucker for all he's worth. So tell me what you had hoped would happen when I found you playing with Master T? I suspect I was being set up to find you playing with him. Was I supposed to start a fight?"

"Absolutely not," she began and likely would have continued had he not leaned over and put his nose right up against her pussy. "Oh my god."

It was good to know he could put her off balance. Laurel almost seemed too competent half the time. She would stand there in her prim little outfits and tell him what she thought he should do. It was usually the exact opposite of what he wanted to do. She liked to change things. He liked things to stay the same. It wasn't that he couldn't accept something new. He was definitely liking his new decoration. And he knew damn straight he wouldn't want to let her go. Ever.

He breathed her in, memorizing the spicy, deeply feminine scent of her arousal. And there was no doubt she was aroused. He could see her gorgeous labia. Her pussy was perfectly shaved and a lovely cream coated her pink flesh. He could see the pearl of her clit. It was poking out of its hood, begging for a lick, a suck, some sweet attention. But he had a couple of questions first. "Would you have let him fuck you?"

Her whole body tensed. "My contract didn't even allow nudity until three weeks in. I was kind of hoping you would wake up in three weeks. And no. I wouldn't have slept with him. I was desperate. I only wanted you. I would never have accepted another Master but you, you jerk."

He had been a jerk. He'd overreacted and taken something from her. Yes, she'd put him in a corner, but he wasn't a child. He hadn't had to fight his way out. He should have made the choice. He should have decided to be her Master or to let her go. Now he had no choice. He would be her Master. "I like to think I would have made a proper decision and that would be to take over and make you realize that you need me. I think I can still do that. But if you even look that cowboy's way, we'll have problems, you and I."

He was sure she would have argued on her own behalf. She would have told him that she wouldn't ever play with Master T, but he didn't give her a chance. He would rather let her know what she would be missing if she did.

He licked her, a long, slow drag of his tongue over her pussy. This was what he'd missed. He'd missed her taste and smell. God, he loved her smell and he fucking needed to know how she tasted when he could really take his time to enjoy her. He wasn't sure how he'd lived without that taste on his tongue. He put his hands on her knees, gently pressing out as he very tenderly ate that sweet pussy. He was careful. Despite what Will had said, he was still nervous about hurting her or the baby. He needed to read up. Research was something he was good at. He would read all he could about pregnancy and sex, but for now he simply licked and sucked at her.

She gasped and wiggled, but he had a good firm hold on her. She wasn't trying to get away, but he would bet she also wasn't completely comfortable with having a man spend this much time at her pussy.

"Relax, Laurel. There's nothing for you to do except let me have my way."

"Mitch, I want you."

"And I want you." He sucked one side of her labia as his thumb started circling her clitoris. Not enough to make her come. He didn't want to do that yet.

"Mitch, I want to have sex."

She was taking a deeply Clintonian definition of sex. "We are having sex."

She'd shaved and her skin was baby smooth and god, she was so wet. He delved inside, fucking her with his tongue, gathering all her cream for himself.

"Mitch, I want your cock. I think we should have intercourse. Penetrative intercourse."

He pulled away. "Then you should have found a different lover, Laurel. I told you how this would go." He hated leaving her. He hated the fact that he wasn't going to get what he wanted, but he couldn't let her move him on this. He'd already given in to her. He knew what he needed and if he allowed her to, she would walk all over him.

Again. God, he was a perverse son of a bitch to need control and always be attracted to women who wouldn't give it to him.

"I think I'll go take a shower. Lisa should be here soon. Do you mind waiting for her?"

Her eyes were wide. Her whole body flushed a nice pink and he wanted nothing more than to give her exactly what she wanted, but he'd played that way before and it didn't work out. "You're leaving?"

His dick was protesting, but he knew what he wanted and it wasn't to be pushed around and told what to do. Definitely not during sex. "You should have read the contract more closely, Laurel. I'm in charge in the bedroom, and you obey me there or you use your safe word if you get frightened or find yourself in pain. You weren't scared and what I was doing couldn't have caused you pain, so you were trying to take control. I'm ending the session. I don't play like that and I've explained that to you on numerous occasions. I've never lied to you about what I wanted."

She shook her head. "No, you haven't, and I want to understand what it means to be your submissive. Please, Mitchell. I'm sorry. You can spank me if you like, but I promise I won't try to take control again. I was excited and I wanted you more than I've ever wanted anything. Please forgive me."

"The punishment was clearly laid out in our contract. When you infringe on my bedroom rights, I withdraw and you're to be left to think about your actions." He'd punished many subs this way. So why did it seem so foolish to punish Laurel? Why did something that once seemed like a game now feel so fucking serious?

Things were changing and he didn't like it. The best course of action would be to leave her for an hour or two and get his distance. Then he could return and they would discuss the infraction.

She hopped off the table and stepped up to him. "Mitch, I'm asking you to change that punishment. You're right. I didn't read it as thoroughly as I should have because I wasn't going to let anything stop me from signing, but I can't do this. I can handle a spanking. I can't handle you withholding affection as punishment. You asked me to never ignore your calls because you wouldn't ignore mine. Well, don't play with my heart this way because I won't ever do that to you. This makes me feel very small."

His former subs would have pouted and sulked, and now he realized why he'd chosen the women he had. To those submissives, everything was a game. He'd been careful to pick women who enjoyed the manipulative aspects, who would give him reasons to punish them because they enjoyed the game.

This wasn't a game for Laurel.

He nodded and forced some unnamed emotion down as he reached for her and drew her close. "I don't want you to feel small, baby. You're not small to me. Forgive me. I didn't mean to make you feel that way."

"And I didn't mean to make you feel out of control." She kissed his jaw and then settled herself against him. She didn't seem to be self-conscious in any way. She was like a happy kitten rubbing against him. "I can handle a lot of things, but I can't handle you being cold to me."

He'd been cold for so long. It was all he knew how to be, but he found himself holding her close and then his mouth found hers. How long had it been since he tossed out his rituals and routines and simply let the sex happen? Well, besides what had happened in his office a few weeks before. Tonight wasn't going to end the same way. Tonight he would end up in bed with her, wrapped up with her.

He kissed her, his tongue finding hers and playing. His hands moved across her skin, exploring. She was his for the time being and she was different from the other subs he'd kept. She wasn't after his money or his connections. She wasn't looking for a free ride.

She was carrying his child.

He hated change, but it was here and he was trapped.

He was surprised to find that didn't scare him the way it should have.

Before he really knew what he was doing, he was pressing her back, taking her down to the couch. He kissed her as his hands fumbled at his belt and then the fly of his slacks. His cock sprang free and he wasn't thinking about anything but getting inside her. He shoved his slacks down and made a place for himself at her core.

Her hands tore at his shirt as though she couldn't stand the clothes between them. He ripped the damn thing off himself, hearing the sound of the buttons pinging on the hardwoods as he tossed it away. It didn't matter. He had twenty exactly like it and he wanted to feel her hands on him.

She sighed as she looked up at him. "You're so beautiful."

She was the beautiful one. "Wrap your legs around my waist. The good news is I don't have to fumble around for a condom. That ship sailed."

The smile on her face would have brought him to his knees if he hadn't already been there. "That ship has definitely sailed and there's no getting off it."

But she was smiling. She was stuck with him and she was still smiling. God, he would do a lot to keep that smile on her face.

He slowed down. He was always in a rush to have her. She pushed him past all control, but that smile gave some of it back. He lowered himself down, giving her his weight. Her legs circled his waist and he kissed her, his cock nudging at her.

He groaned as he thrust inside. So tight. God, she had the tightest, hottest pussy. It fit him like a damn glove, like she'd been made to take his cock.

He buried his face in her neck, breathing her in as he slowly forced his way inside her. She was wet, but it was still a deliciously tight fit.

"That feels so good." Her nails ran over his back.

He kissed her neck and let the heat of her body warm his own. "One of these days, I swear I'm going to get out of my clothes, baby."

He pushed in until there was nowhere else to go, until she'd taken every inch of him and he could feel her squeeze him tight. He flexed inside her and was rewarded with a sexy gasp from her.

He thrust in and dragged back out, feeling her all around him. Her legs tightened, arms circling and nails scoring him lightly.

He didn't have sex like this. Somewhere in the back of his head alarm bells were going off. He controlled the sex. He preferred to have his sexual partner tied up or ordered to remain still, to give her body over to him and he would see to their pleasure. But he couldn't do it with Laurel. He gave over to the primal instinct to mate. He couldn't call it sex. Sex was something he could take or leave, but he wasn't sure he could ever leave this woman, and that was precisely why he'd stayed away from her in the first place.

He was not the man who got lost in freaking passion.

He fucked her hard, not caring to listen to alarm bells or reason. It felt too good to have her around him, to be in the center of her touch, her smell, her heat. He forgot about all the reasons why he shouldn't and let his cock take over. His cock knew exactly what he wanted and he wanted to mark Laurel as his.

Over and over he thrust inside, taking them higher and higher. When she tensed around him and called out his name, he knew this fight was over. The silky muscles of her pussy clamped down and milked his cock. His spine sizzled as he gave up and held himself hard against her, pouring himself into her.

He finally rested, completely spent. Her hands smoothed over his back and there was nothing but the peaceful sound of her breathing, her heart beating as he laid his head on her chest.

He was in deep and he was fairly certain that this time he would drown.

# Chapter Six

Laurel looked around the new Sanctum with a sense of wonder. It was big. Three levels. There was a bar, lounge, and gorgeous locker rooms on the first floor. She'd been surprised to discover she'd been given her own locker complete with a nameplate. When she'd opened it, she'd found her favorite toiletries had already been stocked and there were clothes Mitch had picked out for her hanging there.

He was a thoughtful Master. She'd traded the delicate gold chain she wore during the day for a heavier collar. This one was made of leather, but he'd had it custom detailed with green, glossy leaves.

For a Laurel tree.

The second level was the dungeon. She stood there, looking out over Ian Taggart's own version of heaven, and hoped Mitch didn't have a thing for the human hamster wheel. It was a massive thing and someone had lined it with twinkle lights. Serena and Bridget were giggling as they watched a male sub jogging his ass off in the hamster wheel while a big Dom stood watching, threatening to whip his ass if he slowed down.

"Is that Chris?" Chris was her sister-in-law's best friend. Along with Serena, Bridget and Chris were a trio to be reckoned with at Sanctum. Everyone knew that if you gave them a juicy story it would end up in one of their books.

Bridget gave her a spectacular smile. "Yeah, he told Jeremy he needed help getting fit. He kind of threw a hissy fit because Jeremy can eat whatever he wants and still stay gorgeous. Chris got a little bratty and hence the new sub workout."

Chris's legs pumped harder and faster and the twinkle lights changed from white to green.

"That's right. Get it up to green, sub. Five more minutes or I'll have you on a St. Andrew's Cross and you won't be able to sit down for a week. How many calories will that burn, love? Yeah, don't try to talk. Just run." Jeremy winked at her. "That's the last time he tells me I'm a shitty trainer."

"Tag set it up so the lights change the faster you go," Serena explained. "It's kind of the symbol for the new Sanctum. Pretty and functionally torturous. I can't wait to start writing about it."

Bridget pulled Laurel in for a hug. "I'm so glad you're here. I see Mitch was kind with the clothes."

She was wearing a crop top and tiny miniskirt. No shoes for her. He'd explained that while he liked her heels, he was afraid she would trip in them. She hadn't stopped wearing them to work, but he ruled here at Sanctum. "He's afraid a corset would be confining for the baby. I did not even point out that women wore them for many years and they're adjustable. I've found on some things, it's easier to give in. And I really hope we got all the hideously embarrassing questions out of the way with the first doctor's visit."

Mitch had driven her to Dr. Bates's office and waited with her. He'd helped her change into her gown and listened intently while the doctor had searched for the heartbeat. While she'd gotten teary at the sound, he'd been stoic. He'd simply nodded and squeezed her hand as though he'd read somewhere that was what the expectant father did when the expectant mother cried. He'd shown no real emotion, but boy had he had some questions for the doc.

Bridget laughed. "How bad was it? I happen to know your OB. She's very cool and understands the lifestyle, so I'm sure it's nothing she hasn't heard before."

"He asked if anal sex was okay for the baby. I'm not kidding you." It had been horrifying. He'd had a list of questions for Dr. Bates, most of them about sexual things she never thought she would talk to a doctor about.

"What did she say?" Serena asked. "Because when Jake asked she told us as long as it was my ass he was very gently fucking it would likely be all right, but otherwise he might be in trouble."

Dr. Bates seemed to have come from the Big Tag school of bedside manner. "Yes, that seems to be her patent response. Did Mitchell have to go through an entire list of sexual positions and acts?"

"This is a guy's way of caring. He's nervous about it so he has to find some way of taking control," Serena explained. "Pregnancy can be very difficult for the man. Especially a Dom. He can't control it so you have to find ways to make him more comfortable with the situation. Let him pamper you even when it's annoying. Seriously, a foot rub can get boring after three hours, but it soothed Jake to do it. Adam was definitely calmer until we hit the delivery room. That first blood freaked him out. He wasn't prepared for it to be so bloody and painful."

"Hey, ixnay on the ainpay." Bridget frowned Serena's way.

"Oh, because I should tell her that childbirth is a lovely, pain-free, and completely comfortable experience."

"I'm going to take all the drugs," Laurel admitted. "Every one of them. I'm not a Viking woman."

The pain part scared the crap out of her. So did all the things that could happen. Mitch didn't want her to read the childbirth books. He'd told her they would only scare her, but she'd put a couple on her Kindle anyway. One of them had to be ready. He'd asked the doctor a million questions about their sex lives and not one about the actual pregnancy.

Sometimes she wondered if he'd changed his mind about the baby again. Or was it all about his duty to her and responsibility for the child?

She'd noticed that after their first night together, they hadn't spoken of marriage again. She told herself it was good because she didn't want to have that fight, but she had to wonder if she really wanted to be a single mom.

"Do you absolutely have to play tonight? It's hard walking around without looking at things. I'm going to crash into someone's scene," a familiar voice said.

She turned and there was her brother coming up the stairs with Mitchell and Kai. Will's eyes were firmly planted on the ground.

Kai gave her a smile. "He's trying to avoid seeing you half naked."

"She's actually quite covered," Mitch admitted.

He looked utterly delicious. No matter what kind of problems they might have, there was no denying the fact that this man got her motor running like no other. Sanctum was filled with gorgeous men, but Mitch seemed to stand above the rest. He was so masculine, with his broad shoulders and cut chest on display. She loved how petite she felt when he held her. He seemed to like to show off how strong he was by carrying her around.

Will brought his head up, his eyes opening cautiously. He seemed to relax. "All right. I suppose I can handle that. What kind of scene are you two doing tonight?"

Mitch moved to her side, his eyes going to the collar around her neck. She could practically feel the satisfaction pouring off him in waves. He might not want her as a wife, but she could tell he was enjoying keeping a submissive. "I'm doing a ropes demonstration, and no, you will not want to watch. We're up very soon, so you and Bridget should stay on the east side of the dungeon. I hear Weston and his wife are doing an impact play scene."

"I'm going to find a pretty little pain slut and get my freak on," Kai promised. He looked nothing like his normal self. Kai was usually very intellectual looking. Like the professor at college every girl wanted to date. But with his hair down around his shoulders and dressed in leathers and motorcycle boots, the good psychologist looked dangerous. And definitely ready for some fun. Of course, his idea of fun had to do with pain.

"When are you going to play with Kori?" Mitch nodded to a girl across the room.

Kori was standing with her friend, Sarah. The two were pretty women. With curves for days, they looked ready for play in their corsets and teeny tiny thongs.

Kai frowned. "I'm not and I've made that clear. She works for me. I'm not going to play with my employee. I've so recently seen where that leads." He patted Mitch on the shoulder. "I'm going to find a compatible woman and work very hard to not get her pregnant. You look lovely, Laurel."

"I don't think that's a compliment."

Kai took her hand and brought it to his lips, kissing it gallantly. "It was meant to be. I wish you all the best. And know that my door is always open."

Kai strode away.

"If I didn't know he was offering you a counseling session, I might go kick his ass. I think I want to amend our contract. No one gets to kiss you except me. Not any part of you. I didn't like him kissing your hand." Mitch could get the tiniest bit jealous, but he looked so cute standing there staring after his friend like he wasn't sure what to do.

"Somehow, I think he merely meant it as a friendly gesture. Shall we take a look around? I know all the Doms got to see the place being built, but this is my first time."

He took her hand, threading their fingers together. "I suppose that's why you weren't waiting for me outside the locker rooms?"

She winced. He'd been implicit in his instructions, but then Mitch always was. "I wanted to know what I was getting into."

"You knew where I wanted you."

"Yes, Master." She'd actually thought she could run up and take a peek and then get back downstairs. Then she'd caught sight of that damn hamster wheel and gotten off track.

"I like the way that sounds," he said, satisfaction evident on his face.

"Master?" She hadn't called him by his title before. Maybe it would save her. She gave him her more innocent smile. "My Master."

He shook his head. "That's not going to save you, sweet brat. While we're showing people how to form a rope dress, you'll also receive twenty swats."

Will shuddered. "See, I don't need to hear that. Ever."

Bridget sent Laurel an apologetic glance. "Sorry. He'll get used to it."

"No, I won't," Will complained as Bridget led him off.

Serena went to join her husbands and Laurel was left alone with her Dom.

"I didn't like you not being there when I came out. I would have stood there waiting for you had another sub not come out and explained you had already left. Will told me where you would be. Apparently he knows you better than I do."

"Living with a person for eighteen years will do that to you."

"That's another five for sarcasm."

She should have known he would be more rigid in the club. The play parties they'd attended over the last few weeks hadn't seemed as formal. She lowered her head in deference to her Dom. "I'm sorry, Master. I was very eager to see the dungeon and Bridget was walking upstairs. I went with her. I meant to get back down after I took a peek. I understand and accept my punishment."

His hand came out and he gently lifted her chin up so she saw him again. "I don't like not knowing where you are. It worries me."

Her heart melted a little because he really did worry when she wasn't with him. "I'm sorry."

He leaned over and kissed her forehead. "Don't do it again. I want to be with you when you walk this dungeon. Now, we don't have much time. Let's take a walk and then get to our space. Everything's set up for us so we have a few minutes."

He started to lead her around. There was the heavy thud of industrial music playing. It seemed to thump through the entire floor. There were numerous scene spaces. She saw a well-stocked doctor's office. It looked like Mitch's friend Keith was giving his wife a very deep examination using his penis.

"You're blushing." Mitch stopped on the outskirts of the scene. "How are you going to get through our scene if this bothers you?"

She shook her head. "It doesn't bother me at all. They're happy, consenting adults. I have no problem with it. It's very arousing."

His lips quirked up. "You're aroused, are you?"

She was getting more aroused because he was backing her up, his big body invading her space. She found herself against a wall. "Yes."

His hand found her thigh. "I think I'd like to see how aroused you are. Spread your legs for me."

There had been no panties left in her locker and she definitely hadn't been foolish enough to wear the ones she'd entered the building in. She would wear what she wanted outside, but in Sanctum she dressed to please Mitchell. Her Master had tossed out all her old cotton panties and replaced them with gorgeous silk undies, but he'd been plain about not wearing them at all in the club.

She did as he asked. It was her first time in the club. The play parties hadn't truly prepped her for how it would feel. Sanctum was so big. It gave her the sense that any moment anyone could walk by and see her. Her heart raced a little. The club was full tonight. There was a big party for the grand opening with a gorgeous buffet downstairs, but suddenly she wasn't thinking of food. She was thinking of Mitch's hands on her body. His big palms moved up her thighs, taking the miniscule skirt with them. She felt cool air on her most private part.

"I don't want nudity to bother you, Laurel. Certainly not your own. You're gorgeous and you're mine. I'm going to love showing off your body. I'm thinking about showing it off right now. What are you thinking about, baby?"

He slid the skirt to her waist, completely exposing her pussy and backside. Cool air hit her sensitive flesh and she felt the most delicious chill go up her spine.

"You. Nothing else." It was the nice thing about the time they spent playing. She could let go of everything else. There was no reason to worry. This was the place where she could live in the moment. Every other moment of her life she suddenly had to worry about the future, but here she could simply be Master Mitchell's submissive.

His hand moved between her legs. "Let's see what happens when you think of me."

A finger slide through her labia, parting her pussy and gently curving up. His thumb found her clitoris and pressed down and up and then moved in a sensuous circle.

Her whole body responded, softening, preparing.

"Hands above your head," he commanded in that low growl that always got her motor running.

She moved her hands over her head, holding her right wrist with her left. It brought the shirt she was wearing up to the point that the bottoms of her breasts were showing.

He withdrew his hand, much to her dismay. He brought his fingers up, a grin on his face. "I like the way you think about me, Laurel."

He sucked his soaked fingers inside his mouth, obviously savoring the taste of her arousal. When he was done, he crowded her again.

"You're the only man who could ever get me this hot this

fast." She wanted him to know this crazy piece of her only seemed to be for him. She couldn't imagine standing here in a crowded room with her legs spread wide for all to see with anyone except him. She'd been perfectly vanilla until she'd met Mitchell Bradford, and she would likely go back into her comfy shell if he left her.

"I intend to keep it that way." It was the closest thing he would say about the future. He tugged her skirt down. "Come with me. It's time to get started."

She followed him through the club, well aware that the ache inside, the desperate wanting, was all part of her Dom's punishment for disobeying him. He'd felt how wet she was and he was going to leave her waiting. It was all part of the scene.

In the weeks they'd been living together, she'd gotten used to Mitch's version of play. He was a man of routine. He liked the discipline of holding to a schedule. While that might sound boring to a lot of people, Laurel loved the fact that the man came home every night at six o'clock on the dot without fail. She knew to be undressed and waiting for him, and had never once been left on her knees waiting.

For a girl who never knew if her mother was going to show up at all, it was comforting.

But she did miss his passion. He'd found the routine of discipline and he no longer deviated. While he'd put aside the use of withdrawal of affection as a punishment, he still wasn't exactly chatty. He would listen to her all day but never said a word about his past or their future.

She walked with him, looking around her at all the happy couples. There were a few women she knew from her training classes. Before subs were ever introduced to Doms, they had to go through classes and pass a psych eval. She waved at a couple of her friends who seemed to be flirting with the new Doms.

They briefly stopped at one of the odder scene spaces. She'd passed the classroom space, with its school desks and chalkboards where professors spanked wayward subs who didn't do their homework. This was like a classroom, but an almost medieval one.

She recognized the "professor" in the scene. Jesse Murdoch was wearing a long, dark robe and standing in front of a series of beakers and cauldrons that had what looked like steam coming out of them.

"Miss Grant, this potion is atrocious and not befitting of a witch of your caliber," Jesse said in a dark tone.

She felt her eyes widen as she realized where the scene was coming from. Phoebe Murdoch stood, her hair flowing and eyes wide. She was wearing a robe too, though hers barely covered her backside and she didn't seem to be wearing anything underneath it.

"I suppose you'll have to punish me, professor. For the good of all the wizarding world," she said as she presented her ass to him.

"I don't think that's what J.K. Rowling intended wands to do," she whispered to Mitch.

He shook his head and continued toward the center of the dungeon and the raised stage. She definitely knew a couple of the people in this crowd, but she couldn't tell what kind of scene was being performed.

That was when she saw the rope that had been placed on a table along with what looked to be a ridiculously large anal plug and some lube.

He was not about to…

"Come on, baby." He started to help her to the stairs.

"This is the main stage."

"Yes, and this is a teaching scene. The new Doms are all expected to attend. We wouldn't want to be late, would we?"

There were a lot of people and they were about to watch Mitch tie her up. What was she doing? She was pregnant. She was going to be a mom. She shouldn't be out here.

"Laurel?"

She realized she was standing there and everyone was watching them. Mitch was going to be angry. He'd planned this whole scene and he wouldn't like her messing it up.

"Laurel?" He stepped back down and stared at her for a moment. His eyes were cold and she felt frozen in place.

He was going to give her an ultimatum now. It was what he did. It was how they seemed to work, or rather how he worked. She'd figured out that she had to adapt to him if she wanted to be with him.

Maybe that wasn't the best way to live.

He stepped up close and she waited for him to tell her to get on the stage or accept whatever punishment he was going to give her, and then she would have to make a choice. God, the moment was here and she wasn't ready for it. She wasn't ready to leave him, but she also wasn't sure she wanted to go on that stage.

His hands sank into her hair, but instead of tugging on it and forcing her to look at him, he pulled her close and settled her against his chest. "Baby, there's nothing to be afraid of. Shhh. If you don't want to do this, you don't have to. We can spend the rest of the night watching scenes and then go down and have a nice dinner. It's going to be all right."

"But you set up the scene." He didn't back down. He plowed through. He did what he said he was going to do.

"And someone can take over." His hand smoothed down her hair. "Laurel, baby, what are you afraid of? I would never hurt you and I certainly won't make you do a scene you're uncomfortable with."

He was making everyone wait. He was holding them up so he could comfort her.

"There are a lot of people here," she admitted. "And I thought about the fact that I'm pregnant and I'm going to be a mom and god, Mitch, what are we going to do when the baby gets here? What are we going to do?"

She wasn't sure why it hit her then and there, but it did. Weeks of holding it together culminated in her shaking and crying and making a complete idiot of herself in front of all the Doms in Sanctum.

Mitch swept her up into his arms. "Alex, could you take over for me?"

Now they would have to go home and talk about why she'd ruined the scene. She wasn't looking forward to going into the locker room alone and having to change back into street clothes. She wasn't looking forward to an awkward discussion.

She held on when she realized he was going up and not down. He was heading to the third floor.

A man was stationed at the top of the stairs. He looked up, his eyes registering surprise. "Master Mitchell? I wasn't expecting you for another hour."

"Sometimes aftercare has to come first, Mike. Is there a room open?"

"You're lucky. I already prepped your room. It's number five, but I gotta warn you. The big boss is in four and he will neither turn the music down nor change it."

Mitch nodded and before she knew it, she could hear the strains of a familiar song as Mitch opened the door and strode in. "Sweet Child o' Mine."

She was having a baby.

She found herself on his lap, sobbing against his shoulder. How had she gone from getting all hot and bothered to weeping openly?

He rocked her, his arms encircling her. "It's going to be all right, Laurel. Baby, it's going to be okay. I'm going to take care of you and the baby. You don't have to cry."

He sounded almost as broken as she felt. She wrapped her arms around him and let go completely.

* * * *

Mitch had never felt so helpless in his whole damn life, and there had been plenty of times when he'd felt helpless. But Laurel sobbing in his arms…he would rather pull his heart straight out of his chest than have her so utterly heartbroken.

She'd seemed happy. She'd wanted to come to Sanctum. She'd been looking forward to it all week. But something had happened to her as she stood in front of that stage. She couldn't be afraid of him or the ropes. He loved to tie her up. Sometimes he practiced as they sat together at night. She would sit in front of him and he would weave the rope into her hair or have her lay across the couch and let him bind her legs before he would ease her to the floor and fuck into her from behind.

It couldn't be the ropes. She'd said something about all the people.

"Baby, were you scared of people looking at you?" He asked the question knowing that women sometimes got weird ideas. Laurel was simply the most beautiful woman in the world, but that didn't mean she believed it. She was so sexy he couldn't be in a room with her and not have his dick get hard. Just thinking about her made him erect, but women often didn't see themselves the way men did.

He'd never actually gotten her naked during a scene before. He'd taken it slowly, tried to allow her to adapt. He was well aware she would still be considered in her training period had he not collared her. She would have been given a training Dom who couldn't undress her or do anything more intimate than hug her or let her sit on his lap. He'd gone much further than that. He'd stroked her pussy in full view of the club, forced her to show herself off.

Had that scared her?

She shook her head. "I'm not scared so much as confused. I don't know what happened, Mitch. I got to the bottom of those stairs and I realized that I was pregnant and I don't know what's going to happen. Am I going to be up there getting tied up when I'm as big as a whale? Or is this temporary and I'll only play while I'm still somewhat small and you won't want to play with me when I'm huge. Maybe you'll want another sub. One who can see her feet. Serena told me by the end of her pregnancy she couldn't see her feet."

Yep. He would rather face a team of lawyers in front of the Supreme Court with a no-win case than have to see her cry. He held her close. He was shitty at the tender stuff, but somehow Laurel seemed to bring it out of him. "You'll only get tied up as long as you want to be, baby. I can't imagine wanting another sub. Even one who can see her feet. I'm not all that into feet anyway. And if you want to see yours, I'll hold a mirror up and you'll be able to see them. Baby, don't cry."

That seemed to make her cry harder.

"Or you can cry. You can cry all you like."

He held her and smoothed a hand over her back as he rocked to the music. There was something both sexy and comforting about the beat.

Until he listened to the lyrics.

Where did they go? From here, where the hell were they supposed to go? Should they simply move through life and play house?

He had to face the fact that he wasn't sure he wanted to get married again. He also had to face the fact that he didn't want to live without Laurel.

He didn't even know what to think about the kid, and didn't that make him the biggest shit of all time?

Somehow, they ended up lying together in the big bed as she slowly calmed. He cuddled her close, almost dreading the moment when they would have to talk again because he had no idea what to say. When he was with her, everything felt right, but she was utterly correct. Things were going to change. They would have to.

She sniffled and laid her head on his chest. "I'm sorry I ruined the evening."

The song started up again and he laid a hand on her head. "You didn't ruin anything, Laurel. We're fine. You're just emotional. Don't you have hormones and stuff?"

She nodded against his chest. "Lots."

They would ebb and flow and eventually go away. He simply had to hold on to her through the rough stuff.

*And what about when the kid comes? That's about the roughest stuff possible. No way you can control a kid. You don't even know how to be a dad, and we all know what kind of a husband you make.*

His arms wrapped around her almost as though rebelling against the logic of his brain. She was his. He didn't have to give her up now. Not even for her own good. "You'll see. We'll be fine. And you're going to be gorgeous when you're really big… I mean further along."

Her face was red but her lips had turned up when she looked at him. "I'm going to be big, Mitch. Really big. I'm supposed to gain at least thirty pounds, but when I'm not nauseous I'm hungry, so I might gain more. Unfortunately, this baby doesn't get kale cravings. He wants ice cream. Or she. Either way, this tiny thing obviously has a sweet tooth."

Well, Laurel certainly did. "The good news is I heard Macon Miles made a massive cake for tonight. The midnight buffet isn't far away, but if you need something now, we can make it happen. Pregnant ladies get perks."

Or he would steal some if he had to. He would do anything to keep a smile on her face.

"Mitch, do you honestly think you'll still want to play with me?

I don't see a bunch of pregnant women running around here. I think I'm the only one."

Was that what she was worried about? She'd been in the nursery for most of her time as a trainee, so she'd only seen the moms coming back after they had babies. "Laurel, it's been a freaking baby boom around here. You feel alone because you haven't seen it. Charlotte Taggart was playing up until a couple of weeks before she gave birth. They modified everything for her, but she and Big Tag weren't going to give that part of their life up. From what I hear, Serena and Avery played long into their pregnancies, and so did Sean's wife, Grace. And you won't be alone. I happen to know Keith and Ashley are trying to get pregnant, and so are Jesse and Phoebe. Although they'll probably name their baby after Harry Potter, so I'm praying for that kid. And you know one of these days Will's going to give in and convince Bridget to have a kid."

He feared for a world where Bridget Daley had pregnancy hormones running through her veins.

But he didn't want Laurel to feel alone.

"So no one's going to think it's weird or irresponsible?"

"To play with the father of your baby?" He'd almost slipped and said husband.

She shrugged as though it didn't matter when it so obviously did. "Just to play. Maybe I should only think about the baby."

"Laurel, you don't have to give up your sexuality because you're pregnant. No one here would ever want you to do that. You're beautiful and nothing makes me prouder than to show you off, but if you're uncomfortable, then we'll play privately."

"Do you mean that?"

He would miss coming here, miss the camaraderie. "Yes. My place is with you."

At least he knew that much.

"You love this place."

"But I need to stay with you." There was something else, something he couldn't even think. *I love you more.* "I need to look out for you and the baby. If I can't do that here, then I'll do it where I can. But Laurel, you don't stop being a woman because you become a mom. I've seen it happen, though more on the other side. My mom didn't stop being a woman. Ever. She wasn't much of a mom, but even I know you're different. You can be both because I know you'll never neglect your child. You'll find a balance."

He hoped they would both find it. Somehow, he couldn't see himself being a father and if he couldn't manage it, then he wouldn't be able to keep Laurel. Unlike his mother, she would choose her child's needs. Even if it meant giving up the child's father.

She buried her head in the curve of his neck. "I can't believe I did that. I burst into tears. How am I ever going to walk back out there?"

"Why wouldn't you walk back out there?"

"Because of how embarrassed I'll be."

Now that the storm had passed, it seemed like a good time to take control again. "What would you be embarrassed about? Because everyone here knows you're pregnant. And almost all subs cry at some point. It's expected. No one will think less of you. Now tell me what happened. What really made you cry?"

She sat up and her eyes slid away from his. "It was the thought that I'll be a mom soon and…it's not like I'm thin now. Everyone would see me. You would see me."

What the hell did that mean? It was definitely time to take charge. He sat up beside her. "Laurel, I've seen you naked many times. I see you naked every single night, so you're going to have to explain how my seeing you naked could possibly cause you to cry."

"You haven't seen how your friends might react. Maybe they have prettier subs." She frowned. "I know it sounds stupid, but I'm trying to be honest with you. I might be all right now, but everything is going to change. I'll gain weight, and even afterward I'll have stretch marks and I'll breast feed so my boobs will likely sag, and it's really hard because you keep telling me to live in the moment, but I can't."

"Laurel, I'll still want you." He wasn't sure she would want him. He wasn't sure she wouldn't figure out exactly how many men there were out there with whole hearts and easy tempers.

"How can you know that?"

"I know." It was the one thing he was certain of. "If you're worried about the future, you know what to do." He was also certain that marriage would be best—even if he found the entire idea unsettling. "I've already asked you to marry me. We can get on a flight to Vegas and be married tomorrow."

She stared at him, her eyes wary. "Is that what you want?"

"I think that would be best for our baby."

Her eyes turned down and she seemed to shake something off. When she looked back up there was a smile on her face, though a hint of sadness permeated her being. "I think our baby is going to be fine. And you're right. Living in the moment is for the best. Marriage isn't a promise of permanency. Let's make a pact. Whatever happens, we'll respect each other and be friends."

He didn't want to be her friend. And he didn't want to be her ex. He didn't want to only see her or hear from her when she needed money or wanted to take him back to court. "We'll always be friends."

It was why he hadn't wanted to get involved with her in the first place. Laurel had become essential to him. She was the bright spot in his days, the reason he wanted to get up in the mornings. He truly would have stayed in the background. He would have watched her date and find a good man and get married. He would have watched over her and counted himself lucky to have her in his life.

Friends stayed. Friends stuck it out.

He was almost certain they could never be friends again.

"Sweet Child o' Mine" started up again and there was a banging against the wall. Rhythmic and loud.

Laurel laughed suddenly, her whole face lighting up.

At least it proved a point. He gestured to the wall. "Proof positive that there is sex after children. And hey, we've only got one in there. We're better off than Big Tag and Charlotte, but they seem to have found a way around it."

She stood up and walked over to the closet. He watched her cautiously, unsure of where she was going. She opened the door and he heard her rummage around inside. When she turned, she had a length of rope in her hand. "Mitch, I know I screwed up the demo."

"You didn't screw it up. You had an emotional reaction. It's fine. Alex can handle it."

"Maybe we could at least show off your skills. Maybe you

could make me a dress for the after party."

His dick jumped at the thought. "Come here."

She stepped toward him, offering him the rope. "Do you think that's a good idea? I love the patterns you can make. They're beautiful."

"You're beautiful, but we have something we need to take care of first." He patted his lap. They wouldn't be able to do this for much longer. When she started to show she wouldn't be able to lie on her belly, but he wanted her across his lap while it was still safe. He usually disciplined submissives on spanking benches or in some fashion where he had the most control and the least amount of intimacy. He tended to use crops or paddles. Canes if the submissive was amenable.

But he wanted Laurel over his lap, wanted her dependent on him, needed to feel her squirm and writhe under his hand.

"I thought you didn't care that I ruined the scene."

"This isn't about the scene. You disobeyed my direct command that you wait for me outside the locker room. You're not allowed to run around the dungeon without me."

"Bridget was up there without Will."

"That's Will's problem. Not mine. You're my sub and we have our own rules. So let's get the punishment over and I'll make your top. I won't do a complete dress because I want you to be able to move." He would have to go easy. Though right now there was absolutely no sign that Laurel was carrying a child, he wouldn't bind her tightly. He would form diamond patterns around her torso, force her breasts out, but he would bind her in deference to her comfort. And if she simply couldn't stand it, he would run the ropes over her clothes.

She couldn't know how much he was bending for her. She couldn't imagine how rigid he'd been before. If she ever knew how much power she had, it would all be over. It was better to let her think this was the normal way his relationships went.

"You haven't punished me before."

"You haven't misbehaved before."

A sweet grin lit her face. "You have no idea how unlike me that is." She took a deep breath. "Okay. I did the crime. I can do the time. It's twenty-five, right?"

"Yes. Twenty-five. Take off your clothes. Punishment requires nudity. That's a new rule, too." He went to the closet. The room had been prepped for him and had everything he'd requested, including the item he found waiting with a nice bottle of lubricant. "And you'll take a plug in addition to your dress. That's not punishment though. That's preparation."

"I can handle a plug, Master. You've been making me wear one every night."

"You haven't been spanked while wearing a plug. I believe you'll find the experience stimulating."

When he turned, her eyes had gone wide. "That's a much bigger plug than normal, Mitch."

"Master here, Laurel. I don't require formality anywhere but the club. And yes, it's large, but I fully intend to take your lovely ass very soon, and this will make things so much easier." He brought the prepped plug and lubricant back to the bed and sat down, his cock already straining.

This was what he needed to banish the unsettling feelings he had about the future. He needed to play with her, to reassure himself that at least for now she belonged to him.

It was all he could really ask for. She belonged to him now.

"Yes, Master." She drew the shirt over her head and he let go of his cares.

She was all that mattered now.

# Chapter Seven

Laurel pushed the skirt off her hips and let Mitch help her lie over his lap. Vulnerable. She was so vulnerable in this position. The room had gone quiet, the music ending. She heard a low chuckle and then a door opening and closing. The Taggarts, it seemed, were satisfied. They would be going downstairs to host the party that was soon to come.

The party she would be attending wearing nothing but Mitch's rope over her chest and likely the skirt.

Unless he chose otherwise. She'd promised herself she would give Mitch the rest of the night. He'd already given her so much. She wasn't foolish. She knew his reputation. All of his D/s relationships had been in California, but he'd played with many subs here and they'd all said the same thing. Mitchell Bradford didn't bend. He was uncompromising as a Dom. If she'd been asked what Master Mitch would do if his submissive threatened to ruin a scene he'd prepared for, she would have told anyone that he would simply find another sub for the scene and then punish his own sub.

But he hadn't even hesitated. He'd been tender and kind and so sweet she'd forgiven him for not being able to say he wanted to marry her.

The man had been screwed over so many times before, he wasn't sure what he wanted. He needed time and she intended to give it to him. She also intended to give him her submission for the rest of the evening, even if it meant taking that damn hung-like-a-horse plug.

After all, Mitchell was that.

The leather of his pants was smooth against her belly. His cock was not. It was a hard ridge that proved the man wanted her despite her crazy emotional swings. She relaxed as he smoothed a hand over her back and down to the cheeks of her ass. He'd certainly touched her there before, but she always loved how he paused as though he was taking in the sight. He cupped her, his fingers tracing the seam before he parted her.

She forced herself to relax. He'd been plugging her for days and she'd learned there was nothing truly painful about the experience. Just some pressure and a feeling of being full. She shivered as he placed the lubed tip to her asshole.

"You are so beautiful."

She held on to his ankle as he pressed the plug in. All that training was paying off because the tip eased in with very little prompting. She didn't clench, merely gave over because in this her Master would have his way. Somehow it was easier when she could see how he gave in to her. It was inconsequential things like where to eat. He didn't love Mediterranean food, but he took her to her favorite place and didn't complain. He preferred rock, but turned the station to country when he drove her someplace.

Tonight had given her great hope despite his refusal to speak long-term future with her. Mitch had held her and rocked her and been kind even though he didn't understand. He was educable. That was all she could ask for.

She breathed out as he slid the plug in, forcing her to open. A low groan came from the back of her throat as he stretched her wider than he ever had before. So much pressure, but she'd come to think of it as erotic now. Her big strong Master was playing with her. Her body was his toy in these moments and he was right. She didn't want to give this up. She shouldn't have to simply because she gave birth. She would still be a woman. She would still need to play with him.

She understood why Big Tag had spent so much time and effort and money on this club. For him and his wife, Sanctum was a place where they could simply be a couple, where they could love each other the way they needed to.

"See, you took that beautifully and you're not going to have any trouble taking me." One big hand was on her back while the other caressed the bare flesh of her ass. "Please count for me."

He didn't give her time to brace herself. One second he was asking for a count and the next his hand came down on her. The sound cracked through the air and it took a moment for the pain to register. She gasped as it flared through her.

"I asked for a count, Laurel."

"I hate you."

The bastard chuckled. "That is not a count and give it a minute. I know what I'm doing. I need a count before I can continue."

"Good." He could shove his count up his ass.

"Laurel, if I don't get a count, I'll add another swat for every ten seconds it takes you to give me what I requested. Or you can use your safe word."

After one smack? It had hurt, but now there was a pleasant heat in her backside. She could try a few more. "One."

His hand came down again and she bit back a shout.

"Two."

Again. Pain flashed and then heat. It seemed to sink into her skin. She gave him his count and he continued. She could feel the plug. Every time he slapped her ass, the plug sent a shiver up her spine, odd at first and then electric. Like lightning was flashing through her system. Her body was getting pleasantly warm and she could feel her pussy softening.

"I'm not hearing a safe word from you." His voice was deep. It wasn't his Master voice. Nope. That gravely, low sound was Mitch's sex voice. He was hot and ready, and if that cock under her belly was any indication, more than a bit desperate.

"You won't, Master. You're right. I'm getting used to it. That was twelve. I believe you owe me another thirteen."

"How do you do this to me?" He gave her a hard smack, though she knew he could hit her harder. He was measured and careful, giving her only what was required to heat her skin and give her a flare that turned to a sensual tingle. She counted and he smacked again, this one making the plug vibrate. "All I want to do is fuck you, Laurel. I want to tie you up and fuck your ass. I need it. I don't need anything."

Or anyone. She was sure his childhood and two failed marriages had taught him not to need anyone, but she was going to change that. "Please, Master. Please let me serve you."

Fourteen through twenty-two came like a firestorm. As soon as the number slipped from her mouth, he spanked her again, never letting up. She gritted her teeth, giving him what he wanted because she trusted him. She counted it out.

"Twenty-three." Smack. "Twenty-four." Smack. "Twenty-five."

His hand rested on her and she could hear him breathing. Shaky. He sounded a bit shaky, as though he was trying to get back into control.

Laurel breathed in, allowing the pain to shift deep inside. She could feel how wet she was, but she wanted more from him. If she pushed even a little, he would break and fuck her hard and quick. She would love it and he would chastise himself for losing control.

"Master, please can you tie me? I want to feel your ropes around me."

He helped her up and had the rope in his hands before she could say another thing. She could see the relief stamped on his face. He needed the control, needed it so badly.

Something about her made him lose it and that was great at times. She loved their passion, but this was part of the man, too. He needed to be patient and slow. He needed to rise above his instincts.

She could give him both.

The room was quiet as he worked, wrapping the rope and tying it off. It wasn't super tight and she suspected that was for her comfort. She found an odd peace as she submitted to him. As he wound the rope around her, working it in diamond patterns, she relaxed. Her whole body was humming. Her blood thumped through her system and she was aroused by the feel of his hands on her skin, but there was no hurry.

She loved this quiet time when they didn't have to talk, when they could simply be together. Peace and passion. They could have both if they tried.

"Did you hate the spanking? I haven't had to discipline you before this evening." They were the first words he'd spoken in fifteen minutes. His hands expertly tied two pieces of jute together before he began a row that would end at her hips.

She could feel where the knots were. The way he'd tied her, they rubbed against her skin, but not in an unpleasant way. It was like everywhere the knots sat was another place he touched her. "I didn't dislike it and you know it. I suspect you can tell how aroused it got me."

He breathed in. "I love the way you smell when you want me. And I love how your whole body blushes when I talk about how good you smell."

It was something none of her previous lovers would have dared to mention, but then nothing was out of bounds sexually as far as Mitch was concerned. He might have a million hangups in real life, but once the clothes came off, he didn't shy away from anything. "Like I said, I didn't mind the spanking. And I like this. I like how the rope feels."

He moved to her back, getting to one knee to finish off the pattern. "You look beautiful. I want you to come downstairs with me. Exactly like this. You can put your skirt on, but I want your breasts out. You look like every Dom's wet dream. I want to walk around the party and know they're all looking at my submissive. They're all jealous because my sub is so fucking gorgeous."

And just like that all her inhibitions melted away. The giving was a two-way street. While she truly believed she had something to give to her Dom, he definitely gave back. He gave her the confidence that came from knowing she was the center of his world. "Yes, Master."

She felt him lean over, his lips touching the small of her back and sending shivers up her spine.

"That's what I like to hear. Yes, Master. Do you know how long I dreamed about hearing those words from your lips, Laurel?"

"No. I thought I was more of a nightmare for you."

"Never. I dreamed about you the first day we met." He moved to her front and finished his pattern. "There. You look perfect. Are your breasts all right? Do they hurt at all?"

They ached, but not from the pregnancy. If she gave him any hint she was uncomfortable, he would cut her out in a heartbeat and ruin all his pretty work. He'd wrapped the pattern around her breasts in a way that thrust them up, making them the centerpiece of his artwork. "They're fine. I feel good though I do have a place where I ache."

Her pussy ached. She needed to be filled.

"Is that right?" Mitch asked. He stood up and his hands went to the waist of his leathers. He worked the ties quickly and his cock sprung free.

She nodded. It was completely right. She needed him.

He shoved out of his leathers and she couldn't help but stare, but she was well aware they were in a club, and Mitch could be very formal in a club. "Master, may I touch you?"

He towered over her and took her hand. "Never ask me that again. You can always touch me, always speak to me. It doesn't matter where we are. You're mine and that means I'm yours. I will always want you to touch me, Laurel."

She had to frown because that wasn't the truth as she'd been told. She placed her hands on his chest, loving how warm and smooth the skin was, how the muscles were hard while his skin was soft. "I heard you believed in high protocol. When I asked around, trying to find out what it would mean to be your submissive, I was told you didn't allow subs to touch you without permission. I was told your subs had to ask for permission to speak in a club."

He was still under her touch, allowing her to explore for a moment. "My other relationships have been more hardcore. I wanted my version of a pure D/s relationship with them, and for me that included certain protocols." When she touched his cock, he winced. "None of that, baby. I'll come in your hand and I don't want to do that. Get on the bed. On your knees."

She had to clench around the plug to move on the bed. It dipped behind her as he joined her. "So I don't know what it's really like to be your submissive?"

His hands caressed her hips and she felt his cock lined up at her pussy. "No. This isn't what it's like to be my sub. This is what it's like to be my Laurel."

He pushed his way in.

Full. She was so full. She could feel him everywhere. The ropes hugged her, the texture caressing her skin. The plug was so big. Mitch had to force his cock inside. Every inch was a delicious fight.

Mitch gripped her hips, thrusting inside. "Do you have any idea how perfect you are for me?"

She'd kind of thought he hadn't figured that out yet, but she would take it. She tilted her hips up, willing him to give her more.

"I know you're perfect for me. Master, you feel so good."

He thrust in and pulled back out, taking his time and making her absolutely insane. "You like getting what you want, don't you, brat?"

He said the word with such affection she couldn't argue with him. She was being the tiniest bit bratty. She was moving against him, trying to find the perfect angle that would send her flying. "You know I do."

He pulled out, leaving her empty. "Unfortunately, tonight's not only about you, baby. I'm going to need you to hold on."

"Damn it."

A hard smack hit her ass, sending electric sparks through her. "That's one protocol I'm not giving up. No cursing in the club. I don't curse at you. I treat you with respect."

"I wasn't disrespecting you. I was merely expressing my deepest regret at your choices."

He chuckled. "Oh, I bet you are, baby. I bet you regret what I'm about to do, too. But you won't for long."

She gasped as he pulled the plug out. Empty. She'd been full and now she was so empty. He moved behind her and she heard the sounds of him opening the lubricant and pouring it on. She didn't feel it, so she guessed he was preparing his cock. In her mind, she could see her beautiful Master stroking that thick erection of his. His hand would move from the plum-shaped head to the thick stalk, all the way down almost to his balls. He would already be slick with her arousal, but he would need more for what he was about to do.

She braced as she felt the head of his cock at her asshole.

"Relax, baby. You can take me. We've been prepping for this. You can handle me." He pressed inside, using little strokes to open her up.

So much pressure. He was bigger than the plug, but there was something so intimate about it. This was something she'd never shared with anyone, but then even the acts she'd performed before seemed new with Mitchell.

She wanted him to be her last lover, her only Master, her only husband. When they were together like this, it felt so close to being true.

"I want you to flatten out your back." The words came out of his mouth in a low growl, his hands tightening on her hips. "Take a deep breath and then move against me."

He was right there. He was stretching her and she wasn't sure how much of him she could take. The pressure was crazy but not painful. It was an odd feeling, almost an anticipation of pain that never quite showed its face. She could handle this, she decided. She could handle him.

Deep breath in. She moved like a cat stretching, lengthening her spine, lifting her backside. And he slid inside, filling her to the point that she was gasping for air, the sensation so foreign and complex. One of Mitch's hands slid around and found her clitoris.

Everywhere. He was everywhere. Despite the fact that he was behind her, she felt surrounded by him. All those knots he'd tied were like a hundred hands caressing her. She wanted more, wanted him to tie her up from head to toe and then make love to her. She could be completely under his control and safe. He would worship her with his ropes and then with his cock, and she wouldn't have to do a thing except feel utterly adored by the man of her dreams.

"God, you feel so good. You can't know how good it feels to fuck you. I want you to come back to work for me, baby. I'll call you in when I want you. I'll fuck you on my desk, on your desk, in the break room, in the fucking lobby. There won't be a single inch of that office I don't fuck you in."

She couldn't breathe. He was holding himself still and she was trying to adjust. No amount of taking the plug could prepare her for the feel of hot flesh inside her, burning inside and making her want to move, to see what else he could give her. "I don't think that would be conducive to performance."

He rubbed her clit in rhythmic circles. "It would for me. I'd have you sit at my feet and when I finish what I need to, I'd have you suck my dick long and hard. A treat for staying on task because I never stay on task any more. I'm always thinking about you, always wondering what you're doing and where you are and if you're safe and happy."

That finger circling her made her forget all about the fact that she was stretched to overflowing. Her pussy was humming with his rhythm. "I'm safe, Master. I'm careful."

He started to move, tiny thrusts and retreats, as though his hips couldn't stay still. "I know you are, baby. When I'm not thinking about your safety, I'm daydreaming about fucking you. You're always there. Always in my head."

He dragged back, a long stroke from inside, and her body lit with sensation. She couldn't help it. She tried to stop the moan that came from her throat but it filled the room.

"Yes," he said as he filled her again. "Yes, that's what I want. I want you to crave my cock. I want you to take me anytime, anywhere. I want you addicted to this because I sure as hell am."

He fucked into her again, but this time was easier and she breathed into the sensation. His finger moved on her clit and she felt lit up from within. He pressed down hard and she went over the edge.

It seemed to let him off the leash. He stroked in and out, faster and faster. The heat, the pressure, the pleasure, all swamped her senses as she came again, this time harder than the last. It seemed to never end and then she felt him come. His movements lost their rhythm as he fucked her hard and then held himself against her, giving her everything he had.

He fell on her, cradling her and pulling her into the side of his body as he shifted on the bed. "Never think you aren't the most beautiful creature in the world."

In that moment, she could almost believe him.

# Chapter Eight

"It's a dog and an orangutan. I don't see why that makes her cry. Really cry. She was sobbing over a commercial about animals that would eat each other in the wild. I make one comment about the fact that the tiger and the bear would totally go at it for dominance and she tells me I'm the world's worst human being and won't talk to me for thirty minutes. How am I supposed to respond to that? I can't punish her. She's already crying." Mitch sat back in his office and looked at Liam O'Donnell, Kai Ferguson, and Ian Taggart. Though to be honest, he was pretty sure Big Tag was asleep. Oh, he was sitting upright, but his eyes were behind mirrored aviators and his breathing was perfectly even. It had been six weeks since Laurel had moved in with him, since she'd become his submissive, and every night seemed like a new whirl on the roller coaster.

Since the night in the club, they'd found a happy rhythm to their lives, but every now and then he felt like he was stepping into a minefield.

Kai shook his head. "This is why signing a contract with her at this stage is a horrible idea. It's too much change for you and for her as well. This is a good time to take a step back and reassess both of your needs."

Li groaned. "There's no stepping back now, Kai. You want to make this some sort of an intellectual thing, but you can't. Laurel's pregnant. There's no way she's going to be logical, not with all those hormones running through her system. Do you want to know how to handle her, Bradford?"

Kai leaned forward. "The way to handle her is to treat her like a partner. You two got into this because you weren't thinking. You didn't have a solid contract in place when you started your sexual relationship and it looks like you're treating the one you have now with indifference. This isn't the way to start a relationship, much less one that I know she hopes is going to end in marriage."

"Says the perpetually single sadist," Li cracked back. "Love ain't got nothing to do with logic."

Li was right about Kai. And Mitch was beginning to think there was nothing logical or rational about his sub at this point in her life. Laurel seemed to be running on pure emotion and he had no idea how to handle that. "I'm going with Irish on this one, Kai. How do I handle Laurel?"

"Agree with everything she says. She thinks bears and tigers can be best friends, so do you. Absolutely, my love. Let's go buy two. Trust me, by the time you get around to finding that exotic pet shop she's moved on to worrying about something else. Avery cried pretty much every single day of her first three months. And then there were three lovely months where we fucked like rabbits, and I hid for the last three. That's pregnancy in a nutshell."

"Which is why this is a horrible time to begin a relationship," Kai pointed out. "Laurel isn't capable of thinking properly when she's so emotional and has a ton of stress on her. And starting a D/s relationship is even more risky. I applaud you for taking responsibility for the child, but you might take a step back and concentrate on becoming a father and then later, after the baby is born, then you can work on your relationship with Laurel."

That sent Li into a fit of laughter. "Oh, yeah, you'll have so much time for that after the baby's born. You got no idea what you're talking about, Kai. I know you've got some fancy degree and all, but you have zero idea how the whole marriage and parenting thing works. There's no logic to you. Look at the big guy there. His wife gave birth and the poor sap ain't had a decent night's sleep since. Do you honestly believe he's capable of logic?"

Kai rolled his eyes. "Big Tag is only capable of sarcasm and sitting perfectly upright while he naps. That's actually impressive, but not my point. Look, Mitch, you asked my opinion."

"No. I really didn't. I asked if you were ready to sign the paperwork on the office space and I got a lecture on how I'm screwing up with Laurel. And you know, aside from the whole crying at commercials thing, we're doing pretty good." Better than good. They'd had one fight in the six weeks they'd been together and apparently that was more about her hormones than his being a truly evil person who liked neither animals nor friendship. Her words, not his. After he'd gotten her some mint chocolate chip ice cream and rubbed her feet and watched some horrid show about doctors saving lives in between screwing each other in tiny rooms—she'd cried during that, too—she'd settled down and been the loving, affectionate sub he was crazy about.

They'd found a nice routine, one he'd come to crave. They had breakfast together every morning. He was used to grabbing something on his way into the office, but Laurel preferred to cook. He was getting used to egg white omelets and steel cut oatmeal, but he'd put his foot down when she'd tried to buy turkey bacon. Bacon came from pigs and no one was going to tell him otherwise. After breakfast, they went to work. She came to his office or he went to hers for lunch when they could. And she was always waiting for him when he came home. He would open the door and enter the living room and his gorgeous sub would be waiting there for him on her knees. Most of the time he had her right then and there, but a few nights had come that he could tell how tired she was, and he'd scooped her up and cuddled on the couch with her and ordered takeout so she wouldn't have to cook.

It was the times when he felt almost compelled to change the routine that scared him the most.

Li shook his head. "Kai's being pissy because his house exploded and there's no good place at the new Sanctum for him to live."

"I am not pissy," Kai shot back. "I'm annoyed because the place I lived and worked at exploded in a fiery hell ball and took everything with it, including most of my patient notes. I'm having to reestablish everything and I can't do that without office space. I'm tired of working out of McKay-Taggart. Do you have any idea how not peaceful that office is?"

Li shrugged. "Big Tag wouldn't let him put in a waterfall or some shit."

"It's a reflection pool and it's very peaceful and calming for my patients, all of whom have been through hell. I also would like to make myself clear on how wrong it is to bring the entire club in on one of your missions, Tag. Look what happened the last time and you were hiding Jesse and Phoebe at Sanctum. The club blew up. Letting Tennessee Smith work an op at Sanctum is going to cause trouble. But is Tag listening to me? No. He's asleep. That dude can sleep through anything."

At least Mitch could solve one issue. "Well, I got the paperwork for your new office so you can add all kinds of reflecting pools and stuff and still be close to the club. The building next door came up for sale. It's industrial, so you'll have to do some renovations."

The building next door had already been quietly purchased by Big Tag and his brother-in-law, Simon Weston. They'd come to Mitch with the plan to sell to Kai for a fraction of the price. What Kai didn't know was his loan had also been secured via Weston's relatives, the Malones. A whole bunch of very wealthy people were backing Kai's efforts to help soldiers with PTSD reintegrate into the civilian world. They weren't telling Kai, who was on a "stand on his own feet" kick after the club exploded.

"I'll take it. I need some quiet and I can't get it in that office. I swear I don't know how Eve does it. I can't have sessions because someone is always knocking on my door. And damn but there are a lot of babies up there now. Cute little things but…there is one hallway you don't want to walk down."

"He's right about that. The babies can make quite a stink when they want to," Li explained. "Now, do you want to know what I found out about your case or not? I came down here to give you a report. These two latched on. Kai wanted to nag you and Tag wants lunch at Top. I'm not going to wake him up until someone can shove a forkful of food in his mouth."

"How are you going to get him to Top if you don't wake him up?"

"Oh, he'll sleep walk for ya. You gotta point him in the right direction and he walks fine. And that's why you have to work all this out with your girl before the baby gets here." He pointed to Taggart, who didn't move an inch. "Because this is what you'll be like after. Ain't that right, Tag?"

Taggart made some kind of huffing sound and then went still again.

He didn't even think about what would happen after the baby got here. He tried not to think past the now. Making plans would only screw up a good thing. He passed Kai the documents and all the information on the building he was going to buy. While Kai went over his paperwork, Mitch turned back to Liam.

"Okay, can you tell me what's going on?"

"I've had surveillance on both the Dixon brothers for the last six weeks."

That didn't sound right. "I told you I was only interested in what Harvey Dixon did when he got out of rehab."

Li shook his head. "You did, but I changed up the plan. Look, I have more experience at these things than you do. There's always a bloody twist. So I've been watching both brothers and I did a thorough assessment of Dixon Technologies. The name sounds impressive, and in some ways it is. Harvey was the idea man while Patrick handled the money and the actual business operations. The company itself and the patents they hold are worth roughly three million dollars, but it turns out Patrick is a brilliant investor. He diversified the company a few years ago and now they have assets in excess of nine million. The trouble is there are three siblings involved. Patrick has a twin. Her name is Frances Dixon, and apparently she tends to side with Harvey against Patrick."

"Good for them. None of this explains why I'm getting my ass kicked regularly." The phone calls had started two weeks before. He got robocalls at all hours of the night. They began at precisely ten p.m. and went on until six a.m. He'd turned off his phone after the first few and then changed his number.

"Adam traced the calls back to a computer, but it was at a public library. Someone got on the system and upgraded the thing, so to speak. That's why you only got the calls late a night. They were set up to turn on after the library closed and everyone was gone. Obviously this is something a man of Harvey Dixon's brilliance can do, but it's also something most hackers can handle. I've also used surveillance footage and found the kid who's been vandalizing the building and your car. His name's Austin Hunt. Seventeen. Juvie record about a mile long. I took everything to Brighton and he sent his men out to bring the bugger in for questioning, but the kid's in the wind."

He looked down at the picture Liam placed in front of him. He was a kid, but he was a kid who had fired a gun at Laurel. "So you think Dixon hired this kid."

"I think one of the Dixons hired this kid. The question is which one."

"The real question I have is why any of them would bug me. I'm just the damn lawyer. I'm representing a company that made it to market first. I'm not responsible for the invention. If I drop the case, someone else will pick it up. They can't stop this from happening."

Liam sat back. "No, at the end of the day, there's nothing any of them can do, so I have to either come up with a logical reason for this to be happening or accept that Patrick Dixon is telling the truth and this is all Harvey. Harvey could be paying the kid. According to Derek, Austin Hunt is known for hiring himself out. He's already worked for a couple of area drug dealers and his father had mob ties."

But Liam was suspicious, and everyone who knew the McKay-Taggart boys knew Liam O'Donnell was the one with an almost sixth sense when it came to crime. "You want to dig deeper?"

"I do. I know you want this to be cut and dry, but I don't think it is. I think there's more here and I need to find some kind of money trail. Whether it leads from Harvey Dixon to Austin Hunt or somewhere else, my every instinct is telling me to find the money. It's buried deep, but it's here. In the meantime, you've got the new security system both here and at the house. If it escalates, we'll put someone on you twenty-four seven."

"How is the guard on Laurel doing?" He wanted to forbid her to work at all, but he was smart enough to know that wouldn't fly. However, he'd also known the moment she moved into his house that she would become a target. He'd set her up with an air horn and a bottle of pepper spray, and a bodyguard for the hours he wasn't with her.

She didn't know about the bodyguard. He pretty much hoped she never found out about the bodyguard.

"I've put Remy Guidry on her. He's one of the five professional bodyguards Tag recently hired. Adam and Jake used to do all our close cover, but that's not possible anymore. With the corporate accounts we've recently signed, we've got a lot of bodyguard work."

"Is he any good?" He didn't like the idea of the new guy watching over his sub.

"He's former Navy SEAL. He's patient and very thorough. Talks like a douchebag though."

"He talks like he's from New Orleans, which he is," Kai shot back. "Remy's solid, Mitch. He'll take care of Laurel. He will not take care of you when Laurel finds out you put a six-foot, five-inch Cajun bodyguard on her ass twenty-four seven."

"Hey, if nothing goes wrong then she never has to know." He'd already gone over this line of thinking about a hundred times. "And if it does go wrong, she'll be happy to be alive."

"Keep thinking that, buddy." Kai handed him back the signed paperwork. "Can I get a copy of the file you've got on Hunt? I can take a look at it. I'm sure Eve already has, but fresh eyes are always good. Harvey Dixon, too, if you have it."

"Absolutely. There are also some interviews with business magazines and a couple of stories about the family. Anything you find could be helpful," Li explained. "Could I have a moment alone with Mitch?"

Kai's eyes narrowed. "Sure. Is this a client thing?"

Li nodded. "We do have confidentiality clauses. He might not have a problem talking about this in front of you, but I have to give him a chance to keep it private."

"Kai's cool. He knows pretty much everything. I don't think I have anything to hide." Mitch couldn't imagine what Liam was about to say.

"All right then. While I was looking into the Dixons and trying to see if they had any ties to you we didn't know about, Adam found out that someone is definitely looking for you and it ain't Harvey Dixon."

Maybe it would have been better to ship Kai out. "Are you talking about a man named Flynn Adler?"

Kai sat up. Mitch could guess why. He'd heard the name Adler in connection with Mitch but never Flynn. "Isn't your father's name Adler? John Adler?"

"Flynn is my half brother. I have two. Flynn is Dad's son by his second wife. He's a couple of years younger than me. Chase is in high school, I think."

"You think?" Kai asked. "You have two brothers and you never mentioned them?"

Yep, this was why he'd never brought them up in conversation. "They're my half brothers and I've never spoken to them. They're my father's legitimate children. Liam, I don't have anything to do with my father. He gave me money to start my firm. I didn't want to take it. Margot insisted on taking the money and my father's contacts. The minute I could, I paid the man back so I didn't feel pressure to talk to him. He doesn't want anything to do with me. He never has. Guilt made him loan me that money."

"From what I can tell, it wasn't a loan. Did you know there's a trust in your name? It was started with the exact amount of money he loaned you," Liam explained.

He wasn't even going to ask how O'Donnell had found out about that. There was a reason McKay-Taggart was considered one of the best firms in the world. As for the trust, he wouldn't touch it. "It doesn't matter. I don't need his money. Like I said, it's guilt money. I think he feels it more as he gets older. Now he's sending Flynn after me. I don't read his e-mails and I don't take his calls. As far as I'm concerned, the Adler family doesn't exist."

Li nodded. "All right then. I had to ask. He's been calling you since before the Dixon problems?"

"Yes. The two events are mutually exclusive. Flynn will give up after a while. It's not a problem, but do get back to me about Dixon."

Liam stood. "That's all I have then. I'll keep in touch. Kai, can you bring the car around?"

Kai stared at Mitch for a moment and then sighed. "I don't guess you want to talk about the fact that you have a whole family you've never mentioned?"

"I don't. That's the whole point. I don't have a family." Beyond Laurel and the baby. They were going to be his family. He had to make sure he made things right for them.

"All right. I'll pull up in front of the building." Kai walked out.

Li followed him. "I'm going to watch for him and then I'll come back up to get the big guy to the car. Don't let him fall over or anything."

And he was left with a very still Ian Taggart.

"What the hell would you do, Tag? What would you do if your dad was still alive and wanted to talk to you?" Big Tag's father had walked out on him and his brother, Sean. He'd married again and had two children Tag hadn't met until the year before, and naturally Tag had welcomed them with open arms and sarcasm. Now they worked together, though Mitch was fairly certain Taggart was closer to Theo than Case.

Should he talk to Flynn? He didn't want to. He didn't want to get dragged into their lives. He'd wanted it so desperately at one point and now he wanted to forget the Adlers existed.

What would Laurel say? Why did it truly matter what Laurel would say? It didn't affect her in any way. She wasn't involved and he meant to keep it that way. She never needed to know they existed as far as he was concerned. So why was he wondering what she would think?

"How did you know you wanted to get married?" He kind of liked sleeping Tag. It was like he had a buddy, but one who didn't talk. "How did you know you were in love?"

He didn't like the word. It was imprecise, but Laurel was very soft hearted. She would want to hear it. She would want to say it to him and hear it back. He was coming to the point that he would have to use it.

"Charlie told me." Big Tag stretched and pulled off his sunglasses.

"Sorry. I didn't mean to wake you up."

Tag put a hand over his mouth to cover a yawn. "Hey, I woke up to a whiny manheart question and not the sound of two warrior princesses trying to out wail each other. I'm counting it as a win."

"Okay. I feel better about my life."

"Yeah, you can for the next seven and a half months or so and then you're up shit creek, buddy. You going to marry Laurel?"

"I already asked her." He hadn't really asked her though. He'd told her he would and in an almost grudging fashion. Not the most romantic of proposals. But what could she expect? If she'd wanted romance, she should have found someone else. "I suppose you knew it was the right time to marry Charlotte because she told you to."

"Bingo. If I'd had my way we would have simply signed a contract and I would have kept her as my submissive. I would have put a collar around her throat and shown her off at clubs and been very happy."

"That doesn't sound so bad." It actually sounded kind of perfect. He'd tried marriage. Maybe he and Laurel could try a long-term contract. Once a year they would review and renew it.

"You didn't let me finish. I would have been very happy until she decided she wanted more."

"Why does there have to be more? I've tried this twice, Tag, and it doesn't work for me. Still, I'm willing to give it a try for the kid's sake."

"Does she know that's why you're willing to try?"

He shrugged. "I might have mentioned it. I try to be honest with her."

Tag frowned, his mouth turning down. "That's where you're going wrong. Totally wrong. Honesty is horrible. No wonder she won't marry you. Hey, but that's a good thing because you don't want to get married."

"You didn't want to get married either."

A mysterious smile crooked up the sides of Tag's face. "Didn't I? I don't remember. I'll have to ask Charlie. Well, the good news is Laurel's got a whole family around her and once the inevitable happens, she and the kid will be fine."

This whole conversation was making him antsy. She didn't need her brother or her sisters to take care of her. She had him. "She'll be fine because I'll make sure she's fine. One way or another."

Tag gave him a thumbs-up. "Sounds like you know what you're doing then. No need to worry that you don't have legal ties to her or the kid. I'm sure it will all work out on its own. That's the great thing about relationships. They happen on their own with no work or compromise at all. I'm going to go and eat whatever Sean made. He said it was…" Tag yawned again, looking a whole lot like a sleepy lion. "I don't remember. Meat. It better be meat. I want to put meat in my face before I go back to the office. I've got a meeting with some bigwig computer dude to nap through this afternoon. You'll be fine. Hey, you're totally used to breakups and stuff."

What the fuck was that supposed to mean?

Before he could ask, Liam was rushing into the room. "Mitchell, we need to get over to Laurel's. It seems there's been a break-in at her apartment. I got a call from Derek. Lisa was going over to check on the place and found the door open. She called the police and Derek is on his way."

Thank god Laurel was at work. He rushed out, ready to hurt someone.

* * * *

"Laurel Daley?"

Laurel looked up from her computer. "Yes?"

She had to stop and do a double take because for a moment, she thought she was looking at Mitchell. It took a few blinks to realize this man was younger, a bit less broad than her Master. He was also far better dressed, a thing she intended to address eventually with Mitch. She had to go slow with her Dom, introduce things gradually. She was going to sneak in a couple of pairs of navy-colored slacks. He wouldn't even realize he was wearing them and when he did, she would point out that he'd been wearing them for weeks and the world hadn't ended.

But none of that mattered because she was looking at someone who absolutely had to be related to her Master.

The gorgeous man in front of her was dressed casually in an open-throated black shirt and khakis. His hair was stylishly long, brushing the tops of his muscled shoulders. "My name is Flynn Adler. I'm so happy to meet you, Laurel. I've read an awful lot about you."

That forced her attention away from the fact that he looked like Mitch. She immediately went on full alert and thought about how she should handle this. She didn't know this man, but he knew her.

"I'm afraid you're going to have to explain what that means." She put as much chill as she could into her voice. She was well aware of the situation with Harvey Dixon. If he was now sending someone to intimidate her, she wasn't about to give him what he wanted.

But how the hell had Dixon found someone who looked so much like Mitchell? That couldn't be a coincidence.

The man in front of her frowned. "The private investigator told me you're living with Mitch."

Now she was nervous. Luckily, it wasn't quite lunchtime. The office was still full of people. It gave her some measure of comfort. "Private investigator?"

"I'm sorry. I'm...well, I never expected that Mitch wouldn't tell you about us. He's never mentioned me or Chase?"

She didn't recognize either name. "Who's Chase? For that matter, who are you?"

"I'm Flynn Adler." He placed careful emphasis on his last name, as though it should mean something to her. When she said nothing, he continued. "Of the California Adlers. I'm Mitchell's brother."

Her stomach dropped. Brother? He had a brother and he'd never once mentioned him? Mitchell knew all about her family. She told him everything. She thought he'd always been quiet because all he had was his mother, and they weren't close. Now she found out he had a brother? Only one? "And Chase?"

"He's the youngest. Mitch is first. He's eight years older than me. Chase is significantly younger. He's a junior in high school. Mitch really never told you about us?"

She shook her head. What else hadn't he told her? How did he hide a whole family? And why? Did she mean so little to him that he didn't bother to mention his brothers? "Did he mention you to me?"

Flynn huffed. "Uhm, no. He doesn't talk to me, Laurel. I found out about you through the private investigator. I'm so sorry to invade your privacy this way. I had no other choice. I thought it would be better to talk to you. You're obviously important to my brother."

"I don't know about that. Our relationship is fairly casual." It hadn't felt that way. It felt serious, but she had to question the fact that he'd hidden this part of his life from her. Was he never going to tell her their baby had two uncles?

"I thought you were living with him."

"We're not engaged or anything. Not really looking to do it." Mitch had made himself plain. He would marry her, but he didn't want to. He would do it for the sake of the baby. "I'm not sure how much I can help you. I can give you Mitch's office address."

He held a hand up. "No. I have it. I've tried to contact him about a hundred times over the last twenty years. I've called and e-mailed and sent letters. I'm worried that if I show up at his office unannounced, he'll call the cops. If I show up announced, he'll probably lock the doors and leave me outside. So I thought I would come and talk to you."

"Why won't he talk to you?"

"I have to think it's more about our father than me. I've only met Mitch once. I was a kid. He didn't say more than two or three sentences to me. He was really only interested in talking to Dad about the money to start his firm. Once he had that and Dad had introduced him to some important clients, he dropped us. Well, Dad. He never was interested in me. I sent him a note when Chase was born. Nothing. Not even a card."

Mitch had told her Margot, his first wife, had been the one to go to his father. He hadn't wanted to. Now it seemed like there was more to the story. If her baby had more family, she wanted to know about it.

Sometimes Mitch could be very stubborn. He could let really good things pass him by because he was afraid of the change they would bring to his life. She'd spent weeks thinking about him, weeks trying to dig under the surface and find the real man she knew was buried underneath his pride.

His pride would keep him from his family unless she did something. His pride might keep their baby from knowing his or her relatives, and she couldn't allow that to happen. "Maybe we should talk. How about an early lunch? There's a sandwich place next door. It's not great, but if you stick to deli staples, you'll be okay. Don't try the special."

He smiled. It was what Mitch would smile like if he ever relaxed and let himself be truly happy. "I promise."

Ten minutes later she sat across from Flynn Adler, a chicken sandwich loaded with veggies and cup of tortilla soup on her side. He'd gone for the all-meat special. Another way he was an awful lot like his brother. He was courting heart disease and apparently loved cholesterol. Still, she wasn't allowed to nag no matter how much she wanted to.

Discussing the Master's diet was off limits. So naturally she'd taken to cooking breakfast every morning and dinner every night. She'd gotten a cookbook that taught her how to sneak vegetables into staple meals. It was meant for kids, but worked on Mitch, too.

Sometimes she felt like she had to sneak in her love or Mitch would reject it.

"So why are you here?" She took a sip of her water. It was hard not to see Mitch in his brother.

"I'm here because Dad is dying and he needs to see Mitch. I gave up trying to get to know Mitch years ago. I get it. He doesn't want anything to do with me or Chase. I wouldn't be here for me. I'm here for my dad."

"Your dad, who walked away from Mitch? Who didn't have anything to do with him for most of his childhood?" She knew enough of the story to defend Mitch a bit.

When he raised that singular brow and his jawline got hard, he really looked like Mitch, the Dom. "There are always two sides to a story, and you would do well to remember that. I'll admit that my father was married to his first wife when he had an affair with Mitch's mother. I don't know everything."

"Mitch grew up without him. Isn't that all you need to know?"

"Did you know Dad settled a bunch of money on Nora Bradford? Do you know what she did with it? She moved them out of San Francisco and as far away from Dad as she could get. Once she ran through the money Dad meant for Mitch, she went through a string of lovers and wouldn't allow Dad to see his son without sending a hefty check. After a while, it got too hard to keep up with where Nora had taken him. She moved about ten times before Mitch got to high school."

Chaos. It would have been so chaotic for a child to constantly be on the move. Always the new kid. Always having to adapt to his mother's new man. Never having a family to call his own. His mother, from what she could tell, was always more interested in herself than Mitch. She didn't call him unless she wanted something, usually money.

What had it been like to be Mitch growing up? She'd had a rough childhood. Her mother had been in and out of jail, in and out of rehab, but they'd owned their trailer and somehow Will had always found a way to keep them together and fed. She'd always had Will and Lila and Lisa. They'd given her support and love and stability.

Mitch, it seemed, had none of those things.

"He could have fought for custody. It sounds like he would have won."

"I didn't say my father was perfect. He went through a divorce and married my mother. And then another divorce. I suppose he lost track of Mitchell, lost the will to fight. Like I said, he's not perfect."

She couldn't imagine having a child in the world and not fighting to be his mother. "What does he want with Mitchell now?"

Flynn leaned forward, his eyes on her as though he could will her to believe him. "Laurel, he's dying. He was recently diagnosed with stage four cancer. The doctors have given him maybe a month to live. Six weeks, tops. He wants to make things right with Mitch. He needs this. It's his dying wish."

"And you've written to Mitch?" How could Mitch know his father was dying and not talk about it? She talked about her mother often. He'd even driven her and Lisa halfway across the state the prior weekend to visit their mom in prison. He'd made sure her mother had everything she needed.

But not once had he mentioned his own father was dying.

"Multiple times. I've sent e-mails, letters, left voice mail messages. He changed his number, naturally, and now I can't find it."

He'd changed it for a different reason, but Flynn didn't need to know that. She wasn't sure how much to tell him. "He hasn't talked to me about it. Mitch can be stubborn. I know he feels your father abandoned him."

Flynn's hands were fists as he moved them off the table. "Then Mitch should confront him about it. All my dad wants is to see him.

I don't think it will matter if Mitch needs to yell and scream and let it all out as long as he gives our father a few minutes of his time so he can say what he needs to say."

"Mitch would never yell." He never lost control that way. Except the first couple of times they'd made love. When they made love now, he was very controlled. He brought her an enormous amount of pleasure, but it felt like there was a distance between them. He was thoughtful and she knew she should be grateful for it, but she missed the passion they'd had those first two times.

Mitch wouldn't yell. Not at his father. Not at her. Maybe it was a good thing or maybe he simply didn't care enough to yell.

"He needs to. My father would take it. He knows he hurt Mitch, but how can he ever have any chance to make it right if Mitch won't talk to him?"

"I'm not sure Mitch believes in second chances." It was another thing that frightened her. They were happy for now, but when the pressure hit and she couldn't play the perfect submissive, when she had to be a woman with all her flaws, how would he handle it?

He always said the reason he hadn't wanted a relationship with her was because she deserved better. What if he'd just been kind by saying that? What if the real reason had been he simply hadn't wanted her?

Flynn sat back, his sandwich untouched. "Then there's not a lot I can do. I'm sorry I wasted your time."

He started to push his chair back, like he was leaving. She couldn't let that happen. Flynn had ties to Mitch, knowledge she needed. Flynn was his brother. He couldn't walk away with nothing. She reached out a hand and put it over his.

"Please don't go. I know Mitch won't talk to you or your dad, but I will. I lied to you. Mitch and I are serious. Maybe not about getting married, but we've got a commitment between us and you should know I'm pregnant."

Flynn sat back, a smile covering his handsome face. "That's great, Laurel. It's about damn time, as my dad would say. Mitch isn't getting any younger. When's the wedding? Or are you waiting until after the baby's born? I know that's a popular thing to do. Damn, Dad's going to be happy to hear that. He doesn't have any grandkids."

Why did she always blush when she had to answer the wedding question? It was the twenty-first century. Plenty of people had babies without getting married. She'd grown up in a household where her mother had never married and had four kids. Not that she wanted to follow in her mom's footsteps, but still. "We don't have plans to marry at this point. I'm afraid this baby wasn't planned, though I'm very happy about the pregnancy."

Was she? She wanted the baby. She knew that, but it was hard to be happy about it when Mitch didn't want to talk about baby things. Every time she brought up things like nurseries or baby names, he shifted the conversation to something different, saying they had plenty of time to discuss it. They needed to live in the now and let the future work itself out.

She was getting sick of living in the now.

"That's great. I know you don't know me very well, but I would love to know my niece or nephew."

She sat up straight. Maybe it was time someone knew Flynn Adler. "I would like that, too. Are you married?"

He shook his head. "No. I run the family company. I don't have time to date. We're moving into a couple of new and exciting areas. I always wanted to run R&D, but I was needed in management. Chase is a better programmer anyway. He's incredible. I'm worried he won't make it out of high school. He's had some trouble with drugs. It scares the hell out of me."

Flynn seemed like a man who had the weight of the world on his shoulders. He reminded her a little of her brother. There had been a time when Will had to juggle school and work and being a dad because they didn't have one. "Where is your mother in all this?"

"She's in Monaco with her second husband, who happens to be younger than me. Chase's mom died of breast cancer a few years back. We're all that's left. I seem to be failing at raising a teenage boy. I don't know how to get through to him. I can't make him understand that life isn't high school."

He was alone. "Would it help at all if I talked to your father? I can't promise you that Mitch will, but I can at least tell him about the baby and how well Mitch is doing professionally."

Flynn had his cell phone out in a heartbeat. "I can't tell you how much that would help." He punched in a few numbers. "Hey, Dad. Guess who I'm talking to?"

A few minutes later she took the phone and had a long talk with the grandfather of her child.

# Chapter Nine

Mitchell looked around the small apartment and thanked god Laurel hadn't been here. Someone had kicked in her door and then taken a knife to the place. Her furniture was slashed all to hell, pictures broken, all her dishes smashed.

Lisa walked in, her eyes red. She'd been the one to call the police, and then Derek Brighton had immediately contacted Li. It had been a good thing to let Derek know McKay-Taggart was on the case. Otherwise, it might have been hours before he would have been notified.

Lisa walked right up to him and threw her arms around his waist, crying. "Who would do this, Mitch? Who would try to hurt her like this?"

The good news was he was totally getting used to dealing with crying Daley women. He was sure at one point in time he would have hesitated, but now he simply hugged her back. She was Laurel's sister and he was Laurel's…damn. Well, he was Laurel's Dom and it was his job to comfort her sister and that was that.

How would they view him after a while? He knew the whole Daley family thought they were only months away from a wedding. Would Lisa seek comfort from him if he knew he and her sister were never going to get married?

He pushed the thoughts aside because only one thing mattered now and that was dealing with the problem in front of him. The police were busy, taking pictures, looking for fingerprints.

"This isn't about her. It's about me," he explained to Lisa. "And I'm going to fix it."

She stepped back. "It's about you?"

"Someone doesn't want me working on the contract I'm writing at the moment."

Her jaw firmed and a stubborn light hit her eyes. "Well, screw them. You can't back down."

The Daley women were a bit stubborn too, he'd learned. Oh, they could be sneaky, but they tended to get their way. He wasn't an idiot. He knew the mashed potatoes Laurel served hadn't had a damn potato in them. He suspected cauliflower was the culprit. But she'd looked so excited about it, he'd played along.

He'd specifically requested she stop nagging him about his diet. Not requested. Ordered. And he hadn't even thought about punishing her for lying. He'd smiled like an idiot and eaten every semi-nasty bite, and then found out that Laurel's version of brownies contained something that wasn't sugar, but also wasn't half bad, and he hadn't disciplined her for that either.

"I'm not going to back down. I'm making a lot of money on this contract and I'll need it. Besides, me backing down only sends the problem along to someone else. I'd rather catch this guy and make him pay." He nodded as Derek stepped out of the kitchen with Liam.

"Mitchell, we haven't been able to get hold of Laurel," Derek said. "We were hoping you would know where she is."

She'd texted him and told him she was going to lunch with a friend at the deli close to work. "Her phone was dying. Something's wrong with her battery. It's being replaced this afternoon. She texted me she would be out of pocket for an hour or so right before Liam and Kai showed up. Where are Kai and the big guy?"

"Kai took Tag to lunch. I can't let him go into a meeting hungry. He tends to eat the clients. Derek will give me a ride back to the office," Li explained. "Lisa called it in. She has a unit at the end of the hall. She was coming back from a class and noticed the door was open."

"It was kicked in," Lisa said, sniffling. "I looked past the door but that was all I needed to do. I was too afraid to go inside. I tried to call my sister but it went to voice mail. When I called Will, he told me to call Derek directly and here we are."

"You did the right thing." He worried Laurel wouldn't have. She would have marched in and tried to confront whoever was in her apartment. And why did she still have this place anyway? She was paying rent on a place she didn't live in. Why would she need to do that? They should have packed the place up and moved her stuff to storage.

Derek gestured back to the techs he had working the scene. "We've already got a couple of prints. We need Laurel's and whoever else would normally be here so we can exclude them. This place only has security cameras at the gates. If someone jumped the fence, it's likely we don't have them on camera, but we're going to look."

Which meant they likely wouldn't get much. "I want to know where Harvey Dixon was while this was going on."

"I'm already on it."

He looked around at the mess that had been made. Laurel had brought most of her clothes with her. She'd brought books and some pictures, but she'd left her dishes because he'd had his and there wasn't a ton of room for more. Now he wondered if she'd spent time selecting the pattern. They weren't in one piece anymore but there was color to her dishes. His were a plain white chosen for utility. Laurel would have picked something she thought was pretty or had reminded her of something that made her happy.

Why hadn't he offered to bring her things into his home? Was he still thinking of it as his home? Not theirs?

When he thought about it, the house he'd bought when he moved to Dallas didn't fit Laurel. He'd given the realtor a set of parameters and when he'd found one that met his needs, he'd purchased it. Good neighborhood. Close to work. No big yard upkeep.

Laurel would have liked a yard. He didn't have anywhere to sit in the back and when she'd brought it up, he'd told her no because it would be hot soon and no one sat outside in the Texas heat. He'd told her it was silly to spend good money on outdoor furniture they wouldn't use for more than a few months of the year.

And she'd simply sighed and gone in to cook dinner.

Why had he done that? Why was it bothering him now?

*Because she's going to leave you. Because she's going to find someone who'll move heaven and earth to get her a damn patio set so she can sit outside and have her coffee even if it's only a couple of days out of the year. Because she'll find someone who can make her happy.*

"Are you sure this wasn't random, Mas...Lieutenant Brighton?" Lisa winced. "Sorry, Sir."

Derek put a hand on her shoulder. "It's fine though I notice he's just Mitch to you. No formalities for him?"

She blushed. "He's family. You put a baby up in my sister, you're family. I don't call my brother by a title either. Ever. It's not going to happen no matter who spanks me."

Liam chuckled, but Mitch was thinking it was nice that she didn't even think to follow club rules with him. Because he was family.

"And I think the note left in her bedroom is solid proof that this wasn't random." Derek pointed to the door in the back. "If you're careful, I'll let you come back and see it. Try not to touch anything. Mitch, I'll need your prints, too."

But he wouldn't. "I've never been here before. Lisa brought her a bag for the first week and when we decided she would stay with me, she came after work and picked up the stuff she wanted. I was stuck on a call about a liability claim against a company I represent."

"You've never been here?" Derek asked, stopping in the doorway. "She's lived here for three years."

He'd never been to her apartment because he'd known what would happen if he came here. It had happened anyway. He'd pushed her away back then and now he had to wonder if he wasn't doing the same thing now. He was crazy about her, but he still kept his distance. He still placed that very significant mileage between them.

Did he want it? Did it make him feel safe because she couldn't quite touch his essential self?

He followed Derek. "No. I brought her to my place when I could. She worked for me. Our relationship was kept to the office until recently."

"But she's pregnant. At least that's what I heard."

"Yes, our son or daughter was conceived on my desk." He nodded as he realized certain truths. "I probably should keep that desk. It's kind of historical."

His child—maybe his only kid—had been conceived on that desk. Would it be his only? How much better would his life had been if he'd had brothers or sisters to depend on? What if he hadn't been alone in the world?

How could he get her pregnant again and quickly, so she would need him even more?

God, he was such a shit.

Liam was chuckling. "It's good to keep that handy. Avery and I have a couch very much like that, brother."

Derek laughed and entered the bedroom.

He heard Lisa gasp and felt her move closer to him.

When he saw the far wall, he pretty much wanted to kill someone.

Someone had spray-painted the wall over her bed.

*Bradford's whore*

Oh, someone was going to die.

Lisa gasped and then he heard a low growl from behind him.

"Son of a bitch." Will stepped into the room, his eyes wide and an angry look on his face. "Tell me you're taking care of this, Mitch."

"I'm doing everything I can. I've got O'Donnell on the case." He hesitated mentioning the bodyguard. As sweet as Lisa was, she would absolutely go straight to her sister and tell her everything, and then he would have one very stubborn Laurel to deal with. He tried her phone again. She should be back from lunch by now.

It went straight to voice mail.

"Maybe it's time we thought about getting her out of the line of fire," Will said. "She can come and stay with me and Bridget."

"No." He wasn't giving her up. "I told you, she's safe at the house. My place is far more secure than your building. I've got the rest of it handled. There's a reason he's going after soft targets like this place."

Will stared at him as though he could see through him. He finally nodded. "All right, but the minute he gets anywhere close, she needs to be out of this."

"The contract is finalized next week. A few more days and it's all over. He'll have to find another target for his irrational rage."

"Will, we've got an eye on all of this," Li explained. "And Derek is taking another look, too."

Will nodded and seemed to calm a bit. "I tried Laurel, but I can't get hold of her. I'm going to run over to her office."

Derek smiled and asked Lisa to join him so he could take her statement, leaving him alone with Will and Li.

Li leaned in, making sure Lisa couldn't hear them. "Mitch put a bodyguard on Laurel a couple of weeks back."

Will let out a long breath, obviously relieved. "Thank god. Does she know about the apartment?"

Mitch dialed her again and it went to voice mail. "No. I think you're right. I think we should go and talk to her. Let me check in and make sure she's all right." He punched in a number and a Cajun accent came over the line.

"This is Guidry."

"Do you have eyes on Laurel?"

"That's my job. Though you should know that keeping my eyes on that pretty *chère* ain't no job at all."

Maybe she needed a new bodyguard. He had to hope all of Tag's new employees weren't such flirty asshats. "So she's back at work?"

"Nah, she's taking an extra long lunch today. Must have something to do with her male friend. You said this was a protection job. You didn't tell me she was cheating on you. Do you want pictures or something?"

His blood seemed to chill. "What are you talking about?"

The line went quiet for a moment. "So this wasn't about the fact that she's getting cozy with someone else?"

His blood started to thump through his system. This was a place he'd been in before. It wasn't the first time he'd stood there like an idiot while some professional investigator gave him the rundown of all the ways the woman he was committed to had given her body to someone else. A vision of Laurel in bed with some nameless man assaulted him. The man would be younger, kinder, more giving, he was sure. The new man would be all the things Laurel needed. All the things Laurel had given up when she'd gotten pregnant by Mitch. "Where is she?"

Guidry's voice came over the line. "No, slow down. I was joking around. I was surprised that she was spending so much time with someone I haven't seen before. She usually follows a routine. She eats lunch at her desk or in the break room. Maybe this is completely innocent."

But she hadn't mentioned that she was having lunch with a

man. She'd texted him, as they'd agreed, to let him know her phone wasn't working, but now he had to wonder. Was it truly not working or did she merely want to be alone with someone? She hadn't mentioned any male friends. Laurel loved to talk about work. He knew the names of everyone there. She was friendly with some of the male workers. Maybe that was all it was.

"Is it one of her coworkers? I know she's friends with a Jeremy." That was all. Jeremy was young and good looking, but Laurel told him they were only friends. He forced himself to calm down. He was being an irrational freak. He trusted Laurel.

"No, I've documented all the coworkers. This is a new guy."

"Where is she?" He would go and see for himself. Maybe she was interviewing a client. She took her work seriously and she was a compassionate woman. It didn't mean she was cheating on him.

"She's at the deli next to work. It's not like she's in a motel."

"How long has she been there?"

"An hour and fifteen minutes. Look, Bradford, I really was joking. I was ribbing you. She's been eating and talking." There was another pause over the line. "That's all."

That little pause made him think. There was something else. Something Guidry wasn't telling him. "What else? Damn it, Guidry. You work for me. I'm the one paying the bills, and I want to know what else she's done with him."

A long sigh came over the line. "She hugged him for a while and she seems pretty affectionate with him for a man she just met, that's all. At one point, she held his hand for a little while as they talked. But from what I can tell, she's an affectionate girl."

She was affectionate with her family. She wasn't with anyone else but her lover. No. God, this couldn't be happening to him again.

*Not with Laurel. Please not with Laurel.*

He felt a piece of himself go cold. If Laurel was cheating, he had to go cold. If Laurel was sleeping with someone else, he might never warm up again.

"Call me if she leaves and get photos. I want to know who this man is and I want the information soon. I don't care who you have to get on it. Find out who he is and how long she's been seeing him." He hung up.

"What the hell is going on, Mitch?" Will followed him as he started out of the apartment and toward his car.

He didn't want to have this conversation now. He needed to get there. He needed to see for himself that Laurel was exactly like all the rest. She was looking out for her best prospect, and he'd always known it wouldn't end up being him.

"It's between me and your sister." The last thing he needed was Will coming with him.

"I don't like the look on your face. You need to calm down." Will kept following him.

Mitch made it to his car. He wasn't about to tote her brother around. He was sure Will would make a hundred excuses for her. He had to see it for himself and then he could figure out what to do.

He got in and immediately locked the door, started up the car and backed out. Will stared at him, shaking his head. He immediately got on his phone, very likely trying to warn Laurel that hell was coming her way. Poor Laurel. She'd left her phone behind so he couldn't interrupt her date, and now that action was going to come back to haunt her.

He drove toward her work like a man possessed.

\* \* \* \*

Laurel sniffled as she hung up and passed the phone back to Flynn. "He seemed happy."

Flynn slid the phone in his pocket. "I'm sure he was. You have no idea how much not having Mitch in his life has haunted my father. I think he made a choice at one point. He decided it was too hard to deal with Mitch's mother and Dad gave up. He would send money, but not fight her on seeing him. He thought after Mitch turned eighteen they could start over again."

She could have told him that would never have worked. Mitch was far too stubborn to allow that to happen. Though he didn't talk about his father, she knew Mitch had to be angry with him. How could he not be?

She'd been angry with her mom. Her mother had battled addiction throughout Laurel's childhood, but at the time all Laurel had been able to see was the fact that her mother consistently chose drugs over her children. Now she could look back with more mature eyes and see how hard her mother had it. Nothing was ever cut and dried. There were always two sides to a story and rarely was any one person perfectly good or perfectly evil. Most people tried. Her mother had come from an abusive family and despite her struggles, she'd never gone back, never exposed her kids to her fist-wielding father, though Laurel was sure at some points it would have been easier for her to have gone home. She'd come to peace with her mother, and it had been freeing to not have all that rage in her heart. She wasn't sure how she could go into being a mom without it.

Mitch needed to see his dad. He needed to come to terms with his father before it was too late.

"I'm sure Mitch was stubborn. I'm surprised he took the money your father offered."

"That was all Margot."

He'd met Mitch's ex? "Did you know her?"

Flynn frowned. "Yeah. When I met her I'd recently started college. I was pretty excited to meet Mitch since I'd heard about him all my life. Margot was an interesting woman."

There was something about the way he said "interesting." "I know she cheated on him with his business partner."

Flynn's eyes wouldn't quite meet hers. "I would suspect that was just the tip of the iceberg."

"What happened? Did she hit on you?"

"My father. I walked in once and she was all over Dad. He turned her down, but she was always looking for the best bargain. I remember that's pretty much exactly what she said. She asked why would she go for the imitation when she could have the real thing. Dad tried to talk to Mitch about it but he wouldn't hear anything he had to say. There was a huge fight and a few years later, Margot had Mitch's firm and Mitch pretty much spent everything he had left to pay Dad back. When he started up the second time, he didn't engage my father at all. I never met his second wife."

Mitch had a lot of reasons to distrust relationships. From what she'd managed to uncover, his second wife had cheated on him, too. "His mother had a lot of relationships."

"Oh, yes. From what I understand she went from wealthy man to wealthy man. It didn't matter if they were married or single. If they could take care of her, she was okay with it. She's been married five times, but there were many more men. She moved often. I'm sure that had an effect on Mitch."

He held on to things that didn't matter because he found them comforting. All those places he'd lived and likely not a one of them had been a home. He couldn't trust the ground underneath his feet. It was constantly changing.

She could see him as a child. Alone. Confused. Afraid.

That would not happen to her baby. And it wouldn't happen to Mitch again either. Not if she had any say in it.

The door to the deli opened and she gasped in surprise. Mitch stood there, his face a bright red as he looked over the customers, his eyes finally falling on her. His jaw hardened and a nasty light hit his eyes.

She hadn't had enough time. She needed more. She'd already told herself she could take a few days and figure out how to broach the subject of his father with him. It looked like her time had completely run out. There was nothing to do but brazen through. She smiled his way. "Mitchell, we're over here."

Flynn began to turn, but it was too little too late. Mitch crossed the space between them in a few long strides and had a hand on Flynn's shirt, hauling him up. "You think you can fuck around with my woman?"

"Mitch!" She was horrified. She watched as Mitch's fist came out and connected with Flynn's face with an audible crack. She stood up and tried to move between them. Flynn was stepping back, his hand on his jaw. He stepped between her and Mitch, placing himself between them.

Mitch didn't take it well. As she tried to move around him, Mitch reached out, dragging her to his side. There was a wild look in his eyes as he looked down at her. "You will get in the car and wait for me there while I deal with your boyfriend. Don't even think about walking away from me, Laurel. You won't like what happens if you walk away from me."

"I don't think I like what's happening right now," a new voice said. She looked through tear-filled eyes at the man who had come to stand behind her. He was roughly six foot three, with dark hair he'd pulled back in a queue at the back of his neck. He was dressed in jeans and a black T-shirt that showed off broad shoulders and a chest to die for. He stepped between her and Mitch. "You might be paying me, boss, but you're paying me to protect her, and in my mind that means I protect her from everyone—including you. You need to take a couple of minutes and get your head right before you talk to the lady again."

"What the hell was that for?" Flynn stared at his brother.

Laurel was still trying to process what the guy with the slow Cajun accent had said. He was being paid by Mitch?

"She's taken, asshole. And she probably didn't bother to tell you, but she's pregnant." Mitch stepped toward Flynn, looking like a bull about to charge.

The guy, who was apparently supposed to protect her, gently grasped her elbow and pulled her back from the brothers. "Yes, she's pregnant, and that's a damn good reason to be civil around her, Bradford."

Flynn stopped and stared at Mitch for a minute. "You don't even know who I am. You have no fucking idea who I am."

Mitch didn't know what his brother looked like? She tried to step around the bodyguard she hadn't even known she had, but he was apparently serious about his job.

"Not on my life, *chère*. Those men aren't going to listen to you. Bradford's got his panties in a wad, and the best thing for you to do is let him have his hissy fit."

"I'm not having a hissy fit and you're fired, Guidry. And why the fuck would I..." Mitch stared for a moment. "Flynn?"

She tried to shove around Guidry. "Yes, it's your brother, Mitch. Not that you told me you have one." She frowned at the bodyguard, who still wasn't letting her through. "He said you were fired."

"Ain't no one firing me but the big guy. When Taggart says I can go home, I will. Though I still probably wouldn't. I don't like the look in that man's eyes." Guidry kept his gaze on Mitch, though she was fairly certain she still wouldn't get around the man. "Since this is a family matter, why don't you take this someplace less public, gentlemen? I think all the testosterone is making it difficult for the other patrons to enjoy their lunch."

Mitch turned around. "You're right. Laurel, get in the car. We'll discuss this at home."

She looked back and saw that Flynn's face had fallen. "I think you should talk to Flynn."

Mitch pointed toward the door. "I think you should remember our contract. You don't tell me what to do, baby. You follow orders. Get in the car. I won't ask again and punishment for disobeying me won't be pleasant."

"Punishment?" Flynn stepped up.

God save her from over-dramatic men. "I'm fine. He has never and will never hurt me."

"There's a first time for everything," Mitch said in a low growl.

His panties really were in a wad. What had gotten him to stalk in here like an angry bear? Had he thought she was cheating on him with his brother and a chicken salad sandwich? "I'm not going anywhere until I'm sure you're not going to kill your brother, and you can also explain the Cajun dude who seems to think he's supposed to protect me. How long has that been going on?"

She was pleased with her calm tone of voice. It was obvious none of the men were going to remain calm, so she had to.

Mitch turned and she watched as he visibly forced himself to chill. He reached for her and then stopped, his eyes closing as he took a deep breath and seemed to mentally count. When they opened again, his blue eyes were icy cold. "Laurel, we'll discuss this at home. For now, the police need to talk to you. Someone broke into your apartment and trashed the place. This is Remy Guidry. I hired him because someone nearly killed you and I wanted to ensure your safety. He's watched you when I couldn't. As for my brother, he's none of your business and the fact that you would talk to him behind my back makes me question your loyalty—another thing we'll discuss this evening. Don't be surprised if I ask for that collar back."

The room seemed to still, everything around her moving to the background until there was only Mitch and his cold stare. "Are you serious?"

He was cold as ice as he stared down at her. "You've read the contract. You know what I require and you defy me at every turn.

You sneak in your wants and your desires and I give in. This is what happens. You aren't capable of being my sub and I knew it the minute I met you."

Anger flared through her system and before she could think about it, her hands went to the gold necklace around her throat. They'd selected it together, spending the day at NorthPark Mall, trying on pretty jewelry. He wanted it back? She could give it to him. "Well, I'm sorry I proved you right, Mitchell. We don't have to talk at all."

It seemed they had nothing to talk about. She tossed the necklace at him. He could use it on the next idiot, and there would absolutely be a next one. He was too gorgeous, too sexy, to not have another woman dangling for him. Likely, as soon as they realized he was available.

She turned and walked out the door, tears clouding her vision. This was what she got for her trouble. The minute she didn't do what he wanted, he dumped her.

Except that wasn't exactly what had happened. And she did try to get her way on things he was unreasonable about.

It didn't matter now. And apparently she had to go and talk to the police.

Mitch was on her heels the minute she stepped outside. "Laurel."

Guidry moved in beside her. "I'll drive you to your apartment, and that's not a suggestion. Just because Bradford wants to act like a jealous asshole doesn't mean you're out of danger, darlin'."

God, she wanted to tell them all to go to hell. She wanted everyone to go away and let her mourn. How could she have a relationship with a man who shoved her away the minute things got tough? He didn't even recognize his brother? Would he even bother to call and check on the baby now that they were through? Sure, he'd written it into their contract, but seeing how he avoided his father and brothers, she couldn't know that he'd want anything to do with their baby now.

Mitch was used to walking away.

"Hey, I didn't say I was through talking to you, Laurel. I'll drive you to the police station and then I'll drive you home. We have a few things to work out," Mitch insisted.

She stopped on the sidewalk and looked back. Flynn had stepped out of the deli and he looked positively heartbroken.

That was what she would likely look like in a few months. When Mitch decided he was done with a person, he was done with them.

She should have listened. He'd told her he was bad for her. He'd said it in plain English. He'd tried to stay away.

In the end, she had to be sensible. Someone was out to hurt Mitch, and right now, they thought they could use her to those ends. It might take a few weeks for Dixon to realize there was no place in Mitch's heart for anything, much less her.

"Remy can drive me and I'll be a good client. I understand why he's here and I'll cooperate with him until we're sure it's safe. I'll pick up my things from your place later tonight."

"What do you mean?" Mitch asked. For the first time the chill was replaced with an almost expectant wariness.

He'd really thought she would fall in line? "You say I'm not your sub. So I'll find a place to stay until my apartment is safe. I'll call my brother. His building is secure. I think you should talk to your brother."

"He isn't my brother," Mitch returned, his tone savage. "And don't think this is over, Laurel. Are you forgetting you have something of mine?"

Her hand went to her stomach. "This is a baby and not a piece of property, and don't you dare try to use our baby against me. Go to hell, Mitch."

She turned and started back down the street. This time, he didn't follow her.

"My truck is close. You should probably go in and let them know you won't be coming back this afternoon. I'll call in and let my boss know what's going on. If you're not with Mitch, then I need to stay close to you," Guidry explained.

The last thing she needed was another man watching out for her, but she wasn't about to let her stubbornness get her baby killed. She nodded, walked into the building and explained about her apartment. She was the world's worst employee, but her boss seemed to understand. She grabbed her phone, which had finally charged back up.

They were supposed to get a new battery today. Well, Mitch was. He was going to order a new one and then take her out to dinner. She sniffled as she looked down at the phone. He'd called several times and left her texts about getting in touch with him the minute she could.

Why would the man seem so panicked about a woman he could throw away like a used tissue?

Maybe she was the drama queen.

"I'm parked out back," Guidry explained.

"Of course you are. I might have noticed I was being followed if you'd parked out front." She understood the need, but was irritated Mitch hadn't told her.

But then Mitch wasn't the most reasonable of men.

And pretty much every woman he'd ever cared about had cheated on him.

She turned suddenly and was pleased to see the big strong Cajun stop and look the slightest bit off-kilter. "What did you tell Mitch that had him in a jealous rage?"

To his credit, the Cajun boy didn't flinch. Still, it seemed like he was the honest type. "I told him you were having lunch with another man and you seemed cozy. You hugged him. You seemed close. You aren't openly affectionate with other men. I've been watching you for weeks and the only men you've touched past a handshake are Mitch and your brother. In my defense, I was unaware Mitch had any family at all. Had I known you were spending time with his brother, I likely wouldn't have mentioned the physical affection. That being said, it doesn't seem like Mitch appreciated you spending time with his brother."

"Well, that doesn't matter now, does it?" She settled her purse over her shoulder and started out the back door.

Guidry escorted her to his massive truck and helped her up. "I'll bring you back after we deal with the police. I'll follow you back to Bradford's place and let you pick up your things. You're being more reasonable about this than I thought you would."

She was barely hanging on. She wanted to wail and cry and feel incredibly sorry for herself because she was going to be alone.

She would be alone without Mitch. Or would she? Why should she live the rest of her life alone because Mitchell Bradford was an asshat? She didn't have to be alone. She'd wasted the last year of her life on him and she was going to have a child by him, but that didn't mean she had to be alone.

"I'm always reasonable," she said in a quiet voice. She folded her hands on her lap.

"You're not being very reasonable right now." He turned out of the parking lot and toward the freeway.

"What is that supposed to mean?"

He shrugged as he maneuvered through the streets. "I'm surprised you gave up so quickly."

She didn't like the sound of that. She hadn't given up. He'd told her she wasn't good enough to be his submissive. And he'd never lied to her about wanting to get married. If she wasn't his wife or his sub, she wasn't anything to him. He'd proven that utterly. "It doesn't matter anymore. He made himself plain."

"Did he?"

"Are you always this chatty with your clients?" How the hell had she gotten here? She was moving toward the police department to talk about the break-in at her apartment. Mitch had let her go pretty easily.

But didn't he do that with everything? He let people go all the time. Things were harder for him. If she was an old concert T-shirt, he would hoard the hell out of her.

Objects were the only things Mitch could count on, so he tried to keep them. He simply didn't think he could count on her. His head had immediately gone to cheating. She didn't deserve that.

But wasn't it kind of inevitable?

"We don't have to talk."

"He was horribly rude to me."

"Yes. Men in pain are usually horrible. That boy's got a thorn in his paw and it's not coming out by itself." He was quiet for a moment as he sped up to get on the freeway. "You two seemed pretty happy."

"It was an illusion." He'd always been waiting for her to screw up so he could get her out of his life. He'd been waiting to do it from the moment he'd heard she was pregnant. This was what he wanted, wasn't it?

"If you say so. I'm saying as an outside party, you seemed

pretty happy, and since you two have a baby on the way, maybe it's a little hasty to throw in the towel. Or the collar, as it seems. Men will say a lot of things they don't mean when they're hurting, and finding out the woman they love is seeing another man behind his back would hurt a lot. I've looked into Bradford some and he's the kind of man who hasn't had a lot of support in his life."

He'd had no support. None. She'd been surrounded by family. Yes, they'd been children, but she'd learned to lean on them, to trust and love her brother and sisters.

Mitch had learned that everyone left.

He wasn't completely ignorant when it came to love. But she'd learned long ago that there was a difference between being ignorant and being dumb. Ignorance was merely an absence of education.

Mitch was a smart man. Could he be taught? Did he even want to be?

She was well aware that tears flowed down her cheeks, but she wasn't capable of stopping them. Remy Guidry wanted to be her bodyguard? Well, he had to deal with her emotional state, too. And if he wanted to listen, then maybe she should talk. She'd kept quiet about so many things because she didn't want her family to worry, didn't want Mitch to look bad in front of them. Guidry seemed to know everything, so she could lay it all out there. And it didn't matter because it was over.

Yes, she was seeking counseling from her ridiculously attractive bodyguard. "I'm worried there's nothing for me to do. I can't go back and erase the things that happened to him. I can't right the past for him."

"No, you can't, but you can make him believe in the future."

She'd been trying. How could she make him believe in a future when he was so tied up in the past? He kept things forever. Stupid things like old T-shirts and stacks of comic books he never read or looked through any more. "How do I do that?"

"Oh, that's simple, *chère*. You be you. Don't have to be any more than that. I'm going to ask you a question and it's going to seem silly, but I want you to think about it. Let's say you got this dog and he keeps coming around your house. He's growling and barking every time you come outside. Now, most people would be scared. Most people would know that tangling with a nasty piece of dog is gonna get them bit. But there's a few people in this world who look at that dog and see something else. There's a few people who see deeper. Even though they've never been a mangy dog themselves, they seem to understand what it would feel like. So I'm going to ask you, how would you handle that dog?"

She cried pretty freely in that moment because the minute he'd given her the scenario, she'd known what she would do. "I would feed him. I would put out a dish and then wait. I wouldn't push him the first couple of times. I would put the dish out and then walk away. After he got used to that, I would stand in the door until he learned it was all right for me to watch him."

"You sound like you've done this before."

She nodded. "We had this dog when I was a kid. He was the bane of the trailer park. He was quick though. Believe me, some of the residents tried to shoot him because they said he was too far gone. He'd been abused and they told me once a dog got mean, he couldn't come back."

One side of his mouth tugged up and he smiled at her. "You didn't think so, though, did you?"

"I don't know why, but he spent a lot of time outside our trailer. I guess there was a warm place or something. He would scare the crap out of us when we would go to school. I was afraid Will was going to do something to him. Not because my brother's mean or anything. He just took his responsibilities very seriously. So I saved some of my dinner one night and I brought it out to the dog. I did it the night after and so on. He stopped growling at us. He wouldn't come in the house, but he didn't bark at us anymore. And then one day I opened the door to go to school and he was waiting for me. We had that dog until he died of old age."

"Mitch is growling and barking at you because it's the only thing he knows to do. I promise you that man is telling himself it's all for the best because you would have kicked him in the end. No one will think less of you for moving on to an easier man, *chère*. But he'll be alone because I think you're his one shot at finding something good. You walk away and he won't ever try again. That's something for you to think about."

She watched the streets go by and wondered if she would think about anything else.

# Chapter Ten

"Wow. You are really bad at that."

Mitch stared at the spot where he'd last seen Laurel and only vaguely thought about punching his brother in his movie star, good-looking face. But that would require him to turn around, and he might never be able to do that again. He might spend the rest of his life watching this spot and praying for her to show up again.

Guidry nodded his way as though letting Mitch know he would handle things from now on and then he, too, disappeared into the building where Laurel worked.

She was gone.

*Suck it up. You knew it would happen eventually. It's better that it happen now before you got too deep.*

He was already too deep. God, she was gone and he felt something open deep inside him. A wound that was never fucking going to heal.

"Aren't you going after her?"

Flynn. Laurel was gone, but Flynn was still here. His younger brother. The one dear old dad wanted. It was so fucking good to have a place to throw his hate. He turned and was slightly pleased that Flynn took a step back. He would bet Flynn had never had to defend himself because no one was around to help him. Flynn would have been given the best of everything while Mitch hadn't even gotten fucking scraps. "I would rather deal with you, Adler. You want to explain why you're here fucking around with my submissive?"

Flynn's eyes narrowed. "Submissive?"

Oh this was going to be fun. He was sure Flynn was perfectly vanilla and would be so horrified at big brother's perversions. "Yes. You were flirting with my sub, Adler. When I talked about punishing her I meant pulling her skirt up and smacking her ass because it makes her hot. I've tied her up six ways to Sunday and I didn't leave her untouched, if you know what I mean. You couldn't handle her even if I allowed it, which I won't. Go back to California, you little prick."

Flynn's face went red, but he took a step forward, his fists clenched at his sides. "Yeah, I guess it doesn't surprise me to find out you're an abusive piece of shit."

Like he hadn't heard that before. He turned and started walking to his SUV. He had work to do. He would find a way to get her back. Oh, he'd do it in a nasty way, but she was going to be back in his home, in his bed before she could play around with someone else.

"Mitch." Flynn was suddenly beside him, jogging to keep up. "Mitch, I said that in anger. I'm sorry. I'm not a complete idiot. I watch TV and stuff. I know some people have relationships like that. Hell, I even knew you went to clubs. It was just surprising to hear you say it like that. Which I'm sure was why you did it. You seem to want me to think the worst of you."

Mitch turned. Flynn didn't seem to understand him at all. "I don't care what you think. That's why I avoid you. I don't care about you or Dad or anyone at all, so get the fuck out of my state. Why do you think I left California? It damn sure wasn't to get closer to you. Go back to your cushy life and leave me alone."

Flynn had cost him everything. If the jackass had stayed away, Laurel would have been sitting at her desk and he would be the one taking her to the police station. He would be the one holding her hand and promising her everything would be fine. He would be the one she turned to.

He crossed the street and stalked toward his car, all the while thinking about how he was going to keep her. He was stupid. He knew he'd been a major asshole, but she was in the wrong, too. She knew he didn't talk about his past unless he specifically brought it up, and she'd sat right down with one of the biggest pieces of his past and had lunch. She'd known damn well he wouldn't have approved and she'd done it anyway.

Likely because she thought she could help in some way. Because Flynn had given her some kind of sad story and Laurel had bought it hook, line, and sinker.

He was about to get into his car when something struck the windshield. A rock. He turned and Flynn had another one in his hand.

"What the fuck is wrong with you?"

Flynn threw that one, too. He let that sucker fly and it cracked against the windshield. "Me? What the fuck is wrong with you? You think my life is so cushy? Dad is dying, you asshole. He's dying and the only thing he wants is to spend a few minutes with you. I have no idea why since it's obvious to me you aren't worth talking to, but does he listen to me? Fuck no. I've spent the last five years of my life taking care of him, but he wants you. And I won't even go into what's happening with Chase. I'm going to lose him. Do you even care? You've got a little brother and he's going to die because I can't convince him life doesn't suck. Because for him…for him it does. So I'm going to be alone and miserable very soon, and I'll still be happier than you are because at least I'll have tried."

He wanted to pick up one of those rocks, shove it right back at Flynn, get in his car and leave. This wasn't his problem. Laurel was his problem. Laurel was all that mattered now.

He'd screwed up with her so badly she would likely never come back, so it didn't matter.

It didn't matter that Laurel would want him to have some small piece of empathy for the brother who hadn't asked to be born either. It didn't matter that Laurel would think more of him if he would put aside his pride for two seconds and talk to the man he hated for no good reason except the circumstances of his birth.

Flynn hadn't asked for any of this. He hadn't had a choice in parent or birth order, but he was making a choice by seeking out Mitch.

And Mitch had to make a choice, too, and it didn't matter what Laurel would want because Laurel was gone.

So he was going to smash his brother's face in and that would make him feel better.

For a second the sun caught Flynn, illuminating his features, and Mitch realized he'd seen that face in the mirror. He'd seen the starkness, the emptiness. He'd seen the hopelessness reflected there before he put on his mask for the day.

Damn it.

"How bad is he?"

Flynn's head came up. "Dad has stage four pancreatic cancer. He doesn't have long. I don't know what to do. He asked me to reach out. He wants to talk to you before he dies."

"I don't want to talk to him."

"Please. You don't have to talk. Please just listen. What do I have to do? If you want me to beg, I will."

"Why would I want you to beg?"

Flynn shrugged. "Maybe you would like seeing me on my knees. Maybe it would make you feel better."

To see the chosen child beg and squirm and plead? "No, it won't make me feel better, Flynn. Let me think about it. Can I have a day or two?"

"Yeah." Flynn suddenly looked younger than he had before, his eyes wide. "Of course. Take the time you need, but know he doesn't have a lot of it."

"What did you mean about…" He'd been about to pretend he didn't know his youngest brother's name. He did it out of habit. He did it to show the world he didn't give a damn. "Chase? How old is he anyway?"

Flynn stepped forward, his shoulders sagging a bit. "He'll be seventeen soon. If he makes it."

*Don't ask. Don't. Stay the fuck out of it.* He didn't want to go into this. He liked his life the way it was. Except he didn't. He only liked it because Laurel had been with him, and now she was gone. "Why do you say that?"

"He got mixed up in drugs. He says his overdose was an accident, but I found out he's being bullied by this kid at school. I tried to get Dad to pull him out and let him go to the public school, but they have a problem with violence there. I don't know what to do."

"It's only one kid?"

"It's a group, but you know how these gangs work. One asshole runs the crowd and the crowd runs the school. They outed him. Publically. One of them found out Chase likes boys and catfished him."

"I don't know what that means."

"It's where you make up a false presence on the Internet. He claimed to be another gay kid and they started an online relationship. Once Chase was sure the kid loved him, the group posted every embarrassing moment online."

"Huh. Go after the parents. Go after them hard. Threaten to take them for every dollar they have and I bet the little shit will fall in line."

"They don't want to talk about it. They said it was all kid stuff and Chase should be stronger."

"Did you threaten to sue them and take it all public so their darling baby boy can't show his face at college? I don't know where you've been but most places don't take kindly to bullying anymore. The tide turned a while back. No one takes the side of the mean kid, and threatening to haul them all into court might give Chase some peace. He needs to stand up for himself. A lawsuit could give him that."

"Our lawyers don't do those types of suits. I don't know if I could even convince Chase to consider it. He thinks it's all going to go away. Or he tells me that and then I find him barely breathing. I take him to the hospital and find out he's been buying pills at school."

"Nice. We can sue the school, too." He kind of wanted to. He was sure the school had brushed off the fishing thing as nothing. To them it would be something to work out between the kids. They would likely say that working it out among themselves would prepare them for adulthood, but adults who acted like assholes got fired or shot. There were consequences for adults. "I can talk to him. I can be persuasive when I want to be. It sucks to be a kid."

If anyone did something like that to his kid, they might not get the courtesy of a lawsuit.

"It sucks to be human sometimes."

Maybe Flynn didn't have it so great. "I'm sorry about punching you."

Flynn touched his jaw gingerly. "For a lawyer, you know how to throw a hook."

"I've found beating the shit out of my friends makes me feel better. In the ring, of course, and with rules. A couple of the guys I hang out with work out this way. You should try it sometime. Don't tell your girlfriend though. They get weird about it." It made perfect sense to him. You put on gloves and took out your aggressions and everyone was bruised and happy, but he'd learned to never mention it.

"Like I have time for a girlfriend." Flynn sobered a little. "I'm sorry about yours, man. That was some kind of argument. You should know nothing was going on between me and Laurel. She's a very nice lady and it's obvious she cares about you. Why did you freak out on her like that?"

"I don't know."

"She's not Margot."

"I know that."

"Do you? If I'd been through what you have, I don't know that I would truly understand that Laurel's different."

"I know she's not Margot." But he'd gone to the worst place he could. It had taken him a couple of minutes, but he'd finally arrived at the most improper conclusion he could have about Laurel. He'd basically called her a tramp when she'd only been having lunch with Flynn.

And then he'd questioned her loyalty.

He pulled his phone out. No calls. She hadn't called or texted. Not that he expected her to. She likely wouldn't ever speak to him again unless he forced her to.

Maybe it would be better this way. He wasn't cut out to be a father or a husband. He wasn't ready for any of it. He definitely wasn't ready for her. He'd hurt her and he would do it again if she stayed with him.

What the hell should he do?

How could he let her go? How could he keep her? This was everything he'd feared from the moment he'd met her. He'd known it wouldn't—couldn't—work. He'd known there was no way and now there was a baby involved.

Did he even deserve to be a dad? He had no idea how to be one. Would it be better to let Laurel find someone ready for the job?

"Are you going after her? I think you should. I think you should find her and apologize," Flynn said.

"And after that?" He'd tried to live in the moment but the truth was the future was almost here. Oh, it might be a few months away, but it would catch up to him. It would get him in the end. "No. I need to figure a few things out."

Lonely. He was going to be so fucking lonely without her.

"Like how to sue her so she comes back to you?"

Mitch frowned. When he put it like that it sounded really bad. "We do have legal things to work out."

Despite the thoughts playing in his head, he knew he couldn't do it. He couldn't walk away. Not from her. Not from their kid.

Flynn leaned against the car. "Let's go and get a beer, which I will buy since I kind of damaged your car."

"I damaged your nose." When he thought about it they were kind of even.

"True. You can buy the second round and we can talk about less litigious ways to get your girlfriend back. I might not have a girl right now, but I'm pretty good with them."

"I've ignored you for years. Why would you help me?"

Flynn sighed and put a hand on his back. "Because you don't know this yet, but that's what brothers do."

He wanted to go after her. He wanted to stay away from her.

He wanted…fuck, he just wanted.

He nodded and got into the car because maybe it was past time to confront all his fears. It seemed he had nothing left to lose.

\* \* \* \*

Mitch pulled up to the driveway but couldn't manage to hit the button on the key fob that would raise the garage door. He didn't want to see the empty spot where her car should be. It was funny the things a man got used to. He was used to opening the garage door and seeing her piece of crap nestled in there. He'd fully intended to replace said piece of crap with a car that had all the up-to-date safety features as soon as Laurel would have the conversation with him. She'd been all independent and hadn't budged on it.

Would it have been different if he'd been smart enough to convince her he wanted to marry her in the beginning? Would she have taken the car and his crap for a little while longer?

He turned the engine off and got out. A few hours with his brother had been somewhat illuminating. Flynn didn't seem to have Mitch's "the world is half full of assholes" philosophy of life. He seemed to think if Mitch got on his knees and begged for Laurel's forgiveness, she might think about it.

He'd never gotten to his knees before. Not for any woman. Not for anything.

He needed time. He needed to think about what was best for all of them. Perhaps that meant taking a step back. He was going to write her a very polite note requesting that she keep him up to date on any and all developments with the baby and asking that she honor their contract and allow him to escort her to appointments having to do with their child. He would concentrate on the baby.

Perhaps at some time in the future he and Laurel could be friends again.

He sighed as he noticed a big truck in front of the house. He would have to talk to the neighbors because it was utterly ridiculous that they had guests park in front of his house when they had a massive circular drive.

Hell, he couldn't even work up the will to argue anymore. He was about to put his key in the front door when it opened and Remy Guidry stood in the doorway, a frown on his face.

"You are in the doghouse. Dinner's been ready for damn near thirty minutes and it's cold. You should probably come up with a good excuse right damn now." The big Cajun shook his head. "That woman makes a fine roast. If you're stupid enough to lose her, give me a call. I'll take her."

Mitch stared at him as Remy walked through the doorway and toward the lawn. "What?"

The Cajun kept walking, his keys in his hand. "I'll pick her up at eight tomorrow. The good news is now we're out in the open and I can stay close to her. Night, Bradford."

Laurel was here? Laurel was here.

He could hear the sounds of soft country playing through the house. He'd hated it at first, but now it seemed like the sweetest thing he'd ever heard. He locked the door behind him and set the alarm. He dropped his briefcase and walked through the living room. Slowly. Like this was a dream and he wasn't sure he wanted to wake up.

"Laurel?"

She was standing at the sink, rinsing off one of his boring dinner plates that had no personality or color to them. She was the color in his home, in his life. She looked up. "Hello, Mitchell. Are you hungry? I made dinner."

"Why?"

She set the plate in the dishwasher and dried her hands. "Because we eat dinner at night."

There wasn't a lot of expression on her face. God, she looked tired. He'd done that to her. But still, he needed to understand. He didn't understand her at all. "Why are you here, Laurel?"

"Do you want me to leave? I can call Remy back."

He moved around the bar, almost wanting to block her path. "No. I don't want that. But I thought you left me."

"I can't leave, Mitch. We don't get to throw everything away. I don't know if we can go back to what we were before, but I think being apart is a mistake. So I think we should sit down and have dinner, and later, we'll go to bed and maybe you can make love to me because I had a shitty day."

He stepped up and dragged her into his arms, pressing his lips to hers. He took her mouth in a long, hungry, grateful kiss. She wasn't leaving. She was here with him.

It was enough.

"Maybe dinner can wait," he said against her lips, his hands moving to her blouse.

She sighed against him. "Definitely."

\* \* \* \*

Deep in the night, Laurel looked down at her sleeping...what did she call him now? They still had a contract but it felt broken despite the way they'd ended the evening. They'd avoided all talk about the future like it was a land mine waiting to explode in their faces, and she wasn't sure what to do about that.

She loved him. She simply wasn't sure love was enough in their case.

When he kissed her, when he put his hands on her like he would die if he didn't, it felt like love. The D/s sex they had was over-the-top insane with pleasure and she craved it, but there was no doubt she also needed those times when Mitchell lost control and had to have her without any protocol or rules between them.

That was when she felt like he adored her.

She'd thought a lot about what Remy had told her today. She'd thought about that dog she'd coaxed into the trailer finally. It had taken weeks and weeks. Will had forbidden her to get anywhere near that dog. Come to think of it, Will hadn't been spectacularly excited when he'd realized she was interested in Mitch. It seemed like her brother recognized the destruction capability that lived in both beasts, but she'd seen something else. She'd seen a chance to give something to a creature that had obviously been broken.

The world could break a spirit, but that didn't mean it had to stay that way.

She looked over at him. Why was this man precious to her? Why couldn't it have been someone simpler? Someone happy and whole? Why did he move her?

At the end, it was a mystery and she wouldn't solve it. There were some things that simply were. If it didn't work out between her and Mitch, she would miss him forever. She would move on because she wasn't the type to lie down and fade, but she would always love him.

Why hadn't she told him?

It seemed like the last wall she had, the very last defense.

"You can't sleep?" Mitch's voice rumbled as he turned over. Even with the lights out, she could see the hard line of his jaw, watch as his hand came out to touch her shoulder.

"I'm fine." She wasn't sure what to say.

He sat up. "That means you're not fine. I know that much."

She had to laugh at that. "No, I didn't mean it that way. Physically I'm good. I'm a bit restless, that's all."

He pulled her into his arms, resting against the back of the bed. His warmth surrounded her as he stroked her hair. "Because we're not settled. Laurel, I'm worried you want something I can't give you. Nothing is ever settled. I learned that a long time ago. We can be good one minute and broken the next. There's no guarantee."

And that was precisely why he refused to talk about the future. He didn't believe in it. He didn't trust it.

"I know." It wouldn't do any good to lecture him about it. She felt him sigh.

"I'm sorry about today. Baby, I'm sorry I reacted the way I did. I did the one thing I promised I wouldn't do."

Yes, he had. She sat up and looked at him, an idea in her head. Sometimes ideas got lost in the muddle of communication. People didn't always use the right words to make someone truly understand. Words got filtered through the drain of a person's history, giving them weight or lightness that others wouldn't place on the definition. "You withdrew affection. You promised you wouldn't do that, Mitch."

"I know. I'm very sorry, Laurel. If it means anything to you, they were just words."

And so was the rest of it, but words could drag a man down. A couple could drown in words if they weren't speaking the same language. "Affection is something that can go away."

"No. I don't think so," he argued in a low rumble. "Not this kind. I can't imagine a time when I won't feel this way for you."

Marriage was a hard word for Mitch. Love was a word he didn't even understand. So she would find the ones that would get to him.

"Even when I walked away, I adored you, Mitchell Bradford."

He hauled her close again, his arms so tight around her. "I adore you, Laurel. I don't know why you're still here with me. It scares me, to tell you the truth. I don't trust it."

But he could. He wanted to. He simply needed time, patience. "You don't have to right now. Just know that when we fight, I'm going to be here when it's time for you to come home. I promise."

She let her head rest against his chest, listening to the strong beat of his heart.

"I'll go with Flynn."

He held her tight when she tried to get up. She eased back down, understanding he needed her in his arms. She hadn't expected him to give in on that. Not at all. She'd expected to have to tell Flynn to go home alone. "Why?"

"Does it matter?"

Did it? "Not really. I'm happy. I think it will be good for you. I know it's going to be hard, but I'll be waiting at home for you. You simply have to let your father talk and then you say whatever you need to. I don't want you to have regrets after he's gone."

"I won't. I wouldn't. I'm not doing it because I need closure, Laurel. I'm doing it because I want to make you happy. Tell me this will make you happy."

Mitchell Bradford was a man who took his responsibilities seriously. He followed the letter of their contract and tried to hold her to hers. He was unbending about certain things and didn't lie about them. He'd told her flat out that discussing the past was out of bounds, that she had no place there.

And now he was facing it because he wanted to make her happy.

"Yes. Yes, Mitch. You make me happy, but this will make me even happier."

"Then it's good. I'll go. And Laurel, I think while I'm gone, I want you to talk to a decorator. We should pick one of the rooms for a nursery. It's still a long time away, but we should start making plans and stuff. Babies need lots of things, I think. God knows Tag's kids do. Last time I was at his place, there was baby stuff everywhere. I think we should clean out my office."

His office? His office was a train wreck of things he kept. He loved his office. "Mitch, I can use the guest room."

"Too small. And it's not close. I want the baby close to us. We can get rid of the stuff. Well, I'd like to keep some of the comics. They're worth money, but no more than a box or two."

"Mitch, you love that stuff." She thought it was junk, but it was important to him.

"I want to love the baby more. I need to. I need to not need those things, Laurel. I need for us to be enough."

She held him in the quiet of the night and for the first time, felt real hope for them.

## Chapter Eleven

He had exactly forty-five minutes to get to the airport. He glanced down at his watch. He wasn't more than fifteen minutes away, but in Dallas, one always had to allow for some traffic. "Are you sure you're going to be all right?"

"I'm good, babe. Lisa is spending a couple of days with me and Remy assures me he won't let us out of his sight. I'm actually interested in seeing how Lisa takes to the big guy. She's always had a thing for that sexy Cajun accent."

"You think it's sexy?"

"Absolutely not, Master. I think it's terrible and it makes my ears bleed."

He grinned. Such a brat. "See that it continues to. I'm going to miss you while I'm gone. Why did I talk you into going back to school?"

He'd tried to convince her to come with him, but she was in the middle of saving some tenants from their evil landlord or something. That was his Laurel.

"I believe at the time you hoped I would find someone younger and less broody to turn my attentions to."

He'd been an idiot. "I'm sure that wasn't it at all. You stay safe and I'll call you after we land."

"Bye."

He hung up as Sharon looked in from the doorway. "Mr. Bradford, you have a very insistent man in reception. He does not have an appointment."

He hit *send* on his laptop. The contracts were in place and all negotiations were finalized. He'd just billed one very lucky company a couple of thousand hours. Damn, he was looking forward to that check. He might expand. Maybe it was time to think about taking on a couple of associates. He would keep the core clients for himself, but he could use some help around here, and Laurel was far too happy making the world a better place to ever come and help him sue people for cash. Lots of cash. Heaping wads of lovely cash that he was going to need because babies cost money.

Babies. He'd started to think about babies. Not just the singular. Laurel had a big family. She would want one for her kid. After the long talk with his brother and spending a few days with him while he got ready for the trip, he'd kind of turned around on the sibling thing. Flynn was cool and he seemed to truly care about Chase. He'd been on the phone with Chase, too. They'd talked about handling his problems. Mitch had told him about some of the things that happened to him in school. They'd agreed that Chase should come out to Dallas and spend some time getting to know Mitch during the summer.

After their father…

He wasn't thinking about that now. He would have to later on today, but not now.

"Flynn is going to be here to pick me up any minute now. I've got to be at the airport very soon, so it's going to have to wait."

Sharon shook her head, that brown helmet of hair not wavering at all. It was solidly sprayed down. "I'll tell him." She turned. "Mr. Dixon, he cannot see you now and you're going to have to leave. As soon as the boss goes, I'm heading out of here. My grandson has a baseball game and he forgot his favorite bat. I have to get it to him."

Dixon? What was Patrick Dixon doing here?

He took a step back when he realized the man charging into his office wasn't Patrick. This was a big man, much bigger than his slender, intellectual-looking brother. He was messy, his eyes red, as though he'd gone days without sleep.

Harvey Dixon.

"Sharon, call the police and then get out of here."

Harvey Dixon shook his head. "No, you don't have to do that. Or maybe you should. He's not going to stop. He's going to keep going until one of us is dead. Are you Mitchell Bradford?"

He wished he was someone else. Someone who carried a gun. That might come in handy right now. Hopefully someone from

McKay-Taggart was currently watching his security feed and would be on hand soon.

"That depends. You still planning on murdering me?" He didn't see a gun in the man's hand. Both hands were empty, but that didn't mean he couldn't pull one lickety-split. "You should know I sent off the contracts. They'll be signed in a few minutes and filed with the court system. There's nothing you can do."

"Contracts? For what?"

Great. He was delusional, too. Maybe he should keep him talking until the cops got here. "Why don't you sit down, Mr. Dixon, and we can have a talk."

Or the minute the fucker sat down, he could clock him with his umbrella. Except it was sitting in the stand out in reception because Laurel had put it out there along with a pretty coat stand she'd found.

Laurel's OCD problems were going to be the death of him. If she'd simply let him toss things wherever he liked, there would be an umbrella on the floor right now. If he lived he was so going to spank her pretty ass.

Harvey—who needed a shave—shook his head. "No. I think we should go somewhere else to talk. He could be behind me. By now he knows I got out."

"Out?"

"Of the prison he locked me in while he was setting me up."

"I thought you were in rehab."

"I have never touched a drug in my life. Never. My brother made it look like I did and he somehow convinced Frances I was in danger. This is all about the company. Mr. Bradford, I never meant you harm."

What the hell was going on? "I was told you were trying to kill me because I'm the lawyer pushing through the sale of a certain solar energy technology you feel like you pioneered."

"I toyed with it in the past. I will admit that, but I haven't touched solar in a few years. This isn't about solar. This is about money. I've come up with a device to measure domestic power consumption. It's an inexpensive device that measures energy pull."

Mitch wasn't following. "Energy pull?"

Harvey paced, his boots dragging the floor. "Homes waste

incredible amounts of energy from appliances that bleed it. A refrigerator that doesn't work properly, a laptop that pulls energy even though it's fully charged and off but plugged in. My device could help people figure out what needs fixing and what to unplug completely when it's not in use. People simply pay their energy bills without discovering where they're wasting the most. And they could fix that problem with one machine that reads the electrical currents. They wouldn't even have to walk through testing devices and plugs. I can do it all from one fuse box."

"That sounds great." As a person who'd made a lot of money on start-ups, he would look into that. One of his clients was Keith Langston, an angel investor. He'd taken some of Sanctum's wealthy members and formed an investment pool for promising new technologies. Keith was known for having an almost preternatural ability to find start-ups that would pay off. This was one of those ideas he would float by Keith. "It should make Dixon Technologies a fortune."

"My brother wants the fortune for himself."

Shit. "Patrick wants to sell the idea to an energy company, doesn't he?"

Now that he looked back, he could remember the way Patrick Dixon had sweated the day he'd come in, how his hands had been shaky. At the time, Mitchell had chalked it up to Patrick being upset about what his brother was doing. What if he'd been nervous about selling his brother out?

Harvey nodded. "I didn't know until he had me committed. He hired a police officer on the take to set me up and force me into rehab. He thought he could wrest the company away from me. All it would take was Frances and him forcibly buying me out. Our father put it in our bylaws in case one of us was incapacitated or doing something wrong."

"Frances is your sister. Why didn't she get you out of there?"

"Patrick has her believing I've gone crazy with rage about the solar project. I've been secretive the last two years because I knew Patrick would want to make as much money as possible off this tech. I want to help people. It's all I've ever wanted to do. I want to share this, keep the cost down. Patrick would never let me do that. Somehow, he found the plans and he started talking to an energy company. They're going to bury it. The only reason I'm still alive is he doesn't know where I hid the specs."

"Why would he send people after me? Someone's been making my life very difficult. There's been a campaign of harassment against me and the woman in my life. What's the purpose of that?"

"Our father always taught Patrick to have a contingency plan. If I'm convicted of a violent crime, they split my piece of the company and Patrick can still make his deal. It could be worth millions. It could take much longer to make that kind of money if we take the product to market. Development and retail takes money and time. He wants the money now."

The door opened and Flynn walked through. "Ready to go?"

His brother looked particularly dapper this morning. He'd spent the last few nights in their guest room, getting to know both Mitch and Laurel, and one of the things Mitch had discovered was his brother's penchant for wearing clothes that weren't selected for their utility. Maybe they could shop while they were in San Francisco. Laurel would probably be shocked if he showed up in a non-black suit. Or was it navy he was wearing today? He must be getting old. He never bought navy suits. Were his eyes going?

"Give me a couple of seconds, Flynn." He saw an opportunity. If Harvey was telling him the truth and he wasn't a big old crazy pants who had gotten out of the asylum, then Mitch could help him get his company back, and it looked like old Harvey would be needing a lawyer in his near future. "I'm going to put in a call to Lieutenant Brighton and we'll get this cleared up."

Flynn sighed. "This is a lawyer thing, isn't it? I can already see billable hours lighting up your eyes."

Harvey's eyes widened. "Lawyer. Yes." He reached into his pants, but the pockets were empty.

Flynn seemed to understand. He pulled out his wallet and handed Harvey a bill.

Harvey smiled and slapped a five-dollar bill on Mitch's desk. "There you go. That's a retainer. Now you're my lawyer, right?"

For five dollars? Someone had been watching way too much TV. "That is five dollars. That will retain approximately thirty seconds of my time."

Flynn frowned. "Mitchell."

Mitch shrugged. "I did not go to law school for five dollars, and I've got a baby on the way. Those little suckers are expensive."

"Five dollars now and a promise to let you handle Dixon Technologies contracts and sales in the future. I'm firing every single person who sided with Patrick."

A firm of that size and with those types of ideas would be worth thousands of billable hours…visions of college funds danced through his head. He took the five dollars. "You've got yourself a lawyer. Now let's get some cops here because this is going to get so messy."

Lawyers liked messy. Messy took time. Messy made money.

He wondered briefly how many lawyers actually represented the men who had harassed them. And Harvey better be telling the truth because he damn straight wasn't repping the man who had sent someone to shoot Laurel. He would shove that five dollars so far up Harvey's asshole it would come out his nose.

"I wouldn't dial that number if I were you," a new voice said.

He looked up and his day went to complete hell. Sharon walked in, her eyes wide, tears running down them. Patrick Dixon was behind her, a gun pointed at the back of her head.

"I'm so sorry, Mr. Bradford. This one didn't have an appointment either," she said.

Nope. He really needed some new security to keep the riffraff away. It looked like they were going to have a Dixon family reunion, and he hoped it didn't turn deadly.

\* \* \* \*

"See, I told you he would still be here." Laurel rushed up the steps to the building, Remy following behind her. She had a bag in her hand. Chocolate chip cookies from Mitch's favorite bakery and his earbuds. He'd left them behind this morning. He could buy more, but this particular pair were the ones that fit the best. He always complained that he must have a weird ear canal because most didn't fit.

He wouldn't be comfortable without them. She wanted to make sure he had everything he needed. He didn't particularly like to travel. He was doing it for her, so she was going to go out of her way to make it nice for him.

But she'd wanted to surprise him and get in one last good-bye kiss, hence the subterfuge.

"You're lucky he's on a private plane because the rest of the world has to go through security, and that means getting to the airport two hours ahead of the flight," Remy complained.

Remy, it seemed, wasn't looking forward to a whole weekend of watching two women. He'd seemed awfully flirty until he'd seen the lineup of movies she'd chosen for her sister's sleepover. He wasn't a big fan of the romantic comedy. From what she could tell, Mitch's sudden trip had also screwed up a date Remy had planned, though it had taken him a few minutes to remember the woman's name.

Candy. She was fairly certain Remy had met her at a strip club. Her bodyguard didn't have particularly good taste in women.

"Security isn't so hard to get through. You just have to avoid mornings and weekends."

Remy opened the door for her. "Yeah, it might not be hard for the curvy little white girl who looks like she shits sunshine. Try looking like me and having a metal plate in your head. See how those TSA officers treat you then."

She laughed as she started up the stairs. "I do not look like I shit sunshine. I'm very tough."

"You keep on believing that, *chère*." They had made it to the fourth floor when he stopped. "I've got a call from the office. I'll be right here."

That was all for the best since she intended to have an impromptu make-out session with her man. She'd already given him something to remember her by. She'd woken up in the early morning light with Mitch's hands on her body, his mouth covering her skin with kisses. He'd made slow, lazy, languid love to her. And then he'd taken her to the shower and washed her off, holding her like he never wanted to let her go.

It didn't matter that she could still feel him. She wanted one more kiss before he left.

She walked through the door, happy that he'd gone with the windows. Even when they hadn't been speaking, he'd given over to her wants. The building was still filled with gorgeous natural light.

Sharon wasn't at her desk, but that wasn't shocking. Her purse was still here and that was. She usually took Friday afternoons off for whatever baseball/soccer/school play was going on that day. Sure enough, there was a little slugger baseball bat sitting behind her vacant chair.

She smoothed down her skirt and started back toward Mitch's office. She loved what she was doing now. Because they were a nonprofit, she was allowed to do far more than a paralegal at a big firm would be allowed to do. She loved the feeling that she was making her city a better place to live, but she missed getting to see Mitch all the time. She even missed their silly battles over decorating and what to cater in for lunch. She kind of missed her old office.

"And what exactly do you think to gain by this play?"

She stopped outside of Mitch's office. It sounded like he had a client in there. His voice was hard, like this was a nasty, come-to-Jesus meeting. He had some clients who required a firm hand. Some people thought lawyers were like genies unleashed from their bottles—capable of granting them anything they wished. Mitch tended to put those clients in their places, and very quickly.

"It isn't my fault," a low voice said. "I didn't mean for it to turn out like this. Harvey was supposed to tell me where he hid the designs. He was supposed to give up the designs or go to jail. And Frances was supposed to vote with me."

Who was Frances? He'd mentioned a Harvey? He couldn't be talking about Harvey Dixon. Her heart threatened to stop as she eased to one side and saw through the half-open door that Patrick Dixon was in Mitch's office. He had a gun in his hand and Sharon as a human shield in front of him.

"This should have all been over, but that prick went to Frances when I couldn't pay him anymore," Patrick was saying.

"Austin? The man you hired to kill my girlfriend?" Mitch's voice was practically arctic.

"He wasn't going to kill her. He was supposed to scare her and you into filing police reports against Harvey. Austin was going to confess he'd been hired. He was going to serve some time in juvie and then get out and I would have given him a job," Patrick whined.

"But the little fucker got greedy," Mitch surmised.

She couldn't see him, but from the sound of his voice, he was likely at his desk.

"What did you do to Frances?" The man she had to figure was Harvey Dixon took a step toward his brother.

"Move again and I kill her." Patrick tightened his hold on Sharon, who whimpered.

Poor Sharon. She just wanted to be around her grandkids. What was she going to do? She took a step back, still able to hear everything that was going on.

"I don't know where Frances is. She called me and said she was going to get you out of the facility. She's being detained by my man on the inside. I'll have to get rid of her now, too, and all because you're such a selfish shit, Harvey. All of these people have to die because you won't save your family."

Her family was in there. Her heart raced. She moved to the reception area and pulled out her phone, dialing 911. As quietly as she could, she explained the situation. She could still hear Mitch talking in the background.

"So you think the police are going to believe that Harvey came in here and killed all of us because he was upset that a company I represent stole his solar storage idea?" Mitch sounded so calm, so patient.

The operator told her to get out of the building as quickly as she could. The police were on their way.

She hung up, but she couldn't leave. Where the hell was her bodyguard?

"It will work. I have several people who are more than willing to state that Harvey is insane," Patrick promised. "He's pissed off a whole lot of people in his time."

"What did you do? Did you get in with that bookie again?" Harvey asked.

"Are you even considering all the problems that are going to come up?" Mitch completely ignored the family argument. "First of all, you're not wearing gloves. How are the police going to believe Harvey did this when his prints aren't on the gun?"

The baseball bat. It was sitting right there. She picked it up and took a deep breath because she was so going to get spanked for what she was about to do.

The cops wouldn't come in quietly. She hadn't thought about that. Maybe all those sirens would scare Patrick Dixon into letting everyone go, or maybe they would make him desperate and he would start shooting. She couldn't take that chance.

She took the bat in hand and moved back into the hall. There he was. Patrick was standing with his back to the door. He hadn't closed it all the way. There was plenty of room for her to move into the office and clock the son of a bitch.

"I'll figure out a way to make it work." Patrick screamed suddenly. "You stay back!"

"Flynn, get behind me now," Mitch said, his voice a low growl.

"I'm not hiding behind you," Flynn insisted.

"Me, big brother. You, little brother. Remember that in the future and don't argue with me. You wanted me for a brother. Well, we follow the rules of the pack in this family. Get the fuck behind me now," Mitch ordered. "Anything happens to me and you…"

"Take care of Laurel," Flynn promised.

Oh, he was so not going to like the fact that she was breaking the rules of the pack. She would bet his rules included not putting herself and their baby in danger, but she couldn't let him die. She couldn't live in a world where there was no Mitchell Bradford to growl at her and get irritated when she changed things, and make love to her like she was the last woman on earth.

He couldn't die when he was finally learning what family meant.

She would show him what it meant.

She swung the bat back as she strode through the door and let that sucker go. There was a horrible crack as the bat met Patrick Dixon's skull, and she felt the reverberation all the way up her arms and through her chest.

He dropped to the ground, blood welling from his skull.

The whole world seemed to stop.

"Laurel?" Mitch was standing behind his desk, his eyes wide.

"What the hell?" Remy strode in, his gun in hand as sirens started to blare. He kicked the gun away from Patrick Dixon's still body. "I got a call from Liam that Austin Hunt had been spotted trying to follow Patrick Dixon into the building. I caught him downstairs with an arsenal strapped to his body. He's tied up and out of the way."

"Yeah, well, tell Li he was right," Mitch said as he strode around the desk. "There's always a twist. Meet Harvey Dixon. He's my newest client and not responsible for anything but being brilliant. Make sure Patrick doesn't get back up. Sharon, take next week off. Be with your grandchildren. And I'll get you a new bat."

Sharon shook her head. "Oh, no. I think this one is lucky now. Well, after I get the blood off it. And I'm so glad you mentioned it. I was hoping to take a couple of weeks off. My daughter recently bought a new RV. Grand Canyon here I come."

Mitch frowned at her. "Shouldn't you be more freaked out?"

The older woman kicked Patrick's body. "Mad is more like it. And I've worked for lawyers for a very long time, Mr. Bradford. You people tend to piss off the world. This isn't my first rodeo. I think I'll make a pot of coffee for the nice police officers on their way up."

Mitch took Laurel's hand and led her out. He didn't even look at her. He simply dragged her away from the scene of the crime.

He didn't stop until he got to her old office. He pulled her inside and locked the door.

She held her breath and prayed he wasn't too angry.

\* \* \* \*

Mitch could feel his heart beating in his chest as he looked at her. When he'd realized she was coming through the door with that bat in her hand, he'd wanted to die. Anything could have gone wrong. The gun could have gone off. She could have not hit Patrick hard enough.

She could have died.

"Mitch, I know you're mad at me."

Mad didn't cover it. He was overwhelmed. His body was a riot of emotion and he wasn't sure where to start. He'd been proud because his girl didn't hesitate. He'd been horrified that she was in danger. He'd been so fucking helpless.

But one thing had played out in his head and that was the fact that they weren't done. God, they couldn't be done.

She sank to her knees in front of him. "I know I upset you, Master. I know I scared you and I'm willing to take anything you have to give me."

She hadn't left him the day she should have. She hadn't walked away because he'd fucked up and lost his temper. He'd woken up the next morning and realized that he could get this situation back in hand. He could steer her toward the relationship he was comfortable with. He could go back to being her Master. Hell, if he played his cards right, he could probably train the waywardness out of her. He could likely manipulate her so she was comfortable accepting his dictates. She wouldn't try to sneak things in or go behind his back because she thought she was helping him.

She was proving it right now. She was kneeling before him, her head bowed.

She would be his submissive for the rest of her life, if he wanted.

God, he just wanted her to be his Laurel.

He dropped to his knees and wrapped his arms around her and said the words he'd sworn he would never, never say. "Please don't leave me. Don't ever leave me."

He was five again, clinging to a mother who cared more about parties than a child. When she'd turned him away, he'd stopped asking, stopped hoping, stopped wishing. He couldn't do that anymore. He couldn't live in that world because if he did, he forced Laurel and their baby to live there, too. He had to find a way out.

He had to find a way to believe. He knew only one real thing he believed in and that was her. If he held on to her, if he followed her lead in the things he didn't understand, maybe, just maybe he could be a better man. He could be better for her, better for their children.

Laurel's arms came out, holding him tightly to her. They were on the floor, their bodies pressed together as though they were trying to meld into one. "I won't. I promise. Mitchell, for as long as you want me, I promise I won't leave you. I'll be here."

He tangled his hands in her hair, desperate to be surrounded by her. She was his everything. How had he ever thought he could leave this woman alone? She'd been made for him. "Don't you ever do that again. Don't ever put yourself in danger. I swear to god,

Laurel, you nearly gave me a heart attack."

"I can't promise you." Tears shone in her eyes. "I won't ever let someone hurt you when I can help it. You'll simply have to punish me."

"No punishment, baby." He would do the same for her, and he wouldn't change her in any way. He loved her exactly the way she was. "But you will have to calm me down. I'm going to do something I wanted to do from the moment I hired you."

"Are you going to take me rough and hard on my desk?" She was grinning up at him. "Even though the cops are probably storming up the stairs as we speak?"

Yes, that had always been on his mind, and he was definitely going to do that. Since the moment she'd walked through his doors, he wanted to have the right to come into her office and demand she take him. But there was something else. Something he should have done all along because it had been inevitable.

"I'm going to tell you I love you." He framed her perfect face in his hands. She'd become the most precious thing in the world to him. She was the reason he breathed. "I love you, Laurel. Be my wife."

"Yes." She pressed her lips to his. "Yes, Mitchell."

He got to his feet and hauled her up and into his arms. He hadn't changed a thing about her office since the moment she'd walked out. It was neat as a pin and clean, so he felt zero guilt in setting his fiancée on top of the desk and running his hand up her skirt. His mouth found hers and he kissed her. His bride. He was going to kiss her for the rest of his life.

He heard the Dallas police enter and start asking questions, but it didn't matter.

His life started now.

# Epilogue

Six months later

Mitch stared down at the baby boy in his arms and wondered how he'd managed to get so lucky.

"He's very wrinkly." Chase stood beside him, looking down at the little boy they'd named John William Bradford.

After his father and Laurel's brother. "He's only a few hours old. The whole birth thing can take a lot out of a baby."

His son yawned, and it was the single cutest thing Mitch had ever seen. His tiny mouth opened and his whole body wriggled before he settled back down and blinked his eyes up at Mitch.

Blue. Like his. Like his father's.

"He looks a little like Dad," Chase said. His brother was living in Dallas. He'd decided to finish school here after their father had died. Flynn had packed them both up and moved to the Dallas office where he was running things remotely. He'd said they needed a new start, but Mitch had a suspicion that after John Adler had peacefully passed, they'd both wanted to be near family. Near him and Laurel and their new nephew.

"He does." Mitch had spent time with his dad. It had been easier than he thought it would. Somehow, loving Laurel had opened up possibilities he hadn't expected. He'd walked into his father's hospital room and there wasn't a monster there. He hadn't seen the man who neglected him. He'd seen a man who wished life had gone differently. He'd seen the man he could have been without Laurel.

His father had asked for forgiveness and when Mitch had given it, a great weight had left him. He wouldn't trade the three weeks he'd spent with his father for anything. Laurel had come out and they'd become a family in those weeks before John Adler's death.

He simply wished that had been the only funeral he'd had to attend.

He didn't know the hows and whys. Big Tag didn't talk about ops outside of his team, but Mitch knew that whatever had gone wrong had left McKay-Taggart changed forever, and he only hoped they could rally after losing one of their own.

"Who needs coffee?" Flynn slipped in, carrying a tray. "I've heard you will live off of caffeine for a very long time."

"Thanks, I'll take it. I don't want to sleep. I just want to hold him." He didn't want to let his son go.

"Well, I want to hold him, too." Laurel sighed and sat up, dragging the covers around her.

Mitch stood. "Momma gets dibs. She spent hours giving birth to you."

She looked tired but radiant as he gently transferred the baby to her arms.

"If she's going to breast feed, I'm going back out to the lobby," Flynn promised.

"Wimp," Chase shot back. "It's a normal, natural thing. Baby boy's gotta eat."

"Yeah, well, you're not wired to think it's kind of hot," Flynn admitted.

Chase laughed. "Not in any way. But I'm going to be the best uncle ever."

The kid had turned it around. He seemed happier now, though Mitch knew he missed his father. Mitch often got Chase to talk about their dad.

"I think I'm the best uncle," Flynn argued before putting his arm around his younger brother's shoulder. "Come on. Let's give these two some peace. I know they'll have a flood of visitors soon."

Laurel waved good-bye and then scooted over. "Sit with me."

He didn't hesitate. They'd found a perfect place together over the months of living as husband and wife. They'd continued to play until she couldn't. Mitch had discovered he preferred keeping their D/s life mostly to the club. His Laurel was such a perfect partner he wanted her by his side at all times. And he never, ever held himself back when he was making love to her. He was thinking about doing it now. "You know, after getting caught fucking on a desk by the police, I really think the nurses wouldn't be a big deal at all."

"Oh, you're waiting a while for that, babe." She leaned against him.

He kissed the top of her head. "You're worth waiting for. And the good news is Johnny can go to college. The sale of Dixon Tech went through. Harvey and Frances are making two hundred million each."

"And poor Patrick is making friends in prison. You know it couldn't have happened to a nicer guy," Laurel admitted.

His wife had been a vigilant watcher of Patrick Dixon's trial and relieved when the man had been sent to prison. She was taking some time off from saving the world to spend with their baby, but Mitch knew she would be back at it.

This time, he might help her. After all, he wanted the world to be as perfect for his son as it was for him.

"I was thinking. You know, as long as we're redoing the office at home, maybe I should take a look at your office at work."

He groaned. "You are always changing things. But fine. When you change things, I like them more. And god knows I love you more than my desk."

She smiled up at him. "Oh, no. We're keeping that desk. It's a historical desk. John's lucky he wasn't named Daddy's desk because he was conceived on it."

"We're never telling him that story. He only needs to know one thing about his conception."

"And what's that?"

"That he was conceived in love. I love you, baby. So damn much."

"Back at you, Bradford."

She rested her head against his chest and they watched their son sleep, the world fading around them.

# About Lexi Blake

Lexi Blake lives in North Texas with her husband, three kids, and the laziest rescue dog in the world. She began writing at a young age, concentrating on plays and journalism. It wasn't until she started writing romance that she found success. She likes to find humor in the strangest places. Lexi believes in happy endings no matter how odd the couple, threesome or foursome may seem. She also writes contemporary Western ménage as Sophie Oak.

Connect with Lexi online:

Facebook: https://www.facebook.com/lexi.blake.39
Twitter: https://twitter.com/authorlexiblake
Website: www.LexiBlake.net


Sign up for Lexi's free newsletter at
http://www.lexiblake.net/newsletter

# Also from Lexi Blake

*Masters And Mercenaries*
The Dom Who Loved Me
The Men With The Golden Cuffs
A Dom Is Forever
On Her Master's Secret Service
Sanctum: A Masters and Mercenaries Novella
Love and Let Die
Unconditional: A Masters and Mercenaries Novella
Dungeon Royale
Dungeon Games: A Masters and Mercenaries Novella
A View to a Thrill
Cherished: A Masters and Mercenaries Novella
You Only Love Twice
Luscious: Masters and Mercenaries~Topped
Adored: A Masters and Mercenaries Novella
Master No, *Coming August 4, 2015*


*Masters Of Ménage* (by Shayla Black and Lexi Blake)
Their Virgin Captive
Their Virgin's Secret
Their Virgin Concubine
Their Virgin Princess
Their Virgin Hostage
Their Virgin Secretary
Their Virgin Mistress


*The Perfect Gentlemen* (by Shayla Black and Lexi Blake)
Scandal Never Sleeps, *Coming August 18, 2015*
Seduction in Session, *Coming November 3, 2015*

URBAN FANTASY

*Thieves*
Steal the Light
Steal the Day
Steal the Moon
Steal the Sun
Steal the Night
Ripper
**Addict,** *Coming Soon*

# Master No
Masters and Mercenaries, Book 9
By Lexi Blake
Coming August 4, 2015

Disavowed by those he swore to protect…

Tennessee Smith is a wanted man. Betrayed by his government and hunted by his former employer, he's been stripped of everything he holds dear. If the CIA finds him, they're sure to take his life as well. His only shot at getting it all back is taking down the man who burned him. He knows just how to get to Senator Hank McDonald and that's through his daughter, Faith. In order to seduce her, he must become something he never thought he'd be—a Dom.

Overcome by isolation and duty…

All her life, Dr. Faith "Mac" McDonald has felt alone, even among her family. Dedicating herself to helping others and making a difference in the world has brought her some peace, but a year spent fighting the Ebola virus in West Africa has taken a toll. She's come home for two months of relaxation before she goes back into the field. After holding so many lives in her hands, nothing restores her like the act of submission. Returning to her favorite club, Mac is drawn to the mysterious new Dom all the subs are talking about, Master No. In the safety of his arms, she finds herself falling head over heels in love.

Forced to choose between love and revenge…

On an exclusive Caribbean island, Ten and Mac explore their mutual attraction, but her father's plots run deeper than Ten could possibly have imagined. With McKay-Taggart by his side, Ten searches for a way to stop the senator, even as his feelings for Mac become too strong to deny. In the end, he must choose between love and revenge—a choice that will change his life forever.

# Hades
A Demonica Novella
By Larissa Ione

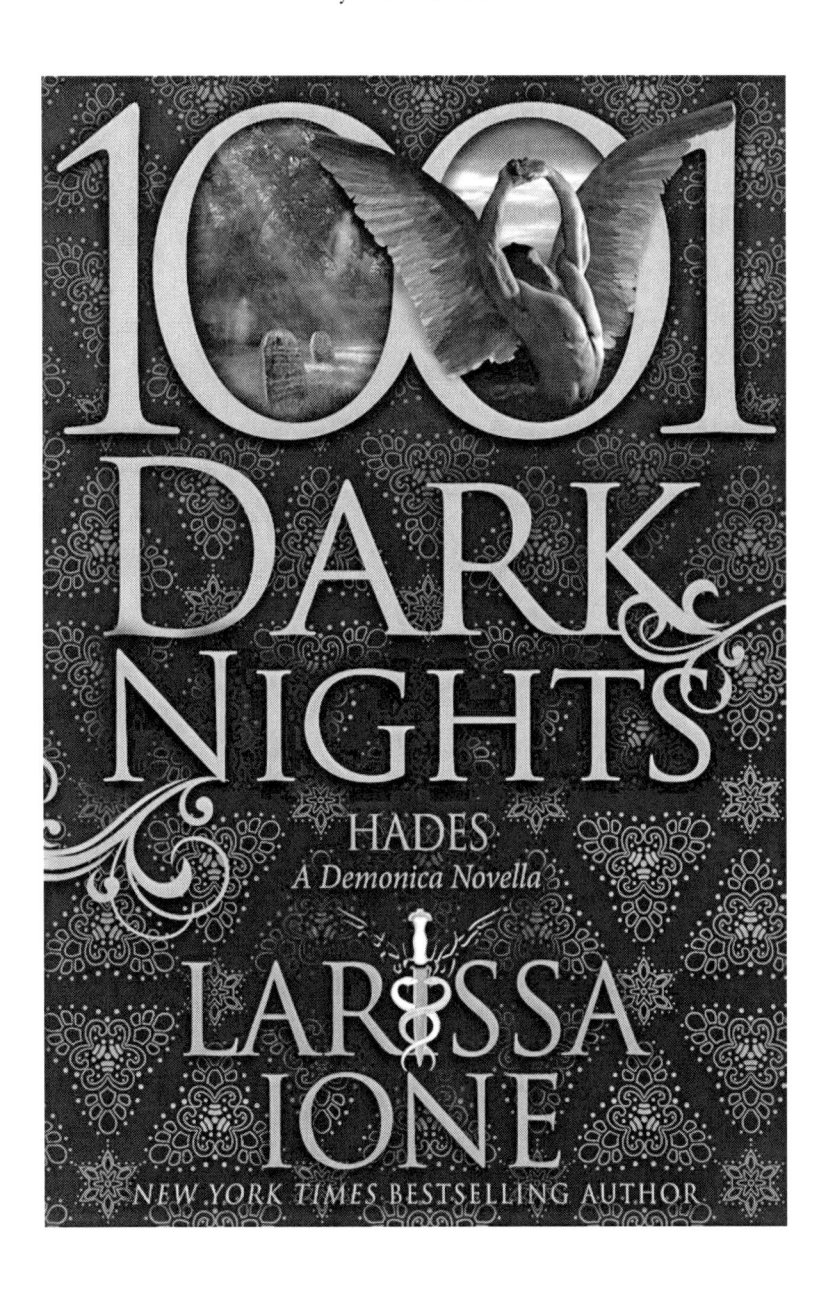

# Author Acknowledgments

Every story presents unique challenges for an author, and every story makes the author appreciate those who help to make a book the best it can be. For the most part, Hades played nice, but I need to thank Liz Berry, Kim Guidroz, and Pamela Jamison for all their hard work in whipping Hades into shape. I love you, ladies! I just wish Hades hadn't liked the whipping so much…

# Glossary

*The Aegis*—Society of human warriors dedicated to protecting the world from evil. Recent dissension among its ranks reduced its numbers and sent The Aegis in a new direction.

*Emim*—The wingless offspring of two fallen angels. *Emim* possess a variety of fallen angel powers, although the powers are generally weaker and more limited in scope.

*Fallen Angel*—Believed to be evil by most humans, fallen angels can be grouped into two categories: True Fallen and Unfallen. Unfallen angels have been cast from Heaven and are earthbound, living a life in which they are neither truly good nor truly evil. In this state, they can, rarely, earn their way back into Heaven. Or they can choose to enter Sheoul, the demon realm, in order to complete their fall and become True Fallens, taking their places as demons at Satan's side.

*Harrowgate*—Vertical portals, invisible to humans, which demons use to travel between locations on Earth and Sheoul. A very few beings can summon their own personal Harrowgates.

*Inner Sanctum*—A realm within Sheoul-gra that consists of 5 Rings, each containing the souls of demons categorized by their level of evil as defined by the Ufelskala. The Inner Sanctum is run by the fallen angel Hades and his staff of wardens, all fallen angels. Access to the Inner Sanctum is strictly limited, as the demons contained inside can take advantage of any outside object or living person in order to escape.

*Memitim*—Earthbound angels assigned to protect important humans called Primori. Memitim remain earthbound until they complete their duties, at which time they Ascend, earning their wings and entry into Heaven. See: Primori

*Primori*—Humans and demons whose lives are fated to affect the world in some crucial way.

*Radiant*—The most powerful class of Heavenly angel in existence. Unlike other angels, a Radiant can wield unlimited power in all realms and can travel freely through Sheoul with very few exceptions. The designation is awarded only to one angel at a time. Two can never exist simultaneously, and they cannot be destroyed except by God or Satan.

*Sheoul*—Demon realm. Located on its own plane deep in the bowels of the Earth, accessible to most only by Harrowgates and hellmouths.

*Sheoul-gra*—A holding tank for demon souls. A realm that exists independently of Sheoul, it is overseen by Azagoth, also known as the Grim Reaper. Within Sheoul-gra is the Inner Sanctum, where demon souls go to be kept in torturous limbo until they can be reborn.

*Sheoulic*—Universal demon language spoken by all, although many species also speak their own language.

*Shrowd*—When angels travel through time, they exist within an impenetrable bubble known as a shrowd. While in the shrowd, angels are invisible and cannot interact with anyone — human, demon, or angel — outside the shrowd. Breaking out of the shrowd is a serious transgression that can, and has, resulted in execution.

*Ter'taceo*—Demons who can pass as human, either because their species is naturally human in appearance, or because they can shapeshift into human form.

*Vyrm*—The winged offspring of an angel and a fallen angel. More powerful than *emim*, *vyrm* also possess an ability that makes their very existence a threat to angels and fallen angels alike. With a mere second of eye contact, a *vyrm* can wipe out a fallen angel or an angel's entire immediate family. Once hunted ruthlessly, they are now a protected class, by mutual agreement between Sheoul and

Heaven, so long as none harm others with their unique power.

*Watchers*—Individuals assigned to keep an eye on the Four Horsemen. As part of the agreement forged during the original negotiations between angels and demons that led to Ares, Reseph, Limos, and Thanatos being cursed to spearhead the Apocalypse, one Watcher is an angel, the other is a fallen angel. Neither Watcher may directly assist any Horseman's efforts to either start or stop Armageddon, but they can lend a hand behind the scenes. Doing so, however, may have them walking a fine line that, to cross, could prove worse than fatal.

*Ufelskala*—A scoring system for demons, based on their degree of evil. All supernatural creatures and evil humans can be categorized into the five Tiers, with the Fifth Tier comprising of the worst of the wicked.

# Chapter One

*The road to Hades is easiest to travel.* —Diogenes Laertius

*Enjoy the trip, because the stay is going to be hell.* —Hades

If Cataclysm had to clean one more toilet in this demon purgatory known as Sheoul-gra, she was going to jump in and flush herself down.

She'd always assumed that when angels got kicked out of Heaven they got to do fun fallen angel stuff. Like terrorize religious people and drink foamy mugs of Pestilence ale with demons. But no, she'd gotten stuck wiping the Grim Reaper's ass.

Okay, she didn't *actually* wipe Azagoth's ass. And if she did, his mate, Lilliana, would have had something to say about it. And by "say," Lilliana meant "behead."

Cat reconsidered that. Lilliana, who was still, technically, a fully-haloed angel, wouldn't do anything quite so drastic. Most likely. But Cat still wouldn't want to get on the female's shit list. Anyone who pissed off Lilliana pissed off the Grim Reaper, and that...well, Cat could think of nothing worse.

Except maybe cleaning toilets.

*Stop whining. You took the job willingly.*

Yes, that was true, but she'd only agreed to serve Azagoth because she wanted to earn her way back into Heaven, and doing that required her to A) keep her nose clean, B) avoid entering

Sheoul, the demon realm humans often referred to as Hell, and C) do something heroic to save the world.

Easy peasy.

She snorted to herself as she carried a tray of dirty dishes from Azagoth and Lilliana's bedroom, her bare feet slapping on the cold stone floor that covered every inch of the ancient Greek-style mansion. He'd surprised Lilliana with breakfast in bed this morning, which was something Cat would have been shocked by a few months ago. Who would have thought that the Grim Reaper was such a softie?

She supposed she should have known better after he gave her a job and a place to live so she didn't have to worry about some jerk dragging her, against her will, into Sheoul for fun or profit.

No, Sheoul was off limits to her. Entering the demon realm would complete her fall from grace and turn her into a True Fallen, a fallen angel with no hope of redemption. As an Unfallen, she had a little wiggle room, but even so, very few angels had ever been given their wings back. In fact, she knew of only two

One of those two, Reaver, was now not only an angel, but one of the most powerful angels to have ever existed. His mate, Harvester, had also spent time as a fallen angel, but her circumstances were unique, and while Cat didn't know the whole story, she knew that Harvester had saved Heaven and Earth, and she deserved every one of her feathers she got back.

The thought of being made whole again made Cat's useless wing anchors in her back itch. Her luxurious mink-brown wings were gone, sliced off in a brutal ceremony, and with them, her source of power. She totally understood why an Unfallen would cross the barrier between the human and demon realms to turn themselves into True Fallen and gain new wings and new powers. But was the evil upgrade worth it? Cat didn't think so.

"Cat!" Azagoth's voice startled her out of her thoughts, and she nearly dropped the tray of dirty dishes as she looked up to see him striding down the hallway from his office.

In the flickering light cast by the iron wall sconces, he didn't look happy. He also wasn't alone.

Hades, Azagoth's second-in-command and the designated Jailor of the Dead, was walking next to him. No, not walking. With the way his thigh muscles flexed in those form-fitting black pants with every silent step, it was more like prowling. His body sang with barely-leashed power, and she shivered in primal, feminine response.

Son of a bitch, Hades was hot. Hard-cut cheekbones and a firm, square jaw gave him a rugged appearance that bordered on sinister, especially when paired with a blue Mohawk she'd kill to run her palm over. But then, she'd kill to run her palms over all of him, and she'd start with his muscular chest, which was usually, temptingly, bare. Not that she'd complain about what he was wearing now, a sleeveless, color-shifting top that clung to his rock-hard abs.

She tried not to stare, but really, even if she'd stood in the middle of the hall with her tongue hanging out, it wouldn't have mattered. He never looked her way. He never noticed her. She was nothing to him. Not even worth a glance. Those cold, ice-blue eyes looked right through her. And yet, this was a guy who laughed with Lilliana, pulled pranks on the other Unfallen who lived here, and played with hellhounds as if they were giant puppies. Giant, man-eating puppies.

Azagoth stopped in front of her. "Cat? You okay?"

She blinked, realized she'd been lost in a world of Hades. "Ah, yes. Sorry, sir. What is it?"

"Have you seen Zhubaal?"

She nodded. "He was heading toward the dorms about half an hour ago. I think he said he was going to be teaching some of the new Unfallen how to be an asshole or something."

Hades barked out a laugh, and she caught a glimpse of two pearly-white fangs. She used to think fangs were repulsive, but if Hades wanted to sink his canines into her, she'd gladly bare her throat and invite him in. She tapped her tongue against her own tiny fangs, the smaller versions that Unfallen grew a few days after being de-winged. For the most part, she'd gotten used to them. She didn't even bite her lip anymore.

"Z is finally teaching them something he knows all about," Hades said.

There was no love lost between those two, but Cat had no idea why. She did, however, know why *she* thought Zhubaal was an ass.

Not that she wanted to think about it, let alone talk about it. She just had to hope that no one else knew.

Because humiliating.

"Thank you, Cataclysm," Azagoth said, dipping his dark head in acknowledgment. "I hear you've been helping out with the Unfallen, as well. Lilliana says you advised them to use their Heavenly names instead of their Fallen names. You know that's forbidden, right?"

Anxiety flared, but she lifted her chin and boldly met his gaze. "Not in Sheoul-gra. The rules are different in your realm. I figured that if they use their Heavenly names here, it'll remind them to stay on the right track if they want to earn their way back into Heaven."

Hades's gaze bored into her, the intelligence in his eyes sparking. No doubt he was wondering why she hadn't taken her own advice, but thankfully he didn't have a chance to ask.

"Very smart." Azagoth's approval gave her a secret thrill, and then it was back to minion-chores as usual when he said, "By the way, my office could use some attention. It's a little...messy."

Azagoth brushed past her, and was it her imagination or did Hades linger for just a moment? Every inch of skin exposed by her blue and black corset tingled, and she could have sworn his gaze swept over her, appreciative and hot. But then he was as cold as ever, walking next to Azagoth as if she didn't exist and never had.

With a sigh, she dropped off the dishes in the kitchen and grabbed her bucket of cleaning supplies before heading to Azagoth's office. Once inside...well, he wasn't kidding when he said he'd left a mess.

She ran a cloth over the stone and wood walls, wiping down the blood mist from whatever demon Azagoth had vaporized. And it must have been a *big* demon.

Apparently, he didn't obliterate demons often; there was a price to pay for destroying souls. But when he did, the mess was considerable.

She went through two bottles of cleaner and dozens of rags before the office no longer resembled a slaughterhouse, and man, she was going to need a long shower. Relieved to finally be done, she started to gather her supplies when a dark spot on the wall behind Azagoth's desk caught her eye. Cursing, she swept her cloth over the stain, scrubbing to make sure she got every sticky bit of gore. But dammit, blood had gotten into a crack, and...she frowned.

Putting down the rag, she traced the crack with her finger, squinting at what appeared to be a round recess in the wall. What the heck was it? Driven by curiosity, she pushed slightly. There was a click, followed by a flood of light coming from behind her.

Oh....*shit*.

She turned slowly, and her gut plummeted to her feet.

A huge chunk of wall had disappeared, revealing a portal from the human and demon planes. A stream of *griminions* filed through, their short, stocky forms escorting the souls of demons and evil humans into the realm of Sheoul-gra. The creepy little *griminions* chittered from under their black, monk-like hooded robes as they marched the souls, whose bodies in Sheoul-gra were as corporeal as her own, through the cross-sectioned tunnel, only to disappear into another portal that would take the demons to their final destination—Hades's Inner Sanctum.

"No!" she shouted. "Stop! Azagoth hasn't approved the transfers!"

But they didn't stop. They kept emerging from the right side of the tunnel and disappearing through the shimmering barrier of darkness to the left. Panicked, she pushed on the lever again, but the *griminions* kept marching. She wiggled it, pushed harder, punched it, and finally, with a whoosh, the portal closed, leaving only a solid wall in its place.

Cat swallowed dryly, her heart pounding, her pulse throbbing in her ears. Maybe she hadn't screwed up badly enough for anyone to know. Maybe no one would notice the souls that got through to the Inner Sanctum without Azagoth's approval.

And maybe she'd just earned herself a place in the Grim Reaper's hall of horrors, the Hall of Souls at the mansion's entrance, where statues made out of the bodies of his enemies were on display for the world to see.

What made it all worse was that the people encased in those statues weren't dead.

On the verge of hyperventilating, she slumped against Azagoth's behemoth of a desk and forced herself to breathe slowly. How did she keep screwing up? And not just screwing up, but *royally* screwing up. Just last week she'd broken one of Azagoth's centuries-old Japanese swords. And a month before that, she'd spilled pineapple soda all over a priceless rug woven from demon sheep wool by Oni craftsmen.

"Did you know that, unlike pineapple soda, fallen angel blood doesn't stain demon wool?" he'd asked in a dark, ominous voice as she'd scrubbed the rug. And no, as a matter of fact, she hadn't known that.

When she'd said as much, he'd merely smiled, which was far, far worse than if he'd just come out and said that if she fucked up again, her blood would definitely *not* stain that damned carpet.

Soda, however, did stain, just like he'd said.

It seemed to take hours before she stopped trembling enough to gather her crap and flee the office, and thankfully she didn't run into Azagoth on her way to her quarters. She did manage to catch another glimpse of Hades as he rounded a corner though, the hard globes of his ass flexing under the tight, midnight black pants.

Maybe she could try talking to him someday. Try saying something more coherent than, "Hi, Mr., um, Hades. Or do you prefer Jailor? Or Lord? Or...?"

He'd looked at her as if she'd crawled out of a viper pit. "Hades," he rumbled. "Easy enough."

And that had been the sum of their conversation. Their only conversation. Ever.

Did he think she had freaking halo pox or demonic measles? And why was she dwelling on this anyway? He was clearly not interested in her, and she had more important things to worry about.

Like whether or not Azagoth was going to *not* stain his carpet with her blood when he found out that she'd allowed unauthorized souls to enter the Inner Sanctum.

## Chapter Two

Hades had a lot of names. Lord of the Dead. Keeper of Souls. Jailor of the Baddies. Asshole.

He owned them all. Ruled his piece of the underworld with an iron fist. Feared nothing.

Correction. He feared nothing except the Grim Reaper. Azagoth was the one person who had proven time and time again that he could turn Hades's underworld upside down and shake it like a snow globe.

So Hades generally despised the monthly meetings between him and Azagoth, but thankfully, this latest one had been refreshingly brief and light on fault-finding. Which was good, because Hades's brain had been occupied with images of Cat.

He remembered the first time he'd seen her when she came to work for Azagoth a few months ago, remembered how drawn he'd been to her energy. She was new to life on this side of the Pearly Gates, and while most newly fallen angels were either terrified or bitter, she was neither. According to Lilliana, Cat was curious. Eager to learn. Enthusiastic to experience new things.

Hades could teach her a new thing or two.

Except he couldn't, could he? Nope, because the curvy redhead was off-limits to him, and panting after her like a hellhound on the trail of a hellbitch in heat would only end in pain.

Pain that would likely come at the end of Azagoth's hand, and Hades had long ago learned that pissing off his boss was stupid beyond stupid...beyond stupid.

Still, it grated on him that he'd been read the riot act about Cat when he was about ninety-nine percent sure Zhubaal had bedded her. So what was up with *that*? Z was a cranky sonofabitch with a short fuse and a stick up his ass, but somehow *that* mongrel was good enough for Cat?

So fucked up.

Hades took one of three portals dedicated to travel between Azagoth's realm and the Inner Sanctum back to his residence, and as he materialized inside his living space a tingle of mayhem skittered over his skin. How...odd. Sure, hell was all about mayhem, but this was different, and it had been different for a few months now. Before, there had always been a balanced mix of order and chaos. Organized chaos. Chaotic organization.

Even here, in Sheoul-gra's Inner Sanctum, where the souls of dead demons came to play until they were born again, there was order. Rarely, there was chaos.

At least, chaos used to be rare. But now that Satan had been imprisoned and Sheoul was no longer under his rule, all hell had broken loose—literally. Sheoul was now operating under a new regime, with a dark angel named Revenant as its overlord, and not everyone was happy about the new leadership situation. Just as with humans, demons didn't accept change easily, and the tension surrounding Revenant's takeover had bled over into Sheoul-gra.

Completely unacceptable.

The tingle began to sting, as if Hades was crawling with hornets. Resisting the urge to rip off his own skin, he stepped into his personal portal next to the fireplace. Like Harrowgates that transported demons around Sheoul and the human realm, some of the portals inside the Inner Sanctum had been built to travel only between two locations, while others could transport a person to one of multiple places by manipulation of the symbols inside the portal's four walls. But Hades could also operate them with his mind, allowing any portal to take him anyplace within the Inner Sanctum he wished to be. Or, like now, to get where he needed to be, he merely had to concentrate on the sensation of mayhem wracking his body, and a moment later, the portal opened up.

He wasn't at all surprised to find himself in a burned-out sector of the 5th Ring, a vast, dreary realm of fog, heat, and despair that contained the evilest of the evil. Before him, demons scattered into the mist the moment they recognized him.

Most demons, anyway. A few stood their ground, their defiance admirable, if not foolish.

A demon who had been a professional torturer before he was killed several years ago by Aegis demon slayers blocked his path. Here, demons could choose their appearance, and this bastard had chosen his former skeletal Soulshredder form, his grotesque, serrated claws extending from long fingers.

"Move." Hades slowed, but he didn't stop. He didn't have time for this shit. His skin burned and his insides vibrated, alerting him to some sort of violent disturbance nearby. And it had to be a whopper for him to have felt it from inside his home on the other side of the Inner Sanctum...which was roughly the distance from one earthly pole to the other.

"Fuck you, Soul Keeper."

Surprise jolted him; few were brave—or stupid—enough to challenge him. But Hades kept his expression carefully schooled. Tension was running high right now, and he couldn't afford to let anyone think he was losing control of the Gra.

From two-dozen feet away and without breaking his stride, Hades flayed the demon with a mere thought. Stripped him of his skin like a banana. The demon screamed in agony, and Hades let him. That noise would carry for miles, warning everyone within earshot of the consequences of fucking with him. Sure, Hades could have "killed" him, but the demon's soul would simply have fled the old, broken body and taken a new form. Handing down pain was much more satisfying.

Hades continued on his way, his boots crunching down on charred bone and wood, and as he strode by the Soulshredder, the demon stopped his annoying screaming long enough to croak, "You...will...fail."

Hades ignored him. Because really? Fail at what? His job was pretty simple and straightforward. All he had to do was keep demon and evil human souls inside the Inner Sanctum until the time came when, or if, they were born again. *How* he kept them was entirely up to him. He could leave them in peace, he could torture them, he could do whatever he wanted. Failure? That was ridiculous. There was nothing to fail *at*.

Really, this place was boring as shit most of the time.

Leaving the asshole behind, he threaded his way past the kind of horrors one would expect to find in a place where the evilest of evils lived, but the bodies, blood, and wrecked buildings didn't even draw his eye. He'd seen it all in his thousands of years down here, and nothing could faze him.

Not even the hellhound crouched in the shadows of the gnarled thorn tree gave him pause. The beasts could cross the barrier between Sheoul-gra and Sheoul, and for the most part, Hades let them. He kind of had to, since their king, Cerberus, had taken it upon himself to be the self-appointed guardian of the underworld—specifically, Sheoul-gra. For some reason, hellhounds hated the dead and were one of the few species that could see them outside of Sheoul-gra. Inside Sheoul-gra, they got their rocks off by ripping people apart. As long as they limited their activities to the 3rd, 4th, and 5th Rings, where the worst of the demons lived, he didn't give a crap what the fleabag hounds did.

Ahead, from inside the ruins of an ancient temple, came a chorus of chanting voices. *Ich tun esay. Ich tun esay. Ich tun esay alet!*

He frowned, recognizing the language as Sheoulic, but the dialect was unfamiliar, leaving some of the words open to interpretation. Somehow, Hades doubted his interpretation was correct and that the chanters were talking about opening a dime store.

He tracked the sound, and as he approached the reddish glow seeping through a doorway in the building ahead, the hair on the back of his neck stood up. What the hell? He hadn't been creeped out or afraid of anything in centuries. Many centuries.

*Ich tun esay. Ich tun esay. Ich tun esay alet...blodflesh!*

What. The. Fuck.

Something screamed, a soul-deep, tortured sound that made Hades's flesh crawl. Something was very, very wrong.

Kicking himself into high gear, Hades sprinted into the fire-lit, cavernous room...and then he skidded to a halt, his boots slipping in pools of blood on the stone floor. A hundred demons from dozens of species were gathered around a giant iron pot hanging over a fire. Inside the pot, a Neethul demon's screams died as his body bubbled in some sort of acidic liquid.

"*Stop!*" Hades didn't give a shit about the demon. What he did give a shit about was the ritual. In Sheoul-gra, all rituals were forbidden and came with a penalty of having one's soul disintegrated, so they didn't happen often. Oh, Hades had come across one or two loners performing religious rituals now and then, but this kind of massive gathering and ceremony? This was a first.

And, by Azagoth's balls, it would be the last.

The mass of chanting demons turned as a unit, their creepy smiles and empty eyes filling him with a sickening sense of doom. Alarm shot through him, and in an instant, he summoned his power and prepared to blast every one of these freaks into the Rot, the prison meant for the worst of the worst, where suffering was more than legend, and where the only release came when Azagoth destroyed your soul.

With a word, he released his power. At the same moment, one of the demons overturned the pot of acid. The liquid, mixed with the goo of the dissolved Neethul, splashed on the floor in a whoosh of steam. Suddenly, as if Hades's power had hit an invisible wall, it bounced back at him, wrapping him in a cocoon of blackness.

As he was transported by his own spell to the prison all demons feared, he heard the chant again. *Ich tun esay alet!*

Oh…shit. This time, he understood.

The demons weren't trying to open a dime store. Somehow they'd acquired a forbidden object or person of power and were attempting to open Sheoul-gra's very walls, to allow millions of souls out into the human and demon realms.

They were looking to feast.

# Chapter Three

Hades had no trouble freeing himself from the Rot, although he'd had a hell of a time trying to convince one of the guards, a fallen angel named Vype, that he wasn't a demon in disguise.

Once he'd talked the guy down, Hades gathered a handful of his fallen angel staff and returned to the site of the demonic ritual. Within a few hours, they'd captured two of the demons who had been there. They'd changed their physical appearances, but Hades could see through their costumes to their souls. Idiots.

After delivering them to the Rot, he went immediately to Azagoth, who was surveying his library's vast shelves of books, some of which vibrated as his gaze landed on them. Hades hung back, a lesson learned after being bitten by one of Azagoth's rabid tomes. Who knew books could bite? Vicious little bastards.

Hades cleared his throat to announce his presence. Azagoth didn't even turn around, simply barked out a curt, "Sit."

The Grim Reaper's voice didn't leave room for argument. But then, it rarely did. So Hades took a seat in the leather chair...leather made from the finest Molegra demon hides.

Azagoth took a seat on the plush sofa across from Hades and reached for a tattered book on the armrest. "So," he said. "What's going on in the 5th Ring?"

Hades didn't bother asking how Azagoth knew. No doubt one or more of Hades's wardens were agents for Azagoth. The guy's spy network extended from the deepest pits of Sheoul to the highest reaches of Heaven.

"Hell if I know," Hades said. "But whatever it is, it's bad. I caught a bunch of assholes performing a forbidden ritual powerful enough to deflect my power and blast me to my own fucking prison."

One of Azagoth's dark eyebrows shot up. "I assume you took care of the situation."

"Once I got myself out of my own jail, yeah. I only found two of the offenders, but I've got 'em strung up and awaiting your questioning. I believe they got their hands on something from outside. The power they wielded was like nothing else I've felt."

"Dammit," Azagoth breathed. "You're losing control—"

"My ass," Hades snapped. "The Gra is becoming overloaded with evil souls. You need to stop reincarnating only non-evil demons and start working on the baddies. Get them back to Sheoul where they belong. I've been spending way too much time moving Ufelskala Tier 4 and 5 demons to Rings less equipped to handle that kind of malevolence."

The Ufelskala, a scale developed to categorize demons into five Tiers based on the intensity of evil inherent to their species, was also one of the tools Azagoth used to sort demons into the five Rings of the Inner Sanctum. Not that the guy couldn't send anyone to any Ring he wanted, but in general, he followed the information laid out in the Ufelskala.

"The 1st and 2nd Rings are clearing out," Azagoth said. "As per Revenant's orders, I'm reincarnating a lot of the non-evil demons on those levels. So do some creative reassigning."

Not only would that be a lot of work, but it would require bringing in more fallen angels to oversee Rings that were going to contain a lot more evil demons, and no fallen angel volunteered to work in the Inner Sanctum. Not when they weren't allowed to leave and their powers were limited. They'd have to be...recruited. By force.

"Sir, this is bullshit," Hades growled. "What the everloving fuck is Hell's new overlord doing?"

Azagoth flipped open the book. "That's not for you to question."

Hades burst to his feet. "My hot ass," he snapped. "I never thought I'd say this, but at least Satan kept order and balance in Sheoul. This new douchebag—"

Burning pain ripped through him, and only belatedly did he realize that he'd been struck by a bolt of hellfire that had streamed directly from Azagoth's fingers.

"Here's the thing," Azagoth said calmly. "Satan didn't give a shit what anyone said about him. But Revenant? He's putting down everyone who speaks out against him. Hell, he's laying out anyone he even *suspects* might rebel."

"That's because he's a paranoid fool. Learning his true identity has made him weak." Apparently, Revenant had grown up in Sheoul believing he was a fallen angel, when the truth was that he had always been a Heavenly angel. How could a true angel, no matter how tarnished his halo, expect to be ruthless enough to rule Hell?

"And yet, he managed to defeat and imprison not only Satan, but Lucifer, Gethel, and the archangel Raphael as well." Azagoth snapped the book closed with a heavy thud. "Respect him."

"He couldn't have done it without help from his brother," Hades muttered.

"Maybe not. But keep in mind that he and his brother have each other's backs. Don't piss off either one of them. Together they are far more dangerous than Satan ever was."

Hades actually liked Revenant's brother, Reaver, who happened to be one of the most powerful Heavenly angels to ever exist. Reaver had spent a little time in the Inner Sanctum as Azagoth and Hades's prisoner, and really, even when the guy had been in pain, he'd been pretty cool.

But Revenant could suck Hades's balls.

The thought of having his balls sucked made an image of Cat flash in his head, which, granted, was way better than thinking of Revenant. But still, off-limits was off-limits. Dammit.

"Yeah, whatever," Hades said, resisting the urge to roll his eyes. "Ever since Rev took over as King of Hell, the Inner Sanctum has been a war zone."

"Which is, in part, because he requested that I only reincarnate Ufelskala Tier one and two demons."

"And the result of that idiotic order is that my domain is filling up with majorly evil fuckheads who only want to cause trouble."

Azagoth's dark eyes flashed as his patience with Hades wore thin. But then, he'd never had much patience to begin with. "Deal with it. Now. Your rebellions are leaking over into my part of Sheoul-gra, and the archangels are starting to get twitchy."

"The *archangels* are starting to get twitchy? I'm the one trapped down there with demons who are desperate to get out."

"Then keep it from happening."

*Keep it from happening?* As if Hades had just been laying around on a beach and drinking margaritas while the Inner Sanctum went up in flames? "What the fuck do you think I've been doing for thousands of years?"

There was a long, brittle silence, and then Azagoth's voice went low. And maybe a little judgmental. "There have been escapes."

"Very few, and never more than one at a time. And come on...there were special circumstances in each case." No demon could escape on his own, not when demons had no power in Sheoul-gra. Escape required energy or objects from an outside source, which was why visitors were very rarely allowed inside the Inner Sanctum. A single feather from an angel could be used in spells to destroy barriers or kill a target. One seemingly harmless vampire fang had once given a Neethul the power to reincarnate himself without Azagoth's help.

"Still, you must be extra vigilant." Azagoth dragged his hand through his black hair, looking suddenly tired. Good. Hades shouldn't be carrying the stress of all of this by himself. "I've never seen Sheoul so unstable."

Vigilant. *Vigilant*, he'd said. As if Hades was a total noob at this. But instead of saying that, he merely gritted his teeth and offered a tense smile. "Yes, sir. Anything you say, sir."

"Good. Now get out. And do not fail me again."

* * * *

Somewhere outside Azagoth's Greek-style mansion, a bird of prey screeched. Cat loved hearing it. Not long ago, Sheoul-gra had been a dead realm, a physical manifestation of Azagoth's emotional state. Dark and dreary, the "Gra," as it was sometimes called, had resembled a toxic wasteland that couldn't support any animal or plant life that wasn't straight out of Hell itself.

But Lilliana's love had changed Azagoth, and with it, his realm.

Now, when Cat strolled outside the palace, the grounds and buildings surrounding it teemed with life, from the lush grass, leafy green trees, and sparkling water, to rabbits, birds, and even the occasional fox or deer.

Smiling, she put down her feathered duster and headed from Azagoth's pool room toward the mansion's entrance, and as she rounded a corner, she collided with a body.

A huge, muscular body.

*Hades.*

An instant, hot tingle pricked her skin as she leaped backward, crashing into something behind her. She heard something break, but at the moment, it didn't matter.

This was the first time she'd touched Hades. The first time her ability to sense good and evil as a physical symptom on the surface of her skin had triggered. At least, it was the first time with Hades.

She'd always suspected he'd give off an intense blast of evil, but she hadn't expected the evil to be tempered by a ribbon of goodness. She also hadn't expected to be so…aroused by the vibes he gave off. Then again, merely looking at him aroused her, so why wouldn't touching him do the same?

He stood there, bare-chested and wearing a skin-tight pair of silver pants that showed every ropey muscle and presented that impressive bulge at his groin like a gift. Criminy, he might as well be naked. She *wished* he was naked.

"E-excuse me," she squeaked.

He looked down at her, one corner of his perfect mouth tipped up in a half-smile. Which was a first. Everyone seemed to get smiles but her.

"You broke Seth."

She blinked. "What?"

He nodded at something behind her. She turned and gasped in horror at the black, waxy hand lying on the floor and the now-handless statue next to it. "Oh, shit. Azagoth is going to be pissed."

This was his Hall of Souls, a giant room filled with mounted skulls and fountains that ran with blood. It was also where people who did especially vile things—or who made Azagoth *really* angry—were turned into tortured statues. Inside, they were still alive, screaming for all eternity. And she'd just given one an amputation that must be agonizing.

She scrambled to replace the hand, but Hades just laughed.

"Don't worry about it. Seth was a demon who passed himself off as an Egyptian god back in the day. He tortured and killed thousands of children. He deserves worse than anything Azagoth or you could do to him."

She stared at the statue, the naked body twisted in whatever agony Azagoth put him through before turning him to stone, his mouth open in a perpetual scream.

"Children?"

"Children."

Sick bastard. She dropped the hand, grabbed Seth's tiny penis, and snapped it off. "I hope he's feeling that."

Hades's booming laughter echoed around the chamber, and she swore the crimson liquid in the center fountain stopped flowing for a heartbeat. "I'll bet you just made every poor stiff in here fear you more than Azagoth. Awesome."

She dropped the nasty appendage next to the hand. "Yeah, well, I'd probably better find some Superglue before he notices."

Hades nudged the pieces with his boot. "I'll take care of it. I'm the one who ran into you, and besides, I live for this kind of thing."

The note of mischief that crept into his voice made her suspicious, and she narrowed her eyes at him. "What have you got up your sleeve? You know, if you had sleeves."

"Don't worry," he said with impish delight, "I know what to do with a cock." He shifted his gaze to her, giving her a roguish once-over that heated her skin even more than touching him had. "So, what's got you in so much of a hurry? Hot date?"

Flustered, because this was the first time he'd spoken to her like she wasn't diseased, she stood there like an idiot before finally blurting, "I heard a bird."

He looked at her like she was daft. "And that's significant...why?"

Heat flooded her face. She must be as red as a Sora demon's butt. "They have wings." Geez, could she sound any dumber? "I guess I miss mine."

"If you miss them that much, you could just enter Sheoul." Massive black, leathery wings sprouted from his back and stretched high enough to brush the ceiling. Blue veins that matched his hair extended from the tips to where they disappeared behind his shoulders, and now that his wings were visible, the veining appeared under his skin, as well. It was as if he were a marble statue come to life.

Cat's breath caught in her throat as she took in his magnificence. He'd transformed, and for the first time, she could see why the demons in the Inner Sanctum would kneel before him.

*I'd kneel,* she thought, *but for far different reasons.*

That image burned itself into her brain, and she wondered if her face went even redder. Then, to her horror, she found herself reaching out to skim her fingertips along the edges of his wings. He went taut, but her body did the exact opposite as shivery, wild sensations jolted her system and coiled between her thighs. Damn, this male was a danger to everything that made her female, and she stumbled back on unsteady legs.

"Sorry," she whispered, hoping her voice didn't betray her lust. "Like I said, I miss them. I want them back, but I want to get them by earning my way back to Heaven, and I can't do that if I become a True Fallen."

"Not joining me on the dark side, huh?" Now that she was no longer touching him, he'd relaxed, probably relieved that the crazy, horny Unfallen was keeping her hands to herself. Shrugging, he put away his wings, and the veins under his skin faded away. Good, because her fingers might have been all about his wings, but her tongue had wanted to trace every vibrant vein on his body. "Suit yourself. More evil cookies for me."

Shooting her a wink, he sauntered off toward one of the portals that allowed travel between Sheoul-gra proper and the Inner Sanctum. Cat watched him—and his drool-worthy butt—until he disappeared around a corner.

Outside, the bird of prey screeched again, but now that she'd seen Hades's wings, she wasn't sure anything else could compare. As she contemplated her next move, she eyed the castrated statue and, unbidden, her mind popped an image of the bulge in Hades's pants. She glanced down at the sad little male appendage on the floor and laughed.

Nope. No comparison.

## Chapter Four

It had been three days since Cat had opened the portal from the human realm and allowed souls into the Inner Sanctum, and as far as she knew, nothing catastrophic had happened. Maybe no one had noticed. After all, there were millions of souls imprisoned in Sheoul-gra. So what if a handful had slipped through without Azagoth's stamp of approval?

Rationalizing the whole thing didn't make her feel a lot better, so she took out her frustration on the floor of the Great-Hall-slash-Hall-of-Souls at the entrance to Azagoth's mansion. Why the hell did she have to polish the obsidian stone by hand, anyway? Did Azagoth not believe in buffing machines?

Okay, in all fairness, he'd never told her to clean the floor. The big jobs, like landscaping outside and maintaining the floors inside, had been assigned to the dozens of Unfallen who, like Cat, had come to live in the safety Sheoul-gra provided to those caught in the gap between Heavenly angel and True Fallen. But footprints on the floor drove Cat nuts, and today, some jackass had tracked in dirt and grass, completely ignoring the new mat she'd placed at the entrance that said, in bold red letters, WIPE YOUR DAMNED FEET.

She thought the play on "damned" was funny, given that almost everyone who came to Sheoul-gra was some sort of demon. Hades had gotten the joke, had laughed when he saw it. She still smiled when she thought about it.

She shot a fleeting glance over at the statue of Seth, which still hadn't been repaired, but at least the two body parts were missing. Maybe Hades was trying to fix them. *Hopefully*, he was trying to fix them.

A tingle of awareness signaled the arrival of a newcomer into the realm – it was kind of cool how anyone who resided in Sheoul-gra developed a sensitivity to the presence of outsiders. It was usually Zhubaal's job to meet visitors, but he was busy, so she leaped to her feet.

Happy to toss her cleaning supplies aside for a few minutes and always curious about who was paying a visit, she hoofed it out of Azagoth's mansion to the great courtyard out front, where the portal from outside was glowing within its stone circle.

And there, striding toward her, was a magnificent male with a full head of blond, shoulder-length hair and a regal stance that could only mean he was a higher order of angel. As a lowly Seraphim, she'd rarely seen angels ranking higher than a Throne, but there was no doubt that this male was at the very top. Perhaps even a Principality, one rank below an archangel.

"E-excuse me, sire," she said, her voice barely a whisper. "Can I help you?"

The big male nodded, his blond mane brushing against the rich sapphire blue shirt that matched his eyes. "I will see Azagoth."

"I'm sorry, but he's busy—"

"*Now.*"

Mouth. Dry. A lifetime of fear of higher angels made her insides quiver, even as she realized that Heavenly angels held no power here. Inhaling deeply, she reached for calm. As a fallen angel in Azagoth's employ, she was actually more influential in Sheoul-gra than this new guy was.

Somehow, that thought didn't make her feel any better.

"This is not your realm, angel," she said sternly. "You can't just poof in here and demand an audience with Azagoth."

"Is that so." The male's voice was calm. Deadly calm. *Scarily* calm.

"Yes. That is so." She was proud of the way her voice didn't quake. Not much, anyway.

A slow smile curved the male's lips, and if it hadn't been so terrifying, it would have been beautiful. "I don't want to cause trouble for you, Cataclysm. So either fetch him or take me to him. Those are your only choices."

"Or?" she asked, and how the hell did he know her name?

Suddenly, the air went still and thick, and massive gold wings sprung from his back, spreading like liquid sunshine far above them both. "Guess."

Holy...*fuck*. He was...he was...a Radiant. An angel who outranked even archangels. And since there could be only one Radiant in existence at any given time, that meant that this was Reaver, brother to Revenant, the King of Hell. That alone would have been enough to terrify her, but making things worse, much worse, was the fact that she had lost her wings because she'd been in league with an angel who had not only betrayed him, but who had attempted to kill his infant grandchild.

Cat's knees gave out, but before she hit the ground, Reaver caught her, landing her on her feet with one arm around her to hold her steady. Instantly, her skin became charged with his Heavenly energy, the magnitude of it rendering her almost breathless.

It was too intense, scattering her thoughts in a way that touching Hades hadn't. As an angel, she'd touched other angels, but it had never been like this. As a fallen angel, she'd had skin-to-skin contact with Lilliana, and while the female had given off a slight positive energy buzz, it hadn't been anything like what she was experiencing with Reaver.

Maybe the fact that she was a fallen angel had made the sensation of goodness too overwhelming for her. Or maybe the intensity had to do with the fact that Reaver was a Radiant. Whatever it was, it made her want to throw up, the way eating too much of a rich food did.

"You okay?" he asked, his voice low and soothing.

She couldn't say a word. But her inability to speak was more than just her reaction to his touch. He was a rock star in the angel world. Beyond a rock star. He was...*the* rock star. *The* angel.

And she'd nearly destroyed his family.

"What the fuck?" Azagoth's voice rang out from somewhere behind her. Dazed, she turned her head to see him walking toward them, his gaze boring into Reaver. "You know that when a high-ranking angel steps foot into my realm, I feel it, right? Like, migraine feel it."

Legs wobbly, she stepped away from Reaver. "Sir—"

A wave of Azagoth's hand silenced her. "I've got this. Reaver is a friend."

"Friend?" Reaver asked, incredulous. "May I remind you that you ordered Hades to hold me in the belly of a giant demon, where I was slowly digested for centuries?"

Cat couldn't believe it when Azagoth rolled his eyes. He wasn't usually so casual with Heavenly angels. But then, Reaver *had* sent gifts for him and Lilliana. "It was three puny months."

"Yeah, well, it felt like centuries," Reaver muttered.

"Good." Now *that* was more like Azagoth. "Are you here to see Lilliana?"

Reaver shook his head. "Unfortunately, I'm here to see you. There's a soul in Sheoul-gra I need to be released."

"Demon?"

"Human."

Azagoth cocked a dark eyebrow. "Really. And why should I do that?"

"Because he shouldn't be there. Your *griminions* took him before his soul could cross over."

"Even if they'd made that mistake, I'd have caught it," Azagoth said, and a knot formed in Cat's stomach.

"You missed this one."

"Impossible."

A bird chirped in the distance, its cheery song so out of place in the growing tension surrounding Azagoth and Reaver. Cat couldn't help but think that the old, lifeless Sheoul-gra might have been a better setting for the confrontation happening right now between these two powerful males.

Reaver stared at Azagoth, his expression darkening with anger. "Seriously? You think Heaven would make that kind of error?"

"You think *I* would?" Azagoth shot back. "In thousands of years, have I ever allowed a non-evil human soul into Sheoul-gra?"

Oh, no. The knot in Cat's belly grew larger as her little incident three days ago filled her thoughts.

"Mistakes happen."

As Azagoth growled, Cat started to sweat. *She* was responsible for the innocent soul being sent into the holding tank. It was the only explanation.

"I don't make mistakes." Azagoth spoke through teeth clenched so hard that Cat swore she heard one or two crack.

"Then someone else did," Reaver said. "I don't give a shit who's at fault. What I do give a shit about is the fact that there's a human soul in the Inner Sanctum who doesn't belong there, and we want him back before he's harmed or someone realizes he's not evil and they use him to break out of Sheoul-gra."

"Um...excuse me," Cat interrupted. "But this person you're talking about...he's a soul, not a physical being, at least not on Earth or in Sheoul, so how could he be used to help demons escape?"

"Here, as in Heaven, his soul is solid," Reaver said. "A soul-eating demon could absorb him, or his soul could be harvested and liquefied to use in spells." As the horror of what could be happening to an innocent human sunk in, Reaver turned back to Azagoth. "You fucked up big time."

Azagoth snorted. "Bite me."

"You have one week."

"And I repeat—"

"Reaver!" Lilliana's voice rang out, and a moment later, she flung herself into his arms. "It's so good to see you."

They started to chat, giving Cat time to slink away. Holy shit, what had she done? Azagoth had given her a purpose, a home, and safety, and she'd just gotten him into some serious hot water with Heaven.

And that poor human. She'd seen firsthand how traumatic dying could be for humans. Even in Heaven it sometimes took them months to adjust, especially if their deaths were violent or sudden. But to die and then find yourself trapped in hell with no idea why or what you'd done to deserve it?

She shuddered as she shuffled along the stone path toward Azagoth's palace. She had to fix this, but how? Maybe she could find the human herself. Her ability to differentiate between human and demon souls from great distances would be an advantage for her, so maybe, just maybe, she could fix this quickly. If she could get in and out of the Inner Sanctum before anyone noticed she was gone, surely Azagoth would forgive her. It was even possible that the archangels would consider the rescue a good enough deed to allow her back in Heaven.

No one noticed her moving away from the group, so she took the steps two at a time and hurried through the massive doors. The moment she was away from prying eyes, she could no longer maintain her cool composure. She sprinted into action, running so fast through the corridors that she skidded around one corner and nearly collided with the wall on her way to Azagoth's office.

As expected, the office was empty. Terrified, but hopeful that what she was about to do would right a lot of wrongs, she hurried to the lever she'd accidentally opened, the one that had started this whole mess.

Next to the lever that opened the soul tunnel was a switch she'd seen Azagoth and Hades use to gain access to the Inner Sanctum. When she flipped it, a section of the wall faded out, allowing a view of a dark, shadowy graveyard set amongst blackened, leafless trees on the other side.

For a moment, she hesitated. In Heaven, she'd always been the first of her brothers and sisters to take risks, to step into the unknown. But none of them had ever faced anything like this. To them, taking risks meant speaking up at meetings or chasing a demon into a Harrowgate.

Her two brothers and two sisters would shit themselves if they ever stood where Cat was right now.

The thought gave her a measure of comfort and even made her smile a little. So, before she changed her mind, she took a deep, bracing breath, and stepped through the portal. Instantly, heat so thick and damp she could barely breathe engulfed her. Each breath of fetid air made her gag. The place smelled like rotting corpses. And the sounds...gods, it was as if people in the graves were moaning and clawing at their coffins.

Why would anyone *be* in the coffins?

Fear welled up, a suffocating sensation that seemed to squeeze her entire body. This was a mistake. A horrible mistake. She had to go back. Had to confess what she'd done to Azagoth. Panicked, she spun around so fast she nearly threw herself off balance.

*Hurry*, her mind screamed. Then it froze mid-scream.

The portal was gone.

Frantic, she searched the wall for a lever of some sort. Or a button. Or a freaking spell that would allow her to use a damned magic word.

"Open sesame?" she croaked.

Nothing.

"Let me out."

Nada.

She pounded on the wall where the door had been. "Open the damned portal!"

The sounds coming from the graves grew louder, and her throat clogged with terror.

She was trapped.

# Chapter Five

Cat spent what seemed like forever trying to find a way back to Azagoth's realm, but the solid wall, which reached upward into a pitch-black sky as far as the eye could see, was apparently endless. So was the graveyard. Why was there a graveyard here, anyway?

Even stranger, the headstones, all different sizes, shapes, and materials, were unmarked. At least, they weren't marked with names or dates. Some had been carved with what appeared to be graffiti, and others were scarred by writing, mainly in the universal demon language, Sheoulic. Several were warnings to not enter any of the five mausoleums that seemed to be randomly placed around the sprawling cemetery.

Unfortunately, she'd heard enough about the Inner Sanctum to know that the mausoleums were the gateways to the five levels, or Rings, as they were officially called, that housed the demons Hades watched over. She had to enter. But which one? None were marked in any way that would indicate which Ring they led to. Was she supposed to just choose randomly and hope she'd picked the right one? Ugh. Yet another reason she wanted to go back to Heaven. There, everything was clearly marked.

She eyed the five mausoleums and finally decided on the closest one. Before she entered though, she found a heavy piece of wood she could use as a club if needed. When she'd lost her wings, she'd lost all innate defensive weapons, but they wouldn't have done her any good down here, anyway.

She really should have thought this out a little better.

*Your impulsiveness is going to get you in trouble someday.*

Her mother's words rang in her ears, and so did her siblings' echoes of, "Told you so," uttered just before her wings had been sliced off.

Cat stared at the mausoleum's iron grate door. Apparently, not even losing her wings had taught her a lesson.

Cursing herself—and throwing in some choice words for her siblings—she pushed open the door, cringing at the rusty creaking noise that made the things in the graves screech. The inside was dark and dusty, but anything was better than the foul dampness of the graveyard. It was also smaller than it appeared to be from the outside, about the size of a phone booth.

The door slammed shut behind her, and she nearly screamed at the clank of the metal hitting the stone. An instant later, it swung open by itself, and she stepped out into a featureless, sandy desert. There was nothing but pale yellow sand and gray sky. Nothing moved. There was no breeze, no sound, no smell...what the hell was this place?

Okay, this might have been a mistake. She spun around to go back to the graveyard and a different mausoleum, but like earlier when she first left Azagoth's library, she found nothing but empty air where the doorway should have been. Panic rose up, but before she could form a coherent thought, she heard a noise behind her. A chill shot up her spine as she slowly turned.

Heart pounding, fingers digging into the wood club, she squinted into the distance, and that's when she saw it—a shimmer in the air that slowly solidified into a number of blurry shapes. And then the shapes took form, and her heart slammed to a sudden, painful stop at the blast of evil that struck her.

At least fifty demons of several different species formed a semicircle around her, a wall of fangs, claws, and crude, handmade weapons. The crowd parted to allow one of them, a seven-foot tall, eyeless thing with tiny, sharp teeth and maggot-colored skin, to come forward. In his slender, clawed hand, he held a chain, and on the other end of that chain, crawling on all fours like a dog, was a human male, his hair matted with blood, his skin bruised and bleeding, one ear missing.

This was the very human she'd come for. Relief quickly gave way to guilt and horror at what had been done to him. And at what might *still* be done to him. To both of them.

"Aren't you a tasty thing," the maggot demon slurred, his voice mushy and sifted through sharp teeth.

Terror, unlike anything she'd ever experienced, clogged her throat. Oh, she'd been afraid before, plenty of times. But this was different. She'd never faced so many demons, and she'd certainly never done it while holding only a stick of wood as a weapon.

Raising her club, she found her voice, shaky and squeaky as it was. "Demon, I am a fallen angel on a mission from Azagoth himself," she lied. "You are to hand over the human immediately."

Maggot-man laughed. "Foolish *kunsac*." Her Sheoulic was rusty, but she was pretty sure he'd just called her a rather nasty slang term for a demon's anus. "You bluff. And you will die." He grinned, flashing those horrid teeth at her. "But not before we get what we want from you."

Another demon stepped forward and made a sweeping gesture toward the others. "What we *all* want from you."

*What they wanted from her?* How had they even found her?

They came at her in a rush. She swung her club, catching one in the jaw hard enough to knock a few teeth out, but as she swung again, something struck her in the head. She tasted blood and heard a scream, but only later did she realize that the scream was hers.

* * * *

"My lord."

Inside one of the hundreds of tiny cells in the Rot's lowest dungeon levels, Hades turned away from the broken body of one of the two demons he'd captured three days ago. Silth, the fallen angel commander in charge of the 5th Ring, stood in the doorway. "Tell me you've located the rest of the insurgents."

Silth inclined his blond head in a brief nod. "Yes, but—"

"I trust you've dumped them into the Rot's acid pit?" That was one of Hades's favorite punishments. The demons would splash around as their bodies were dissolved slowly and painfully, until only their souls remained.

That was when things got fun. Exposed souls were delicate, and the acid was even more agonizing on their raw, tender forms. The demons would take another physical body, and then the acid went right back to work, starting the cycle again. It usually didn't take more than a few days before the bastards started talking.

And if that didn't work, dropping them into one of the graves in the cemetery for a couple of decades would.

"Of course." Silth shifted his balance nervously, making his chain mail rattle, and Hades stiffened. "A situation requires your attention."

A dark, slithery sensation unfurled in Hades's gut at both Silth's words and the grim tone. "Tell me."

"The entire 5th Ring is becoming unstable, and the violence is spreading into the 4th Ring. Intelligence indicates that a large-scale escape from Sheoul-gra is in the works."

"Bullshit." Hades kicked at the straw on the floor and watched a hellrat scurry into another filthy pile. "There's no way they could gather enough power to accomplish something like that."

Silth, who Hades had personally chosen as the 5th Ring's warden because he was an evil sonofabitch who liked pain and feared nothing, suddenly looked as if he'd rather be anywhere but here. He even took a step back from Hades, as if he expected to be slaughtered.

Which meant the guy had some fucking bad news.

"Somehow," he growled, "they got hold of an Unfallen."

Hades blinked. "An Unfallen? Like, a living, breathing fallen angel? How? Azagoth wouldn't have allowed anyone inside without telling me." No way. Any living being who was given access to the Inner Sanctum had to be escorted and contained to prevent exactly what appeared to be going on right now in the 5th Ring.

"I saw her myself," Silth said.

"Her?" Hades frowned. "Who?"

"I know not. I caught but a glimpse," Silth said, reverting back to what Hades like to call his "medieval speak." The dude had fallen from Heaven in the late 900's and had spent way too much time messing in human affairs and picking up their annoying habits. "When I captured one of the rebels, he admitted that she was an Unfallen being used in a ritual that would break down the Inner Sanctum's walls."

The hellrat poked its head out of the straw and took a bite out of the unconscious demon on the floor. They were cute little buggers.

"Something's still not right." Hades tore his gaze away from the rodent. "It would take more than a single Unfallen to unleash the kind of magic that would destroy the Inner Sanctum's boundaries. What else do they have?"

"Unknown. But I fear that if we don't act now, it won't matter if the walls fall or not. The uprising is spreading, and if it reaches all of the levels..." He trailed off, knowing full well that Hades understood the seriousness of the situation.

A large-scale rebellion might not result in the destruction of the Inner Sanctum's walls, but it would force Azagoth to halt the admission of new souls into the Inner Sanctum, resulting in a backup that would affect both the human and demon realms. Azagoth had even theorized that a large enough riot could blow out the inner barriers that separated Azagoth's realm from the Inner Sanctum, resulting in a wave of chaos that would destroy everything Azagoth held dear.

Not that Hades gave a shit what Azagoth held dear, but any threat to Azagoth was a threat to Hades, as well. If Azagoth fell, so would Hades, no matter how connected he might be to the Biblical prophecy laid out for Thanatos, the Horseman known as Death.

*And I looked, and behold a pale horse; and he who sat on it was named Death, and Hades followed with him.*

Yeah. That.

Hades had already helped out the Four Horsemen on several occasions, but he had no idea what was in store for him down the road. No doubt, it wouldn't be good. The Horsemen had a way of getting themselves into trouble.

Hades brushed past Silth and started down the narrow, torch-lit hall, the fallen angel on his flank. "Where are the insurgents holding the Unfallen?"

"My boys and I battled them on the 5th Ring's Broken Claw Mountain." Silth paused as they stopped at the armory, where Hades grabbed a leather harness loaded with blades fashioned from materials found in the Inner Sanctum. Anything from outside was strictly forbidden except inside Hades's home. "The survivors fled into the canyon with the female. I believe they're holed up there."

Hades snorted. "You think they're what, cornered? Waiting to be slaughtered?" Testing the edge of a bone blade, he shook his head. "They have a plan."

"You think it's a trap?"

"Hell, yeah, it's a trap." He grinned because as shitty as the turmoil in the Inner Sanctum was, there was a bright side. Thousands of years of monotony had worn thin, but now there was a little excitement. Something to challenge him, to make him feel alive.

He thought of Cat and how, when she'd run into him in Azagoth's Hall of Souls, he'd had a moment where he'd felt more alive than he had in centuries. It had been enough to make him forget, just for a few minutes, that she was off-limits to him. His pulse had picked up, his body had hardened, and he'd wanted so badly to wrap himself around her and revel in skin-on-skin contact.

But that wasn't going to happen, so he'd have to settle for the next best thing.

A good old-fashioned fight.

# Chapter Six

It turned out that Silth hadn't been exaggerating when he'd said that the 5th Ring was in chaos. In the canyon where the Unfallen was supposedly being held, Hades found himself having to fight his way through hordes of demons simply to get within sight of the staging area where the leaders were chanting and dancing and sacrificing demon critters for their blood.

As Hades and his team of fallen angels battled an endless stream of demons, he kept an eye out for the idiot Unfallen who had somehow landed herself in a shit-ton of trouble. Because even if the demons didn't kill her, Hades would.

And he was going to have fun doing it.

He threw out his hand, sending a wave of disruptive power into the crowd of demons in front of him. They blew apart as if they'd been nuked, leaving a path of meat and blood ahead of him. Hellhounds rushed in to feast and snap at the souls rising from the ruined bodies. It wouldn't be long before they reoriented themselves and generated new flesh-and-blood bodies again, so Hades had to hurry. Although only Hades and his fallen angel wardens possessed supernatural powers down here, the demons still had size, strength, teeth, and claws in their arsenals, not to mention sheer numbers. If Hades and his team were overwhelmed, things could get bad. Real bad.

Worse, he'd gone back to his place to contact Azagoth only to find that communications were down, and they must have been for hours. Azagoth always sent a message for a status update at precisely midnight, but for the first time in thousands of years, there was nothing. He probably should have popped into Azagoth's office to see what was up before charging into battle, but dammit, the Grim Reaper's Darth Vader-ish warning to not fail him again was still sitting on his mind like a bruise, and he didn't feel like poking it. Still, it might have been helpful to know how the hell an Unfallen had gotten into the Inner Sanctum.

Whatever. Regrets were for douchebags.

"There!" Silth pointed to a crude wooden crucifix near the site where animal blood ran thick from a stone outcrop in the cliffs. "The Unfallen."

Hades sprinted toward the crucifix, dodging a volley of spears raining down from demons perched on the rock outcroppings of the canyon's walls. He wished he could use his wings, but flying would make him more of a target. For now, he was safer in the enemy crowd.

He kept his eye on the crucifix as he ran. From this angle, he could make out the slim body of a female hanging limp from the crucifix, arms tied to the cross-board, her head falling forward, her face hidden by a mop of bright red hair. A spark of recognition flared, but it snuffed like a squashed firefly as an axe struck him in the head. Pain screamed through him as shards of bone from his own skull drove into his brain.

"Bastard" he snarled as he wheeled around to his attacker, a burly Ramreel with a black snout and glowing red eyes. "You fucked up my Mohawk." At least, that's what he thought he'd said. The words were garbled. Clearly, the bone shards had also fucked up the part of his brain that controlled speech.

One eye wasn't working, either, but his ability to draw and quarter a demon with a single thought was still intact, as he proved a heartbeat later.

Head throbbing as flesh and bone knit back together, Hades made a run for the Unfallen female. Lightning flashed overhead, and electric heat sizzled over his skin. That lightning wasn't natural. He looked past the giant wooden crucifix, and his hackles raised.

An Orphmage, one of the most powerful sorcerer-class demons that existed, was moving toward the female, a bone staff in his hand. And from the staff, tiny bolts of lightning surged.

Impossible. *Im-fucking-possible*. No one but Azagoth, Hades, and his wardens could wield power here. No one. Not without a source from outside the realm. He supposed the demon could be drawing energy from the Unfallen, but she wouldn't have enough for the kind of magic he was brandishing.

No, something much, much bigger was in play here.

Hades lunged, sending a stream of white-hot electricity at the demon. The Orphmage flipped into the air, avoiding Hades's weapon like he did it all the fucking time. As he landed, he whirled, and in a quick, violent motion, he stabbed the Unfallen in the chest with the sparking end of his staff. She screamed, a sound of such suffering that it somehow drowned out the violence of the battle and reduced the cries of the wounded to muted whispers in the background.

Hades froze. He finally recognized that voice. And that hair. And, as her scream began to fade into a tortured rasp and her body went limp, he recognized her clothes. Faded, torn jeans. Black and emerald corset. Bare feet.

Cat never wore shoes.

The Orphmage stepped back, his head covered by a burlap hood, but Hades could make out a sinister grin stretching his thin lips into a hideous slash. He raised his staff to strike Cat again. With a roar, Hades hurled a series of fireballs at the demon even as he charged toward him. Somehow the demon blocked the fire, but the force of their impacts against his invisible shield still knocked him backward with each blow.

In Hades's peripheral vision he saw one of his wardens go down, his body going one way, his head going another, and dammit, Geist might have been a sadistic tool, but he'd served Hades well for nearly a thousand years.

Quickly, Hades put the dead fallen angel out of his mind and charged up the rocky slope, using his mind to continue throwing shit at the Orphmage. A crude arrow punched through Hades's arm, and as he yanked it out, several more pierced his legs and back. Gritting his teeth against the pain, he hauled himself up the incline and leaped onto the plateau where demons had been making their sacrifices and where Cat was hanging limply from the crucifix.

"Cat," he breathed. "Cat!"

He ran toward her, ignoring the volley of projectiles raining down on him. Pain wracked him, blood stung his eyes, and his battery of powers was draining, but none of that mattered. He had to get to Cat. She was only about thirty yards away, but it felt like he'd run miles by the time he unsheathed a dagger and sliced through the ropes holding her captive.

Awkwardly, he threw her over his shoulder and reached out with his senses to locate the nearest portal. It wasn't far, but naturally, a horde of well-armed, giant demons were standing between him and the way out.

"Hellhounds!" he shouted into the flashing sky. From out of nowhere, two inky canine blurs shot up the side of the canyon toward him. "Make a path!"

Instantly, the hellhound veered toward the group of demons and went through them like bowling balls through pins. Hades followed in the beasts' wakes, reaching the portal as a demon with a missing arm swung a club at him. With relish, Hades sent a blast of power into the bastard's head, exploding it in a fabulous gore-fest.

The portal swallowed him, and an instant later, panting and exhausted, he stepped out of the 5th Ring's mausoleum at the graveyard. He flew the short distance to the wall where portals to and from Azagoth's part of Sheoul-gra were laid out and triggered by only his and Azagoth's voices.

"Open," he barked. Nothing happened. Frowning, he tried again. "Open."

Again, nothing. What the hell? Reaching out, he smoothed his hand over the dark stone surface. It felt the same as always, so why was it not opening?

"Open!" Gods, he might as well have been talking to a wall. He snorted. Sometimes he cracked himself up. "Damn you, fucking *open!*"

Given that the passage was the only way to get out of the Inner Sanctum, this was not good. Had Azagoth sealed the door on purpose? Was this a weird glitch? Or had the demons in the 5th Ring had something to do with this?

Hades wasn't sure which scenario was the better one.

Cat groaned, and shit, he needed to get her someplace safe where she could recover from whatever the Orphmage had done to her. And as soon as she was able to talk, she had some serious explaining to do.

## Chapter Seven

Everything was gray. Light gray. Dark gray. And every shade of gray in between.

Cat blinked. Where was she? Squinting, she shifted her head from side to side. She was lying down, apparently inside some sort of lidless stone box. It was huge, about the size of a king-size bed, and like a bed, it had blankets and pillows. Who the hell slept in a giant box?

She sat up, but she was so weak that it took two tries, and as she peered around the room, her head spun.

"Ah, Sleeping Beauty awakens."

Cat turned to the owner of the voice, and she would have gasped if her breath hadn't clogged in her throat. Hades? What was he doing here? Of course, it might help to know where "here" was. "Here" appeared to be a room constructed from the same stone as the box she was sitting in. Iron sconces on the walls gave off a gloomy light, but the fire in the hearth kept the place from being completely horror-movie chic.

"Where am I?" Her voice sounded cobwebby, which seemed appropriate, given that the room looked like a tomb.

"My place." Hades walked over to the far wall where a pot steamed over the fire's roaring flames. He was shirtless today, and the light from the fire flickered over his skin, the shadows defining every glorious muscle as he went down on his heels and ladled something into a cup.

Gods, she was confused. Why was she here? What had happened? The last thing she remembered was being in Azagoth's office...no, wait. She'd gone to the Inner Sanctum to find a human. But everything was pretty cloudy after that.

She rubbed her eyes, which were as blurry as her memories. "What happened to me?"

Hades came over, moving in that way of his, like a panther on the hunt. Not even the chains on his massive black boots made a sound when he walked.

"That's my question for you." He held out the cup, which was really more of a bowl. That looked suspiciously like the top of a skull. "Drink this."

She eyed the contents as she took the bowl, nearly splashing the clear yellow liquid on her hand. It seemed safe enough, wasn't full of floating eyeballs or anything.

"Smells good," she said as she put it to her lips. "What is it?"

"It's a healing broth. Made it myself from the skin and bones of a Croix Viper."

Cat tried not to gag even though the liquid actually tasted decent, like spicy chicken soup. "Thank you." She tried to hand it back, but he shook his head.

"Drink it all. It'll heal the rest of your wounds."

She looked down at herself, but there wasn't a mark on her. Her jeans were dirty, and there were splashes of what might be blood on her feet, but it didn't appear to be hers, and otherwise, she seemed to be in great shape. "What wounds?"

He picked up one of several blades he'd laid out on a crude wooden table and began wiping it down with a rag. "You were pretty messed up when I found you. I have the capacity to heal minor physical damage, but the other stuff is beyond my ability."

"The other stuff?" She watched him slide the blade into a leather harness hanging off a chair.

"Psychic wounds," he said gruffly. "The kind you get when an Orphmage thrusts his magic stick in you."

She drew a sharp breath. "Magic...stick?"

"Not *that* kind of magic stick. Seriously, you ever seen an Orphmage's junk?" He snorted. "I figure they use their staffs to compensate for their tiny dicks."

She'd have laughed if she wasn't so confused about why she was here and what had happened to her. She hadn't spoken to

Hades much, but she'd seen how he interacted with others, and she loved his sense of humor. He was so inappropriate and nothing like the people she'd dealt with in her sixty years of life in Heaven. She was pretty sure most angels had *magic sticks* up their asses.

"Maybe I could get out of this..." She looked around at the box she was sitting in. "This...um, coffin? Am I in a freaking coffin?"

"It's actually more of a sarcophagus." He grinned. "Cool, huh?"

Actually, yeah. Hades, guardian of the demon graveyard, had a sarcophagus for a bed. He really lived the part, didn't he?

He offered her his hand, which she took, relishing the hot static buzz that skittered over her skin as she allowed him to help her to her feet and out of the giant coffin. And man, his hand was big. And strong. And it made her wonder what his fingers would feel like as they caressed her skin.

This was the second time they'd touched. She liked it. Wanted more. Being this close to a male was rare and strange, and aside from the unfortunate incident with Zhubaal, she'd never really had more than casual contact with the opposite sex. In Heaven, many angels were all "free-love" and "if it feels good do it," but Seraphim tended to be conservative, determined to use ancient practices like arranged matings in order to preserve the inherent abilities that made Seraphim unique among angels.

She'd always thought Seraphim customs were a drag, even though her parents hadn't been as militant as most others. Even so, just before she'd been booted from Heaven, they'd started to nudge her in the direction of suitable mates.

Now she was on her own, curious, and frankly, she was horny. Her brief encounter with Zhubaal had been ill-conceived and had only left her more sexually frustrated. Although, if she were honest with herself, she could probably lay some of her frustration at her own feet since she hadn't been shy about asking Lilliana about sex with Azagoth.

Lilliana had been shocked at first, but they'd grown close, and soon Azagoth's mate was confiding in Cat, sharing what they did in the shower, with the spanking bench, out in the woods... Cat shivered at the thought of doing some of those things with Hades.

The desire to feel more than the buzz she was getting through their clasped hands became a burning need, and she stepped closer to him, drawn by his bare chest and thick arms. If she could just smooth her palm over his biceps or abs—

Abruptly, he released her and leaped back, almost as if she'd scorched him. A muscle in his jaw twitched as he stood there, staring down his perfectly straight nose as if she were an enemy. And yet...there was an undercurrent of heat flowing behind the ice in his eyes.

Could he read her mind? And if he had, wouldn't her naughty thoughts have made him want to touch her more? She didn't know much about the males of her species, but she knew it didn't take much to get them interested.

"Make yourself comfortable," he said gruffly. "I don't have a lot of visitors, so..." He shrugged as he gestured to one of two chairs in the small space.

Right. So...pretend that neither one of them had been affected by the brief moment of...well, she didn't know what to call it. Maybe avoidance was for the best.

She cleared her throat in hopes of not sounding like a moron. "This is your home? I wouldn't have expected you to live in a one-room...what is this? A crypt?"

"Ding, ding," he said, his voice dripping with sarcasm but not malice. "Give the girl a prize. More snake soup, maybe?"

She held up her still-full bowl. "Thanks, but I'm good." The crackling fire drew her attention to the carved gargoyles on the ends of the mantel and the faded painting of angels battling demons in a cemetery hanging above it. Okay, maybe Hades was taking the graveyard guardian thing a little too far. "So, why do you live in a crypt? Surely you could have a mansion if you wanted."

"You'd think, right?" He gestured to the chair again. "Sit."

It didn't occur to her to not obey, so she sat carefully in the rickety chair that must have been put together by a five-year-old child. As far as she could tell, it was constructed of branches and strips of leather.

Hades folded his arms over his massive chest and stared at her until she squirmed in her highly uncomfortable seat. As if her discomfort was exactly what he was waiting for, he finally spoke.

"Tell me, Cat. What did you do to piss off Azagoth, and why

would he send you to the Inner Sanctum without telling me?"

Shit. She was a terrible liar, and she had a feeling that Hades would see through a lie, anyway, but the truth...man, it was probably going to get her punished in a major way. She stalled by sipping the snakey soup.

"Also," he pressed, not missing a beat, "what do you know about communications being down and the door between Azagoth's realm and the Inner Sanctum being locked?"

She choked on the broth. "It's locked for you, too?" At his nod, her mouth went dry. This was bad. Really bad. "I tried to go back, but I couldn't. I thought I screwed something up."

"You screwed up, all right," he said, "but you couldn't have gone back. Only Azagoth or I can operate the doors." He tossed a log on the fire. "Why did you come here?"

Dread made her stomach churn, as if the soup had morphed back into a snake in her belly. "Before I answer your questions, I need to ask something."

"Sure," he drawled, arms still crossed over his chest. "Why the fuck not."

Well, that didn't sound promising. "Azagoth has the ability to destroy souls." She shuddered at the very idea, at the sheer *power* one must possess to undo what God himself had done. "Do you?"

One corner of his perfect mouth tipped up. "You worried?"

"A little."

"Seriously?" He lost the smile. "What the fuck did you do?" His eyes narrowed, becoming shards of angry ice. "Azagoth doesn't know you're here, does he? You entered the Sanctum without his knowledge. Holy shit, Cat, do you know what I'm supposed to do to intruders?"

She could guess, but she really didn't want to. The bowl in her hands started to tremble. *Calm down. He probably won't kill you. Probably.*

"Cat!" he barked. "At least one of my wardens is dead because of you, so I need some answers. *Now.*"

She couldn't look at him, so she concentrated on her feet and said softly, "I accidentally let some souls into the Inner Sanctum."

"Accidentally?"

"Of course it was an accident," she snapped, annoyed that her motives were in question. "Who in their right mind would open the tunnel without Azagoth's permission? I didn't even know *how* to open the thing. I was cleaning, and I accidentally—"

"Okay," he interrupted. "I get it. It was an accident, but that doesn't explain why you're here."

She set the bowl on the edge of the coffin and blew out a breath. "I wanted to fix my mistake. I know it was stupid. I changed my mind, but the portal closed and I couldn't get back."

"So you traveled to the 5th Ring?" he asked, incredulous. "What kind of dumbass move was that? What the fuck were you thinking?"

"I was thinking that I needed to find the human," she shot back, feeling a little defensive. She might be impulsive, and she might not have made the best decision ever, but she had been trying to make things right. "But I swear, I'd barely stepped out when demons surrounded me."

"That's because you're different. You are, for lack of a better word, alive. They can sense your life-force in a way my wardens and I can't." He scowled. "Wait. Human?" He moved a little closer, and she suddenly felt crowded. "What human?"

Ah, yeah, this was where things got really sticky. And bad. "One of the souls that got through...it was human."

"So?" He picked up another of his wicked knives off the table and ran his thumb over the blade. "Evil humans are admitted to the Inner Sanctum every day. The souls you allowed through would have made their way to one of the five Rings...which isn't a catastrophe. Eventually we'd have figured out that they were in the wrong place. *If* they were in the wrong place. So why did you worry about it? Because you were afraid of Azagoth's wrath? Not that you shouldn't be afraid," he threw in. "He peeled me once. *Peeled me.* Do you know what it feels like to be fucking peeled? I'll give you a hint. It's not as fun as it sounds."

Er...she didn't think it sounded fun at all. And geez, she knew Azagoth could be terrifying, but she'd also seen his tender, caring side, and she'd never known him to be needlessly cruel. Then again, by all accounts, Lilliana had softened him considerably. Cat wouldn't have wanted to know Azagoth pre-Lilliana.

"I'm...not sure how to respond to that." But she was sure as hell more afraid of Azagoth than ever. "I mean, yes, I was worried about Azagoth's reaction, but the problem is that the soul was mistakenly brought here. He's human, but not evil. He was reaped by mistake."

"A mistake? How do you know all of this?"

"Because Reaver paid a visit to Azagoth. He wants the human back in a bad way."

Hades went silent, spinning around to pace, his heavy boots striking the floor with great, tomb-shaking cracks. "When did this happen? When did you send the human into my realm?"

She didn't *send* the human into the realm, but she wasn't about to quibble about terminology at the moment. "Three days ago." She reconsidered that, since she didn't know how long she'd been held captive by the demons. "Could be a little longer."

Hades let out a low whistle as he ran his hand over his Mohawk. "Damn, Cat. Just...fuck."

"I know," she said miserably.

"No, you don't know. It all makes sense now. The ritual I came across a few days ago. The Orphmage wielding power. The human was fueling all of it. The damned human is why all of this shit is happening, and with the comms down, Azagoth had no way to warn me."

"What shit?"

"The riots down here. The rebellion." He hurled the knife to the table. The tip of the blade punched into the wood and vibrated, the noise filling the small space with an eerie echo. "The magic."

She shook her head, completely lost. "I don't understand. There have been riots? What magic?"

"The magic that severed communication with Azagoth and sealed the exits out of the Inner Sanctum."

"Sealed? Not just locked? Like, there's nothing you can do?" She couldn't believe that. How could one dead human cause so much trouble? "You're Hades. Surely—"

"No, Cat. That's what I'm trying to tell you. The exit is sealed. We're stuck here, and if the demons are clever enough, they can use the human to reveal the location of my home as well. And once that happens..." He trailed off, and she swallowed. Hard.

She knew she shouldn't ask, but as the psychotic angel she

used to work for once said, she was "fatally curious." "Once that happens...what?"

"We'll be overrun by millions of the evilest demons on the Ufelskala scale. They'll kill us, Cat, and if we're lucky, they'll only spend a couple of days doing it."

## Chapter Eight

Hades could not believe this shit. In his thousands of years of presiding over the hellhole that was the Inner Sanctum, not a single soul had entered by mistake. Both he and Azagoth had been very careful about who—and what—passed through the barrier. The consequences of the smallest foreign object or unauthorized person entering the Inner Sanctum was precisely why not even his fallen angel wardens were allowed to leave once they started work here. Hades himself couldn't bring anything in, except under certain circumstances, and only with Azagoth's permission.

Made it tough for a guy to get a pizza.

And now, in a matter of days there had been at least two unauthorized entrances, and the full extent of the resulting damage had yet to be seen.

Cat shoved to her bare feet, which were decorated with purple nail polish. Cute. He'd been ordered not to touch her sexually, but would sucking on her toes count?

"So you're saying that we have no recourse?" Her hands formed fists at her sides, and he wondered if she was attempting to keep from punching something. "There's no way to contact Azagoth?"

"I've been trying. My phone has no signal, and even our old methods of communicating through ensorcelled parchment and blood isn't working. I'd been wondering why Azagoth has been so quiet."

"You have a phone down here?" She glanced around as if seeking said device. "A phone that works?"

"I know you haven't been a Heavenly reject for long, but never underestimate the ability of demons to hijack and tweak human advancements." He gestured to a cabinet in the corner. "I have TV, too. Do *not* mess with me on *The Walking Dead* night."

Her delicate, ginger eyebrows cranked down in skepticism. "Are you saying that demons are smarter than humans?"

"I'm saying that demons think outside the box and are a lot more creative." He shrugged. "Plus, most of them aren't limited by stifling moral values."

Cat appeared to consider that, her blood-red lips pursing, her pert, freckled nose wrinkling as she thought. "Okay, so we find the human. They must be using his non-evil energy to fuel the spell that cut off the Inner Sanctum from the rest of Sheoul-gra."

He liked that she was thinking this through without freaking out. And as stupid as her decision to enter his realm might have been, he had to admit it was bold—and brave. How many people would have done the same? And how many could have gone through what she had and still be not only mentally intact but willing to keep trying to fix their mistake?

"Maybe," Hades said. "But what did they want with you? Do you know?"

She closed her eyes, her long lashes painting shadows on her pale skin. "I'm not sure. I thought they were going to hurt me, but if they did, I don't remember much of it."

Good, because Hades remembered enough for both of them. Oh, he hadn't witnessed everything that happened to her, but he knew she'd taken a beating at some point. He still couldn't get the bruises and welts that had marked every exposed inch of her body out of his head.

A growl threatened to break free from his throat as he thought about it. Even as he'd laid her carefully in his bed and channeled healing waves into her, he'd sworn to hunt down every one of her attackers and introduce them to his favorite knives.

"Did they say anything to you?" he ground out, still angry at the memory of what had been done to her.

She licked her lips, leaving them glossy and kissable, and he was grateful for something to concentrate on besides her now-healed injuries. "The Orphmage talked about using me to usher in a new world order. Or something crazy like that."

"That sounds about right. Orphmages *are* crazy. But it's a mad scientist kind of crazy that's dangerous as fuck because they can make their insane ideas come to life." Which actually sounded pretty awesome. "Man, if I ever get to be reincarnated, I want to come back as an Orphmage."

"Fallen angels can only be reborn to other fallen angels," she pointed out, as if he didn't know that. "Also, you're twisted."

"Which doesn't stop you from panting after me every time you see me at Azagoth's place." He got a kick out of the way her face went bright red, and he wondered if she was going to deny it.

He wasn't an idiot; he'd seen the way she looked at him. The way she got all flustered when he was near. He loved it. Had come to crave the attention whenever he was visiting Azagoth. He supposed that intentionally seeking her out just so he could get a reaction he couldn't return in kind was a form of self-torture, but hey, torture was what he did, right?

"W-what?" She sputtered with indignation. "I don't do th—"

"You do."

"Don't."

"Do." He laughed. Felt good, but not because he didn't laugh a lot. He just hadn't had a laugh teased out of him by a female in a long time. "It's okay. There's no shame in wanting me. I *am* hot, after all."

She huffed, making her breasts nearly spill out of the tight black and emerald corset she wore. "Whatever," she mumbled. And then she smiled shyly. "I didn't think you noticed."

He nearly swallowed his tongue. He'd been teasing; he hadn't expected her to be bold enough to admit to wanting him. Time to change the subject, and fast, because he wasn't entirely sure he had the willpower to withstand any coy come-ons. He hadn't been with a female in years, not since the last time Azagoth let him out of Sheoul-gra. Everyone inside the Gra, including demons, were off-limits to him, and always had been.

*That's what you get when you mess with the Grim Reaper's family.*

Yeah, he'd brought his punishment on himself, but fuck, he'd made that mistake thousands of years ago. Hadn't he paid his debt by now? He'd asked Azagoth that very question just recently. As it turned out, Azagoth had a long memory, held a grudge, and wasn't the forgiving type.

Shoving thoughts of past mistakes aside, he changed the topic.

"So what made you think you could enter the Inner Sanctum and find the human?"

Disappointment at the subject change flashed in Cat's jade eyes, but she covered it with a casual shrug. "I possess a particularly powerful ability to sense good and evil."

"You still have it? Even after you lost your wings?"

She glanced around the room, and instead of answering, she asked, "You got anything to drink? You know, that isn't made from snakes?"

"Sure thing." With a flick of his wrist, the wall behind the TV slid open, revealing a small kitchen that looked like something straight out of *The Flintstones*. Except he had demon-installed electricity. Yay for refrigeration and hot stovetops.

"Huh," Cat said. "I did not expect that. You got a secret bathroom, too?"

"Other wall." As he walked to the kitchen, he heard the wall behind him slide open, heard her murmur of approval.

"Happy to see the shower. Not so happy to see a...what is that, a toilet *trough?*" Her dismayed tone amused him. "That looks like something pigs would eat out of."

"I'm old-fashioned." His amusement veered quickly to shame as he reached into the cupboard for his only two cups. As he plopped them onto the pitted stone counter, he cursed his stark living conditions. They'd never truly bothered him before, but now, seeing how he lived through Cat's eyes had lifted the veil a little, and he didn't like it at all. So instead of going for the rotgut moonshine made right here in the Inner Sanctum, he reached for his prized bottle of rum that Limos, one of the Four Horsemen, had given him three decades ago. "Rum okay? And you haven't answered my question."

"What question? Oh, right. Um, yes, rum is fine, and as far as my ability, it's not as strong as it was before I lost my wings, but I can still feel the difference between good and evil from a greater distance than most haloed angels or True Fallen."

As he splashed a couple of fingers of rum into each cup, he realized that for all of the times he'd seen Cat and asked questions about her during his visits to Azagoth, he knew very little about her. Oh, he'd heard the story of how she fell from grace, how she'd associated with Gethel, the turncoat angel who sold her soul to have Satan's child. He also knew Cat had been brave enough to admit to her mistakes instead of trying to cover them up.

Admirable. Not the route he'd have gone in her situation, but hey, he'd never been a shining beacon of light even when he'd still rocked a halo.

Swiping up the cups, he turned back to her. Damn, she was beautiful, standing in the middle of his living room, barefoot, her jeans ripped in several places, a narrow strip of flat belly peeking between her waistband and her top. But the real showstopper was her hair, that glorious, wavy ginger mane that flowed over her shoulders and breasts in a tangle of wild curls. She looked like a warrior woman plucked from Earth's past, and all she was missing was a sword and shield.

And all he was missing was a brain because those were thoughts he shouldn't be having. He strode back to her and handed her a cup.

"So, with that kind of specialized ability," he began, "what did you do in Heaven?"

"You mean, what did I do before I started working for a traitor who got me booted out of Heaven?" Her voice was light, sarcastic, but there was definitely a bitter note souring the soup.

Of course, if he'd been tricked into nearly starting an apocalypse, he'd be bitter, too.

"Yeah." He raised his sad little bone cup in toast. "That."

She gave him an annoyed look. "I'm a Seraphim. What do you think I did?"

As a Seraphim, who Hades knew was one of the lower angel classes despite what human scholars thought, she would have been required to work closely with humans. "Guardian angel stuff?"

She snorted. "Seraphim don't work in the Earthly realm. We mainly do administrative work for humans who are newly crossed over."

He hoped it wasn't too rude to cringe, because he did. "Sounds boring as shit."

"It is," she admitted. "But because my ability to distinguish good and evil was so strong, my work was a little more interesting."

*She* was interesting. "How so?"

"Well, all humans are a blend of good and evil, but they're mostly good. They almost immediately cross over to Heaven when their Earthly bodies die." She sank down in the chair again, gingerly, as if it would splinter. It might. Hades had made it himself, discovering in the process that he was a better Lord of Souls than he was Lord of Furniture. "The evil ones are collected by Azagoth's *griminions* and brought here. But if there's any question at all about their level of evil, *griminions* are supposed to leave them alone so they can either remain in the human realm as ghosts or cross over to Heaven on their own. People like that are a very specific mix of equal amounts of good and bad. And others, the ones humans call sociopaths, are even more complicated."

Huh. Hades had never really thought about that. Yes, he knew there were more shades of good and evil than there were stars in the sky, but it never occurred to him that there would be those who walked such a fine line that they would be difficult to place in either Heaven or Sheoul.

"So you worked with the oddballs?"

"We called them Neutrals. Or Shuns." She sipped her rum, her freckled nose wrinkling delicately at that first swallow. "And yes, my job was to feel them out, I guess you'd call it."

He'd like to feel *her* out. It was probably best not to say as much. "How did you do that?"

She smiled and gestured to her bare arms and feet. "Our skin is our power. We can't discern good and evil the way animals, some humans, and other angels do, like a sixth sense. For us, awareness settles on our skin. That's why I cover as little of myself as I can get away with, and what clothes I do wear need to be tight, or sensation can't get through and I feel like I'm suffocating."

Now *that* was interesting. He'd never met anyone who shared his affection for form-fitting clothing. Most people thought tight clothes were binding, but Hades had long ago found that garments that fit like a second skin were more freeing and allowed him to feel the world around him. The air. The heat or cold. The touch of a female...when he could get it.

He took a swig of his rum. "So did you perform your job naked?"

Her eyes caught his, held them boldly, and damn if he didn't stop breathing. He'd been teasing; she was not. "Some of my colleagues did." She reached up and twirled a strand of hair around her finger, and he swore it was almost...playful. "I preferred our standard uniform of what humans would call a tube top and miniskirt."

He pictured that and got instantly hard. But then, he liked her in the ripped jeans and belly-revealing corset she was wearing now, too. He watched her lift the cup to her lips almost in slow motion, watched her throat work as she swallowed.

Damn. He threw back the entire contents of his cup, desperate to get some moisture in his mouth. "And what does good and evil feel like?" he rasped. "On your skin, I mean?"

"I'll show you." She moved toward him, every step popping out her hips and making her breasts bounce in a smooth, seductive rhythm. His mouth went dry again, but then it began to water as she reached out and placed her palm in the center of his chest.

Very slowly, she dragged her hand along the contours of his pecs, her touch so featherlike that he barely felt it, and yet, he was hyper-aware of every move her hand made, every centimeter of skin her palm passed over.

"Goodness and light," she said softly, "is like bathing in Champagne. It's tingly and effervescent. It wakes you up even as it relaxes you."

"Like sex," he murmured. "With someone you like."

"With someone you like?" She blinked. "Why would you have sex with someone you *didn't* like?"

A rumbling purr vibrated his chest. "Baby, it's like fighting, but with orgasms."

"And less blood, I suppose."

"Not if you're doing it right." He waggled his brows, and she rolled her eyes. "So what does evil feel like to you? If good feels good, then does evil feel bad?"

"That's the funny thing." She inched closer, adding another palm to his chest, and he gripped the cup so hard he heard it crack. More. He needed more. And damn her for making him crave it when he'd been perfectly fine being alone for all these years. "It's as seductive as good, but in a different way." She shivered delicately. "It's hot. If good is like bathing in Champagne, evil is like bathing in whiskey. There's a burn, but it's almost always a lovely burn."

Yeah, he felt that lovely burn where she was touching him. As she talked, it spread across his chest and into his abdomen, then lower, to his pelvis and groin. Everything tightened and grew feverish with lust.

"Seems to me," he said in a humiliatingly rough voice, "that bumping up against evil would be an incredible temptation for angels like you."

"It is," she purred. "Which is why we aren't allowed to leave Heaven except under certain circumstances, and even then, we must have an escort. It's one of the reasons I know I can't ever enter Sheoul. To become a True Fallen would be to have my full powers of detection restored, and I'd be skewed toward evil. The few Seraphim who have become fallen angels are like drug addicts, seeking out the most evil beings they can find, to serve them, to just be near them."

He wondered how having a Seraphim fallen angel as a warden in the Inner Sanctum would play out. Then Cat dragged her palms down his chest to his abs, and he forgot all about everything except what was happening right now, right here in his home.

"And what do you feel when you're near me?" He knew he shouldn't ask. Knew he was encouraging something that shouldn't be encouraged, but holy hell, he was starving for female contact. Maybe this little bit would be enough.

And maybe he was lying to himself.

Closing her eyes, she inhaled. "Like I want to climb your body like a tree so you can wrap yourself around me."

Hot...*damn.* He wasn't sure if the rum had gone to her head or if she was affected by his inner evil, but what she'd said made him want desperately to play giant oak for her so she could do whatever she wanted with his hardwood.

Giant oak. Hardwood. Man, he cracked himself up sometimes.

His amusement fled as her fingers brushed his waistband and reality crashed down on him, splintering the tree fantasy. She was clearly not in the right state of mind to understand the consequences of getting physical with him, while he understood far too well.

*Cataclysm is off limits to you.*

Azagoth's deep voice echoed inside Hades's ears. He'd gone to Azagoth a few months ago, hoping he'd grant Hades permission to see Cat. Hades would have been happy to just talk to her, to get to know her, but Azagoth had been immovable. And then, when Hades had asked Azagoth why, after thousands of years of service, he couldn't even take a walk in Sheoul-gra's lush forests with Cat, the unsatisfying answer had been, *You know why.*

Yeah, he did. *And what if I disobey?*

*Do you remember the last time you disobeyed me?*

As if Hades could forget. The very memory still made Hades's testicles shrivel. Reluctantly, he stepped back from Cat, but she moved with him, her hands splaying on his torso as they caressed him in slow, sensual circles.

So. Fucking. Good.

Gods, he felt like he'd been deprived of air for so long that he no longer knew how to breathe, and now someone was offering him an oxygen mask but he wasn't allowed to take it.

"Is this really what you want?" He forced the question from his mouth, because dammit, this was really what *he* wanted. He just wanted to take a breath. "To get me worked up?"

"Didn't you just accuse me of panting after you?"

He had. He'd been teasing, but there was nothing funny about this anymore. Her flirtation had been cute and flattering, but it had to stop. For both of their sakes.

"Yes," he drawled, reaching for the cockiness that had served him well when things got too serious. "But to be fair, all females do."

A slow, seductive smile curved her mouth, and it took a lot more restraint than he cared to admit to keep from dipping his head and kissing her senseless. "I'd tell you that you're arrogant, but I'm sure you already know that. And I like it."

Man, he had no idea how to handle this little vixen. She seemed both innocent and experienced, and he wasn't sure which was the truth.

Maybe it was time to find out.

# Chapter Nine

Cat's heart was pounding so hard that she wondered if the surrounding tissue was going to be bruised. After months of trying to catch Hades's eye, she had him all to herself. She had his ear, his eye, and with luck, she'd have him in that coffin-bed.

Yes, there were pressing matters to attend to, but in this moment, they were in background because all she cared about was the foreground. And what a foreground it was.

The problem, she realized, was that she had no idea how to proceed. Things with Zhubaal had gone disastrously wrong, so she didn't want to repeat the mistakes she'd made with him. She just wished she knew what, exactly, she'd done.

Gods, this had better not be a replay of her incident with Z.

Closing her eyes, she let herself feel Hades's unique blend of good and evil on her skin. She'd made the comparison of good feeling like sparkling wine, while evil felt like whiskey, and Hades was a swirling mix of both. Carbonated whiskey. Might taste funky, but her skin felt alive with a tingling heat that spread to her scalp, her toes, and everything in between.

It was especially concentrated in her feminine parts.

So delicious.

"Hades—" She'd barely gotten his name off her tongue when his mouth came down on hers.

"Is this what you want?" he growled against her lips. "I'm not one to question motives when it comes to females who are willing to fuck me, but you have me confused as shit."

She wasn't confused at all. Zhubaal…he'd been an experiment. A means to an end. Oh, she'd liked him, she supposed. He was gruff and rude, but he was never cruel. At least, not that she'd seen.

But Hades was unique. From his clothing to his hair, he blew other fallen angels out of the water. And where most other fallen angels were all serious and dour, Hades was playful, even silly at times. Once, when Thanatos, one of the Four Horsemen of the Apocalypse, had come to Sheoul-gra with his toddler son, she'd watched Hades chase the squealing boy through the courtyard before tackling him gently and then tickling the boy's belly with his Mohawk.

She'd been fascinated to see a legend like Hades, a male whose job it was to make life miserable for millions of demons, handle a child with such tenderness. And he did it with such exuberance, without a care who was watching. How many times had she seen male pride get in the way of fun, as if enjoying life and showing emotion was wrong or weak?

No, it took strength to live the way Hades did and still be able to laugh at a joke or enjoy a child's giggle.

That was the fatal moment in which Cat had decided that she needed to get to know Hades a little better. It was also the moment in which she decided she wanted to feel that blue stripe of hair tickle *her* sensitive spots.

Before she could tell him as much, he spun her, put her hard into the wall, his body against hers. She gasped at the feel of his erection as it pressed into her from her core to her belly. Oh, sweet Heaven, how was that going to feel inside her?

"Most females want me because I'm a monster." He arched against her, and she moaned at the erotic pressure against her sex. "Is that your game? Fuck the underworld's most notorious jailor and earn some bragging points?"

A note of bitterness crept into his voice, but she couldn't tell if he was bitter because of what he was...or if he was bitter because he thought she only wanted him for bragging rights. Either way, it made her want to hug him.

Not long ago, she'd have thought him a monster, but even if she hadn't seen him playing with a child or pilfering bread from Azagoth's kitchen to feed the doves, Lilliana's stories about Azagoth's redemption had touched her. Azagoth had been perched on the precipice of the kind of evil one couldn't come back from, but Lilliana had lured him away from the ledge. Oh, there was still darkness in him—the kind that had made Cat sick for days after accidentally touching him. She had a feeling that if anything ever happened to Lilliana, Azagoth would fall into that black, evil hole and would never return.

But Hades, for all his evil deeds and all the malevolence that surrounded him, had somehow avoided becoming toxic. So, no, he wasn't some sort of fiend, and he wasn't going to convince her otherwise.

She lifted her leg and wrapped it around him, trying to get closer. Trying to get some friction going on. "I don't believe you're a monster."

He scraped his teeth over her ear. "Why not?" he growled, so softly that the crackling flames from the fire nearly drowned him out.

She could have told him the Thanatos story. She could have told him how beautiful he was when he laughed with Lilliana. She could have mentioned the time she saw him smiling as he watched a couple of foxes playing on the edge of the forest just outside Azagoth's mansion. But for some reason, she wanted him to know why her opinion of him was so personal.

"Because I worked with Gethel," she whispered. "She was a traitor who plotted with Pestilence to slaughter a newborn baby and start the Apocalypse."

He brought one hand between them to feather his fingertips across the swell of her breasts, and she went all rubbery in the knees. "So you're saying that in comparison, I'm a saint."

"No." She nipped his lip. "I'm saying you are nuanced. You're evil, but there's good in you, as well."

"You don't know that."

"Expose more of my skin, and I will."

She felt his chest heave against hers. Once. Twice. And then, as if he'd given himself permission, he reached around behind her and ripped her corset off. Thank Heavens she'd chosen the one with the Velcro closure today.

"Now tell me," he breathed into her hair, "do you feel me?"

"Yes," she moaned, undulating her entire body, desperate to get as much skin-on-skin contact as possible. Her nipples, so sensitive they were almost painful, rubbed against the hard planes of his chest. She hadn't known they could ache like that.

"Shit," he rasped. "Too much. This is too much."

Too much what? It wasn't *enough*, as far as she was concerned. "I like touching you."

"No one ever touches me." He took a deep, shuddering breath that somehow sounded...pained, and not in a good way. "Nothing but the wind and rain ever does."

Wind and rain? Was that why he often went bare-chested? He liked the feel of something caressing his skin because people wouldn't? Or maybe he wouldn't let them?

She couldn't imagine living like that. She liked to touch and be touched. To show him how much she enjoyed it, she shoved her hand between them and found his erection as it strained against his pants.

Oh...my. She could feel every ridge and bump through the thin fabric as she ran her fingers along his length. Her strokes, made awkward by her inexperience and their position, still managed to elicit a tortured moan from him. The sound emboldened her, and she gripped him more firmly. His thick length pulsed, the hot blood pounding in her palm, and his shout of pleasure filled the room.

Then, suddenly, he was standing near the portal door and she was slumped against the wall, which was the only thing holding her up. How had he moved so fast? More importantly, *why* had he moved so fast?

"I have to go." For a split second he looked frazzled, his chest heaving, his nostrils flaring. Then he smiled, a cocky lopsided grin that did *not* fit the situation. "Hanging with you was great, but I have people to torture and shit. You can..." He looked around the room. "I don't know. Clean or something."

"*Clean?*" Sure, she was still disoriented from the fog of lust and the surprise of him breaking it all off so quickly, but still...*clean?* "I work for Azagoth. Not you."

He shrugged. "Then sleep. Cook. Watch TV. Whatever. Just don't leave this crypt."

"But I have to find that human."

Reaching behind him, he palmed the symbol carved into the portal door, and it flashed open, turning into a shimmering arch of light. "I'll do it."

She pushed away from the wall, hoping her wobbly legs would

hold her up. "I can help."

"No." His tone was harsh, but he softened it as he continued. "The demons were using you for something. Until I know what, we can't risk you being out in the general population. Stay here. I'll be back soon." Before she could protest, he stepped through the portal and disappeared.

"Bastard," she shouted after him.

She swore she heard laughter echo from out of the portal.

* * * *

Lilliana strode through the halls of the building that, just a few short months ago, she'd thought of as her prison. Now it was her home, and the male who ran it was the love of her life.

She found him in his library, standing in front of the fire, his big body outlined by its orange glow. He didn't turn when she entered, even though she knew he'd heard her approach. Coming up behind Azagoth, she wrapped her arms around his waist and pressed her cheek against his broad back.

"Hey."

He covered her hands with his. "My love," he purred. She adored that, how he saved certain tones and words for her and her alone. "What's up? I thought you were busy with the new Unfallen recruits."

"I was, but I couldn't get Cat off my mind."

"Cat? Is she okay?"

She sighed. "I don't know. Have you seen her?"

"Not today." His voice rumbled through her as he spoke. "But I've been busy trying to figure out why Hades won't respond to my messages and why the fucking portals to the Inner Sanctum are sealed."

Yeah, Azagoth hadn't just been busy with that mess—he'd been obsessed. Something was terribly wrong in the Inner Sanctum, and with Heaven breathing down his back over the human stuck inside, Azagoth had been going nonstop. Between researching ways to open the portals and requesting help from the best demon engineers alive, he'd barely had time to eat, let alone sleep.

"You haven't made any progress, I take it?" He made a hellish sound she was going to take as a no. "I'm sorry," she whispered, and that fast, he relaxed a little.

"S'okay." Within the cage of her arms, he turned to her, his gaze intense but concerned. "Now, what's going on with Cat?"

"Did you send her on an errand to the human realm?"

Concern creased his forehead. "No. What's this about? Is she missing?"

"For two days." She stepped away from him, needing room to pace off her nervous energy now that she knew her friend was truly missing. "I didn't worry until today because you sometimes send her off with messages or to fetch things. But she's never been gone this long."

"And you've looked everywhere? The forest? The dorms? The old buildings? You know how she likes to explore."

True. Lilliana had never seen anyone so inquisitive and curious about the world around her. When Cat had first arrived, her constant, prying questions had irked Lilliana until she realized that Cat was simply trying to learn and experience.

"I've scoured all of Sheoul-gra," Lilliana sighed. "I suppose she could be hiding, but there's no reason to do that."

"Maybe she got tired of working here."

She shook her head. "She feels safe here. And even if she did decide to leave, she wouldn't have done it without saying good-bye first." A bad feeling tightened her chest. "Could someone have hurt her?"

He stiffened a little, just a slight shift of his broad shoulders, but Lilliana knew him well enough to recognize genuine unease. "You think one of the Unfallen living here has done something to her?"

God, she hoped not. It had been Lilliana's idea to use the old outer buildings to house Unfallen who didn't want to enter Sheoul, who wanted a chance to make amends for whatever had gotten them booted from Heaven. If one of them had harmed Cat, she'd never forgive herself.

"I don't know," she said. "But I'm telling you, she wouldn't have gone this long without telling one of us. And Sheoul-gra is huge. I searched for her, but there are a lot of places where a person could hide a body or hold someone captive."

Azagoth's eyes went stormy, and Lilliana was very glad the tempest of fury wasn't aimed at her. "If anyone has dared to so much as *touch* a female under my protection," he growled, "I will create a 6th Ring in the Inner Sanctum just for them, and I will fill it with every nightmare they've ever had. They will spend eternity alone, running from the things that scare them most, and just when they think they can't take it anymore, *I* will become the thing they run from."

She shivered. And how twisted was she that she found his threats sexy? Not long ago she'd have thought him a fiend. Okay, he was still a fiend, but only to those who deserved it...and with them, he showed not a shred of mercy. Not even Lilliana would dare get between him and someone he set his vengeful sights on.

So Heaven help anyone who touched Cat, because Azagoth sure as hell wouldn't.

# Chapter Ten

Cataclysm spent the next few hours rummaging through Hades's house-crypt. It was probably all kinds of rude to sort through his things, but it was also all kinds of rude to get her worked up and then suddenly back out, tell her to clean his dusty tomb, and then take off. So she didn't feel too bad about snooping through his stuff.

And what interesting stuff it was. Hell, his entire crypt turned out to be a treasure trove of mystery. In addition to the hidden kitchen and bathroom, there was an office, but instead of it being concealed behind a wall, it had been camouflaged by sorcery. His desk, a blocky monstrosity that appeared to have been carved with a pocket knife, sat just inches away from the rickety chair she'd sat in, but she never would have seen it—or bumped into it—if she hadn't picked up the hollowed-out book she found on a shelf. The simple act of opening the book had revealed the hidden desk and file cabinets.

Unfortunately, the cabinets were locked, presumably by more sorcery. But the contents of his desk were more than enough to keep her occupied. She found building plans for an expansion of the 1st Ring, an accounting of the prisoners in some fortress called the Rot, and a list of every fallen angel warden employed in the Inner Sanctum. Then there were the knickknacks on his desktop.

She ran her finger over an egg-sized stone carving of a hellhound, laughing every time she touched its tail because the carving would come to life and snap at her before freezing again in its snarly, crouched stance. Then there was a framed photo of a blue lake nestled between snowcapped mountains. It was beautiful, but why did he have it?

As she went to put it back on the desk, she bumped her elbow, and the picture fell to the floor. Glass shattered, sending shards skidding all over the place.

*Shit.* Hades was going to kill her.

As she scrambled to clean up the mess, the portal Hades had gone through opened. Of course. Apparently, Hades had the same impeccable timing as Azagoth when it came to her breaking stuff.

"I'm sorr—"

"Who are you?" The deep, unfamiliar voice made her yelp in surprise.

She leaped to her feet, and her surprise veered to terror. A huge male strode into the room, his craggy face shadowed by a filthy, hooded cape that flapped over boiled leather armor as he walked. The necklace of teeth around his neck and the string of ears dangling from the belt around his waist said he was pretty damned comfortable with cutting things off, and she hoped the gore-crusted halberd he carried in one gloved fist wasn't going to be the weapon he used to cut *her* things off.

"W-who are *you*?" she asked, her voice trembling as fiercely as her hands.

As he strode toward her, crusty stuff fell off his boots with every step, and wasn't it crazy that she wanted to yell at him for leaving a mess?

"I'm a warden in the 4th Ring, and you"—he seized her by the throat—"you are an intruder."

"No," she gasped, and then she just tried to breathe because he squeezed harder, cutting off her voice and her air.

His lips peeled back from blackened teeth and a wicked set of fangs as he put his face in hers. "The 4th and 5th Rings are in chaos, and do you know why? There are reports of unauthorized beings in the Inner Sanctum, and it looks like I caught one of them." He grinned, and if she hadn't been struggling to breathe, she'd have screamed. "Do you know what we do to intruders, female? I dare you to imagine the worst because I promise the reality will look far, far more horrible."

His meaty fist filled her vision, and then there was blackness.

\* \* \* \*

Hades was balls deep in a demon horde. The 5th Ring had literally been set on fire, and all around, smoke and flame erupted from crude bombs and fire arrows.

He and every 5th Ring warden had been fighting for hours, and they hadn't come any closer to finding the human. Reports of violence were coming in from the 3rd and 4th Rings, as well, and just moments ago, Silth had brought extremely troubling news.

He'd found a weak spot in the membrane that separated the Inner Sanctum from the rest of Sheoul-gra. If the spot wasn't shored up, and fast, demons would overrun Azagoth's realm, which could result in a catastrophic destabilization and allow the souls to escape, flooding human lands.

At least Cat was safely ensconced in his home, although he'd come to realize there was nothing "safe" about her. She might have been an angel once, but he wouldn't be surprised if there was a little succubus in her family tree.

He whacked an ugly-ass demon on its scaly head with his battle-ax and shot a lightning bolt at another. The bolt bounced around the crowd of demons, taking out another dozen before it fizzled away. Shit, this sucked. He'd always liked a good fight, but this was on a scale he hadn't seen since...well, ever.

Panting with exhaustion, he took advantage of the brief reprieve from charging demons. They were all around him, but they were busy fighting wardens, so he figured he had about thirty seconds to breathe.

"My lord!" A towering warden from the 4th Ring powered his way through the crowd and jogged over, his sword dripping with blood. "Malonius sent me with a message. He needs you at the Rot right away."

"Do *not* tell me we're dealing with prison riots, too," Hades growled.

The warden, Rhoni, wiped grime out of his eyes with the back of his gauntleted hand. "No, sir. He captured an intruder."

He frowned. "Someone else was able to get into the Inner Sanctum?"

"Apparently, sir."

*Yes.* The portals must be operating again. Azagoth must have realized something was wrong and had people working on the problem from his side. Finally. Now he could get Cat back where she belonged.

An uncomfortable sensation caught tight in his chest. He wasn't ready to give her up yet. Sure, he couldn't have her, not in the way he wanted, but now that he'd gotten a taste—so to speak— he wanted more. Her bravery and impulsiveness fascinated him, and her unique blend of artlessness and seductiveness enchanted him. He loved the way her kisses were eager but unpracticed, and her emotions were so unguarded. Such a rare thing for a fallen angel.

Yes, she was newly fallen, and no doubt she'd lose that innocent patina eventually, but only if she was exposed to ugliness. Something inside him wanted to protect her from that ugliness, the way he'd protected humans back when he'd been an angel.

Back then, he'd gone too far in his desire to protect the innocent, and it had cost him his wings and his soul. But how far would he go to protect Cat?

He knew the answer immediately. He'd stop at nothing. Which meant that, if the portals were open, he had to send her back. With only one exception, the Inner Sanctum was ugly, and Cat deserved better. She deserved to not lose her shiny.

The whisper of a spear passed too close to Hades's ear for comfort, jolting him back to the ugliness around him. The kind he needed to protect Cat from.

"How are things in the 4th Ring?" he asked.

"They're bad," Rhoni said, "but not this bad."

Hades clapped the guy on the shoulder. "Get back to it. I'll head to the prison."

Extending his wings, he launched into the air, spinning and diving to avoid projectiles. The icy burn of some sort of weapon ripped through one wing, but a few heartbeats later, he punched through the portal and was striding down the Rot's dark, damp halls to the processing center where all guests were interrogated before being sent to either a cell or a torture chamber. When he arrived in the chilly antechamber, Malonius greeted him.

"She's in Jellybean," he said, his breath visible in the freezing air. "Seems her greatest fear is spiders."

From its pulsating walls to its seeping ceiling, Jellybean was a room that fed on fear and came alive when someone was locked inside. Once it got hold of someone's fears, it made them real. He'd once seen the room fill with jellybeans while the demon inside screamed in terror...hence, the name of the room.

Malonius had shoved an orange bean up the guy's nose, and the demon had confessed all of his considerable sins. *Freaking jellybeans.*

"Wait. She?" Hades asked, every internal alarm clanging as what Malonius said sank in. He opened his mouth, but whatever he was about to say fled when he saw the pile of clothes on the table behind the other fallen angel.

A pair of faded, ripped jeans and a corset.

*Cat.*

*Fuck!* Wheeling around, he tore out of the room and charged down the hall, his pulse pounding in his ears even louder than the strike of his boots on the stone floor. Holy hell, if she was hurt, someone was going to pay in blood and bone and pain, and Hades was going to be the one to collect.

Up ahead, a warden stood guard outside Jellybean. "Open that fucking room!" Hades shouted.

The guy jumped, fumbled at his side for the key, but before he could unlock the door, Hades was there. He wrenched the key from the warden's hand and knocked him aside.

His fingers shook as he jammed the heavy iron skeleton key into the lock, but somehow he managed to open the door. He whipped it open, and a wave of spiders of all species and sizes skittered out, spilling over his boots.

"*Dach niek!*"

The Sheoulic command put the room to rest, and the arachnids disappeared. He burst inside, and his knees nearly gave out at the sight of Cat huddled in the corner, naked and shivering. Her arms covered her head as she rocked back and forth on her heels. Bruises marred her pale skin, and fury made his blood steam.

"Cat." He knelt next to her and laid his palm gently on her shoulder, cursing when she flinched. "Cat, it's me. It's Hades."

A shudder wracked her body, and she made a sobbing noise that pricked him in the heart he'd long ago thought immune to pretty much anything emotional.

He lowered his voice, shooting for something that might resemble soothing. "The spiders are gone. They weren't real. It's okay."

Very slowly, her arms came down, and she peeked at him through splayed fingers. Her bloodshot, red-rimmed eyes were a punch in the gut. "Hades?"

"Yeah." He cleared his voice of the hoarseness that had crept into it. "It's okay, I promise."

She lowered her hands, but her gaze shifted and her eyes went wide as the sound of footsteps indicated that someone had come into the room.

"My lord," Malonius began, his voice pitched with fear, proving he wasn't completely stupid. Clearly he realized he'd fucked up in a very, very big way. "I found her in your crypt...she'd ransacked the place...I thought—"

"I know what you thought," Hades snapped. He didn't turn to look at the male because if he did, he wouldn't be able to control the murderous rage pounding through his veins. "And that's the only reason you aren't hanging by your entrails right now."

As much as he wanted to blame the warden for this, it was ultimately Hades's fault. He hadn't thought to tell all of his staff about Cat, but that was a mistake he wouldn't make again.

"Tell the others," he said. "Tell them that this Unfallen is mine, and she's not to be harmed, or ogled, or even fucking *breathed on*."

"Yes, sir." Malonius tossed Cat's clothes to Hades, and a heartbeat later, they were alone again.

"Cat? I'm going to take you home...ah, I mean, to my place."

He started to pull her into his arms, but he jerked back at the sight of the gore streaking his arms. Cursing, he looked down at himself, realized he must look like he'd showered in a slaughterhouse. The fact that he was covered in blood wasn't the most unusual thing ever, but after what Cat had just been through, she didn't need this, too.

*So much for protecting her from the ugliness of the Inner Sanctum.*

Guilt churned inside him like a living thing, and this thing had teeth. It gnawed at his heart and clawed at his soul because this could have been prevented.

Cat's teeth began to chatter, so he let the guilt monster feed as he gathered her in his filthy arms and tucked her against his grimy chest and got her out of there, snarling at everyone who got in his way. Or who looked at her naked body. Or breathed in his general direction.

He reached the exit portal in record time, but as he stepped inside, he wondered what else could possibly go wrong.

# Chapter Eleven

Face buried against Hades's powerful chest, Cat clung to him with all her strength, which seemed to be in short supply. She couldn't stop the shaking, but when Hades held her tighter and whispered comforting things in her ear, the wonderful whiskey-fizz sensation he gave off wrapped around her like a warm blanket and helped ease the trembling a little.

She didn't open her eyes to see where they were going. She didn't care. As long as she wasn't trapped with spiders in that horrible room with pulsing walls and the faint sound of a heartbeat, she was thrilled. Besides, she trusted Hades. He'd given her no reason not to. More importantly, he worked for Azagoth, and no one in their right minds would do anything to intentionally harm anyone in the Grim Reaper's employ.

Hades let out a hardcore curse, grumbled, and cursed again. She didn't look. Whatever had pissed him off wasn't something she wanted to see. He started moving again, and then suddenly, she felt a cool, fresh breeze on her bare skin. The scent of freshly mown grass and flowers filled her nostrils, and riding on the raft of air was the faint tang of the ocean.

Where in the world were they? Had they escaped the Inner Sanctum?

Still, she didn't peek, not even when he spoke to someone in Sheoulic, dashing her hopes that they'd gotten free. A few moments later, she heard a door close, and the mouthwatering aroma of roasting meat and baking bread finally had her cracking her eyelids.

Her mother had always joked that nothing could make her come running like the ring of the dinner bell, and it was so true. She loved food. Loved to cook. She secretly enjoyed when Azagoth or Lilliana asked her to whip them up something in the kitchen, even though they had several full-time chefs. Sometimes she even helped out in the kitchen that served the dozens of Unfallen who lived and trained in Azagoth's realm.

She wondered how long it would be before she could do that again.

"Where are we?" Her throat, raw from screaming, left her voice shredded.

Holy eight-legged hell, she hated spiders. And, as she'd discovered in that horrible room, demon spiders made every species of arachnid in the human realm seem like cuddly puppies.

"We're with friends. They're letting us take their house for as long as we need." Hades's hand stroked her hair gently. "I'm going to put you down on the bed. Is that okay?"

She nodded, and he set her down carefully on a mattress she suspected had been filled with straw. Before she was even out of his arms, he covered her with a blanket and tossed her clothes onto a small table next to the bed.

They appeared to be in some sort of Tudor-era hut that, while being primitive in comparison to modern-day standards, was pristine, as if brand new. The furniture and decor was simple but elegant and had clearly been fashioned by talented hands. A small, doorless bathroom had been built into one wall, but like Hades's place, the toilet was crude, a mere hole in a stone and wood box she was guessing emptied through some sort of pipe and away from the home.

He sank down beside her on the mattress. "I'm sorry about what happened. I'll be having a little chat with Malonius later."

"Don't," she said, surprising herself. Earlier, she'd cursed that male from here to Mars until she had to stop cursing in order to scream. "He caught me going through your things. I can see why he thought I was an intruder." She shuddered. "The spider room was overkill, though."

"You're a lot more forgiving than most people would be...wait, going through my things?" His voice was teasing and light, so unexpected, and so welcome. How did he know exactly what she needed?

"I was bored. And I wanted to get to know you better." She rolled her bottom lip between her teeth, wondering at what point curiosity became intrusion. "I saw the picture on your desk. The lake in the mountains. Is it someplace special?"

He grunted. "Crater Lake. I've always thought it was one of the most beautiful places in the world, and I need a reminder now and then. Especially since most of the Inner Sanctum is craptastically ugly."

That was so...sweet. And again, unexpected. Who would have thought that the guy who operated a demon holding tank would want something beautiful near him?

"I'm going to go get something for you to eat." Hades reached over and squeezed her hand, but when he glanced down at the way their fingers were entwined, he jerked away from her. "Sorry...I'm covered in...I was fighting before I went to the Rot...fuck." A blush spread over his cheeks as he popped to his feet. "Will you be okay by yourself?"

"I'm not afraid of a little dirt and blood," she said tiredly, "and I'm not a child who can't be left alone." That said, she still checked out the room for spiders. And she couldn't get that infernal heartbeat to stop echoing in her head.

"I know." There was an odd note in his voice...admiration, maybe? The idea that he, a powerful Biblical legend, admired anything about her, a disgraced Unfallen with few survival skills, gave her a boost of much-needed energy. "I'll be right back."

She waited on the bed, the scratchy wool blanket wrapped tightly around her. Soft voices drifted back and forth from the other room, and a few minutes later, he returned with a pottery mug and a bowl of steaming meat and bread swimming in gravy. Her stomach growled fiercely, and she didn't feel the slightest embarrassment when she snatched the plate and crude metal spork from him.

Completely setting aside polite manners, she shoveled a bite into her mouth and chewed. "Oh, damn," she moaned. "This is amazing. But I'm not going to ask what kind of meat it is."

He chuckled as he set the mug on the stand next to the bed. "I can tell you that it's not demon snake."

"Good," she muttered. "I've had enough of that for a lifetime." She took another bite, chewed, swallowed. "So why aren't we at your place?"

"Because Malonius locked the portal to my crypt to protect it, and I can't open it without him. I can break through his lock eventually, but I didn't want to waste time. Besides, I figured you'd be more comfortable here."

She licked gravy off the spork and decided she wanted the recipe. "Where is here?"

"We're in hell's version of Cloud Cuckoo Land."

"Say what?"

"Don't you watch movies?" He shook his head, making waves in his Mohawk. "We're in a recently-built realm Azagoth and I created for demons who don't really fit into any of the five Rings."

She frowned. "But I thought the Rings coordinated with the Ufelskala."

"They do." He moved over to the window and peered out, his expression watchful but not tense, which relieved her more than she'd care to admit. She'd always thought of herself as being tough, but the last couple of days had tested her resolve, and she was ready for a break. "But the 1st Ring didn't seem suitable for all good demons. There was no reward for demons who have done more than simply exist. Who have contributed to society for the greater good."

As an angel who spent her entire life in Heaven, she'd been raised on stories of the depravity of demons, so while she had no trouble believing that there were demons who were "less evil" than others, she wasn't convinced that "good" demons existed.

"Good demons?" she asked, not bothering to hide her skepticism. "Really?"

He turned away from the window, his big body partially blocking the eerie orange light from outside. "You said yourself that humans come in a wide range of good and evil, so why wouldn't demons? God has always wanted balance, so for every evil human, there exists a good demon."

Cat scooped up a bit of bread and gravy. "Makes sense, I guess. But what kinds of good demons are you talking about?"

The muscles in his shoulders rippled as he shrugged, and her pulse kicked. When she'd clung to him earlier, her lips had been *right there*. She could have kissed him. Licked his skin to see if it tasted as smoky as it smelled.

At least, she could have done all of that if she hadn't been occupied with trying to keep from curling up into a weeping ball of spider-trauma.

"Kinds like the ones who work at Underworld General Hospital." He propped one booted foot against the wall behind him, his pose casual, but deadly energy remained coiled beneath the surface, so tangible that Cat swore she could feel it dance on her skin. He might say they were safe, but he was prepared for anything. So *he* might not feel safe, but she did. Nothing was going to get past him.

"Or the ones who live among humans and do nothing more than try to fit in," he continued. "Before this expansion, they went to the 1st Ring, which is still a pretty hellish experience. Here demons can actually enjoy their time until they're reincarnated. Which, thanks to Revenant being Sheoul's new overlord, happens pretty quickly."

Someone who looked human walked past the window, a ball in his hand. Hades didn't even glance at the guy, but Cat had a feeling he was well aware of every step the male took.

"I'm curious," she said after the guy disappeared. "In Heaven, humans choose their appearance, but everyone can still 'see' each individual as the person they'd always known, even if they knew them on Earth as a twelve-year-old boy, but in Heaven they appear as a twenty-five-year-old female. Is it the same here?"

Hades dipped his head. "Essentially. Demons in the Inner Sanctum do choose their appearances, but people don't always recognize them. I think it's because they're rarely born twice as the same species."

Huh. It hadn't occurred to her that a Seminus demon wouldn't be born again as a Sem. "How does that work?"

He cocked an eyebrow. "Do you really want to talk about this?"

"It's your fault," she said around a mouthful of bread. "You piqued my curiosity."

"Well then," he said with a lopsided grin and an impish glint in his eyes, "I guess I'll have to satisfy your…curiosity."

*Oh, yes, please. Satisfy anything you want.*

She swallowed about a million times to keep her mouth from

opening and those exact words from falling out.

Hades didn't seem to notice the lustful distress he'd caused, continuing his demonic reincarnation lesson as if he hadn't just teased her with sexual undertones. "Demons here are generally reborn as a member of a species that fits within their soul's Ufelskala, but every once in a while a level one will be reincarnated as a species that rates a five, or vice versa. It's why you'll sometimes encounter a Soulshredder that wants to help others, or a Slogthu that likes to kill."

That made sense, she supposed. Anomalies happened in every species on Earth, so why not in Sheoul? "So how does all of this work? How do you keep everyone in line?"

"That's the reason the Rings are all based on the Ufelskala. No matter your score, you can travel to any level that is higher on the scale, but never lower. So an Ufelskala Tier Two demon can travel between the 2nd, 3rd, 4th, and 5th Rings, but they can't go to the 1st Ring. And no one from any Ring can come here."

She considered that for a moment. "But as you said, the Ufelskala scale is based on a species' level of evil as a whole, and not every individual is representative of their breed."

"Which is why Azagoth and my team review every person who comes through the gate." Hades bent over and yanked off his boots. "Now, if you don't mind, I need to clean up."

She scooped up another bite of gravy-soaked bread. "Go for it." Oh, wait...was he going to use the open—*very* open—bathroom? He strode over there, his fingers working at the ties on his pants. Oh, boy, he was going to—

He dropped his pants, and she nearly swallowed her tongue along with the bread. With every silent step, the muscles in his legs and ass flexed, making her fingers curl with the desire to dig into his hard flesh.

Hades hit a lever, and water streamed from a wide slot in the stone wall. He stepped beneath the steaming waterfall, closing his eyes and dipping his head back. He was a living, breathing work of art. Angel and demon all wrapped up in a package of physical perfection. Her mouth watered, but now it had nothing to do with the food. She wanted something much more tasty.

Wanted it desperately. And the thing was, lust had driven her wants before, but something had changed. Yes, when she looked at him, lust was a writhing, burning entity inside her, but there was also a flutter of attraction to the male inside that magnificent body.

But did he want her? He'd spent months avoiding her—or, at least, it seemed that way. And back at his crypt, he'd taken off just when things had gotten hot. But things *had* gotten hot. And he'd sort of flirted a couple times, the way he had a moment ago when he talked about satisfying her…curiosity. So there *was* something there. Right?

She needed to know for sure. Her curiosity had always driven her, even when she should have minded her own business, but a wereleopard couldn't change its spots, could it?

Gathering all her courage, she stood, letting the blanket fall to the floor. His back was turned to her, so he didn't see her moving toward him, her pulse picking up speed with every step.

"Need help washing your back?"

He whirled around, eyes wide, his lips parted in surprise. A blush crept up his neck and into his face as his gaze traveled the length of her body. Between his legs, his sex stirred, swelling and lengthening as he took her in. Between *her* legs, she went wet, and she hadn't even stepped under the water yet.

"I…ah…I'm doing fine by myself…" It was adorable how flustered he was. Big bad Hades was completely off balance. She was so taking advantage of that.

"You missed a few spots." Stepping into him, she gripped his biceps and forced him back around. The tingly, whiskey heat of him immediately sparked on her skin, giving her that contact high that had been so incredibly seductive back at his crypt.

She soaked up the sensation as she palmed the hard bar of handmade soap and began to wash him, starting on the back of his neck and working her way down. Damn, his body was firm, his skin smooth. She'd never touched a male like this, and she made a mental note to do it again. Hopefully with Hades.

Intrigued by this new experience, she committed everything to memory, like the way his muscles leaped under her touch. Like the way the water and suds sluiced over hard flesh that rolled with every one of his rapid breaths. Like the way his fingers dug into the stone wall as if he was trying desperately to hold himself upright.

"Cataclysm," he said roughly. "This might not be the best idea."

Pulse fluttering in her veins, she dropped her hands lower, skimming his buttocks as she scrubbed in wide circles.

"Why not?" She hoped her words came off as light and teasing, that the sound of the water hid the tremor of insecurity. What if he rejected her again?

Taking a deep breath, she went lower, so she was gliding the soap over his firm ass and hips.

"Because."

His voice, husky and dripping with male need, made her bold. "That's not a reason," she murmured as she tucked the soap in the crack of his butt and slid her hand downward, her fingers reaching between his legs—

His hand snapped back to grasp her wrist, and then he was turning into her and pushing her back against the wall. "I think," he said, as he pressed his body against hers, "that it's my turn."

*Yes!* He did want her!

Dipping his head, he captured her mouth as he wrested the soap out of her hand. His kiss was hotter than the water pouring on them, and his hands, oh, sweet hell, his *hands*. They roamed her body with finesse, his touch alternating between light and firm, teasing and let's-do-this-thing serious. Every pass of the soap over her breasts and buttocks made her groan, and when he dropped the bar and dipped his fingers between her legs, she cried out in relief and amazement. She'd never been touched so intimately before, but now she was glad she'd waited. Hell, she'd have happily given up her wings for this one, beautiful moment.

"You like this," he said in a deep, guttural rasp. "I like it too. I shouldn't, but I do."

There was a strange note in his voice, a tortured thread of...regret? Before she could think too hard on that, he did something sinful to her clit, and she nearly came undone. His fingers slid back and forth between her folds, the pressure becoming firmer as her breath came faster. He changed the rhythm every few strokes to rub circles around her sensitive nub or to slide the pads of his fingers past her opening, hitting a sensitive spot she didn't know she had.

"Please," she begged, not even sure what she was begging for. She wanted everything he could possibly do to her, and thanks to Lilliana, Cat knew a *lot* of things were possible.

He smiled as he kissed a path from her mouth to her jaw and down her neck. Arching her back, she let her head fall against the stone wall to give him as much access as he wanted. He grunted in approval and nipped her throat, the tiny sting adding fuel to the fire that was building inside her.

Another pass of his fingers had her panting and pumping her hips into his hand. Then he slipped one inside her. Yes, oh, damn...*yes!*

He worked her for a moment, wringing sighs and moans from her before adding another finger. The burn of her tissue stretching yielded to pleasure within a couple of heartbeats, and she surrendered herself to his masterful play.

His fingers pumped as his thumb circled her clit, and too soon she exploded, her first climax with a male coursing through her body in an uncontrolled free fall. When she still had her wings, she would sometimes climb high into the air, tuck in her wings, and let the fall take her skimming close to mountaintops and deep into canyons. The orgasm Hades gave her was like that. Freeing, life affirming...and dangerous.

She knew herself well enough to know that for her, sex and emotion would be tightly linked. It was a horrible character flaw, one that had the potential to hurt badly. She supposed it was a good thing Zhubaal had rejected her, but now she thought that maybe Hades should have, too.

He brought her down slowly, his touch growing lighter as she became sensitive to every waning sensation.

"You're so beautiful." His smoky voice rumbled through her like a second climax, sparking a new wave of pleasure skimming across her skin. "God, the sounds you make when you come."

"I need to hear you," she said, taking him in her fist. "Let me."

He gasped, his body going rigid as she squeezed his erection. She'd never touched one before; she and Zhubaal hadn't gotten this far. Not even close. The skin was so silky, the shaft textured with veins she wanted to trace with her tongue.

Suddenly, he seized her wrist and shoved her hand away.

Confused, she glanced up at him. He didn't meet her gaze as he backed out of there, leaving a trail of puddles on the wood floor. "I have to go."

What the hell?

"Don't do this again." She shut off the water. "Please, Hades. What's wrong?"

Someone knocked on the door, and she swore he jumped a foot in the air. "Who the fuck is it?" he yelled.

"Silth. I have news you're going to want to hear."

The urgency in Silth's voice said the news wasn't good, but Hades seemed relieved. Was he happy for an excuse to get out of the bedroom? "I'll be out in a second." He didn't bother drying off, simply jammed his feet into his pants. He didn't look at her as he said, "In this part of the Inner Sanctum, and only this part, you can clothe yourself in whatever you want, with just a thought. But the second you leave, the clothes will disappear."

Cool, but clothes were the least of her concerns right now. "Can you slow down for a second?" She reached for one of the folded cloths on the shelf next to the shower. "We need to talk."

"Talk," he said sharply, "doesn't seem to be what you want from me." He held up the hand that had, just moments ago, given her so much pleasure. "I gave you what you wanted, didn't I?"

Stung by his sudden, inexplicable anger, she lashed out. "No, you didn't. Not even close. You think I sit around fantasizing about your *hand?*"

Said hand formed a fist at his side. "Sorry to disappoint, babe." He yanked open the door with so much force that the iron handle broke. "But I'm sure Zhubaal will be happy to give you whatever it is you fantasize about."

"Wow," she said quietly. "I can see where your reputation as a master torturer comes from. You know exactly where to plunge your dagger, don't you?"

He jerked as if she'd struck him, and then he stormed out, leaving her to her fantasies. Which, right at this minute, included smacking Hades in his stubborn, infuriating head.

## Chapter Twelve

*What the fuck have I done?*

Snarling, Hades slammed the bedroom door and strode into the hut's living room, his hard cock pinching in his pants and his regrets piling up with every step.

He never got this moody, but right now he was strung tighter than a vampire stretched on the Rack in the Rot's dungeon. Sexual frustration combined with the anger from the situation with Cat and the bullshit going on in the Inner Sanctum had damned near reached critical levels. He considered himself to be a pretty laid-back, easygoing guy, especially for a fallen angel, but damn, when he was with Cat it was as if he was mining desires and emotions he'd kept buried, and now he'd hit a vein that ran thick with fury and hopelessness.

It had been centuries since he'd last succumbed to the kinds of feelings that usually signaled an impending catastrophic bout of self-destructiveness.

He either wanted to kill something, or he wanted to fuck something...and the latter something was Cat.

*Stupid, Hades. It would be so fucking stupid to start a relationship that can't go anywhere, not to mention the fact that Azagoth will break you in half like a wishbone.*

Oh, but didn't he already board that stupid train when he made her the brunt of his anger at not being able to make love to her? She hadn't deserved any of that. Then he'd made it worse by bringing up Zhubaal, which had only served to throw jealousy and shame into the toxic mix brewing inside him right now.

He'd hurt her when he'd sworn to protect her. He'd done what he did best; find a soft spot, slip a blade in it, and give it a good twist.

Fucking idiot.

Water dripped down his back, reminding him of how Cat's gentle fingers had caressed him in the shower. He'd felt like a map and she was the explorer looking for interesting places to go. He'd wanted so badly to let her. Her touch was a gift, a connection he hadn't had with anyone since before he fell. Even then, his relationships hadn't been serious. He'd been young and impulsive, and females had been a fun distraction from his crappy job and his priggish, cold parents.

Since his fall, the few females he'd been with had been sexual partners and nothing more. How could they be anything more when the total of his time outside of Sheoul-gra could be measured in hours instead of days?

Gnashing his teeth, he stopped in front of Silth and tried to keep his tone civil. "What is it?"

"We captured the Orphmage who was holding the Unfallen female you rescued," he said, and Hades's heart leaped. Finally. Maybe he would get to kill someone after all.

"He's alive, I take it."

"Yes, sir." Silth fingered the hilt of the sword at his hip, his chain mail armor tinkling softly as he moved. "We have him at the Rot. But I had a chance to interrogate him at the site where we captured him."

"He talked?"

"After I reached into his chest cavity and started breaking off ribs."

"Nice." Hades nodded in approval. "So what did he say? Did you get the human?"

"No, sir. But he did say that when he jammed his staff into the Unfallen, he released an enchantment inside her."

Hades's heart stopped leaping. "Her name is Cat. And what kind of enchantment?"

"The kind that drains her life force."

Oh, fuck. His heart started beating again, but in an erratic, schizy rhythm. "For what purpose?"

"To open holes in the barriers between the Inner Sanctum and Sheoul, as well as the barrier between the Sanctum and Sheoul-gra."

Not unexpected, since demons were always trying to get out of the Inner Sanctum to wreak havoc as ghosts in both Sheoul and on Earth. But they'd been trying to do that for eons, so what made this attempt different?

"I'm still not clear on how that would work," he said. "What role does the human play in this?"

"They're draining him, too. Both the Unfallen, ah, Cat, and the human are timed to drain at the same time."

Hades's gut was starting to churn. "And how much time do we have before this event takes place?"

"Approximately twenty hours. But it could happen sooner if both the human and the Unfallen are beheaded simultaneously. When their souls flee their bodies, perforations will appear in the barriers, and demons will escape."

Holy shitmonkeys. "Find a hellhound," Hades said. "Quickly."

Silth's upper lip peeled back, revealing two shiny fangs. Like pretty much everyone else, he hated hellhounds. "Why must I track down one of those filthy mutts?"

"Because I need a message delivered to their king. Tell the hellhound that we need Cerberus's help. We can use every hellhound they can spare to find the human."

Silth's curse told Hades exactly how he felt about dealing with the beasts. "And if that fails?"

"Then we'll need the hellhounds to patrol the borders. We can't let a single demon escape, let alone millions of them."

And there was no way he could let Cat die.

"There's one other thing, sir."

Of course there was. "What is it?"

"The enchantment inside the Unfallen...it can be used to track her whereabouts."

Mother. Fuck. "She can't be left alone."

"Do you want me to stay with her?"

Oh, hell, no. Silth was a nasty motherfucker, but he was movie-star handsome and had an insatiable sexual appetite. He wasn't getting near Cat, who had shown herself to be very open about her own sexual appetites.

Gods, she was a dream female. Beautiful and kind, if a little reckless, and when it came to being physical, she wasn't shy...and yet, there was that pesky innocence about her that intrigued him.

And made him crazy, as his outburst in the bedroom had proven.

"My lord?" Silth prompted, and Hades realized he'd gotten lost in his thoughts. "Shall I stay with her?"

"No," Hades said quickly. "I've got it for now. Send the message to Cerberus, and then contact me once we have hellhounds searching the Rings. Cat can help look for the human, but I don't want her out there until we have the hounds for protection."

Silth gave a shallow bow and took off, leaving Hades to wonder what to do in the meantime.

One thing was certain, he wasn't going to tell Cat any of this. She'd been through enough already. Now he had to figure out how to stay with her while not giving into his desire for her. Somehow, he had to pretend that being with her was easy, no big deal, when the truth was that being with her without being inside her might be the hardest thing he'd ever done.

# Chapter Thirteen

The longer Hades was gone, the angrier Cat got.

Yes, she understood he was handling business. And given the state of...everything, it was probably serious business. But the way he'd backed out of the shower and run out of the room had been insulting. Of course, his insults had been insulting, too.

Was he playing a game with her? Was he getting a good laugh over the Unfallen panting after him while he remained distant? Was she just a toy for his amusement?

Cursing to herself, she finished drying with the rough linen cloth she'd assumed was meant to be a towel, and then she tried out the "thought clothes" Hades had mentioned. Instantly, she was clothed in jeans and a corset identical to the real ones on the bed. Huh. She changed the colors, turning the corset to bright orange and the jeans to black.

Neat.

But maybe she should try something different. Something that would knock Hades off balance. He thought she should go to Zhubaal to get what she wanted, so maybe she should show Hades exactly what he'd be missing.

But what?

*If you want to get a male's attention, give him something to look at.*

Lilliana had told Cat that while picking out an outfit to distract Azagoth from some sort of bookwork he'd been poring over a few weeks ago. Hours later, if the spring in Azagoth's step had been any indication, Lilliana's choice of clothes had been spot on.

What the hell, Cat thought. She replicated the outfit, going for a red leather miniskirt and a leather bra top, finishing it off with matching stilettos. Looking down at herself, she smiled. Let Hades resist *that*.

As if on cue, he opened the door. But to her frustration, he didn't so much as glance at her as he crossed to the window.

"Silth found the Orphmage." He brushed back the curtains. "It shouldn't be long before he gives up the location of the human."

Great. Terrific. She should probably say something about that, given that she'd kicked off this entire mess when she came to the Inner Sanctum to find the human.

Instead, she opened her mouth, and something else came out. "What is up with you?" she snapped. "I have been flirting my ass off, and you act like I'm trying to sell you stewed maggots."

"Hey," he said with a wave of his hand. "Don't knock stewed maggots. With enough spices and tomatoes—"

"Argh!" She spun away from him, too angry to continue this. And she hoped like hell he didn't notice her nearly break her ankle on these stupid shoes that clearly didn't work to catch his attention. Nothing did. Maybe it was time to give up and stop being pathetic. "Never mind."

A hand clamped down on her shoulder, halting her in her tracks. A heartbeat later, Hades was in front of her, his expression serious. "Trust me, I'm not immune to your...feminine wiles."

"First of all," she said, shrugging away from his touch, "I don't have any wiles. Second, you're a big, fat liar."

"Baby, you're *wearing* fucking *wiles*." He grabbed her wrist, and before she could resist, he ground his erection into her palm. "And does this feel like I'm immune? Did I look like I was immune when I was in the shower and you were stroking me?"

Holy shit. She stood frozen to the spot, her hand cupping Hades's massive erection. Finally, she looked up at him, her breath catching in her throat at the glow of heat in his eyes.

"I—I don't understand. If you want me, why have you been such a colossal asshat?"

One corner of his mouth twitched in a smile. "Asshat? I like that."

With a huff, she stepped away from him. "It wasn't a compliment."

"Your hand was on my dick. Anything you said would have been a compliment."

How had he gone from being a jerk to being all charming so

quickly? "You still haven't answered my question."

"You want the truth?" Reaching up, he ran his hand over his hair and blew out a long, tired breath. "You're off limits to me."

"Off limits?" she asked incredulously. "Says who?"

"Azagoth."

She scowled, searching her brain for a reason Azagoth would say that, but she came up blank. "Why would he tell you I'm off limits?"

"You mean, why would he tell me that when he didn't seem to give a shit that Zhubaal fucked you?"

*Ouch.* Flustered, she opened her mouth. Shut it. Opened it again. "That's not what—" She cursed. "How did you know about me and Zhubaal? What did he say?"

"He didn't say anything. That bastard is as tight-lipped as a Ghastem."

Seeing how Ghastems had no mouths...yeah. "Then how did you know? And why do I have to keep asking the same question twice?"

He shrugged, his bare shoulder rolling slowly. "Dunno."

She was going to kill him. "How. Did. You. Know?" she ground out.

"*Griminions* love gossip. Those little suckers live for it. When they aren't collecting souls, I'm pretty sure they hold tea and knitting parties or something."

Hmm. Maybe the reason things with Z had been so disastrous made sense now. Because he'd taken her to his chambers, but then he'd refused sex with her. She'd been pissed, but what if the reason for his reluctance was because Azagoth had forbidden him to be with her?

Sighing, she wished away the shoes and padded barefoot to the wooden chair at the end of the bed. "Is he punishing me, do you think? I keep breaking stuff, and I've missed some cobwebs in corners, and once, I even tracked ashes through his library." She sank down on the chair, her stomach churning. "He's going to send me back to the human realm, isn't he?"

She'd be in danger there, defenseless, easy prey for angel-hating demons and True Fallen who made it a sport to drag Unfallen into Sheoul. Even worse, she'd lose Lilliana as a friend. And she'd never see Hades again. At least, not until she died and came back to the Inner Sanctum as a soul waiting to be reincarnated.

Groaning, she rubbed her eyes with the heels of her palms. She could lose everything, and wasn't that a laugh given how little she actually had. Feeling suddenly very vulnerable, she wished herself new clothes that covered everything. She didn't even mind the suffocating feeling of having so much skin hidden. Right now, the clothing was much-needed armor.

"He's not punishing you," Hades said, his gaze fixed somewhere outside.

"How do you know? Obviously I've angered him somehow."

"Trust me, if he was angry with you, you'd know." He shook his head. "No, Cat, this isn't about you. It's about me." Reaching up, he rubbed the back of his neck. "I'm the one he's punishing. All females in Sheoul-gra are off limits to me, including servants and his daughters. And trust me, when the Grim Reaper tells you his daughters are off limits...you listen. I looked at one of them too long, and he impaled me. Big stick right up the ass and out of the top of my skull. I still pucker when I think about it." His tone was light, breezy, as if his pain was no big deal, but when his gaze caught hers, she sucked in a harsh breath at the sadness there. "I want you, Cat, and if all it would cost me was a pointy stick up the ass, I'd pay that price. But it wouldn't stop there. And I don't know what price you'd have to pay, as well."

Stunned by his admission, she just sat there, unsure what to say. All she knew was that Hades wanted her after all, and that should have made her happy, but the only thing it did was make her miserable.

\* \* \* \*

So much for playing it cool.

Hades felt like a total jackass. He shouldn't have said anything about his punishment, about wanting Cat, about anything at all. The only way he stayed sane was to let everything slide off him like lava rolled off a Gargantua.

He wondered if the owners of this hut had alcohol stored somewhere. He could use a drink. Or ten.

"Hades?"

He gazed out the window at the lily pad-choked pond out back and braced himself for a bunch of pity. "What?"

"Is that why you live in the Inner Sanctum? Because Azagoth doesn't want you to be tempted or something?"

"Nope." He watched a crowd of people tossing a ball around in a nearby yard. He hated this place. It was too...human. Too bright and cheery. It reminded him that his life was all gloom and doom and asshole demons.

"So you choose to live in the Sanctum? In what's little more than a hovel?"

He turned back to her, drawing a quick, surprised breath at her clothes. While he'd been looking out the window, she'd changed into tights and a long-sleeved, form-fitting T-shirt. There were even socks on her feet. Since her skin was a gauge for good and evil, she must not want to feel those things. She must not want to feel *him*.

Not that he blamed her, but he still felt a pinch of hurt that made his voice sharper than he'd intended. "What, you were expecting a palace?"

She stared. "You live in a crypt and sleep in a coffin. They make these things called beds now."

What a joke. "Azagoth limits my comforts. You know what I miss most about that? Peanut butter. And chocolate. Limos introduced me to them when they first appeared on the human scene, you know? I always raid Azagoth's kitchen while I'm on that side, but usually I fill up on shit like pizza and Doritos."

Cat had been reaching for a miniature wooden arrow on the shelf next to her, but now she froze, her brows cranked down in confusion. "Azagoth won't even let you bring decent food to your place?"

"Oh, he will. He just won't help me get it. I have to call in favors. Or blackmail people. Limos brought me gelato once, but it was melted by the time Azagoth let it through."

Cat gasped. "That's awful."

He laughed. "It was gelato. Hardly a global disaster."

"Azagoth is an asshole," she snapped. He probably shouldn't love that she was angry on his behalf. "Why is he doing all of this to you?"

"Long story."

She picked up the arrow and gently stroked her fingers over the smooth surface. "Well, we don't have much else to do while we're waiting for the Orphmage to give up the human."

He could think of a lot of things they could do. If he wasn't forbidden by Azagoth to do them.

Anger and frustration threatened to boil over. He'd put up with Azagoth's asshattery for thousands of years, but now...now it felt like he was at a crossroads, at a place where he couldn't stand it anymore. Hadn't he paid for his sins for long enough?

Growling to himself, he stormed out of the bedroom and searched the hut for liquor. Soft footsteps followed him, but he ignored Cat as he popped the cork out of a clay jug of what smelled like extremely potent bloodwine.

Cat drifted into his peripheral vision as she checked out the knickknacks on the walls. Demons loved their wood and bone carvings. "So how did you end up here, anyway?"

He chugged a few swallows of the tart bloodwine, relishing the hot tingle as it burned its way down his throat. "You're a fallen angel, too. You know all about dirty laundry."

A wisp of pink swept across her cheeks. "My fall wasn't entirely my fault."

"You're still going with that story, huh?"

Her chin lifted. "It's true. I told you how it happened."

He snorted. "And Seminus demons hate sex."

She snatched the jug from him and took a swig. He had to hide an amused smile when she coughed. "So you own your fall?" she wheezed as she sat down at the kitchen table.

"Yup." He took back the jug. "I fucked up royally." He brought the container to his lips, pausing to say, "You really want to hear this? You want to know how I got here?"

At her nod, he lowered the jug. He hadn't told anyone this. It wasn't that he gave a crap who knew. It was just that he never really talked to anyone. Not about himself or his life. This was new, and he wasn't sure it was a good thing.

Finally, he propped his hip on the table edge. "When I was still an angel, my job was to process new humans arriving in Heaven after they died on Earth. It was boring as shit, and every time someone came through who had been slaughtered by another human, it pissed me off. So I started spending my time in the human realm, stopping sinners before they committed sins."

"Stopping them? How?"

"At first, I caused distractions. Earthquakes, sudden rainstorms, swarms of mosquitoes, whatever it took. Then I came across some vile bastard in the act of raping a young woman. I didn't think, didn't pause. I flash-fried him with a lightning bolt. And the weird thing is, I didn't feel an ounce of guilt. I knew I was going to be punished because, with very few exceptions, angels aren't supposed to kill humans."

He expected her to show some revulsion, but she merely propped her elbows on the table and leaned forward like a kid hearing a bedtime story. "Did you? Get punished, I mean?"

He shook his head. "Nope. Guess no one was paying attention. So the next time I found an evil human committing an atrocity, I whacked him. Damn, it felt good." So. Fucking. Good. "And that's where it all went wrong."

"Ah," she murmured. "You liked to kill."

Damn straight, he had. "It didn't take long before I wasn't just killing evil humans, but bad humans." There was a difference, a very *important* difference. Evil couldn't be repaired. Couldn't be forgiven. But bad could. "I made no distinction between those who were evil and those who were just assholes. I felt the need to punish, and I was made bolder by the fact that I didn't get caught. Not until I went after a son of a bitch who was famous for his torture methods. Turned out that he was Primori."

"Primori are people whose existence is crucial in some way," she mused, and then her eyes shot wide. "Which means he had a Memitim angel to protect him. And all Memitim..."

"Are Azagoth's children," he finished.

"Oh, shit."

"Yeah." He took another healthy swig from the jug. "The Memitim dude came out of nowhere, and we got into a nasty fight that ended with him dead."

"What did you do?"

Despite the fact that this had taken place over five thousand years ago, Hades's gut sank the way it had way back then when he'd realized what he'd done. He'd killed a fellow angel. Nearly killed a Primori. And worse, he hadn't cared all that much. His concern had been for himself, and for thousands of years, nothing had changed.

Until now. Now his greatest concern was making sure Cat was safe. His own fate was unimportant.

"I knew I'd get caught," he said, "so I ran for a while. Lost myself in the human population. But my parents were both professors of Angelic Ethics, and I'd had their teachings drilled into me since birth, so when the angels started closing in, I figured I'd earn points for turning myself in voluntarily." He curled his lip. "Turns out, not so much. I was relieved of my wings, but instead of being given a new name and booted out of Heaven, I was handed over to Azagoth."

At first, he'd thought the archangels's decision to let him keep his name and send him to Azagoth had been done purely to make the Grim Reaper happy, but once the Biblical prophecy tying him to the Four Horsemen appeared, he understood that he was meant for more than just being Azagoth's plaything.

Not that being a Biblical legend had helped him avoid pain. At all.

"Wow." Cat's already pale skin went a shade paler, making her freckles stand out on her nose and cheeks. "I'm shocked that he didn't kill you."

"Azagoth doesn't kill people." Hades reconsidered that. "Mostly. He's a big fan of eternal torment." No, Azagoth didn't take the easy way when it came to revenge. Or justice. He definitely wasn't the forgiving sort. "He needed someone to run the Inner Sanctum, so he gave me wings and power, making me the only Unfallen in history to be able to enter Sheoul without becoming a True Fallen." He smiled bitterly. "But he also made it his mission to make my life a living hell. And for thousands of years, he did."

She sat back in her chair, her lips pursed in thought. "Is your living situation part of that?"

"Yup." He shrugged. "He's only recently started letting me out of the Inner Sanctum for short periods of time. It's only been in the last fifty years or so that he allowed me to have luxuries from the outside if I can get anyone to bring them to me."

"Like the ice cream Limos brought you."

The pity creeping into Cat's voice made his jaw tighten. "Yeah."

"But you said you can go outside now. How often?"

"I've left Sheoul-gra five times in the last hundred years, and it cost me each time." Even when the Four Horsemen had gotten him sprung to help with a massive battle a few years ago, he'd paid dearly despite the fact that he'd fought for the good guys. For that, Azagoth had taken away Hades's only real friend, a demon who had been living in the 1st Ring for two thousand years. Azagoth had reincarnated him, leaving Hades with only his asshole wardens for company.

"So I'm guessing you don't do much dating if you can't leave, huh? You said females in Sheoul-gra are off limits, but what about here in the Inner Sanctum?"

He laughed. But it was a bitter, hard sound, even to his own ears. "Everyone is off limits to me, Cat. My wardens can screw whoever they want in the Inner Sanctum, but me? Remember the peeling thing I told you about? Yeah. Celibacy and me became really fucking intimate."

"You must have been so lonely," she said softly.

He blinked. Lonely? That thought hadn't occurred to him, and he didn't think it would occur to anyone else, either.

Although, now that he thought about it, yeah, there had always been a strange tension inside him that he couldn't identify. That he'd always written off as being sexual in nature. But now that he'd spent time with Cat, it was killing him to know that it was only a matter of time before he lost her company and her soothing touch. Fuck, he couldn't think about it, because if he did, he'd lose it.

Redirecting his thoughts, he flipped back to his default setting of deflection. "I don't know if I was lonely, really, but I was definitely horny."

She muttered something that sounded suspiciously like, "I know the feeling."

A scream from outside jolted them both to their feet. He rushed to the window and signaled for Cat to stay back, out of sight of anyone who might have a ranged weapon.

"What is it?" she asked. "What's going on?"

Awesomeness, that's what. Turning to her, he grinned. "Ever

seen *The Lord of the Rings* or *The Hobbit?* You know how the giant eagles always turn up to save the day?"

She jammed her hands on her hips. "Are you going to tell me that big birds are helping to search for the human?"

Outside, people were still screaming. "Better. The hellhounds have arrived."

"Hellhounds eat people," she pointed out.

"Hilarious, right?" He held out his hand. "Come on. I'll introduce you."

"To the hellhounds?"

"Not just the hellhounds," he said, grasping her hand in his. "To the king himself. Let's go say hi to Cerberus."

## Chapter Fourteen

Cataclysm had seen a lot of scary shit in her life—most of it in the last few days—but the massive, two-headed beast standing outside, surrounded by hounds that were as large as bison but still half his size, was one of the most intimidating creatures she'd ever come across.

Black as night, with glowing crimson eyes and teeth that would make a shark jealous, Cerberus used one massive paw to rake deep grooves in the grass. Steam rose up from the damaged earth, turning everything around it to ash.

"Hey, buddy," Hades said. "'Sup?"

The two heads snapped at each other before the left one put its ears back and lowered to eye level. A deep, smoky growl curled up from deep in the beast's chest.

Hades turned to her. "He said his brethren are sweeping the Rings for the human, and he apologizes in advance for any accidents."

"Accidents?"

"Most hellhounds hate angels, fallen or otherwise. Ol' Cerb here barely tolerates *me*. So we can expect some casualties among my warden ranks." He picked up a stick and threw it, and two of the hellhounds took off in a blur of black fur. "Also, he didn't really apologize. It was more of a description of how he thinks they'll taste."

She couldn't tell if he was serious or not, and frankly, she didn't want to know.

Cerberus's other head made some snarling noises, and Hades snarled back. The two of them went back and forth, until finally, Hades held up his hand and turned to her again.

"I...uh...I failed to mention something earlier."

She glared at Hades. She hated being kept in the dark about anything. "Dammit, Hades, what did you not tell me?"

"The Orphmage who captured you is using your life force to fuel the spell that will open the Inner Sanctum's barriers. He did the same thing to the human. Cerberus thinks that if we can get you close enough to the human, you'll be able to detect him. It should also unlock the doors between the Inner Sanctum and Azagoth's realm. Basically, the mutt wants to use you to track the human. Funny, yes? How it's the opposite of in the human realm, when humans use dogs—"

"I get it," she blurted. And criminy, could this situation get any worse? "But I can't believe you were keeping this from me. My life force? Seriously?"

"I'm sorry," he said, but he didn't sound very contrite. "I didn't want to worry you. Especially not after I was such a dick to you earlier."

Well, at least he admitted to being a dick. "I'm not worried," she explained. "I'm mad. We need to be out looking for the human. I have to fix this so the world isn't overrun by demon spirits and so Azagoth won't expel me from Sheoul-gra." She watched the hellhounds grab the stick and start a game of tug-of-war. "And fixing this could go a long way toward earning my way back to Heaven."

Hades's head jerked back as if he'd been slapped. "Why the everloving fuck do you want to go back to people who kicked you to the curb?"

"Heaven is my home," she said simply.

Even with the growls and snarls coming from the hellhounds and the shouts of people yelling at the beasts from a safe distance, Hades's silence was deafening.

Finally, he said quietly, "Seems to me that home is where the people who want you are."

For some reason, his words knocked the breath out of her. "And who would that be?" she asked. "Azagoth? I clean his house. And not very well. Anyone can do that. He's probably going to fire me anyway, once he learns that I was the one who got the human sent here in the first place. Lilliana? I consider her a friend, and I hope she feels the same about me, but she'd be fine without me.

The other Unfallen living in the dorms? Sometimes I cook for them. They'd miss my brown butter vanilla bean cake, but aside from that..."

She shrugged as if it was all no big deal, but the realization that she was so insignificant hurt. Making matters worse was her status as an Unfallen. She had no powers, no status, no identity. Maybe she should have entered Sheoul and turned herself into a True Fallen. At least then she'd have wings and power.

But the cost would have been her soul.

Suddenly, Hades's hands came down on her shoulders. "*I* want you, Cat. I want you more than I've wanted anything since I fell."

Her heart pounded with joy, but a blanket of sadness wrapped around it, muffling the happiness. "And what good does that do either of us if Azagoth is so bent on revenge?"

"Cat—"

She pulled away from him. "Don't make things worse. We need to find the human, and I need to get back to Heaven. Can we do that, please? Before all of my life is drained?"

A chill settled in the air, so noticeable that even the hellhounds looked around to see where the cold front was coming from. Cat didn't bother searching.

An icy glaze turned Hades's eyes cloudy and his expression stony. Blue veins rose to the surface of his skin, which had lost a few shades of color, the way it had back at Azagoth's mansion when he'd shown her his wings. A darkness emanated from him, making her skin burn, and it struck her that this was the Hades who came out to play when things went to hell. *This* was the Jailor of the Dead. The Keeper of Souls. The Master of Torture.

"Tell me, Cataclysm." His voice had gone deep, scraping the craggy bottoms of Hell's fiery pits. "How did you get your name?"

Oh, God. *He knew.* Humiliation shrunk her skin. "It doesn't matter. We should go." She spun around. The door to the hut was just a few steps away—

A hellhound blocked the path, drool dripping from its bared teeth. Clearly, Hades wasn't done with this conversation, but she wasn't going to give him the satisfaction of turning around to face him.

"Did you choose your name?" She jumped at the sound of his

voice, so close to her right ear that she felt his breath on her lobe.

"You know I didn't," she ground out, her humiliation veering sharply to anger that he'd chosen to go there. But then, he was the Master of Torture, wasn't he? He'd proven earlier that he knew where to strike in order to extract the most pain from a victim, and names could be an extremely sensitive subject for fallen angels.

When an angel lost his or her wings, they usually got to choose their new names. Heck, a fallen angel could rename themselves over and over, although they were never to use their angel names again...except inside Sheoul-gra.

But sometimes, the archangels chose a person's fallen angel name. As a punishment, or an insult, or a lesson...whatever their motivations, when they selected a name for a disgraced angel, it forever rendered one unable to refer to oneself as anything but the name the archangels chose. If they'd wanted Cat's new name to be Poopalufagus, she would be compelled to use it. Hell, she couldn't even *speak* her angelic name if she tried...and she had. The name always got clogged in her throat.

"Why did the archangels choose to call you Cataclysm?" His lips grazed her ear as he spoke.

"Because I was a disaster." Her voice cracked, and she hated herself for it. Hated Hades for making her revisit the worst moment of her life. Hated him more for forcing her to confront a truth she wasn't ready to face yet. "I helped nearly end the world, and they wanted to remind me of it forever."

Silence stretched, and she sensed Hades withdraw. When he finally spoke, his voice was back to normal, but somehow, she knew that nothing would be normal ever again.

"And those are the people you want to go home to." He brushed past her and shooed the hound out of the way. As he threw open the door to the hut and gestured for her to enter, he smiled coldly. "Then, by all means, let's not waste any time getting you back there."

\* \* \* \*

Hades spent over twelve hours with a pack of ravenous hellhounds and one fiercely silent female as they searched the 5th

Ring for the damned human. Granted, he hadn't felt like talking, either, because ultimately, what did he and Cat have to talk about? Her desire to go back to Heaven, to people who saddled her with a name that would haunt her forever? His selfish desire to prevent that?

Ultimately, there was nothing he could do to convince her not to go back to Heaven if she was given the chance. She didn't want to be here, and even if she did, they couldn't be together. Not if Azagoth was still determined to punish him.

He looked over at Cat, who was standing about thirty yards away on a cliff above a river of lava. In the distance, a blackened volcano spewed smoke and steam as reddish-orange veins of molten rock flowed down its sides. She was dressed in her jeans and corset, and when Hades made clear they were going to be dealing with scorching terrain, she'd agreed to wear a pair of boots loaned to her by a the demons whose hut they'd stayed in.

Hellhounds surrounded her, keeping her safe. The demon canines were unabashed killers, but when given something to protect, they took their job seriously. There was nothing on the planet more loyal than a hellhound. There was also nothing more ravenous, as the half-dozen hellhounds tearing apart some hapless demon nearby proved.

Hades signaled to Silth, and the guy jogged over from where he'd been using a divining rod, fashioned from the thighbone of the Orphmage who had captured Cat, to locate the human. The stupid mage had refused to talk, so they'd gone with Plan *B*. Or, as Hades called it, Plan Bone.

"My Lord?" Silth asked as he climbed the jagged lava rock hill to get to him.

"The hounds want to phase us to another region." Which was awesome because Hades hated this one, despised the heat and the smell. The only upside was that few demons lived here. Which made it a potentially great place to store a human. "But I want you and a few hounds to stay."

"You suspect something?"

Hades couldn't put his finger on it, but there was a sense of wrongness here that went beyond simply not liking the area. They hadn't found anything suspicious, but—

"Hades!" Cat came running toward him, hellhounds on her heels. "I think I can feel the human."

One of the hellhounds with her had something in its mouth, and as she drew to a halt in front of Hades, the hound playfully tossed it at her. She caught it, yelped, and dropped it.

"Hey," Hades said, "he likes you. He just gave you the finger." Of some kind of demon.

She gave him a look of disgust. "How can you joke about that? It's not funny."

"Nah," he said. "It kind of is."

"Gross." She kicked at the digit, and the hound snatched it up, swallowing it in short order. She grimaced and then rubbed her arms. "Like I was saying, I'm sensing something nearby. It's a feeling of good, which shouldn't be here, right?"

"In the 5th Ring? No way." His pulse picked up as the idea that they might be close sank in. "It's gotta be the human. Can you narrow it down to a direction?"

She shook her head. "It's weird, like a thread of good woven into a massive evil cloth. There's too much evil around it to get a bead on it."

"Uh...boss?" Silth held up the wobbling divining bone. "Got something."

As Hades watched, the thing went from barely moving to vibrating so intensely that Silth had to use two hands to hold on.

"Shit." Hades wheeled to the hounds. "Call for backup! Now—_"

An arrow punched through his chest. Agony tore through him, but as a hail of arrows fell on them, all he could think about was getting Cat to safety. A fierce, protective instinct surged through him as he took her to the ground and covered her with his body while the hellhounds charged an army of demons pouring out of fissures in the ground that hadn't been there a moment ago.

"Son of a bitch!" Silth, pincushioned by a half a dozen arrows, shouted in anger and pain, but he didn't go down. Palming his sword, he leaped into the fray.

"Let me up," Cat yelled against Hades's chest. "The human is close now. If I can get to him—"

"They're trying to draw you out." He held her tight, cocooning them both in his wings as he peeked between hellhound legs. "They need to behead you both simultaneously to open the holes in the barrier."

"*Behead* me?" she screeched. "Maybe you could have shared that little factoid sooner?"

"Maybe," he said, keeping it light to hide how fucking terrified he was for her. "But nah." He signaled to one of the hounds who had arrived at the hut with Cerberus, a scarred son of the hellhound king Hades knew only as Crush. "Take her to the graveyard. If I'm not there in ten minutes, take her back to the hut."

"What?" Cat punched him in the arm and struggled to her feet. "No. I can help!"

He didn't have time for this, but he gripped her shoulders and shook her. "There are thousands of demons coming at us, all with one goal; to behead you."

"But what about you? If you're not there in ten minutes—"

"Then I'm dead." Before she could say another word, he kissed her. Hard. And he poured as much emotion into it as he could. Because whether they won the battle or not, this would be the last kiss they shared.

Quickly, he stepped back and signaled to the hound. A heartbeat later, the beast was gone, and with him, Cat.

Even above the sounds of battle, he heard her scream, "*Noooooo*," as she faded away.

# Chapter Fifteen

Cat and the hellhound materialized in the weird graveyard where she'd started this bizarre journey.

Damn Hades! She eyed the mausoleums that corresponded with the five Rings, but even as she zeroed in on the one she'd originally entered that went to the 5th Ring where the battle was going down, the stupid hellhound got in her way. It even snarled at her.

"You're an asshole," she snapped.

It cocked its big head, raised its pointy ears, and looked at her as if it was expecting her to throw a stick or something. Then it burped. And dear God, what had the thing eaten today? She tried not to gag as she turned around and searched the wall for the opening to Azagoth's realm. Yes, she knew it was locked, but it couldn't hurt to try. It wasn't as if she had anything better to do, since clearly, the gassy hellhound wasn't going to let her go back to the 5th Ring.

*Hurry, Hades.*

His kiss still felt warm on her lips. Her skin still burned from his touch. She missed him, and they'd only been apart for a couple of minutes. What would happen when—and if—she finally got out of here? How could she deal with knowing he was just a doorway away?

Maybe it would be better if she got to go back to Heaven. He wouldn't be a temptation to her anymore. And besides, being accepted back into Heaven meant her family would take her back, right? Her friends would forgive her. She could forget the terrible things they'd said as she'd been dragged to the chopping block.

*Traitor.*

*Satan's whore.*

*You're no daughter of mine.*
*You sicken me.*

Yes, she could forget. With enough demon bloodwine, anyway.

An electric tingle charged the air, and the hairs on the back of her neck stood up. She pivoted around as Cerberus materialized, his black fur shiny from blood, one of his massive jaws clenched around a broken, bleeding human.

And dangling limply from the second set of jaws was Hades.

Oh, shit! She sprinted to the giant hellhound, who dropped both bodies to the ground. Sinking to her knees, she gathered Hades's lifeless body in her arms.

"Hades? Hades!" She shook him, but there was nothing. He wasn't even breathing. How could this be? How could he be dead? He couldn't be, right?

"He's only mostly dead."

She wrenched her head around to see Azagoth striding toward them, a trail of *griminions* on his heels.

"M-mostly dead?"

"Haven't you ever seen *The Princess Bride?*"

It took her a second to realize he was making a joke. Mr. Serious, the Grim Fucking Reaper, was *joking*.

The opening in the wall must lead to an alternate reality.

The *griminions* gathered up the human and scurried back through the doorway where Lilliana was waiting.

"Come on," she called out. "Leave Hades to Azagoth."

Cat hesitated, and when Azagoth barked out a curt, "Go," some secret, dark part of her rebelled. She'd just spent what was likely days in a hell dimension with a male who wanted her, a male she wanted, and the person who was keeping them apart wanted her to leave.

Screw that.

She held Hades tighter and boldly met Azagoth's gaze. "I'm staying."

Azagoth's eyes glittered, but his voice was calm. "What I'm about to do won't work if I'm not alone with him, so if you want him to live, you'll go."

Lilliana held out her hand. "Trust him."

Swallowing dryly, Cat nodded. Very gently, she eased Hades's head onto the ground, stroked her hand over his hair, and said a silent good-bye.

Why was this so hard?

"Azagoth," she croaked. "The human and I…the demons enchanted us, and unless it's broken—"

He cut her off with a brisk hand gesture. "Whatever was done to you will lose its power when you leave the Inner Sanctum. So go. *Now.*"

Sensing he'd reached the limits of his patience with her, she reluctantly shoved to her feet. She managed to keep it together until she was inside Azagoth's office. The moment the door closed, she started bawling, and Lilliana pulled her into a hug.

"I'm so glad you're okay," Lilliana said, and was she crying too? "I knew something was wrong days ago, and then when we tried to operate the doorway to the Inner Sanctum and it wouldn't work, we feared the worst." She pulled back just enough to eye Cat, as if making sure it was really her, and then she hugged her again. And yes, she was crying.

"I'm sorry," she murmured into Lilliana's shoulder. "I screwed up, and when I tried to fix it, I only made things worse."

"It's okay," Lilliana said. "We can hash it out later." She wrapped her arm around Cat's shoulders and guided her toward the door. "Let's get you cleaned up and fed. You must be exhausted."

Cat cranked her head around to the closed portal door. "But Hades—"

"There's nothing you can do for him. Azagoth will update us when he can."

Cat wanted to argue, to rail against being led away, but Lilliana was right. "What about the human?" she asked as they walked toward her quarters. "What happened to him?"

"The *griminions* took him to the human realm where he'll be met by angels and escorted to Heaven."

Good. When most humans died, their souls crossed over to the Other Side on their own, but this poor guy had gone through the worst nightmare imaginable, and if anyone deserved a Heavenly escort, it was him. He'd definitely be sent to a Special Care Unit where humans who died as a result of trauma went to allow them time to adjust. Cat had a feeling he'd need an eternity. She just wished she could do more for him.

Cat was so lost in guilt and worry about Hades that she barely noticed when they arrived at her small apartment. The fragrance of her homemade crisp apple potpourri snapped her out of her daze, and she wasted no time in showering off the remains of the Inner Sanctum. She tried not to think about the fact that Hades was part of that. Gone was the smoky scent of him on her skin. Gone was his touch. His kisses.

She tried not to cry again as she dried off and dressed.

When she was finished, Lilliana was waiting with a tray of food and a pot of hot tea.

"Thank you," Cat said as she took a seat. The food looked amazing, but she couldn't eat. Not until she knew Hades was okay. "It's weird to have *you* serve *me*."

"It's what friends do," Lilliana said. "Also, Azagoth sent word that Hades is fine." Cat nearly slid off her chair in relief. "Like he said, Hades was only mostly dead." She grinned. "I've made Azagoth watch *The Princess Bride* about a million times now. He bitches and moans, but he laughs every time."

*That* was hard to imagine. "What does 'mostly' dead mean?"

"It means that Hades was killed, but *griminions* grabbed his soul and brought it straight to Azagoth." Lilliana shoved a cup of tea at Cat. "If Azagoth can get a soul to a body fast enough, he can sort of...reinstall and jumpstart." At what must have been Cat's expression of amazement, Lilliana nodded. "Yeah, I didn't know about that until today, either." She propped her elbows on the table and leaned in, her amber eyes glowing with curiosity. "So. What's going on between you and Hades?"

Cat wasn't going to bother asking how Lilliana knew. It was probably written all over her face. She stalled for time though, sipping her tea until Lilliana tapped her fingers impatiently on the table.

"Nothing," Cat finally sighed. "There's absolutely nothing going on with Hades." Saying those words made her heart hurt far more than she would ever have suspected.

"Why? Doesn't he share your feelings?"

"That's not the problem." Man, she was tired. She shuffled to the bed and sank down on the edge of the mattress. "The problem is your mate."

Lilliana's hand froze as she reached for a grape on the platter of food. "What do you mean?"

"You should probably ask him." Cat's lids grew heavy, and she felt herself sway. "Why am I so sleepy?"

"The tea." Lilliana helped ease Cat back on the bed. "It's made from Sora root. It'll help you rest."

Rest would be good. Maybe in her dreams she and Hades could finally be together.

* * * *

The thing about dying was that it made a guy think about his life. What he'd done with it. What he could potentially do with it in the future. And as an immortal, Hades's future could be really long. And really lonely.

The thought of living one more day the way he'd lived the last five thousand years made him want to throw up as he prowled the length of his crypt until he swore the soles of his boots cried out for mercy.

Azagoth had left him hours ago with all kinds of assurances that Cat wouldn't be harshly punished for what she'd done. But Azagoth's idea of "harsh" was a lot different from Hades's. Well, not usually, but for Cat, definitely.

Hades just hoped Azagoth hadn't suspected that anything had gone on between them. Technically, Hades hadn't gone against Azagoth's orders, but the Grim Reaper wasn't a fan of technicalities. And if he did anything to punish Cat for what Hades had done, Hades would fight that bastard until he was too dead to fix.

Snarling, Hades threw his fist into the wall. Never, not in his entire life, had he felt this way about a female. Hell, he hadn't felt this way about anything. Oh, he'd always been passionate about meting out justice, but this was a different kind of passion. This was an all-consuming desire to be with someone. To be something better *for* that someone.

He hadn't known Cat for long, but in their brief time together, he'd shared things he'd always kept private. He'd given comfort and had been comforted. He'd wanted, and he'd been wanted back.

*She wants to go back to Heaven, idiot.*

Yeah, then there was that. The chances of going back were extremely slim, given that in all of angelic existence, only a handful of fallen angels had been offered the opportunity. But just the fact that she wanted to go was troubling.

Oh, he understood. Who would choose to live in the grim darkness of the underworld when they could flit around in light and luxury? But dammit, Cat was wanted down here. Could he make her see that?

Closing his eyes, he braced his forehead on the cool stone wall he'd just punched. Pain wracked him and not just because he'd broken bones in his hand and they were knitting together with agonizing speed. That pain was nothing compared to the ache in his heart.

He needed to be with Cat, but how? He supposed he could try reasoning with Azagoth. Sometimes the guy wasn't completely unbending. Especially now that he had Lilliana. She'd leveled him out, had given him a new perspective on life and relationships.

But would it be enough?

Because one thing was certain. If Hades couldn't have Cat in his life, then Azagoth had saved it for nothing.

# Chapter Sixteen

Cat dreamed of Hades.

It was so real, so sexy, that when she woke, she was both heartbroken to find herself alone in bed and turned on by the things they'd done in her dream. She let her hand drift down her stomach, her mind clinging to the images that had played in her head like an erotic movie. She could almost feel the lash of his tongue between her legs as her fingers dipped beneath the fabric of her panties.

Oh, yes. If she couldn't have him right now, in her bed, she could at least—

Someone knocked on the door, and then Lilliana's voice filtered through the thick wood. "Cat? Are you awake?"

Cat groaned. "No."

Lilliana's soft chuckle drifted into the room. "Azagoth wants to see you in his library."

A cold fist of *oh shit* squeezed her heart, and so much for her libido. It was more dead than Hades had been yesterday.

"I'll be right there," she called out.

It took her less than five minutes to dress in a pair of cut-off shorts and a tank top—she wanted as much skin exposed as possible in hopes that she could sense Azagoth's level of anger in the form of evil. Not that knowing would help her any, but it could at least mentally prepare her for disintegration or something.

Gut churning, she hurried to his library, finding it empty. She took a seat in one of the plush leather chairs, and just as she settled in, Azagoth entered.

She trembled uncontrollably as he took a seat. "Hades told me what happened," he said, getting right to it. "I know that letting the unauthorized souls into the Inner Sanctum was an accident. What I don't know is why you didn't tell me when it first happened. We could have prevented all of this."

"I know," she whispered. She tucked her hands between her knees as if that would stop them from shaking. It didn't. "I should have. But I was afraid. I thought I could fix it on my own, but then I got trapped and couldn't get back...it was all a big mistake."

One dark eyebrow shot up. "A *mistake?* It was a colossal fuckup that could have caused destruction on a global scale. And after the recent near-Apocalypse, having millions of demonic spirits loose in the human world would have damned near started another one."

Her eyes burned, and shame in the form of tears ran down her cheeks. "Are you going to kill me?" Or worse, give her a place of honor in his Hall of Souls, where she'd scream forever inside a frozen body. She wasn't going to ask about that, though. No sense in giving him any ideas.

Azagoth gaped. "Kill you? Why would you think I'd kill you?"

Was he kidding? "You're sort of known for not giving second chances. And for disintegrating people who piss you off."

He appeared to consider that. Finally, he nodded. "True. I've never denied that I'm a monster." He jammed a hand through his ebony hair and sat back in the chair, his emerald eyes unreadable as he took her in. "You're a terrible housekeeper, Cat. You're always breaking and misplacing things, and I doubt you even know what a vacuum cleaner is—"

"I'll do better," she swore. "I'll try harder and work longer hours. Please don't—"

"Let me finish," he broke in. "Like I said, you're a terrible housekeeper. But you're an excellent cook. Zhubaal and Lilliana have watched you with the Unfallen, and they both agree that you're also a great teacher. You're eager and enthusiastic, and I don't think I've ever seen anyone try as hard as you do to get things right. It's that quality that led you to fix the mistake you made by letting the human into the Inner Sanctum. I admire your determination, and I like having you around. So no, I won't kill you. Besides," he muttered, "Lilliana would mount my head on a pike if I did that."

Cat sat, stunned. He admired her? Liked having her around? Even more unbelievable, the Grim Reaper was *afraid* of Lilliana. "I-

—I don't understand. What are you going to do to me?"

"Nothing. I think you've punished yourself far more than I ever could." He smiled, barely, but for him, that was huge. "I can hire someone else to clean if you'd rather do other work in Sheoulgra. Just let Lilliana know, and she'll arrange it."

Relief flooded her in such a powerful wave that she nearly fell out of her chair. She could barely function as Azagoth came to his feet in a smooth surge. "I'm glad you're back, Cataclysm. Lilliana was inconsolable."

Inconsolable? Warmth joined the flood of relief. Lilliana truly cared about her. Oh, Cat had had friends in Heaven, but no one had worried about her. Okay, sure, they didn't worry because Heaven was a pretty safe place, but even when she'd gone to work with Gethel, no one had expressed concern. When she'd been found guilty of colluding with a traitor in order to start the Apocalypse, her friends and family had been sad, angry, and embarrassed, but to say that they'd been distraught or inconsolable would be a huge overstatement.

"Thank you," she said, her voice thick with emotion. "But before you go, can I ask you something?"

He gave a clipped nod. "Ask."

She cleared her throat, more to buy a little time than to get the sappy emotion out of her voice. "I want something from you." Azagoth cocked a dark eyebrow, and she revised her statement. "I mean, I would like something from you."

"And what's that?"

"Let Hades have some furniture."

Clearly, Azagoth hadn't expected that because the other eyebrow joined the first. "Furniture?"

"He's been sleeping on a hard-ass slab of stone and using scraps of who knows what for other furniture. He made his own playing cards from bits of wood."

"So?"

She shoved to her feet, ready to go toe-to-toe with him over this. Hades deserved as much. "Don't you think he's been punished enough?"

"You know what he did, yes? You know he slaughtered my son?"

"I'm aware," she said gently...but firmly. "I know that must be painful for you. But I'm also aware that he's been paying for that for thousands of years."

Crossing his arms over his broad chest, Azagoth studied her. His green eyes burned right through her, and she wondered what he was searching for. "He wouldn't ask for these things. So why are you?"

"Because it's the right thing to do."

"Is that all?" he asked, and her stomach dropped to her feet. *He knew.*

"I care for him," she admitted. "And he deserves better—"

"Than how I'm treating him?"

Oh, hell, no, she wasn't falling into *that* trap. "Better than how he currently lives."

When Azagoth smiled, she let out the breath she didn't realize she'd been holding. "Fine. He can have whatever he wants for his home."

She almost pointed out that his home was a damned crypt, but she figured that would be pushing it. So for today, she accepted the victory.

But she wasn't done. Hades had fought for her, and now it was time for her to do the same for him.

First, though, she had someone to see.

# Chapter Seventeen

"Can I talk to you?"

Cat stood in the doorway of Zhubaal's office in the Unfallen dorms, her stomach churning a little. She really didn't want to be having this conversation, but curiosity had always been her downfall. Like a real cat.

Zhubaal had been gazing out the window at the courtyard below where several Unfallen were playing a game of volleyball, but now he turned to her, his handsome face a mask of indifference. "About what?"

"I want to know why, ah..." Man, this was awkward. "That day, in your chambers..."

Leaning against the windowsill, he crossed his booted feet at the ankles and hooked his thumbs in his jeans' pockets. "You want to know why I refused sex with you."

Her cheeks heated. That had been a seriously humiliating thing. "Yes. Did I do something wrong?"

"You didn't do anything wrong. I had my reasons."

She probably shouldn't ask, but... "Can you tell me those reasons?"

He stood there for a long time, his expression stony, his mouth little more than a grim slash. Finally, when it became clear that he wasn't going to say anything, she shook her head and started to turn away.

"It's okay," she said. "I had no right to ask."

She headed down the hall, made it about ten steps when he said, "I'm waiting for someone."

Oh. She pivoted around to him as he stood just outside his office door. "Someone you know? You have a lover? A mate?"

He averted his gaze, and she realized that in all the months she'd known him, this was the first time he'd shown any vulnerability. "Not exactly."

Not wanting to ruin the moment, she took a few slow, careful steps toward him, approaching the way she might a feral dog. "Did…did Azagoth warn you to stay away from me?"

"No."

That seemed strange, given that he'd read Hades the riot act. "Why not?"

Gaze still locked on the floor, he replied, "Because he knows about my vow."

"What vow?"

"That," he said, his head snapping up, "is none of your business.

Touchy. But now she was curious. What kind of vow? She recalled his interactions with the resident Unfallen and all the visitors to the realm and realized that she'd never once seen Zhubaal with a female.

"Are you gay?"

He snorted. "Hardly."

Come to think of it, she'd never seen him with a male, either. So what was his deal? He was waiting for someone…someone specific? Was his vow—

She inhaled sharply. "You…you're a virgin, aren't you? You rejected me out of honor."

His gaze narrowed, and his lips twisted into a nasty sneer. "Do not confuse my lack of sexual experience with innocence or kindness, and especially not honor. Not when you tried to use me to rid yourself of your own virginity."

"I didn't know. I'm sorry. I'll just go now. But Zhubaal…I hope you find whoever it is you're waiting for."

As she hurried away, she swore she heard a soft, "I hope so, too."

\* \* \* \*

Zhubaal watched Cat disappear around a corner, his heart heavy, his body numb. She had been his single moment of weakness, the only one in nearly a century.

It had been ninety-eight years since his beloved angel, Laura, had been cast out of Heaven. Ninety-eight years of searching for her in Sheoul and getting his own Heavenly boot in the ass in the process.

Cat had come to him in a moment of weakness, on a day when he'd despaired that he'd never find Laura. But even as he'd kissed Cat, touched her, started to undress her, Laura had filled his thoughts.

As young angels, he and Laura had made a blood-pact to be each other's firsts, and he'd kept that vow, even after she lost her wings. He'd searched for her, eventually losing his own wings, but still, he remained faithful. And then, even after he discovered that she'd been slaughtered by an angel, he'd held onto that pact like a toddler with his comfy blankie. After all, her soul had been sent to Sheoul-gra, and he'd figured he could find her there, even if he had to get himself killed to do it.

At least they'd have been together in the Inner Sanctum.

But fate had intervened in the form of Azagoth, who had needed a new assistant, which gave Zhubaal access to privileged information about the residents of the Inner Sanctum.

Then fate threw him a curve ball.

He was too late.

Laura had, indeed, been a resident of the Inner Sanctum's 1st Ring. Until Azagoth reincarnated her thirty years ago.

Pain stabbed Zhubaal in the chest. His Laura was out there somewhere. She was a different person with a different name, but she was still his, and he wouldn't break his vow until he found her.

Unfortunately, he was now bound to Azagoth with a vow just as binding as the one he'd made with Laura. He could leave Sheoul-gra, but only for a few hours at a time, which made searching for Laura—or whatever name she went by now— next to impossible. Especially since Azagoth refused to give any specifics regarding her status, her parents, or even her species.

As a fallen angel, she should have been born only to a fallen angel to become either *emim* or *vyrm*, but Z had learned long ago that there were very few rules that couldn't be broken. For all he knew, his Laura could be feeding on offal and lurking in garbage piles as a Slogthu demon.

The big question was whether or not he'd recognize her. Surely their bond had been strong enough that he could see his Laura in whoever she'd become. And if she'd had the rare good luck of retaining her soul-memory, she could remember bits of her previous life. If so, *she* might even be searching for *him*.

Sighing, he went back inside his office, but he didn't feel like working anymore. He wanted to be out in the world, scouring the realms for Laura. He was a fool and he knew it, but dammit, he'd made a vow, and even if he couldn't have the angel he'd fallen in love with, he wasn't going to break the pact with someone he didn't love. He'd hurt Cat, and he felt a little bad about that, but he hadn't loved her. Cat deserved better. Laura deserved better.

He wasn't sure what he deserved, but he knew what he wanted.

He was just losing faith that he'd ever get it.

# Chapter Eighteen

Cat spent the next two days plotting ways to convince Azagoth to lighten up on Hades. Lilliana had volunteered to help, and Cat gladly took her up on her offer. The trick, Lilliana said, would be to make him think it was his idea. As Cat had suspected, he could be incredibly thick-skulled when it came to certain things, like offering second chances.

She opened the door to her apartment, intent on paying Lilliana a visit. But instead of facing an empty hall, she found herself standing mere inches away from Hades. Heart pounding with surprise and excitement, she stared.

"Hades," she gasped. God, he looked good, so good he stole her breath. Wearing nothing but form-fitting, color-shifting pants and black boots, he filled the doorway, his massive shoulders nearly touching the doorframe. "What are you doing here? You'll get in trouble—"

He was on her in an instant. His mouth came down on hers as he swept her into his arms, crushing her against him. His hand came up to tangle in her hair, holding her in place for the erotic assault. Forbidden, shivery excitement shot through her, and her core went molten.

"I don't care," he said against her lips. "I need you. I *burn* for you."

She moaned, her heart soaring at his words as he pushed her toward the bed. But as her knees hit the mattress and they both fell onto the soft covers, she wedged her hands between them and pushed him off.

"I can't," she said, and oh, how it hurt to say that. "I can't watch you suffer because of me."

Hades cupped her cheek in his warm palm. "I was going to go

to Azagoth first, but I know him. He'll say no."

"All the more reason to not do this." She heard the sound of the plea in her voice, the weakness in the face of Hades's desire. She needed to be stronger, but she wanted him so badly she shook with the force of it.

He leaned forward and brushed his lips across hers in a feathery, tender kiss. "All the more reason to do it. How does that old saying go? Better to seek forgiveness than ask permission from some asshole who's going to tell you no?"

Damn him, this wasn't funny. "Hades—"

"Shh." He silenced her with another kiss. This one deeper. Harder. "Just this once, Cat," he murmured. "I need this to hold onto when I'm alone at night."

She might have argued some more. She might have shoved him away. She might have done a lot of things if he hadn't slid his thick thigh between her legs as he untied her corset and freed her breasts. If he hadn't dipped his head to take one aching nipple into his mouth.

"Hades," she moaned.

He opened his mouth fully over her breast, his hot breath flowing over her skin as he worked the buttons of her jeans. His tongue teased her as he dragged it low, under the swell of her breast before laving attention on the other one.

Against her thigh, she felt his immense arousal pressing into her, a hot, unyielding presence that she'd never felt in the one place she needed it to be. Arching, she twisted so his erection settled between her legs, but her damned jeans and his pants—

As if Hades was thinking the same thing, he reared up and made fast work of removing her pants. "I love that you don't wear shoes," he said, his voice all breathless and needy. "Nothing to catch your jeans on."

He tossed them to the floor, kicked off his boots, and then stripped away his own clothing, leaving him beautifully, gloriously, naked. His cock jutted upward from the plump sac between his legs, the broad head glistening at the tip. Unbidden, her hand reached out, but he seized her wrists and pinned them over her head as he stretched his body over hers.

"Not yet," he said as he nuzzled her neck. "If you touch me,

I'm a goner. Embarrassing, but true."

Okay, she'd let him off the hook. For now. But later, she wanted to touch him. Smell him. Taste him. She had a lot to learn, and she was going to use whatever time they had wisely.

"There you go," he murmured. "Relax. Close your eyes. I'll make this good for you."

Relax, huh? It was weird how her body felt wound tight and liquid at the same time. In the dark behind her eyelids, she imagined the expression on his face as he kissed his way down her body.

His tongue circled her navel, and the tightness ramped up a notch. Anticipation made her squirm, but he put a lid on that quick, clamping down on her hips to force her into blissful submission. Her limited ability to move jacked up the intensity of every sensation until she was clawing at the bedspread and silently begging him to make her come.

But no, Hades was indeed a master of torture, and he took his time scooting lower, his tongue trailing along her abdomen and skimming her mound. She jerked upward, her body instinctively following his mouth as he kissed the crease of her leg.

"You okay?" His voice was a deep, sexy growl that sent stabs of pleasure shooting through every nerve ending.

"Uh-huh," was all she could manage.

He chuckled as he spread her legs and settled between them. The brush of his hair against the sensitive skin of her inner thighs made her hiss in pleasure, and then that soft, prickly Mohawk shifted, finding her center. She moaned as Hades bobbed his head up and down between her legs.

"Oh...my," she breathed. "How...naughty."

He nodded, sending a silky caress over her sex. "There is no part of me that can't bring you pleasure," he purred, the vibration adding to the amazing sensations that cascaded over her in an erotic wave.

His hands slid up and down her legs, circling her ankles and tickling her calves as he brushed his hair over her sex in slow, decadent sweeps. Tension built, a writhing knot of need that grew hotter with every erotic bob of his head. She needed more, and he knew because his head came up and his tongue came out and her eyes went wide when she realized what he was about to do.

"Yes, please," she whispered.

With a raw, erotic curse, he spread her with his thumbs and dipped his head. His mouth met her core, engulfing her in heat as his hot breath fanned the flames. She cried out at the first tentative touch of his tongue. The tip flicked whisper-light over her oh-so-ready knot of nerves before he used the flat of his tongue to lick all of her at once, from core to clit.

She fell back with a strangled moan and drove her fingers through his silky hair to hold him there, to keep him doing exactly what he was doing so perfectly. He lapped at her, starting with long, lazy licks before changing up and swirling his tongue between her folds. But when he pushed his tongue inside her and curled it firmly as he pulled back, she bucked so hard he had to pin her with his hands on her thighs so he could do it again.

Relentlessly, he drove his tongue inside her and licked his way back out, over and over, until the steam building up inside her exploded. The orgasm he'd given her in the shower had been amazing, but this...this made her not only see stars, but join them. The supernova of ecstasy sent her hurtling into the heavens—where she'd never felt like this.

The pleasure rolled over her in great waves, and just when she thought it was over, Hades did something with his fingers and tongue that sent her spiraling out of control again. She heard a distant shout...his name. She'd screamed his name...

Somewhere deep inside her it occurred to her that someone might have heard, but as Hades brought her back to Earth with a series of gentle, slow licks, the danger they faced slipped away until all that was left was the big male prowling back up her body, his lips glistening, his eyes smoldering with the promise that there was more to come.

* * * *

Hades had never in his entire life been this turned on. As an angel, he'd had a couple of sex partners, but he'd been overeager and underexperienced. The encounters had been nice, but all these years later, he could barely remember them.

As a fallen angel, he hadn't had much opportunity to get down and dirty, but when he had, he'd taken advantage of it. The rare times when Azagoth allowed him out of Sheoul-gra, he'd hit every succubus he could find, visited every demon pleasure palace he could get to in his allotted time.

He'd learned a few things, for sure, but one thing he'd never learned was to care. To take the time to enjoy a female with not only his body, but his mind and soul. Maybe because he'd always known he couldn't get attached to anyone, so he'd kept his distance, used jokes and a carefree attitude to breeze through a one-hour stand.

But Cat changed all that. She'd wormed her way into his heart like a dire leech, and all he could do was hope she'd drain him.

Bracing himself on his fists, he looked down at her as she lay panting, her face flushed, her lips parted to reveal just a hint of pearly teeth and tiny, pointed fangs. As the tip of his cock prodded her wet opening, she gasped and rolled her hips, inviting him in.

"I've never done this before," she said. There was no shyness, no self-consciousness, just a plain and simple fact that left him speechless for a second.

"But...Zhubaal," he finally blurted.

She shook her head, making her hair shift in shiny red waves on the pale yellow bedspread. "Nothing happened."

Oh, great, so he'd been a jealous jackass for nothing. It was probably a good thing he hadn't given in to his desire to rip Zhubaal's head off and shove it up his ass every time he saw him, too.

Hades looked into her gorgeous, guileless eyes, loving that she was trusting him to be her first. Pride swelled, but close on its heels was shame. This might be the only time they had, and to take the gift of her virginity, knowing they might never again—

"Knock it off." She dug her nails into his shoulder, the little pricks of pain snapping him out of his train of thought. "I can see your mind working, and I know what you're thinking. I'm capable of making my own decisions, and even if we can't be together again, I want to always have this, same as you."

Ah, damn, she was a gift. This was going to be worth anything Azagoth put him through as punishment. Anything.

Reaching between them, he gripped his cock to guide it inside her, but once again, she clawed him. "Wait. I want to..." She trailed off, a burst of pink blooming in her cheeks. "I want to taste you."

At those words, his cock damned near humiliated him. It jerked in his hand, all, *yes, please, and do it now.*

"Okay," he said, proud of how he didn't sound completely strangled with lust, "but only for a second. You've got me way too worked up."

Her cocky grin made him regret agreeing to this as he climbed up her body and kneeled next to her head. He barely had time to push his unruly erection down when she lifted her mouth to it and flicked her tongue over the bead of pre-come at the tip. He hissed at the contact, hissed louder when she did it again.

And then the crazy little angel swallowed his cock from the head to the base and sucked like she'd been born to do this. A sound somewhere between a shout and a bark escaped him as she slid her mouth upward and swirled her tongue around the crown. Holy hell, she was no tentative kitten lapping at a bowl of milk. This was a she-tiger with an appetite for man, and—

He pulled back and squeezed his cock so hard he lost his sight for a heartbeat. A hot climax pulsed in his balls and his shaft, and there was no way he was blowing down her throat. He needed to be skin-on-skin with her, body to body, sex to sex.

For the first orgasm, anyway.

"Not nice," he scolded, but she just gave him a wide-eyed doe look he might have bought if he hadn't just experienced the rabid carnivore she really was.

"I thought I was being *very* nice." She batted her eyes, still playing innocent, which only made his cock throb harder.

Time to teach her a lesson.

In a quick motion, he flipped her onto her belly and dove between her legs again, lifting her hips for prime access as he stabbed his tongue into her dripping sex. She cried out in surprise and pleasure as he licked her, this time not even trying to be gentle. He growled against her core, nibbling and feasting as he ground his cock against the mattress to keep the bastard happy.

Then, just as her cries and breaths signaled that she was on the edge, he rolled her again. Her legs flopped open, spreading that beautiful pink flesh wide for him. He wanted to lick her some more, but the foreplay had set him on fire, and the bed-humping had fanned the flames.

Time to burn.

He positioned himself between her thighs and pushed against her opening. She arched, giving him even more access, and his head slid into her warmth.

"Tight," he groaned. "Ah, damn, you're tight." Her eyes caught his, held them as he pushed in a little more. Like many angels, she didn't seem to have a barrier, but the invasion still couldn't be comfortable. "Does it hurt?"

"No," she breathed. "It just feels...right."

She couldn't have said anything better. Throwing back his head, he thrust deep. At her cry, he panicked, but the expression on her face wasn't pain. It was bliss. She was so ready, so eager, and he was so damned lucky.

He pulled nearly free of her body and slid back in, keeping an eye on her, gauging her reactions in case he hurt or frightened her, but she was gloriously free of inhibition, fear, or discomfort.

"More," she begged. "Don't hold back. I want it *all*."

It was the same strength of character she'd exhibited in the Inner Sanctum, the drive to get what she wanted at all costs, and this time, he was going to give it to her.

Dropping to his elbows, he kissed her as he pumped between her legs, his thrusts growing faster and harder as his climax began to tingle at the base of his spine. The wet slap of their bodies grew more furious as she clung to him, wrapping her legs around his waist with more strength than he'd imagined she had in her entire body.

She met him thrust for thrust, both with her hips and her tongue. He heard the bed banging against the wall and sliding across the floor with the fury of their joining, and shit, he was close, so close that when she came, all he could do was hold on for the ride.

Her sex rippled along his shaft, wringing the climax from him in long bursts that bordered on agony. Sweet, sweet agony. He couldn't think, couldn't see as he came once, then twice, the second sending his entire body into spasms of ecstasy. He filled her, but she filled him, too, with emotion he'd never known.

And as he collapsed on top of her, his skin coated in sweat, his lungs struggling to pull in enough air, he wondered if he should tell her how he felt about her. Would she believe he was capable of love? He hadn't thought so, but what else could explain his inability to stop thinking about her? What else could explain his willingness to disobey Azagoth? Would it be fair to tell her he'd fallen hard for her?

They had, after all, only known each other for a short time. Worse, Azagoth might kill him.

And then, as if just thinking about the male was a curse, the door slammed open. The Grim Reaper burst inside, the whites of his eyes swallowed by inky black, swirly pools. Massive, leathery wings brushed the ceiling, but it was the set of ebony horns sprouting from his forehead and curling over the top of his skull, that filled Hades with dread. Azagoth only took out his horns when he was pissed.

Yep, Hades was dead. And this time, he had a feeling the "mostly" part wouldn't apply.

# Chapter Nineteen

This was a nightmare.

Terror winged its way through Cat as Azagoth strode into her little apartment, black horns jutting from the top of his skull. Lilliana had once said that when the horns came out, so did his temper.

Which was bad, considering that he did most of his killing while being perfectly calm. She didn't even want to *try* to imagine what he'd do while seriously pissed off.

She and Hades leaped off the bed, and while she scrambled for a robe, he very coolly pulled on his pants. Azagoth had the decency to avoid looking at her, but his eyes burned holes through Hades. Who, for his part, showed no emotion at all, although he did keep himself between her and Azagoth. It was sweet of him to want to protect her, but she had a feeling he was in far more danger than she was.

"Azagoth." Hades held his hands up in a placatory gesture, but Azagoth kept moving toward them in a slow, predatory gait. "This isn't—"

"Isn't what it looks like?" Azagoth's words, sounding as if they'd been dredged in smoke, were a dare, and Cat hoped Hades didn't take it.

"No," Hades said, standing his ground and looking completely unruffled. "It's exactly what it looks like. But it isn't Cat's fault. *I came to her.*"

Tugging her robe closed, Cat stepped next to Hades. "Please, Azagoth," she begged, and she'd go to her knees if she had to, "don't punish him. He saved my life."

Azagoth halted a few feet away, clenching and unclenching his fists at his sides. Claws at the tips of his fingers shredded his flesh, and blood began to drip from his hands. "And you felt grateful enough to sleep with him?"

"Of course not. This started before he saved me." Cat immediately realized her mistake when Hades groaned and Azagoth growled. Quickly, she added, "It was all my fault. He kept telling me he couldn't, and I kept...seducing him."

"You expect me to believe that?"

"It's the truth," she said, "so, yes."

Azagoth turned to Hades, and was it her imagination or had his horns receded a little? "And what have you got to say?"

"She's telling the truth. But..."

"But what?"

"But I could have resisted more. I chose not to." He took her hand. "I want her."

"I see." Azagoth scrubbed his palm over his face, leaving behind smears of blood like evil war paint. "Lilliana has made me soft," he muttered. He dropped his hand and studied each of them in turn before focusing his laser gaze on Hades. "Will you fight for her?"

Hades growled. "I would fight Revenant himself for her."

Azagoth's upper lip peeled back to reveal a set of huge fangs. "Would you fight me?"

"I'd rather not, but if forced to, yes."

The expression on Azagoth's face became stony, sending a chill down her spine. "Will you beg?"

Beg? What a strange question. But it seemed to get a rise out of Hades, because he stiffened. "I...have never...begged."

"I know."

Hades dropped to the floor so fast and hard his kneecaps cracked on the stone tile. "Please, Azagoth," he began, his gaze downcast, his hand clasped against his thighs. "I've served you well, but if you want me to do better, I will. If you want to torture me every day for the rest of my life, I'll gladly submit. All I ask is that you allow me to see Cat between sessions." He lifted his head, and she had to stifle a cry at the liquid filling his eyes. "I am sorry about your son. His death must sit on your heart like a bruise, and if I could heal it, I would. I can only keep trying to make it up to you, but without Cat, I don't know how long I can survive to do that.

Please, my lord, let me find the same happiness that you've found with Lilliana." His voice cracked with emotion. "*Please.*"

Cat lost it. Truly, hopelessly, lost it. Sobbing, she sank down next to Hades and wrapped herself around him, needing to comfort him as much as she needed comfort. Her heart ached and her throat closed, and her skin tingled with the sense of goodness that radiated from Hades. Right now, he wasn't a fallen angel who ruled a demon purgatory. Right now he was a male, in pain and vulnerable, whose intentions were truly pure.

"Yeah, yeah," Azagoth muttered. "Fine. Get up. You have my blessing. That wasn't so hard, was it?"

Cat nearly burst with happiness as Hades blinked up at Azagoth. "Holy shit, so that's all I had to do was beg for your forgiveness?"

"Yep."

"So I could have done that centuries ago?"

"Yep." Azagoth's voice took on a haunted quality that struck Cat right in the heart. "All I ever wanted from you…after enough pain, of course…was an apology for taking my son's life."

Cat's eyes watered anew as Hades swallowed hard. "I am truly sorry, Azagoth."

And that fast, Azagoth's appearance returned to normal, the blood gone, his eyes glinting like gems. "I know."

Then, in a move that left Cat speechless, he offered a hand to Hades. Clasping Cat's hand first, Hades reached out with the other and allowed Azagoth to bring them to their feet. The two males locked gazes for just an instant, but in that brief, intense moment, something passed between them. Something she could only describe as mutual respect, and by the time Azagoth stepped back, she knew that this was the beginning of a brand new relationship between the two.

Hades tugged Cat close. "You know, I'm glad I didn't beg sooner, because if I had, I wouldn't have Cat."

"Yeah, well," Azagoth said wryly, "you *did* have Cat, and let me tell you, everyone in Sheoul-gra knows it."

A hot blush spread over Cat's face. Now she knew how Azagoth had learned about them. As the blush worked its way down her body, Hades planted a kiss on the top of her head, and the blush turned instantly to fierce, uncontrollable desire.

"I think," she said, "that everyone is going to know it again."

Azagoth cringed. "I'm out of here." He paused. "Before I go, do either of you know why my Seth statue is fucking itself?"

Cat nearly choked on her own saliva, and Hades held his hands up in denial. "No idea what you're talking about."

"Really." Azagoth's dubious expression said he wasn't buying it. "So you have absolutely no idea who glued Seth's penis to his ass?"

"Nope." Hades slid his hand to Cat's butt and gave her a playful pinch. "Didn't you say you were leaving?"

Muttering obscenities, Azagoth hotfooted it out of the apartment, and Cat turned to Hades with a sly smile. "You are very naughty."

Hades's eyes glittered as he trailed a finger along her cleavage. "You think?"

"I know." She went up on her toes and brushed her lips over his. "What do you say? Should we show everyone why they need to invest in earplugs?"

Hades tore open her robe and tugged her to him. "Earplugs? Baby, we're gonna need to soundproof this room after what I'm going to do to you."

"And what," she said, as she cupped his swelling erection, "would that be?"

"Everything."

"Promise?"

He reached around and slid his fingers between her cheeks as he lowered his mouth to hers. "Promise."

As it turned out, Hades kept his promise. And as it also turned out, everyone knew it.

\* \* \* \*

"Hello, Cataclysm."

Cat yelped in surprise as she whirled around to face the newcomer who had flashed into the courtyard in front of Azagoth's manor. She'd just been on her way to the Unfallen dorms to help Lilliana set up a new training program after spending an entire day in bed with Hades, and if she hurried, she could get back in time to join him in the shower.

"Reaver," she breathed. He stood there next to the fountain, his angelic glow radiating around him. "It's good to see you again. Azagoth is—"

"I'm not here for Azagoth." His deep voice rumbled through every cell in her body. "I'm here for you."

Her heart skipped a beat. Then another. And another, until it felt as if the organ was nothing but a shriveled husk in her chest. What if he was here to finally punish her for her stupidity in helping Gethel conspire against him?

"Me?" she croaked. "Why?"

"Because your actions in preventing the escape of millions of evil souls has earned you a reward." He smiled, his blue eyes sparkling. "I'm here to give you your wings back."

She sucked in a harsh breath as relief and joy filled her with such happiness that her body vibrated. He wasn't here to destroy her! But...why not?

"I don't mean to sound ungrateful, but...surely you understand what I did to you and your family. You know my history with Gethel, yes?"

Dark shadows flashed in his eyes, and she instantly regretted bringing up the evil bitch who had tried to start the apocalypse. "I am very well aware of your role in Gethel's machinations. But I also know you didn't realize the depths of her depravity until it was too late." The shadows disappeared. "She's paying for what she did, and you've paid the price as well."

"I'm not sure I have." She looked down at her bare feet as if her fresh blue nail polish would help her out. "I haven't apologized to you, either. I'm so sorry, Reaver. I didn't know what Gethel was planning, but I knew it wasn't good. I tried to go to Raphael, and he swore he'd look into it, but—"

"He didn't."

She shook her head miserably. "No."

"That's because he was tangled up in a million different plots to overthrow Heaven and screw me over," Reaver said. "I've always thought your sentence was too harsh, but once I learned that it was Raphael who sentenced you, it made sense. He wanted you out of

Heaven because you knew too much."

"But I didn't know anything," she protested.

"I know. But he couldn't take any chances. Forcing your name on you was unnecessarily cruel, but not exactly a shock. He was, as one of my Seminus demon friends would say, a major dickmunch." He smirked. "Raphael's gotta be hating life right now."

No doubt. Thanks to Reaver and his brother Revenant, Raphael was sharing a ten by ten cage with Satan, Lucifer, and Gethel for the next thousand years. Wasn't long enough, in Cat's opinion.

A rabbit scampered across the courtyard. It might have been one that Reaver had brought to repopulate what had once been a dead realm. "So anyway," Reaver said after it disappeared under a bush, "you're forgiven. Come home, Cat. You'll even get your name back."

Once again, joy engulfed her, as if she'd been swallowed by the sun. The fact that Heaven wanted her back was all she'd wanted when she'd first arrived here, scared and lonely and full of regret. But now...now she was happy. Happier than she'd ever been in Heaven.

"Thank you, Reaver," she said. "But I'm afraid I'll have to turn down your offer."

One blond eyebrow shot up, but given that she'd just refused to get her wings and halo back, she thought he'd have been more surprised. "It's Hades, isn't it?"

Now she was the one who was surprised. "Ah...how did you know?"

"It makes sense." He cocked his head and looked at her with an intensity that made her feel positively naked. "Are you sure you want to stay here as an Unfallen? Your powers are muted, you're nearly as fragile as a human—"

"I'm sure. I don't need powers down here, and with people like Hades, Azagoth, Zhubaal, and Lilliana around me, I don't need to worry about my safety."

He nodded. "Cool. But know that if you change your mind, the offer will remain open as long as you don't do anything to betray Heaven or Earth. And you do understand that you could accept my offer and still be able to travel in the human and heavenly realms while living and working here in Sheoul-gra, yes?"

"I understand. But Hades resides in the Inner Sanctum, and as a fully haloed angel it would be far too dangerous for me to live there with him." She laid her hand on his forearm reassuringly but pulled it back before his Heavenly goodness burned her skin to ash. "Being Unfallen puts me at a serious disadvantage everywhere but here. Here, it's actually more protection than if I were an angel. I'm okay with it, Reaver. Really. Not everyone has to have badass superpowers to be something special."

"Can I at least give you the ability to choose your own name? Or give Nova back to you? It's a beautiful name."

A lump formed in her throat. That was the first time anyone had spoken her Heavenly name in months. It brought back memories, so many of them, both good and bad. But it was her past, not her future.

"Nah," she said. "I'm happy with who I am now. Raphael tried to shame me when he gave me my fallen angel name, but I won't let him do that anymore. I'll keep it to remind me to make wise choices."

"Then so be it." He pulled her into a brief embrace. "Be happy, Cataclysm."

Then he was gone, and she was holding empty air.

# Chapter Twenty

One month after moving in with Hades, their new "crypt" was finally finished.

Azagoth had completely removed all restrictions on Hades, and they now had a decent house that matched the ancient Greek style of the rest of Sheoul-gra. Unfortunately, Hades had been so busy meting out punishment to the demons who had participated in the uprising that he hadn't had much time to enjoy it.

She'd taken today off from her new job working with the Unfallen, and she was going to make Hades do the same. They needed some quality time together, and she had the most amazing picnic planned.

He was at the Rot, as usual, which, besides their home, was the only place she was allowed to go in the Inner Sanctum. He'd taken her once to Cloud Cuckoo Land so she could thank the demons who had loaned her and Hades their home, but he'd made it clear that it was far too dangerous to do it again.

She finished dressing in a cute violet and black plaid skirt and a black tank top and gave the little wooden dog on Hades's desk a stroke along its back and tail, laughing when it snapped at her. It was a silly little ritual she'd developed every time she left the house. Hades had promised to make her a tiny cat to match, but he'd see if he could enchant it to purr instead of bite.

Rubbing her belly in a futile attempt to quell the anxious flutters, she stepped into the portal and arrived at the Rot a heartbeat later. She hated this place, couldn't help but think of the spider room every time she was there.

Malonius was at the entrance, and he gave her directions to some sort of classroom in the prison's upper tower where Hades was supposed to be dealing with a group of unruly incubi. She could only imagine what kind of punishments would be doled out to sex demons.

She climbed the narrow, winding stone staircase and found Hades sitting on a stage before a horrified audience. As she entered through the door behind the stage, Hades spoke, reading from a book in his hands.

"Fill me with your filthy pee stick." He paused for dramatic effect. "And lick my lush, melon-like boobies."

She tripped over her own feet. Pee stick? Boobies? What the hell?

"Come on, boy," Hades drawled, his voice pitched high as he read from what was clearly a woman's point-of-view. "My old pussy needs some young meat."

Cat cleared her voice to announce her presence, although, really, it was more like choking. Hades looked over his shoulder, his face split in a wide grin.

"Baby! Hey, it's good to see you." He waggled his brows as he gave her outfit a once-over. "It's especially good to see you in that."

She looked out at the roomful of demons, all human in appearance, as they sat in their too-small chairs, their eyes wild, their faces pale. Clearly, they were miserable.

"What *are* you doing?"

Hades held up the book. "I'm reading bad porn to a captive audience."

"Bad porn? *Bad?* That's a compliment. Whatever it is you're reading is horrifying. Whoever wrote it should be roasted slowly over a bed of coals."

Hades's grin widened. "I like the way you think." He waggled his brows. "Wanna play with my pee stick?"

She did, but not until he stopped calling it a pee stick. "Is that an actual offer or are you just having fun saying 'pee stick'?"

"Tell you what," he said, bounding to his feet. "What do you say we head back to my place, and I'll whip us up a nice pot of mac and cheese—the good kind in the blue box—and you can tell me what you like to call dicks."

"Does this mean we're done?" someone called out from the audience. "Please?"

Hades snorted. "Stay put. I'll get a sub in here." He glanced at his watch. "You only have twenty days and three hours left of listening to atrocious porn, and then you can go back to being the perverts you are." He waved, and they groaned. "See ya."

"That was kind of cruel," Cat said as they headed toward the portal that would take them to the house.

"But funny." He threw his arm around her and planted a kiss on the top of her head. "So? What's up? Are you breaking me out of prison for something good?"

"Yup." They entered the portal, but instead of passing her hand over the symbol that would take them to his place, she took them to Azagoth's realm. As they stepped out into the receiving room off the kitchen, she explained. "We're having a picnic."

He scowled. "Here?"

"Hardly." Taking his hand, she led him through the mansion and outside to the portal that could whisk them to the human realm. Azagoth had released his restrictions on Hades's travel, but so far, Hades hadn't taken advantage of his newfound freedom. It was past time he did.

He kept silent until they arrived at a sunlit meadow surrounded by mountains and looking out over a vast, azure lake. A bald eagle cast a shadow on the water as it flew overhead in search of a meal, and somewhere in the forest, a coyote yipped.

"Crater Lake." He inhaled the fragrant air, a bouquet of pine and summer wildflowers. "It looks just like the picture."

She'd done a lot of scouting to find the exact location where the photo had been taken, and Reaver had escorted her to keep her out of danger. Heck, Reaver had even arranged for her parents to meet her here a couple of days ago. They'd been sorry for the way they'd treated her, although her father had still been a little cool. But then, he'd always been a bit stuffy.

They'd been horrified by the thought of their daughter hooking up with the Jailor of Souls, had tried to make her reconsider going back to Heaven, and when she refused, they'd promised an open line of communication. Even her brothers and sisters had agreed to contact her. It was far more than she ever would have hoped for.

"Come on." Squeezing Hades's hand, she led him to the bottle of wine and basket of fried chicken, potato salad, and fruit she'd laid out on a red and white checkered blanket. Thanks to Reaver and a little invisibility spell, animals had left everything alone.

Hades sank down on the blanket, extending one leg and propping up the other to rest one arm casually across his knee. He looked absolutely edible like that, more at ease than she'd ever seen him.

"I've never been on a picnic before," he said as he peeked into the basket.

"I know. You told me once." Kneeling next to him, she poured two glasses of red wine and handed one to him. "My coworkers and I used to do it all the time in Heaven. Everything is so beautiful that it makes you want to be out in nature, enjoying every minute of it."

His gaze dropped, and even his blue hair managed to look sad. "Do you miss it?" he asked quietly, as if worried about her answer. "You gave up so much to be with me."

"No," she said fiercely, reaching over to tip his chin up so she could look him directly in the eyes. "I would have given up far more if I'd gone."

"I love you, Cat," he whispered. "I don't know what I did to deserve you, but I hope you know that I'd do it all over again to be with you. Thousands of years of loneliness was worth every second you've been in my life."

Something caught in her chest. Tears stung her eyes. That was the first time he'd told her he loved her.

"I love you, too," she rasped. "I can't believe I ever thought that Sheoul-gra couldn't be my home. You were right. Home is where the people who want you are."

"Mmm." He looked at her from over the rim of his glass, his gaze heating, focusing. Holding her in place.

Very slowly, he set down the glass and shifted so he was on his hands and knees, prowling toward her like a tiger with prey in its sights. Excitement shot through her. Electric, shivery excitement.

"Do you want me?" He pushed her backward, lowering his body over hers.

"Yes," she hissed as he scraped his fangs over her jugular. "Oh, yes."

One hand slid beneath her skirt and found her wet and ready. "Then take me home."

With so much love she thought she might burst, she very happily welcomed him home.

# About Larissa Ione

Air Force veteran Larissa Ione traded in a career as a meteorologist to pursue her passion of writing. She has since published dozens of books, hit several bestseller lists, including the New York Times and USA Today, and has been nominated for a RITA award. She now spends her days in pajamas with her computer, strong coffee, and fictional worlds. She believes in celebrating everything, and would never be caught without a bottle of Champagne chilling in the fridge…just in case. After a dozen moves all over the country with her now-retired U.S. Coast Guard spouse, she is now settled in Wisconsin with her husband, her teenage son, a rescue cat named Vegas, and her very own hellhound, a King Shepherd named Hexe.

For more information about Larissa,
visit www.larissaione.com.

# Also from Larissa Ione

~ DEMONICA/LORDS OF DELIVERANCE SERIES ~
Pleasure Unbound (Book 1)
Desire Unchained (Book 2)
Passion Unleashed (Book 3)
Ecstasy Unveiled (Book 4)
Eternity Embraced ebook (Book 4.5) (NOVELLA)
Sin Undone August (Book 5)
Eternal Rider (Book 6)
Supernatural Anthology (Book 6.5) (NOVELLA)
Immortal Rider (Book 7)
Lethal Rider (Book 8)
Rogue Rider (Book 9)
REAVER (Book 10)
AZAGOTH (Book 10.5)
REVENANT (Book 11)
HADES (Book 11.5)

~ MOONBOUND CLAN VAMPIRES SERIES ~
Bound By Night (book 1)
Chained By Night (book 2)

# Base Instincts
A Demonica Story (M/M)
By Larissa Ione
Coming Late 2015

According to the news, the weather system bearing down on Damon Slake was a proven killer.

But then, Slake was also a killer, and he could guaran-damn-tee that he was far more lethal than a thunderstorm.

Rain and hail pelted him as he stood outside one of several secret entrances to Thirst, a vampire nightclub that operated in the shadows of a human goth hangout called The Velvet Chain. Like most upscale vamp clubs, this one catered to all otherworldly beings, as well as humans who were willing to give themselves up as a snack for those who fed on blood. And, like most upscale vamp clubs, this place even had a medical clinic. Reputation was everything, and no club owner wanted to deal with a bunch of human deaths from overfeeding, or demon deaths from a drunken bar fight.

Which was smart, especially now, when the recent near-apocalypse had revealed the demon world to humans, causing tension, fear, and chaos. Humans were now in extermination mode, while demons were dealing with some sort of political shakeup in Sheoul, the realm humans called Hell. Slake had no idea what was going on in Sheoul, and frankly, he didn't care. He had a job to do, and he always completed his tasks.

After a lot of time and effort, he'd tracked his prey here, and it hadn't been easy. The wily succubus had covered her tracks well over the last couple of decades, but Slake had a knack for ferreting out secrets, and as good as the female named Fayle was at hiding, Slake was better at finding.

He entered the dimly-lit club, his status as a demon providing him with the ability to enter through a doorway only supernatural creatures could see. Instantly, the blare of rock music, the stench of sweating, dancing people, and the electric, sensual energy of sin assailed him. If he hadn't been on the job, he'd revel in the club scene, would be scoping out potential partners to take home for the night.

Partners like that sexy-as-hell medic propped against the wall near the medical station, his gaze sweeping the crowd with the intensity of a battle-wise soldier in enemy territory. Even from across the room, Slake could see the alertness in the guy's green eyes and the readiness for anything in the subtle tautness of his body.

And what a body it was. His black uniform stretched tight across his shoulders and abs, the rolled sleeves revealing thickly-muscled arms made to pin his partner to a mattress.

Slake had no idea if the dude was into males, females, or both, but the guy practically oozed confidence and sex. The medic crossed his arms across his broad chest, giving Slake a prime view of a sleeve of tattoos winding from his fingers to where they disappeared beneath his uniform at his biceps and reappeared at the top of his collar. The pattern ended just below his jaw, although Slake couldn't make out the individual designs. Damn, Slake loved tats.

He wondered what species of demon the guy was. He wasn't human; Slake's ability to distinguish a blue human aura from an orangey-red demon one made that clear. Not that Slake was picky when it came to bed mates, but he drew the line at fucking any species of demon that rated a five on the Ufelskala scale of evil. Fours were bad enough, but with a five, you never knew whether or not your partner was going to kill you after you came.

Or *before* you came, for that matter.

Reluctantly tearing his attention away from the medic, Slake strode through the club, his eyes peeled for his target. There were approximately a million and a half females milling about, but none resembled the petite, black-haired Asian in the picture he'd been given two months ago by his boss at Dire & Dyre, the law firm that employed him as an Acquirer. Yup, if someone wanted something or someone, Slake was the one sent to acquire it.

Except this job was different. This job was the one that would determine the course of the rest of his life.

And the rest of his *after*life.

But hey, as his boss pointed out, it was *only* his *soul* on the line.

The jackass.

He spied an empty booth near a little-used exit to the sewers and made a beeline to it, growling at a burly green-skinned demon who tried to slip into the seat ahead of Slake. The demon cursed, but one look at Slake's arsenal of weapons peeking out from beneath his leather jacket gave the guy second thoughts. Probably third thoughts, too.

A waiter brought Slake a double whiskey, neat, and he settled in, hoping his prey would show her pretty face. In the meantime, though, he didn't see any harm in checking out the medic at the rear of the club a little more.

That male was something special. Even his coloring was perfect. Not too tan, but not pale, and given the guy's reddish hair, shorter in the back than in the front, Slake would bet that close up, there would be some freckles waiting for the caress of a tongue.

Slake's mouth watered at the thought, and he had to shift to make a little more room in his leathers, but he didn't let his lust distract him from his mission. No, not when success meant freedom…and failure meant kissing his his soul goodbye.

He downed half his drink and reached for his cell phone just as the thing vibrated in his coat pocket. The name that flashed on the text screen was exactly who he'd been wanting to hear from for days. Hoping for good news from his favorite underworld spy, he tapped out a message.

*Hey, Atrox, it's about time. Tell me you have an update on our prize.*

He waited an unbearably long time for the reply. Atrox's fat fingers and long claws weren't exactly compatible with touchscreen keyboards. The reptilian demon had to use his knuckles to type, which Slake had found to be funny…until lizard boy used those knuckles to knock Slake on his ass.

Finally, the phone beeped with Atrox's incoming text. *Got a lead. One of the dudes I grilled last night is a regular at Thirst. Said he's seen the succubus several times in the company of a male with red hair and a sleeve of tats on his right arm.*

Well, now. Slake looked up at the hot medic and grinned.

This assignment had just gotten interesting.

# Ravaged
An Eternal Guardians Novella
By Elisabeth Naughton

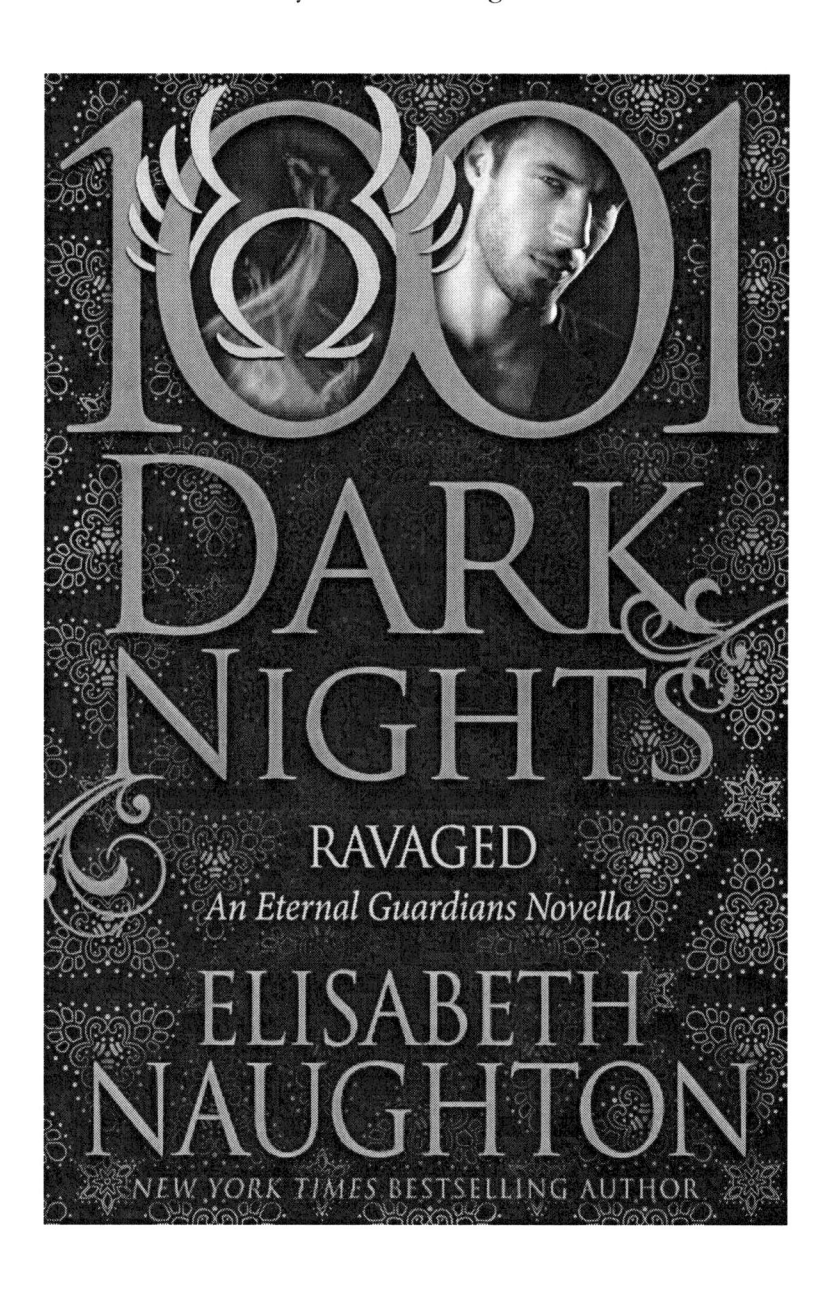

*"There will be killing till the score is paid."*
— Homer, *The Odyssey*

# Chapter One

Time was irrelevant on Olympus. Something Daphne was grateful for today.

The sun set low on the horizon behind the shimmering white marble of Zeus's palace as she lifted the magical bow and arrow all Sirens wielded, pulled the string back for the umpteenth time, and zeroed in on her target a hundred yards away. Holding her breath, she released the string. A sting echoed in her finger, and she jerked her hand back and winced as the arrow flew through the air toward the trunk of a tree carved into the face of the god of the Underworld.

A *thwack* echoed across the space. The arrow grazed Hades's right earlobe.

Daphne frowned. She'd been at this for three hours and still couldn't hit the stupid god anywhere deadly, let alone between the eyes where she was supposed to tag him.

"Better." Sappheire, Athena's right-hand Siren and the leader of Zeus's female warrior army, nodded at Daphne's side. "You keep practicing and you'll get there."

Daphne wasn't so sure. All Sirens went through rigorous training in a variety of different areas—combat, seduction, warfare, strategy—and she'd passed each section with high marks from her trainers. But she couldn't take her final Siren vows until she conquered the marksmanship exam. And at the moment, her aim wasn't even close to one-hundred percent, which was why she was out here now, on the training field behind Siren headquarters, working on her shot long after the other recruits had retired to the mess hall for dinner. So far she'd failed the test three times. Until she could hit a target repeatedly dead center—without injuring herself—she was SOL. Which meant her dream of being a full-fledged Siren kept hovering in the distance, just out of reach.

"That's a nice thought," she said, lowering her bow and shaking out her hand. "I'm not sure how realistic it is, though."

"Persistence will pay off." Sappheire's luxuriously sleek mane—a mixture of blonde and chestnut and ginger locks—swayed as she turned Daphne's way, and those brilliant blue eyes for which she was named sparkled. "If this is your calling, it'll happen. Just don't give up."

Dressed in form-fitting black pants, a tight, black, low-cut tank that showed off her cleavage and muscular arms, and kick-ass stiletto boots that elongated her legs, Sappheire pressed the button at the end of her bow, shrinking the weapon down to a six-inch metal bar. She'd lost the leather breastplate and arm guards she usually wore in the field, but she still looked as menacing as any warrior. And not for the first time, Daphne was glad this Siren had taken a liking to her instead of harassing her as she did some of the other recruits.

Slipping the weapon into her boot, Sappheire added, "Athena's been watching you."

Watching her fail? Daphne winced. She wasn't sure she needed to know that, not when she already felt like a major loser.

Daphne shrank her own weapon. She was dressed the same as Sappheire—tight black pants, fitted black tank, crazy high boots it had taken her years to learn to walk in—but where Sappheire wore the outfit with confidence and grace, Daphne still felt awkward in the take-notice-of-me-now getup. "Well, if nothing else, I'm sure she's entertained."

"Perhaps." Sappheire peered back toward the white painted building of Siren headquarters, less stately and ornate than the structures on Olympus, but still intimidating. "I think you're being summoned."

Daphne's gaze followed as she slid her bow into her boot, then focused on two figures standing on the back porch of the building. One she knew on first glance. The goddess Athena and head of the Siren Order flicked her curly chestnut locks over her shoulder and waved her hand in a come-this-way move. She was striking and gorgeous and every bit the goddess Daphne had imagined her to be as a child. But it was the other figure that made Daphne's pulse skip. The seven-foot tall, dark-haired god at Athena's side, commanding all with just his stately presence.

Zeus.

"Don't stand there dumbfounded, girl." Sappheire nudged Daphne toward the building. "The last thing you want to do is keep the king of the gods waiting. Go already."

Right. The king of the gods...

Swallowing hard, Daphne put one foot in front of the other and headed for the building. Behind her, the sun dipped below Zeus's palace until the sky above was nothing but a warm pink glow, but she didn't even notice. She was suddenly too scared that Athena and Zeus had finally figured out she wasn't Siren material and were going to kick her out of the Order.

She stopped at the bottom of the steps and looked up at the gods. Steeled herself for the inevitable. "My king." She bowed, then nodded toward his companion. "My lady Athena. You called for me?"

Zeus, every bit as handsome and muscular and intimidating as always, rested his enormous hands on his hips and peered down at her. "She's not been altered."

"No," Athena replied. "This one did not require any special enhancements."

Heat rushed to Daphne's cheeks as Zeus's gaze rolled over her breasts, slid down her waist to the flare of her hips, then followed the line of her legs to her feet. She wondered if he remembered her. Doubted that he did. Though Zeus occasionally came to the training fields, he rarely paid her any attention. In fact, she'd bet he didn't even remember meeting her as a child.

Slowly, as if he could see through her clothing to her nakedness beneath, he raked his eyes back up her body until every inch of her skin was hot and trembling. "This is even her natural hair color?"

"Yes," Athena answered. "She was born with the dark mahogany locks. No makeover necessary."

"Hm...." The king of the gods moved down the three stone

steps and circled Daphne. Her pulse shot into the stratosphere and her stomach caved in as he examined her from every angle. "Curvy. I like that. Nice ass, small waist." He stopped in front of her and stared at her tits, desire flaring hot in his black as sin eyes. "And these. Enticing."

Daphne kept her arms at her sides. Didn't flinch. Didn't show any response. But her nerves kicked up even higher. It was normal for her to react to an attractive male. All nymphs did. But this wasn't a male she was even the least bit interested in, and not for the first time she cursed her overly sexual lineage.

"Ahem." Athena cleared her throat. "The matter at hand?"

Scowling, Zeus turned to look up at the goddess. "Seduction training?"

"Completed," Athena answered. "She received high marks from her instructor."

Zeus looked back at Daphne, and once again, his lusty gaze scalded her body. "I'm sure she did. She's a purebred Naiad. The spitting image of her mother."

So he did remember her. Images of her mother and the day Daphne had lost her filled Daphne's mind and tugged at the heart she kept carefully closed off.

"Marksmanship has proven to be a limitation for her." Athena moved to stand at Zeus's side and crossed her arms over her chest in a clearly perturbed manner. "If you'd rather see some of the others—"

"No." Zeus held up a hand but didn't once look away from Daphne. "This one will do. Tell me, female, have you taken a new name since being on Olympus?"

They were finally talking to her. Daphne had no idea what was going on, but so far it didn't sound as if they were going to kick her out of the training class. And as much as she hated the mention of her mother, especially in combination with Zeus's lusty looks, she knew the probability of the god-king propositioning her was slim. She wasn't her mother, even if she did resemble her. And Sirens, thanks to Athena, were the only females that were off limits to Zeus. "No, my king. I go by my given name, Daphne."

"Ah, named after the nymph who was rescued from my son Apollo's unwanted advances and changed into a laurel tree. Tell me,

Daphne, do you wish to become a laurel tree like your namesake?"

"No, my king."

"I should hope not. Your skills would be extremely wasted in tree form." He clasped his hands behind his back and eyed her carefully. "Sappheire has had nothing but good things to say about you, and so far your training scores have been stellar. Aside from marksmanship, that is."

"I'm improving," Daphne said quickly. "I'm working very hard. If you just give me a little more time—"

"Relax." Zeus held up a hand. "What we need from you does not involve marksmanship."

Daphne's gaze darted between Zeus and Athena. "What you need from me?"

Athena shot a frustrated look at Zeus, but he didn't bother to glance her way. "We're in need of a Siren with your talents for a special mission. Are you interested?"

She had no idea what kind of mission they were talking about, but something in her gut said never to say no to the king of the gods. "Yes, of course."

"She's too naïve," Athena mumbled.

"That's exactly why we're going to use her." Zeus's eyes flashed. "You've heard of the rogue Argonaut loose in the human realm? The one they call Ari?"

Daphne's mind skipped over snippets of gossip she'd heard from her Siren sisters. "We all have. He's a monster."

"Yes, he is." Zeus's jaw clenched. "A very dangerous monster that needs to be stopped. Unfortunately, our conventional attempts at dealing with him have not worked. Which is where you come in. We want to send you in undercover for the Order."

Daphne stared at the god's face for several seconds, sure she had to have heard him wrong. "Me? But I-I'm not even a Siren yet. I haven't taken my final vows. I'm—"

"You are a nymph. A voluptuous, alluring nymph, like your mother. Aristokles has but one weakness: sexy, vulnerable nymphs. You will pretend to be in jeopardy, let him take you back to his lair, and when he least expects it, kill him."

Daphne's heart beat hard, and her hands grew sweaty. This was a suicide mission. She'd heard horror stories about the crazed

Argonaut and what he liked to do to Sirens. "But...my king...he tortures and kills Sirens. I'll not make it past—"

"You are not a full Siren yet," Athena cut in. "You have not been inducted, you do not bear the marking, and because of your nymph heritage, your body was never altered. He will not sense that you are a Siren, because you are not one...yet."

"If you succeed in this mission, however," Zeus added, "you will be inducted immediately upon your return. Regardless of your marksmanship scores."

Daphne's pulse roared in her head. This was her chance to belong. To finally be one of them. Her stomach swirled with excitement and apprehension. "Wh-what would I need to do?"

"Kill him, of course," Zeus answered. "But before you do that, I need confirmation of something. I suspect the Argonaut has a very special marking on his body. Not the Argonaut markings on his forearms. This is different. Before he's terminated, I need you to search his entire body and either prove or disprove the appearance of the marking."

"What kind of marking?" Daphne asked.

Zeus glanced toward Athena. A silent look passed between the two gods before Zeus refocused on Daphne. "We're not sure. But the marking disappears at the time of death, so you cannot kill him and then look for it. You must find it while he is alive."

So all she had to do was get close enough to the mass-murdering psycho to check every inch of his skin for some unknown marking. Yeah. That sounded easy.

*Not.*

"I-I'm not sure how I would do that," Daphne said hesitantly.

"This is where your nymph background comes in handy." Zeus lifted his brows in a "duh, it's easy" move. "Use your seduction skills. Charm him. Get him to drop his guard. Earn his trust so he least suspects your mission."

Daphne's eyes widened. "You don't mean—"

"Yes, you'll have to fuck him," Athena said. "Probably several times." An irritated expression crossed the goddess's face. "You sailed through seduction training, Daphne. This shouldn't be that difficult for you."

Unease rippled through Daphne. She'd only been twenty when

she'd been plucked from her foster home and brought to Olympus to train with the Sirens. Barely old enough to come into her sexuality, and the males she'd fooled around with as a teenager didn't count. Yes, she'd made it through seduction training easily, but only because she'd had an amazing instructor, a minor god who hadn't forced her. One who'd taken plenty of time to teach her about her own body and the powers of sex. That didn't mean she had any real experience seducing males—she'd been here for seven years, for crying out loud. And she had zero experience with savages like the psycho Argonaut Aristokles.

"We need an answer," Zeus said. "Either you are with us—"

"Or you are without us," Athena finished.

Daphne's gaze slid from one god to the other. She knew what they were saying. Either she did this and became a full-fledged Siren, or she didn't and was banished from the Order forever.

"Well?" Zeus asked.

Daphne bit her lip and nodded. Then prayed she made it through this alive. "I'll do it."

# Chapter Two

"This is as good a place as any." Sappheire nodded toward the log resting along the edge of a small stream in the mountains of the Snoqualmie National Forest.

"Here?" Shivering in the cool, damp air, Daphne crossed her arms over her belly and rubbed her biceps to stimulate blood flow. There was nothing but trees and moss and a scattering of snow in the dark forest of Northern Washington for as far as she could see. Nothing to indicate anyone besides them was even in the area. "Are you sure?"

"His hunting patterns indicate he'll come through this region soon." Sappheire looked toward the redheaded Siren at her side. "Rhebekah, take her jacket."

Without a word, Rhebekah stepped forward, tugged the jacket from Daphne's shoulders, and pushed her to sit on the log.

Grunting, Daphne reached for the wood beneath her to keep from falling over. Her stomach swirled with apprehension as she looked up at Sappheire, waiting for some kind of reassurance—any kind of reassurance—from her mentor. But just as she'd done while they were preparing Daphne for this mission and while they'd traveled to this location, Sappheire refused to look at her or offer any words of advice.

That apprehension turned to a wave of fear. Did the Siren know something Daphne didn't? Had Zeus lied? Was this really—she swallowed hard—a suicide mission after all?

Daphne's mind spun with possibilities, but she couldn't come up with a legitimate reason for Zeus to have lied. He clearly wanted the Argonaut dead. Ari had been wreaking havoc on Sirens for years. Regardless of Zeus's connection to her mother, she had to make this work. But Zeus's order that Daphne find a mark on the Argonaut's body—a vague mark which he hadn't bothered to explain—sent another wave of worry rushing over her.

Stealing her nerves, Daphne looked from Sappheire to Rhebekah and back again, focusing on what came next, not what she had to do down the line. "But why would he be here? There are no Sirens in this area. Except for, well, us. He doesn't know we're here. He certainly didn't know we were coming."

Sappheire nodded toward Rhebekah. "It's time for us to leave."

"Wait." Daphne pushed quickly to her feet. "How will I know where to find him?"

"You'll not find him," Rhebekah answered. "He'll find you."

Before Daphne could protest again, the Sirens disappeared, flashing back to Olympus without her.

In the silence, Daphne shivered and lowered herself back to the log. As she wasn't a full-fledged Siren, she couldn't flash after them, which meant from here on out, she was on her own.

Glancing around the forest, she tried not to freak out. Dusk was quickly moving to dark. In a matter of minutes it would be pitch black, not even a moon to guide her.

She wrapped her arms around her waist and rubbed her bare skin in the hopes of scrubbing away the fear. The dress Athena had made her wear was flimsy and white, with tiny cap sleeves and a hem that barely hit mid-thigh. The matching shoes were nothing but ballet slippers. She knew the outfit was meant to be alluring, but no female in her right mind—nymph or not—would be caught out in the cold in this getup. And right now she was more worried about freezing to death than what any crazed Argonaut was doing out here in these woods.

*Don't think about Aristokles. Think about what you need to do next.*

She rubbed her arms again. Tried to think clearly. She had no coat, no blanket, nothing to stay warm, and no idea how long she'd be here. It could take hours for the psycho Argonaut to venture her way—*if* he was really out here. In the meantime, she needed to find shelter and a way to stay warm. Needed—

A howl echoed somewhere through the trees. She jerked in

that direction, her heart rate shooting up even higher, sending blood pulsing through her veins.

Okay, maybe cold wasn't her biggest problem right now. Her Siren sisters hadn't just left her without a coat, they'd left her without a weapon to defend herself.

A twig cracked off to her right. Lurching to her feet, she scanned the ground and spotted a downed branch, as long and thick as a baseball bat. Grasping it in both hands, she swiveled toward the sound and slowly backed up, her hands shaking.

Long seconds passed. Finally, a rabbit jumped out of the brush, spotted her with big brown eyes, and quickly scurried away.

Daphne released a heavy breath and dropped the branch to the ground. She was flipping out for no reason. If that didn't prove she needed to pull it together, nothing did. She was a Siren, for crying out loud. Not a wimpy female.

Or...she would be. As soon as this mission was over.

A shiver rushed down her spine, dragging her awareness back to the cold once more.

Shelter. That's what she needed to focus on. Not some stupid, irrational fear that wasn't doing anything but making her nuts.

She straightened her spine and glanced around the forest again. The ground rose steadily to the north. Through the trees she could see what looked to be some kind of rock outcropping. Deciding that was her best bet, she headed in that direction. If she could find a cave, she could at least get out of the elements and decide what to do next.

The air grew progressively colder the closer she drew to the rocks. Rubbing her hands vigorously against the bare skin of her arms, she tried to keep her teeth from chattering as she picked her way around stones and branches and roots sticking out of the ground that bruised her feet in the silly shoes. Just as she moved past a boulder the size of a car, a growl echoed in the steadily darkening forest, drawing her feet to a sharp stop.

The hair on her nape stood straight. Her heart rate shot into the triple digits. Slowly, she turned in the direction she'd just come and stared in horror at the creature moving out from behind the rocks to stand in her path.

It was at least seven feet tall. A mixture of goat and lion and dog and human, with the body of a man, sharp teeth, horns, and glowing green eyes like something straight out of a nightmare.

A daemon. One of the Underworld's monsters. She stumbled backward.

"Nymph." The daemon drew in a deep whiff and growled. "Now this is a treat. What is a nymph doing out in these woods all alone?"

Daphne's mouth fell open, but words wouldn't come.

Before she could think of an answer—before she could think of something to *do*—another daemon stepped out from behind the boulder and growled. "The nymph is mine."

Fear shot Daphne's heart straight into her throat. The first daemon turned to the second and roared a menacing, aggressive response. The second bared his fangs and lurched for the first. Bones and fists and claws clashed as the two tore into each other.

Daphne swiveled and ran. Made it ten feet into the trees before another daemon jumped out from behind an old growth Douglas fir, right in her path. She skidded to a stop. Tried to lurch out of the way. He roared, reached out with claws as sharp as knives, and caught her across the side and abdomen, sending her flying into the brush.

A burn like the heat of a thousand suns lanced her side. She smacked into a tree, then dropped to the ground with a thud. Pain spiraled through every inch of her body, but she knew she had to get up. Had to run. She clawed at the dirt and tried to stand, but the wound in her side gushed blood, twisting her to the ground in a cry of agony.

The daemon growled and advanced. With the forest spinning around her, Daphne looked for something—anything—close to use as a weapon. Her vision came and went. But through descending darkness, she spotted a rock the size of her fist with sharp edges.

She dug her fingers into the ground, used every ounce of strength she had left to crawl in that direction. Another roar echoed at her back. She whimpered through the pain and tried to move faster, but it was as if she were crawling through mud. Just when she was sure she would never get there, her hand closed around the rock. She tugged it close, then rolled to her back and stared in horror at the sight before her.

A man—no, not a man, she realized—an Argonaut, battled back not one, but all three advancing daemons. His shoulders were broad, his arms muscled, his waist tapered to strong legs. And he moved like a seasoned warrior, swinging the blade in his hand like a ninja swings nunchucks. She watched in disbelief as his blade sank deep, he pulled it free, then swung out and decapitated the first daemon before moving to the second and third. In a matter of seconds, the fight was over, as if the daemons were paper dolls rather than living, menacing monsters.

The Argonaut turned Daphne's way. Daphne's vision flickered, but one look was all it took to send her scrambling backward in a haze of pain. A nose that had been broken more than once. Puckered scars that covered the left side of his jaw, ran down his neck, and disappeared under the collar of his long-sleeved T-shirt. And mismatched eyes—one a brilliant blue, the other a deep green—blazing and focused directly on her as if she were the next threat.

The Argonaut kicked the daemon's body out of his way and marched toward her. Blood and some kind of vile green goo covered his clothing, and that wild, fevered look in his mismatched eyes told her he was no friend, not to her.

It was him. The crazy Argonaut.

Aristokles.

Fear caused her to jerk back, but her head hit something sharp, stopping her momentum. Pain shot across her scalp, and she cried out, but the sound gurgled in her throat. He knelt beside her and reached one bloody, dirt-streaked hand her way.

She gripped the rock tightly, but before she could lift it to protect herself, everything went black.

* * * *

Ari carried the injured female into the living area of his home high in the mountains and laid her on the couch.

"Holy Hera," Silas said, grabbing a blanket from the back of a chair and laying it over her limp body. "She's a nymph. What in Hades was a nymph doing out in the wilds unprotected?"

"I don't know." Ari moved back as Silas knelt close and

worked on the female. In his old life, Silas had tended to the sick and injured of his village. Now he tended to Ari, which Ari knew was the most thankless job on the planet. "I didn't seal the wounds. If it was an archdaemon who did this, I didn't want to make things worse."

"Smart." An archdaemon's claws held a dangerous poison that could prompt infection. Silas peeled the female's torn dress back over her ribs so he could see her wounds. "But the chances she was attacked by an archdaemon are slim. I'm gonna need rags and hydrogen peroxide from the kitchen."

It took several seconds for Ari to realize Silas was talking to him. Tearing his gaze away from the female, Ari turned out of the living room with its high-beamed ceiling, roaring fireplace, and leather furnishings and headed for the kitchen. He was still covered in blood and slime from his battle with those daemons, tracking mud through the house Silas worked hard to keep clean, but couldn't think about anything other than the nymph lying half dead in the other room.

Silas was right. There was no reason for a nymph to be alone in those woods. She'd clearly been running. From who though, he didn't know. Before he could stop it, Ari's mind tumbled back dozens of years to another nymph he'd found alone and injured in the wild. To a moment that had cursed his existence for all eternity.

His vision darkened, and a flood of emotions that would only mess with his control threatened to overwhelm him. But he slowly beat them back. This was the reason he chose to isolate himself. Because he was unpredictable. Because he'd been cursed by the gods. Because some days, he was as much a monster as the daemons he'd sworn to destroy.

"Ari! The rags! She's bleeding, man!"

The sound of Silas's voice penetrated Ari's consciousness. He grabbed the items Silas had asked for then moved back into the living room. After handing Silas the materials, he stepped away again and watched as Silas cleaned the wounds then held his hands over the female and used his sensing gift to search for infection.

Long seconds passed. Finally, Silas eased back on his heels and lowered his hands to his thighs. "It wasn't an archdaemon. You can seal these now."

When Ari didn't make a move forward, Silas turned to face him. "I can't do this part myself. You know that. It has to be you."

The claw marks across Silas's face seemed to dance in the firelight as he stared at Ari, waiting for a response.

Scowling, Silas pushed to his feet. He was tall—over six feet—with broad shoulders and sandy blond hair in need of a trim, but he was no match for Ari. Thanks to his link to the ancient Greek gods, Ari was taller, more muscular, bigger everywhere. And he was never intimidated.

Except now. Right now, Ari wished he was anywhere but in this room, not only near a nymph but being forced to touch one.

"She'll die if you don't do something," Silas said. "You know this."

Still Ari didn't move. Didn't trust himself near a nymph. Nymphs were as dangerous to him as Sirens. Nymphs left him just as unbalanced and reminded him of a life he'd left behind without a second look.

"You brought her here," Silas said, stepping forward. "You could have left her in the woods to die, but you didn't. She's just a female, Ari. Show her the same mercy you showed me."

*Just a female...* She was. Ari had used his gift to heal dozens of females *and* males over his years. This female was no different.

History tried to hold him back, but that damn duty inside pushed him forward. Silas stepped to the side as Ari moved toward the couch and looked down. The nymph's head was tipped his way on the throw pillow, long, dark lashes feathering her alabaster skin, her dirty hair falling over her bruised shoulder and the remnants of her bloody dress. But even injured and unconscious, Ari could tell that she was attractive. Alluring. A nymph created to torment any male who crossed her path.

A heat he hadn't felt in years stirred low in his belly. One he didn't like and definitely didn't want. The fastest way to get rid of her was to heal her. Then forget he'd ever stumbled across the female in the first place.

He lowered to his knee and avoided looking at her face or the swell of her breasts pushing against the thin, once-white fabric, and focused on the red, bleeding wounds. Laying his hands over the gashes, he focused his strength until heat and energy radiated from his palms, permeating the skin beneath and knitting the wounds back together.

The nymph didn't even stir, even though it was a process he knew caused intense pain. She laid still, her eyes closed, her body deep in sleep. Soft. Vulnerable. Minutes later, Ari lifted his hands and pushed to his feet, intent on getting as far from her as possible.

He stepped back from the couch, turned so he didn't have to look at her longer than necessary, and moved for the archway that led to his wing of rooms. "As soon as she's alert and able to travel, I want her gone."

"Ari." Silas sighed. "Maybe she's—"

"As soon as she's able," Ari repeated, not waiting to hear Silas's protest. He knew what Silas was thinking. That a female in the house might do him some good. But Ari knew only bad could ever come from this situation. "I'll not have her here disrupting my schedule. Not a minute longer, Silas. Get rid of her. That's an order."

He disappeared through the doorway, but at his back he heard Silas mutter, "Maybe a little disruption's what you need, dipshit."

# Chapter Three

Daphne blinked several times and tried to make sense of her surroundings. She definitely wasn't on Olympus.

Slowly, she pushed up on her arm, wincing at the sting in her side. A soft bed lay below her. An eerie gray light shone through the window across the room. Sitting back in the pillows, she glanced around the bedroom with its dark furnishings and high-beamed ceiling and tried to figure out where the heck she was.

Her memories were a foggy mess. She remembered talking with Athena and Zeus. Remembered being in the woods with Sappheire. Remembered those daemons showing up. Remembered running and being struck in the side. Remembered...

Her eyes grew wide as her mind flashed back to the warrior she'd seen battling those daemons. To his mismatched eyes. His wild look. And the way he'd focused on her as if she were his next victim.

Throwing back the covers, she pulled up the long shirt she was wearing and checked her side. Four thin, red lines crossed her skin from her hip to just beneath her breast.

Confusion tugged her brows together. She brushed her fingers over the sealed wounds that should have killed her and tried to remember what had happened but couldn't. Tried to figure out how long she'd been out of it but drew a complete blank.

Her gaze drifted to the bed beneath her, the floor, then finally to the window. Cringing at the pain in her side, she pushed to her feet. Her breath caught as she pulled back the curtain and gazed out at the snowy forest and acres of mountains that disappeared in a dark gray sky.

No other houses. No other signs of life. Just miles and miles of wilderness and snow as far as the eye could see.

Her heart pounded as she let go of the curtain and turned to look around the room again. The walls were made of logs. Dark, scuffed hardwood floors ran beneath her bare feet. The sleigh bed she'd been sleeping in was old but more than comforting.

*Think, Daphne.*

Her hands shook as she pressed them to her cheeks. The crazed Argonaut had obviously brought her here, wherever *here* was. He must have sensed she was a nymph. Zeus had said he had a weakness for nymphs, and that meant she was over her first hurdle—finding him and not getting killed. She wasn't sure how he'd healed her, but just the fact he'd bothered meant she was halfway to her goal. And that meant all she had to do next was make nice and…and seduce the psycho so she could complete the second half of her mission.

Feeling lightheaded, she lowered to the bed so her legs didn't go out from under her. Squeezing her shaking hands into fists against the comforter, she drew a deep breath then let it out. She could do this. She'd trained with the best, after all. And when it was done, she'd finally be a Siren. He was a monster, right? Just because he'd saved her from a horde of daemons didn't mean anything. It just meant Zeus was right and that his brain turned to mush near a nymph.

*That* she could use to her advantage. Rising again, she stepped toward the door only to realize she was wearing nothing but a male's white button-down shirt. The tails hit at her knees, and the sleeves were so long, they'd been rolled up several times to her wrists.

He'd changed her clothes. He'd seen her naked. Her stomach swirled with that realization.

*That's not exactly a bad thing considering your mission.*

Straightening her spine, she pulled the door open, then peered down a long, dark hallway. Sconces lit the passageway on both sides. Her stomach continued to toss and roll, but she moved as quietly as possible through the corridor. Doors opened on both sides of her, but she didn't look to see where they led. Her focus remained fixed on the light ahead and what she had to do next.

The hallway opened to a balcony that overlooked an enormous great room with more antique furnishings set near a giant stone fireplace that rose to the ceiling. Drawing to a stop at the railing, Daphne glanced over the empty space and tried not to be completely awed by the three-story windows that looked out over a wide deck and across a snowy valley. A frozen river meandered far below, and though she couldn't be sure, she had a feeling those black dots down there weren't people but elk or deer wandering across the frigid earth.

Her gaze drifted up and around. The enormous lodge-style structure seemed to be tucked into the side of a mountain and built on the edge of a cliff. The perfect place to wait and watch. If anyone tried to attack this place, they'd be spotted long before they could even mount an offense.

And that meant if things went bad for her, she wasn't getting out of here unseen.

Pushing down the unease, she headed for the curved staircase. Escaping was five steps down the line. After she completed her mission. When he was dead. Until then, she had other things to focus on.

A twinge in her side made her stop near the bottom step and draw another deep breath. She pressed her hand against the wounds and fought back the wave of nausea that seemed to want to pull her under.

So, okay, maybe she wasn't totally ready for seduction just yet. Her body was still clearly healing from that daemon attack. But she could find her target and at least see what was up. Flirt a little. Play the damsel in distress. And start this plan in motion.

Determination firmly in place, she wandered from one massive room to the next. An enormous kitchen opened to a dining area that led to an office and another set of curved stairs. Still finding no sign of him, she headed down the steps and slowed when she heard voices.

"Your first mistake was accepting my challenge," a deep male voice said. "Your second was turning your back on me."

A *thwack* echoed, then another male said, "You've been practicing."

"Damn right I've been practicing," the first responded. "I'm tired of getting my ass handed to me."

A chuckle echoed up the stairs.

Daphne stopped midway down the steps where she could see into the gigantic room below. This one wasn't furnished like the rooms above. It was wide and open, with dumbbells and weight-lifting equipment along one whole side. Tall windows looked out over another deck and the sweeping valley view, but what held her attention were the two males in the middle of the room, both dressed in nothing but low-riding, dark pants, both carved and muscular, both circling around each other with reddened fists and bruised faces.

The first she didn't recognize. He was tall and broad, with sandy blond hair, sharp blue eyes, and a series of scars across his face. But the second she knew in an instant. Dark hair, legs the size of tree trunks, the unique Greek lettering etched into his forearms, and a wild look across his features that said he'd locked on yet another target.

A trickle of blood ran from Aristokles's temple down his scarred cheek and neck, but he didn't seem to notice. A wicked grin curved his mouth as he continued to circle the other male. "It's about time. You've been getting soft doing all that housework."

Aristokles lunged forward, but the other male ducked out of the way, swiveled to avoid being nailed by the Argonaut's fist, then rolled across the floor. Popping to his feet, he kicked Aristokles's legs out from under him.

The Argonaut went down with a grunt, but before the male could pounce, Aristokles did a backward roll and jerked back to standing. "You've really been practicing. I guess it's time I stopped going easy on you and—"

As if he sensed her, the Argonaut's gaze darted toward the stairs and focused on Daphne. And in those mismatched eyes, interest immediately flared.

Daphne's first instinct was to shrink back into the logs behind her, but unfortunately she didn't possess the power of camouflage. Her second was to run, but her legs wouldn't let her. Because as the Argonaut's heated gaze washed over her, her traitorous body was already responding—her nipples pebbling beneath the thin cotton shirt, her belly warming and sending waves of heat straight between her legs, her skin craving a dangerous touch she shouldn't want.

Her breaths grew shallow, her head, light. But this was more than just responding to an attractive male. This was instant arousal with just one look. Arousal on a scale she'd never experienced before, not even with a god.

The male Aristokles had been sparing slammed his fist into the Argonaut's stomach. Aristokles pulled his gaze from Daphne, grunted, then wrapped his arms around his belly and doubled over.

The other male stood upright and turned toward the stairs with a surprised expression. "Ah, you're awake. We expected you'd sleep at least another day."

*We.* Daphne had no idea who he was or what that meant, and she wanted to ask, but her gaze darted right back to the Argonaut. Aristokles shot the male a hard look, then stood upright and crossed to the far side of the room. After swiping a towel over his face, he reached for a shirt from a bench near the wall, tugged it on, and muttered, "You know what to do."

The second male looked Aristokles's way, but the Argonaut didn't meet his gaze. Didn't even turn to look at Daphne again. Just disappeared through a doorway on the far side of the room and was gone.

The heat in Daphne's belly slowly cooled, and a shiver rushed down her spine.

"Sorry about that." The male turned toward her and grimaced. "He lacks basic social skills."

His words seemed to snap her out of the trance she'd fallen into. Daphne cleared her throat and gripped the banister at her side. "I..." No, that wasn't how she wanted to start this. She needed to play it cool. Whoever this guy was, hopefully he could help her. "Where am I?"

The male crossed to the bench and pulled on his own T-shirt. "Stonehill Hold. Don't worry. You're safe here. No daemons can get to us. And if they did"—he nodded toward the door Aristokles had exited through—"he'd sense them."

Sense them. Right. Argonauts could do that. One of their many awesome hunting skills, ironically bestowed on them by the very god who wanted Aristokles dead.

Remembering she needed to play the damsel in distress,

Daphne brushed the hair out of her eyes. "Stonehill Hold? I've never heard of it."

"Not many have." He moved to the base of the stairs and looked up at her five steps above. "How do you feel?"

"Fine," she answered hesitantly. "Tired." When his gaze dropped to her side, she remembered her wounds. "Sore."

"I'm sure you are."

Daphne couldn't help but notice the angled scars that ran across his features. A series of thin, white lines that stretched from one cheek, across his nose, to the opposite jaw. Claw marks, she realized.

She wanted to ask about them but decided now wasn't the time. Instead, she tried to figure out who he was. He wasn't an Argonaut like Aristokles. She would have picked up on that. As an otherworldly creature, she had the power to sense a being's race, and she already knew he wasn't a god or a nymph like her. But to be here with the psycho Argonaut and not be intimidated meant he had to be someone important.

Her eyes widened when his lineage finally registered. "You're a half breed."

He moved up the steps toward her. "We prefer the term Misos."

Misos. The race of half-human, half-Argolean beings. Argolea was the realm established for the descendants of the ancient Greek heroes, a utopia of sorts, one Daphne had studied during her time with the Sirens. But many Argoleans didn't remain there. They often traveled back and forth between the human realm and their own, and whether they'd intended to or not, they'd created an entirely new race. The Misos. Because of their link to Argolea and the heroes, each Misos was born with a special gift, and their lifespans were longer than those of mortal beings, but they weren't immortal in any sense of the word. As far as Daphne knew, they weren't even that special.

"I…" Words faltered on her tongue. If anyone knew what it was like to face a daemon, surely he would. Half breeds had been hunted by daemons for years simply because they were different, and to daemons that meant weak. "I didn't mean any disrespect."

"Don't worry. Where you come from, I'm sure Misos are few

and far between."

That was true. He was the first Misos she'd ever met. But that didn't mean she condoned stereotypes. In the otherworldy universe, nymphs were considered less than the other races, interested only in sex. She hated that perception. It was part of the reason she'd worked so hard to become the best Siren she could be.

Even if she wasn't all that great.

*That's why you're here. To fix that point.*

He stepped past her and motioned for her to follow. "I'm sure you have a million questions. I'm starving though. We'll talk while I cook."

Daphne couldn't seem to stop herself from glancing toward the doorway where Aristokles had disappeared. "What about him?"

"Ignore him. He's being moody."

She had no idea what the male meant, but she wasn't sure she was *with it* enough to go exploring on her own just yet. She followed the Misos back up the stairs and into the massive kitchen.

"Have a seat." He nodded toward the hand-carved barstools near the counter. "I'll get you something to drink. I remember being extremely thirsty when I first awoke."

Daphne's mouth was suddenly bone dry. As she pulled out a chair and sat, she licked her lips, thankful someone seemed to know what she needed because right now, she had absolutely no clue.

He handed her a glass of clear liquid. "Drink."

Daphne drained the entire glass, then lowered it to the counter and swiped the back of her hand over her mouth. "I didn't realize how thirsty I was. Thank you..."

"Silas."

"Thank you, Silas. I'm Daphne."

He opened the refrigerator and pulled out lettuce and other salad fixings. "How is it you came to be out here in the wilds all by yourself, Daphne?"

She'd known the question would be asked, she just hadn't expected it to be asked by anyone but her target. Either way, she needed to relay the same story Zeus had suggested because it might trigger a useful reaction in the crazed Argonaut. "I was... escaping."

"From?" Silas reached for a tomato.

She thought about lying. She didn't know this male. He could be Aristokles's henchmen or even his slave. But he didn't act like either. His shoulders were relaxed, and there was a look of contentment across his scarred features as he worked. And when she thought back to what she'd seen of the two sparring downstairs, it was clear he wasn't afraid of the Argonaut.

She suddenly didn't want to lie. It wasn't in her nature to lie anyway. But she couldn't tell the truth either. She figured a half-truth was her best bet. "There's a god who wants something from me. I was in the wilds because of him."

"Running from him?"

Daphne definitely wanted to run from Zeus. His lecherous gaze put her at instant unease, and she hated the way he kept referencing her mother. In a way, accepting this assignment was running from him, wasn't it? "You could say that."

He sliced through another tomato. "If it was a god, I'm guessing you came through a portal."

"I did."

"Which explains the dress you were wearing when Ari found you."

*Ari*... Her body warmed just thinking of the Argonaut. He'd been the one who'd found her. Rescued her from those daemons. Brought her here and stripped her of her shredded garments.

Arousal stirred in her belly all over again, but as her gaze drifted to the knife in Silas's hand, it cooled. He sliced through the flesh of the tomato. Juice spurted across the cutting board, instantly reminding her of that daemon's claws slashing through her skin.

"Thank you," she said softly, "for taking care of me."

"You're welcome. But I didn't do much aside from make sure you were comfortable. Ari's the one you should thank. Without his healing gift, you'd be dead."

Daphne stared at the Misos's scarred profile, unsure she'd heard him right. The Argonaut. He was implying that the Argonaut hadn't just rescued her from those daemons, but healed her as well.

That went against everything she knew of the monster.

Silas glanced up. "I take it from your reaction you didn't expect that."

"I..." Heck no, she hadn't expected that. "I recognized the markings on his forearms. He's a warrior, not a healer."

Silas looked down at his vegetables. "He is. But Ari also has a healing gift. One he doesn't often use. Only when the situation is dire."

What situation would the crazed Argonaut consider dire? Daphne's gaze swept back over Silas's scars. "He saved you as well?"

Silas nodded.

"Why?"

A smile pulled at the corner of Silas's lips. "Because it's in his nature to help those in need."

Daphne's brow wrinkled. "I'm not sure I understand."

Silas moved the diced tomatoes to a salad bowl. "The Argonauts are duty-bound to protect the human world. My people are part of that world."

"Yes, but...if he lives here instead of in Argolea, he no longer serves with the Argonauts."

Silas looked up again, only this time when his eyes met hers, they narrowed. The knife in his hand hovered above the cutting board. "Now that, I know, you did *not* pick up from the markings on his forearms."

Oh Hades. A quick shot of fear rushed down Daphne's spine.

*Think...quickly.*

"I..." Her mind spun. "No, I-I didn't. But in my circle, I've heard whispers of a rogue Argonaut. One with mismatched eyes who no longer serves with his Order. I just assumed—"

"Naturally, you assumed the worst." Silas's jaw clenched as he went back to slicing. "Not everything those gods you surround yourself with say is true. Ari might not serve with the Argonauts anymore, but that doesn't mean his duty is any less."

An odd tingle spread across Daphne's nape. She'd offended the Misos. Her memory skipped back to the laughter she'd heard from the lower level. The two were friends. She opened her mouth. Closed it. Wasn't sure just what to say.

After several awkward seconds of silence, Silas said, "My village was attacked by daemons. We lived in a remote area high in the mountains. Kept to ourselves; were a peaceful community. We thought we were safe. Turns out we weren't. A daemon horde attacked us in the night. The raid was bloody and vicious, and before we could defend ourselves, it was all but over."

"I..." Daphne didn't know what to say. She knew what it was like to lose her entire village, too. "I'm sorry."

"Nothing to be sorry about. It happened." He moved all the salad fixings to a bowl, cleaned off the cutting board, then stepped toward the refrigerator again and pulled out a casserole dish covered in tinfoil. "I made peace with it a long time ago. Ari found us after. He'd been patrolling the area as he often does. He tried to heal as many as he could, but in the end, I was the only one who survived."

A humming sounded in Daphne's brain. Everything she'd been told about the Argonaut seemed at sudden odds with what she'd just learned. She wasn't sure what to believe. All she knew for certain was that the Argonaut could have killed her. He could have left her for dead in those woods. But he hadn't. He'd saved her, brought her here, and healed her. And though she wanted to chalk that up to his weakness for nymphs, she was starting to wonder if that was true. Because he'd done the same for Silas.

Her gaze drifted toward the open door. She had no idea where the Argonaut was or what he was doing, but her mind skipped back over that moment in the woods. After he'd killed those daemons. When he'd stalked toward her, knelt at her side, and reached for her. She'd been too afraid to listen then, but now two words echoed in her mind. Two words she hadn't realized he'd whispered until right this very second.

# Chapter Four

Daphne wandered through the halls of Stonehill Hold late in the evening while Aristokles's words continued to ping around in her mind. It was late, well past midnight, but she couldn't sleep.

*You're safe...*

Had she ever felt safe? Maybe as a child with her parents, but they'd been gone so long she barely remembered what safety felt like. She'd never truly felt safe with her foster family, even though they'd been nice. She'd been too afraid something bad was lurking around the corner. And she'd certainly never felt safe on Olympus. Even with all her years of training, she still worried daily that someone would see she didn't have what it took and kick her out. Every day she struggled just to fit in. And every day she knew she really didn't.

Hating where her thoughts were heading, she ran her fingers over the spines of a series of books in the library. Tomes from all over the world filled the shelves, covering topics from gods to history to woodworking. Daphne had always loved books. As she glanced over the titles in front of her, she couldn't help but see the irony.

Books separated man from the animals. Learning kept him from becoming a savage. And the savage Zeus wanted her to kill was obviously very well read.

Turning on a sigh, her gaze drifting over the fireplace, the comfy seating area, and the table near the window holding a globe.

After dinner, Silas had given her a tour, explaining that Stonehill Hold had been nothing but ruins when Aristokles had found it over fifty years ago. Silas was the one who'd pestered the Argonaut into rebuilding the fortress. Silas was probably the one who'd collected all these books.

She froze when she realized she wasn't alone, and her heart rate shot up. Seated in a high-backed chair in the corner of the room, a book in his lap, the Argonaut she'd just been thinking of watched her with wild, mismatched eyes.

Warmth gathered in her belly. A warmth that was both unwelcome and painfully arousing. He didn't speak, only continued to stare at her from the shadows, and with every passing second, her adrenaline surged higher and that warmth trickled lower, awakening places she wasn't willing to think about just yet.

*Say something. Anything.*

"I-I didn't realize anyone was here."

Aristokles didn't move a muscle, didn't look away, still didn't speak. And his face was so shadowed, she couldn't read his expression. All she could see were his eyes, fixed only on her.

Nerves bounced all over in her belly, and she pulled her gaze from his, glanced around the room, and tried to sound nonchalant when she said, "This is a fabulous library. I'm always so tempted by books. I hope you don't mind if I borrow a few. I'm not used to the quiet here." She wrinkled her nose. "Kinda hard to sleep."

When he still didn't answer, she fought back a wave of unease. "I'm sure you're used to being here. I mean, why wouldn't you be? This is your house, after all. It's a great house. Just a little big for me. And cold. You must like the cold though. I mean, to have a house way out here in the mountains, you'd have to, right?"

Oh gods, she was babbling. She'd spent years on Olympus training herself *not* to babble like she used to do as a child.

He didn't answer. Didn't move. Pressing her lips together, she twisted her arms behind her back and clasped her hands. One quick look toward the dark corner told her he was still staring only at her.

Sweat broke out along her spine. His hand resting on the arm of the chair was so big, she knew it could crush her skull in a matter of seconds. But even as fear churned in her belly, she held on to the fact that he'd saved her life. If he wanted her dead, she'd already be there. That meant he wanted her for something else.

Seduction. She needed to be a seductive, alluring nymph, not a rambling fool. *You trained for this, idiot.*

Right. She had. This was the easy part.

Straightening her shoulders, she unclasped her hands from her back and cocked her hip. The movement accentuated her breasts, which she knew were her best feature. Flipping her hair over her shoulder, she rested her hand at her waist and looked right at the Argonaut as she licked her lips in a move she knew would draw his attention right to her mouth.

"But enough about me." Lowering her voice to a throaty whisper, she added, "Is there anything here that tempts you?"

For a heartbeat, the Argonaut didn't move. Then very slowly, he unfolded himself out of the chair and rose to his full height.

Her pulse pounded. Arousal stirred low in her belly. He crossed the room and stopped mere inches from her, the scents of fresh pine and citrus wafting around her. Scents, she suddenly realized, she'd smelled before.

When he'd rescued her in the woods? She wasn't sure. And right now she couldn't think. Because this close, he was bigger than she'd first thought. Broader across the shoulders, more muscular everywhere, so tall she had to tip her head back to look up at his face. And hot. His body heat sizzled across the distance between them, seeping into her skin until that arousal slinked lower and her thighs trembled.

She didn't fight the arousal this time. Told herself it was because her arousal would produce pheromones that would draw him in. And drawing him in meant she could finish this job, maybe tonight. But something in the back of her consciousness knew that was a lie. She wasn't fighting it because he excited her. Because a wicked place inside her wanted to know what it would feel like to be devoured by a savage like him.

He stepped forward, and though Daphne wanted nothing more than to feel his skin brush hers, she moved back. Two steps were all she had until her butt hit the bookshelf behind her. The Argonaut lifted both large hands, and her stomach caved in, waiting for his touch, wondering where he would start. But instead of his skin grazing hers, he rested his hands on the shelf near her head, boxing her in.

His mismatched gaze skipped over her features. Heat surrounded her as he leaned in, jacking her arousal up even higher, making her forget the Sirens, her reason for being here, even her own name.

Her body instinctively swayed toward him. Her eyelids lowered. She lifted her head toward his, her lips trembling in pure anticipation.

He stopped millimeters from her lips and whispered, "Can't sleep, huh?"

His warm, minty breath brushed her sensitive skin. Her mouth watered, desperate for a taste. Without even realizing it, she eased even closer. "No. I'm not the least bit tired. I think I may need help with that."

"Help, huh?"

His words were a throaty purr, his massive legs so close they skimmed her own, making her sex ache. It was all she could do to keep from reaching him, but Sappheire's voice—something she didn't expect—whispered that he needed to make the first big move so she knew she could completely draw him in.

She didn't want to think about Sappheire right now. Didn't want to think about the Sirens or her mission. She just wanted to be taken. By this savage? Oh yes... She didn't even care what he'd done anymore.

He leaned toward her ear, his warm breath fanning her neck, sending tingles straight down her spine. His lips just barely brushed her lobe, and her eyes slid closed. "Here's your help, little nymph," he whispered. "Lock yourself in your room where it's safe because if I see you out here again, I won't be held responsible for my actions. I'm unpredictable. And not in any way you want a male to be."

A tremor ran down Daphne's spine, dimming her arousal. Cool air washed over her as the Argonaut drew back. Slowly, she opened her eyes, but the instant she looked up, she knew the Argonaut wasn't the least bit turned on like her. His jaw was hard, his eyes icy and cold. And when she heard the wood crack behind her where he still gripped the shelf, she realized what she'd missed thanks to her stupid excitement.

He was every bit the savage Athena had claimed him to be. His eyes were wild. His skin flushed. And it wasn't just arousal dragging him to the edge of control. It was something else. Something she knew instinctively she should be afraid of.

"I'm no hero, nymph. Don't invade my space again."

He let go of the shelf, turned, and exited the room without another word.

Daphne sagged back into the bookshelf and drew in a shaky breath. But fear didn't come. Because as soon as she was alone, she realized what she'd missed moments before.

He hadn't been icy until just the last moment. When she'd obviously tried to seduce him. Before that, when he'd been watching her and she'd been her silly, rambling self, his expression had been one of noticeable interest, just as it had been when he'd looked at her downstairs in his gym.

He was attracted to her. Very attracted. He just wasn't attracted when she used her Siren skills. That meant straight up seduction wasn't going to work. She needed to finesse the situation, make him trust her. She just wasn't sure how to go about doing that.

She pushed away from the bookshelf and remembered Silas. Silas could help her. She'd talk to the half breed and figure out the best way to get close to Aristokles.

Then she'd finish the job she'd come to do. And forget about the sexy savage who made her body ache.

* * * *

Ari found Silas in the lowest level of the hold, a dark, windowless room carved out of the cliff that they used for storage.

Dressed in jeans and a long-sleeved T-shirt, Silas stood on the far side of the room, making notes on the clipboard in his hand as he checked supplies on the shelves that lined the walls. "We're almost out of wine," he said without turning, obviously hearing Ari's footsteps. "You drink too much of it, you know. I'm pretty sure I replenished that stock two months ago."

Ari wasn't in the mood to talk about his drinking habits. He wasn't in the mood for anything except getting that nymph far, far away. Resting his hands on his hips, he glared toward the Misos. "If she's well enough to wander around the hold, she's well enough to leave."

Silas made another mark on his paper. "I thought you'd appreciate having something prettier to look at than me."

"How pretty she is has nothing to do with this."

"Ah." A mischievous smile curled Silas's lips. "So you did notice."

Ari's frustration shot up. Yes the nymph was pretty, but his opinion would be the same if she were Aphrodite beautiful or Medusa ugly. Stonehill Hold was his one and only refuge, and he wasn't about to be bullied by a nymph in his own home.

"I want her gone," he said. "I'll be back by nightfall tomorrow. When I return, she'd better not be here."

"Daphne."

"What?"

Silas turned to face him. "Her name's Daphne, not she. And what you want and need are two very different things, Argonaut."

Ari's jaw clenched. "Don't pretend to know what I need. I'm no good for any female, especially that one, and we both know it." He stomped back up the steps, refusing to give in even an inch. "Tomorrow, Silas. No excuses."

"What you need," Silas muttered, "is a two-by-four to the head." Then louder, "Get some wine while you're out. It does wonders for your personality."

Ari ignored the smartass comments and moved back to the main level where he headed for his rooms. The entire west wing of the hold was his domain. An office complete with desk and chair he'd carved by hand opened to a bedroom suite filled with a bed, side tables, and a sitting area flanked by a wide stone fireplace. Crossing toward the closet on the far side of his room, he pulled out a backpack and set it on the bed.

His gaze slid over the empty wine bottle on the nightstand. Scowling, he looked down at his pack and checked the supplies he kept inside for his patrols. So he drank to fall asleep. Big deal. A lot of people did that. A lot of *normal* people did that, and he was way past normal. Normal people didn't have to deal with his curse. Normal people didn't have the blackout episodes he did. *Normal* people didn't have random flashes of the horrible things they'd done while in the midst of one of those episodes.

Needed a woman? No way. Sure, he had desires just like the next guy, and he had no problem fulfilling those desires when he was out on his scouting trips. There were always willing females if you knew where to look. But the last thing he needed was one infiltrating his personal space.

More frustrated than before, he snapped the top of his pack, pulled on a jacket, then slung the straps over his shoulders. Screw Silas and his opinions. Ari didn't need anything but himself. He'd been getting along just fine alone for dozens of years.

He headed for the door and the frozen wilderness beyond. And hoped he ran into another pack of daemons. A good bloodletting would take his mind off that nymph. But something told him it wouldn't be enough to make him forget that she now had a name.

\* \* \* \*

Daphne hadn't slept well. Her dreams were a mixture of Ari and the Sirens and her long-destroyed village.

She climbed out of bed and yawned as she dressed in the sweats and T-shirt Silas had given her after dinner. The clothing was huge. She had to roll the pants down at the waist several times just so they stayed up, and the light-blue T-shirt wasn't much better—hanging like a dress almost all the way to her knees. After tucking it in as best she could, she fluffed her hair and told herself she could still make this work. She'd aced her strategy training. She simply had to think outside the box where Aristokles was concerned.

She turned out of her room and moved barefoot through the hall. When she reached the kitchen on the lower level, she found Silas filling a backpack on the table with supplies—water, bandages, gloves.

She approached slowly, not sure what he was doing. "I hope you're not running away."

Silas glanced up and smiled, his hair damp around the collar from a shower, his light-blue eyes sparkling, making her almost forget about the scars on his face. "Good morning. Sleep well?"

"Fine," Daphne lied as she pulled a chair out at the table and sat. "Are you going somewhere?"

Silas shoved a bag of granola into his pack. "Supply run. We're low on several things."

Panic clawed at her chest. "How long will you be gone?"

"Three, maybe four days. I'm supposed to take you with me."

Shit. She couldn't let that happen. "Um—"

"I don't think you're well enough to leave, though."

Daphne's gaze shot to his. The male's blue eyes sharpened when he added, "And call me selfish, but I think you can do some good here while you finish healing."

She didn't know what he meant but as he pushed his pack to the end of the table, pulled out a chair, and sat across from her, she found herself hanging on his every word. "Ari left on a scouting trip. He'll be back later tonight. He'll likely be ticked you're still here, but he can just deal with it. He *needs* to deal with it."

"Why?"

"Ari thinks it's better for everyone if he isolates himself."

"Why does he believe that?" she asked, playing dumb.

"Because he's bullheaded," Silas answered. "But I fear this self-imposed isolation of his is slowly catching up with him."

"You care about him." The realization hit before she could stop the words from spilling from her lips.

"Of course I do." Sighing, Silas shook his head and leaned back in his chair. "It's more than the fact he saved my life. I'd heard rumors about the crazed Argonaut just as you, but I quickly realized he's not what everyone says he is."

"And what is he?"

Silas didn't immediately answer, and in the silence, Daphne thought back over everything she knew of Aristokles. The stories she'd heard from Zeus and Athena contradicted with what Silas had told her last night. And after spending a few minutes with Ari in the library, she didn't know who to believe.

"You know the story of the Argonauts, right? How each are given a soul mate?"

Daphne remembered a story her mother had once told her. "Hera cursed them. Because of Zeus's affection for his son Heracles. She was jealous that Zeus had created a realm for

Heracles's descendants, and she cursed him and all the Argonauts with a soul mate." She frowned. "I never understood how that could be a curse though."

"It's a curse because the soul mate in the equation is the worst possible match for that particular Argonaut. The person he's forever drawn to but who will torment his existence. Some Argonauts never find their other half. Some do. Ari found his, fifty-odd years ago, in the human realm while on patrol with his Order. She was a nymph, like you. Young and beautiful. And she was running from Zeus."

Silas leaned forward to rest his forearms on the table. "Olympians can't cross into Argolea. It was the one safeguard Zeus put in place, to protect the Argonauts from Hera's wrath. But that safeguard turned out to be a source of frustration for Zeus. See, Ari took the nymph to Argolea. He tended her wounds, gave her a place to live, and eventually they fell in love. But when Zeus discovered Ari had stolen his prize, he was livid. Since he couldn't cross into Argolea himself, he sent his Sirens to get her back. There was a confrontation. In the struggle, Ari's soul mate was killed."

It was the same story Daphne had heard from the Sirens. With one minor change: in the telling she'd heard, the nymph hadn't loved Ari. He'd recognized her as his soul mate, kidnapped her, and she'd been trying to escape his clutches when the Sirens arrived to rescue her.

"Ari lost it then," Silas went on. "The death of a soul mate is like losing half of who you are. He withdrew from the Argonauts, went into isolation in the human realm, struggled to deal with his grief. Months passed, but he couldn't find the strength to return home. His son Cerek wouldn't give up on him, though. Cerek tracked him down, tried to bring him back, but Ari refused to go. When it became clear to Ari that Cerek was never going to give up on him, he faked his death. You saw those scars on his neck?"

Daphne remembered the scars she'd seen up close last night in the library. "Yes."

"They cover the whole left side of his body."

"From what?"

"A fire. One he set on purpose. His son thinks he's dead. Most everyone does."

Everyone but Zeus and Athena and the Sirens. Daphne tried to imagine the scene but couldn't. Tried to imagine what it would take to isolate one's self so dramatically, but came up blank. Even in her darkest moments, she'd never wanted to be alone, which was why she'd jumped at the chance to become a Siren when she'd been chosen.

"It wasn't until after all this that Ari started having his episodes," Silas said.

"Episodes?" Daphne looked back at the male across from her.

"Spans of time where he completely blacks out. He's not aware of what he's doing while in these episodes, but he has flashes of them afterward, and of the things he's done while in them. From what we've been able to discern, the episodes are usually triggered when he senses Sirens close by."

Daphne's head was suddenly spinning. Zeus and Athena had implied he killed Sirens in his crazed need for revenge, but if that were the case, he would have started killing them as soon as his soul mate died. What Silas was describing made it sound like Ari's "episodes" began after he'd left the Argonauts. Months after his soul mate was already gone.

That didn't sound like revenge at all. It sounded like...a curse.

Daphne opened her mouth to ask more, but before should get the words out Silas went on.

"For a while, he kept himself locked in this hold. Thought if he isolated himself, he could stop the episodes. But his duty was too strong. The need to protect is engrained in his Argonaut DNA. He now runs his own missions, hunting daemons and safeguarding the people he swore to defend ages ago. But any time he has a blackout, it weighs heavily on him. Thankfully, they're few and far between these days."

Daphne's brow wrinkled again. Zeus had made it sound like Ari's attacks were stepping up, not lessening.

Silas shook his head. "Things changed a few months ago, though, when one of Ari's friends called asking for his help. Nick is one of the few people from Ari's old life who knows Ari's still alive. I was hesitant about Ari traveling to Mexico. Offered to go with him but he wouldn't let me. You see, he hasn't had an episode in quite a while, and I was worried about how he would react. Turns out Ari didn't encounter any Sirens on his trip, but something did happen there. When he came back, he was different. Sullen. Moody. No longer laughing and lighthearted as he'd been when we were renovating this place." He looked up and around again. "He's never said exactly what occurred, but I think seeing his old friend made him realize what's missing in his life—friendship, family…love."

Daphne's head grew light. Did she have those things? Definitely not love. She'd never known a male deep enough to fall in love. And with her parents gone, she had no family left. She had friends, though, didn't she? Her Siren sisters were her friends. But even as she tried to convince herself of that fact, she knew it was a lie. The way Sappheire had left her in the woods without a single word of comfort or encouragement proved she wasn't a true friend in any sense of the word.

"He reacts to you in a way I haven't seen him react to anyone else," Silas said. "He's nervous around you. Not in a dangerous way, but in an interested one. I'm not trying to set you up, just to be clear. That's not my goal. I simply think your being here is good for him. It forces him to see that he can be around others and not flip out. And he needs that. He needs to see he isn't the monster everyone believes him to be."

Daphne stared down at the table, taking in all this new information, trying to process it, trying to fit it into what she'd been sent here to do. He still killed Sirens. That fact was irrefutable, and she couldn't ignore it. But if he didn't know he was doing it, if he really was cursed in some way, then that made a huge difference to her.

She needed to spend more time with him. Needed to figure out if Zeus or Silas was correct. Then she'd know how to proceed.

"I don't want you to think he's dangerous," Silas said. "He can be a grouchy pain in the ass sometimes, but he's never had an episode while he's been in the hold, and as I said, the only ones at risk when he does are Sirens, which you are clearly not." A half smile curled his lips then faded. "But yes, I'd like you to stay. If you're amenable to the idea. At least until I return."

She was. But not for the reasons he wanted.

Knowing she couldn't agree too quickly, Daphne bit her lip. She still needed to play the damsel-in-distress role. No matter what she decided to do about the Argonaut in the end, she couldn't let her cover slip. "He won't want me here. Especially if you're gone. He pretty much told me last night to get lost."

"I know." Mischief filled Silas's light-blue eyes. "That's why I have an idea. The question is simply whether or not you're brave enough to go through with it."

# Chapter Five

Daphne wasn't sure about Silas's so-called plan. He wanted her to take the damsel-in-distress façade one step further and insist Ari teach her self-defense. She had to admit it wasn't the worst idea out there, but she wasn't a hundred percent sure she could pull it off. Sure, she sucked at marksmanship, but she knew full well how to take care of herself.

*Like you did with those daemons?*

She scowled at a book on the shelf in Ari's library. Told herself no one stood a chance alone against a horde of daemons—especially unarmed and wearing those stupid shoes Athena had given her. But even as she tried to justify it to herself, a little voice in the back of her head whispered, *You're not Siren material, and you know it.*

Shaking off the voice, she wandered through the library, looking at books and trinkets on the shelves. Silas had started a fire before he'd left, and even though the room was warm and cozy, she couldn't seem to relax. Reading didn't sound the least appealing, she didn't feel like tackling a puzzle, and she was too keyed up to sleep. Nerves humming, she wandered from room to room, wondering when Ari was going to return. Wondering how he'd react when she proposed her little "you teach me to fight and I'll agree to leave you alone" plan.

She stopped outside the wing that led to his suite of rooms. Drew a deep breath. Knew she shouldn't invade his privacy but wanted to know what he kept locked behind this door. To her surprise, the handle turned with ease.

A hallway led to a wide-open bedroom suite complete with a simple bed, another fireplace already burning thanks to Silas, a sitting area, closet, and a door partway open to a bathroom. The room was sparse, nothing hanging on the walls, only two pillows and a plain white blanket on the bed. No pictures or trinkets or anything that personalized it as his. She moved to the closet, flipped on the light, and eyed the scattering of clothes hanging on the rack. All rugged. All made for being in the elements. All boring colors and way too functional fabrics.

Turning out of the closet, she looked over the room again and couldn't help but feel a twinge of sadness for how boring his life must be. Silas had said he kept himself closed off from people. This room was a reflection of him—simple, empty, lonely.

An image of her room back on Olympus filled her mind. White walls, white furnishings, white bedspread and pillows. No pictures on her walls either. The only thing of personal value in her room was the stack of books she'd collected.

Telling herself she wasn't anything like the crazy Argonaut, she headed back for the hallway that led to the door. The last thing she needed was for him to find her snooping in his space. But just before she got to the hall, she noticed another door she hadn't spotted in the shadows when she'd first entered.

She pushed that door open and stepped inside. Darkness surrounded her. Feeling along the wall, she found the switch and flipped it on. Light flooded the room from above. She let her eyes adjust, then scanned the space. A scuffed wooden desk took up the middle space. A couch sat across the room. Shelves stuffed with books lined three whole walls. But her attention landed and held on the fourth wall, on the giant world map stretching from one corner to the other.

Her brow lowered as she stepped closer and looked at the tiny red flags stuck in various locations across the earth. They were scattered all over Europe, Asia, North and South America, even the Arctic. But it was the symbol on each flag that made her eyes widen and her stomach draw up tight. A bow and arrow cut by the Greek symbol for sigma.

"What in Hades are you doing in here?"

Ari's voice boomed at her back, but Daphne didn't turn to look, didn't move, couldn't take her eyes off the map.

"You're supposed to be gone." He moved back to the door,

mumbled, "Skata," then yelled, "Silas!"

Daphne's gaze swept over the map, both disbelief and dread swirling in her belly to form a hard, tight knot. "You're tracking Sirens."

"Where the fuck is Silas?" he demanded.

She couldn't believe it. Silas had made her think Aristokles didn't hunt Sirens on purpose, but this map proved otherwise.

She whirled on him, no longer caring if he was upset she'd invaded his space. He was wearing jeans and a sweatshirt, his face flushed from the cold outside, his dark hair mussed, his bare feet insanely sexy against the hardwood floor, but she ignored the way he looked and focused on the facts. "Why are you tracking Sirens?"

His gaze narrowed. "How do you know what I'm tracking?"

She pointed toward the map. "Because I'm not stupid. I know the Siren symbol. You are hunting them."

A steely look crossed his features as he stepped slowly back into the room. "What do you know about anything I do?"

"I know—" Her mouth snapped closed when she realized she was about to give everything away. "I've heard stories. About an Argonaut who hunts Sirens. It's you, isn't it?"

He glanced toward the map with all its little red flags, then back at her. But he didn't say a word.

"Answer the question," she demanded.

He still didn't speak. Just stared at her with hard, narrowed eyes. And she knew instinctively that he wasn't going to answer, but she needed the truth once and for all.

Crossing her arms over her chest, she glared at him, no longer caring how this impacted Silas's silly plan or what Zeus wanted. "Silas is gone. He left to get supplies. Why are you tracking Sirens?"

"Stupid half breed," Ari muttered. He glanced toward the map. Still didn't seem to want to answer, but after several long seconds said, "Not that it's any of your business, but this is for avoidance, not tracking."

"Avoidance of what?" she asked skeptically.

"Sirens. I have a personal distaste for their Order. I started mapping their movements years ago so I could stay well out of their way. That's why I picked the Snoqualmie National Forest as my home base." He pinned her with an annoyed look. "Happy now?"

No, Daphne wasn't happy. She glanced back at the map. There was only one Siren flag in the Pacific Northwest, south of their location, but still close enough to Stonehill Hold where he could get to the location quickly if he wanted. "What happened to those Sirens?" She looked back at him and pointed toward the map. "The ones marked there in Washington?"

He scrubbed a hand over his forehead. "I'm not going to get rid of you, am I?"

"Not until you answer my questions."

He dropped his hand to his side. "I'm going to fucking kill Silas."

When she only continued to glare at him, he scowled. "I don't know why you care but there was only one Siren in that location, and I never personally ran into her. She, luckily, was too interested in a different Argonaut to taunt me."

Sirens didn't taunt. They lured. But Daphne didn't bother to explain the difference because she knew it would be lost on him.

She looked back at the map, taking in the flags all over Europe, following the intricate lines he'd created of the Sirens' movements, thinking of the hours and months and years it must have taken to compile this information. But her awe drew to a shuttering stop when her gaze landed on a collection of flags marking a location in Northern Greece.

"What is this?" She stepped toward the map, her eyes growing wide. "Why are all these flags grouped together in the Pindus Mountains?"

"What are you looking at now?" he muttered.

Fabric rustled, indicating he'd moved further in the room, but she didn't care how close he was. The pressure pushing on her chest was all she could focus on. "Here." She pointed. "Marking this tiny village."

"Because Sirens were there. Just like every other mark."

"I get that," she said calmly when all she really wanted to do was scream. "But why so many? And what does the black flag in the middle mean?" Her gaze skipped over the rest of the map. There were only a few other black flags on the map, randomly scattered over the continents, but if there was a pattern to their marks, she couldn't see it.

"Black means they wiped it out."

Everything inside Daphne went cold. "Wiped what out?"

"The entire village."

Daphne's heart felt as if it skipped a beat, then picked up speed until it was a whir in her ears. Her hands grew sweaty. Her legs swayed. He couldn't be right. The map blurred in front of her eyes, but somehow, she found her voice and asked, "H-how?"

"Gods, you're curious." His feet shuffled. "If I tell you, will you go?"

"Yes! What happened?"

Panic was rising in her voice. She could hear it herself. Several minutes of silence ticked by, but she didn't turn to look at Ari. Couldn't because she was too afraid of what she'd see. Truth? Lies? She wasn't sure which she wanted at the moment.

"It was like twenty years ago," he said at her back. "Zeus has always had a thing for nymphs, and this village was made up of nothing but nymphs. There was a female there he wanted. Simple thing. Wasn't interested in Olympus or the gods. But you know Zeus. He always gets what he wants. He pursued her, but she repeatedly turned down his advances. When he grew aggressive, she threatened to call the Argonauts in to protect her."

"Argonauts aren't sworn to protect nymphs."

"They're sworn to protect the human realm from otherworldy threats. Zeus can be a definite threat. Anyway, Zeus didn't like the ultimatum. He backed off, let her think she'd won. When enough time had passed and she'd let down her guard, he sent his Sirens to teach her a lesson."

No. No, *no, no, no, no.* It couldn't be true.

"I heard they burned the village, top to bottom," Ari said. "When they were done, there was nothing—and no one—left. Nice girls those Sirens, huh? Now you know why I avoid them."

The room spun around Daphne. It couldn't be true. It couldn't be.

"You seem shocked by this," Ari said. "Sirens have killed hundreds of thousands over the years. Anyone Zeus wants gone. What does one little village in the middle of nowhere matter to you?"

The map blurred. Flames flared in Daphne's memory, cries for help echoed in her ears. Hot, burning tears threatened, followed by a wave of pain she thought she'd put behind her long ago.

"I..." Pushing away from the desk, she bolted for the door, rushing past him, needing space, needing to think, needing to figure this out before the memories swept her under and devoured her. "Get out of my way."

* * * *

Ari was cold, wet, and more than a little frustrated. He'd spent the last twelve hours tracking a horde of daemons across two ridges before losing them in the snow. All he wanted was a hot shower, food, and a few good hours of sleep—in that order—so he hadn't been happy when he'd stumbled into his rooms and found the nymph who was supposed to be long gone invading his space.

Only now, food and sleep were the last things on his mind. Now all he could think about was the way she'd bolted out of this room as if she'd just relived a nightmare.

He looked at the map again, eyed the flags marking the location where that village used to be, then pictured Daphne's sickened face. And finally put two and two together.

"Skata."

He turned out of his room before he thought better of it. Was on the stairs before he even realized where he was heading. And pushed her bedroom door open before he could stop himself.

The room was empty.

For a fleeting moment, he thought maybe she'd left, then realized there was nowhere in this wilderness for her to go. He turned out of the bedroom and headed back for the staircase. Halfway down, he caught a flicker of movement through the tall, arching windows across the great room and stopped.

She was out on the deck. He watched her hair blow in the wind for several moments and told himself she wasn't his concern. He could go back to his rooms. Forget about the nymph. Forget everything but sleep. The sooner the nymph was out of his life the better. But that stupid duty inside him wouldn't let him walk away like he wanted.

He crossed the great room and pulled open one side of the

double glass doors. The nymph stood at the railing looking out over the dark valley, snow already collecting in her thick locks. Her feet were bare, and dressed in nothing but the T-shirt and baggy sweats she had to have gotten from Silas, she was already shivering, though he doubted she even noticed.

"Come inside," he said.

She didn't move. Thinking she might not have heard him, he stepped out into the snow, the cold immediately penetrating his own bare feet. "Come inside before you freeze to death."

For a long moment she didn't answer. Then softly, so softly he barely heard her, she said, "Were you there?"

She was talking about the village. *Her* village.

Skata. *This is not your concern. You don't have to answer.* "No."

"It was the middle of June. So hot I could barely breathe. I asked my mother if I could run to the creek to cool off. She didn't want to let me go, but I persisted. Finally, she agreed, but only if I took Argus with me."

Dammit, he'd been right. Though he wanted nothing more than to run now as she had then, his feet wouldn't let him. "Argus was your dog?"

She nodded as she continued to stare out at the darkness. "I lost track of time. When I realized how late it was, we ran back as fast as we could. I knew my mother was going to be so mad that I'd stayed late." Her eyes drifted closed, and pain etched her features. "I heard the screams first. By the time I cleared the trees, everything was in flames. I was seven."

Ari knew what it was like to lose everything—your hopes, your dreams, your future. And as much as he wanted to stay indifferent to the nymph, now he couldn't. "I'm sorry."

It was a feeble thing to say. His Argonaut brothers had all told him they were sorry when his soul mate had died, and it hadn't changed a thing. He watched as she stared out at the black swirling storm. Her face was as stony as the rocks in the cliff below them. Except for the tears that slid down her cheeks in silence.

"And you're sure it was Sirens?" she asked quietly.

"Yes."

"But you weren't there. You can't know for certain."

Her protest didn't surprise him. As a nymph, she'd probably

been taught that the Sirens kept the gods' peace. Denial was the hardest hurdle to clear. He knew that better than most. "There was one survivor, besides you. A boy. Eton, I think was his name. He was gathering firewood at the time of the attack. He saw what happened from the ridgeline and ran. After, he sought refuge in a Misos colony in Eastern Europe. He confirmed it was Sirens."

"I knew him." Daphne's eyes slid closed. "He was a few years older than me."

She stood still several long minutes, the wind whipping her hair, snow collecting on her dark locks, her clothes, her face, her arms and legs. And as much as Ari knew she needed this time to deal with her grief, the inch of snow that had collected near her ankles since she'd come out here told him it was time he got her inside. "Daphne—"

Abruptly, she turned back for the hold. "I have to go."

Thankful she was heading back in, Ari moved into the great room and shut the door at his back. But instead of heading for the stairs and the solitude of her room as he expected, she rushed for the entry to the hold.

She shoved her feet into the first pair of boots she found, then reached for the massive door handle. It took only two seconds to realize what she was doing.

Ari slapped his hand against the hard wood before she could pull the door open.

"You're not leaving like this."

"Get out of my way." She pushed his hand away from the door and yanked. "You wanted me gone, so consider me gone."

Cold air swept into the hold. But before she could get two steps outside, he captured her around the waist, pulled her back against him, then shoved the door closed with his foot. "I said you're not leaving."

She dug her fingers into his forearms and struggled against his grip. "Let me go!"

She was a strong little thing. Stronger than he expected. Twisting her around, he pushed her back against the wall and closed in at her front, bracing his arms on the walls near her head so she was trapped with nowhere to go. "Running after them won't do any good."

"How would you know?" She pushed at his arms but he held them still. "You don't know anything about where I'm going."

"No, I know everything about where you're going. I've been where you are right now. I've wanted them dead for what they did. But I also know there is no such thing as revenge against Zeus's army. The Sirens are too many."

Her struggle slowed. She looked up at him and glared, and in her heated look he knew that he was the closest target for her pain. But as their eyes met, the glare slipped away and was replaced with a sea of emotion. And he noticed for the first time that her eyes were a deep, emerald green. As green, he guessed, as the woods around her lost village. And completely and utterly mesmerizing.

"My mother's name was Eleni." Tears filled her gemlike eyes, and she blinked rapidly to hold them back. "I saw Zeus in our village days before it happened, talking with her, but I never put it together. I didn't know she was the reason…"

Her voice trailed off as tears overtook her. She lifted her hands to her face, her slim shoulders shaking with her sobs. And before Ari realized it, she leaned into him and rested her forehead against his chest.

For a moment, he stood stone-still. Didn't know what to say. Didn't know what to do. But when warm wetness seeped through his shirt and penetrated his skin, that duty took over, and he closed his arms around her, holding her while she cried.

She was small, the top of her head barely reaching his shoulder, soft and curvy, fitting perfectly against him. He didn't know a lot about comfort, had never been good at accepting or giving it, but he held her any way as she worked through her emotions. And though he told himself he was just being supportive, that there was nothing sexual about the situation, he couldn't stop his body from reacting to her.

His blood warmed. Tingles rushed across his skin wherever they touched. She smelled like vanilla, her scent rising in the air to make him lightheaded, and her damp hair was silky soft wherever it grazed his flesh. He forced himself to remain still, but the longer he held her, the more he had to fight the urge to slide his hands up and down her spine, back and over the curves pressed into him. And the more he tried to fight that, the more all he could think about was tangling his hands in her curly mass of hair, tipping her head back, and claiming her mouth with his own.

She shivered against him, and the movement snapped his brain back to the moment. In a rush, he realized the wetness pressed against him wasn't just from her tears. Her T-shirt and sweats were soaked from standing on the deck in the storm.

"You're cold." He drew back enough so he could lift her into his arms. The enormous boots on her feet slid right off to clomp against the floor. "You need dry clothes."

She didn't fight him when he carried her into the great room and headed for the stairs. Just sniffled and swiped her arm across her nose. "I don't have any other clothes. These were the only ones Silas gave me."

Ari stopped at the bottom of the steps. Skata. She was right. That dress she'd been wearing when he'd brought her here was nothing but rags now.

He moved for the hallway that led to his rooms before he thought better of it. She didn't say anything as he carried her in, set her on the bed, then pulled a blanket from the foot and wrapped it around her shoulders. "I'll find you something dry."

Still she didn't answer. Just clutched the blanket around her and stared off into space, her damp hair hanging around her face, her bare feet dangling above the hardwood floor.

She looked wrecked. As wrecked as he felt most days. Telling himself it wasn't the same, he moved into the closet and stared at the shirts hanging from the rack.

But he didn't see them. Suddenly, all he could see was the way she'd looked pinned against the bookshelf in his library last night. The way her breasts had lifted with her shallow breaths. The way her leg had trembled against his when he'd moved in close. The way her lips had parted and she'd lifted her mouth to taste him, an offering he'd been too afraid to accept.

His blood warmed all over again, and arousal flickered through his belly then rushed into his groin. It was wrong, so very wrong considering how vulnerable she was at the moment, but he wanted her. Wanted her spread naked before him. Wanted her writhing in pleasure. Wanted to feel her close around him as he slid into her from behind. She was a nymph built for sex, and he was a virile warrior who'd been locked away for far too long. It was basic biology that he should want her this much. But a little voice in the back of his head whispered now—right now—part of that wanting had very little to do with sex and everything to do with the fact wanting, craving, *taking* could make both of their pain and memories disappear. If only for a little while.

Skata. He blinked several times when he realized he was trying to justify it all to himself. Aside from the fact he hadn't been the least bit civil to her since she'd arrived, he'd just told her the truth about her village. She was in the next room falling apart *because of him.* There was no way in this world or the next that she'd ever want him again. And that was assuming she'd even been interested in the first place.

Disgusted with himself, he chose a long-sleeved henley he knew would be way too big for her and hide her trim little body from view, then headed for the bedroom. After she was dry and dressed, he'd shuffle her off to her own room and forget this night ever happened. And tell himself it was a good thing he'd come to his senses before it was too late.

Plan in place, Ari stepped back into his bedroom, then stilled. The wet shirt and sweats she'd been wearing lay in a heap on the hardwood floor. Blood pounded in his ears as his gaze skipped to the right, where she sat cross-legged on the sheepskin rug in front of the fireplace, the blanket wrapped tightly around her, her faraway gaze staring into the flames.

*Naked. She's naked beneath that blanket.*

Blood rushed into his cock, making him hard in an instant. But he fought back the arousal and told himself to hold it together a few more minutes as he walked toward her.

He held the shirt out. "I found you something dry to wear."

"Does it ever go away?" She didn't turn to him. Didn't reach for the garment. Didn't even look up. Just continued to stare into the flickering flames. "I thought it did. I thought I was past it. But knowing all of this...it's sharper than before."

She was talking about pain. The pain of loss, the pain of heartbreak. The pain of betrayal. He knew all three intimately.

He didn't answer. Didn't move. Focused only on keeping his emotions trapped behind the wall he'd erected to stay semi-sane.

But the hitch in her voice hit him hard, right in the center of his chest.

Unable to walk away like he knew he should, he laid the shirt over the arm of a side chair and sank to the floor next to her. "It gets easier."

"Silas told me it's been fifty years. It's not easier for you."

Ari rested his elbows on his updrawn knees and stared into the fire, irritated Silas had told her about his past, thankful at the same time because it meant he didn't have to talk about it now. He thought about those fifty years as he watched a flame dance over the log and wished he had sage advice for her, but knew he really didn't. "If you're lucky, you learn to live with it. And you don't let it define you."

"But yours defines you."

"My situation is different."

Daphne continued to stare into the flames. "What was her name?"

Ironically, it was no longer pain that consumed Ari when he thought of his soul mate. It was emptiness. Emptiness for a life he'd never have again. "Penelopei."

Daphne was silent several seconds. Then softly, she said, "'Duty crumbles to ashes in the fires of love.' My father said that once. He wasn't a nymph. Just a human. Caught between two worlds. He left his job, his responsibilities, everything for my mother." She shook her head. "I don't know anything about that kind of love. Not like them. Not like you."

Ari held back a huff. "I don't know much about love either. Penelopei sure as heck didn't love me."

Daphne finally turned his way, her soft green eyes no longer tormented by the past, but filled with a thousand questions. Questions that made his belly tingle. "But she was your soul mate. Silas said—"

Gods, she was gorgeous. More gorgeous than she probably knew. And he had no right being anywhere near her. He looked back at the fire so he didn't do something stupid. Like grab her and never let go. "Silas likes to romanticize the entire thing. I think it makes him feel better about choosing to stay here with me."

She stared at him, eyes wide and curious, waiting for more.

And though he didn't look at her, though he knew he shouldn't go on, that he had no reason to tell her any of this, for the first time in forever he found himself wanting someone to know the truth.

"Silas told you I found her on one of my missions in the human realm, didn't he?"

She nodded.

"And that she was injured?"

"Yes."

"When I came across her, her dress was ripped to the thigh, her leg scraped and bleeding. She begged me to help her. Told me Zeus had been chasing her. That she was trying to get away. I believed her. Took her back to Argolea, knowing she'd be safe from him there, and tended her wounds. Penelopei was..." He watched a flame devour a branch and couldn't help but see the similarity in the way Penelopei had devoured him. "She was like wildfire, consuming everything in her path. When she wanted something, she didn't let consequences influence her desires."

Disgust rushed through him when he remembered how he'd dropped everything for the female, even his duty. How he'd so easily walked away from his family. He shook his head. "As thanks for saving her, she seduced me. It was then I realized she was my soul mate. This may sound silly but sex is a powerful medium. Every Argonaut in the history of Argonauts has found his soul mate that way. What I should have keyed into, though, was the fact a soul mate is a curse, not a blessing."

"You're talking to a nymph," Daphne said softly. "I know how powerful sex can be. I've seen it firsthand. Zeus's desire for it destroyed my village."

And Ari's desire had destroyed not only his life, but his son's as well.

Guilt crept in. A guilt he'd tried so long to ignore, but it was there. It was always there, hovering in the background, telling him there was no way he could ever make up for the pain he'd caused his son because of his blinding desire for Penelopei. For a soul mate who'd never truly seen him as anything other than a pit stop.

"Penelopei quickly grew bored of me and life in Argolea," he went on, "and when Zeus's Sirens showed up to take her back to the god, she was more than willing to go. To her it was all a game.

Jumping from one male's bed to the next."

He sounded bitter. And maybe part of him still was. Because thanks to Penelopei, his whole world had shifted. Not because he'd loved her and lost her but because a stupid curse had made him crave a manipulative and shallow female.

"When the Sirens arrived at my home outside the capitol city of Tiyrns," he went on, "I wasn't willing to let her go. I was blinded by the soul mate connection and convinced if I could just get her to stay, everything would work out. A standoff resulted. The Argonauts came to my aid. But she didn't want to stay and struggled against my hold. The Sirens thought I was going to harm her. Before any of us could stop it, a battle broke out. In the chaos, Penelopei was killed."

And there was the crux of the rest of his guilt. Knowing that because he hadn't been able to control his desire, not only had he abandoned his son, but a female had died. "It wasn't my blade that struck her," he finished, "but I killed her just the same. If I'd let her go, she'd still be alive."

"Maybe." Daphne looked back at the fire. "If I hadn't gone to the creek that day, maybe my parents would still be alive too. Then again, maybe not. We'll both never know. And maybe that's the point. Maybe we're not meant to know. When I was a child, my mother told me that life was a series of events that make zero sense at the time, but which come together to reveal a greater good in the end. I forgot that until just now. Maybe what happened to you stopped Penelopei from tormenting another male. Maybe Zeus's fascination with her—and you—stopped him from ruining another family's life, like he ruined mine. Maybe everything happens for a reason."

He turned to look at her, at her profile set against the flickering flames. There was strength inside her. A strength he wasn't sure she knew was there. There was also simplicity. Something he craved in his confusing, fucked up, crazy world. "Are you saying you believe in some unseen Fates pushing us around like pawns on a chessboard?"

"I don't know." She shrugged. "I just know that if someone had told me a week ago I'd be sitting here like this with you, I would have laughed and said they were insane. Everything's changed in a short amount of time, and not by my doing. There has to be a reason for it."

He glanced back at the fire. He didn't believe in reasons. He didn't believe in the Fates. Where were the Fates when his world fell apart? Where were they when he started having blackouts and went nuts? No, he believed in what he could see and touch. And right now, what he could see and touch was way too close and much too vulnerable, especially when his arousal was still up and his own vulnerability hovered on the edge. "Be careful. People call me insane, and they're not far off the mark."

"Those people don't know you. I'd say you're way more sane than I am."

He huffed. "You haven't seen me at my finest."

"Yes, actually, I have." She leaned close and kissed his cheek.

Her lips were soft and sweet and gone way too fast. And though he knew he shouldn't, he turned to look at her. "Why did you do that?"

"To say thank you for stopping me from going after Zeus and his Sirens. I wouldn't have gotten very far in the snow without a coat. You saved my life, Argonaut. Again."

Their eyes held. Heat and electricity crackled in the air, warming his skin all over, sending a rush of heat straight to his belly. He didn't know if she felt the charge the way he did, but as the firelight danced over her smooth features and she continued to hold his gaze, her eyes slowly darkened and a warm flush grew in her cheeks, telling him she was feeling something. Something dangerous. Something wicked. Something he might not be ready for.

"Don't worry," she said softly. "I'm not going to seduce you to extend my thanks."

A wave of disappointment washed over him even though he knew he had no right. But then she leaned close once more, and he sucked in a breath, afraid to move, afraid to hope, afraid to do anything but go stone-still.

Her luscious mouth stopped millimeters from his own, more sweet and hot and tempting than any mouth had ever been. And in a husky whisper, she said, "I can't, because you've already seduced me."

# Chapter Six

Daphne knew she was playing with fire, but she no longer cared. Before Ari could push her away, she pressed her lips to his.

He tensed against her mouth. Every muscle in his body went rigid. And though she tried to keep it back, doubt rushed in. Doubt that she'd misread the look in his eyes. That he wasn't attracted to her like she thought. That his being nice to her here was simply that: politeness and not motivated in any way by the same desire she'd been fighting ever since she awoke in this hold and realized the sexy, rugged, wounded Argonaut had saved her life.

Slowly, she eased back, breaking the kiss. He didn't speak. Didn't move. Just stared at her with those mismatched eyes that seemed to flicker just like the firelight. And in the silence her mind tumbled for excuses, for something she could say to ease the sudden awkwardness. She was a nymph, trained in the art of seduction by Sirens. Awkwardness wasn't supposed to happen to her. But then *he* wasn't supposed to happen to her either, and here she was, hoping for something that had absolutely nothing to do with her mission. Wanting—

"Where do you think you're going?" His arm snaked around her back and pulled her in close to the heat of his body. "That wasn't nearly enough."

Daphne drew in one quick breath before Ari's mouth closed over hers, but relief filled her lungs, seeped into her body, and made her more lightheaded than any wine. She opened instinctively, drawing his tongue into her mouth, groaning at the sweet, masculine taste of him filling her senses. His lips were soft, his mouth wet and alluring, and when he leaned closer and kissed her harder, she knew she was lost.

She let go of the blanket, pressed her hands against his chest, then shifted her weight and straddled his hips. The blanket fell to her waist. He didn't break the kiss, continued to nip and suck and lick like he couldn't get enough. Inching forward, she slid her fingers up his pecs then across his soft, scruffy jaw. His hands found her waist, tugging her even closer. His mouth turned greedy beneath hers. Hot. Wild.

Settling herself on his lap so she could rub against his rock hard erection, she let him take the lead, wanting only to taste him deeper, to feel him everywhere.

"Daphne." He pulled his mouth from hers and pressed kisses along her jaw as he swept his rough fingers up her back. "Daphne," he whispered again before nipping gently at her earlobe.

Desire enflamed every inch of her skin. She groaned, tipped her head back so he could trail his wicked teeth and tongue down the length of her neck, rocked her hips against the thick line of his cock straining to be set free.

He flattened his hands against her shoulder blades, trailed his lips down her neck and across her upper chest, then pressed forward with his forehead, forcing her to lean even farther back. "I know I shouldn't, but, gods, I want you."

She lifted her head. Watched as arousal danced across his flushed features. Wanted only that and more. Wanted to see him on the edge of control, like she was now. "Then take me."

His mismatched gaze slid back to hers. Held. Didn't once waver. And the way he watched her, as if she were the only thing he ever wanted, only made her heart beat faster in anticipation. He looked back down at her breasts. "You don't know what you're offering."

Oh, yes she did. Suddenly, she knew exactly what she was offering. And it had nothing to do with Zeus or the Sirens. It had only to do with him.

Capturing his face in her hands, she tipped his eyes back up to hers. "I know exactly what I'm offering. You're not the monster people say you are, and I'm not afraid of you. If I was, I wouldn't be here now. I wouldn't be wet just from the thought of you."

A growl rumbled from his chest, one filled with lust and

hunger and need. Sliding his hand up her back to cradle her head, he pulled her mouth toward his and devoured her. She moaned and kissed him back. His fingers found the blanket at her waist and yanked. Then he rolled her onto the plush sheepskin rug and climbed over her.

*Yes, yes, yes...* Her legs fell open as he licked into her mouth. Her hands trailed to his shoulders and thick arms. He pressed kisses down her neck again. Kisses that made her hotter and wetter, and she arched her back, offering more, wanting everything. Gripping the fabric of his shirt, she pulled, needing heat, wanting skin. He eased away long enough so she could tug the shirt over his head, but when she reached for the snap on his jeans, he captured her hands.

"Not yet." His bare chest grazed her oversensitized nipples as he pinned her wrists to the floor above her head with one hand. "I'm not done exploring." He let go of her wrists, his lusty gaze scraping every inch of her skin, making her strain for his touch. "Don't move these. Or you'll regret it."

It was a warning, not a threat. And she hadn't lied. She wasn't the least bit afraid of him, not after the way he'd saved her life, healed her, and tonight shown her more compassion than she ever deserved.

A smile pulled at her mouth, and she wriggled against the carpet as his fingertips grazed her ribs and skimmed across her hip. "How will you make me regret it?"

He laved his tongue over her right nipple. "I won't let you come."

Her eyes slid closed. She arched against his wicked mouth as he did it again. Was already so close she was pretty sure he couldn't stop her.

His hand drifted across her thigh. The softest touch between her legs made her groan and lift her hips. "Oh, do that again."

He moved to her other breast, licked and laved, applied more pressure between her legs and swept his thumb over her clit. "Like that?"

"Yes." She rocked against his hand as he teased her breasts, desperate to feel him inside. "More."

He released her breast, slid down her body. "More here?"

The first swipe of his tongue along her steamy center sent tingles all through her body. The second raced along every nerve ending until she trembled. He licked and suckled, devouring her like a feast, and when electricity raced down her spine, she grasped his head and arched up to meet his tantalizing tongue.

He pulled away just before the orgasm hit. Gasping, Daphne reached for him, but before she could touch him he flipped her over, wrapped his arm around her waist, and lifted her hips off the rug.

"Stay there."

Daphne's hands landed against the carpet, and she pushed up, but his palm landed against her shoulder blades, holding her down. "I said stay there. You have trouble listening to directions, little nymph."

There was humor in his voice, and a hunger that supercharged her arousal. Fabric rustled behind her, telling her he was finally losing his clothes, and just knowing he was nearly naked sent white-hot excitement pulsing through her veins all over again. Curling her fingers in the rug, she pressed her cheek against the carpet and held her breath.

One bare knee nudged her legs apart. His fingers slid through her wetness again, making her groan. "Do you want more, little nymph?"

"Yes," she panted. "More."

He pressed his thumb against her clit. "How much more?"

She bit her lip to keep from crying out. Her fingers tangled tighter in the carpet. "You. I want you."

The thick head of his cock pressed against her opening. They both groaned as he filled her, at the tight slide as he drew back, at the friction when he plunged deep once more. His fingers dug into her hips. She braced her forearms against the carpet as she pressed back against him. They picked up a rhythm, one that made her see stars, one that pushed her closer to her release.

"Gods," he groaned. "This is how I imagined you."

His large hand slid up her spine and into her hair. Knowing he'd fantasized about her made her that much hotter. Her climax screamed toward her. White light flooded her vision. She opened her mouth to cry out. But just before she reached the peak, his hand closed around her hair and pulled. Not hard enough to hurt, but enough for a sharp sting to echo in her scalp and shoot down her spine, keeping the orgasm hovering just out of her reach.

"Not yet, sweet thing."

She gasped. Groaned. Rocked back into him, wanting more, needing everything. He wrapped his arm around her waist and pulled her upper body away from the carpet until her back was plastered to his chest. Letting go of her hair, he trailed his wicked hand down her chest and over her breasts.

"Wait for me, Daphne."

Sweat drenched Daphne's skin. She couldn't find the words to answer as he plunged inside her. All she could do was grip his forearm and brace her knees against the carpet.

"Just a little longer," he breathed against her, "and it'll be so good."

His fingers slid down her belly and into her wetness. She dropped her head back against his shoulder and groaned with every thrust, with every flick of her clit. He grew harder, pressed deeper, reached places she hadn't known existed. And when he drew her earlobe into his mouth and suckled, when he hit that most perfect spot, the orgasm she'd been chasing crashed into her and exploded.

He buried his face in her neck and kept thrusting while she rode the pleasure, driving deep again and again and again. Electricity raced down her spine, through her sex, and then it was there, another blinding orgasm, consuming her, dragging her down, making her melt. He whispered frenzied words she couldn't make out. His thrusts grew faster, harder, longer. And then he plunged deep and held, spilling himself inside her and quivering with his own release.

Daphne fell forward, the soft carpet almost painful against her sensitized skin. She turned her face toward the fire, dragged air into her burning lungs and tried to catch her breath. Ari's sweat-slicked skin slid along her back, then he collapsed next to her, struggling for his own breath as he wrapped an arm around her waist and drew her back against him.

She didn't fight the tug, didn't have the strength, didn't want to. His chest pressed against her spine, his hips to her ass, and though his flesh was hot, kicking up her body temperature, she didn't care. She liked the way he fit against her. Liked the way he held her. Liked the things he could do with his wicked hands and tongue and that super sexy hero body.

"You...are...a surprise...little nymph," he said in ragged breaths. "A very pleasurable...surprise."

He was too. A delicious surprise she never expected. She had no idea what she was going to do next, but she knew for certain that she wasn't finishing her mission or going back to the Sirens. And no matter what, she wasn't letting anyone else finish it either.

Smiling, Daphne reached for his hand at her waist and drew it to her mouth so she could press soft, wet kisses against his fingers. Sliding her tongue along his index finger, she drew the digit away from the others, closed her lips around the tip, and sucked.

He groaned behind her and pressed his awakening erection against her ass. "A very wicked surprise."

Daphne's lips curved around his finger before she let go. She shifted around and looked up at him. "You like wicked? I can be wicked."

Sitting up, she pushed her hand against his shoulder and rolled him to his back. A lusty, heated grin curled his mouth as she climbed over him. His hands landed on her hips. "I'm almost afraid to ask what you have in mind."

She settled on his lap, then braced her hands on the ground near his head and leaned forward. "Everything. I have everything in mind for you, warrior."

His smiled faded. He slid his hands into her hair as his gaze skipped over her face and he looked at her, really looked at her, as if seeing her for the first time. And though she couldn't read his expression, she knew he was as moved by all of this as she was. And that something important had happened here tonight. Not just sex, but a connection. One that had the power to change everything.

"Show me," he whispered.

She leaned down and kissed him. And planned to do exactly that.

\* \* \* \*

Wind howled past the windows of Stonehill Hold, but the chill didn't reach inside. Wrapped around a sleeping Daphne on the carpet in front of the hearth, Ari stared into the dying fire and watched wood crumble to ashes.

A pillow was tucked under his head, and a blanket covered their legs, but the warmth Ari felt came directly from Daphne, snuggled against him, her head resting on his bicep as she faced the fire, her hand clutching his at her waist. He knew he should wake her, carry her to the bed where she'd be more comfortable, but he didn't want to move. Moving meant he had to think, and thinking was something he was trying to avoid. Because thinking meant facing reality. And reality was hard and cruel and deadly.

The charred log slipped and fell into the smoldering coals, sending burning ash into the air. Ari watched a flake float and cool, turning from red to gray and finally white powder as it hit the stones of the hearth.

*"Duty crumbles to ashes in the fires of love."*

Daphne's voice echoed in his head. She was wrong. It wasn't love that destroyed duty, it was lust. Lust was the true deceiver, messing with the mind, fooling the heart. Lust for a female who'd never truly wanted him had destroyed everything Ari had held dear. And now, if he wasn't careful, lust had the power to destroy another life. Not his this time, but Daphne's.

He looked down at her sleeping against his arm, watched her eyelids flicker, and wondered what she was dreaming about. Wondered if she was dreaming of him. Her skin was like alabaster, her hair a warm mahogany that curled around his fingers like silk. His gaze slid over her cheek, down the long, lean line of her neck, to her succulent breasts he'd licked and laved and worshipped. And though all he wanted to do was worship her all again, a place deep inside his chest—a place she'd set free—knew he couldn't.

Bit by bit, Ari's good mood slipped away. Gently, so as not to wake her, he untangled his hand from Daphne's and carefully slid his arm out from under her head. A soft, sweet grunt slipped from her lips as she adjusted on the carpet and rolled to her other side. When her breathing lengthened and slowed, he pulled the blanket up to her shoulders then rose to his feet.

He tugged on his pants and headed for his office. After flicking on the lamp, he lowered into the chair and stared at the map on the wall across the room.

The sum of fifty years' worth of work. An obsession he'd prefer to forget but couldn't. He looked from flag to flag, marking the Sirens movements, and knew that even though he didn't want to, he'd go on tracking them. It was the only way he could stay semi-sane. He'd told Daphne about Penelopei, but he hadn't told her about the aftermath of Penelopei's death and what losing his soul mate continued to do to him even fifty years later. And as much as he liked Daphne's companionship, as much as he enjoyed being with her, he didn't want her to ever see him in the throes of one of his episodes. He'd barely survived seeing the horror in his son's eyes when Cerek had witnessed it.

There was only one way to keep that from happening. Rising, he walked to the window and looked out into the darkness. The wind had died down. By morning the storm would be gone. There'd be fresh snow, but he knew how to traverse the snowy landscape. And no matter how much he wanted to stay hidden in this hold, this time he couldn't.

Because by this time tomorrow, Daphne needed to be nothing but a memory. Not just for her sake, but for his as well.

\* \* \* \*

Daphne awoke with a start. Blinking several times, she looked up only to realize she'd been shaken out of sleep by a firm hand.

"Sorry to wake you." Ari set something next to her on the floor and pushed to his feet. "The storm's broken. I took these from Silas's room. You should be able to make them work."

Groggy, Daphne watched him disappear into his closet. He was dressed, wearing jeans, a long-sleeved T-shirt, and boots, and he'd showered, the tips of his hair still damp where they brushed his nape. But he should still be lying next to her, not up and moving around.

She glanced at the items he'd left beside her and realized they were clothes. Clean clothes. Confused as to what he was doing and why, more importantly, he seemed to be avoiding eye contact, she pushed up on her arm and scanned the dimly lit room.

The fire beside her was nothing but smoldering embers. A backpack sat near the door, one that looked as if it had already been packed.

Apprehension slid down Daphne's spine. Tugging the blanket up to her chest, she ran her fingers through her hair, then pushed to her feet and wrapped the blanket around her. She moved toward the closet and leaned against the doorjamb as she watched him pull a box from the shelf above the rack and flip off the lid.

"You're up early," she said, trying to sound nonchalant. Nonchalant had never really been her specialty, but if there was one thing she'd learned from the Sirens, it was that morning-after awkwardness killed the mood like nothing else, so better to avoid it altogether. "Any chance you made coffee? I don't operate well unless I have caffeine. Well, food too. We burned off so many calories last night, I definitely need food."

She was rambling. But this time she didn't care. He seemed to like it when she rambled.

He pulled a black knit hat out of the box, replaced the lid, and set the box back on the shelf. Handing her the hat, he stepped around her and said, "I'll find you a coat."

Two things hit Daphne at once. He was definitely avoiding eye contact—or any contact for that matter. And he was getting her dressed for outside weather.

"A coat for what?" She snagged the sleeve of his shirt before he could get all the way past her. "What's going on, Ari?"

He gently pulled his sleeve from her fingers and moved back a step. "I'm taking you into town. You need to get back to wherever it is you came from and I need to get back to the way things always are for me."

He was pushing her away. The realization hit like a punch to the gut. Last night *had* meant something if he was kicking her out like this. She stepped away from the wall. "I liked last night, and I know you liked it too. I don't want to leave."

"Well, you don't get a say in it." He moved for the door. "It's safer for you if you just go."

*Safer*... Safer, she realized...from him.

She darted around him, stopping in the hallway, preventing his exit. "Silas told me about your blackouts. I'm not afraid of them. I know you wouldn't hurt me."

He turned his mismatched eyes on her. But unlike last night, they weren't soft and dreamy. They were hard and icy. "Silas should learn to keep his big mouth shut."

He tried to move past her again, but she stopped him with a hand on his chest. "He cares about you. That's why he told me. And they're not your fault."

Those steely eyes narrowed. "You don't know what they are, and you don't want to be around when they happen." He grasped her wrist and pulled it away from his chest, then stepped around her. "This isn't up for negotiation. We're leaving in fifteen minutes whether you're dressed or not. It's cold outside. I suggest you listen."

He stomped out of the room before Daphne could stop him, but as soon as he was gone, her stomach sank and all the excitement she'd felt last night leaked out of her like a balloon deflating. Dropping down to sit on the hearth, she clutched the blanket at her chest and tried to stop her silly heart from aching.

If he wanted her gone, there wasn't anything she could do to stop him from kicking her out. She wasn't strong enough to intimidate him, sex clearly hadn't worked to seduce him, and Silas was gone, so she didn't even have the half breed on her side to talk some sense into the Argonaut. But what really hurt was the fact she'd failed. Not at her mission—she'd decided last night she wasn't about to let Zeus manipulate her into doing his dirty work ever again—but at convincing Ari he wasn't the monster everyone thought him to be.

Her gaze drifted to the rug where they'd slept tangled together, then to the clothes he'd left for her. And as both blurred in front of her eyes, she realized something else.

Without the Sirens, without a purpose in her life, she had no idea where she would go from here.

# Chapter Seven

The howling wind was nothing but a dull hum lost in the roar of the engine as Ari maneuvered the snowmobile around a tree. Unfortunately, it wasn't enough to distract him from the simmering heat at his back.

He tried to focus on the solid handlebars beneath his gloves, on his knees pressing against the seat between his legs. The machine was an extension of himself, the skis slipping over the pristine snow with ease, familiar and comforting. But the warm circle around his waist where Daphne held on for dear life kept distracting him. And the pressure of her thighs against the backs of his legs, the press of her breasts along his spine—even through the thick jackets they both wore—definitely wasn't comforting. It was arousing as hell, and every time she flexed her arms and moved even closer to hold on tighter, he remembered what it had felt like to have her wrapped around him last night. Naked and begging for his touch.

He zigzagged around trees, heading down the mountain toward the small town at the mouth of Lake Shannon. He had plenty of money to give her. From there she could catch a bus into Seattle then hop a plane wherever she wanted to go. Bottom line, though, was that where she went from here wasn't his concern. He was doing the right thing by making her leave. Getting her to safety before he snapped and did something he'd regret.

A heavy hand knocked into his shoulder. Realizing she was trying to get his attention, Ari turned his head, intent on telling her to sit still until they got to their destination. But one look was all it took to realize she was focused on something off in the trees.

Ari slowed the snowmobile. Before the machine came to a complete stop, she jumped into the snow and tugged off her helmet.

He quickly pulled off his own helmet and grasped her by the sleeve. "Where do you think you're going?"

"I saw someone." She tugged free of his grip and darted into the trees before he could stop her, her too-big boots sinking into the new powder with every step.

"Skata." Ari dropped his helmet on the seat and followed, his own boots sinking all the way to his ankles. Someone could be some*thing*. She could have seen a damn daemon for all she knew. Yeah, she was ticked at him for making her leave, but this wasn't ticked. This was stupid. "Come back here, before I—"

His words cut off when he passed a large tree. A trail of blood stained the snow and led from the tree around a large boulder. A warning tingle slid down Ari's spine. He reached for the dagger he'd strapped to his thigh before they'd left the hold. "Daphne, come back to me right now."

A grunt echoed from behind the boulder. Ari gripped the dagger and bolted around the rock, then slowed when he saw the horror.

Daphne knelt next to a female leaning against the rock in the snow, the front of Daphne's pants and jacket red with blood.

His heart lurched into his throat, and he rushed forward. "Holy gods. Are you—?"

"It's not me," Daphne said quickly, tugging off her gloves. "It's not my blood."

She pressed her hands against the female's shoulder. Blood gurgled between Daphne's fingers, ran down the female's arm, and dripped onto the snow at her side. "She's hurt. We have to help her."

Relief that it wasn't Daphne's blood whipped through Ari, slowing his steps, but that relief waned when he turned his attention to the female. She was dressed in knee-high black snow boots, slim black pants, and a thin jacket. Nothing someone who spent a lot of time in the snow would wear. Her thick mane, a mixture of blonde and brown and red, hung past her shoulders in a sleek wave, and her brilliant blue eyes were guarded as she stared over Daphne's shoulder toward him. On the ground beside her injured hand, lay a very unique, very intricately carved bow. A bow Ari had definitely seen before.

*Siren.*

The word ricocheted in his head like a marble zinging around a track. He waited for the rage, for the blackness to overtake him, but nothing happened. Looking out over the trees, he searched for anyone else, but the snowy forest was cold and silent.

"Ari," Daphne said, her voice dragging his attention back to her. "She needs help."

Ari watched the blood bubble through Daphne's fingers. She wanted him to help a Siren, the same being he hunted.

Except...he wasn't hunting this one. He hadn't even known she was in the area, which totally went against everything he knew and understood.

"Ari," Daphne said again, looking over her shoulder with pleading eyes. "She's going to die if you don't help her. Please."

That duty that was ingrained in his DNA kicked into gear, forcing his feet forward before he could stop them. He knelt on the Siren's other side and rubbed his hands against the thighs of his pants. The female whispered something to Daphne he didn't catch. In response, Daphne said, "Shh... It's going to be okay. Trust me."

Ari wasn't so sure. He didn't know what would happen when he touched the Siren, but that duty wouldn't let him leave. Regardless of what she was, she was injured, and he had the healing gift that could save her. To Daphne, he said, "Move your hands."

The Siren's jacket was shredded in three long, angled lines, blood seeping through the garment and running down her arm. Ari reached for the Siren's ripped collar. The female's eyes grew even wider, and she jerked back against the rocks.

"He's not going to kill you," Daphne said, scooting forward and placing a hand on the Siren's arm to steady her. "I promise."

The Siren looked from Daphne back to Ari, and though fear reflected deeply in her eyes, she stilled.

She knew who Ari was. She'd probably been in these woods to kill him, and here he was about to save her life. The irony wasn't lost on him, and for a split second he considered getting up, dragging Daphne with him back to the snowmobile so the Siren could die as she deserved, but as soon as the thought hit, he knew he wouldn't do it.

"Damn duty," he muttered. Then louder to Daphne, "We need to get this jacket off. I can't reach the wound like this."

Daphne grasped the ripped fabric in both hands and pulled, tearing through the Siren's jacket so they could peel it away from the wound. Three large claw marks ran in a diagonal pattern over the Siren's shoulder and down past her collarbone.

"A daemon," Daphne said, staring at the wound.

That was exactly what it looked like to Ari. And where there was one, there was always more. He shifted closer to the Siren, intent on getting this over and done with fast.

"How many?" Daphne asked the Siren. "And what happened to them?"

"Th-three," the Siren answered. "We killed two. The third"—she cringed in pain and adjusted against the rock—"the third took...Rhebekah...into the woods."

Daphne closed her eyes for a quick second, then opened them. "Was she alive?"

The Siren shook her head. "I...I don't know."

Two Sirens in the area, and he hadn't sensed either. Ari didn't know what the hell was going on, but when Daphne turned to look at him with pleading green eyes, he knew they were done wasting time.

He reached for the Siren's shoulder. "Hold her still. This will hurt."

The Siren tensed, but Ari laid his hands over her wound before she could jerk away again. Heat gathered beneath his palms, penetrating the wound and stitching it back together. A warm yellow glow radiated from below his fingers and palms. The Siren cried out as the heat and energy shot through her body, but Daphne held her down, preventing her from moving and disrupting the process. Seconds later, it was over, the wound sealed. The glow subsided, and Ari lifted his hands to check the result. Nothing but thin red lines remained on her skin.

"Will she live?" Daphne asked, looking at what he'd done.

Unfortunately for him, yes.

Knowing Daphne wouldn't want to hear that, he pushed to his feet. "Her wounds weren't nearly as bad as yours." He glanced at the Siren. Her head was tipped against the rock, her damp hair stuck to her temple, her eyes half-lidded as she breathed through the remainder of the pain. "In an hour or so she should be fine."

"Thank the gods," Daphne breathed.

Ari didn't thank the gods for anything. But as he studied Daphne's profile, the strong jawline, small nose, and the determined chin, he remembered her horror last night at learning Zeus's Sirens had destroyed her village and killed her parents. She, of all people, should want to see a Siren dead, but here she was, relieved that he'd saved one.

That icy space in his chest that had warmed and expanded because of her grew even wider, making his heart beat harder, making his fingers tingle with the urge to reach for her, to drag her close, to ask her what the hell she was doing to him. But he knew this wasn't the time or the place, and he definitely didn't want to have that conversation in front of his archenemy.

"Stay here." He tugged off his jacket and laid it over the Siren. "I'm going to have a look around."

He made it three steps away before Daphne's hand captured his arm. Before he could ask what she wanted, she rose on her toes and pressed her cold lips against the scruff on his cheek. "Thank you," she whispered. "Thank you for helping her."

She let go of him, knelt back by the Siren, pulled his jacked up to the Siren's neck and whispered words Ari didn't catch. And as he watched, that cold space deep inside heated until only warmth remained.

\* \* \* \*

"What the hell are you doing here?" Daphne whispered when Ari disappeared into the trees. "And what in Hades happened?"

Sappheire adjusted against the rocks, sitting more upright. "Athena sent us to find out what was taking you so long. We were looking for you."

Unease filtered through Daphne's belly. If Athena had sent Sappheire and Rhebekah, she could easily send more Sirens. She needed to think fast. "I hit a snag."

"No shit," Sappheire grunted. "What's going on, Daphne? Why did he heal me? He has to know what I am."

Daphne fixed the jacket over Sappheire's bare shoulder then sank back on her heels. "He does. I could tell by the way he looked at you. But he's not what you think."

Sappheire's brilliant blue eyes narrowed. "I don't understand. He should have killed me already."

Daphne brushed her hair over the shoulder of her jacket and braced her hands on her thighs. "He's not crazy, Sappheire. Not like they want us to believe. They lied to us—Athena, Zeus, all of them. He's not the monster they say he is. You've seen it for yourself."

Sappheire's eyes grew skeptical. "He's got you under some kind of spell. What have you been do—"

Ari's shout echoed through the trees, cutting off Sappheire's words. Frustrated that Sappheire so easily believed the lies they'd been fed, Daphne whispered, "There's no spell. I've simply opened my eyes."

She turned toward the trees where Ari appeared, stomping through the snow.

"I found two dead daemons and a trail of blood." He wiped his blade against his thigh, then sheathed it at his hip. "The third's no longer a problem." He looked down at Sappheire. "Your friend was dead by the time I got there. I'm sorry."

Daphne's heart pinched as she looked back at Sappheire. Daphne hadn't known Rhebekah long, but Rhebekah and Sappheire had been close. Emotions ran over Sappheire's face as she glanced around the snowy forest, clearly not seeing any of it. "I..."

"Are you sure there were only three?" Ari asked.

Brow drawn low, Sappheire finally looked up. "Three?"

"Daemons. Did you see any others?"

"No." Sappheire shook her head and swallowed hard. "No, only three. They surprised us. We heard voices over the ridge and went to look. It...it must have been them."

Ari glanced toward Daphne. "Voices could mean more. I can handle a handful of daemons on my own, but not an entire horde, not with you both here, and not with fresh blood in the area. We need to go."

Fear wrapped an icy hand around Daphne's chest and squeezed. She remembered all too well the horror of being caught with those daemons. She pushed to her feet. "Can the snowmobile hold all three of us? I can—"

"I'm not going with you."

Daphne's gaze snapped to her mentor. "Of course you are. You can't stay out here, especially if there are more daemons in the ar—"

"I'm not going with you," Sappheire said again. "I know how to get home on my own."

"But—"

"No buts." Gritting her teeth, Sappheire pushed up to standing. Her arm hung limply against her side as she leaned back against the rocks, but it was clear Ari's healing powers had worked. She looked past Daphne toward Ari at her back. "Thank you. For killing that last daemon. Where is she?"

Ari nodded toward the trees. "Fifty yards that way. You'll see the rocks. She's behind those."

Sappheire eased away from the boulder and took a step past Daphne.

"Wait." Panic pushed at Daphne's chest. They couldn't just leave Sappheire out here, not if there were more daemons in the area.

"I'm fine." Sappheire pinned her with a hard look. "I'm getting Rhebekah and taking her home. Go, Daphne, before anything else appears."

*Before any other Sirens appear.* Daphne heard the warning loud and clear. Sappheire was letting Ari go. But Daphne had no idea if the Siren meant to bring other Sirens back or if she'd tell Athena what she'd witnessed.

A new sense of urgency gripped Daphne. "She's right." She grabbed hold of Ari's sleeve and pulled him toward the snowmobile. "We need to go."

She picked up her helmet as they drew close, grabbed his and handed it to him. He was watching her curiously as she sat on the snowmobile and snapped her chinstrap, and she knew he was wondering what the hell had just happened, but she didn't have an answer, and she didn't want to get into it now. Now they just needed to put as much distance between them and this location as they could, in any direction.

"Come on," she said when he only continued to stare at her. "I thought we were going."

"She called you Daphne." His eyes narrowed. "I don't remember saying your name in front of her. Do you know that Siren?"

*Oh shit...*

Daphne's stomach drew tight as a drum, and her mind spun as she tried to think of an answer—any answer—that would make sense. But before she could latch on to one, Ari drew in a deep whiff through his nose and growled.

Startled, she looked up. And a new sense of fear consumed her.

His gaze was fixed on something far off in the trees. Every muscle in his body was tight and rigid. But more importantly, his eyes were no longer the mismatched green and blue she'd come to love. They were black. Deathly black, and one-hundred percent possessed.

"Sirens," he growled in a low, unfamiliar voice.

Daphne lurched to her feet and glanced over her shoulder. Six females—six Sirens—emerged from the trees. They were dressed in knee-high boots, slim pants, and tight, sleeveless shirts. All carried the familiar bow and arrows from Olympus, and all were as gorgeous and built as Sappheire. But a tingle of unease spread down Daphne's spine as she looked over the group. None of the females were familiar to Daphne, and she'd met every Siren on Olympus, even the newest recruits. More than that, though, the look in each of these Siren's eyes was both dark and evil. And it was a look she'd never seen from any of her sisters.

"Something's not right." She reached for Ari's forearm.

He pulled his gaze from the Sirens and looked down at her. And for a moment, the crazed, dark look faded and his eyes shifted back to their normal mismatched colors.

An arrow whirred through the air. Ari pulled Daphne off the snowmobile and shoved her to the snowy ground. Against her ear, he growled, "Stay down."

Her heart beat hard. Another arrow whirred through the air.

Ari jerked to his feet before she could grasp him, that crazed look darkening his eyes once more and twisting his features until she barely recognized him.

"Ari." She reached out to draw him back to her. "Stop."

But he was already was gone, racing toward the females she knew instinctively had never been her sisters.

# Chapter Eight

Ari was in hell. Burning in the fires of Tartarus, unable to escape from the heat. He turned, kicked, punched out at the flames, but they snaked over his body and danced toward his face as if he hadn't even moved.

He was going to die. Suffocate from the heat. From the smoke. And he deserved it after all the horrible things he'd done. After he'd left Daphne bloody and alone in those snowy woods. After he'd lost control and—

He bolted up, gasped in a breath, and stared into the flames across the room. A log rolled off the pile and sent a flutter of ash and sparks upward in the fireplace. Sweat slid down his temple and dripped along his spine as the crackle of wood echoed in the air, drowning out the sound of his heavy breaths, bringing consciousness slowly back into place.

His bedroom in the hold. He looked down at the soft bed, at the covers tangled around him. Kicking them free, he swung his legs over the side of the mattress, leaned forward, and dropped his face into his hands.

In. Out. He breathed deep as his heart rate slowly came down. He didn't know how he'd gotten here or what had happened, but that was nothing new. Whenever he had one of his episodes, he couldn't remember shit. All he knew for sure was that he was alive, he was naked except for a pair of boxers, and he was alone. But as soon as he closed his eyes, images flickered through his mind. The snowmobile. The Sirens. Arrows flying through the air. Daphne covered in blood, lying in the snow.

He jerked upright, walked across the room and back again so he didn't completely lose it, and racked his brain, trying to remember what had happened. He could only see bits and pieces, not the entire scene, and his mind kept tripping over Daphne in the snow, blood staining her hands and shirt and pants, reaching out for him, telling him...

He stopped. His brow dropped low. Telling him what?

*"Ari, stop."*

Her voice echoed in his head, the sound of her plea squeezing his chest so hard pain radiated outward from the spot. She'd been telling him to stop. To stop hurting her.

Bile slid up his throat. The walls closed in until he could barely breathe. Glancing quickly around the room, he spotted a pair of sweats he'd left on the chair days ago. With hands that shook so hard they barely worked, he pulled them on, needing air, needing to breathe, needing to run until the pain of disgust and regret loosened its hold.

He flung his bedroom door open, stumbled down the hall toward the great room and the wide deck beyond. Darkness pressed in through the tall windows. He had no idea what time it was, but he didn't care. All he could focus on was freedom. All he heard was Daphne's voice, echoing in his head.

*"Ari, stop..."*

"Oh my gods, that's it. That's...holy Hades, that's it."

His feet slowed just past the open library door. The first words had definitely come from his mind. A memory from the snowy forest. But the second...

He moved back to the library door and peered inside. A fire crackled in the fireplace, and in the middle of the floor, surrounded by books and notebooks, a slim female with dark, curly hair hanging past her shoulders sat cross-legged and scribbled on a piece of paper.

"Daphne?" he whispered.

Her head came up, and when her gaze met his, her green eyes twinkled. "Oh, you're awake. Good. There's something I want to talk to you abou—"

She wasn't covered in blood. She wasn't lying dead in the snow. Heart in his throat, Ari crossed the floor in three steps, grasped her at the shoulders and hauled her to her feet. The notebook and pen flew from her fingers. She yelped but he didn't let it deter him. He closed his arms around her and held her tight.

"Um. Okay." Her arms shifted around his back until they rested softly against his bare skin. "I guess that means you're happy to see me."

Relief was sweeter than any wine. He closed his eyes, breathed her in. Reveled in the fact she was whole, alive, not a single hair on her head out of place. And that she was here. With him. Waiting for him to come out of his nightmare.

He eased back, but he didn't let go of her. Wasn't ready yet. His gaze searched her face for answers. "How?" He drew away just enough so he could look down her body, so he could see for himself that she wasn't injured. Dressed in nothing but one of his long-sleeved T-shirts, the hem hitting mid-thigh to show off her shapely legs, she didn't just look healthy, she looked perfect. His gaze lifted back to her face. "What happened? The last thing I remember is seeing you bloody and hurt in the snow."

"I wasn't hurt." She slid her hands to his forearms, over the Argonaut markings he'd been born with. "That wasn't my blood. It was Sappheire's."

"Sappheire?" His brow wrinkled. "Who the hell is Sappheire?"

"The Siren you healed. She's upstairs. In my old room. Asleep."

A Siren was in his hold? He tuned into his senses. Didn't pick up a thing. If a Siren was close, he should know. He should be flipping out already.

Daphne's soft fingers landed on his jaw, tugging his face back toward hers. "Ari, you're not crazy. It's a curse. It's not your fault."

She was talking about his blackouts. His psychosis. Holy gods, she'd seen it. He let go of her and stepped back, for the first time realizing the kind of horror she must have witnessed.

"I know." He turned toward the fire, unable to face her. "It's the soul mate curse. Whenever I sense Sirens I can't stop myself. The need for revenge is too strong. I can't control it. I didn't want you to see that. I didn't—"

She stepped in front of him. "No, it's not the soul mate curse. It has nothing to do with your soul mate's death. If it did, you wouldn't have healed Sappheire. You'd be going after her now. And look at you, you aren't. There's not a crazed thing about you."

There wasn't. He felt as in control as ever. But that just meant his curse was growing more unpredictable, and unpredictable meant even more deadly. "I remember sensing them. I remember the rage and—"

"They weren't Sirens."

"They were Sirens. I was there. I saw them." He opened his eyes and stared down at her, ready to tell her to stop being so naïve, but the excitement in her gemlike eyes halted his words.

"Come here." She grasped his hand and pulled him around to her books, then drew him to the floor. "They weren't regular Sirens."

Her grip was strong, and he was still wrecked from his episode. He let her tug him to the floor. She grasped a book from her stack and handed it to him.

"Look here." She pointed toward a passage on the page. "They looked like Sirens. When they showed up in those woods, I thought they were. But then I realized they were different."

Ari glanced down at the book. A drawing of a female warrior dressed in leather breastplates, armbands, and boots, holding a weapon graced the page. "Different how?"

"At first it was the look in their eyes. There was a darkness there I'd never seen before on a Siren. But then I looked closer." She flipped the page. Another drawing of yet another female warrior filled the page. She was dressed the same as the first, except this one wore a sleeveless tunic. "It's subtle, but if you look closely..." She pointed toward the marking on the female's right bicep, flipped back to the first drawing. No marking there. She turned the page again. "Two S's in the shape of snakes, head to tail. Those females had this marking."

Ari was more confused than ever. "If they weren't Sirens, what were they?"

"I think they were the Sirenum Scorpoli. Zeus's secret band of Sirens. The ones he culls from the Siren Order to do his dirty work."

"That's no different from any regular Siren."

"It is different. The Sirens are tasked with policing otherworldy creatures in the human realm. Zeus's own private army. He can't control the Argonauts and what you do, but he can control the Sirens. The Sirens, however, are headed by Athena, the goddess of wisdom and war, so he can't use them in all the ways he wants. Enter the Sirenum Scorpoli. He can do what he wants with them, can command them to carry out any plot he deems worthy. And no one can stand in his way. Not Athena, not the Argonauts, and especially not his wife."

"What does Hera have to do with this?"

"Everything, I think." Daphne paged through the book in his hands until she came to a chapter on the gods, specifically a passage about Hera, Zeus's wife. "'And the Fates decreed,'" she read aloud, "'that no person—mortal or immortal—shall be subjected to more than one curse by any god at any time.'"

He stared at the words, still unable to see her point. "You've lost me. What does this prove and why is it important?"

"It proves you're not hunting Sirens." When he glanced up at her, still completely confused about where she was going with this, she shook her head. "It means what happened to you isn't related to the soul mate curse. If it truly were the soul mate curse making you hunt down Sirens in revenge for your mate's death, you'd have gone crazy as soon as Penelopei died. But you didn't. Silas told me that you didn't start having these episodes until long after you'd faked your death and were living in the human realm alone."

Ari looked down at the page. That was true. His episodes hadn't started for several months after Penelopei's death.

"These blackout moments don't happen when you're around regular Sirens," Daphne added. "I think they happen only when you sense the Sirenum Scorpoli. And if that's the case, then I think it's highly possible Hera took advantage of your pain and depression after you lost your mate and cursed you a second time."

"You just said a person can't be cursed more than once by any one god. Hera is the one who established the soul mate curse."

"Right. But once an Argonaut's soul mate is dead, there is no more curse, now is there?"

Ari studied her smooth face in the firelight. Her eyes were filled with hope and promise, but he was wary. For fifty years he'd been fighting the soul mate curse. Hadn't he?

"I hear what you're saying," he said cautiously. "But there's no way to prove it. Just because I didn't flip out on the Siren upstairs doesn't mean anything. It could just be that the soul mate curse is changing, adapting, I don't know, fucking with me so I go even more nuts."

"I might have believed that myself until I saw the marking on your calf."

"What marking?" He reached for the edge of his sweats and pulled them up to his knee. "I don't have a marking on my leg."

"It's faint. I didn't notice it until I helped you out of your wet clothes and put you into bed. Here." She placed her hand on his leg and twisted so he could see the back of his calf. And the very faint mark, two inches long, so light and in a place he never thought to look, he'd never noticed it.

A feather. A peacock feather.

"The peacock is a symbol for Hera," Daphne said. "I looked it up. No other Argonauts have that marking. Which means this mark, this curse? It's unique to you."

Ari stared at the marking, his mind tripping back over every encounter he'd ever had with Sirens. He couldn't remember them. Couldn't see their faces or the markings on their arms. But even if Daphne's theory was true, it didn't change anything.

He set the book down, what little hope he'd foolishly built up crumbling at his feet. "Whether they're Sirens or this Sirenum Scorpoli, it makes no difference. I still hunt and I still kill and I still can't remember why."

"It makes all the difference." She grasped another book from the floor and set it in his lap. "According to this—this ancient text from Olympus that I found in your own library—the Sirenum Scorpoli are responsible for instigating most of the wars in the human realm. They stir up religious zealots. They prey on differences between cultures and emphasize those differences until people want nothing more than to kill each other. These pages are filled with accounts of the Sirenum Scorpoli stimulating one natural disaster after another with Zeus's magic, for causing diseases like the black plague and AIDS. Think about it, Ari. Zeus thrives on chaos. Chaos creates instability and instability leads people to pray. To pray to the gods. And that, more than anything else, is what he uses the Sirenum Scorpoli to do. To make people turn back to praying to the gods. Because the more humans who worship Zeus, the stronger his powers grow.

"Ari," she said softly, "You're not hunting unsuspecting good guys. You're hunting the bad guys. The Sirenum Scorpoli cause more bloodshed and death than any daemons. They're daemons trussed up like models."

Ari's chest vibrated with both hope and doubt. He looked down at the book she'd set in his hand. Didn't remember bringing it here. Didn't know where it had come from. Closing the book, he looked at the cover. The same double-S marking Daphne had seen on those females' arms in the woods was stamped into the leather.

A memory flashed. Bits and pieces of a battle he couldn't piece together. "I took this from them," he muttered. "After a fight. When they were dead."

"That's what I assumed. There's no other way you could have gotten your hands on something from Olympus." She glanced up and around the library. "It's been here a while. You had the knowledge the entire time. You just didn't know it."

A sliver of hope tunneled its way into Ari's chest, but he was too afraid to let it grow. "If this is true, why would Hera use me? What did I ever do to her?"

"Nothing. You did nothing to her. But if she saw you struggling with your grief after your soul mate's death, I'm guessing she saw a way to use you. To curse you again in a way you'd never know. To make you think it was simply an extension of the soul mate curse, when in reality, it was her way to get back at her husband. The god who's done nothing but humiliate her to the world."

Ari's heart beat hard and fast against his ribs. If what Daphne said was true, then he'd been used as a pawn in an immortal chess game. He'd lost his life, his home, his son, all because of the whims of the gods. But ironically, he didn't care. Suddenly all that mattered was the fact he might possibly be free.

He reached for Daphne's hand, warmth and hope filling his chest, making him feel light and alive. More alive than he'd ever felt before. "How did I get here?"

Daphne smiled as he pulled her toward him. A sweet, beautiful, electrifying smile that made his whole body tighten in anticipation of her touch. "I brought you here. Sappheire helped. She heard the commotion through the trees and came running to help. When she saw the Sirenum Scorpoli, she opened a portal and helped me get you through before anything happened. I told her how to get here."

He hadn't hurt anyone. Not even those evil Sirens. "And she just...saved me? Even knowing how many Sirens I've killed over the years?"

Daphne's eyes softened. "She saw what I saw, Ari. And she realized the same truth I already figured out. That she'd never known a Siren killed by you. She's served with the Order for nearly three hundred years. She's Athena's right-hand Siren. If you were really killing Sirens like Zeus and Athena want everyone to believe, she would have met at least one."

Ari glanced toward the fire and watched a flame dance over the log. Remembered his dream of burning in the fires of Hades. He wanted to believe Daphne's claim. Wanted to believe he'd been doing good all these years instead of bad, but something held him back.

"How do you know so much about the Sirens?" His gaze drifted to the shelves. "I haven't been asleep that long. You can't have learned it all from these books or the Siren upstairs."

A nervous look passed over Daphne's face. "That's the other thing I want to tell you." She pulled her hands from his, pushed to her feet, and crossed toward the fire. "Oh man. I can't believe I'm about to do this."

Ari's brow dropped low as he watched her, and a low buzz sounded in his ears. One that set his nerves on edge. One he didn't like. Sliding the book on the ground beside him, he slowly rose to his feet. "Do what?"

"Ruin everything," she mumbled.

Before he could ask what that meant, she turned to face him and straightened her spine. "I know about the Sirens because a week ago, I was on Olympus training to become one. I wasn't in that forest by accident, Ari, and our meeting wasn't by chance. Zeus sent me here to find you. He sent me to find you, to seduce you, and then, when you let down your guard, to kill you."

* * * *

Ari didn't say anything. Just stared at her from across the room with blank, unreadable eyes.

Urgency pushed Daphne's feet forward, her stomach swirling with both dread and fear. Not fear that he would hurt her, she knew he'd never do that, but fear that she'd lose him if she didn't tell him everything fast.

"I was close to being inducted into the Order. I thought that's what I wanted. When Zeus gave me this mission, I couldn't say no. If I didn't do it, they would have kicked me out, and you know I have no family left. So I said yes, and I came here looking for you, and I pretended that I was running from a god, when the truth was, I was doing what he and Athena told me to do. But I quickly realized that you aren't at all what they said you are."

She knew she was rambling but she didn't care. All that mattered was making sure he understood the truth. "I didn't seduce you. I realized early on that I wasn't any good at seduction. I mean, I was trained in it. All Sirens are. But I guess none of it really stuck because when I tried to use it, you totally walked away. The only time you even seemed interested in me was when I was being my normal, rambling self, which, by the way, the Sirens do not like. I can't even begin to tell you how many times Sappheire's told me to shut the hell up. And I'd already decided that I wasn't going to do what Zeus and Athena sent me to do, but then I saw the map in your office and I learned what they'd done, and you were so nice and you comforted me, and...and I knew even more that you weren't the psycho they said you were."

She swallowed hard and met his eyes. They were guarded now, his gaze narrowed. And she still couldn't read what he was thinking. But those mismatched eyes of his were locked on her, and she took that as a good sign.

"I didn't sleep with you because I was trying to seduce you," she went on. "I slept with you because I wanted to. Because I'm attracted to you. Because you're the sexiest male I've ever laid eyes on. I mean, let's get real." She held out her hand toward his chiseled abs and muscular arms. "You're like...carved from marble. My knees went weak the first time I saw you in the gym downstairs, and that was when I thought you were a lunatic and when you didn't even want to have anything to do with me. I slept with you because you excite me. Because I'm crazy about you. Because..."

Heat burned her cheeks when she realized how insanely she was rambling now. But she forced herself to go on. "Because I...because I care about you."

No, she didn't just care. She loved him. The truth burned through her chest, stole her breath, and knocked her back a step. She'd heard that nymphs fell fast and hard when they met that perfect someone—her mother had once told her she'd fallen in love with Daphne's father in a matter of days—but Daphne had never experienced love before so she didn't know what to expect. Now, though, she did. Now, when her head grew light and her legs trembled, she knew exactly what it was from.

The room spun around her. Backing up, she reached out to steady herself but knew it was already too late.

Strong arms closed around her and pulled her against a hard chest before she hit the floor. Blinking several times, she gazed up into Ari's handsome face as that whoosh of emotion sped all through her chest again.

She really did love him. So much she no longer saw the scars on his jaw and neck, no longer saw the menace she'd first noticed in his mismatched eyes. She just saw a hero. Her hero. The only true hero she'd ever known.

She also saw someone who wasn't drawing her into him and professing his feelings right back.

He shook his head. "You're crazier than I am, you know that?"

Crazy. He'd said crazy, not beautiful, not amazing, not alluring, not dreamy. Just *crazy*.

Heat rose in her neck and enflamed her cheeks. A hard knot rolled through her stomach with the realization that she'd just made a giant fool of herself.

Pushing against his arms, she found her feet and stepped back, just enough so she could catch her breath. Just enough so she didn't humiliate herself even more.

*Pull it together, Daphne. So he doesn't love you. Big deal. You still believe in him. You can still help him.*

"So what if I am? Crazy, at least, is real. I could be all seductive and mysterious if I wanted, but I don't want to be. Just like I don't want to be a Siren. I never really wanted to be a Siren in the first place, but you can't say no to the gods, at least I didn't think I could. Now I'd tell them all to fuck off."

An amused expression crossed his features. One that only kicked her embarrassment up even higher. "And why are you smirking at me? Is what I'm saying funny? None of this is funny. I'm trying to tell you the truth. I'm trying to tell you—"

"Daphne." He grasped her by the shoulders and pulled her into him. "Stop talking, okay? I believe you. Any time you ramble I know there's no way you're lying."

Butterflies took flight in her stomach. "You do?"

He nodded, lifted one hand to her cheek, and brushed the hair away from her face. "And you are seductive and mysterious, and yes, even crazy. I've lived with crazy long enough to spot it." He slid his fingers into her hair and cupped the back of her head, pulling her toward him. "Which is probably why I can't get enough of you. Even when I know I'm the last person who should ever touch you."

"Oh..."

His lips brushed hers, and she groaned, immediately opening to his kiss. The taste of him rocketed through her body, bringing hope back to life. Tipping his head the other direction, he kissed her sweetly, slowly, with so much passion her head grew light. And, wanting only this, wanting only *him*, she dug her fingers into his biceps and just held on.

He broke the kiss. Rested his forehead against hers. Breathed deep as his thumb grazed her cheek. "All these years... All this time, and you're the first person who ever saw past the monster." He lifted his head and looked into her eyes. "Why did you even try?"

Tears filled her eyes. Tears filled with joy and love. "I didn't have to try. I just had to open my eyes. And when I did, I knew with you is the only place I ever want to be."

He groaned and kissed her again, his tongue sliding along hers, his mouth absolutely devouring her. She moaned, lifted to her toes, and wrapped her arms around his shoulders, giving him anything he wanted.

His hand slid from her hair, down her back and over the swell of her backside. He stepped into her, forcing her backward. Cool air tickled the fine hairs along her spine as he continued to kiss her, to drive her wild with his tongue, and she knew he was grasping her shirt, that he was pulling it up, that in seconds she would be completely naked. And she wanted that. Wanted more. Excitement pulsed through her. Excitement and heat and a desire that would never get old.

He broke the kiss long enough to tug the long-sleeved T-shirt she'd snagged from his closet up and over her head. The garment landed somewhere on the floor behind him. She didn't look to see where. Was too lost in the fiery heat in his eyes to care.

"This," he whispered as he slid his knuckles down her breast and around one straining nipple, "is all I want." He lowered to his knees in front of her. "Don't move."

Her stomach quivered as she looked down at him, and she remembered when he'd pinned her hands to the ground in front of the fireplace in his room and told her the very same thing. "Or what?"

He looked up at her, and mischief flashed in his mismatched eyes as he pressed his fingers against the inside of her right knee, forcing her to step open. "Or I'll tie you up and make sure you don't move."

A wicked thrill rushed through her just as he exhaled a breath of hot air over her mound. Her eyes slid closed, and she rocked forward, seeking his touch. She'd never been into the whole bondage thing, but with him she knew she could be. With him she had a feeling she'd be into everything.

His tongue parted her folds, slid along her center and flicked her already sensitive clit. Daphne groaned and pushed her hips against his mouth, wanting more. He did it again, this time flicking faster, circling the sensitive nub, then drawing it into his mouth to suckle.

Heaven. His mouth was pure heaven. His hands sliding over

her skin absolute paradise. When he suckled her again, she groaned and dropped her hand on the back of his head, pulling him into her. Pleasure arced through her body. Before it could consume her, though, his fingers closed around her wrist. He pulled her hand away then twisted it around her lower back and pinned it to her body.

His threat echoed in her mind, and that naughty thrill whipped through her once more. But then he flicked his tongue against her again and it faded. She rocked her hips again and again, losing herself in the ecstasy. Her orgasm barreled close. She slid her other hand into his hair and pulled him in again. Pleasure rippled along her nerve endings and shot down her spine.

He jerked away before it could consume her and quickly rose to his feet. "I warned you, little nymph."

Daphne gasped, stumbled. Reached out for him. But Ari ducked down, and before she realized what was happening, he wrapped his arms around her legs and threw her over his shoulder. A grunt passed her lips. She pushed a hand against his back, opened her mouth to tell him this wasn't what she wanted—that she wanted his mouth, his hands, *him*—but the words never made it out. A whoosh of air brushed her spine, and the grunt turned to a screech. Then her back hit the couch cushions, and she stared up at his handsome, naughty, playful face.

Desire burned in his eyes. A desire that heated her blood and supercharged her need. "You like being in control, don't you?"

He smirked, a sexy, one-sided grin that made him look downright delectable. Straddling her hips, he pressed one knee into the cushions, leaned over her, and reached for the lamp on the end table beside the couch.

Unsure what he was doing, Daphne twisted against the cushions and looked over her head. He grasped the lamp at the base, pulled until the cord snapped free of the lamp and the light went out, then tugged the end out of the wall socket.

Daphne's gaze shifted back to him. Firelight danced over his features, making his skin look darker and his eyes even wilder. "You just ruined that lamp."

"I know." Grasping her hands at the wrists, he tugged them over her head so they hit the arm of the couch, then wrapped the lamp cord around her wrists and secured the cord to the leg of the table. "Does that hurt?"

Unrestrained lust consumed her when she realized what he'd just done. And though a little voice in the back of her head screamed giving up control was so not a Siren thing to do, she ignored it. Because she wasn't a Siren. And because she was so wet from just the thought of him having his way with her, she could barely think. "No."

"Good." His eyes sparked with heat. "Now, you can't move."

*Oh yes...*

Her gaze slid down his chiseled abs, directly in her line of site, then over the waistband of his sweats, sitting dangerously low, the V at his hips making her mouth absolutely water. "What do you plan to do with me?"

He leaned down toward her mouth but stopped a millimeter from kissing her. "Everything."

She lifted, aching for his kiss, but he drew away. His hand lightly skimmed her belly and moved across her mound. She whimpered. Then his talented fingers finally slid along her heat and pressed deep inside, and she groaned.

Her eyes slid closed. Energy raced along every nerve ending. She arched her back, tightened around his fingers, twisted against the cord pinning her hands over her head. Sweat gathered along her spine. Her orgasm rushed right back to the surface. Pleasure overwhelmed her. But before it could crest and drag her under, he pulled away once more.

"Oh gods." Fabric rustled somewhere close. Daphne pulled against her restraints. Frustrated. Hot. Aching. "Come back. I need—"

His lips captured hers. His chest grazed her sensitive nipples. His tongue dipped inside her mouth until she was breathless and right back on the edge. "You need me."

"Yes. Gods, yes." She tore her eyes open, stared up at him through hazy vision. His face was flushed with arousal, his muscles straining beneath his skin. Capturing her leg, he hooked it over his hip, then raked his lust-filled gaze down her naked body until he was staring at her sex.

Her body quivered at the heat she saw in his eyes. She bit her lip as his hand closed around his thick cock. He leaned forward, and unable to look away, she lifted her head and watched as he rocked his hips forward, as the blunt tip of his cock slid through her wetness and over her clit, as he groaned at the sight.

Fire rushed down Daphne's spine. She dropped her head back and moaned. He slid his cock through her wetness again, then circled her clit until she saw stars. Until she was rocking against him, growing hotter with every stroke. Until she was so close her body trembled.

"Not yet, little nymph." He pressed his lips against hers and then was gone. His cock slid down and pressed against her opening. "With me."

She cried out at the delicious fit. Lifted to hold him in. Groaned when he slid out then speared inside once more. He braced one knee on the couch between her legs for leverage. Drove deep again. Every thrust was heaven. Each slap of skin divine. Leaning close, he kissed her again, taking control of her mouth the same way he controlled her body.

His hand skimmed her ribs. He pinched her nipple between his thumb and index finger. Rested his forehead against hers as he drove her closer to the edge of oblivion. "Gods, I love being inside you. Could stay like this forever."

Daphne moaned at the thought, lifted her mouth back to his and kissed him crazy, wild for more. He skimmed his other hand up her body and grasped her wrists in his long fingers, squeezing to hold her arms still. His lips released hers. Sweat dripped from him onto her as their bodies picked up speed. And it was good—so good—but she wanted more. Wanted all of him.

"Surrender to me," he growled.

She wanted to—gods, she wanted to—but she didn't know how to do that. She tightened around him, lifted to meet every stroke, tried to grasp his hand with her fingers pinned beneath his hold against the arm of the couch. She was close. So close. And she knew if she could just go over she could drag him with her. But—

He pinched her nipple again. Pain ricocheted through her entire body, wiping away every other thought. She arched and cried out. But before the sound was even out of her mouth, the pain transformed into pure, mindless pleasure.

Daphne moaned and sagged into the cushions. Ari's cock grew even harder as he pushed into her deeper, faster, hitting that perfect spot again and again. She let go of the tension in her muscles, gave herself over to his thrusts and wicked touch. And the moment she did, she had a split second of clarity. Of his need to overwhelm her. To consume her. To own her so she was his. Which was everything she needed too. The orgasm exploded inside her without warning, a sea of white-hot, blinding light that absolutely devoured her.

Long moments passed, but slowly consciousness seeped back. Shaking, Daphne dragged air into her lungs. Her muscles felt like gelatin, her body a pile of bones under a heavy weight. Prying her eyelids apart, she looked up, but all she saw was skin.

Ari lay over her, one hand still closed over her bound wrists, his slick body resting on top of hers while he fought to catch his own breath. Tingles erupted everywhere they touched, warming her skin, bringing it back to life one millimeter at a time.

"I'll move," he breathed in her ear. "Just...give me a second."

His body was as limp as hers, and the realization made Daphne's lips curl in a self-satisfied smile. She'd done that. She'd completely and utterly wrecked him. As thoroughly as he'd wrecked her.

Slowly, he eased back and looked down at her. His mismatched eyes were still glazed from his own pleasure, but a look of pure contentment softened his features and smoothed the scars on the lower half of his face.

He glanced toward the table above her head and chuckled.

"What's so funny?" She twisted so she could see what had captured his attention, then gasped.

The table lay in pieces on the floor, the lamp shattered against the hardwood.

She whipped back to face him. "Did I do that? Oh my gods, I don't remember that. I'm sorry."

His grin widened. "Why? I like a female who can relinquish control so completely and forget about everything around her." He pressed his lips against hers and rocked his hips, proving he liked it a lot. He was already growing hard again inside her. "I like it so much, I want to make you do it again."

Oh... She wanted that too. Right here. Right now. Every day

for the rest of her life.

*"I'm the last person who should ever touch you."*

His words echoed in her head. Groaning, she lifted to his kiss and lost herself in him all over again. He was wrong. He was the *only* person who should touch her. The only one who made her feel alive.

And somehow, she promised herself, she'd find a way to make him believe it too.

## Chapter Nine

Ari lay in bed, his arm wrapped around Daphne's back, her naked body draped over his as she trailed her fingers along his ribs. Firelight from the hearth flickered over the ceiling in his bedroom, and he watched the shadows dance and move as he played with the ends of her hair and tried to convince himself keeping her with him was not a bad idea.

Nymphs were highly sexual creatures, free with their bodies in ways other races weren't. He wasn't stupid. Sex with Daphne would have been mind blowing regardless of the situation, but the fact she'd shared her feelings made it all the more sweet. Nymphs weren't known to declare their emotions. Penelopei hadn't once told him how she felt, and they'd been together for months. Then again, Penelopei had been manipulative and selfish, and Daphne wasn't. Even though Daphne had trained with the Sirens, she was the most selfless person Ari had ever met.

She rolled her luscious body on top of his, rested her palms on his chest, and looked up. "You're awfully quiet, Mr. Argonaut. What are you thinking?"

She was also highly perceptive. Something that struck him as odd because Penelopei hadn't once keyed in to his moods in all the time they'd spent together.

He brushed the hair over her shoulder so it ran down her sexy back in a sleek mass. "Sorry. I was thinking about home."

"Argolea?"

He nodded.

"You miss it, don't you?"

He toyed with the ends of her hair. "Yes, I do. I miss the mountains and the ocean and the white marble of Tiyrns. But mostly I miss the people."

"Silas said you have a son."

"Cerek." His chest pinched with a familiar sense of guilt. "He'd be about a hundred and twenty-five years now."

She pushed up on his chest and stared down at him with wide eyes. "Good gods, your son is a hundred and twenty-five? You must be ancient."

Smiling, he rolled her back in the pillows and kissed her neck. "That's right. I'm older than dirt. You just got fucked by a senior citizen."

She giggled and slid her fingers into his hair. "Thank the gods your ass isn't saggy. How old is dirt, anyway?"

He moved to her earlobe. "Really old."

"Give me a number."

He stilled against her ear. She was only in her twenties. Nymphs had long lifespans, but not as long as Argonauts. Even though they both had roughly five hundred years left to live, he didn't want to shock her.

He also didn't want to lie. Not after the way she'd been so honest with him. He pressed a kiss to the soft skin behind her ear. "Two hundred and twelve."

Her hand shoved against his shoulder, knocking him back into the mattress. Sitting upright, she stared down at him with even wider eyes. "Holy Hades. It's a wonder you didn't break a hip with that last acrobatic stunt you pulled."

She had an adorable way of lightening the mood. One that put him at instant ease. Tugging her down onto his chest, he wrapped one leg around hers, locking her tight against him. "I have a stockpile of acrobatic stunts saved up." He lifted his head and kissed her. "And I heal fast. So if you break my hip, little nymph, I'll be good to go in only a few hours. Don't worry."

Laughing, she relaxed into him again, then laid her head back on his chest. "No wonder you're so attracted to me. You need someone to keep you young."

He sifted his fingers back through her hair and realized she was right. Isolating himself the way he'd done had only aged him beyond his years. Every day he felt the weight of loneliness wearing on his body and mind. He hadn't realized how much until Daphne had come into his life like a breath of fresh air, reminding him he was still a relatively young male.

"So when was the last time you saw Cerek?" she asked, drawing a lazy circle on his chest with the pad of her index finger.

His stomach instantly tightened, and an image filled his mind. A flash of that last day, when he'd set that fire. "Fifty years ago."

"In Argolea?"

"No. The human realm."

She didn't ask, but he knew she was waiting for more. And even though talking about it only brought back painful memories, he owed her answers after everything she'd given him.

"After my soul mate was killed, I wasn't much fun to be around. I was living in the human realm then, just trying to get from one day to the next. Cerek kept popping over to check on me when he should have been focused on his new position with the Argonauts."

"He took your spot after you left?"

"Yes."

"Do you have other children?"

"No. Just Cerek."

"And you miss him."

It wasn't a question but a statement, one that hit him hard beneath her hand where it rested on his chest. A lump formed in his throat. One he'd spent fifty years trying to get rid of but never quite could, one that made it hard to form words. He nodded.

She was quiet for several seconds, then said, "Since you said you were only with your soul mate a few months, and Cerek's way older than fifty, I'm guessing his mother wasn't your soul mate?"

He breathed out a sigh of relief, thankful they'd moved on from what a shitty father he was. "No, she wasn't."

Daphne looked up at him with narrowed eyes. "It's very hard to get information out of you, Mr. Super Secretive Argonaut."

There she went again, relaxing him when no one else ever really had. He brushed his hand down her hair, smoothing it over her lower spine. "It was right after I'd joined the Argonauts. I was young. She was interested in hooking up with a Guardian. It wasn't serious. When she discovered she was pregnant, we both knew our relationship wasn't going to last, but we remained connected through our son. We stayed friends."

"Does Cerek see her often?"

"She died when he was about ten. This was back when the borders of Argolea were more fluid. She and some friends crossed into the human realm and were attacked by a horde of daemons."

"I'm sorry."

He sighed and looked up at the ceiling, another whisper of guilt rushing through him because he hadn't been able to stop Gia. Hadn't been able to save her. "It was a long time ago. When she died, I mourned her, but it didn't break me. It was harder for Cerek. I had the Argonauts. He didn't. Somehow, no thanks to me, he got through it."

Ari's chest squeezed tight. Cerek had been dealt a crappy hand, and it was all Ari's fault. He hadn't done a thing to make life easier for Cerek, and when it all got to be too much, he'd walked away, leaving Cerek to pick up the pieces of a shattered family. That was Ari's greatest regret. That his son had paid for his mistakes. Was *still* paying for them.

"No," Daphne said softly. "I'm sure it's *because* of you that he got through it."

Startled by her words, Ari looked down at her. Her eyes were a soft green, her face filled with so much emotion, the pain in his chest slowly seeped away. She didn't know Cerek, didn't know how cocky and arrogant Ari had been back then, didn't know anything about his old life except what she saw now. And even after all of the horrible things she knew about him today, she still believed the best of him.

"Why do have such faith in me?" he asked quietly. "I'm not worth it."

"Do you really have to ask? I have faith because I love you."

For a moment, he was sure time stood still. Of all the things he'd expected her to say, that wasn't it. His heart beat hard against his ribs as he searched her face for the lie he knew had hidden somewhere inside her. But in her shimmering gemlike eyes he saw nothing but truth.

"Daphne." His pulse turned to a whir in his ears. "I'm pretty sure I'm not capable of love."

Bracing her hands on each side of his shoulders, she straddled his hips and leaned forward so her lips brushed his in the sweetest, softest kiss. "I don't believe that for a second. I can tell by the look in your eye and what you don't say that you love your son. And something tells me you didn't fake your death so Cerek would stop pestering you. You left to spare him from seeing his father in the throes of a nightmare he didn't understand. You can love, Ari. You already do."

She moved back to his side, rested her head on his chest, and curled into him. "Love is a blessing, not a curse. You just have to choose it."

Her breaths slowed as she drifted to sleep beside him, but Ari knew he'd find no sleep. Because as he looked into the flames on the far side of the room and her words of love echoed in the air around him, he knew he couldn't keep reality at bay any longer.

Zeus would never let her live. Not with the way she'd sacrificed her duty for his enemy. By now his Sirenum Scorpoli had probably already shared what had happened in those woods. And that meant every moment she spent in this hold put her life in that much more danger.

His chest pinched so hard it stole his breath. Rolling to his side, he wrapped his other arm around her and pulled her in tight to his chest. Gods, she awed him again and again. She believed in him when she had no reason to. Cared for him when others would turn away. Loved him even when he didn't love himself.

She was wrong. Love wasn't the blessing. *She* was the blessing. And he would do whatever he had to do to keep her safe.

Even if that meant becoming the savage she didn't believe him to be.

* * * *

Daphne slid out of bed at dawn, tired but in need of caffeine.

She hadn't been able to sleep much, thoughts of the Sirens and Athena and Zeus and the Sirenum Scorpoli sifting through her mind. She knew that wasn't the last they were going to see of Zeus's secret sect, and as much as she hated to leave Ari naked and asleep in that big bed of his, she needed to talk to Sappheire about what their next move should be.

She found one of Ari's huge button-down shirts in the closet, tugged it on, and headed for the hall. Voices echoed from the kitchen, and her brow lowered as she tried to figure out who Sappheire was talking to.

"And I bet that's something you do regularly on Olympus," a familiar male voice said.

"Actually," Sappheire answered, "it's not. I can't tell you the last time I went out on a date. The only males on Olympus are gods who aren't interested in anything but casual sex. And, no thanks, I don't need to be another notch on an immortal's bedpost. The males I encounter in the human realm won't even come near me when they discover what I am."

The male chuckled, then the refrigerator door opened and closed, and as Daphne listened, she realized it was Silas, back from his supply run a few days early. "Maybe it's not what you are but the way you look. Gorgeous females are more than a little intimidating to the average guy."

"It's not real," Sappheire said. "It's part of the whole Siren gig. Immortal glamour to create the perfect female. The old me isn't anything like this, believe me. Daphne's the only female I can remember in all the recent classes who wasn't altered. Nymphs are so genetically blessed. It's disgusting."

Silas chuckled again. "Something tells me you're wrong. Zeus doesn't pick the homely girls for the Siren Order. I'm sure he was fully impressed before your transformation."

"Well, I did always have great tits. Those didn't change."

"See?" The sound of a knife hitting a cutting board echoed from the kitchen as Daphne drew close, but it was the smile she heard in Silas's voice that piqued her interest. "There you go."

"Are you agreeing with me?"

"I'm definitely not arguing. They're more than nice from where I'm standing."

They both looked up when Daphne stepped into the room, Silas from the stove where he was cooking, and Sappheire from the counter where she sat on a stool sipping a cup of coffee with a silly grin. The Siren was still wearing the same pants she'd had on yesterday, but the light-blue T-shirt hanging off her toned shoulders had to be Silas's.

"Oh, there you are." Sappheire's smile wobbled as she set her mug down. "I was just telling Silas here about your irritating genetics."

Silas grinned. "She doesn't give her own genetics enough credit. Nice shirt, Daphne."

This wasn't one of the shirts Silas had picked out for her before he'd left, which meant he knew where she'd gotten it. And how. Daphne knew she should be a little embarrassed, but she wasn't. Not at all.

"How's the patient?" Sappheire asked.

"Fine." Actually, he was better than fine, but Daphne didn't want to share that with her friends. Some things were meant to stay private. She crossed to the far side of the kitchen, pulled a mug from the cupboard, and poured herself a cup of coffee. "He was more than surprised to learn you were here though, Sappheire."

"I bet he was," Sappheire mumbled, lifting her cup again. "Not as much as this guy though."

Silas chuckled. "You shocked me, I'll admit it."

"But it was a nice kind of surprise," Sappheire said with a smile in her voice. "Wasn't it?"

Daphne turned. Sappheire sipped her coffee, and looked right at Silas with that same silly, mischievous grin. His gaze held hers, and he smiled too, then went back to chopping. "Yes it was. A very nice surprise."

They were flirting. Daphne looked between the two, amused and, yes, surprised herself. Ari's caretaker and Daphne's mentor. Who would have guessed? In all the years Daphne had known Sappheire, she'd never known the Siren to flirt. Sappheire didn't even use seduction on her victims, like the other Sirens in her Order. Just arrows.

Silas's grin faded, and he turned toward Daphne. "Sappheire filled me in on what you discovered about Zeus's secret Sirens. It makes a lot of sense. Makes a shit ton of sense."

The secret Sirens. Right. Daphne needed to remember why she'd come in here, not get caught up in someone else's romance.

"The question is what are we going to do about it?" Sappheire asked. "No one's ever confirmed the Sirenum Scorpoli actually exist. That tells me right there that anyone who knows about them is dead. Which means we're at the top of Zeus's shit list. It's only a matter of time before he finds this place."

"I was thinking the same thing." Daphne bit her lip then looked toward Silas. "Ari's not safe here. The only place where Zeus can't get to him is Argolea."

"But his Sirens can," Sappheire pointed out. "That won't protect you or me from Athena's retaliation, or any of us from Zeus's evil bitches."

"No." Silas braced his hands on the counter. "It won't. And if Zeus sends his assassins into Argolea, it'd turn into a blood bath. Thousands of innocents would die."

Silence settled over the room as each of them considered. Finally, Daphne said, "We could contact the Argonauts. Ari's son serves with them. I know they would send help if they knew he was still alive."

"No one's contacting the Argonauts." Ari's voice echoed from the archway to the hall.

He'd pulled on loose-fitting jeans and a black T-shirt that stretched seductively across his broad shoulders, and as Daphne took in the sight of him, her skin warmed and all the delicious things they'd done to each other last night rolled through her memory. But there was a hardness to his mismatched eyes she hadn't seen last night, and remembering their conversation about his son, something in the back of her mind whispered not to push him too hard too fast. "It's the smartest option we have, Ari. I know you're not ready to go back to Argolea yet, but if Zeus comes here—"

"Then I'll deal with him." His gaze didn't waver from hers. "The same way I've dealt with his secret sect all these years. But you're right. The three of you need to leave." He looked toward Sappheire. "Take her back to Athena. If you tell her what happened, I'm sure Athena will protect her."

Oh no. He wasn't sending her away. Not now. Not after everything that had happened between them. He'd tried that once before and this time she wasn't leaving.

She set her mug on the counter, moved behind Silas, and crossed to stand in front of Ari, still in the doorway. "You're not getting rid of me that easily. If you're staying, I'm staying."

"This isn't up for discu—"

His words died as he lifted his head. Every muscle in his body went rigid. Before Daphne could ask what was going on, his eyes shifted from their mismatched blue and green to deathly black.

"Oh shit." Her stomach clenched with fear. For him. "Ari?"

He darted to the window and looked out at the early morning light.

"What's going on?" Sappheire slipped off the barstool. "Do you sense something?"

Ari darted to the next window, his gaze scanning the cliff beside them, then shifting to the valley far below. A low growl built in his throat. "Sirens."

Silas and Sappheire exchanged worried glances, but Daphne was too focused on Ari to care what they were thinking. Rushing to his side, she reached for his hand. "Ari, stay with me."

He rounded on her so fast she gasped, and when he looked down at her with those crazed eyes, his features twisted with fury, fear shot through her chest. But in her heart she knew this was the same male who'd touched her and loved her so thoroughly last night. And she wasn't about to let him forget.

She gripped his hand tighter. Forced him to look at her. "Stay with me. You can fight it. You fought it yesterday. Focus."

He squeezed her hand so hard, pain shot up her arm. But she didn't pull away. Instead, she watched his eyes for her cue. Held on. Said his name over and over. His eyes flickered between black and blue and green. Then slowly they shifted to the familiar colors she knew so well.

"Yes," she whispered, squeezing his hand, knowing she had him back. "I'm right here."

Before she could wrap her arms around him, he pulled his hand from hers and looked toward Sappheire. "Take her back to Athena *now*."

Panic pushed at Daphne's chest when she realized he meant to stay here and face Zeus's evil Sirens alone. She darted in his way, blocking his exit toward the hall. "I'm not leaving you."

He glared down at her. "Too fucking bad. You don't have a choice in this."

He tried to step around her but she moved in front of him again. "Yes, I do. I said I'm not leaving, and I'm not."

His jaw clenched down hard. His eyes flickered. She could feel the insanity bubbling just under his control, but she wasn't backing down. She hadn't been there when her village had been attacked. She wasn't leaving Ari now to the same fate.

"I'm not going anywhere without you," she said again.

"Yes, you are." His eyes flashed to black and held. "The Sirens trained you well, female. You were a good fuck and a decent distraction, but I don't have time for your games anymore, and the last thing I need is another person hanging on me, hoping for something I don't have the power to give them. I ditched my son for way less than you, so don't think for a minute that you're anything special. I don't want you anymore. Deal with it and get lost. All of you."

Daphne's mouth fell open, but he stepped past her before she could stop him.

Long, silent seconds passed. No one in the room spoke.

"We can't go to Olympus," Sappheire finally said quietly. "Athena will never side with us, not against Zeus. Not even if she knows about his secret sect. We wouldn't be safe there."

"We can't stay here," Silas said.

"No, we can't," Sappheire answered.

"I know who can help us." Strength gathered inside Daphne as she turned to face them. A strength she hadn't even known she possessed until just this very moment. "A Siren who would never say no to an Argonaut in need."

Sappheire's brow lowered. "You're talking about Skyla."

Daphne nodded.

Sappheire's jaw clenched. "She hates me."

"Doesn't matter. She's bound to an Argonaut. She'll be able to get the help we need."

Sappheire and Silas exchanged glances, then Sappheire looked back at her. "Are you sure about this? If we do this, they'll find out he's still alive, and he clearly doesn't want that."

"I'm more than sure. That little speech of his was complete bullshit. He might say he knows what he wants, but I know what he needs. We're not leaving him to Zeus alone."

"Well done, nymph." A slow smile spread across Silas's face. "Very well done."

# Chapter Ten

"Come on." Cerek tapped his palm against his bare chest then held his arms out wide. "Hit me. Ever since you and Skyla were bound, you fight like a pussy."

A low chuckle rumbled from Orpheus across the mat, rising in the ancient gymnasium toward the upper seating levels of the oval-shaped stadium that showcased some of Tiyrns greatest sporting matches. The Argonaut tipped his head and shot Cerek a pointed look. "I know you're scared of females and all, big guy, but let me tell ya a secret. Pussies don't fight. The good ones give nothing but pleasure."

Cerek swiped the sweat out of his eyes with the back of his marked forearm and scowled. He wasn't afraid of females. His reasons for avoiding them were his own and no one else's. But just the fact Orpheus seemed to make it his personal mission in life to razz Cerek about his lack of female companionship only fueled Cerek's desire for blood. "Fine, then you fight like a fucking girl."

"My girl's a Siren." Orpheus grinned as he dropped his bare shoulder and shifted his feet on the mat. "Or was. She'd take that as a compliment."

Orpheus charged and plowed his shoulder into Cerek's ribs. Locking his arms behind Cerek's back, he lifted Cerek off the floor. Air whooshed over Cerek's spine just before he cracked hard into the mat. Pain spiraled across his back, but before Orpheus could get the upper hand, Cerek flipped Orpheus to his stomach, grabbed the back of Orpheus's head, and slammed the Argonaut's face into the ground.

"Son of a fucking..." Orpheus shoved his elbow hard into

Cerek's ribs, knocking Cerek back a step. "That's my godsdamn nose, you prick."

"Let me guess." Skyla's voice echoed from the doorway that disappeared beneath the spectator area. "My mate was giving you a hard time."

Cerek pushed upright and glanced toward the former Siren. Skyla's blonde hair hung in a sleek wave past her shoulders, and her green eyes sparkled with amusement as she watched her mate roll to his back and pinch his nose to stop the gush of blood.

"I warned you not to taunt him," Skyla said to Orpheus. "Clearly, you didn't listen. Again."

A goofy grin slid across Orpheus's face as he peered up at Cerek. One that told Cerek loud and clear that the bastard had intentionally pushed him right to the edge just for the fun of it. "It's not really a workout if it doesn't get the blood pumping."

*Fucking idiot.* Orpheus was a deadly warrior in battle, but he liked to stir the shit at home. He always had.

Cerek held his hand out to Orpheus and pulled the Guardian up. "Next time I'll break your arm."

Orpheus flashed bloody teeth. "Next time I'll get my *girl* to break yours."

Skyla sighed. "My hopes for either of you to grow up just crashed and burned. Listen, children, we have a situation."

"What kind of situation?" Cerek's gaze snapped to Skyla, his focus zeroing in on the Siren and her real reason for being here.

"A very serious one." A female wearing slim black pants, boots, and the baggiest T-shirt Cerek had ever seen stepped up next to Skyla, her auburn hair, streaked with gold and brown, hanging past her shoulders like a luxurious mane. Beside her, another female moved into the room, this one much shorter, with long, dark hair, dressed in nothing but a man's oversized shirt.

"Whoa," Orpheus muttered. "Siren."

"Both of them?" Cerek's brow lifted in surprise. Sirens didn't often visit their realm. In fact, he could only remember one time in the last ten years that any Siren other than Skyla had shown up in Argolea.

"No, just the one on the right," Orpheus muttered. "The other's a nymph."

Cerek's gaze ran over the nymph, and his back tingled when her focus locked solidly on him. He'd never met her before but something about her made the hairs on his nape stand at attention and a whisper of worry rush down his spine.

"Don't get any ideas, daemon." Skyla shot her mate a pointed look. "The nymph's already spoken for." She turned toward the nymph. "Don't worry. He's harmless."

Grinning, Orpheus stepped off the mat and slid an arm around Skyla's waist, then leaned down and kissed her cheek. "Totally harmless."

"Ew." Skyla grimaced and leaned away from him. "You're covered in blood and sweat."

"Never bothered you before."

Skyla rolled her eyes. The Siren beside her looked Orpheus over with speculation. "*This* is the male you left the Order for?"

Skyla frowned up at her mate. "Yes. The one and only. Sometimes I can barely believe it myself."

Orpheus held out his hand toward the Siren. "Orpheus the great and powerful."

Skyla crossed her arms over her chest and huffed. "In your dreams, daemon."

Orpheus's bloody grin only widened. The Siren returned his handshake cautiously. "Sappheire."

"Whoa." Orpheus's stupid smile faded, and he looked back at Skyla. "The same Sappheire who—"

"Yes," Skyla answered quickly, turning toward Orpheus and widening her eyes in a shut-the-hell-up signal only a moron could miss. "The same Sappheire I served with on Olympus. Amazing, isn't it?"

From his spot on the mat where he watched the banter, Cerek couldn't help but chuckle. Even Cerek had heard Skyla's stories about the Siren who'd constantly challenged Skyla's status as Athena's right hand on Olympus. Leave it to Orpheus to stir the shit for his mate when the female in question was standing in the same room.

Orpheus looked back at Sappheire, his gaze sliding over her baggy shirt. "What are you doing here? That's not a sanctioned Siren uniform."

"No, it's not," the nymph said, finally speaking. "We're here because we need Cerek's help."

"Me?" Cerek glanced at the nymph once more, confusion tugging at his brows. "Why me?"

"Because Aristokles is in trouble." Her green eyes narrowed only on him. "Your father's alive, Cerek, but he won't be for long unless you help him."

\* \* \* \*

*Please don't let him die. Please, please, please...*

As she traveled through the portal toward Stonehill Hold with the handful of Argonauts who'd joined them, all Daphne could think about were the multitude of ways they would find Ari's lifeless body.

*Don't let him die. Please don't let him die.*

She wasn't stupid. She knew why he'd said the things he had. Not because he meant them but because he was trying to get her to leave him so she'd be safe. But what he'd been too stupid to realize was that the only safe place for her was with him.

Her nerves vibrated as her feet connected with the frozen ground. As they couldn't flash through solid walls, they'd chosen a location on the hillside outside the hold. She said another prayer that they'd gotten here before Zeus's army, then opened her eyes and gasped.

The entire structure was on fire. Dark smoke rose to the gray sky above. Female bodies littered the ground, some missing their heads, others stabbed through the heart by random blades, even more burned as if consumed by flames.

"Oh my gods." Fear wrapped an icy hand around her throat as she scanned the destruction.

"Way to go, Ari," Silas said at her side.

Daphne whipped toward him with wide eyes, but when the half breed met her gaze, she discovered he wasn't horrified like her. He was impressed. "Why—?"

"Booby traps," he said. "Ari wired this place up good in the event we were ever attacked." He pointed toward a dagger sticking out of a dead female's chest. "A rain shower of blades. Dirty bombs." He glanced toward the charred remains on the hillside beside them. "Barrels of oil he could light on fire."

Daphne looked back at the burning structure, a new sense of terror ripping through her. "Are you saying he set this fire himself?"

"Maybe. Hard to know. Zeus could be trying to smoke him out of the safe room."

"Is there no other exit?" Cerek moved up next to Daphne, his features tight, his eyes a little wild. Wild, Daphne knew, because she'd told him his father was alive, and they'd just walked into a nightmare.

"If Ari's in the safe room, he can get out." Silas pointed toward the south. "A tunnel runs from there, through the mountain, and exits in a ravine on the other side of the ridge."

Hope leapt in Daphne's chest. She scanned the snowy hillside.

Cerek took a step in that direction, but Theron, the massive Argonaut with shoulder-length dark hair Daphne had learned was the leader of the Argonauts, stepped in his way and pressed a hand to Cerek's chest. "Be careful. If what the half breed said is true and Ari's in one of his episodes, he could be dangerous. Even to you."

Cerek's back tightened. "He's my father. I'm not afraid of him."

"I know you're not, but—"

"He can control it," Daphne said. They both turned her way. "He just has to focus. If I can get to him, I can help him."

The skepticism in Theron's eyes said he wasn't convinced. "Let's hope you're right, female." He glanced toward the other warriors who'd flashed in just after them, standing behind Cerek. "Zander, Demetrius, and I will take Silas around the south side of the building and check the hold. Skyla, you and Sappheire go with Cerek and Daphne to where the tunnel lets out and see if you can find him. Orpheus, Phin, and Gryphon are coming up from the west where the path leads down the mountain in case anyone's coming or going that way. I sent Titus to find Nick. He and Cynna are on holiday, but if we run into Zeus, we're going to need our own god on our side. Let's hope we get out of here before that happens. Everyone clear?"

Heads nodded. Blades were drawn. As a light snow began to fall, Daphne looked from face to face, both awed and relieved that so many had come to Ari's aid. He thought no one cared. If he knew what they were all willing to do for him—

"Good." Theron stepped past Daphne and headed for the burning hold. "Let's wrap this up before anyone gets hurt."

"That dumbfuck better be alive when we get to him," Zander muttered as the group parted and he followed Theron down the snowy hillside. "Or I'll kill him myself."

Cerek turned to Daphne. "Come on."

Daphne had so many questions, about the Argonauts, about their relationships with Ari, about Cerek and what he'd been through these last fifty years, but now wasn't the time to ask them. She and Cerek had spoken briefly regarding Ari before they'd left Argolea, about who she was to Ari and how she'd known to go to Argolea for help, and though she knew Cerek had a million questions of his own, he didn't ask them either. Both of them were lost in thought as they hiked through the snow.

Her throat grew tight and her hands trembled as she stepped around trees and boulders, trying not to sink into the snow, trying not to let fear get the best of her. Sappheire and Skyla were silent as they followed. But the closer they drew to the ravine, the harder it was for Daphne to keep her pulse steady and her breaths slow and even.

The sound of metal hitting metal reached Daphne's ears first. Her heart rate shot up when she realized blades were striking. Her legs pushed into a sprint.

"Daphne," Sappheire hissed.

But Daphne didn't stop. Couldn't. Her heart lurched into her throat.

Breathless, she reached the edge of the ravine and looked down. Ari stood in the bottom of the small, snowy valley, his blade clanging against the dagger of a Sirenum Scorpoli as she lunged and tried to slice him. His arms were a whir of black menace, his blade a violent weapon that beat her back. And though Daphne couldn't see his eyes, she knew they were black and crazed. Could tell by his jerky motions that he was in that moment where all he craved was blood.

Screams echoed from the other side of the ravine. Daphne's gaze jerked that way, toward the dozen or so Sirenum Scorpoli sliding down the snowy incline. Her heart rate went stratospheric.

"Holy gods," Cerek muttered at her side.

She didn't have time to respond. Before she could look his way, he was over the edge, sliding down the snow, yelling Ari's name and swinging his blade as he sliced through Zeus's assassins like paper dolls.

Skyla and Sappheire quickly followed him down into the ravine and joined the fight. She was trained for this very thing, and Daphne knew she should join them, but all she could focus on was getting to Ari. On grounding him before he turned his blade on the wrong person and did something he couldn't undo.

Dagger gripped tightly in her hand, Daphne slid down the hillside. The sounds of blades slicing through flesh and bone echoed in the small valley, but she shut them out and focused on her target. Twenty yards ahead, Ari arced out with his blade and caught the Siren he'd been fighting across the jugular.

The female hit the rocks with a crack. Blood gurgled from the wound, choking her to death.

"Ari." Daphne raced up on Ari's right and gripped his forearm with her free hand as tight as she could. "I'm here, Ari."

His eyes were a sea of black, as possessed as she'd ever seen them. As if she hadn't spoken, he jerked his forearm free so he could move on to his next kill, but she knew if that happened, he might attack the wrong person. Frantic to get through to him, she dropped her blade on the rocks at her feet and grabbed on to his arm with both hands.

"Ari, dammit. Look at me."

Using every bit of strength she had, she jerked him around to face her. His crazed eyes couldn't seem to focus, skipped everywhere as if looking for the threat. But she held on, not letting go, and said his name over and over again. Until those black pools landed on her eyes. Until the glossiness started to fade. Until his eyes flickered from black to blue and green and back again, telling her he was still in there. That if she didn't give up, he could come back to her.

"That's it," she said softly while the battle continued to rage behind him. "I'm right here. Focus on me, Ari."

"D-Daphne?"

"Yes, it's me." Relief swept through her, stealing her breath, making the muscles in her legs grow weak. "I'm here."

His familiar, beautiful mismatched eyes skipped over her features. "What the hell are you doing here? I sent you to Olympus where you'd be safe."

Oh, she'd been so right.

"I'll never be safe on Olympus. Not when anyone who looks at me can see I'm in love with you. Did you really think I was going to let you do this alone?"

"Do what alo—" He turned to look over the ravine, then froze. "Holy skata."

Daphne glanced past him, toward Skyla, pulling her arrow out of a dead Sirenum Scorpoli, then to Sappheire, shaking her head at a body on the ground at her feet. Each and every one of Zeus's assassins who'd come over the side of that ravine was now dead. But Ari's shock had nothing to do with their victory.

His reaction had only to do with the fact his estranged son was striding right for him with a bloody blade held tightly in his hand.

\* \* \* \*

Ari tensed. Cerek was exactly as he remembered. Fifty years hadn't changed the color of his eyes, or the slope of his nose that was so much like his mother's, or the square cut of his jaw that came directly from Ari. He was just as big as he'd been before, the same height and size as Ari, and his sandy brown hair was just as rumpled as it had always been when he was a kid. Even the small scar on his upper lip, the one he'd gotten when he'd fallen out of that tree, was exactly the same.

But he wasn't the same. Fifty years had aged him in a way that didn't show on his face, but reflected deeply in his light-brown eyes. Eyes that were now guarded and filled with disbelief.

Cerek stopped two feet away, his wide-eyed gaze skipping over Ari as if he'd seen a ghost. A splatter of blood was smeared across his cheek. His jacket was torn at the shoulder, and the blade in his hand dripped crimson red droplets onto the dirty snow. But Ari didn't move. Didn't speak. Didn't know what the hell he could say to make up for fifty empty years.

"I didn't think it was true," Cerek muttered. "I can't believe it's you. All these years..."

Ari's pulse whirred in his ears, and his hands grew damp against his side. He wanted to turn, to run, to disappear, but he couldn't. Not this time.

*Say something, shithead. Do something. He's your son.*

He swallowed hard. "Cerek, I—"

The blade in Cerek's hand clanged against the snowy rocks at their feet. Then he moved so fast, Ari barely had time to brace himself. But instead of the right hook to the jaw Ari deserved, Cerek closed his arms around Ari's shoulders, pulled him in, and held on tight.

The snow, the ravine, everything seemed to swirl around Ari as he stood still, embraced by his son. He heard Cerek's voice. Knew the boy was talking to him, but couldn't make out the words. Except for one. One got through and wedged its way solidly inside that heart he thought he didn't have.

*Pateras.*

Every mistake he'd made, every wrong choice over the last fifty years no longer mattered. With tears stinging his eyes, Ari wrapped his arms around his son and hugged him back.

"I'm sorry," Ari managed, his throat thick with regret. "I shouldn't have left. I was wrong. I—"

"I don't care." Cerek drew back and clasped Ari's face in both of his big hands. Tears shimmered in Cerek's eyes as he shook his head. "You're back. That's all that matters to me." A beaming smile pulled at his lips. "You're back."

He hugged Ari again, so tight the air felt as if it were squeezed right out of Ari's lungs. But Ari didn't care. He didn't deserve redemption, but his son was offering it, and he wasn't about to let it pass him by.

Cerek finally let go and swiped his forearm over his eyes. "But you're an idiot for not contacting us sooner. What the hell were you thinking taking on Zeus's assassins alone? Good thing Daphne's smarter than you."

*Daphne...*

Ari's chest warmed at just the thought of her, and he turned quickly, desperate to find her. He didn't have to look far. She stood off to his right, her hair twisted into a knot on the top of her head, her body covered by slim black leggings, a fitted hip-length jacket, and boots that elongated her legs and reminded him what it felt like to be surrounded only by her. And her eyes, her beautiful, honest, innocent eyes, were focused right on him, shimmering with both love and forgiveness. Two things he didn't deserve. Two things that were now part of his life, all thanks to her.

He reached for her, slid his arms around her waist, then lifted her off the ground and buried his face in her neck. "I love you," he whispered. "I love you, I love you, I love you. Forgive me."

Her arms closed around his shoulders. "There's nothing to forgive." Her breath was warm against his skin, her words the sweetest thing he'd ever heard. "I knew you were just trying to protect me. I'm not stupid."

He couldn't stop the smile that spread across his mouth or the kiss he pressed against her cheek. "I know you're not. You're the smartest female I've ever met. Way smarter than me. Even my son knows that."

Her gemlike eyes sparkled as she eased back and looked up at him. "Don't forget it."

"I won't. No way I ever could."

"I should have known you were too much of a rat bastard to die," a male echoed from somewhere close.

The familiar voice ricocheted through Ari's mind, and he released Daphne just enough so he could turn and glance behind him. Zander, the oldest of the Argonauts and the Guardian Ari had served with the longest, strode across the snow toward him, all blond-headed and Adonis-beautiful, just as he'd been for the last eight hundred years.

Ari let go of Daphne and pushed her a step away, bracing himself for Zander's legendary rage, just in case. Behind Zander, he spotted other Argonauts, but he didn't have time to look closely. Because Zander captured him in a tight hug before he could, then slapped a hand on Ari's shoulder and drew back.

"You're an asshole, you know that?" Zander grinned and shook his head, that rage nowhere to be seen. "I fucking missed you man. Holy hell. I can't believe you're really here."

Friends Ari had thought he'd never see again stepped close,

hugged him, then let go. Words of happiness echoed around him but he was too dazed to decipher what was said. He recognized his Argonaut brothers—Theron, Demetrius, Gryphon, Phineus, and Titus. Spotted a couple people he'd never met but who were now obviously part of the group—like the blonde holding a Siren's bow and the guy at her side with dark hair and mischievous eyes. And he saw others still—like Silas and Nick and Daphne and Cerek—people who were familiar. Whose friendly eyes and warm smiles told him that no matter where he'd been or how long he'd been gone, he was home.

Emotions closed his throat, and tears—joyous tears—filled his eyes. Wrapping an arm around Daphne's shoulder, he pulled her in to his side and smiled. Really smiled. In a way he hadn't smiled in at least fifty years.

She laughed at something someone said and slid her arm around his waist. But instead of the warmth he expected to feel, a chill slid down his spine and everything inside him came to a screeching halt.

"Ari?" Daphne's worried voice echoed close but he couldn't look at her. Because his mind was suddenly focused on only one thing.

"Sirens..."

The world seemed to spin in slow motion. Ari turned and looked up. A Siren stood on the top of the ravine, her venomous gaze pinned on him. She pulled the string of her bow back. The arrow whirred through the air. Screams erupted. Ari lurched to his side. His arm caught Daphne by the waist, and he dragged her to the ground. A grunt echoed from her lips. Opening his eyes, he expecting to see the arrow, zinging toward him, but a body darted in the way.

The arrow struck flesh and bone with a *thwack*. Cerek dropped to the snowy rocks with a crunch only feet away.

No. Ari's eyes flew wide. *No!* He scrambled from the ground and skidded to Cerek's side.

"Cerek..."

Someone screamed his name. He looked up just as the Siren on the edge of the ravine pulled another arrow back. Another whir sounded, but this one didn't come from the Siren's bow. Just before she released the arrow, a dagger struck her in the throat. Blood spurted from her neck, and the bow fell from her fingers. Her body hit the ground and slid down the side of the ravine.

Ari's head swiveled to the side, and in a daze, he realized Daphne had thrown the dagger. She rushed to his side, dropped to her knees next to him, and looked down at the blood drenching Cerek's shirt. "Oh gods."

Air clogged in Ari's lungs as he looked back at his son. He had to fix this. Grasping the fabric where it was torn, he ripped Cerek's shirt open, then wrapped his hand around the arrow and pulled, but it wouldn't release.

"Ari." Panic lifted Daphne's voice. "Ari look."

His eyes shot to the wound. To the blood that was already drying, and the gray lines streaking outward from the spot where the arrow was embedded into Cerek's flesh.

Ari placed his hand on the skin near the wound. It was hard. Hard and cold, like stone.

"No." He focused on his healing power, placed his other hand over Cerek's chest. Energy gathered beneath his palms, but it wouldn't permeate Cerek's skin.

He tried again, but still nothing happened. Voices muttered near him. Feet shuffled. Someone dropped to the ground on Cerek's other side. But all Ari could see was his son lying in the snow in front of him, his body slowly turning to stone with every inch those lines traveled.

"No." Ari's vision blurred. He moved his hands to yet another spot, only his healing powers weren't getting through. "This can't be. Someone help us. Someone—"

"*Pateras.*" Cerek's hand closed over Ari's on his chest. "Dad," he said in a weak voice, "it's okay. Stop."

Ari stilled his frantic movements and looked at Cerek's face.

"I'm okay," Cerek said. "There's nothing you can do. I'm... You have to let me go."

"No." Tears swam in Ari's vision. He pressed his hands harder against Cerek's chest but it was already hard and cold. *"No."*

"I'd do it all again for you," Cerek said, his voice fading. "Promise me...you'll finish what we started. Promise"—the streaks crept up his neck—"you won't let our line fail."

Tears slid down Ari's cheeks. He'd said those very words to Cerek just before he'd faked his death and disappeared. He'd wanted Cerek to take his place with the Argonauts, to fill the slot meant for his kin as the chosen descendants of Theseus. Never in a million years did he expect to hear his son say the very same words back to him.

"I...I promise," Ari choked out. "I won't let our line fail."

Cerek closed his eyes and drew a shallow breath. "That's...good. That's...the way it should b—"

The streaks crept over his chin and up his cheeks, hardening his lips mid-sentence. Ari grasped Cerek's stone shoulders and screamed "No!" but the streaks spread up his face until his skin cracked and hardened and what life force was left inside him turned to solid stone.

"Holy Hades," someone muttered.

"Gods Almighty," someone else said.

Through tears, Ari stared down at Cerek's lifeless body, unable to believe what he was seeing. There had to be a way to fix this. There had to be someone—

His frantic mind caught on Nick. Nick was a god now. Kronos's son. Ari had seen Nick's face only moments before. He turned quickly, scanned the crowd through blurry vision, screamed, "Nikomedes! Do something! Do something now!"

"Ari, man." Nick stepped close, his face drawn and somber, his dark gaze skipping over Cerek's stone body. "I'm so sorry. I can't—"

"He can't bring anyone back from the dead," a cold voice said from the top of the ravine. Ari's head jerked around, and he looked up to where Zeus stood staring down at their group with contempt and victory in his black as sin eyes. "No god can. Thank your fucking Fates for that, Argonaut."

"You." Ari's vision turned red. "You did this. You killed my son."

"Technically," Zeus answered, "my very special Sirens killed him. Their arrows were dipped in Medusa's venom. I'd much rather one struck you, but since your friends consistently choose war over peace, I guess I'll take any dead Argonaut I can get."

"You bastard." Ari lurched to his feet.

Zeus's eyes flashed. "Careful, Argonaut. The laws of the Fates don't allow me to kill you with my powers, but if you come at me, I'm more than happy to rip your head from your pathetic body."

Ari jerked forward, but Nick captured him by the shoulders and stepped in his way. "He's right. Dammit, Ari." Ari struggled against his hold. "You can't win against the king of the gods."

The other Argonauts moved between Zeus and Ari. Disgust filled Zeus's features. "Circling the wagons. Such a mortal thing to do. You needn't bother. I'm done here." He turned his soulless gaze on Daphne. "You'd all be wise to remember who caused this tragedy, though. Had the nymph finished the job I sent her to do, I'd have what I want and your son, Argonaut"—he looked toward Ari—"would still be alive."

Zeus disappeared in a poof of white smoke. Smoke billowed around the ground near Ari's feet as well. Startled, he looked around, wondering where it was coming from. Then Daphne screamed his name.

He swiveled and looked down, and as the smoke cleared, he realized the ground where Cerek had just laid was empty..

"He's gone." Daphne's wide-eyed gaze lifted to his. "He's just...gone."

"Fucking bastard," someone said. "He took him. He took all of them."

Ari glanced over the battlefield. The dead Sirens were all gone too, only blood-stained snow left in their wake.

Ari turned back to Daphne, his mind a mess of what, where, how... But the tears spilling over Daphne's lashes brought reality to a hard, gasping breath.

His son was dead. Cerek was dead. And there was nothing he could do, no way he could bring him back. He'd healed so many across the years, but he couldn't save the one person who mattered most.

The finality of the moment hit Ari so hard, the pain dropped him to his knees in the snow as if someone had stabbed him straight through the heart.

"I'm sorry." Somehow, in the sea of misery, Daphne was there, wrapping her arms around his shoulders and holding him close. "I'm so sorry. It's all my fault. I shouldn't have gone to him. I shouldn't have gone to Argolea. I—"

"No," he choked out even though just drawing breath hurt like the pain of a thousand daggers. "No, it's not. This wasn't you. This was...me. This was...oh gods..." That pain turned to a burn that consumed his entire chest. "If I hadn't taunted Zeus all those years, if I hadn't killed his Sirens—"

"No." Daphne grasped his face so he could look into her eyes. "That was Hera. Don't you dare blame yourself for this."

Her voice penetrated the pain. She was his strength, his rock, his last lifeline. And he wanted to reach for her, to hold on and never let go, but the guilt wouldn't let him.

"She's right, Argonaut."

Daphne turned toward the female voice and gasped. And when Ari found the strength to look, he glanced past Daphne and spotted the same thing she had—the elderly woman dressed in a diaphanous white gown who'd poofed out of nowhere and now sat perched on a snowy boulder.

The woman brushed her silver hair over one shoulder with wrinkled hands. "Hera cursed you to destroy her husband's secret sect and the power he wields through them and with them. It had nothing to do with you, Guardian. You were but a vessel for Hera's revenge."

Voices whispered behind Ari. Someone muttered, "That's her. It's Lachesis." But he didn't turn to look. Couldn't because the Fate who spun the thread of life was focused solely on him.

"I know you hurt for what you have lost." Lachesis's gaze skipped to the group behind Ari. "I know you all do. And I know you cannot see the purpose. But in time you will understand. All things happen for a reason. Cerek's sacrifice will have rippling effects. Ones you will realize before the end."

She looked back down at Ari. "I also know your heart, Guardian. I know you want revenge. But now is not the time. Now is for healing. And healing is power. Use that power and you will not fail."

She pushed to standing, but her feet didn't hit the snow. They hovered over the ground as if she walked on air. "I cannot remove Hera's curse, but know this. Every curse can be a blessing if viewed in the right light. I have faith you can put this curse to use for the greater good. If, that is, you follow through with the promise you made to your son." Her gaze drifted to Daphne, and a slow smile spread across her wrinkled lips. "This one, I have no doubt, will help you. Hold on to her, hero."

The Fate disappeared as if she'd never been there. And though her words drifted in the cool air, easing a little of the pain, the only comfort Ari wanted—the only person he needed—was already hugging him again, pulling him in and never letting go.

"I'm here," Daphne whispered. "I won't let you fall. I'm not letting you disappear from the world again. Cerek wouldn't want that."

"No." Ari sniffled. "He wouldn't."

"You can do this."

He wasn't sure. But for Cerek and for her—for the two people he loved and who believed in him enough to love him back—he was willing to try.

"Only with you." He rested his forehead against hers and gripped her arms at the elbows as he drew in a steadying breath. "I'm nothing but a savage without you. You brought me back to life. Stay with me, Daphne. Stay with me and be my strength. Help me honor Cerek and my promise."

She brushed the hair away from his temple and drew back just enough so she could meet his eyes. Love and duty twisted together in her shimmering gaze, giving him strength, telling him that even in death, there was life.

"Always," she whispered. "I will always be right where you need me."

# Epilogue

The wind whipped Zeus's hair back from his face as he walked along the windy path up the slope of Mt. Olympus. "So he's rejoined the Argonauts."

"Yes, my king." The Argolean who fed him information on the Argonauts' movements stumbled over a rock then regained his footing as he hurried to catch up with Zeus's long strides. "He's taken the Argonaut Cerek's spot in the Order and vowed to finish his son's work. They've welcomed him back with open arms."

"Of course they have," Zeus muttered. "The prodigal son has returned and they all act as if he never betrayed them. What of the nymph?"

"She remains in Argolea. The two were recently bound."

Zeus's jaw clenched down hard as he walked. Had Daphne completed her mission, he'd planned to bring her into the Sirenum Scorpoli. He wanted her. Still wanted her. Her beauty and sexuality were unmatched, and since her mother had refused his advances, he *deserved* her. But she'd fallen for that asshat Aristokles, and now all his plans to have her writhing and moaning beneath him were ruined.

The Argolean stumbled again. Rocks spit over the side of the cliff that dropped straight down into the clouds. The pathetic male glanced downward with absolute fear. For a moment, Zeus considered pushing him over just to watch him scream, but restrained himself. He needed his spies.

"They—she—" The Argolean regained his balance and looked up at Zeus. "Everyone in the realm is enraged that you took the Argonaut's body. The funeral pyre releases the soul to the afterlife.

He cannot join his ancestors."

"No, he can't." Smug victory rippled through Zeus as they rounded a bend in the path. A cave opened three hundred feet ahead, a slow, red light spilling from the opening. "And what of the Siren? Sappheire?"

"She remains in Argolea as well, my king."

His vision darkened with the familiar rage of betrayal, but it cleared as he eyed the cave. Soon he would have his just revenge. Soon the walls of Argolea would crumble and he would control not only the human realm, but the world of the heroes as well. And all who dwelt there.

"That is all." He held out his hand. "Bring me more information when you have it."

The Argolean's eyes brightened with an evil glow as he reached for the gemstone in Zeus's palm that glowed with a shimmering blue light. "Yes." He bowed, then scurried backward, closing the magical stone in a tight fist. "I will. I absolutely will, my king."

Zeus snapped his fingers, opening a portal for the spineless maggot. Energy popped and sizzled. The Argolean stepped through, then the portal closed with a crack.

Alone, a smile spread across Zeus's lips. The idiot thought he had a prize he could use for his own nefarious purposes. What he really had was one more element that would aid Zeus in his quest.

He moved through the cave, heading toward the red hue. The tunnel twisted through the mountain, the rocks absorbing the light and all but humming with energy. Rounding the last bend, he drew to a stop three steps from the stone altar where the female with fire-red hair spilling down her back in endless curls stood staring at flames crackling in a bowl set on a tall golden pedestal.

Zeus cleared his throat.

"I sensed your approach." Circe, the strongest witch in all the kingdoms, met his gaze with piercing eyes. "Your little friend's pathetic snuffling could be heard for miles."

Zeus ignored the comment about his spy and narrowed his eyes on the witch. She was drop-dead gorgeous, always had been. Her body was long and lean, her breasts heaving and perfect in the flowing green dress that matched her eyes. A wide ballet collar showed off her toned shoulders and milk-white skin, the stitching accentuated her slim waist, and the long skirt flowed around her feet on the ground like an offering, making her look even taller than her seven feet. Bell sleeves cradled her slim wrists and fingers. And the choker at her neck with the large oval red stone in the middle, one Zeus swore fueled her power, accentuated the long, feminine line of her throat.

Her beauty was unmatched, her sexuality greater than that of all the nymphs. But both came with a price. The red sorceress was the most venomous black widow he'd ever faced, and Zeus had learned long ago never to mix business with pleasure in his dealings with her.

She flowed down the stairs as graceful as water, the scent of jasmine floating in the air as she stepped past him, warming both his blood and libido. "You've come to check on your prize."

Of course she knew why he was here. The female knew everything. Reminding himself not to be drawn into her web, Zeus followed her through a dark archway and into another tunnel. "What of your progress?"

"Patience, my king." She stopped at a door, pressed her hand against the steel, and turned to look at him. "Good things are bestowed on those who wait."

Waiting was a virtue Zeus sorely lacked.

She pushed the door open. White light cast illumination all over the black stone floor and walls and shimmered in waves over the still gray body lying on the table in the center of the room.

*Fucking witches...* Zeus's vision darkened as he crossed to the body and knocked his knuckles against the gray stone. "This isn't what I'm paying you to do. I thought you'd have this situation remedied by now. I need to know the truth. Can you bring him back?"

Circe moved to the other side of the table and batted insanely long, gorgeous eyelashes. "I can bring anyone back. But as I said, magic takes time. And what you've asked for here..." She looked down at the stone face. "This is going to require more than just time. Reprogramming is not a simple process."

Time was something Zeus had plenty of. But he preferred to have things done on his timetable, not anyone else's. This, however, would turn the tides in his war against the Argonauts for good. And for that, he was willing to wait as long as it took.

But he didn't like it. He pinned her with a hard look. "I want this fixed. You know I'm an impatient god, and you know what happens when I don't get my way."

Her eyes flared red. "And you know what happens when witches are pushed and magic goes awry. Do not threaten me, *king*, or your magic will turn to ashes in your hands."

Energy gathered in Zeus's palms. The desire to unleash it on her overwhelmed him. But then he looked down at the stone body between them. And told himself to save his fury for the Argonauts.

Their time would come. It would come soon.

He turned out of the room. "Just get it done."

# Eternal Guardians Lexicon

**archdaemon**—Head of the daemon order; has enhanced powers from the Underworld

**Argolea**—Realm established by Zeus for the blessed heroes and their descendants

**Argonauts**—Eternal guardian warriors who protect Argolea. In every generation, one from the original seven bloodlines (Heracles, Achilles, Jason, Odysseus, Perseus, Theseus, and Bellerophon) is chosen to continue the guardian tradition.

**Council of Elders**—Twelve lords of Argolea who advise the king

**daemons**—Beasts who were once human, recruited from the Fields of Asphodel (purgatory) by Atalanta to join her army.

**Fates**—Three goddesses who control the thread of life for all mortals from birth until death

**Fields of Asphodel**—Purgatory

**Isles of the Blessed**—Heaven

**matéras**—Mother

**Misos**—Half-human/half-Argolean race that lives hidden among humans

**Olympians**—Current ruling gods of the Greek pantheon, led by Zeus; meddle in human life

*__patéras__*—Father

**Siren Order**—Zeus's elite band of personal warriors. Commanded by Athena

*skata*—Swearword

**Tartarus**—Realm of the Underworld similar to hell

**Titans**—The ruling gods before the Olympians

**Underworld**—Hell. Ruled by Hades

# About Elisabeth Naughton

Before topping multiple bestseller lists--including those of the New York Times, USA Today, and the Wall Street Journal--Elisabeth Naughton taught middle school science. A voracious reader, she soon discovered she had a knack for creating stories with a chemistry of their own. The spark turned into a flame, and Naughton now writes full-time. Besides topping bestseller lists, her books have been nominated for some of the industry's most prestigious awards, such as the RITA® and Golden Heart Awards from Romance Writers of America, the Australian Romance Reader Awards, and the Golden Leaf Award. When not dreaming up new stories, Naughton can be found spending time with her husband and three children in their western Oregon home. Learn more at www.ElisabethNaughton.com.

# Also From Elisabeth Naughton

Eternal Guardians
*(paranormal romance)*
MARKED
ENTWINED
TEMPTED
ENRAPTURED
ENSLAVED
BOUND
TWISTED

Aegis Series
*(romantic suspense)*
BODYGUARDS IN BED
FIRST EXPOSURE
SINFUL SURRENDER
EXTREME MEASURES
LETHAL CONSEQUENCES

Against All Odds Series
*(romantic suspense)*
WAIT FOR ME
HOLD ON TO ME

Stolen Series
*(romantic suspense)*
STOLEN FURY
STOLEN HEAT
STOLEN SEDUCTION
STOLEN CHANCES

Firebrand Series
*(paranormal romance)*
BOUND TO SEDUCTION
SLAVE TO PASSION
POSSESSED BY DESIRE

# Twisted
Eternal Guardians, Book 7
By Elisabeth Naughton
Now Available!

**NICK** – Leader of the half-breeds and the last true hero. He's spent his life fighting a dark pull toward the gods. A pull he now knows is linked to his father Krónos and the Titan's plan to escape from the Underworld.

But Nick's hidden powers are coveted by more than just his father. Imprisoned by Hades, Nick battles every form of torture imaginable as the sadistic god schemes to break him. Only one thing is keeping him sane. One woman who gives him the strength to fight the relentless darkness. She has a dangerous plan of her own, though, and as Nick's powers grow stronger, even she might not be enough to alter his destiny.

As the fate of the world hangs in the balance, Nick's allegiances are tested. And no one knows whether he will choose to fight for good or succumb to the sinister lure of evil. Not even him.

\* \* \* \*

The guards swung the steel door open and pushed Nick into his cell. No windows, no light. A torch on the wall illuminated the damp space made up of nothing but rock walls and the pile of blankets where he slept in the corner.

They maneuvered him around until he was standing in the center of the room, facing the door. One guard uncuffed his wrists, and for a moment, Nick thought of taking them down. But voices were already resonating through the corridor, growing stronger, coming closer. And one stood out, causing his stomach to tighten and arousal to rush through his body, bringing every other thought to a halt.

The click of heels sounded as the guards hooked chains to D-bolts in the ceiling, then reached for his arms. As they attached the first chain to his left wrist, stretching his limb up and away from his body, he winced, the injury in his shoulder sending a sharp shot of pain across his muscles. They grasped his other arm and locked him to the chain, then closed the metal cuffs around his ankles, kicked his legs shoulder-width apart, and chained those to hooks in the floor as well.

Cynna appeared in the doorway to the room.

The pain dissipated as Nick focused on her. She was wearing the same revealing outfit she'd had on when she'd watched his fight in the training ring, and it distracted him from what was going on around him. Excited him. Sent a wicked thrill through the dark part of what was left of his soul.

"Mistress," the injured guard said, standing straight. "The prisoner is ready."

Cynna's gaze flicked over Nick, over his bare torso and the small white towel covering his awakening erection, then up to his face to hover on the scar on his left cheek. Without sparing a look toward the guards, she said, "Leave us."

Her voice was like sandpaper and velvet, a voice made for sin, just like her body. In her hands she held a jar.

Two females—no, nymphs—rushed into the room as soon as the guards left. One was blonde, the other with short dark hair. They were both petite, both submissive with their eyes cast downward, and both were wearing flimsy pale pink dresses made from thin fabric that barely hid their bodies from view. They were also wearing metal collars. Collars he'd seen on other submissives in the tunnels. Collars that marked them as sex slaves.

Nick's stomach tightened. His gaze skipped past the females, toward the steel door, which was now closed, and through the small window to see who was watching.

Darkness reflected in the glass. But that didn't mean they were alone. Zagreus was always somewhere watching Nick's torture. Feeding off it. Waiting for him to break.

Turning to the dark-haired nymph on her right, Cynna handed the female the jar and said, "Use this. But do not touch him anywhere save where he bleeds."

The nymph nodded and approached, her cheeks a deep cherry red, her breaths shallow. She unscrewed the lid and set it on the rocks at her feet, then gathered a scoop of whatever was in the jar and lowered to her knees in front of him.

Nick sucked in a breath. She was inches away, his groin hidden only by the small towel. Her fingers grazed the wound on his thigh, a tickling sensation that made his muscles tense, but the healing balm was cool where it coated the gash. He relaxed as she rubbed the balm into the wound, feeling the jagged skin already knitting back together, feeling his body healing faster than it would on its own, feeling a heat he didn't expect warming his skin.

"Enough," Cynna said. "Now the other one."

The dark-haired nymph pushed to her feet, still didn't look Nick in the eye, and moved around behind him. Again he felt her fingers gliding over his skin, and he tensed, then the balm slathered the wound in his shoulder, slowly warming his skin, repairing the damage and relaxing him from the outside in.

Cynna's deep brown eyes remained blank as she watched the nymph work. No emotion crossed her face. No pleasure or excitement over what was to come, as Zagreus always showed. Nothing but emptiness. An emptiness Nick had gotten used to seeing on her flawless face.

Only...that wasn't true. When he'd been in the ring earlier, when he'd dropped his weapon in defiance of Zagreus's desire to make him fight, he'd seen something in her eyes then. Something that had looked a lot like panic.

"That's enough," Cynna said.

The nymph's fingers lifted from Nick's skin, and she stepped back. Moving around him, she knelt to pick up the lid, recapped the jar, then sank back against the far wall near the other nymph.

Cynna moved forward, her eyes never wavering from Nick's, and the scent of jasmine hit him as it always did when she drew close, filling his senses, messing with his mind. She was tall for a female, at least five ten, and in those ridiculously high-heeled boots, only a few inches shorter than him. Today her blonde hair was swept over one shoulder, a blue streak near her temple contrasting sharply with her caramel skin. Her face was heavily made up, her eyes rimmed in thick black, making her look every bit the dominatrix. And though he knew he should be anxious over whatever she and Zagreus had cooked up for him next, he wasn't. Because there was something about her that interested him.

Perplexed him. Made him want to know more.

He'd never admit it, but the mystery of who she was and how she'd come to be here had saved him. Saved him from going mad or giving in to all that dark energy Zagreus was waiting to claim.

"You just...won't...break."

Her words were a whisper, a frustration, a surprise. She never spoke to him. Though he'd spent more time with her than anyone else in this hellhole, she never addressed him directly. She gave the commands to her grunts, and they did her dirty work. She never even got near him.

Something about today was different, though. A tiny voice in the back of his head screamed what was about to happen in this cell was on a whole different level from what he'd been through before.

She stepped close, so close he could feel her heat but not close enough to touch, then moved to her right, slowly making her way around him. His stomach tightened, and that blistering arousal came rushing back.

"This isn't a game." Her warm breath fanned his nape, sending a shiver across his bare skin. And in his wounds, where the nymph had spread the balm, heat gathered and grew, radiating outward, heading for his belly. "You cannot beat Zagreus. No one wins against the Prince of Darkness."

Nick's arms flexed, and the chains rattled above his head. He didn't want to beat the fucker, he only wanted to destroy him. Not just for what he'd put Nick through during the last few months, but for what he put everyone in this wretched place through—Cynna, his gut told him, included.

"I can't stop what he has planned for you." She circled around and stopped directly in front of him again. "Give in, and you save yourself the torment. Give in, and this ends now."

"Give in," Nick repeated, staring into her dark eyes. But unlike before, they weren't empty. They weren't dead. There was something there. Something that looked a lot like...desperation.

Was she warning him of something horrendous to come? Why would she do that? She was Zagreus's puppet. Or was she simply afraid of what would happen if he didn't break?

"You want me to give in?" he asked.

She didn't answer. Only stared at him.

"The way you gave in?"

The desperation in her eyes faded and was replaced with that lifeless, vacant look, the one he'd seen so many times when she'd ordered Zagreus's satyrs to torture him. Without a word, she stepped back, but she didn't break eye contact.

"You were warned," she said in a low voice. "Females?"

# Naughty Little Gift
Temptation Court, Book 1
By Angel Payne

# Author Acknowledgments

A few thank-yous!

To Thomas…for the best adventure ever: our awesome life. I love you.

VERY SPECIAL THANKS TO…
Goddesses Liz Berry and MJ Rose, for this incredible opportunity.
It means the world!

Shayla Black: for believing since before the beginning.
Your friendship and support have been boundless and beautiful, and I am grateful.

Victoria: For being there, always, with the special treasure of your friendship.
The journey is so much sweeter, happier, and joyous with you, my beautiful friend!

Melisande: For going "above and beyond" to make this one shine.
I cannot form words to tell you how much your guidance, expertise, and cheerleading
have meant on this one.

Susan: My sweet, beautiful sister in more than just blood—but in heart.
Thank you for all the wonderful love, support, and kayak trips! Here's to more dolphins…

Gratitude beyond compare…
for each and every blogger, reviewer, reader, and supporter
who has taken the time to support, believe, and love Arcadia and the Cimarrons.
Without you, Temptation Court would not have been born! Thank you!

"The declaration of love marks the transition from chance to destiny,
and that's why it is so perilous…"
*--Alain Badiou*

# Chapter One

*MISHELLA*

"Dear, sweet Creator. That man's ass needs its own web page."

"Right?"

"Maybe it already has one. Have we tried looking it up? What would that search string even be?"

"Cassian Court's Glorious Glutes?"

"Sounds about right."

I scowl at the exchange between my best friend and my princess of a boss. Debate adding a huff, though that might make them giggle harder. As it is, Vylet lifts her head, lets the wind blow her black waves as if she is shooting a scene for a movie, and slowly bats the thick lashes framing her huge lavender eyes.

"Is there an issue, Mistress Santelle?"

Her purposeful drawl on the s's turns her query into a tease—though before I can properly purse my lips, she is answered by a long, snorting laugh. I add a groan to my own response, stabbed at the sound's source. Brooke Cimarron, Princess of the Island of Arcadia, might have the loyalty and love of thousands across our land, but her royal in-laws are not in that legion—and outbursts like that are no help to her cause at all.

The groan might be forgotten but the sigh is not. Even after three months in her employ, my work is still clearly cut out for me. In my princess's own words, I am to do everything in my power to "whip the royal decorum into shape." Some days, the task is easy. Some, like today—are entries in the Sweet Creator Help Me journal.

I have one of those. Literally. Though on the outside, as I observe right now, the book simply says Action Items.

Despite the lists taunting me from the pages of said journal, there are many more checks in Brooke's "plus" column than not. Brooke has a good heart, a willing spirit, and a loyalty to Arcadia rivalling that of many native-born to the island. If I can only work out a way to keep Vy from enabling the woman's snarky American side…

Not likely anytime soon.

Most certainly not during this week.

Cassian Court's arrival in Arcadia has sealed that certainty solidly enough.

Cassian Court. Just rolling my mind over the man's name jolts me with such intense heat, I wonder if the Earth has rolled too quickly on its axis, shifting my chair into the sun instead of beneath the table on the Palais Arcadia lawn. That only forms the start of how he has upended my world in just two days.

Two. Days.

Cassian Court.

I cannot help myself. The syllables are synonymous with so many other expressions. Engineering genius. Corporate wizard. Billionaire icon. Consultant to kings. Yes, that includes the leader of our land, Evrest Cimarron, who has invited his friend for a "modernization think tank" with Arcadia's leaders. Yanking a kingdom forward by two hundred years in two days is no small feat.

Two. Days.

World. Upended.

Not to mention my thoughts. And my bloodstream. And the very wiring of my nervous system…

"Mishella?"

Vylet's playful prompt is perfectly timed. "Hmm?" I am grateful to leave behind a memory that has been taunting, of the man in his formal wear from the party King Evrest threw for him last night. Out of respect for Arcadian tradition, he wore a doublet-style jacket with his tailored Tom Ford pants, everything flawlessly fitted to his tapered torso and long legs. The black garment had featured one modern touch: a moss green zipper instead of buttons, drawing out the same shade in his eyes. Matching zippers had adorned his hip boots, making him look very much "at home" in the ballroom's courtly crowd…

"You truly have no comment?" The edges of Vy's lips curl up.

Little wench. She knows I would sooner watch a storm come in over the sea than have to look at the body part they've referred to on Cassian Court's incredible form.

Incredible.

And magnificent.

And breath-stealing.

And in just two days, has made me painfully aware of how small my island home truly is. The man and his magnetic pull have actually made me yearn for a land as big as his, though the expanse of America still does not seem big enough for all these new feelings he inspires—sensations that sweep in again, as I gaze upon him training at swords with Jagger Foxx on the palais lawn.

Dizzy.

Giddy.

Hot.

Needy.

No.

I cannot. I will not.

Instead, I compress my lips harder. Swing another censuring look at my friend. "I was being courteous, in deference to Her Highness."

"Oh, here we go again," Brooke mutters.

Vylet hides a laugh behind her elegant fingers. "But Mishella wants to practice her protocol, Your Highness."

Brooke glowers. "Am I going to kick your ass about this now, too?"

"Not in that pretty tea frock, missie."

"Oh, even in this rag, ho-bag."

"Who you calling ho…ho?"

"Say it twice because I own that, baby." Brooke swirls then stabs an index finger. "Especially after last night's marathon under that man of mine."

"Ohhh!" Vy roller coasters the syllable with knowing emphasis. "And I thought you were just walking funny from the platform pumps."

"See how I did that? Gotta have a cover, girl."

They snicker harder than before. I fume deeper than before. Attempt a prim glance down at my lap, but only get two seconds of the reprieve. A fresh punch of testosterone hits the air, swinging all our stares back up.

By everything that is holy.

The masculine energy is well supported. Even a hundred feet away, the two men are like gladiators of old, shirtless bodies lunging, gleaming muscles coiling. Jagger Foxx, the Arcadian court's lieutenant of military operations, does not give his American guest an inch of visitor's courtesy—a handicap Court would take as an insult anyway.

The result is…

Glorious.

Slanted forward, his body forty-five degrees from the lawn, Cassian Court is a breath-stealing study of sinew, strength, might, and motivation. His thighs, clearly etched beneath his white fencing pants, wield the force of a stallion. His torso, the color of a lion in the sun, coils with equal power.

Their blades clash. Metallic collisions zing the air. Jagger stumbles back. Again. Grunts hard—though not as deeply as the man besting him. Just like that, Cassian Court turns into an even more exhilarating sight. His beauty is meant for the glory of physical triumph.

All the heavens help me, I cannot stop staring. Or wondering. What would it feel like…to be held by those massive arms? What would it be like, to lie beneath that beautiful body? To spread my legs, allowing his hardness against my welcoming softness…my tight readiness…

My throat turns into the Sahara. I swallow, coughing softly as the moisture clashes with the dryness.

"Holy hell," Brooke murmurs.

"Which has to be where I'm going, after what I just imagined about that man."

Vy's confession welcomes new knives of confusion. Logically, I should be reassured. My reaction to Court is not unique or special. But another part, new and foreign, fights the urge to think otherwise. To scratch her eyes out for sliding into my territory.

As Brooke would eloquently put it: what the hell?

Men are a complicated subject in my life—contradicted by their very simplicity. They are like clothing or cars or office tools:

needed but not coveted, functional but not desirable. Yes, some exist in higher-end form, but I do not think of them longer than the time it takes to interact with them. I do not dare. Father and Mother will eventually use me as a pawn to gain what they want from one. It might be the 21st century, but politics are politics—and world-changing decisions are still made by the heads between men's legs, not the ones on their shoulders. I have to be grateful for reaching my twenty-second year without having to bother with it yet.

But I will.

And lingering lustings for Cassian Court will not make it any easier.

"Pffft." Brooke flings the comeback at Vy while reaching across the glass table for her sun tea. At least Brooke looks like a princess today, the pale blue tea dress coaxing matching sparkles in her eyes, the daisy yellow sweater matching her platform pumps. Shockingly, she has listened to my suggestion of wearing a pearl necklace and earrings with the ensemble. "We're mated, not entombed." But looks can be deceiving. Her saucy smirk proves it. "Besides, neither of us is the treasure who's caught Mr. Court's eye—and likely some other body parts."

Mortification. While I debate whether to let it curl me into a ball or send me under the table, Vy erupts in laughter. "True that, sistah!"

At least that helps with the decision. No shrinking now. I fire off a new glare. "Have you two gotten into the nectar?" I am half serious. Nipping at the Arcadian fruit wine, followed by sitting in today's ruthless sun, would be a reasonable explanation for their giddy moods.

"Right." Brooke leads on the response, laughing wryly. "We could only wish."

Vy echoes the snicker. "Word to the princess."

They collide fists in a punching motion, followed by fanning and wiggling their fingers, prompting my fresh fume. It is a joke. I know that. I also admit these are confusing times for everyone in Arcadia. Our country is emerging from two hundred years of self-imposed separation from the world into a reality where nearly everything has changed. The adjustment is unsettling at times, even to Brooke, who was born American but has lived here for the last seven years.

Now, she wears the gold band on her left hand declaring her legally married to Prince Samsyn—a detail Vy enjoys forgetting whenever they get together. That turns me into the reminder police.

"Do not forget your place, Vylet Hester. Brooke is your princess."

I delete the part about Brooke having been the kingdom's actual queen for a week—seven days she never wants to remember again, though they have brought one joyous result. At the time, she needed a secran as soon as possible, so I entered her employ—and found a purpose I never thought possible for my life. For the first time, I am no longer Fortin Santelle's pretty trinket of a daughter, or even a faceless Arcadian court clerk, filing and typing my days away. Brooke depends on me. Confides in me. Relies on me for input on everything from appropriate clothing choices to modern political issues from a native Arcadian's point of view. It is a serious responsibility, and I never take it lightly—despite the fact that she sometimes does.

"Okay, listen up, missie." The woman herself sets her drink down so hard, some of the tea sloshes out. "If you don't loosen that caboose and relax a little, I'll have to personally hunt up some nectar for you."

And sometimes, she completely forgets. Like now.

"Yes! Do it!"

"No. No."

My response overlaps with Vy's, doubling our volumes into an outburst across the lawn—enough to freeze the men in mid-clash. But only one of them adds a concerned glance, giving his opponent a crucial second of advantage. It is the only second Jagger needs. With a shout, he plunges. With a grunt, Cassian goes down.

With a gasp, I lurch to my feet.

Just as swiftly, I sit back down. Too late. The damage is wrought. My chair has certainly sprung flames, since they waste no time climbing to my face. Vy and Brooke give me no mercy, either. They actually clap as I sit there, drowning in embarrassment, and continue the racket so long, the men obviously assume the praise is for them. Well, Jagger does. As soon as he helps Cassian up, turning both their bodies into gleaming masterpieces of sun-drenched muscle, he sweeps a gloating bow.

Brooke and Vy laugh even harder.

Shockingly, my lips twinge. Their joy might be a little contagious…and the day is perfect, with the breeze carrying salty moisture bites off the ocean, along with jasmine and orange from the trees. A little laughter cannot be such a crime. Perhaps it is…therapeutic. I am not a prude—I grew up in the back halls of the Arcadian Court, after all—but talking about lust and experiencing it firsthand are two separate things. Entirely. I have spent the last two days as skittish as a toddler at her first swimming lesson. Everyone has to get in and paddle sometime, though taking oneself too seriously can only be dangerous.

A perfect reassurance—

Until I swing my sights up, to watch Cassian Court approaching across the grass.

Striding like a king.

Rippling like an Olympian.

Staring like a hitman.

At me.

Laughter, meet shredder. Throat, get back to the desert. Composure…

Composure has gone rogue—doing whatever it bloody well wants. My mind is frozen but my sex is incinerated, cranking the intensity with every smooth, sure step with which the man dominates the lawn. By the time he and Jagger stop beneath the table's wide umbrella, my hands are a rigid ball in my lap, and my breaths are rapid pumps against my flower-print dress—which is suddenly, completely, too tight. Oh sweet Creator, how he makes my breasts throb…and ache.

And tingle?

"Oh…my." I keep it to a whisper for my ears alone. Miracle. My hand flies up to assuage my racing heartbeat. I easily disguise the action by fiddling with the polished piece of Minos Reef coral suspended around my neck. Usually, the purple trinket lends me focus and strength. Not now. Not even close. Not with Cassian Court continuing with his unflinching stare at me…his unyielding examination. I cannot help but note every nuance of his gaze. Even in this blazing heat, it is the color of cool forests. I am drawn to thoughts of waterfalls and lagoons in those glades…and him swimming in them, drenched and naked.

By the powers…

When his features crunch, horror sets in. I've blurted it aloud. Can he read the thought that has prompted it too? Does he know the lewd turn of my mind—and his importance in it?

Oh crap oh crap oh crap…

And now, I am as guilty as Vy of borrowing the vulgar Americanism. But that is where I have descended. Where he has made me fall.

"Miss Santelle?"

And just like that, with just two words, has me flying once more. Takes me higher, as I lift my gaze to meet his. Shivering on a breeze of awakening, as I absorb the regal angles of his face, contrasted by the tumble of his dark gold hair and the contemplative indents of his dimples.

"Are you all right?"

I feel my mouth open. Know sound of some sort needs to follow. "I…"

"She is fine." Vylet's tone is playful but her gaze watchful, installing an invisible tether between Cassian and me with the back-and-forth concentration. As if one is not there already…

"At least she will be," Brooke adds. "Forgive her, Cassian. It's this thing called sunshine. New concept for my sweet little secran." She tosses a huff at me then twirls a hand at the palais. "She's always cooped in that place. Day and night, busy as Cinderella in those dark castle halls."

Jagger snorts while shrugging into a black T-shirt. Tosses one to Cassian. "And what does that make you? The evil stepmother?"

"Dude, I'm a wicked stepsister—in all the best ways."

Vylet masks a giggle behind a hand. The tiny nick in her front lip, betraying the cleft repaired when she was a babe, still makes her insecure when men are near—yes, even Alak, her completely smitten betranli. "Corrupting her prince, one day at a time."

"Only when it comes to attending his royal balls."

Jagger and Vy fill the air with their laughs. Yes, I fume again. How can I caution the princess about making comments like that when our friends reward her for them? Jagger, now Prince Samsyn's key aide in running the security forces of the kingdom, cannot be expected to know better—but I need more support from Vy.

And maybe I am simply being a toddler at the pool again.

I drop my head, wrestling with the thought.

Until muscled thighs in white pants kneel in front of me. And a hand, powerful and long-fingered, slips over my knee. And another hand, warm and firm, tilts up my chin.

And that stare, dark and majestic, wraps around me again. Into me.

"Out of the cinders, Ella." His murmur is formed of the same perfect velvet. "It's time to live in the light."

Survival mode. Now.

Lungs, inflate.

Heart, keep going.

Survival may be overrated. Extremely. Dear sweet Creator, all I want is the blissful release of giving in to his sensual hunt...

Ugh.

Can I get any stupider? Princes like him do not chase backward bumpkins like me. They might pretend to...for a little while. Toy with them. Are perhaps amused by them, until the island novelty wears off and they return to the heights of Mount Olympus—also known as New York City—to bed nymphs and marry goddesses.

And despite that entire diatribe, I bear my gaze just as deeply into his—before rasping ridiculous bumpkin words.

"Maybe I like the dark better."

Stupid. Stupid. Stupid.

I expect more giggles from the girls—but they are busy bantering with Jagger, leaving room for the bubble around Cassian and me to thicken. For the world around us to fall away...

For his nostrils to flare, as if catching my scent.

For his lips to part, as if anticipating a bite into his prey.

For my whole body to quiver, as if wanting to let him...

Through one exquisite moment.

Another.

Before being ripped from our reverie by a hand at my elbow. Twisting in, issuing a silent command to get on my feet. I obey before looking, for that grip belongs to just one person in my world—the sole person I expect least right now, and dread most.

"Paipanne." My dutiful murmur is a thread of disguise. Surely he can see every illicit thought that has been possessing my mind and body.

"Mishella," he levels, from between tight teeth.

Once more this afternoon, my throat convulses on a dry gulp. He has seen. Creator help me.

"High Councilman Santelle." Cassian's tone comes as a surreal interjection. He is not a stupid man. Surely he sees how Father's quiet fury wrings the joy from the air, though he smiles as if exchanging niceties about the weather. "What a pleasant surprise. Thought I'd have to wait for the pleasure of greetings until this evening."

My nerves flee. No. Wrong. They double. Ice in one's veins is tricky that way. "Th-this evening?" I dare a glance up at him, forcing my features to neutrality—not an easy task when the wind plays with the edges of his hair, and molds his T-shirt against the steely planes of his pectorals.

"Yes." Father's tone modulates to match Cassian's—on the surface. Likely, nobody but Vy and I detect its lingering tension. "It is Mr. Court's last evening on the island, and your maimanne thought he might be tiring of the rich palais food. He and his retinue shall be dining with us at seven."

"I—I did not know."

"Because you were dressed and out the door before we could tell you this morning."

"And you must be so proud." Vylet slices out the statement before Father can issue another accusation. If I am not tempted to kiss her feet for that, her finishing look is the decider. Few are experts at sweet-but-deadly like my rule-breaking friend.

"I'll back that up," Brooke adjoins. "Your daughter works harder than anyone I know, High Councilman. My life would be a mess without her."

Paipanne colors. A little. "You are too kind, Highness." Dips his head with a thin smile. It assures me little, for his initial agenda, whatever that is, lingers in his steel gray eyes. "Her maimanne and I are certainly proud of her. On that note, I must have needs to 'borrow' her for a moment. About tonight, you know."

"Of course." The distrust in Brooke's eyes cannot be missed from a hundred feet away, but I sneak a reassuring nod in her direction. Father will not be able to wreak too much damage right here, without all of them watching and noticing. He will restrict the blows to verbal form only; I am sure of it.

And to that, I am well accustomed by now.

*CASSIAN*

The craving is as shocking as it is sudden.

But sure enough, I long to smash in every inch of Fortin Santelle's self-righteous face.

Why not? He's an ass.

But you've known that from the beginning.

Still, he's the ass willing to vouch for my ass with the decision-makers about Arcadia's new infrastructure needs. So yes, I'm conflicted. But—perhaps this has nothing to do with Mishella. Not really. I'm just trying to reconcile doing business with a rung-grabbing bastard. Replacing my discomfort about a future in professional bed with the man by breaking—translation: snapping in half—one of my own hard-and-fast rules. Pushing my nose into his personal affairs. Actually caring about the fact that he treats his own daughter like a puppy to be disciplined.

Stay out of it. Personal ties become business pigsties. Didn't you learn that the hard way? And you haven't dealt with thousands like him before? Even the man you once called father-in-law?

A huff escapes me, thick with relief. At least now I have an explanation. Displaced emotions, courtesy of the shit storm known as old baggage. It makes sense—meaning now I can compartmentalize and cope.

Until I look once again at her.

Mishella.

My little Ella.

The words embed into my psyche like diamonds stirred into concrete. She has changed the structure of my being. But how the hell? I've seen her exactly six times in the last three days, including what was supposed to be a "casual" welcome reception at the palais but turned into the cataclysm of my first sight of her—and I remember every moment of every encounter since. Even just passing hellos with her make it happen all over again—the world fading away, the senses captivated by her—and just like that, my interest is amplified in the island girl with hair like spun gold and eyes like a toy store collector doll.

Interest?

No. I'm not "interested" in her.

I'm fascinated by her. Entranced. Maybe a little obsessed. Maybe a lot more than that. Worse, I have no idea how to explain it—which should scare the living fuck out of me, but doesn't.

She feels…right. Secure. Even safe. Yet she's the most exhilarating adventure of my life, a high-wire walk with a view of the entire world.

Just don't look down.

"Christ." I grit it to myself while bending down, retying a perfectly secure shoelace. It's a quick fix; I can keep eyes locked on Fortin and her, but hide the growing erection she has inspired.

Yeah. Inspired.

What was the word Samsyn used with me last night after dinner, when describing how he'd felt the moment he met his Brooke? It was an Arcadian phrase, unique in its blend of Turkish and French influences…

Soursedias.

Yeah. That. It's goddamn perfect, coming close enough to even the English word for what that woman has done to me.

Sorcery.

Yeah. That has to be it. She's an island enchantress, empowered by the Arcadian spirits to wrap my mind, soul, and body in a searing, clinging erotic spell. And fuck, is it working. I want to give in to the rest of it, just to know how high and hot she'd take me…

And how far I'd take her. Claim her.

How greatly would her gorgeous innocence change…transformed by lust? How much wider could I make those big blue eyes? What would her pretty bow lips look like, formed into an O of raw desire? What would her refined voice sound like, panting in the spasms of a mindless orgasm?

I break a shoelace.

Snap back to reality.

I have to get off this damn island.

It will happen—first thing tomorrow morning. I'll wrap up the talks with Santelle tonight—not looking in his daughter's direction while doing so—then tell Mark and his crew I want the plane ready by daybreak. That'll allow time to check numbers in the foreign markets, call my key project managers in New York, then get out of here before Mishella Santelle can weave any more wonderful witchery into my willing soul.

Witchery.

Who the fuck am I kidding?

She's not a witch. Fairy, maybe. Perhaps an angel, or a mermaid given legs. The certainty hits harder as I stare at her again. She holds herself as regally as any of those, even as her father continues quietly berating her—I cannot label it anything else, if the expression on his face is to be believed—and even in how she sways after he pivots, heading back inside.

But only one sway.

After that, she returns to the queenly stance, holding it despite the wounds Fortin has inflicted. Not physical cuts, but damage just as torturous to bear. Somehow she does, returning to the table with astounding composure. Keeping her shit together even while Brooke and Vylet peal with laughter at some joke from Jagger.

For a moment, I am incensed. How can her two closest friends not see her pain?

Realization. Massive. Maybe she doesn't want to see it.

An answer I'll likely never have—and shouldn't want to. Rescuing knight, I sure as hell am not. Repulsive giant in the clouds? There's the fit.

And it is well past time for me to climb back up the beanstalk. To remember that counting beans is the only magic left in my life now. No more turns at sorcery. I've had my turn at that shit already. Sucked up my life's ration of magic. Neither of them exist for me anymore.

There's only tonight's dinner to get through first. With the sorceress and her family.

God fucking help me.

# Chapter Two

MISHELLA

"Hold. Still."

Though Mother murmurs the words, the command in them is as clear as the directives Father growled at me this afternoon.

Know your place, girl—and stay in it.

Know your purpose, daughter—and stick to it.

I struggle not to wince as she stabs another pin into the bun atop my head. Three pins later, she grunts softly: an approving sound. "Better."

Translation: I look as nondescript as a push-pin. Perfectly acceptable, as far as I am concerned. I have even assisted the effort, selecting a basic black sheath with a demure square neckline and a mid-calf hem. My low heels imbue the ensemble with a tiny stab of class—enough to honor my paipanne without disgracing him—which I apparently accomplished by "fawning" over Cassian Court this afternoon.

With effort, I control the color threatening to invade my cheeks again. I do not dare give Mother any more fuel for her irked fire, which has only increased in the months since I chose to stay on as Brooke's secran. She and Paipanne barely understood my enthusiasm about the position when Brooke had been queen; now that she is a mere princess again, my decision is seen as close to walking the streets a whore.

At first, the dichotomy puzzled me. In the palais, I was happy, productive, and certainly protected. But one day, a conversation with Vy shifted my view.

*This is not a matter of controlling your virtue, shella-bean. It is a matter of controlling you.*

I'd scoffed, even gotten defensive with Vy, refusing to see my own parents in that light—but more and more evidence has surfaced to support the assertion. Incidents and attitudes I've ignored before, perhaps written off as their love expressed in the only way they knew how…but if that were the case, why does it manifest in that form only with me? How is Saynt so different—or has he received the same pressure since Father and Mother pushed for an early end to his school studies, followed by immediate entry into Arcadian military training? At this rate, he will surely be an officer within a few years—though even that timing does not seem swift enough for them.

But there is no chance to steal away for that intimate sibling chat tonight, in light of the events planned down to the second. In that regard, I have an easier assignment than Saynt—a truth Mother reminds me of now, meeting my gaze in the mirror.

"Just cocktails and dinner, hmm?" She arches brows in subtle expectation. "Neither of us needs the fat calories in dessert, anyway."

"Of course, Maim—"

I am interrupted by my own astonishment, when she reaches into my jewelry box and withdraws the amethyst drops from my last birthday. My brows lower. The gemstones are not the plain pearls I would have predicted as her preference—and honestly, they make me squirm a little. They are beautiful but entirely too bright. They are—

"The perfect touch." Like the direction on my hair, it is an order, not a suggestion. She finishes it by holding them against my ears. "Ahhh, yes. Definitely. Perhaps you can talk about how they were passed between each generation in our family…to celebrate our prosperity."

I lower my gaze. It is a sweet story—if only a word of it were true. But Father and Mother are not above "sliding" on the small facts to justify larger gains. As far back as three years ago, before the crown of Arcadia shifted and Evrest Cimarron officially reopened the island to the outside world, they saw Arcadia's future as a major player on the world economy's stage—and did not miss a chance to seize the opportunities from it. A single chance. As a result, they have become nothing short of obsessed with the Santelle family holding major strings in the new Arcadian economy.

Now, Saynt and I are expected to shovel into that locomotive too—and long-gone are the days when we were given any preference about our contributions. Saynt is learning to face our enemies, even take a bullet, for the family name. And I'll learn to spread my legs for the man they point me toward.

And oh, yes—to keep my mouth shut on everything but rehearsed lines until then.

Like the propaganda about my earrings.

"I—I shall try." I add a game smile at Maimanne for effect. She does not have to know that just the idea of lying to Cassian sits on my stomach like rotting fish. It feels too close to lying to myself.

The flash of revelation bursts another into life.

Cassian. When he is near, I somehow feel closer to...

myself.

To parts of myself beyond "the physical obvis," as Vy would call them. Things far past the racing blood, the lightning nerves, the throbbing womb...

Things that are even better.

Things of wonder.

Anticipation.

Feelings brand-new, tied to desires as old as the ancients.

Needs I have to lock away. Now.

Stuff into a place deep inside, as firmly as I seal my pearls back into my jewelry box. Bury deep beneath my gaze, glittering too brightly from the mirror as I secure the amethysts on my ears. Conceal behind my face, lashed into serenity, as Maimanne tilts a last look from the doorway. That will do, her eyes seem to say—the closest thing I shall receive in the way of praise.

"That will do." I repeat it to my reflection, fighting for a shred of its reassurance. Press my clammy hands to my flushed face, praying for an infusion of composure. Beseech the Creator for the strength to get through the next three hours, pretending I feel nothing for the man—and his money—who is so important to our family's future.

Because, despite everything, I love them. And know—pray?—

in my deepest heart, that all of Father and Mother's maneuvers are for ultimately for Saynt and me. I can support them without having to lie to Cassian about the earrings—or anything else, for that matter.

Except how I feel about him.

Except how two days and six encounters—not that I am keeping track—have transformed the man from a complete stranger into the very nucleus of my thoughts, center of my heartbeats—

And apparition on my balcony?

"Guuhhh!"

Stealing more slang from Vy is better than surrendering to my first option of a reaction: a throat-razing shriek. As I choke the sound all the way down, I thank the Creator his hair is slicked back from his face, tamed into waves catching the outside lights as he swings over the wrought iron rail from the bougainvillea trellis he has just scaled. Sweet Creator, his hair. As long as I live, I will not forget it. Thick as molten gold, streaked with honey straight from the hive—a dangerous thought for all the dangerous things he makes me feel, especially now…flinging open the balcony's double doors, locking his gaze to mine once more—

And bringing pure fire back to my world.

## CASSIAN

*Will this woman ever not set me completely on fire?*

The question is as mystifying as the one before it: the demand that hounded every inch I just clawed up the goddamn trellis. It went something along the lines of: *you swore you wouldn't look at her tonight, yet now you're scaling a wall in the dark, hoping you've pegged the right bedroom as hers?*

Even if there *are* answers, I care nothing for them. I don't care about much of anything, other than the euphoria of knowing I was right. The pastel and cream décor I glimpsed from the ground is hers—and now she is standing in it, a stark contrast in her classic black dress and shoes. Not a hair on her head breaks free from its bun. The look should bring severity to her face but accomplishes the opposite. Every angle of her impeccable beauty is brought out in bold relief, turning her into something close to fine art. I half expect to look down and see a *Do Not Touch* sign attached to a rope around her waist.

Thank fuck there isn't one.

Because I need to touch. *Now.*

One step. Another. Then a stop, wondering if she'll shy back, like this afternoon…like the wiser one she is in this whole thing. She knows the truth, more than me. She understands that these threads between us can only ever be that. Threads, like cocoon floss. Gossamer. Temporary.

But she doesn't move. Simply closes her eyes as my hand raises. Releases a shaky rasp as I curl fingers over her full, beautiful cheek. Finally whispers words like the faint furrows that crinkle the top of her elegant nose.

"How did you…"

I laugh softly. "Damn lucky guess."

"Why…"

"Do you really have to ask that?"

Her eyes open. She swallows hard. "We cannot do this. Mr. Court, I—"

"And do you really have to call me *that*?"

"We are both supposed to be downstairs—where *you* will complete business with my *father*. This is *not* part of the plan."

"The *plan*?" I slide closer to her. God*damn*, her scent. Her skin exudes something exotic, like island flowers. Her hair, while yanked back with some shiny styling product, betrays hints of jasmine and vanilla. "How do I know it's not?"

As I anticipate, her stare snaps up, full of incensed fire.

"It's a fair question." I half-abhor myself for venturing down this path. But as long as we're here… "I need your father's influence on this island, but he needs my money. How do I know he hasn't dangled his daughter to sweeten the deal for himself?"

Tears join her fury. Just a sheen—enough to show me the threads are about to break. Her hand swings up. Flies back. When it's at full height, I snap a grip around her wrist. Use the hold to circle her around, pinning her to the wall behind her terrace door. The shadows of the corner envelop us, making her gritted teeth glow, setting even more fire in her huge sapphire eyes.

"Damn you." Her syllables are more like sobs. They jab my

gut, reaffirming that all my stress about doing business with a jackass is pretty stupid. *Like attracts like.*

It's not a new revelation. But right now it sears like pure acid, and I have to halt the damage—no matter how desperate the measure.

"I'm sorry." All right, maybe I *am* desperate. In the last five years, those words have only left my lips once before—on an occasion I'm determined not to dredge up. Not now. "Sshhh, Ella. *I'm sorry.*"

She huffs through her nose. Several more times. "Let me go."

I concede, despite the harsh twist of my gut.

Unbelievably, she stays put. Lowers her arm into a protective wrap around her waist, but doesn't move beyond that.

Like an idiot, I brush fingertips up to her face again.

Like a miracle, she lets me.

"I'm a moron. And I *am* sorry." It's the truth. I hope she can feel it in the pressure of my thumb, slowly tracing the strong line of her jaw. God, she's so warm and smooth. "I'm also trying to make logical sense out of this. Out of…us."

Her laugh is quick—and strangled. "There *is* no 'us'."

"Oh, there's an *us.*" And in another bonehead move, I drag her hand away from her body…sliding it beneath my blue silk tie, against the dress shirt covering my sternum. "You know it as well as I do, Mishella. You feel it too. You feel it…right here…don't you?"

Her lips work against each other. "What I feel does not matter. What *either* of us feels—" She lets her hand drop. Blinks slowly, her lashes shimmering with new salty drops. "I am not free to *feel,* Cassian. You must know that by now. You have spent two days exposed to my father's determination and will. He desires your money, but only because it will bring him something greater."

"Power." I could have supplied the answer from a coma. It was the Holy Grail of the elite, a high better than multiple zeroes in a man's bank account. And in the hands of fools—worse, in the hands of arrogant fools—it could end the entire planet.

"And my brother and I…are additional tools in helping him gain that power." She looks down, using her dress as a visual aid in her argument. She has no fucking idea that the staid color and the conservative cut, accented only by the gemstones on her ears, have only stoked my imagination more. It's a battle not to visualize peeling the garment away from her sleek curves, her creamy skin contrasted by the dark fabric…and showcasing the marks of my grip. "I am to be the ultimate prize for the man at court who helps our family rise the highest. Any 'dalliance' before that time, especially with an American investor who was only here for three days, would wag enough tongues to lower his asking price for me."

I don't even try to contain a disgusted growl. "Like a fucking virgin offered to a dragon." When her reply is nothing but extended tension, my head jerks up. "Wait. *Shit*. Because you really *are* still a…" Her eyes confirm it in a second. God*damn*…her eyes. Those wide blue depths, such a turn-on for me from the start, ignite me to shaking lust now. Openness and honesty, because she *is* open and honest.

And a virgin.

A thought—like so many others that have struck about her—that should horrify the hell out of me.

But doesn't.

Holy hell…just the opposite.

The idea of being the first man to fill her…to bring her to the bliss that will convulse her walls around my cock, make her scream my name as I pump my hot release deep inside her body…

*Crap. Shit. Fuck.*

*You've had enough, sailor. Time to close out the tab and wobble on home.*

Somebody needs to tell that to the breathtaking blonde now pushing from the wall and pressing her body against mine, that gaze again betraying so many of her thoughts. At least the ones betraying the exact match of her fantasies to mine.

*Crap. Shit. Fuck.*

*No.*

"I want to give it to you, Cassian." She slips her hand up to my neck, working those slender, seeking fingers beneath my shirt. "You know that, yes?"

*Hell.*

Now she curls her heated touch into the ends of my hair, awkwardly at first, as if she's just learned the move from movies and is shocked that it works…that such a small gesture has pierced my entire body, slicing into my cock—pulsing heavily between our bodies. Her lips part on the sexiest gasp I've ever heard. The flare of her gaze ensues, making my dick swell again.

"Creator's sweet stars," she whispers. "Would it even fit?"

"Holy *fuck*."

It's all I can say—fortunately, all I *have* to say. She opens her mouth before I even descend, an invitation to plunge with every wet, needing inch of my tongue, embedding her taste into me...gifting me with her soft supplication. And goddammit, I take it. Every inch, every drop, every taste I can possibly steal.

Because it's all I'll get to take from her.

All I'll allow myself to take.

Because despite how much I want her, I refuse to ruin her. Refuse to even think of what her life could be like, if she is of no use to her father's master plan of Arcadian commercial dominance.

Pathetic bastard.

Will he even listen if I tell him it's a losing track? That he'll attain his goal, only to want something beyond it? *Right.* Shaking a spider in its web often just makes the spider work harder—making life hell for its prey.

With a rough moan, I tear myself from her kiss. On legs that shake, step back from her. Then again. Force my hand into a quivering claw, pulling her grip off my neck. But before I set her fingers completely free, I push my face against her palm and impale her gaze with the unmitigated fire in my own.

"It would fit, sweet Circe."

She smiles, acknowledging the illicit imagery I invoke—but winces, recognizing what I do. We'll never act on the words. "Circe." she finally echoes. "The Greek sorceress? The one who transformed her enemies into animals?"

I answer with a growl into her hand. She tries to hide the answering quiver down her body. Fails miserably.

"But you are not my enemy."

"But you have turned me wild."

Her breath catches. In the exquisite silence that follows, sneaks her tongue between her lips.

"*Cassian.*"

My own name has never brought me more heat, more tension...more arousal. Two syllables, and my whole system is heated by another ten degrees…and my cock now throbs against the plane of her belly.

I groan. She whimpers. But the temptation to shove her back, hike her dress to her waist and take her right here, against the wall, hits my gritted restraint. This woman isn't just a whim. She's not a fuck-then-flee socialite, or remotely close to my other preferred social distraction: haute couture bimbo, sans panties. In my jacket pocket is a phone with hundreds of those women on it, willing to be ready the moment my plane touches down in New York once more.

The thought of it makes me ill.

It will pass—it always does—but as I dip toward her, needing one more taste before giving her up forever, I give in to the illusion that it won't. That Mishella Santelle has pulled a real Circe on me, and accomplished the impossible.

Transformed me.

Changed me back into a creature I recognize. A man I respect.

Impossible.

*Impossible.*

I am so screwed.

# Chapter Three

*MISHELLA*

My eyes itch. My back aches. The indents in my palms are likely permanent by now, considering the hours my fingernails have been digging into them. How many hours, I have no idea. At this point, time has been slammed into the same category as my physical comfort level. Irrelevant.

I sit in a stiff chair in Father's study, scooted forward, hands tucked in my lap, knees at a ninety-degree angle. I focus on my toes, flat against the floor, peeking from beneath my sleep pants. Distractedly, I note how they have changed color through the hours, going bluish at the brink of dawn. Living in Sancti, the warmest part of Arcadia, still means ocean breezes that chill the air at night.

Winds capable of lifting Cassian's hair off his high, straight forehead…

Of teasing that hair into his eyes, changing like ripples across a lagoon with his rising desire…

Of infusing wild new scent across his skin, so taut and tanned over all the hard ridges of his body…

"Salpu."

Not even whispering the profanity against myself is effective against the relentless images of him. And maybe, as awful as the torture is, it is for the best. The pictures are all I will have now.

He is gone.

And I am a selfish salpu for lamenting the bizarre sense of loss in my heart, when so much more has walked out the door with him.

New memories assault, making me grimace. That moment, having let down my hair and climbed into bed, when the door of my chamber burst open...then my gape when Father filled the portal. Luckily, the curse I had prepared for Saynt was not yet at my lips. I had expected nobody else, since Mother retired to her own quarters after we bid good night to Father and Cassian, immediately following dinner. I had not diverted from acceptable decorum during the meal, despite the yearning to do exactly that—cheese soup, crème fraiche, and stuffed chicken breast gained new meaning when one dined across the table from Cassian Court's intense gaze—but when Father stormed in, rage mottling his face, I discerned the awful truth before he spat it.

*Did I not tell you, two damn days ago, not to throw yourself at the man like a common rospute? Do you know what you have done, Mishella? Do you know what you have ruined?*

"Tell me again." Mother's mandate jerks me back to the present—though it is no less agonizing than the flashback. "Word for word, Fortin—what Court said before he left, and when."

Father growls. "I do not fathom how this will—"

"Tell. Me. Again."

"Woman."

"Husband." She jerks the edges of her dressing robe tighter. Firms her stance. She doesn't need to say more. Even with a bare face and tangled hair, etched in the unforgiving gray of early morning, Selyna Santelle's golden beauty arrests a whole room.

Suddenly—strangely—I feel sorry for her. Father and she are children of equally ambitious court schemers who married them off for political gain. For many years now, it has been plain that little connects them but a mutual drive for more. And, I suppose, Saynt and me. They love us, in their bizarre way—which might be the only way they know how.

"He is likely preparing his plane for takeoff as we speak," she persists with the same steely calm. "So if I am to help with salvaging the damage,"—a glance in my direction gives chilling clarity about her definition of damage—"I must visualize it again. He said he was 'unable' to commit to the agreement 'as is'?"

"Yes," Father bites out.

"Not that he refused the terms outright?"

"He said what he said, Selyna. I did not have time to dally with semantics."

Mother waves a hand like his snarl is a persistent fly. "But he took the time to issue the last of it? It was issued in the parlor, not tossed over his shoulder in the front drive, on his way out?"

Father expels a breath. Finally mutters, "Yes. In the parlor. After he turned down cigars, had one bite of the trifle, and excused himself to take a discreet shit."

Mother cocks her head. "And you are certain that was it?"

"Certain what was what?"

"The shit. That was what he excused himself for?"

Exhaustion. Shock. Not the best combination for containing frantic laughter. A tight choke helps me at the last minute. Is there any ground forbidden in the path of their ambition?

Father's loose shrug confirms the answer. "I gathered so," he mutters. "I very well did not listen at the door, though he was gone long enough, so I assumed…"

He trails off with a tense scowl—though it has nothing to do with spying on Cassian's bathroom business. Assumed. The word alone implies one of their cardinal sins, as bad as laziness or murder. In this case, it brings just as heinous an outcome—if I correctly interpret the messages beneath their extended, silent exchange…

What if he wasn't spending the time on that private matter? What if he went to the bathroom for other reasons—such as the chance for second thoughts? Why has he backed out of signing the contract so suddenly?

No answers of logic or comfort come forth.

The only thing that has changed in the last four months, since Father and Cassian first communicated about this deal, has been—

Me.

I can peg the millisecond my parents reach the same conclusion. My head jerks down as theirs swing around, though that helps not in battling the weight of their scrutiny.

I want to cease breathing. Not an exaggeration. Every breath I take is a sharp slice between my ribs; like the air itself is contaminated by their disappointment—and disgust.

They know.

I have been circling the ugly words, unwilling to accept them, but now they sting as sharply as the cold on my feet, and throb as hard as the pain behind my eyes. I drop my gaze to the floor. Wish for a way of lasering an escape hole through the polished wood.

Am I supposed to say something now? What on Earth do they expect?

But I know the answer to that already.

It is me. I am the one who derailed it all. Who ruined any respect he had for our family by flirting with him, making stupid eyes at him. Letting him into my bedroom...and letting him do other things there.

And Creator help me, I liked it.

A lot.

And I made him like it.

At least I think I did.

Sweet Creator...did he like it? And why am I stopping to even wonder about it? Or to care?

But I do. If hell takes me for it, then so be it. My virginity is still pristine, and I shall never again see the man who tempted me to change that, so I cling to the memories of the feelings...all the passionate, exquisite perfection of those moments with him. It is shameless and selfish and for one sublime moment, I do not care. For a collection of perfect breaths, I am again simply a woman letting a man climb up her balcony then kiss her senseless...render her breathless...arouse her to that perfect place called mindless...

All too soon, it is over.

With the stiffness in Father's shoulders, as he abruptly turns away.

With Mother's censuring glance, before she rises like an empress. "What happened after that? When Court returned from the tuvalette?"

A blush attacks. The Arcadian word makes the subject sound prettier, though the gritty reality remains. And the guilt. Always the guilt. While I hate their bald zeal on so many levels, I crave their parental pride and approval. My flirtations with Cassian did go too far—perhaps the "romantic" breach into my room was even his way of testing my character—making my overnight moping about it even more pathetic. And how many times have I replayed his kiss in my mind, shamelessly using it to keep myself awake, while my parents watched their plans vanish like a sandcastle under a wave?

In Vy's terms, I suck as a human being.

In Brooke's terms, maybe you've earned the suckage, girlfriend.

Father gets up. Walks to his desk. Slumps into the chair behind it before drumming impatient fingers atop the unsigned contract in front of him. "He did not say much more than that," he finally states. "'Unable to commit.' Those were his exact words. Then he said he would be 'taking some matters into advisement' and would 'be in touch soon.'"

Not much is different than the first twelve times he has told it—but this time, the words click differently. I jerk up my head to look directly at him—a penance I have avoided for the last six hours. Crazily—perhaps insanely—it drives words to my lips too.

"'Be in touch'," I echo. "That is not a full no…right?"

Father does not answer. His features are fixed, frozen and dispassionate, as Mother answers me instead—by digging a scalding grip into my ear. I gasp in place of a scream. The woman has perfected ear twisting to such an art, Saynt still bears a tear at the back of his lobe from the day he skipped school as a boy.

"Stand. Up," she seethes. "You know nothing of these matters, girl—and now you will admit that as you apologize to your father, who might be able to salvage the mess you have made of this."

A thousand needles stab the backs of my eyes. I grit them back while trying to nod, but her fingers feel sewn to my flesh. Her grip is unyielding. And maybe it is what I need. Maybe I am just a stupid girl, playing with fire much too golden, beautiful, and hot for me to ever handle safely. Maybe, Creator help us, my lustful idiocy has not torched everything they have worked for. Maybe Father can fix it…if I get out of his way. If I am humble and prove it by being truly sorry.

It feels right, this simple acceptance of their truth…of my fate. Fighting it, doubting them…it has been exhilarating and exciting—and exhausting. Now a sad peace sets in, like a field mouse surrendering to a hawk's grip, simply letting the end happen—

Until Maimanne jerks to a stop.

I save my ear by skidding short with her—or have my senses been my saviors, sizzling from the blast of new electricity on the air?

Oh…my.

Every neuron in my body is fried from it, letting the energy in—recognizing it at once.

Knowing him at once.

By the Creator.

He has returned.

But my joy is instantly shadowed—by mortification. Cassian Court has come back—to find me being led around by the ear, clad in nothing but my sleepwear. And there go any lingering thoughts for him, at least the good ones, about our passion last night…

Though all I behold on his face right now is—

Fury.

Taut, defined, and clear, all across his perfect, noble features—

And all directed at Mother.

"Let her go."

I blink. Again. Yes, the words have emanated from him—inducing Maimanne's incredulous sputter. Then her forced, tinkling laugh. "Ahhh, Mr. Court! What a delightful surprise. Did you have to let yourself in? I apologize; good help is so hard to find on this tiny island, and we were not aware you would be—"

"Mistress Santelle." Every syllable is a scimitar, bleeding even her conjured civility from the air. "What wasn't I clear about?"

He steps over, readjusting a black messenger bag over his right shoulder, making me wonder if there's a gun stowed inside. He looks like a man intent on drawing a firearm—and using it.

I shiver, boldly afraid. Then gasp, blatantly stunned.

Dear Creator. Has the fear…aroused me?

Though Mother drops her hold, everything still feels surreal. Never has a man said such things on my behalf…been so enraged on my behalf. Or is that it at all? What in Creator's name is going on? Cassian's energy is so different now. While he has changed into more relaxed attire—a white cable-knit sweater and tailored khaki slacks—his demeanor is more high protocol than at any court event I have attended. And I have been to many.

The same curiosity governs Father's face as he rises. "Cassian." His extended hand is given a mechanical shake in return. "To what do we owe the pleasure of your return?"

One of Cassian's tawny brows hikes up—which, of course, makes more of me quiver. Even the forbidden parts. "You weren't expecting me to?"

"In a word," Father rejoins, "no."

Bizarrely, that nicks Cassian's armor. He chuffs without humor. "Then you've misread the business, Fortin. In this case, luckily, it hasn't cost you the business too."

My jaw almost plummets. No one has ever dared this kind of thing with Father. Reproving Fortin Santelle like this, even disguised as "casual" conversation, would drop jaws up and down the halls of the palais. Father has even struck servants for less.

But the look on Cassian's face...as if he is nearly enjoying this...

My nerve endings go icy. By the powers...I actually afraid for him.

Until a new recognition sets in.

Father cannot call on a single recourse against this man. Before him stands Cassian Court: an equal individual. A leader from the most cutthroat kingdom on Earth. New York City.

My lungs clutch. What will Paipanne say? Do?

"Ah. So we still have business?" His desperation is hidden beneath the diffidence, but Cassian sees through it...is utterly beautiful about it. I am only aware of movie stars through pictures Vylet brings up on her computer—when the Arcadian internet chooses to function—but I easily imagine the man as the chiseled star of a high-stakes spy thriller, detecting every weakness in his opponent in the space of a glance.

Cassian himself only fuels that vision—perhaps even enhances it, with a study of Father that reminds me of straight-from-the-mine emeralds. He is...breathtaking. "I said I needed to take advisement, not my complete leave."

Father stiffens again. "You also said you could not sign the agreement."

"I said I couldn't sign *that* agreement." Out from the messenger bag, in his impossibly long fingers, comes a sheaf of papers. "This one, I'll sign."

Mother snags the air with a caught breath. Father balances her, barely flinching. But his gaze goes to work, descending in another silent assessment of Cassian…searching for weakness. He will be out of luck. Cassian remains a perfect, unreadable wall: a hotter, steelier version of Jason Bourne, Jack Ryan, Ethan Hunt, and all their friends put together. He stands tall and determined, legs braced in a solid *A*, locking hands firmly as soon as Father takes the papers…appearing like he has all the time in the world to wait for feedback.

It does not take nearly that long.

Less than a dozen seconds, to be exact.

Which has to be a record for transforming my father from practiced deal broker into stunned gaper.

"We discussed a loan of twenty million."

"Correct," Cassian replies.

"This offer is for twice that."

"Also correct."

Maimanne gasps again. I join her. Forty million dollars? Am I doing the math correctly? I cannot be certain, since every cell in my brain is short-circuited.

"And you cut the interest rate…in half."

As Mother and I now struggle against fish gawks, Cassian's face is unchanged. "Also correct," he states.

"As well as a finder's fee for any additional opportunities in Arcadia that arise within the next year."

"Yes."

I almost beg Mother to pinch my ear again—or anything else, to ensure this is not a dream. The only thing holding me back: the look on Father's face. His gape is gone, replaced by a troubled scowl—shot at me then Cassian, in that order.

My heartbeat stutters all over again. By the powers, what have I done now? More precisely, what kind of concessions has Cassian demanded in return for this astounding new deal? The contract is practically Faustian—except the Devil looks like an angel, moves like a prize fighter, and enthralls like a wizard.

"All for this sole condition?" Father presses.

Mother practically leaps forward. "Accept it! Whatever it is, Fortin, say yes!"

Father looks at her for a long moment. Then once more at me, his gray gaze suddenly hazy—like that of a field mouse in a hawk's talons.

"The acceptance is not mine to give."

*CASSIAN*

"This is insanity."

It's the eighteenth time she's blurted it. Yes, I'm counting—wondering if she'll hit the internal estimation I set during the drive back over here, after having the new contract printed up in one of the palais offices. Somehow, Doyle found a security guard to open one of the rooms for us at four in the morning. Not that I'd ever planned on sleeping, after walking out of here consumed by the proposal now outlined in the pages in her hands.

Proposal.

That's one way of putting it.

In the last half hour, she's come up with quite a few more—though insanity is the favorite, as I'd predicted. Doyle—I make a mental note to give him a massive bonus, after the miracles he's pulled to make this happen in less than six hours—clearly has some more for the list. His stare, filled with have-you-lost-it perplexity, burns from the shadows of the wingback in the corner. I don't earn myself a reprieve by jerking my head, motioning him out the door—not the one beyond which the Santelles are waiting in suspicious silence. It's the one opening onto a small patio with the morning sun now glittering in a small fountain flanked by padded chairs.

Doyle's eyes narrow tighter.

I nod toward the patio again.

With a grunt, he rises. Fortin has all but ordered him to witness every second of my conversation with Mishella, but we're not going to move past the next "this is insanity" at this rate. The dynamic in the room badly needs to change—and D has to know that too. On paper, the guy is my valet, but that bullshit flies as much as saying the same thing about Kato and the Green Hornet. Doyle and I finish thoughts, sentences, and cheeseburgers for each other. He's the closest thing I have to a sibling. At least one who's alive.

As soon as D steps outside, my theory proves out. A rush of relieved breath leaves Mishella.

Just as rapidly, she pulls one back in.

Wheels on me so fast, her loose hair tumbles over her shoulder—

And her breasts pucker beneath her pink sleep shirt.

She's so fucking sexy, I can barely think.

But I must. Force myself to, with willpower I'm now grateful to have fortified over the years…the only thing riveting me in place as blood rushes to stupid places in my body.

"This is insanity!"

So much for theories.

"You must know that," she continues, once more pacing the length of the room. "You—you have to know that."

I can reply right away—I actually have known that since leaving this mansion the first time—but I don't. Instead I lean against her father's desk, bracing hands to the wood at my sides, giving her the full thrust of my gaze, the full recognition of my intent—

The full truth of my spirit.

"It feels more crazy to think of leaving without you."

It's a bomb drop even to me, but I don't try to mitigate the blast. I don't want to. The shrapnel cuts in, and I let it. I welcome the blood; the sensation that I'm watching my heart fall on the floor. For a second, I simply revel in watching it pump. For so many years, I've had my doubts.

I'm braced for the twentieth reference to lunacy but she turns instead, brow tightly knitted. In a rasp, she asks, "Why?"

I quirk a small smile. "After the last two days, do you really have to ask? Wait." I push up, a move easily carrying me into the steps remaining between us. "After last night, do you have to ask?"

She tilts her head up. I'm certain she must hear the thunder in my chest, now so close to her stunning face, as I take in her flash of joy. She hasn't just remembered what happened in her bedroom. She's relived it as many times as I have.

Which doubles my confusion about the new mask she slams down over that bliss. "Cassian—"

"Ella." Yes, I use the name intentionally. With just as much purpose, grip her by both elbows. I don't shirk the hold, even when she stiffens against it.

"Why do you insist on calling me that?"

"Why do you insist on pretending you don't like it?" When she relents, just for a moment, I seize the chance to move an inch closer. Nearly fitting our bodies against each other… "Why do you insist on acting like you're not pleased with my revised proposal to your father?"

"Proposal." She twists both arms free, stumbling back. "That is what you have titled it?" The arms fold back in. She spits a bitter laugh. "And I thought Arcadia had been missing out on so many miracles of the modern world. But if buying a human being is still simply relegated to a piece of paper—"

Okay, slow down." I half-expected her to go here. I didn't expect the vehemence with which she'd do it—or the pain in her eyes as she did. "Nobody is getting 'bought,' Mishella."

"Right," she retorts. "Désonnum. So sorry. My big bad. You do not wish to purchase; you simply want to rent."

"What?" I want to be angry but shock makes that impossible. "Where do you get—"

"Six months." She sweeps a hand toward the contract. "I have that correct, yes? Is it not all completely spelled out in your pretty papers? You agree to invest forty million dollars in Arcadian entities recommended by my father, in exchange for getting to have me on call to you for the next six months."

A band of pain clamps my head. I step back before snarling, "Not on call." It's no less crude than her inflection.

"Oh?" One of her hands hitches to a hip. "What, then? Forty million dollars' worth of companionship? A 'plus one' for social affairs? A movie buddy? A dog trainer?"

One side of my mouth kicks up again. "You want a dog?"

Her eyes widen. I swear that inside, she's just regressed to the age of six. "Do—do you have one?"

"I can get you one."

The six year-old disappears. The woman is back, head tilting, going for what she perceives to be cynicism. "Cassian, are you seriously saying you expect me to return to New York with you…and not fuck you?"

Well, hell.

I'd anticipated that question too—hello, obvious—just not

those words for it. And those words, flowing in her musical voice…what they instantly do to me…

Damn. Damn.

Everything in my body tightens. The skin around my cock does not get a free pass. The fucker just got charged double fare, and he's not happy about it. The insult to the injury: that tiny tick of her auburn eyebrows, which might as well be fist pumps in some unseen boxing match to which she's challenged me.

Okay, sweetheart. You take that victory dance. I'll wait riiiight here.

I've never looked forward more to surging off the ropes.

And I do.

One unwavering step—two—then I'm right back next to her, screwing propriety, manners, and personal space, molding our bodies exactly as they'd been in the recesses of her bedroom. Just as intoxicating as those shadows is the Arcadian morning sun, surrounding us…warming her lips for a kiss I long to brand on her, into her, through her. But I don't. I lean until only the tips of our mouths touch, enlivening those areas so exposed yet so erotic, making us breathe together—me out, her in, then reversed—until she shudders harder than the motes in the rays around us.

"Mishella."

Her eyes drag open. Just a little. "Hmmm?" Then pop wide, as I drop both hands around her ass. Wider as I jerk her body tighter against mine.

"You're not going to fuck me in New York."

"I—" For a moment, before she attempts to hide it, she looks dejected. "I'm not?"

"I'm going to fuck you."

She swallows. "Oh." Pulls in trembling air. "Um…oh."

I roll my hips, making sure the layers of our clothes don't cushion the erect enforcer of my meaning. Complete backfire. My dick rails it at me, screaming to be set free in the hot, soft valley between her lush thighs. Somehow, I'm still able to get words out. Hoarsely.

"You know what else?"

"Wh-what else, Cassian?"

"You're going to beg me for it."

Bigger gape. So goddamn captivating. I could get lost in every facet of her huge sapphire eyes. "I'm—oh."

Her helpless rasp warms my neck. The heat from it reverberates, echoing along my muscles and tendons, my blood vessels and skin cells, an assault of demand to give her a preview of exactly what I'm talking about. But another element shimmers in her breath…and now in the gaze she lifts at me.

She's still afraid.

And I refuse to push her…until she's afraid of only the good things.

With gritted effort, I loosen my hold and step away. My hand finds one of hers. I lead her over to the wingback Doyle was moping from. She looks much better in the thing, the golden tumble of her hair contrasted by the dark leather. Her posture is pristine, though her gaze doesn't miss an inch of my actions. Christ, she's beautiful. My misplaced Cinderella, complete with the princess pink PJs.

"All right," I state, hunkering before her. "Perhaps we should step back."

Her stare clouds. "But you just made me sit."

I quell a chuckle through supreme effort. Lift an indulgent smile—not an effort at all. "Just an American expression, *favori*."

The Arcadian endearment is clearly a surprise—but her small smile confirms it's a pleasant one. "What does it mean?"

"That we should look at this with the body parts above our necks."

She flushes. "A wise idea." Nods. "And a good term. I shall have to journal it."

More of my chest warms. Her journals—one of the first things that fascinated me about her, after recovering from the blow of her beauty—are so much a part of her, it's strange seeing her without one. She keeps them about everything, as if afraid facts will slip into nothingness if she doesn't harness them on paper.

Or maybe they're tangible proof that she controls something in her world.

I tuck away the observation—and my anger from it—to the Deal With This Later file. Just like the surges I battled during dinner last night, when once more she was spoken to like a dog to be curbed, the emotion has no place or use here. Instead I focus on the gentle trust in her grip, while softly prompting, "You remember the most important point, don't you?"

She nods like a child pulling up multiplication tables. "There are three signature lines on the new contract. Yours, Father's, and mine. The contract is not valid without my agreement."

"Which means what?"

"Which means the ultimate choice about this is mine."

"Good."

My voice is serrated and I don't hide it. God help me, even her earnestness is a turn-on. I'm a bastard for fantasizing about what it could be when used for carnal purposes, but my guilt is balanced by conviction. She's the pure air my life has needed for so long. The fresh start I didn't even know I craved, until two days ago.

"What else?" I manage to continue. She fidgets a little. Then more. How the hell has a woman with such light been forced to hide it so thoroughly? "Ella, it's all right. It's just us. I'm listening."

I'll always listen.

"This—this is not you 'buying' me," she finally mumbles.

I let my hands slip free. Lean back on my haunches, sensing she needs the distance. "But you don't believe that."

Her lips purse. "It is a non-negotiable part of the contract, Cassian. What would you have me believe?"

I firm my own features. It's the hardest goddamn thing to do around her, screwing on my "business" brain, but I cinch the fucker tight and go on, "Because your father would be open to considering the courtship of an American otherwise?"

"You underestimate my father's open-mindedness when money is part of the equation."

"I don't underestimate it one bit. But for all intents and purposes, at least in his eyes, I'll be carrying you off then ruining you." I have to force the next words out. "Making your involvement an 'option' gives him an opening for sneaky bullshit. I wouldn't put it past him to double-dip on this opportunity."

Her nose crinkles. "I do not understand. Double…dip?"

"He'll take my money, but still sell off your greatest asset to some horny Arcadian courtier who's stupid enough to believe some made-up line about your absence, like you've been on the other side of the island on a 'research trip' for Brooke." I raise both brows. "There are men that gullible in the Arcadian court, Ella. If *I* can discern that after two days here—"

"I know, I know." Her eyes squeeze shut. "Your assessment is—" A wince takes over. "Correct," she finally concludes. "You are…correct."

More than she wants me to be. The slew of truths has stabbed her, as I knew it would—but this is why I've ordered her parents from the room. If they were still here, she wouldn't feel safe to speak this honestly. "My 'greatest asset'," she finally echoes, blinking at me with aching eyes. "Is that what you are after too, then? Have all the shops on Fifth Avenue run out of shiny virgins, that you have seized the chance to snap one up as a souvenir from Arcadia?"

Her defiance marks each word but she ends with a ragged inhalation—already expecting my righteous fury. Silly, sad, heartbreaking woman. If she only knew that righteous and I have never claimed to remotely know each other—such an abiding truth, her question was one of my first considerations when drafting the new contract.

Battling the urge to yank her close, I settle for locking her in by leveling our gazes. "Ella, if I'd met you here as a hooker in the Sancti marketplace, it wouldn't have mattered." I stop for a second, considering that. "Though I'd likely be on my knees in your pimp's living room instead of here…"

"Having an easier time of it."

We laugh at her finishing my thought. We sigh because that feels as natural—and as exhilarating, and as intense—as the rest of what has happened between us. We sober because the enormity of it hits again too. The mutual recognition that if this is what everything feels like after two days, I shouldn't be pushing fate's favor by forging a contract for six months.

Six months.

Not. Nearly. Enough.

I shove aside the sentimental bullshit. It's enough, you mooning ass. Long enough to get my fill of her, but not so long that I tire of her. More importantly, not long enough for her to start tugging at the threads…asking all the wrong questions…

The threads don't get tugged.

The secrets don't get revealed.

It's for the best, no matter how hard she gets my cock or complete she makes my spirit. In the tapestry of her life, I'll become just a thread as well. The way it should be. The lover who took her virginity, but gave her a bigger gift in return.

Her freedom.

And there's the ultimate ace card in my deck.

The one element she cannot obtain on her own…just six months within her grasp. I watch her start to understand it, her eyes eagerly glittering, even before I speak again.

"Now tell me the third stipulation, Ella. I need to know you understand it."

She responds inside a beat. Imagine that.

"After six months, I shall return to Arcadia. My job as Brooke's secran will be returned to me…and I shall be free to wed a man of my choosing, for whatever reasons I deem acceptable." An incredulous smile flows over her lips. "Even for love."

"Yeah. Even for love."

I fight to ignore how good it feels to hear her say it.

And how fucked-up it feels to force my lips around the same words.

And how confusing it is to watch shadows invade her gaze again.

"Of course…I can also choose not to marry at all." She pulls a corner of her lip under her teeth. Toys with the rivets in the chair's arm. "Perhaps…simply…take a string of lovers."

I don't miss how she finishes it. Her surreptitious glance, darted through her tawny lashes, is a cock-grabbing mixture of question and flirtation. Why deny her the show she's looking for? The instant strain through my whole body. The leap of peeved color up my neck, into my face.

She releases her lip—but instantly wets it. Blinks heavily, clearly perplexed again. Goddammit. My jealousy is actually turning her on, and she doesn't even realize it. The little sorceress has bewitched herself.

Maybe she needs a jolt of clarification. Maybe we both do.

Torch to my kerosene.

I surge forward, slamming into her, submerging us in the depth of the chair, mashing our mouths in a burst of passion and heat. Not waiting for permission, I lunge my tongue inside too. Mate it with hers in complete, carnal intent. There's no ambiguity; she knows what I'm thinking: if she signs that contract, the next six months are going to be about purging this from both our systems, in whatever ways it takes. Whatever the fuck this is…

Right now, I don't want to explore the options around that answer.

Right now, I push my knees apart, opening a space for myself between her legs. Our crotches slide and thrust; even through our clothes, the fit is perfect.

Right now is for ensuring she receives one message only—with complete clarity.

"Ella…"

"H-huh?"

"Why don't we focus on you enjoying your first lover?"

# Chapter Four

*MISHELLA*

I blink.

Once more, very slowly—almost wishing everything around me would click into the same speed. That button is not working. I am caught one step behind, watching as my worldly possessions roll by, stuffed into three suitcases down the narrow strip of asphalt Arcadia calls a tarmac.

Is this happening?

This cannot be happening.

I have surely not done this. Agreed to this.

I take it back. I take it back!

The words are so shrill and loud in my head, surely everyone—and I do mean everyone—can hear them, even over the revving engines of Cassian's private airplane.

I have never traveled in anything that moves faster than a jeep.

Ohhhhh crap crap crap crap.

I gulp hard. Vylet squeals, her face alight with joy. She is accompanied by Brooke, who wears a smile so wide, she has officially inducted herself as the third member of our "sis-friend-hood." They haul me into a three-way embrace, where our dipped heads form seconds' worth of a private chat room. The two of them do not waste the time.

"You know the only reason I'm even agreeing to this is because Samsyn and Evrest vouched for this bozo," Brooke asserts.

"And the only reason I agree is because she does."

A giggle spurts out. I am not sure if it is due to sheer nerves, their wonder twins of protectiveness thing, or both, but I am grateful for the respite from decorum. "So you both have reminded me. Repeatedly."

"Good," Brooke volleys. "That means you remember the rest of it too."

"Sure does." Vy hip-bumps me. "Give us the rest of it, Mistress Santelle." When I give nothing but a psshh, she nudges harder. "The rest of it."

I squeeze her as hard as I can. She knows I need to be irked, in order to fight off the tears. It is only six months. It is only six months. I can do this. At least I think I can.

"Shella-bean!"

I jump a little before girl-growling—but continue to hold her tight. "If the bozo goes bonzo, I call the sis-friend-hood hotline." That is their nickname for our online video chat room.

Brooke nods in approval. "You call it any time, girlfriend. Day or night. Seven hours isn't that huge a time difference."

"Says the girl who has not been roused in the middle of the night by the hotline buzz?" It really is one of the most obnoxious sounds I have ever heard—but it can rouse Saynt from a dead sleep, so I know it works.

"Not yet," she jokes back. "Maybe this is our chance to really test it out."

And maybe it should not be.

Why am I going to do this? How am I going to do this? I will be living in a world without them—a world as foreign to me as Antarctica, with but a thousand Arcadian dollars in my purse, three suitcases full of belongings, and the promises of a man I barely know.

No. Also not true.

A man…I do know.

A man I have known from the moment our eyes met and our hands joined. As if we had just been two ends of a drawbridge, waiting to be dropped back into place, leading the way back to the castle of us.

A man who, even now, as I dare a glance up, seems to know exactly what I need in this surreal moment.

It is not the strength of his stance, nor the determination in his eyes. They help, but they are not the key.

They are not his nod.

One movement. A sole dip, as forceful as the motors behind him, as clear as the sky into which we are bound, that gives me all the truth of his purpose once more. That infuses me with the bursting belief in it.

That reminds me of exactly what Brooke said, during the hour she and Vy had helped me pack.

I married Samsyn three hours after I was asked, girlfriend—by his freaking brother.

Neither Vylet nor I pointed out that his brother was also her king, and that the reason—at the time—was for Arcadian national security. I do not possess even half as good an excuse, but nor am I committing to Cassian Court's ring on my finger. It is only six months.

"By the powers," I mutter, solely to myself.

Six. Months.

When I return, it will be to stand as a maide attendant for the "real wedding" Brooke and Samysn are starting to plan: a grand double ceremony with Evrest and Camellia's.

When I return, Saynt will be keeping watch over that event—as a full-fledged soldier in the Arcadian Army.

When I return…so much will be different.

Especially me.

I am terrified again. Not even another nod from Cassian fixes it, especially as I turn to my brother, who clenches his jaw and blinks suspiciously shiny eyes. I tug his chestnut hair free from its tie and mess the strands until they're tangled, but that does not prevent the crushing ferocity of his parting hug.

"I took Court outside while you were packing," he says into my ear. "Told him that if he hurts you in any way, or lets any fucker in that crazy city hurt you, that contract is null and void—and I will come get you myself."

I pull back by a little, not sure how to react. I go for the honesty of my curiosity. "Wh-what did he say?"

"That it would not be necessary." Reluctant grunt. "That he plans on treating you like the treasure you are—and that if you do not feel as such and desire to come home, he will put you on the plane himself, anytime."

I threaten a sisterly smack by narrowing my eyes. His handsome face does not falter. "He really…called me a treasure?"

"Why do you think I am not blocking your way to the stairs?"

I crush him close again. Emotion floods me, and I shake from the force of it. I am a…treasure. Not just to the guy who has to feel that way because of genetics, but to the man who looks on, emerald gaze gleaming, the rest of his face seeming like a knight reverently waiting for his lady…

Returning his stare, I smile. In my mental journal, I record the metaphor, for it fits. Knightly passion, while perfect, was never intended to last. What kind of perfection ever was?

Six months is an ideal time limit for perfection.

The conclusion lends me the steel for the last of my goodbyes. Maimanne and Paipanne.

I turn, dutifully ducking my head before them both. Mother is the first to tuck me close, pressing quick kisses to both my temples, before scooting back and murmuring, "You are to use that money only for emergencies. You have it stowed safely, yes?"

I lift my head. Search for the sheen in her eyes like Saynt's, indicating she's muttering about money to cover deeper emotions, and that she worries about me leaving for a city with a population ten times that of our island…

Her eyes are hard as flint.

I suppress my disappointment as Father steps over. Perhaps they have agreed he will handle the emotional overtones of the farewell. Makes sense. Mother is not a "public display of affection" type—actually, she is not an advocate of the practice in private either—meaning Paipanne has surely been assigned the parental parting duties.

I lift a new smile at him, giving it an I'm-being-brave-but-do-not-feel-it wobble. He leans over—and bestows the same dual kisses on my forehead, with the same formality as Mother. Tilts my head up, so I am impaled by the similar granite of his stare.

"Do not disgrace our family."

So this is what a fist in the heart feels like.

I step back, struggling around the blow for breath that needs to come. The pressure surges, jerking my shoulders back and my head up. As I look one last time, I borrow a heavy scoop of stone from both of them—one for my left eye, one for my right.

"Have not a worry, Paipanne. I know exactly what is important to you."

## CASSIAN

"What is it?"

The words are out the second I guide her into the leather chair next to mine, then cinch her seatbelt. The syllables are damn near a demand by this point but maybe that's for the best. Whatever force of fate has spurred my inner caveman for this woman has intensified tenfold by watching her board the plane like a zombie, her steps full of wood and her eyes full of loss.

"Mishella."

Her head jerks up—and for a second, she terrifies me. Her gaze takes me in as if she's been jerked out of a dream. Worse, as if we've never met.

Second thoughts?

Dammit...no.

"What. Is. It?"

Suddenly, she's back—honing her gaze into me as if she wants to laser me open. Pressing fingers to my face, and infusing it with the same penetrating force. I battle—in vain—to keep those beams from searing my cock. Lasered. Game over. Hasn't it been from the start with her?

"You...really care how I answer that."

She doesn't phrase it as a question but I hear her bewilderment, responding with a slow nod. I don't want her to stop touching me.

"But that does not matter," she finally murmurs. Expels a long sigh, as if making room for the fresh infusion of sadness over her lush features. "Just get me out of here. Now. Please."

# Chapter Five

MISHELLA

For a second—perhaps many more than that—I regret letting go of my rage in favor of ogling Cassian like a hormone-drenched teenager. Can I be blamed, after the ferocity of his stare, the press of his lips to my knuckles, and the way he barks, "Wheels up" into a phone in the bulkhead? Just as it has been since we arrived at the airport, every move is about my needs and comfort…

Even now, when a lot of my comfort is beyond his control.

A lot of it.

With the exception of the juncture of our hands, my whole body twists from the race of my bloodstream, the heave of my lungs, the tripled pumps of my heart. Was I actually congratulating myself on the tarmac, for thinking the engines' roar was the scariest part of this "flying" thing? Now, with the whole plane shaking as it gains momentum, faster and faster down the runway, I clamp my eyes shut, grit my teeth, and pray to the Creator I will survive—

"Ella."

How can he sound so gentle, in the middle of such violence?

"What?"

"You need to breathe."

I yearn to hurl a glower—but opening my eyes is not a viable option. "No."

"Favori."

"Do not speak at me with sweets."

"You mean…try to sweet talk you?"

"Now you laugh about it?" The glare cannot be helped.

Neither, it appears, can his dimpled grin, making me rip up all my mental bookmarks—even the one I have all but glued to the page marked Cassian Court: Arrogance in the Air.

The air.

We are…in the air.

My breath clutches to a brand-new stop—as I watch the runway disappear, giving way to the aqua expanse of the sea. Then a wisp of a cloud. Another.

"Holy shit!"

Cassian laughs from his belly but I do not care, nearly scrambling over that part of him to gape out the window. A sound escapes me, unlike any I have made before, because it is born of sensations I have never felt before. Fear, yes—but now churned into something beyond. Exhilaration duels with ebullience. Anxiety, but tempered with a new awareness altogether. Something light, like the dandelion seed the plane now feels like. Possibility in the space of a breath.

Is this…freedom?

The knowledge is a crash inside, breaking apart a shell I have never consciously admitted to—but now let myself step from, hatched into something new. Someone new. She is a stranger to me, and I long to crawl back right away into the safety of the tiny world behind me, to the security of the tiny girl who lived there.

Who lived there.

And I realize…

There is no "taking it back."

I have agreed to let Cassian show me how good those words can be. Signed my name on his paper, giving him the right—and the power—to do so. Power not just over where my body physically goes…but the vistas my mind, soul, and senses are taken to, as well.

And I think an airplane take-off has been the most terrifying part of my day?

What in Creator's name have I done?

The query makes me tilt my head—toward the man in whose lap I am practically perched. I am not surprised to find Cassian already staring at me. The intensity on his face is another element entirely.

Arrogance in the Sky. He is still that—only now, Mr.

Confidence is subdued to silence. Perhaps even humbled. The green glass shards in his eyes spike with the crowning truth atop that. Because of you.

I have no idea how to answer that…save with one set of words.

"Merderim, Cassian Court."

One side of his mouth hitches up. "Thank you, Mishella Santelle."

More of the shell shatters.

As more of me steps free, my spirit moves toward the one path in this new world that makes sense…and the perfect, emerald-eyed guide waiting to lead me on it.

My fingers lift to his jaw.

The other side of his mouth raises.

I push my fingers in a little more. Pull tenderly at his jaw.

I want that mouth on mine.

With a ragged grunt of acknowledgement, Cassian obliges.

## CASSIAN

How could just a brush of lips be the best fucking kiss of my life?

There are no answers for that.

There are a million answers for that.

My mind implodes on the conflict—the same way it explodes from merely a memory of that sweet, inexplicable touch of her mouth…

Now nearly three hours ago.

I continue gazing at her in sleep, where I fixate on the plush pads that have tossed me into this chaos. Doesn't help a goddamn bit. With Doyle snoozing in the small bedroom at the back of the plane, I'm alone up here with my sorceress—who has me as baffled, bewitched, and just as stunned as I was after kissing her.

And tasting her…

and breathing her in…

then fighting to push her back out.

A lot of good the effort yields me.

She has beaten me.

Good business means admitting when one is defeated, as well celebrating when one is victorious.

And isn't that the rub?

Mishella Santelle is not good business—or so nearly all my teams inform me. Flying all the way to Arcadia, searching for the angles to maneuver Fortin Santelle and save money, don't match what I'm returning with: a contract at double the budget and a "houseguest" for the next six months. What the hell else am I supposed to call her? Like the explanation will fly for one second with Prim and Hodge—both of whom I will put off thinking about until we're much closer to home. A "treat" to look forward to, if Doyle's dour looks have been accurate prophesy—and they usually are.

I don't give a fuck.

I would've paid four times as much for her. Been just as glad I had, for the payback of that kiss alone—though karma now carves her pound of flesh right out of my libido.

That kiss.

I crave so much more.

Goddammit, I've paid for it.

No. You've paid for the right to explore this with her, not take it from her. Dial it back, asshole. You've only brought this torture on yourself.

The woman herself helps with the meaning of that final pronoun, sighing sleepily...stretching until her pink sweater set is yanked tightly across her sleek figure. I watch the fabric slide across her breasts, mentally filling in the basic white bra that undoubtedly covers them.

Suddenly, every lace-clad temptress I've been with before is a dim memory behind Mishella's hot-as-fuck take on that Doris Day goodness. Is she wearing matching panties? And is she still so soundly asleep, she won't notice if I try confirming with a peek under her skirt?

Sick. Fuck.

"Mmmm."

While her moan kills off my Peeping Tom, it wakes up my Ready-To-Go-Randy. I shift in my seat, adjusting the wood to a more tolerable angle.

Her eyes open halfway, then take me in fully.

"Hey there, little Ella."

She curls a drowsy grin. "Bad princess. I fell asleep in the carriage—even after the prince's kiss."

Hell. She has to mention the kiss. "I'm no prince, Miss Santelle." *Especially after what you've done to my thoughts in the last three hours.*

"Well, thank the Creator." The moment it spills, she clearly can't believe it has. With a dogged shake of her head, she peers out the window. "It is...still light outside."

There's a question in her voice. "Ah. Yes." I follow her gaze, to where the dark orange rays glint against the plane. "We're chasing the sun—for another hour, at least." Unable to rein back the action, I run a hand down the back of her head—intending to do only that. *Slow the fuck down. You have six months.* But when I pull it back, she chases my touch with her head. Burrows so deeply against my hand she ends up pressed against my chest. After the discernible click of her seatbelt, the rest of her follows, sitting fully on my lap—

And I sure as hell don't stop her.

"Do you...mind?" She glances up, adorably sheepish. "I can see the sunset better from here."

"And I can see you better from here." I let a full grin escape. Goddamn, it feels good. "So it's a win-win."

I hope for a smile in return, perhaps even one inviting a new kiss, but her nose crinkles, and her gaze remains somber. "This decision...the new contract..." She traces the pattern in my sweater with the tip of a finger. "It is not a 'win-win' for you, is it?"

"That's not for you to worry about."

Tighter nose crunch. "To be plain about it, Cassian, that is bullshit."

I struggle not to laugh. "Is that so?"

"I have a mind," she asserts. "And two ears that work."

"I never doubted either, *favori*."

"I know what Father's voice sounds like, when he is trying to justify a business choice to a colleague. Yours sounded the same way during several calls on your cell phone today. You have walked out in a tree because of this."

"Walked out in a—?" Deep frown. "Do you mean…gone out on a limb?"

She huffs. Waves an impatient hand. "You have taken a risk. A huge one." Her hand slides up, sneaking a little beneath my sweater, caressing the side of my neck. Once more, the breath I've just regulated is a wind storm in my chest. Outwardly, I suck it in as calmly as I can…praying to God the tempest between my legs is equally obedient. "I want to be worth that risk for you, Cassian."

I swallow hard. Run a hand along the back of her arm, up to her neck, around to her nape. "You already are."

"Bullsh—"

I kiss her into silence, but with lingering tenderness. "Ssshhh. We're not even halfway through the flight." She draws breath to speak but I yank it right back out of her with another kiss—still lingering, not as patient. "We have time," I grate. "Lots of time, all right? Let's just—"

And suddenly, I'm the one being cut off with a kiss. Correction: a kiss, borrowing my idea but very little else; incinerating my temperance on the sacrificial pyre of her passion. Correction: her passion. She is a fireball in my arms: a groaning, grabbing, greedy burst of need, twisting her slender fingers into my hair until our mouths are meshed, our chests are fitted, and our crotches are grinding with inescapable heat…and lust.

Annnnd, the discreet hard-on is officially in my rearview. Who the hell have I tried to fool about that, anyway? Discretion is my Dulcinea when she's near. A glorious, impossible dream.

A soundtrack for another time—definitely not when my balls pulse like this, rocketing my shaft to a solid ten on the pain scale. The fucker fills and lengthens, punching at my fly in response to her incredible little mewls and erotic little writhes. She is going to kill me, and right now, I can think of no better way to go.

When she finally relents, we are both breathing like goddamn freight trains—but she barely waits before pulling my hand free from her nape then guiding it down, down, down, until it's formed to her inner thigh. With our gazes still bound, she rolls her hips…sliding her soft flesh against my trembling touch.

But that's not my undoing.

Her awkward little swallow. The tentative flick of her tongue along the seam of her lips. The questioning glint in her eyes, so unsure about what she is doing but trusting herself—trusting me—enough to follow the instinct of her desire, and do it anyway...

"Wh-what if...I do not want to waste any more time?"

Now I kiss my restraint goodbye.

With a long, slow, growl, I dip my head back down while inching my fingertips up. There's a method to the madness—and with her, it feels like madness—of being able to read her better through her lips. Their stillness or hesitation will tell me that despite what her brain dictates about honoring my "risk," her body is on an entirely separate page.

So far, we are very much on the same page.

Holy fuck, what a page.

As I sweep deeper into the heat of her mouth, my hand explores the silken valley between her thighs. Her skin is soft and shivery beneath my fingertips; her muscles bunch as she undulates in ready response. Pain pricks my scalp as she clings to me tighter, tighter still. "Yes," I hiss, blowing the sound along her lips. "God, yes. Make me feel it, woman. Every shred of it."

She moans and shakes...as I trail my touch higher.

Every. Fucking. Shred.

She arches up. Strangled sounds vibrate in her throat. I kiss down that strained column, reveling in her tension. She's a drawn bow, coiling deeper as I glide a path toward the erotic triangle at her apex. It's shielded by modest panties. I palm her mound through them, my lips hitching as she gasps.

"C-Cassian!"

I growl again. Rub fingers along the fabric's center panel. "Wet panties, sweet Ella. They feel so fucking good."

"Mmmm," she stutters. "I—I am glad you—ahhhh." She jerks upward as I circle my fingers. I can feel her clit even through the barrier, trembling...hardening.

"Tell me they're white."

She shoots a confused stare. "Wh-what?"

"Your panties," I clarify. "So help me God, if we were in this airplane alone, I'd be hiking up your skirt to look for myself, but for now, you'll have to let my imagination do the work." I let my gaze grow heavy hoods while running fingers along the inner seams, never delighting in teasing a woman more. She's slick with perspiration and arousal. She smells like tropical flowers and honey.

The crown of my cock is wet now too.

"Color," I manage to command again. "Tell me the fucking color, Mishella."

She gulps again. "Wh-white."

I hiss, exposing my bliss. Knew it.

"Ohhhh." It's the only option of a response I give her, working my fingers inward, against her bare flesh. "By the Creator. That is…that is so…"

I watch it all take over her face—the wonder, the awe, the heat, the passion—in a transfixed state of my own. Though my cock throbs, damn near screaming for emancipation, it isn't as important as the horizon to which I'm guiding her. "Yeah. It is, isn't it?"

"Cassian." She sighs. "Oh…my…"

"My gorgeous girl." I swipe my thumb in, testing the taut bundle at her very center. She jolts then mewls, fisting my sweater. "You're a virgin to this too, aren't you? Nobody has ever touched you like this before…right here?"

"Oh!" Her head snaps back. "Oh, by all the powers!"

"Tell me, favori. Has anyone—any man—ever stroked you here? Made you this wet and hot?"

"N-no," she finally blurts. "Nobody, Cassian. Only you have touched me like this."

I kiss her softly, conveying my approval. "Now tell me…the naughty way. Tell me how you like my fingers in your pussy. How your wet, succulent clit likes my strokes. How you want me to play with the edges of your tight, virginal tunnel…like this."

"Yes!" It is more rasp than exclamation, though I'm still grateful Doyle has the bedroom door closed. But another part of me mourns the fact, wishing the ass could hear every note of her gasping arousal…wondering if he'd glare at me now for the crazy contract commitment. "I—I like your fingers there. Want you…stroking me…touching my clit…"

"And playing with your entrance?"

"And—and playing with my entrance."

"With my cock getting harder, as I think of fucking you there? Ella?" I charge it when her lips go still. She's back to remembering the white panties instead of the gorgeous vixen beneath them. But finally she pulls in a harsh breath, squeezes her eyes shut, and forces the obedient words out.

"Yes," she blurts. "Yes—all right—I like it when you think a-about f-fucking me." She breaks in on herself with a moan that has to be the most erotic sound I've ever heard. Curls my sweater tighter in her grip, using the hold as leverage for her whole body, shoving herself against my fingers. It's completely unnecessary. Her fever has infected me too. I flick her erect pearl as fast as I can, snarling in satisfaction when her eyes reopen and her mouth drops in arousal.

"Oh, I'm thinking of fucking you, Ella. Be sure of it." I thrust up my hips until the swells of her ass embrace the head of my cock, and we groan together from the torturous friction. My boxers are soaked, a cruel reminder of how badly I want to be pumping like a heathen inside her tight core. "Hard and hot and deep. You'd be feeling me in your eye sockets. Screaming for me. Pleading to let you c—"

She lurches her head up to deliver the kiss—or maybe yanks mine down, as if it matters—joining our mouths as our bodies crave, an unthinking collision of fire and fervor and flesh as she writhes toward a climax that has me breathing just as hard...needing just as much.

"Let me come, Cassian. Oh, by the sweet fucking Creator, make me come now!"

# Chapter Six

MISHELLA

This is not me.

It cannot be.

These are not my words. Not my lips, rambling with these filthy, wanton things; certainly not my body, pulsing with desire I never dreamed possible…heat I never knew existed…

It is all so good.

Too good.

Not me. Not me. Not me.

Not true.

For as Cassian swirls his thumb in then presses it there, punching the hot bundle at my core, I slam back into myself like a soul returned from the dead. I know all of myself, suddenly seeing the past and the present and even the future, for time ceases to exist or matter. Only sensation does, pure and perfect. As my sex screams with ecstasy, my blood is made of stars. My vision is made of light.

My spirit is flown to completion.

"Fuck! Yesssss!"

I ride wave after wave of the silver-white miracle, now unable to utter a sound. Cassian carries me through with words in a baritone gone husky, keeping me from drowning with his strength and his touch. He is my rock…my haven…my all.

The thought is like an icy tide.

Too soon. It is much too soon.

And yet, I cannot deny it.

He bought me. For the next six months, everything I am is his. Yet every new moment with him brings me closer to…

me.

Whoever that is.

Do I even know? Do I even want to? Will she be a woman I find, only to be forced to hide upon returning to Arcadia? Not being bound to an arranged marriage does not excuse the rest of Father and Mother's proprieties…the remaining walls of their boxes.

Even more terrifying: what if she is a person I do not like?

Questions that must remain secrets. I ensure that by dragging my eyes shut as I lift my head, a rag doll in reverse—appropriate, since my body is now limp as one. Cassian assists the feeling by gently massaging my thigh while pulling out from beneath my skirt. His other hand duplicates the pressure along my shoulders. Soon, my head droops to his chest, my senses tempted back toward subconsciousness. I fight them, despite his disciplining growl.

"Sleep, Ella. You need it, favori."

"Mmmm. Noooo." I sound slurry and silly, the rag doll animated…sort of. "You," I insist. "I need to…take care of…you." Despite the lethargy, I am all too aware that his body is still the stiff opposite of mine—especially the part nestled right against my backside. And yes, even in my partial coma, I am aware of how deliciously good it feels.

"I'll be fine."

"That is why you sound like a jungle snake is strangling you?"

He grunts. "Why don't you let me worry about the snakes?"

I trump his sound with a giggle. "Or maybe one snake?"

His laugh rumbles beneath my ear. "Dirty girl. Are you trying to corrupt me?"

"Hmmphh? No…no corruption. Education."

"Ohhhh. Hmmm. Right. Education. I can…understand that."

"Have to know the differences between snakes, Cassian." I nestle a little deeper against him. As a yawn takes over, so does a distant memory. Maybe not so distant. Was it just yesterday, about this time, that I sat drinking sun tea with Brooke and Vy, being subjected to my own lesson in corruption…and snakes?

"Is that so?" His murmur is warm in my hair. "And what about them?"

"Well, according to Brooke and Vy—"

"But of course…"

"Some are small and harmless," I go on, disregarding his wry tone. "And others are anacondas."

"Huge and dangerous?"

Little frown. "But you are not dangerous."

My dulled logic delays my mortified gasp, though not his chuckle. He tilts up my face, lowering a soft kiss on my nose before murmuring, "Sleep, my little armeau. You have a bigger adventure ahead than you think. The anaconda agrees with me, whether he likes it or not."

His firm tone demands obedience—and I am too tired to push back anymore. But his sarcasm also dictates a laugh, and on that, I am unable to deliver. *I* am the one choked now—by a thrill that curls down to my toes.

Armeau. He's deliberately labeled me with another Arcadian word.

It means...

Gift.

## *CASSIAN*

I've lived in New York for nearly ten of my twenty-eight years. Have taken this journey back into the city more times than I can count, gazing at the manmade forest across the Hudson before the Lincoln Tunnel makes the skyline disappear—but over the years, have come to think of those buildings as just collections of rooms with collections of people who have nothing but collections of meetings, contracts, conference calls, action plans, presentations, power plans...endless demands of me. Endless lists for me.

The work that rescued me from grief four years ago has become my Manhattan cage.

Until now.

Until, through the eyes of Mishella Santelle, the forest has become magic again. And those eyes, huge as serving platters made from the blue quartz on her island, don't miss a damn thing. Practically bouncing from one side of the limo to the other, scrambling over the bench seat we share to see it all, she is a conduit of enchantment—a sorceress given new powers, courtesy of New York City.

"How do all those buildings *fit?*"

"How many kinds of cars *are* there?"

"What are the yellow ones called?"

"Can we take a ride in one of those big ones with the seats on top?"

"The horns are like music. So pretty."

"Wait. It is…a tunnel…*under the water?*"

"So when the lights turn red, everyone just…*stops?* What if someone does not agree to that?"

"All those people, moving together…they are like pods of dolphins, only on the land…"

She trails into rapt silence after that one. Freezes in place, crouched like an awed kitten over my lap. I rip my gaze away from the perfect curves of her profile, following the line of her stare. It's a quarter to six, so the crowds along 5th are still dominated by business suits and headphones, but she watches the scene as if memorizing every face she sees. I am filled with the same feeling, only my focus frames only one face. I need to remember this moment. *Everything* about it. The azure glitter in her eyes. The twilight breeze in her long curls. The way she's yanked off my blinders and made me see the poetry in New York City crowds.

*Don't forget this. Don't forget this.*

Especially not now, as she angles her gaze back to me. Blushes a little, as if discerning exactly what I've been up to. "It is incredible, Cassian."

I don't tear my stare from her. "It certainly is, Ella."

She laughs softly, and sucks in her bottom lip in that go-to move she has for awkward times. *Little siren*; she doesn't realize that shit makes me yearn to replace her teeth with mine—and use that as only the first place I'll bite her. Maybe one day, I will.

Maybe right *now* I will.

I reach a finger up. Tug at that strawberry-colored pillow, still caught beneath her teeth. Let my gaze dip there, fully informing her of my intention.

I'm going to kiss her. Hard.

"Welcome home, Mr. Court!"

I refrain from lunging out of the car and driving a fist into Scott's cheerful grin. The kid isn't responsible for me losing all track of time and place; I should be grateful he didn't yank open the door and get an eyeful of me lunging down Ella's throat—and maybe up her skirt. *Likely* up her skirt.

I clench my jaw, forcing a smile, before climbing out. "Thanks, Scott. Good to be home."

Things become more fun when his grin turns into curiosity, clearly wondering why I hang on to the back door instead of letting him close it. Scott's love for the Jag XJL is no secret; he exploits every chance to caress his "car baby." Inside five seconds, he's actually a little antsy.

Until I reach back inside, and help Mishella step out.

And suppress a chuckle, witnessing the normally smooth college kid become a puddle of astonishment.

If Ella notices the influx of Shar-Pei in his brow, she doesn't show it. Instead, extending a hand with openness and grace, she says, "*Bon sonar.* I—uh—mean, good afternoon. My, what a lovely tie."

Scott runs a hand down the strip of navy-colored satin—and his puffed chest. "Well, thank you." I throw a smug smirk from behind her. If he's not going to mention the tie is part of his required uniform, neither will I.

"Mishella, this is Scott Gaines. He's usually around to drool over the car." I cock a trenchant brow. "And *not* a lot of anything else."

Scott clicks from astonished to stunned. Plenty of women have disembarked from this car before—there's no getting around that, especially with Scott—but to this day, I doubt if the guy knows any of their names. I'm irked with myself about that, until confronted with one irrefutable fact. None of them have stopped to compliment his tie, either.

"So nice to meet you. I am—"

"May I present Mishella Santelle, of the Island of Arcadia." The caveman has stomped in, inspiring my interruption, but I'm not sorry. Handling the introduction allows me to answer the rest of the questions in Scott's gaze. "She'll be staying at Temptation for…a while." Though I am the one who set it, the idea of a time limit on her stay is suddenly repellant—but I accept the twist in my gut. It's likely the first of many to come.

"Oh." At first Scott's response is pleasant. Why wouldn't it be, when basking in the sun of this woman's smile? A second later, my statement sinks in. "*Oh*. Really?"

"Yeah." I arch both brows now. "Really." Translation: *deal with it and behave yourself.*

"Well." The guy bounces on his toes before swooping up Ella's hand, then bowing low over it. "In that case, welcome to Temptation, and consider me at your service."

Mishella laughs. Giggles, really, though she is not a typical giggler. Even that girlish indulgence gets her musical infusion…the kind of harmony that shoots straight to a man's cock, as he wonders how to incite it even more. "*Merderim. Bennim honeur*," she murmurs back before translating, "Thank you. It is my honor."

I give Scott two seconds to be charmed by the Arcadian poetry. *One. Two.* Then I step back around, grasping her hand with open possessiveness. "All right, all right. I've got it from here, whelp." Instant gloat, as the melody of a giggle again sprinkles the air—for me.

Scott accepts the trounce with a good-natured bow. "Of course, Mr. Court. I'll take care of the car now."

"I'm sure you will."

I say it while gathering Ella's hand closer. Tucking it under my elbow, and resting her elegant fingers along my forearm. It feels so fucking good to have her there. So right. I guide her past the entrance door, set into the brick wall I had installed when renovating this place five years ago. The entrance disguises what lies beyond: a circular forecourt, also made of brick, leading to a marble staircase that swoops up to the mansion's main entrance. Urns with modern lines counteract the gothic impact of it all—and the memories of the woman who loved this place because of that.

Now, for the first time, I see the space through Mishella's marveling gaze. It's new again. Beautiful once more.

My chest rips in conflict.

In remembrance…

I am glad when Mishella stops to peer around more. Use the chance to turn, fisting the center of my sternum. The cavity beneath has been so dark for so long, these new feelings are like a fucking heart attack.

*I'm sorry. I'm sorry, my blossom...*
*but maybe it's time for new memories.*

"Cassian?"

I spin back around, probably looking as if a ghost has shown up. *And maybe she has.* Lily always did like being the center of attention...

"Hmmm?"

Her eyes find mine—and just like that, my world is filled with nothing else again. The huge blue irises, evoking the sea and skies of her island, bathe me with more warmth and hope and completion than the first time we met. "This—is yours?"

I smile. There's nothing else to do in response to the pure amazement in her voice. "Yes. It is."

"The whole thing?"

I can't help a soft chuckle. "Well...yes."

"It's like a *palais!*"

"Not quite."

"It has,"—she pauses, her finger in the air, counting the floors—"six levels." Her gaze returns to me, narrowing. "The palace in Sancti has only two more, including the beach and private residence."

I shrug. Instantly recognize the lame excuse of a move—but what other option do I have? "A lot it sits empty." *Fondness for the metaphors today, man?* "I bought it to prove something, at a time in my life when I needed that. But the neighborhood is good, and the views of the Hudson are excellent from the turrets." Not that I'd made the time for reflective moments lately.

"There are *turrets?*" Her head rocks back as she searches the building once more. Watching her like that, hair tumbling down her back, creamy neck exposed, makes me instantly think of her inside one of those towers—hands fogging the windows as I pound into her from behind...

"There are two." I clear the croak from my throat. "They're on the other side."

Her smile lights up her whole face. "Can we go in them?"

"Of course." I add hurriedly, "Well, one." Force a casual shrug. "The other is used for storage. Probably a mess."

*A mess.* That's a safe way of putting it.

She pops her hands together, enough to serve as proxy for excited applause. "One is just as perfect."

"Then I am at your service." I give Scott's words a deliberately husky inflection. Her smile drops just enough that I know she's heard…and comprehends.

But first things first.

Introducing her to everyone else.

We cross the ornately tiled vestibule at the top of the stairs and are headed for the waiting elevator, when she stops again. Reads the Art Deco letters etched into the granite over the lift doors.

"Temptation." Her forehead purses. "The building is…actually called that?"

I nod. "It was built in the early twentieth century, in honor of the original owner's wife, whose name was actually Temperance."

"When did irony rear its funny head?"

"Nineteen thirty-three, when the government repealed the Prohibition Act. As soon as that happened, the *new* owners had the first three floors turned into a multi-level supper club. They'd already been operating the basement as a speakeasy for years."

Her frown deepens. "Why would people go to a place just to speak easier?"

"They do it all the time, *favori*. It's called therapy." When my joke doesn't register, I simply go on, "It's a slang phrase, once used to describe an illegal tavern."

"Illegal?" she retorts. "Why?"

"They just were. As a whole, selling and consuming alcohol was—for many years. Many people thought the stuff was evil."

"But declaring something outside the law…does that not just make it more enticing?"

Fucking great. She has to go and issue one of her little insights now, in that insanely sexy accent, as the lift doors close and we're sealed in for half a minute.

Half a minute is all I need.

I sweep around, pinning her against the elevator's cage, before dipping and taking her lips beneath mine. I'm not savage about the move, though I yearn to be. The contrast of her soft curves against the ornate steel…and thinking of taking her hard enough to embed the pattern into her flesh…

Fuck. *Fuck.*

What is this woman doing to me?

I pull away enough to stare into her impossibly gorgeous eyes. In the dimness of the lift, they've turned the color of smoke. "For the record," I rasp, "You're forbidden to say 'enticing' again, unless we're alone."

A slow smile teases at her lips. "And if I do not heed your...decree?"

I dip my head in a mock threat. "Punishment. Merciless. For certain."

"I shall make a note of that."

"In what journal would that go in?"

"Oh, I think a new one shall have to be created." Her fingers toy at my sweater. Her smile flirts with my gaze. "'Cassian's Disciplines?'"

"God*damn.*" I push closer, letting *her* crotch feel what that does to *mine*. "That has a very nice ring to it..."

I'm inches away from smashing another kiss on her, devil take the consequences, when the lift *thunk*s to a stop at level six—and surprise, surprise—Lucifer himself is waiting with a glare for us, right through the steel mesh. All right, so Hodge is a close enough comparison, and that's before Prim arrives on the scene. She has to be near; obviously Scott called upstairs the second Ella and I left his sight.

Sure enough, as soon as the door opens and I help Mishella onto the landing, Prim rounds the corner from the kitchen. Her blonde dreadlocks are twisted into a high bun, making it even easier to note the fiery shade of her gold eyes. Fury will do that to a woman—especially this one.

Despite Prim's ire spiking the air, Mishella slips her hand free from mine then reaches out, as amiable as she was with Scott. "Hello. It is good to meet you. My name is Mishella. And yours?"

Prim glares as if Ella's fingers are scorpions—until her eyes snatch up to meet mine, as I have known they would. I return the scrutiny with a sole, silent message. *Play nice. We'll talk later.*

Her pierced nose flares a little. *You bet your ass we will.* She makes short work of accepting the handshake then stating, "Prim Smith. And before you ask, it's not short for anything. And before you start laughing, I like my name fine."

"Why would I laugh?" Ella's nose crinkles. "I like it too. It is unique. And pretty."

"Thank you."

There's civility in it. Just a toss. I still grab it for the win. My little sorceress has melted *Prim* after just thirty seconds. *Alert the press.*

While the advent is significant, it confuses the hell out of Hodge. My burly curmudgeon of a houseman collects his paychecks from me but signed his heart away to Prim at least a year ago—not that she'll ever notice. Still, Prim's not jabbed the expected iceberg into Ella's *Titanic*, clearly causing his internal debate. "So…uh…Boss, are there bags to handle? I think Scott said some are coming up on the service elevator?"

Ah. Conflict handled with the man's default to practical hospitality. I accept *it* for the win too. "He's correct. Just put them in the master bedroom."

"Sure thing, Boss."

"The master bedroom?"

I ignore Prim's snip, turning Ella's attention toward Hodge. "This is Conchobhar Hodgkins, houseman and engineer extraordinaire—but we call him Hodge for obvious reasons. He'll be your call for anything from heavy lifting to rewiring the lights."

"And an occasional green smoothie." Hodge jams hands into his back pockets and nervously toes the floor. He's not used to bantering socially, but is clearly falling under Ella's spell as quickly as Scott did—though has held out twice as long as *I* was able.

"Oh." Her smile widens. "That sounds delicious."

"If one enjoys drinking the lawn for lunch," Prim mutters.

Mishella laughs, but kills the sound off when struck by Prim's cold fish of an attitude. I'm tempted to locate my own inner mackerel and show Prim what a real seafood smack-down is like, but am thawed once more by the hand curled beneath my elbow, and the eager smile beaming past my shoulder. In this moment, I'm certain the woman can probably talk me out of a kidney. Probably both. Suddenly, the wars fought over Helen of Troy and Ann Boleyn don't seem so idiotic.

"So do I get my tour now?"

I tuck her hand in tighter. Return her grin like a goofy fool—and perhaps I *am* one. At least she's not asking for a war—or a kidney. "You bet."

"Even the turret?"

"The turret!"

Prim's outcry turns me back around—along with the look I've been rehearsing for her since the takeoff from Arcadia. Because I knew this moment would arrive. That there'd be *one* chance to communicate this message in the space of a stare.

*Mishella Santelle is staying for six months, whether you're happy about it or not. Which means we're cooling it about Turret Two, also whether you like it or not.*

Prim's nostrils flare again. Her lips jam into a line of resignation. I nod and declare to Mishella, "We can *start* with the turret, if you like."

She really indulges a laugh now. "Let us begin with wherever *you* like. I want to see it all, so it does not matter."

As I guide her toward the main living room, it's not without a parting stare from Prim—and the knowing truth attached in those deep amber irises. And the sadness layered beneath that.

*She wants to see it all, hmmm? Well, good luck with figuring* that *one out, Cas.*

But Prim knows the answer to *that* already too.

There will be no "figuring that one out."

Because in the end, even Mishella Santelle doesn't get to see it all. Not every corner of my home…*not* every room in my heart…and *not* the fucking ghost who lives in both.

Not the parts of me that are best left in that grave with her.

It makes sense now: the decision I made back on Arcadia, to call this thing at six months. It's enough time to savor the heaven…without fearing the hell will rise up. Because, as I already know all too clearly, hell has a way of doing that. But for six months, I can bribe away the demons. After that, they can have my soul again. I'm sure the damn thing will never be the same after this, anyway.

# Chapter Seven

MISHELLA

Curious.
Even thousands of miles from home, midnight feels exactly the same.
The sounds are different: a wilderness bustling with cars and trains and people instead of wind and waves and birds. The smells are different too: steam and steel and the foods of a thousand cultures, instead of the island aroma that has always brought reminders of only one thing: the water. This is not a complaint; I love the sea; it is the Creator's perpetual gift to Arcadia—but it has always, simply, been there. Then again the next day. And the next. And the next.
This island…is a new world every other minute, even at midnight. Beyond the turret's windows, I watch it all: the people bustling, the horns honking, the trains whooshing, the sirens screaming. The chaos seems to mesh, becoming a peace of its own. A manmade ocean.
It is the respite I need.
The synergy giving me shelter from thoughts that will not stop taunting.
From the memories…
Of that conversation.
The one I was not supposed to overhear. Cassian and Prim, hiding themselves in the pantry off the kitchen after dinner, clearly thinking I was still enraptured by all the technical doo-dads of the living room. Granted, the temptation was certainly there—so many

wonderments to play with, hidden cleverly by the wood, glass, and leather décor—but manners are always more important than amusement, so I got up to help clear the table.

Only to wish I had not.

"What the hell were you thinking, Cassian?"

"Prim—"

"Wait. Wrong question. You're always thinking. Just which head was it with this time?"

"Goddammit. This is about more than that."

"And you don't think I'm afraid of that too?"

"Now what are you about?"

"Oh God, Cas. Have you thrown up the blinders that high—or do you see it and just choose to ignore it?"

"I'm not 'ignoring' a fucking thing!"

"Of course not. Which is why you flew that girl home from the middle of the Mediterranean, then moved her right into the master with you. Let me guess. She was wasting away in the cinders somewhere, and Prince Charming had to ride in with the magic slipper. Wait; no. Perhaps she was a wilting flower, ready to bloom. Eliza Doolittle, filthy island style. Enter Professor fucking Higgins, ready to make that rain in Spain fall mainly on the plain."

"Yeah. Right. That's it exactly."

"Are…are you laughing about this? Why the hell are you laughing?"

"Because you're not making any sense."

"I'm making perfect sense. Dear God, more sense than I want to make. She doesn't just punch one button for you, does she? She punches both. That's why you didn't come home with just the T-shirt."

"The…what?"

"You went to the island. Banged the local wahine. You should've come home with the damn T-shirt. Instead, you came home with the girl. God. You are such a moron."

"Dammit, Prim. Keep it down. And for the record, I didn't bang her."

"You mean you haven't yet. I'll take that lovely silence as a yes. And after you do, what do you think will happen? That she'll happily hop on a plane back home, without asking for a cent in 'compensation for services rendered?'"

"It's not like that, either."

"So you are compensating her?"

"All right. This conversation is over."

I did not linger to confirm if it really was or not. Had the damage not already been done? That answer vibrates throughout the clamp remaining on my chest—that has been there ever since making my excuses from staying for Prim's "famous tiramisu" to retire early, feigning exhaustion from our traveling.

At least it bought me time to prepare for bed—in all the awkward senses of the word—for my first night in a man's bed. It did not halt my mind from racing with every possible, horrible, incredible scenario that might come. Would he seduce me gently? Taunt me with another version of what he did to me on the plane? Or simply launch into bed and fuck me wildly?

Oh. Yes. Option number three…please?

A brutal breath sucks through my lips. A flush invades my neck and breasts. Heat surges between my thighs. Even my mouth aches, craving the dominance of his once more…as it has since the moment that he finally did come to bed…

Then, after but a few minutes, fell into a drained slumber.

After that, as Brooke would say, my choice of action was a no-brainer. The second his breaths evened into deep sleep, I was out of bed, into my slippers, and headed for this exact spot. The turret is my favorite part of his tour from earlier, perhaps because he's restored it to its art deco grandeur rather than installing the high-gloss look prevailing over the rest of the building's interior. Granted, the first three floors of the place are satellite offices for Court Corporation, modern by necessity—but the other areas feel "off" to me, as if the design is a deliberate attempt to shut out the past.

More disturbingly, especially after my accidental eavesdrop on Cassian and Prim's argument, I sense there is actually a past to shut out.

The recognition brings a heavy sigh.

"I'd offer a penny for those thoughts, but it sounds like they're worth a dollar."

The commentary from a few feet back, roughened by recent

sleep, is a surprise because it is not a surprise. The air I breathe in for the sigh is the same air that shifts, making room for his presence. Just like it did in the palais back on Arcadia…and has ever since.

Only all those times, I was not trying to inhale around a vice in my chest.

I do not turn, not wanting Cassian to see my grimace. Idiot. Why should he not see it…and know the conflict weighing on me? Prim made no secret of hers.

"I…could not sleep. Time difference, I suppose." *Or the hundred ways I keep wondering why Prim's input is such a priority to you.*

"Is that all? Just the jet lag?" He stretches on the floor next to me, leaning on an elbow as opposed to my stomach-down recline. The reading chaise behind us is comfortable enough, but being closer to the city's energy is a better fit for my spirit tonight. He sees that too. I discern it in the forests of his eyes.

*Does he see the rest of my thoughts?*

His query has not made that clear. I worry that he does…and that he does not.

"You must be just as thrown out of your kilt as me," I finally offer—to be met by a chuckle that should not be as sexy as it is.

"Off kilter?" he offers. "Though I'm not opposed to kilts or taking them off, if that's the request." He sobers a little while tugging at his hair, which tumbles lushly into his eyes. "Scottish is somewhere in my mutt mix, which is why my hair turns a little red in the sun…or so Mom tells me."

"Your Maimanne?" This new revelation tempers my jealousy about Prim—for the moment. "Are you two close?"

A smile remains on his face but changes. Softens. "Yeah. You could say that."

"Why?" I return. "Why…could I say that?"

His smile evaporates. "We've been through a lot together. A lot." His shoulders stiffen. "Perhaps it's best we leave it there."

"Of course." I swivel my head, resting it atop my hands, again attempting to put aside the petty hurt in my heart. "You have others to confide in, after all."

So much for attempting—or even kidding myself that I did.

But the dig is vague. He has as much right to toss it aside as I did to make it. If he does, then at least I know exactly where I stand. If he does not—

He definitely does not.

Bracing a hand around the back of my neck, he jerks my stare back up to him. The gesture is an unsettling mix of command and calm—reminding me all too clearly of how he took over things in my bedroom, back on Arcadia. Was that just two nights ago? Only a heartbeat has passed since then, right?

No.

A forever has passed.

"You heard," he grates. "Didn't you? Prim and me. In the pantry." He shakes his head. Gets down a leaden swallow. "Never mind. I know you did. I felt you there. Standing at the sink."

Forget about unsettled. I am suddenly frightened—gripped by spectral shivers, such as the ones I have known while working late in the palais and glimpsing the building's famous ghosts in my periphery. Only now, the otherworld does not hide in the shadows. It is here, in the air between us…in the dazzle of emeralds in Cassian's eyes, in the promise of fire in his touch…in the confirmation that he knows me, senses me, feels me just as I do him.

In the magic of us.

"Prim is a good friend, Ella. Nothing more."

But you have history with her. A lot of it.

I cannot bring myself to utter it. "She has the right to feel…what she feels."

He grunts. Retorts through his teeth, "The fuck she does."

"She cares about you. It is a glaring truth, Cassian, from the first second she gazes upon you." I curl a hand against his cheek, as if I can actually soothe his ire. "I do not blame her."

He presses his hand over mine. Runs it down to my elbow with nearly punishing pressure. "I don't want to talk about her right now."

"But…"

"But what?"

I push to a sitting position. Pull my arm down—as far as he will let me. His hold on my elbow remains firm and determined.

"Am I just a 'rescue project' to you, Cassian? The Eliza Doolittle you yanked from the slums, and—"

He shoves to his feet. I almost expect him to punch one of the walls or windows but he becomes scarier, not moving, his posture impossibly erect. "Is that what you believe?" Every word is so low, they are almost drowned by a pair of emergency sirens down on the street, their wails growing.

"I…I do not want to."

I let my head fall, but that brings even more bizarre sensations. Sitting here, my gaze filled with his bare feet, I feel…intimate with him. Stripped for him.

Connecting…

I lean forward. Just enough to touch his knee with my forehead. He's only wearing white cotton pants, and I realize he must have yanked them out of his luggage. They smell the way he did on Arcadia: his cedar and soap blended with ocean wind and oranges…

And there's something else now. A smell unique to New York. Musky. Masculine. Really erotic.

Before I can breathe it in again, he is next to me. Next to me, plummeted back to the floor. Both his hands dig into my hair, forcing my gaze up into his.

Connecting…

"Don't you see?" he rasps into the inches between our lips. "Can't you see?" And then his mouth is on me, molding me…needing me. Then rasping, "Mishella. My favori. My perfect armeau. I brought you here because I'm a selfish bastard who hasn't had anyone like you in my world in…" He stops, shaking his head, gaze glittering once more, a thousand shades of confusion. "In a very long time.

"Mishella Santelle…it is you who have rescued me."

## CASSIAN

What the fuck have you done?

My head machetes me with the words. My gut gladly joins in.

But my heart and my soul have never felt more perfect. Yeah…for the first time in my life, perfect and petrified are happy pals, powering their way into the arms that crush around her, the body that fits against hers…

The cock that swells between us.

"Cassian." Her whisper is high and ragged, verbally interpreting the tears that hovers so beautifully in her eyes. I gaze hard into their glimmer, willing the wetness to break free. To cleanse me, rescue me all over again. To grant me permission for what I've been craving since the moment my skin first touched hers, during that formal reception back on Arcadia. She knows it too. I see it in the quiver of her lips, in the choppy pulse in her neck, in the little trembles of her fingers, all ten raising up, bracing my jaw.

Finally, they thicken, brim…and escape.

My perfect invitation.

I crash my mouth back down.

Invade hers without hesitation. Claim her without compunction. Kiss her like she's my last fucking breath.

As our mouths continue to chase and tease and caress and conquer, our bodies slide all the way to the floor. When we break apart for air, I drag my gaze open to feast again on the sight of her, now awash in the glow of the streetlights and the moon. She's wearing a light blue sleep set tonight, coaxing out dazzling sparks of silver in the stare she returns to me. My beautiful gift.

I dip in, kissing her once more. With reverence this time.

With thanks.

When her fingers caress down to my chest, I don't feel so reverent anymore. Keep it together. Keep. It. Together.

The mantra pounds my blood, even as my dick throbs against her hip. Harder still, as she glides her touch across me, a look of wonder in those blue-silver irises. My nipples stiffen for her. My abs tauten, cinching in my breath.

Go lower. Oh fuck…don't go lower.

I seize my sole moment of self-control, grabbing her wrist, slowly lowering it to the floor on her other side. With our stares still latched, I rasp, "You know what they say about turn-about…" Actually, I'm not sure if she knows—but the anticipation of what she'll transform it into already enchants my mind, and takes my cock along for the ride.

"Mmmm." She lifts a modestly flirty look—quite possibly the

only woman on the planet who can. "That is one I know."

Her start-and-stop sigh finishes it—as I yank on the ribbon enclosure of her top, baring her breasts to my view.

And what a fucking view.

She's more exquisite than I imagined. Round, firm, and full, with flesh a shade paler than the parts of her that get year-round Arcadian sun…a perfect contrast to the sweet strawberries of her nipples, jutting from dusky, tight areolas. They pucker right before I lean in, worshipping her with soft nips and licks, until she's writhing beneath me—

And then I use my teeth.

"Oh! By the powers! Cassian."

I palm the breast I'm attending. Constrict it a little, forcing more blood into her throbbing tip, before I bite again. As she screams, I suckle away the pain. When I shift to her opposite peak, she mutters something in Arcadian and drives her hand through my hair, forcing my mouth down harder.

It drives me crazy. In all the good ways.

Too many ways.

I reach up, snaring her hand again. Swing it over her head, until it's pinned to the floor there. In the same violent sweep, I thoroughly embed my thighs against hers. Push up, notching the bastard of a ridge in my pants against the sweet, wet patch in hers, until we're dry-humping like kids stealing a quickie between classes, fast and fierce and feverish.

"Fuck. Me."

"Take. Me."

"You're so…hot."

"You are so…huge."

"I—we—have to—slow down."

"Wh-what? Why?"

"Can't…hold back. Not for much…longer."

"Then do not. For Creator's sake, Cassian, please!"

I rear up. Try to shake my head. That's a big fucking try. "No. There's no do-over on this. I'm going to make this good for you, dammit." In my head, I already have a vision of how this should go. Candlelit bath, champagne by the fire, and then the roll in the sheets, going as gently as I can. Nothing in there about screwing her senseless in the turret, in the middle of the night, with half of Manhattan watching. Okay, Manhattan probably doesn't care, but that's beside the point. "It's going to be the best for you. It's going to be—"

Her laugh cuts me short, so manic it's cute. "Cassian, if it is more 'the best' than this, you will kill me from sheer pleasure."

I let a taut growl go free. "With all due respect, favori, let me worry about your death-by-pleasure."

Her nose crinkles. It disappears into a stare of pure resolve—an unnerving sight, for the second I'm still able to think—before her hand is under my pants and all over my erection, milking the pre-come I've somehow kept at bay. Not anymore. I turn into one groan after the next as the drops escape, searing and perfect—and torturous. With every one of my moans, her smile kicks up a little higher, until I'm not sure what's snipping the neurons in my brain quicker: her perfect touch or her incredible beauty.

"Stop!" I finally groan it out. "For the love of Christ, Ella, stop or I'll come all over your hand."

Her eyes darken. Her teeth catch her bottom lip. "And how would that not be 'the best,' either?"

My growl lengthens. Little minx, goading me on to more. Notation for my own journal: my proper little Arcadian likes filthy verbal foreplay.

A detail that deserves a little more…testing.

With a commanding yank, I tug her hand back out. With a brutal sweep, slam it again to the floor. Our bodies slide back together, hard to soft, pulse to pulse, arousal to arousal. Her chest surges up, stabbing her nipples against mine. Her mouth falls open on another gasp, nearly begging for my kiss.

I don't give it to her.

Instead, I linger inches above her, savoring the taste of her anticipation, giving her something even better. The words. "Do you like this, favori? Do you like being flattened on the floor beneath me, trembling and aching for me? Do you like my erect cock against you, leaking come in its need for you?"

"Oh," she grates. "Oh…yes."

"Oh yes is fucking right." I dip my lips to her neck. "I can feel it in your pulse, Ella. Taste it on your skin. And I treasure it…everywhere."

I emphasize that with another roll of my hips. Rejoice in the answering buck of hers, adorable little jerks responding to nothing but her most primitive instincts. Have I ever been with a woman like her, so open to feeling everything and thinking about nothing? Have I ever known anyone like her, so transparent about her desire, uncaring that her hair isn't "fanned out" just so, that her feet aren't "daintily pointed," that the sounds bursting from her throat are awkward and rough instead of a mewling porn kitten?

She is a revelation.

A sensual, incredible burst into my psyche. Into my world.

My logic defaults to the only possibility. My lips burst with it, while continuing to suckle her delicious skin. "Sorceress. Dear fuck…that has to be it. You're a sorceress, woman, and I've become your willing slave." I lock her other wrist down with my grip. Rise up, deliberately exposing my muscles and might against her silken skin and curves. "Look at this. Look at you. Do you know what power you have over me, even in your shackles? How your beauty—" I stop, needing to fit breath around the space now occupied by her. "You command me, Mishella. Goddamn…you possess me."

Her own chest pumps, matching the desperate cadence of mine. "Cassian."

I shake my head again. My hair falls into my eyes but I drill a solid stare through the mess at her. "Look at you…begging me. But I'm the one who should be pleading with you."

"Oh…no. Oh…yes…"

"You rule, me, woman. You…destroy me."

As the confession soughs out, I scrape both thumbs across her pulse points. Slide them up, until they dig into the centers of her palms. Deeper…deeper…

Holy Mary, Mother of God, pray for this sinner…because he wants to sin like he's never sinned before, and the only redemption is the sin. The only heaven left is her…

"Tell me." Now I'm the beggar—and it finally feels perfect. "I need to know. I'm your convert. Your slave. What do you bid of me, sorceress…goddess…?"

Her fingers curl around mine. Her back arches, her thighs

constrict...her pussy softens. "Destroy me too," she whispers. "Cassian, please...take me. Fuck me."

My own muscles shake—fighting the surge of heat her plea brings. I breathe raggedly. I've expected the words, so why do they make me feel regressed to sixteen again? Why does air feel like fire as I force it in down my nostrils? Why am I an all-thumbs idiot after rising to pull off her pajama bottoms, then mine?

And now, why does the sight of her mound make my cock drip all over again?

I stare at the rigid fucker, finally admitting my bewilderment. I've always been a Brazilian fan: the football teams, the food, and definitely the bikini wax. But Arcadia is nowhere near Brazil, and the reality here is, again, as I expected—except for one astonishing difference. Beholding Ella's unshaved "wilderness" has turned up my desire—especially when the evidence of her lust forms glittering beads on her tawny curls.

"Fuck. Me." My snarl only hints at the toll she and her enchantress pussy already take. Need to—get in there—so bad.

"A wonderful idea." Her throaty rasp more perfect torture—to which she adds a coup de grace, kneading her breasts until the tips are stiff and red. "Cassian. By the creator—I need you now."

My dick throbs against my palm. Hell yes, it screams—

To be countermanded by my brain. And its evil sense of humor.

Evil.

"You need me, hmmm?" I line myself up, pointing my glistening crest toward her exquisite entrance. "This, right here? You need...this?"

Her whole body tremors. Her hands work her flesh harder. "Yes," she pants. "Oh yes!"

"Not yet." I chuckle in answer to her moan of despair. "First, not without this." Thank fuck I remember Doyle's stash of condoms in the table next to the chaise. This is probably the first time I'm thankful for being aware of the "accessories" he likes to leave behind all over the house. "And second," I continue while sheathing up, "not without you showing me more of...this."

My free hand illustrates the point, running through the slickness between her thighs. Though it elicits a higher cry, she manages to stammer, "Th-this? Wh-what…do you…mean?"

"I mean show it to me, Ella. With both hands. Take them off your tits. Slide them into your pussy. Rub them on your lips then spread yourself with them. Let me see the gorgeous cunt I'm going to fuck."

Without another question, she obeys. Dear God, so perfectly…proving I was wise to make that mental journal entry in ink. This woman, and her gorgeous passion, thrive on nasty words like a flower in the sun. As she blooms for me I grow for her, my flesh filling the rubber…straining for the slick, tight tunnel beyond her dripping curls.

The depths I'll mark for the first time.

The place I'll have in her soul…forever.

The virginity I'll claim…and cherish.

"Damn." Great. That's eloquent. But nothing else is possible in the moment I fit myself to her opening, and push into the impossible softness…the resistant walls.

I halt when she winces. "It—it is all right," she protests. "I—I am all right. Probably just a little…" A sheepish shrug, a stunning blush. "Scared."

I dip my head, kissing her. "It's all right to be scared. But it's also all right to breathe, *favori*."

She laughs. For a moment. "Oh. Yes. That."

I take advantage of her distraction to push deeper. Clench back a groan, letting that privilege belong to her. "Good, Ella. You're doing good, my little beauty." Brilliance strikes. "Try to bear down a little. Just pretend it's a couple of your fingers, only fuller."

"My—my fingers?"

Okay. Screw the brilliance. "Fuck," I mutter, punctuating with another laugh. "Well, that explains things a little."

"A little…like what?"

"Like why you're so goddamn tight…and good." I've used the conversation for the same nefarious purpose: now, I'm nearly two-thirds in.

And blindingly ready to give her the rest.

"So."

A small test thrust.

"Fucking."

A deeper one.

"Good."

She doesn't scream.

She does try to tear off a layer of my back flesh, as her body accepts the last inch of mine. My mouth opens, needing to tell her to relax, but I selfishly savor one more second of her tension, and what it does to the suction power of her walls.

Pray for us sinners...

Now, and at the hour of our death...

Yeah. That's it. That has to be. I've died, and this is heaven, and—

She really has destroyed me.

"Ella." There's nothing left on my lips but her name. Nothing left in my senses but her, surrounding me, consuming me—propelling me to an ether comprised solely of that place in space and time where our bodies pulse together, our hearts hammer together. "Mishella," I whisper this time, squeezing the globes of her ass, forcing her tighter around me. "We're there. You're there. Feel me, favori. Feel all of me..."

"Mmmm." It's not a pleasant hum. It's the I'm trying sound, and I don't fucking like it. But the moment I withdraw even a millimeter, she scratches once again. The sorceress has claws. Sharp ones.

She pulls her arms in, shifting her hold to my jaw. Forces my lips to hers in a kiss that's so searing, it's haunting. As our mouths mesh and our tongues swirl, I am suddenly able to feel her soul, to see inside her heart...for they are the same as mine. Remember. This. The tastes of it, passion and salt and need. The smells of it, sex and skin and jasmine. The sounds of it, roaring in my ears and throbbing through my blood. The feeling of it, a magic that will follow me until those suspended moments between life and death, when all the best moments of my life return...and I pray more of them await me on the other side.

Unless that moment is now.

As she begins to rock her hips, working her body around mine.

As she arches her head back, releasing a sibilant sorceress sigh.

As she cries out, in the second I slide my touch between our bodies, to finish her first.

And she dies too…convulsing through the most perfect end I've ever witnessed. The orgasm strains her muscles, bulges her eyes…and squeezes every inch of her pussy.

Dear. Fuck.

Over and over she seizes me, her body signing the death warrant for mine. I am executed in a hot, consuming flood, life pouring from me, immense and primal…

And perfect.

"Do not…stop. Oh please, Cassian. I think I might…oh, again. Do not stop!"

"Never." I grate it into her neck while continuing to pump her pussy and work her clit. "Never, sweet armeau."

When I take the throbbing little nub and pinch just the tip, she finally gives me her scream. She vibrates, wild and unthinking, gripping me in desperate need, like the fucking angel leading her to heaven.

She has no idea…of how things really are.

That she's the angel. The enchantress gifted from the clouds…to lead me back from hell.

Morose thoughts—for much later. Now, I only want to think about her laugh in my ear, the mix of melody and husk that brings satisfaction as complete as her climaxes, making my resolve official. This really is where I want to die. Right here, right now. Surely, no other moment in my life is going to equal this perfection.

"Oh…my…high…holy…Creator." She lets her arms sprawl, limp as noodles, straight out to her sides. I chuckle my way into a new kiss, letting my grip slide along them, until our fingers are again twined.

"Certainly took the sting out of jet lag."

"Jet lag." She repeats it softly, her face remaining dazed. "So…how long does that last?"

I laugh again, not missing the hopeful lilt with which she finishes. "Not sure."

"Why not?"

"Usually too keyed up to pay attention to it."

"Hmmm."

It's the hum I'm used to—on the other hand, hope to never be used to, because it's so damn adorable. Half of it is barely audible, since she's already dedicated half her brain to at least eight layers of deeper thought. The exciting part is watching her cycle through them, and wondering what she'll say to make the wait worth it.

"Perhaps we should try to find out."

Definitely worth it.

After grinding a slow, savoring kiss into her, I answer, "Perhaps we fucking should."

# Chapter Eight

*MISHELLA*

By now, I am fairly certain there is no such thing as a three-day, debilitating case of jet lag—at least not in Cassian Court's world. But right now, it is not a point I care to argue. Or think about. As if I am capable of either, with my gaze consumed by the sight of his dark gold hair spilling over my lower belly…and the ecstasy of his tongue stabbing into my intimate hole, over and over and over…

My abdomen clenches. My backside pinches in.

Oh, dear Creator…

Close.

A few more. Please…

Close.

I am not even aware of the words spilling off my lips, until his growl interjects—and his head pulls up. "Not yet, armeau. Not…yet."

I whine, protesting and almost angry, reaching back to grab the pillows. There have to be a dozen of them on his big bed, and for a fleeting second, I wonder why I do not know the exact count. I have barely left these sheets for seventy-two hours. Surely there was time to count all his pillows at some point…

But there was not. Not between sleeping and…things like this.

Lots and lots and lots of this.

The most perfect three days of my life.

Consumed with giving myself to the most perfect man in the world.

His body like a gold marble god, taut and defined as he rolls on a condom. His face lined with fierce passion, as he gazes over my spread nudity. His eyes, shimmering and sharp, as he scrapes fingernails down my thighs, to my knees…

And slams my legs wide.

"Keep them like that," he orders. "The whole time I'm fucking you." A moment later, he prompts, "What do you say to that?"

"Y-yes, Cassian."

He knows I'll barely get it out. He knows what his rougher, filthier side does to me. How all his dirty words affect me, incinerating the bonds of propriety that have been the hallmarks of my existence for so long. With the words, he gives me no choice about leaving them behind…about becoming his perfect little investment.

And I do feel perfect.

Adored.

Desired.

Worthy.

His face tightens as he positions himself at my entrance. His body is hard…everywhere. I raise my arms, anxious to learn its formidable landscape once more, but he growls, "No. Leave them where they are. Grip the pillows. It lifts your luscious tits…so perfectly." He sucks and bites one then the other, still taunting my entrance with his cock. "You like that, don't you? When I make your nipples erect like this? When you know exactly what it does to my dick?"

I struggle for breath. "Oh…y-yes, Cassian."

"And does it make you hot too, little Ella?"

"Yes, Cassian."

"Does it make your tunnel wet? Turn you into my horny, sweet sorceress, ready to be fucked?"

"Yes, Cassian."

He lifts back up. Digs his hands into my hips, pulling my body another inch around his, opening the view to his heated gaze—and mine. The sight of his shaft, absorbed into the softness of my core, is as mesmerizing as the rest of him. Muscles straining. Power coiling. Passion building. He is beautiful, rippled…stunning.

"Then use the words." He intensifies his grip along with the dictate. "Tell me what you want...with the words *I* want."

I swallow hard. There will be no getting away with a gentle morning screw. This explosion is going to be nuclear...for both of us.

"Take me," I rasp. "Please...deep inside...with your cock. Take your payment back from my body, until I cannot see straight. Until I scream from being filled by you—"

Then I do scream, as he plows me hard and hot. No inch of my sex is left wanting. He handles me like a piece of clay, subjected to the pound of his ruthless hammer. In a sense, I am. Less than a week after even meeting the man, I am a being recreated...an artwork unveiled with every slice of his chisel...

Then shattered.

Blown apart into a thousand pieces of being, of feeling, of frantic, perfect fulfillment...

"Take it."

"Yes, Cassian."

"All of my cock."

"Yes, Cassian."

"In your perfect cunt."

"Yes...yes...yes!" The pieces of me explode into dust. "Cassian!" I am nothing but sensation, climaxing hard, senses rejoicing as he dissolves with me, coming deep inside me.

And for the fiftieth time in the last week, I wonder if I truly will ever be the same.

Or if I want to be.

Before I can delve into the morose possibilities for answers to that, Cassian's phone vibrates on the nightstand—for the twentieth time this morning. He groans. I giggle.

"I knew I'd regret telling the world I'm back on the grid."

"I think our jerk is up, Mr. Court."

For some reason, that quirks his lips. "Jig."

"Now?" I glance down. At the moment, dancing in any form is rather out of the question.

He explains only by popping a quick kiss to my forehead, before reaching for the device with a brisk swipe. "Rob. Good morning."

Between getting his hands on–and in—me, the man has at least divulged that "Rob" is short for Robin, who, in an even more confusing twist, is a young man in his first job out of college. From what I can tell, Rob is succeeding. In the last seventy-two hours, Cassian has entrusted him with everything from changing security passwords—a weekly ritual at Court Enterprises—to things a little more personal, like scheduling a physician appointment for his boss today.

That being known, Cassian still earns a new dose of my amazement with the tone, as if he's standing in a board room instead of prone in bed, still buried inside me. "Better, thanks," he continues. "Scheduling that fast turn-around for the Arcadia trip was probably too aggressive. I'm current on emails and the latest reports though,"—he shrugs at my when-did-that-happen gawk—"and I'll be coming in today. That face-to-face with Flynn Whelan is too important. Have his people confirmed for lunch? Good. Make sure the catering team brings up that Italian water he likes. Any other notable calls?"

It sounds like Rob hesitates, but delivers the reply in a businesslike tone. Cassian matches the timbre—on the surface. Beyond the new shutters over his expression, I see the same discomfort that first stopped Rob—though he quickly cloaks it. I am not sure whether to be relieved or angry. The resulting confusion makes me restless. I shift, pull away, and leave for the bathroom—as if the sliding wood door can keep out the river stone perfection of his voice, smoothness and power beneath each baritone syllable.

"No. You responded as you should have, Rob. She's been fishing for a definitive on the Literacy Ball for a few months. Jumping up the chain and turning in the RSVP herself...well, I'll applaud her for the guts, if not the intelligence." Heavy huff, through a definitive pause. "Call Yolanda Wood at the Literacy Guild. Clarify my RSVP is for two, but I'll phone myself with my guest's name by EOB today. It will definitely not be Amelie Hampton's."

I finish my business, debating whether to follow my original plan and start the shower, or find a journal and note the name Amelie Hampton. The knot in my belly supports the latter. It is not simply the stress she has brought to Cassian—whoever she is—

though that is a start. It is the discomfiting questions now raised in my heart—and the anger that rises in their wake.

Did you think he was living a monk's life before you arrived?

Did you think because he moved you into his bedroom, he planned on keeping himself out of others?

Did you think he doesn't have a hundred other "Amelie Hamptons" across this city? This country?

I shake my head, forcing the funk away. With a short huff, crank on the shower. Climb in under the wonderfully hot spray, deliberately turning from the granite seat upon which my backside has been planted numerous times over the last few days—for the most erotic of reasons. Right now, it is best to deal strictly with the steam from the water instead of those salacious visions—and how many women from Cassian's past share the exact same memories.

Too late.

As he enters the bathroom, clearly finished with Rob, it is too easy to imagine him walking in on another girl, in another time, and tossing his condom in the trash with the same laser accuracy. It is even more effortless to think of him turning and peering through the stall glass, the same dimpled smirk on his face...with the same dreamy follow-through.

"Why'd you start in there without me?"

Oh, yes. All the others have surely felt just like this as well—body newly tingling, senses freshly awakened, tongue perfectly tied—as he plants those long fingers against his corded hips, purposefully pulling attention to that magnificent appendage at their juncture...

I. Will. Not. Look. I. Will. Not. Look.

I steal a small glance. Just one. Dear sweet Creator, why did you build him with such magnificence? Especially there?

I manage to hitch a little shrug. Whether it hits the mark on the nonchalance I am aiming for is hard to discern—especially because his face has transformed to the opposite. I avoid that new intensity to explain, "You...sounded busy. I did not want to be..."

I let it trail off as he enters the stall, seeming to do so in one masterful sweep. I am sure he opened the glass door, even stepped over the tile lip at the shower's edge, but those sort of movements always seem to simply flow into the powerful prose of his body...

And now the unblinking force of his stare.

"You did not want to be what?"

His tone, just as unflinching, pulses more parts of me to life again. But we are discussing his conversation with Rob, and recalling that brings back composure. At least a little. "In the way," I supply. "Or interfering…with…important subjects."

A worm on a hook would be more graceful. I am certain my face flushes, beyond what color the steam has already brought. The man is no bloody help, tilting my face up with a finger then softly but thoroughly kissing me. Before I can help it, my arms twine around his neck, my body molds against every gloriously hard inch of him—only when I expect him to swoop in with the full force of his lust, he steps back. Then again. Literally looks down to make sure his lengthening sex is not touching me in any way, before finally speaking again.

"Let's make something clear." He jogs his head in the direction of the bedroom. "That is all the 'interference.' That's all the 'getting in the way' crap. This,"—he traces a finger in the air between our chests—"and this,"—then between our foreheads—"is the 'important subject' you need to be worrying about."

I only swallow hard. There is nothing to say. And everything. And I am more flummoxed than ever.

"Mishella."

"What?"

"Look at me." His stare awaits, ready with forest darkness. "Yeah. I thought so."

"Thought so…what?"

"You don't believe me."

"Because I do not have to." I grab his hands. "Cassian, you had a life before I arrived. And you shall have one after I leave—"

"So you're already that anxious to go?" The forests flare with angry fires. I try to understand—anger is fear's child, so what is he afraid of?—but cannot surpass my own uncertainty to see it. I am thousands of miles from home, in a land where even the stupid light switches are new to me, and he is playing at the jilted insecurity?

"Are you truly asking that?" I seethe. "After the last three days? After I gave you my virginity?"

"Which I paid for," he retorts, "as you cannot seem to stop reminding me."

"Because it is the truth!"

"Because that 'truth' is your safety."

He does not stop at the accusation. Uses his body as judge and juror, convicting me with the physical lunge that not only closes the gap between us, but flattens me against the shower's granite wall. His body, tightening and flexing, is now a hard, imposing intruder. His shoulders bunch, ropes of muscles playing against his wet flesh, as he meshes our fingers against the granite.

"Look at me," he growls again. "Look. At. Me." When I do, he lowers his face until I can see my reflection in the beads of water down his straight nose, along his clenched jaw. "You don't get to be safe here, Ella. Neither of us does. We can keep talking about the money, keep pretending it's the chasm that's protecting our castles—or we can just admit the truth." His hands screw tighter into mine. His body pushes harder…so much bigger… "I'm in the fucking chasm, woman—and I'm careening. Tumbling. Every moment I'm with you, next to you, inside you, it gets deeper. Darker. There's no bottom in sight—nor do I want there to be."

I work to get air. Very little comes. My balance tilts. My senses swim. He is the only anchor; my new reality. I whimper, lost in the force of his rough words…the magic. Wanting to believe magic really exists…

but…

"Wh-what about…her?"

His gaze glitters. He shakes his head, confused. "Her who?"

Before the answer is even out, I feel like a petty salpu. "Amelie," I clarify, feeling as if I must. "Hampton. Remember? The woman who responds on your behalf to social engagements?"

"Because she was torqued at me for going to Arcadia without her. Because she also doesn't know how to express herself like, let's say, a mature adult." He pulls away. His shoulders dip as if a weight has been slung across them. "And also, because I've let her get away with it before." Measured huff. "Look…I won't lie to you, Ella. I've let several women get away with it before—because I haven't really cared before."

My turn for the irked exhalation finally comes. "So…what does that mean..."

...for me.

I let the words remain implied. He is not a stupid man. He shows me so by settling his gaze firmly back into mine. "It means that I care now." He lets go of my hands, closing them both in to frame my face. "That I'm not going to that goddamn event with anyone on my arm but the most beautiful woman in New York." His dimples reappear, deep as craters, as I crunch a questioning frown. "You, my pahaleur armeau."

For the first time in my life, I roll my eyes at a man.

Partly because he deserves it.

Partly because I know I can.

Mostly because it feels so, so good.

In return, his own eyes go dark with sage smoke. "Christ. Did you roll your eyes at me?" When I do it again, the desire takes over the rest of his face—and his cock slots against my most sensitive tissues, zinging heat to every nerve ending in my body. "You know what I want to do with that expression, don't you, young lady?"

The grate in his tone brings me more boldness. I toss a flirty glance up, tugging at my lip with my teeth—and his erection with my fingers. He hisses. I clutch harder. By the Creator, I love touching him. Everywhere—but especially here. Feeling him pulse beneath my palm. Watching his jaw clench. Savoring the power that I, for once, have over him...

"Hmmm," I murmur. "I...have no idea. Maybe it is best that you show me, Mr. Court?"

His throat vibrates with a low, snarly sound. "Maybe it's best that I do."

My breath clutches. Holds. I hope, perhaps too desperately, for my backside and the shower seat to become best friends again. Instead, Cassian shifts his hold to my shoulders, urging me down. The action is too brusque to let me trail him with kisses, but I am able to take a tactile exploration. My hand travels the hills of his abdomen, glides into the indent of his hip, savors the perfect plateaus of his thighs. "Beautiful," I rasp. "You are...so beautiful, Cassian."

He lifts his hands, burying them in the wet tangles of my hair, as I kneel before him. With his hold digging into my scalp, he grates, "Then wrap your beauty around me."

I cannot refuse. I do not want to. In my most illicit dreams I have already imagined doing this for him…and for me. Taking over him like this, hoping I can enthrall his body as he does mine…I am flushed all over, intoxicated and afire…all my senses swirl, aroused and alive.

"Fuck." His groan is as tight as the sinew of his legs, clenching as I grasp them, pushing him deeper inside me. His flesh, musky and wet, pushes at the confines of my mouth. So huge. So delicious. His hands brace the back of my head, soon setting a pace for each new lunge over his pulsing length. "Beautiful…favori…take me…take me…"

His words are like the steam, curling around us, dissolving my thoughts into nothing more than particles on the air. I've evaporated, now just a swirl myself, my actions completely controlled by his passion…his will.

"Touch yourself, Ella. Stroke your clit."

I obey at once. Release a moan around his girth.

"Touch me with your other hand. Around my balls. Yes. Like that."

I moan louder. So does he. He rams into my mouth at a quicker pace. The sac beneath my hand throbs and writhes. His cock grows, testing the limits of my throat.

Faster.

Hotter.

Sucking.

Stroking.

Climbing.

Coming.

As the zenith hits my pussy, I scream—welcoming the ropes of cream he gives my throat. I drink burst after burst of his perfect completion…his beautiful passion. And embrace all the beauty he sees in me too…

And am glad the water cascading down our bodies can mask the sheen of my tears, born of an exquisite, inescapable realization.

In being owned by him…

I have been set truly free.

Leaving only one insane dilemma.

How will I ever set him free now?

## CASSIAN

I have to turn from Ella while buttoning up my shirt.

First, the sight of her in the chair next to the window, dressed in nothing but my bathrobe, is too fucking tempting. She's only five feet from the bed I yearn to throw her back onto, keeping her captive for three more days.

Second—my fingers are shaking.

Trembling.

Me.

Like a fucking cat in the rain.

And I never want it to end.

The same way I never wanted to leave that bed. Or the shower—dear fuck, that shower—or the magical wrap of her arms, her eyes, her body.

How the hell am I ever going to set her free?

Because in another five months and three weeks, she'll be properly purged, man. Spoiled and fucked into perfect oblivion. With any luck, she'll even be like all the rest: another Amelie, ready to stomp all over your space with the social engagements, the photo ops…perhaps even the pre-business trip hissy fits…

The argument has merit.

Except for one major snag.

I like thinking of Mishella Santelle in those scenarios. Yeah, even the hissy fit one. If there would ever be any need to leave her behind on a trip, and if she ever found the need to launch such a tantrum, defusing her anger might be more fun than stoking her passion. The woman's pretty damn adorable when she's miffed. Her gaze turns to blue fire, her neck cords with tension, and she turns all Queen Victoria proper, practically using the royal *we* on everybody.

*We are mad at you, Mr. Court…*

*We would like you to keep sucking on our nipples…*

*We would like to suck on your cock…*

*We would enjoy coming for you…*

Yep. Shaking.

I finish with the damn buttons. Not a miracle yet. That comes when I remember how to secure a Windsor knot…that is, when I recall where I put the fucking tie…

My search doesn't last long. It ends with a punch of violent feeling, at finding the strip of red silk trailing from elegant fingers that I long to kiss once more—and do. Ella's smile fills her eyes before her lips, a sequence reaffirming my newfound buy-in to Arcadian voodoo, before she loops the tie around my neck and focuses on the knot. I'm actually jealous of the thing, watching the attention it receives for the better part of a minute, until a more disturbing thought sets in.

"How'd you learn to do this?"

Translation: what man did you learn it for?

She smirks. My subtext isn't the subtlest, and I don't give a fuck. "My brother." She tugs softly, taking her time, and I sense the quiet intimacy of the moment means as much to her as me. "All the kids on Arcadia wear school uniforms until our last year of secondary level. Saynt never perfected his knot, at least not to Maimanne's satisfaction, so I just did the job and let her believe what she wanted."

More emotion wallops me. This time, fierce protectiveness. It pushes my hand up, clasping one of her wrists. When she looks up, I don't ease back on my probing stare. "Would an imperfect knot have been that much of a sin?"

I expect her to drop her gaze. When she doesn't, for a very long moment, she lets me see in…allows me to really view the panorama of her life up until now. It is filled with shifting sands, fickle winds, even a fear of where the next step may take her. Steps that have, until now, all been orchestrated by her parents—down to the threads in her and Saynt's clothing.

Finally, she looks away. Her arm drops too. "And perfection was not expected of you, Mr. Court?"

Clearly, my sadness has come off as pity—not a surprise, if the filter of her pride is considered—so her defensiveness isn't a shock. Nor is the logic behind her words. I've tracked her parents' "research" into Court Enterprises. Undoubtedly, they've told her I didn't inherit the money behind all this. In her mind, two and two are now snapped together—and sum up to a pair of demanding parents.

Little Ella. If only the world were so tidy.

"Perfection," I echo, arching a brow. "Of course it was expected of me. Every day."

She nods, face full of I-knew-it.

"By the guy in the mirror."

The nod halts. "But your mother—"

"Was usually at work by the time I got up for school." I square my shoulders. It's not a new move, even with the onslaught of those distant memories—things not even her parents' probe could have divulged about me. Mom prefers to let me live the public life, and now enjoys the garden she never had while I was growing up, in her dream house out in Connecticut. The way it should be. "She had to take a bus and two trains to get to the Four Seasons on time for clock-in." I cock my head. "You know those rich New York farts. They all don't have much patience when their toilets have to be scrubbed."

She doesn't bite on the levity. Instead mutters, confused frown in place, "But your father surely—"

"Wasn't around." I manage to get it out smoothly.

"A brother or a sis—"

"Wasn't. Around." Not so smooth this time. By half. But Damon is nobody's business. Ever.

"So...it was just you?"

Yes. In an apartment smaller than this room, with the cocaine addicts on one side and the schizophrenic lady on the other. At least the crackheads were quiet in the mornings.

"This isn't the right time for this discussion, Ella."

She nods once more. The I-knew-it is gone but I instantly wish for its return. Anything but the terse lurch into which the action has become. "Of course it is not. I...apologize."

"Dammit." I seethe it beneath my breath, to myself more than her, before wheeling back, grabbing her, and tucking her close. "No apologies," I utter into her hair. "Ghosts are just better left buried; that's all."

"I understand."

But she doesn't. Not really. After courageously unlocking her emotional gates for me, she has met padlocks and guard dog growls from me in return. Not a damn thing I'm going to do about it either.

I tried exposing the pain once before. Forced the gates open.

Was given just another ghost to bury.

Headstone carved with flowers to match her name…

Fresh dirt over the plot, contrasted by the February snow over the graveyard…

I grit the memories away. Gaze over the top of Ella's head, out the window. It's May but the morning sky roils over the city, thick with thunderheads, as if even the big guy beyond them challenges my call. Go ahead, bastard. Give it a try. You turned my secrets into sunshine once, then ripped the sun away. Now, the secrets stay with the ghosts. Buried. For good.

I pull in a deep breath. Normally, it's enough for fortification. Not now. I dip my head, seeking the solace of her warmth, her kiss—but as soon as our mouths meet, I revise the descriptor. This isn't just solace. It's healing. She might hate that my gate is closed, but she accepts it…and simply fixes what she can from where I do let her stand.

She really is a gift.

I've never considered it hell to stop kissing a woman before. Today marks that first, giving new meaning to the words fuck and no. Somehow she deciphers it properly, and giggles a little.

"Off with you, Mr. Court." She adjusts my tie one last time, giving me an accidental eyeful of her cleavage. "The sooner you get done ruling the world, the sooner you can come h—" She barely snatches back the rest, but it's enough to shatter our pretense of domestic bliss as she revises, "The sooner you can get back." She lifts a little smile over eyes turning rich turquoise. "And remember, you have a physician's appointment today."

Oh. Yes. That.

I step back, guiding her hands into mine—deciding to just broach the subject, now that she's gone there anyway. Clearly, the more "formal" moment for which I've been waiting is not coming soon—especially with her standing there, soft and scrubbed and naked in my robe.

"I had Rob make that appointment,"—I deliberately engage her gaze—"for you."

Nose crinkle. Slow blink. "Me? What? Wh-why?"

No better tactic than a direct one. "It's with Kathryn Robbe. She's a friend. And a gynecologist."

"A gyne—" She's confused more than upset. Good sign. "But Cassian, you know my history. Well, my lack of one. You are my first—"

I stop her with a kiss. It's as much for me as her. Hearing her speak it out loud, that I'm the only man who's ever been inside her, fires primeval urges I don't even want to subdue. After a long minute of claiming her with my tongue, I pull back far enough to speak my full, transparent intent.

"It's just to make sure everything's working fine, favori."

She spurts a little laugh. "After the last three days, you are not sure it is?"

"And to talk to Kathryn about birth control."

More blinks. But no more frowns. Just a gorgeous little O of her lips, followed by the same sound in a rasp. "Oh," she repeats. "You...errmm...that is what you want?"

I lower my head. Inhale deeply. Attempt to absorb the clinical scents between us, not the sensual. Toothpaste, deodorant, shirt starch—not body cream, vanilla soap, even the sexy place at the curve of her nape, where her citrus shampoo blends with beads of her perspiration. So many more places like this on her to discover. Marvelous places...

"What I want,"—Christ, what I need—"is to get my body inside yours whenever and wherever I want." Her all-over shiver conveys I've made the point, but my imagination's off and running again. "For instance, I'd be able to tear this robe off of you. Kind of like...this."

"Oh." Her mouth is a rose around the syllable now...dark as the areolas sprouting her erect nipples. Her hair cascades around those lush swells, turning her into my very own Aphrodite...ready to be claimed by her worthless mortal once more. "And—and then what?"

The dusky cue in her gaze is all I need. "And then...I'd be able to spin you around, and march you to the window seat." I twist her hair around a hand and push her forward. When we're in front of the bench built into the curve of the window, I angle her over until her cheek is pressed down—and her ass is presented high. "Like this."

"Oh…my." She wriggles a little, spreading her legs for better balance…exposing the tight entrance now gaping on the air, its glistening layers begging to be filled. Because denying myself air would be easier than rejecting her needs, I give the sorceress what she wants. With one finger, then two…and three. "Cassian!" she cries. "Oh, by the Creator…"

"If you were taking protection, Ella, I could unzip my pants…like this. Then pull out my cock…and line it up to your weeping little cunt…"

"Please," she begs, when I only follow through with the first half of that promise. Instead, I let her listen as I fist my length and begin to pump, in perfect cadence with the three digits inside her sex. "Please!"

At first I say nothing, letting her arousal spiral with mine, continuing to fuck my fingers into her, keeping a perfect rhythm. But then I pivot my hand, letting my thumb hook up, toying with the rosette between her ass's perfect spheres. "I could play here, too…while I fuck your sweet pussy. Spread your gorgeous ass, then press into it…like this…"

The filthy scene, playing out in both our minds, brings on a mutual shudder. I delve my fingers deeper into her pussy…and her other entrance, so tiny and tight.

"Yes," she keens. "Oh, yes…take me…"

"In both places?"

"In both. I need it. I need you. Cassian…Cassian…"

There are more words, long strings of them, but the Arcadian spills from her in such a heated slur, I can only assume she's continuing the dirty theme. At least that's what my cock wants to believe. Engorged and pulsing, pre-come slicking the length, the beast roars through my fist, over and over again, screaming for release as desperately as Mishella does.

And Christ, does she scream.

Openly.

Gloriously.

"Ardui! Faisi-banu-ardui!"

I can translate only the last word but it's enough.

Harder.

My enchantress's wish is my command.

We orgasm together, her gasps mating with my roar. Her walls squeeze around my fingers. My fist milks my cock. Streams of my essence fall across her back, like white chocolate poured against vanilla ice cream. Though I am spent, the sight of it keeps me hard…craving to lean over and fill her with my dick instead of my fingers.

Instead, as our breathing normalizes, I force myself to step back. Scooping my robe back up, I improvise it into a towel, cleaning her back and my cock before scooping her back up against me…yearning to hold her like this all damn day.

Well, not exactly like this.

Doing it in bed would be so much better. Naked and sated, limbs twined, heads sharing a pillow…

For a moment, I consider it. Strongly. Nothing sounds better right now than fucking the day's demands—but even amenable Rob will point out that canceling on Flynn Whelan is professional poison. The man has clout with both the Greek and Croatian governments, contacts we'll be needing once operations in Arcadia move forward in full force. And right now, staying close to the Arcadians has leapt high on my priorities list.

Close.

It's never felt like a flimsy word—but right now, drawing Ella even closer, it comes nowhere near to what I crave to share with her…what I still burn to have beyond this. I've just compared her to a decadent dessert, and stuffed my senses full of the damn thing, yet I'm ravenous for more. So much more.

But will it ever be enough?

I hope so.

Dear fuck, I hope not.

The breath I fan into her neck is full of that rough conflict. She responds with a quiver, rolling down through her whole body, making her skin pebble beneath my touch. I firm my roaming caresses, partly to warm her, partly to memorize the feel of her nakedness. Something has to get me through the day, goddammit.

She finally breaks our silence with a hitched murmur. "Cassian?"

I wrapped myself tighter around her. "Yeah?"

"I will go to the appointment. With your friend."

I tilt my head in. Press lips to her temple. "Thank you, armeau."

She cocks her own head. There's an impish smile on her lips. "You can thank me later. In very thorough detail."

I growl lowly. "Yes, ma'am." Then set about proving how I fully intend to follow through—by stealing that smile off her lips with the attack of my own.

# Chapter Nine

*MISHELLA*

Scott drops me off at the front door of Kathryn Robbe's medical office, which is attached to her home somewhere in a neighborhood on the other side of Central Park. It is far from the sterile environment I spent the morning dreading, and I am more relaxed than I ever thought possible—under the circumstances. There is even a little cartoon bubble taped to the ceiling overhead, emblazoned with the words I Hate This. It eases the discomfort, perhaps a little, of having my womb examined from the inside out.

"Okay, then. All finished." Her tone is crisp but friendly as she pulls out the speculum, and I release my breath in a relieved whoosh. Does any woman ever "breathe normally" through a pelvic exam? "Why don't you get dressed then join me in the other room?"

"Of course."

The "other room" is a cozy office reminding me a little of similar spaces in Palais Arcadia at home. The furniture is just as grand, though made of darker woods. A pair of Turkish carpets overlap on the polished wood floor. Bookshelves line an entire wall, and the big desk looks like the workspace of a busy but happy person.

A few elements not like home: the pair of plush chairs in the center of the room, also formed of dark wood but cushioned in cream velvet. The upholstery matches the colors of an ornate tea table, centered between the chairs.

"Do you like tea?" Her eyes, the color of sherry, smile as much as her lips. Her hair, pulled into a stylish French twist, is almost the same hue. She would be described as a handsome woman, and looks enough like Cassian that she could pass as his older sister. "If not, I can grab some lemonade from the fridge." She motions to a kitchenette, off to my left.

"Tea is fine." I smile as I sit, folding my hands in my lap and crossing my ankles. "And those cookies look even better." There have to be at least three dozen of the assorted confections, arranged on a multi-tiered tray.

"Ohhhh. Someone else with a sweet tooth." She winks. "Cas told me I'd like you."

Cas?

I hide the jealous spike with an answering smile. "Thank the Creator I ate a filling lunch." A salmon filet, served by a sedate Prim—who has decided to warm to my presence, inch by agonizing inch. I think she even stopped scowling, for a flash, when I complimented her about the meal.

"Well, these are light. And calories consumed during business don't count." She shrugs and chuckles. "And I kept the lab coat on, so we can consider this business, right?"

I try not to smile too brightly. If she only knew how close to "business" this really is for me. Or maybe...she does know. By the powers, how much information has "Cas" supplied her with?

I lick my lips. Decide to borrow a gutsy page from Vy's book, and "suck it up" with the direct approach. It is not graceful—but sometimes in life, one simply cannot be.

"So...exactly what is your relationship with...Cas?"

She concludes a sip of tea. To my pleasant surprise, gives a smiling nod. "Bull by the horns. Now I really like you."

That is not my answer but I feel far from pressured to point it out. Sure enough, as soon as the woman finishes nibbling a pink macaron, she replies, "Do you mean am I a lover? Or an ex?"

I take a fortifying bite of cookie for myself. To quote my best friend again, Gawd...delish. "I suppose that is what I mean."

Once more she nods, that atta girl sparkle in her oh-so-American eyes. "The answer is no, and no," she offers. "I went to university with Cassian. We went on one date, which nearly ended in disaster."

I scowl. "How so?"

"Depends on who you ask: him or me."

"Well, you are sitting here."

"But he's at the front of your mind." She arches knowing brows at my confirmation of a blush. "Long story short: the man is too damn serious."

I practically choke on my next bite of cookie. "You are speaking of…Cassian? Cassian Court?" The man with the charm that will not stop captivating me? With the smile that will not let up on assaulting my heart, and the laugh that flips my stomach each time it takes over his lips?

"Six feet-three? Eyes like the Emerald City skyline? Hair so perfect, it belongs on a kid half his age auditioning for a boy band? That Cassian Court?"

We laugh together. That is a very good thing, since it disguises my urge to wistfully sigh at her description instead. I finish with a curious cock of my head. "And yet…you fought with him on your first date."

"On our only date." She settles back a little further, crossing her legs at the knee, absently circling her raised ankle. "Half of one, at that—thank God." An impressive eye roll gets inserted. "All that damn intensity, in one man. He was out to set the world on fire before we were able to legally drink. 'Relax' definitely wasn't a word in his vocabulary, even with dorky bowling shoes on his feet and beer disguised as soda in his hand."

"Bowling…shoes." A frown sets in before I can help it. Racking my brain for the Arcadian translation of the word equates to a blank screen—but this "bowling" must be important. They even have special shoes for it.

Kathryn breaks into another laugh. "Hard to believe, right? The man of Kiton and Berluti, kickin' it casual with a girl in a beat-up bowling alley on a Friday night?" She rests her head against a raised hand. "Neither could he."

"Ambition is not an awful thing." I almost cannot believe the words are coming out—even in defense of Cassian. Firsthand, I have seen ambition's toll on a person—two of them—and on a marriage that was really never a marriage. But thanks to Cassian and the benefits of his drive, I shall never be prisoner to that loveless cage. It is all my choice now—and in a flash, I recognize there is a good chance I will never choose it. Not if I cannot have—

What?

What you have with Cassian? What you are only going to have for six months?

Forever is a long time to be alone, Mishella.

"Of course it's not." The woman's murmur, lined with sincerity, saves me from the miserable turn of my thoughts. "But in this city, it's a drug as lethal as crack or meth—in some cases, more addictive."

I swallow hard—letting my mind follow her lead. Hating myself for every step into that dark, uncomfortable place. "In Cassian's case?"

She barely blinks before answering quietly, "I was starting to fear it…yes."

"Why?"

At that, she does blink. "I think he's still purging demons."

I gulp again. No use. My throat is tight and dry—because I feel the truth of her words. I know it. "Wh-what demons?"

Kathryn lowers her leg. Scoots forward. Pulls in both elbows to her knees. Murmurs as if apologizing, "They're not my stories to tell. And I don't even know all of them. But…they're there, Mishella. Spurring him. Haunting him." The faraway lilt in her voice is suddenly counteracted…by the new smile edging her lips. "Well, they were. Until today."

I straighten. "Huh?"

"Until today," she repeats. "Actually, just an hour ago—when he called, right before you got here, and all but ordered me to take great care of you."

Tiny zings of pride and warmth chase each other through my chest. "Oh," I blurt.

"Yeah," she returns, adding a new chuckle, "oh. The man who never attempted his bossy-boss act with me since the bowling alley catastrophe…" The chuckle mellows. "But now, because of you, he's pulled out his full Smokey the Bear again. It gives me hope."

I don't even hear her last words. "He has a bear?" I recall the moment, in Paipanne's study, back on the island. He had offered to buy me a dog but said nothing about—

"Why don't we make sure he doesn't have a cow, much less a bear." She returns to her soft laughter, clearly proud of herself for the "humor," but sobers when I cannot even feign understanding of the line. Not for the first time in my life, I yearn for a transplant into Vylet's body. The woman is able to laugh even at watching grass grow—and actually has.

"Most excellent of plans."

It is cheerful enough to earn my "game face" as punctuation, seeming to center Kathryn too. Back into doctor mode she rises—literally—standing with brisk efficiency. "Well, I think you're an excellent plan, at least where it concerns my friend Cassian." The strange shadows flit across her gaze again. "He's been by himself for far too long."

I return to my feet as well. "But...surely I am not the first 'friend' he has sent to see you."

She does not placate me with a denial, which would also be a lie. But what she does say is just as huge a seed for disconcerting thoughts—and even deeper emotions.

"Giving a man 'friends' for his body doesn't do a damn thing for his soul." She pulls in a prolonged breath. "And fighting off the alone doesn't mean you're taking care of the lonely."

The words dig into the sides of my mind, refusing to leave even after Kathryn handles the "business" of why I have come, then wraps our visit with a heartfelt hug. It clings as she taps her "digits" into the new cell phone Cassian has purchased for me—and even during her invitation for a "girls' lunch" soon. Though her kindness imparts me with needed confidence, the dark disquiet about Cassian continues to creep in.

Intensity. Ghosts. Lonely.

Beneath the man's rapier swagger and ruthless business cunning, is he truly a haunted beast in a solitary tower? And what—or who—put him there?

The queries overshadow even my awe about New York's nonstop pageantry as Scott drives me back to Temptation—only the trip seems exceedingly short. As we roll to a stop, I peer through the tinted windows in wonder. We are not back at the house. Instead, I look out at wide cement sidewalks, buildings blocking the very sun, and edges of chrome and glass everywhere.

"Errrmm...Scott?"

But Scott is no longer in the driver's seat. He suddenly appears, having opened the limo's back door, extending a hand to help me out—

Onto the sidewalk before a set of massive glass doors—
gliding open like the gates of a modern palace...

Court Towers
Court Enterprises Incorporated

...with its very own, breath-stealing, king.

My lungs cease working at the mere sight of him. That transforms the journey toward him into an interesting experience—knees liquid, heart thudding, palms gummy—while my gaze works to connect a single thought within my brain.

I was naked with that king. Four hours ago. In his bed. In his shower. On his window seat...

The memories lend me fortitude. I need it. I must attempt a feat so outside my comfort zone, only borrowed words from Vy explain it.

Sizing up my competition.

I have always hated the vulgar words, but right now, there is no better phrase for the dozen women and three men who are just as fixated on Cassian as I am—who, I am certain, lust after the same experience I do. To explore the proud body beneath that luxurious suit. To dive fingers into that thick honey hair. To learn if the glints in those emerald eyes are really hints of deeper, hotter desires...

Perfect timing for that thought. Cassian surely reads it in my eyes as we approach each other—then again while taking my hands and yanking me close. Now our bodies are nearly flush...and I almost think he will follow through with a crushing kiss.

For a moment, even here, I wish he would.

Instead, with a tight grunt, he behaves. Lowers his face until only I am privy to his quiet murmur, delivered from barely moving lips. "Dear fuck, armeau. Does that light in your eyes mean what I hope it does?"

I giggle. Just for a moment. "You mean the desire I share with nearly every other woman in this lobby?" Stolen glance one way, then the next. "And a few of the men too."

"Sucks to be them." His fingers twist tighter around mine. His stare dips to my lips. "Because the only thing I can think about is where to get you private and alone."

"I am certain Flynn Whelan might find that an interesting show."

He growls then huffs. "The only 'show' Flynn Whelan cares about is the Canine Classic."

"The...what?"

"Dogs," he explains. "Greyhounds, to be exact. They're his only passion besides his businesses." His gaze swoops down again, teasing tingling energy into the bodice of my pink cotton dress. "But if you're that into putting on a show...we can talk later on tonight."

I sigh as his head lifts again. His gaze is a thousand shades of thrilling, so many verdant colors colliding. I am a heated, pulsing mess, craving the audacity to pull him close then plead for one of his thrilling bites on my neck...

"Behave." I issue it to myself as much as him. We force ourselves back to the respectable hand hold—though his eyes remain hooded, and I can see his clenched teeth past the slight part in his lips.

When a long minute passes without him adding anything verbally, I prompt, "So..."

His dimples make an appearance. Heart. Thud. "So?"

"Ummm...why am I here, Cassian?" I resist adding a crack about showing me his etchings. The man is likely to take me seriously—and I refuse to be the reason for him missing the key meeting with Flynn Whelan.

"Does there have to be a reason?"

Heart. Thunk. And...mortifying blush. "I...I guess not."

"Guess I just needed to see that," he murmurs.

"See what?"

"That blush." His thumbs brush my knuckles. "I've missed it."

A discreet laugh sneaks past my lips. "As Vylet would say, Mr. Court...you are full of shit."

"Good thing my cock isn't already half-hard for Vy, then."

Heart. Melt. Taking the rest of my body with it.

"How'd everything go with Kathryn?"

"Good." I sound breathless and smitten. Who am I fooling? I am breathless and smitten. And now that the subject has shifted to us soon being able to act on our lust anywhere we want…a little sheepish. "Good, good," I rush out. "Everything is…errrmm…working fine. And safely." I already know he is. Even the memory of holding his clean lab results rushes more heat to my face. I must be the color of a ripe tomato by now.

Cassian shifts a little closer. "Did she…give you a prescription?"

"Better." I lift a coy smile. "An injection."

"Ah. Good…good." He sounds as flustered as I am but when he lets out a long exhale, the force of his lust possesses every molecule of the air. "Ella."

"Y-yes?"

"How soon can I be bare inside you?"

My gaze is snatched back up to his. My whole mouth goes dry. Somehow, I manage the response. "T-twenty-four hours."

His hands slide to the backs of my elbows. His stare returns to its green fire, razing into me…through me. By the Creator, my thighs clench at its incursion. My sex throbs, feeling weighted but empty. So empty. Especially after he leans in, whispering words so molten, I am grateful he supports my wobbly walk to the car afterward.

"Twenty-four hours. And starting now, I'm counting every fucking minute."

\* \* \* \*

It only takes ten minutes to drive from Court Towers to Temptation—but in that time, I must swing through just as many emotions. Everything from desire, need, and teen girl-style giddiness is mixed with a soul-deep recognition of the ghosts Kathryn so eloquently explained to me earlier. Of course I have observed the darkness in Cassian's eyes before; I simply have been lacking a way of identifying them…perhaps even seeking an excuse for them, like extended jet lag or simply deep-seated concern about business matters.

No more pretending now.

No more simple veils or innocent oversights.

But Kate has given me no more to go on. They're not my stories to tell, Mishella.

And yet, confronting Cassian about them was simply not an option during our ten minutes together—in glaring public. Letting him make goo-goo eyes at me was one thing; bringing up Kate's cryptic words another. A huge "another."

So now I stand, in the middle of his home, knowing what I know—but unable to do anything about it. Knowing that there are, in Kate's words, things that have haunted him so wholly, he has been obsessed with nothing but work excellence and professional success...

For how long?

For what reasons?

And to what purpose?

In the last week, I have locked stares with the man so many times, there is no more counting them. Every time, it is the closest I have felt to twining my soul with another's...to knowing the heart that is also my own. When I take him inside my body, it is like welcoming myself home...a shore drawing the tide close...

Has it all been an illusion?

Do I not know Cassian Court at all?

And how, in the space of just a week, can I not bear to live with that information as my truth?

Hodge and Scott are downstairs, detailing the cars—Cassian owns three more besides the Jaguar, all prettier and more demanding of upkeep—and Prim is in the kitchen, baking things that make me want to declare dinner will be nothing but dessert tonight. I use the solitude to wander the rooms of the main living floor...not knowing what I plan to find, but hoping it will be some kind of clue about the secrets Cassian keeps behind such high walls in himself.

With every step, I battle myself.

You met him a week ago.

"A week in which our lives have completely changed," I defend in a whisper.

Most couples barely know each other's middle names after a week.

"We are not a couple." I smile from that one. My inner Vylet even high-fives me for it.

He will not even share every secret with Kathryn.

"And the silence is shredding him!"

My whisper has not made it any less a melodrama—making me wonder why I still cannot laugh about it. Perhaps that is because of the twisting, deep in my belly, confirming that even melodrama can carry truth.

The thought gives me conviction. I walk through each room once again, searching for the tiniest sliver of understanding about who Cassian Court really is. About the secrets that don't just motivate him…

They're there, Mishella…haunting him…

I still find nothing.

I peer harder at the sleek walls, glass accents, and elegant furniture, all seemingly custom-crafted for each of his main living spaces. Every inch practically screams of the money spent on it—and the effort expended to separate it from the scrollwork and romance of the building's exterior. Even the décor pieces are carefully crafted to fit the look: slick, clean, neutral.

None of it matches him.

Not the man I have talked with, laughed with, opened up to, and seen into for the last three days. Not the person to whom I feel more connected than anyone in my life, including Vy and Saynt. Not the lover who has given me himself in return—or so I have thought.

I have sensed them…those missing pieces of him…or rather, felt the empty spaces in him sometimes. The unexplained moments of stillness. The searching casts of his gaze, toward a horizon that does not exist…maybe for a person that is no longer there.

Ghosts.

Spurring. Haunting.

I should be patient. Let him come to me, in his time…

But he has known Kathryn since college—nearly ten years—and he still only gives her the shadows.

I cannot accept the shadows.

Ella…it's time to live in the light.

I want his light too.

I have six months with him, not ten years.

Fortune favors the brave.

It feels like destiny to remember the words, a favorite expression often used by King Evrest back home. Evrest even credits their importance in helping his journey toward true love—though that is far beyond my ambition right now, and must remain that way.

It must remain that way.

I have no idea where Cassian and I are bound with each other. I only know that he has helped me at least see my light—and now, if I can help him step toward his too…

Determinedly, I search the spaces again. Living room. Game room. Movie theater. All three guest bedrooms. Even the gym. Still nothing. No mementos from travels, nor artwork that is not abstract. No knickknacks that are not completely curated or more than a few years old, and everything in sync with the out-of-a-movie décor.

I only find one photo, atop the desk in the study that is as sterile as a research laboratory. The image depicts a younger Cassian, between childhood and adulthood, probably twelve or thirteen. He hugs a woman with the same thick gold hair and piercing green eyes. If she is not his mother, I am the Queen of Persia.

Is she one of his ghosts?

I lower into one of the chairs in front of the desk—the leather is so stiff, I wonder if my backside is the first to ever touch it—and stare at the picture, fighting a helpless despair.

"Tell me what to do," I whisper to the woman in the photo. "I am certain I want the same thing as you. I just want him to be…happy."

Deep inside, I wish her sweet smile would order me to leave everything alone. But it does not. It delves to something even deeper…confirms what my gut has already told me since the conversation with Kate.

Satisfying his body comes nowhere close to reaching his soul.

To do that, I must find the ghosts.

"But where?" I beseech it of the room itself now, sending the plea upward as my head falls back. I close my eyes and loll the gray matter to the left. Reopen them—

To find my focus yanked like a weight across a thread. Pulled out the study's entrance, across the central hall, through the breadth of the living room—

To the handle of a door.

Leading to the stairway up to Turret Two.

I know this as a fact, because there's an identical door on the other side of the living room—the one Cassian has led me through, that will forever hold one of the best memories of my life. But he has all but commanded me to forget Turret Two, dismissing it as "the joint's required junk room." Like a proper, smitten lover, I believed him. I still do.

But is not "junk" often another word for "the past?"

And in the past, there are ghosts.

I rise. My heart pounds at the base of my throat. This is it. The *X* on the treasure map.

On quiet steps, I cross to the door. Half-expect it to be locked. Exhale in relief when it is not.

The air beyond the portal is different than that of Turret One. Chilled and dusty, though my feet do not leave any imprints on the wooden stairs as I start to climb. Thank the Creator.

But there are creaks.

I wince, wondering why I did not notice the sounds when ascending the other turret. Because *you were not trying to sneak someplace you do not belong?*

A scowl replaces the wince. Cassian has not expressly "forbidden" me to come up here. And I am not "sneaking." I am searching. There is a difference—

Which thoroughly explains why I jump like a criminal as someone rushes up the stairway behind me. Why my blood turns to ice and my cheeks flame with accusation, as Prim's infuriated form comes into view.

"What the hell do you think you're doing?"

*CASSIAN*

"Mishella. What the hell were you doing?"

I clench my jaw to stop the query from spilling into accusation. She's already been subjected to that treatment; a minute into the phone call from Prim has betrayed that much already. While still on the line with her, I'd ordered Rob to cancel the rest of my day and used the Court Enterprises on-call car to get home, instead of waiting for Scott and the Jag.

Wasn't fast enough.

Prim's wrath has already taken its toll. I see it along the taut slashes of Ella's shoulders, in every glimmering sapphire surface of the gaze she'll no longer lift to mine. Instead, she stares across the study and out the window, perched on the edge of that damn chair—reminding me all too much of how stiff and scared she'd been back on Arcadia, that morning when I'd returned with the new contract.

Only now, she's afraid of me.

My jaw clamps harder. I get down a hard inhalation, battling the bizarre twist in my gut: the beginning of a tornado so distinct, it startles me as much as it terrifies me. I've only endured the tornado twice before. Once for Damon, once for Lily. This—thing—with Mishella is nothing like either of those times.

Is it?

I drop my head. Pinch my nose so hard, vessels are likely broken. I can only hope. A bloodbath from my nose is a thousand times better than a hemorrhage from my soul—which this cannot be. Not after a goddamn week…

You sure about that?

Are you absolutely sure that seven days ago, you didn't walk into that reception hall on Arcadia, behold this woman, and feel every tangle in your brain fall free? Every sprint of your spirit reach its finish line…every hunger of your heart find its fill?

Hasn't everything since then…just made sense?

Except…that it doesn't.

"I—I just wanted to know more about you, Cassian."

And dammit, how it should.

If she were with any other man, it would.

"I know." Both words are growled, drenched in my defeat. I hate this. Hate that the secrets I must keep have made her feel like the one on trial here. I hate that Prim has become so obsessed with keeping those secrets, she's turned into the Temptation guard dog. I hate that she and Ella aren't up on the terrace right now, drinking wine and giggling about—whatever the hell women giggle about. Probably their men. In that case, Prim's giggles should be about Hodge, and Ella's should be about—

Not you, asshole.

But the thought of any other man making her smile, much less giggle, turns my ire into barely contained rage—an anger I have no goddamn right to. She's mine for only six months—and there's no room in that timeline for dredging up ghosts. She'll go back to Arcadia with memories of fire, passion, magic, and romance, not with the miserable stories of how fate, helped by two drug addicts I was stupid enough to love, has fucked my ability ever to trust words that mean even more than those. Words like commitment. And promises.

And forever.

Words she fully deserves in her life.

Not the goddamn misery. Or worse, her pity.

Sure as hell not with the story of how my wife threw herself out Turret Two's window—and how I haven't been able to leave her ghost behind for four damn years.

She sneaks another furtive glance up at me. Squirms but sits straighter, like Lily herself is lurking nearby, and gleefully wiggling the phantom flagpole up Ella's spine.

"I...I am sorry, Cassian."

"It's all right."

She stands in a rush. "No."

"Ella, really—it's all right."

"I mean no, I am not sorry."

Her fists bunch, pulling at the hem of the sweater she must've changed into when returning from Kathryn's—and visiting me. Best five minutes of my fucking day. Her lips twist but she firms them before jogging up her chin once more.

"I—I am starting to...care about you, Cassian. Probably...more than I should." She works a bare toe against the floor—making me long to reach up, strip the gray leggings from her, and screw the rest of her unsteady questions right out of her eyes. Yeah, right here. Yeah, right now.

"I care about you too." My hands drop into their own tight balls. My jaw tautens again. None of it goes undetected by her darting gaze. By now, she has to discern the bottom line. I'm dancing around the real subject as much as she is. "Yeah," I finally add. "Probably more than I should."

Another damn placeholder. I've never just "cared" about this woman—unless the term encompasses a connection so strong, every circuit of my psyche has felt snapped into hers from the moment our eyes first met. Our mainframes completely synched—

Without any backup drive in place.

Fuck. So dangerous.

"So why is it a crime to want to know you better?"

"It isn't." When her brows jump, I emphasize, "It isn't. Prim reacted the way she did out of—"

"Love?"

I square my shoulders. "Yes." Pull in another breath. "Out of love. But not in the way you think." Hell. Could I get any more cliché? The sad answer is yes, because now I have to attempt an explanation about the bond to Prim, without ripping back the scab over the wound named Lily. "You know the funny bit girls have, about friends being a rose garden?" When she gives a small nod, I finish, "Well, Prim and I aren't a garden. We're a briar patch. We both bleed a lot—"

"But it would hurt worse to leave."

Is it a shock that she concludes the thought so perfectly? Rhetorical question. It's also no news alert when my chest clenches from the aftermath: the look on her face depicting the briar thorns she's clearly still picking free from her spirit.

Dammit.

I need to fix this.

Disconnecting the mainframe isn't an option.

"Ella—"

"Cassian." She takes a measured step back. "I—I understand, all right?" Her gaze turns dark and watery. "You have had years with her. I have had barely a week. She was right in reminding me of my place."

"Your place?" I rush forward. She retreats again, nearly

skittering now. Real smooth, idiot.

"It is fine. Truly."

"No." The boulder in my chest is now a quarry, piled with chunks of tension. "Ella…no. Your place here…" I barely hold back from even reaching for her. "You belong in every place." *I need you in all of them.*

"Except Turret Two."

I stab a hand through my hair. "It's just not—safe—up there, okay?"

Truest thing you've spoken all day, mother fucker. She knows it too. Knows it. I feel her perception on the air like a mist before rain. "So we are back to where we started."

She folds her arms. I spread mine out.

"If you want to know things, I'm right here. Just ask me, *favori*."

Her dash of a hopeful glance injects something close to joy. Maybe this hurricane will be just a passing storm after all. With Hodge calming Prim with a run through the park and the door to Turret Two now soundly locked, the spark of trust in Ella's eyes is my light in that storm. If all it takes now to get there is sharing my favorite color and some inane stories from my childhood, so be it.

"All right." Ella lifts her head and nods. Sets her gaze steadily to mine. Despite the bid for confidence, she nervously wets her lips. "After my exam, Kathryn and I talked for a little while."

I smile and mean it. "Good. I knew you'd like her."

"Well…"

"Well…what?"

"She told me some…things."

Continuing the smile isn't an effort. Even if Kate spilled all her "things"—which I highly doubt, knowing Kate and her ethics—they wouldn't be all the things. Nobody has all of it. Silo the explosives, and no one has the power to blow the world up.

"Things like what?" It's still conversational. Okay…this really isn't that hard.

"Like about how you two fought on your first date."

I even let a full chuckle fly. "You mean our only date?"

"Because you were too serious."

"Fair statement."

"She says you still are."

"Which is why I'm the only one laughing about this?"

"She also said intense."

I widen my stance enough for a comfortable heel rock. And a heated turn of my stare. "Intensity can be a good thing…in many situations." Just like that, I fixate on her leggings again—but she doesn't follow the gist. Her brows are knitted, her gaze still clouded.

"She says you are driven to be that way…by ghosts."

Fuck.

The quarry stacks up again—in my gut. Outwardly, I cop a cool-ass Clint Eastwood, bravado bullets across my chest, teeth clenched on an invisible cigar. "Ghosts," I finally repeat. "Was she specific? Gory ones with red eyes or cute cuddly Caspers?"

Ella doesn't flinch.

I'm not sure whether to be encouraged or unnerved.

Clint, don't fail me now.

She diverts her gaze from me. Dips a nod at the photo frame on the desk. "Is she one of them? The woman in the photo with you?"

Her redirected sights give me a second to regroup my expression—and my thoughts. While there's nothing to hide about the picture itself—it's sitting in the open, after all—I predict the shot's surface values will be just the start for my curious little Arcadian. Quickly, I start strategies for where she'll take this.

Because as far as I've let her in…

she can't be allowed to go all the way.

"That's…my mother." I feel my lips kick up as I lift the frame. "Her name is Mallory." I trace a finger around Mom's face. "She lives in Connecticut now, in a little place I bought her, with a garden and room for her cats."

"But this was not taken in Connecticut."

Still not a damn thing wrong with the sorceress's instinct. Right now, because things are still easy, I give her what she wants. "No. Not Connecticut. This was taken at the Jersey shore."

Suddenly, I'm there again. Maybe it's the way Ella always smells a little like the sea or the memories-on-demand corner I'm in, but for one incredible moment, I'm just a kid again, on a grand adventure with my mom and big brother…

"We were there on vacation," I murmur. "Just something last-minute Mom threw together. She did shit like that all the time." I laugh softly as the recollection takes deeper root. "We stayed in this...dump...Christ, the walls were so thin, we heard everything the couple next door was doing. Let's just say I got a crash course in the birds, the bees, and the entire animal kingdom."

"Oh, my."

For a moment, I simply gaze at the new flags of color across Ella's cheeks. She steals my fucking breath. "Oh, yeah. Probably the best two nights of my life up to that point." When she smacks my shoulder, I laugh. "Hey, you wanted to know!"

When her nose crinkles, my breath returns—in time to ignite my chest's fucking fireworks show. "Indeed I did. But I believe the proper term here is...TMI?"

"Too Much Information?" I slide a sly smirk. "Nah. Too much information is bragging that my arm-fart of the national anthem kicked ass all over Damon's. Even Mom agr—"

The abort button is five seconds too late. Ella's curiosity is already in full bloom, though it's still the open, did-I-miss-something kind, not the what-the-hell-are-you-hiding kind.

"Damon?" Her innocence cinches the fresh twist in my gut. Dammit, was I really that careless? "Who is that?"

For a second—maybe more than one—I weigh the merit of a simple lie. Simple? Really? How?

Fine. Maybe half the truth. He went with us to Jersey a few times. I was close to him in childhood.

Both statements are completely true. But neither is the full truth.

"He was my brother."

And sometimes it's just better to lie in the fucking bed one makes.

She would've learned this part sooner or later. Something would've given her more than a passing clue, then she'd mention it to her 'net-savvy little friend over in Arcadia, who'd hunt deeper than the basic wiki and biography websites from which Legal has managed to suppress the information so far. This way, I'm controlling the feed—and exactly how much of my soul is lobbed off in the doing. The wound will be repairable. A more invisible scar after she's gone.

"Your...brother." Her murmur is dotted with bewilderment. "Oh. I—I did not know—"

"Few do." My stomach clenches by another notch. I cloak the discomfort in a haven cold but familiar: the corporate photo pose. Powerful lean against the desk. One hand braced against the top, knuckles down. It says impenetrability. It says back the hell down.

But to someone like Mishella Santelle, it only says here's your pause for more questions.

"Well, does he live in Connecticut now too? Is he older or younger than you?"

And fuck it, all my heart wants to do is answer—as my soul screams from the incision.

"Older," I finally grit. "By two years." My fist grinds so hard against the desk, I expect cracks to fissure the glass plane. "At least...he was."

Her breath clutches—the sound I've been dreading. And now hate.

"W-was?"

I twist my lips. Focus my stare out the window, onto something as innocuous as possible. A crow sits atop a chimney half a block away, a black sentinel against the late afternoon sky. Why is that bird so still? And aren't crows supposed to be magical symbols of something?

"Cassian?"

I swivel toward her. It's torture but I'm unable to fight it. Magic. It's not in the crow; it's right here in her searching gaze, her quiet concern, her soft sorrow...

No. Not sorrow.

Pity.

Fuck.

I am the subject of nobody's pity.

"This isn't something I want to talk about anymore, Mishella."

Her throat vibrates on a heavy swallow. Still, her chin jolts up before she replies, "Is that why the only sound louder than your fist against that desk is the grind of your teeth? Why you look as if you yearn to collapse where you stand, but run as fast as you can at the same time?"

I jerk upright. Shove to my full stance. Pivot away. "This conversation isn't going to happen. Period."

I had to go and nickname her after the princess who walked home from the ball carrying a pumpkin and a bunch of mice. Her hand, persistent and elegant, wraps around my forearm from behind. "I think this conversation is long overdue."

"Then you think really wrong."

"I do not want to hurt you."

A laugh twists out of my constricting throat. "Christ, Mishella." All too fast, the laugh becomes a moan. "Don't you see?" I focus outside again—seeking the crow. Needing it to get out in a snarl, "You. Will. Incinerate. Me."

Pumpkin. Mice. This damn, tenacious woman flattens herself against my back, her cheek like a flare to my whole spine…my whole being. "Maybe it is simply time to live in the light again."

Her arms circle my waist. She feels so fucking good…

I clutch her wrists. Bring her in closer. "But you like the dark better."

"Maybe the world needs both."

The husk in her voice follows the fiery path she has already ignited…up my spine then back down. Spreading lower. Lower…

I shudder. She presses tighter.

"Cassian, please. I just want to help."

Her presence penetrates deeper. Makes me consider, if only for a moment…

What would it be like…to surrender? To really talk about it all? To let someone into the darkness again?

Like you let Lily in?

My breath rushes out, full of relief, as the thought slams in. It's the steel door I need. The clarity I crave. The passage back to the space I can best keep Ella too. Indeed, like a beacon, it guides my hands atop both of hers. Shoves them down until she's cupping me. The inferno of my thoughts turns into the perfect fire between my thighs.

"Then help me," I grate…pushing harder into her grip. Filling her fingers, which now follow my lead. She grips and sprawls and stretches, taking in the width of my bulge…

Her breath quickens against my back. "Oh. By the powers.

Oh."

"Yes. Fuck, yes..."

"No!"

It's just a gasp but breaks us apart like a scream. I wheel around but already know I shouldn't be—that my glare, spawned by disgust for myself, is going to look more like impatient fury. Like the expression of a man who expects to get his forty million dollars' worth out of the woman in front of him. The woman at whose feet he should be falling instead.

The woman who stumbles away, lips trembling, eyes entirely too bright.

"Well." Her chin jerks high again—while her hands wrestle in front of her stomach. "I suppose apologies are in order. I am...sorry, Cassian. Truly."

My throat squeezes. "What the hell? You're sorry?"

"You were right. This conversation really is not happening." Her eyes drop like a subject being judged by her king. "And now that I am enlightened about everything, it will not again. I give you my promise about that."

A strange weight slams my chest. "Promise?" I repeat. "Enlightened? I don't...understand."

"It is all right. *I* do." And why the hell is she smiling now—with such open serenity? "What you really wish for in all this is a bedmate."

"A bed what?"

"A fuck friend?" She cocks her head. "Is that more comfortable for you? Or do you prefer a calling booty?"

I unlock my teeth long enough to snap, "You are not my goddamn booty call."

"Hm." The sound is clipped as her smile taps out. She drops her head again—though not quickly enough. The shiny tracks on her cheeks are unmissable. "That is...an interesting point of view."

Another sensation invades my chest. It's not like the normal ache when I'm with her. It's worse—like my lungs are wrapped in rope and a dull knife is relentlessly sawing to get through. Or to get out?

"Mishella." The dagger's in my voice now, an entreaty for understanding. But will that matter? She wants things I can't give.

She wants the past. She wants the truth.

She wants too much.

She lets my plea fall into silence, as she turns and leaves on slow steps.

I watch until she disappears—

and then I can watch no more.

I spin back toward the desk, toward the window through which I crave to drive my fist—especially now with the crow on its sill, smugly eyeing me as darkness takes over the city behind him.

# Chapter Ten

*MISHELLA*

"Black."

"Blue."

"And red all over?"

I watch, a little stunned, as my quip elicits the same wide eyes and dropped jaws from my two best friends. Their matched reactions are not strange because they have dialed into the video call from different locales in Arcadia, but because they agree on something for the first time in thirty minutes. Granted, half that time has been spent studying the fifty evening gowns I have strewn across the largest of Temptation's guest rooms, and I am in the worst mood of my life not brought on by my parents, but the tension flowing from the two has been palpable—until now.

"Did she just…make a joke?" Brooke ventures.

Vylet cocks her head. "I think so."

"Everyone hold the line. I need to circle this day in red—somewhere."

"Hmmm. Maybe America is a good influence on you, missie thang."

I groan my way into a face palm. "Two weeks, Vy. I have been away for two weeks, and 'missie thang' is already out for some vernacular exercise?"

"Two weeks and three days," Vy asserts. "Almost four. And I'll give up 'missie thang' when you get rid of 'vernacular exercise'."

Brooke, who has given us a backup soundtrack of soft giggles, suddenly sobers. "Sorry, M. I've let her slide a little. Things have been a little…strange around here lately."

"Strange?" I push aside a few of the dresses, needing to sit down. "That does not sound…good."

Understatement. All the strain I have sensed from them is not my imagination—and I shiver just from wondering why.

"Oh, now you have her going, Brooke."

"Have me going where?" I demand. "And why?"

"It's nothing." Brooke waves a hand in front of her awkward frown. "It's probably nothing."

"Probably?" My chest feels rubber-banded. "What does that—" I cannot finish. Coming from Brooke, who is married to the head of all Arcadian security forces, it could mean anything—but I force my mind away from the direst scenarios. The ones left behind are not the most comforting either. "Should Cassian be ordering the plane to take me home instead of sending me more dresses?" Because there will be more—of that, I have no doubt.

"All right. Hold on and chug a chill." Vy throws up a speak-to-the-hand too, with much more purpose than Brooke's fly swat. "The heightened security watches could just as well be practice drills, and—"

"Heightened security watches?" My optimistic resolve crumbles. My thoughts race, bringing up the period that changed so much for Arcadia three and a half months ago—thanks to the vigilante group who forced King Evrest to fake his own death, thrusting Samsyn onto the Arcadian throne. Thank the Creator, the movement was swiftly put down—though not the outside forces suspected of inspiring and funding it. "Are the…Pura…back?" I grimace, loathing even having to utter their name.

"No," Vy protests.

"We don't know," Brooke says at the same time.

"Saynt." His name shoots off my lips, an arrow off the bow of my fear. He is technically not a soldier yet, but desperate times beget desperate measures. Where is he, even now? It is a new day on the island. Is he getting ready for one of those watches? Surely he is not getting done with one. They would not place him on a dangerous night watch so soon. In so many ways, he is still just a boy…

"He's fine, girlfriend." Brooke's words are jabbed with conviction, confirming she has checked that veracity herself. "If anything, he's jonesing for action a little too hard for Samsyn's liking." She inhales with meaning. "But I know how the kid feels."

Slowly, a smile returns to my lips. I hope she can see the gratitude behind it. I miss my feisty former boss—even her daily grumblings about the grind of being a princess instead of a warrior.

"Well…keep him in line," I reply good-naturedly.

"We both are," Vy assures. "Just like his big sistah would."

"Speaking of keeping males in line…" Brooke exaggerates a brow waggle. "Can we get back to the subject—or should I say the confusing jerk—at hand?"

"And the fact that the blue gown will drive him more insane than the black?"

The dress Vy refers to, a sparkly pale blue sheath, is nearly the color of my eyes—not that Cassian will notice my eyes with its plunging neckline. Brooke's top choice is a flowing black creation with an equally dramatic bodice: newly arrived from Milan, according to the curious little woman who has come every morning with fresh batches of gowns, per Cassian's directive—or so she tells me. The man himself has not given me more than twenty words since our "discussion" in the study last week, choosing to work late and eat elsewhere—sometimes even just spending the night at the office. I have little hope that this Literacy Ball is going to change anything, but vow to give it a go.

And yes…perhaps there is a small part of me who wants to really be a princess for a night. Just this once…

"Show us both the dresses again." Brooke's request tugs my mind back to the present—away from its empathy with the sobbing sky outside. Like my spirit, the New York weather has been nonstop on the soggy for days. I welcome the chance to flip the smart pad screen, panning it across the bed. As I do, she emits a low whistle. "Daaammmn, girl. You know I'm not into apology by foof, but that man is trying to tell you something."

"Concurred." I change the screen back, to let them see my little shrug. "He is trying, I think…in his own weird way."

Brooke laughs. "What man doesn't have 'his own weird way'?"

"Mine," Vylet retorts. "What you see is what you get with Alak

Navarre, thank the Creator. And for the record, I am keeping the hell out of him, so neither of you get any ideas."

I move to the window seat. Gaze over the labyrinth of wet streets below, the streetlights and neon signs blended by the rain into a giant watercolor. I would have much the same view from Turret One, which is one floor directly above—but I have not returned to that space, perhaps in subliminal protest to the continued lockdown of the other tower. As long as it stays shackled, I cannot help but feel a similar weight, invisible but just as formidable, on my spirit.

"Can you just lend Alak out for a while?" I venture. "How long do you think it would take for him to rub off on Cassian, just a little?"

Brooke sighs. "I think that lesson has to come from you, girlfriend."

Vylet smirks. "Which, coincidentally, might be best with a little…rubbing."

Brooke peels off a giggle. I groan. Like old times.

Perhaps too much.

I bite my lip. Too late. The backs of my eyes burn. "Creator's toes," I whisper. "I miss you both so much."

Stunningly, Vy is the first to sober on their end. Even more astonishing, her next words aren't then just come home. She gives four even better.

"We are already there."

As Brooke nods, her eyes are shiny too. "She's right, shella-bean. We haven't gone far…the same way you aren't ever far from us."

Now the rain falls inside too. I grip the smart pad as the flooding love of their friendship hits, a storm my heart has desperately needed. One awful sob overcomes another and another and another. They wait as only best friends can, their silence as perfect as a pair of hugs.

"I—I d-do not know wh-what—to do." The confession finally stutters out. "I—I feel so much for him…"

So much. The new understatement. But I am so afraid of saying more. Saying it will make it real. Too real. And too much…

"I told you, B," Vy murmurs after a pause. "Did I not?"

"Sure did," Brooke replies.

"T-told her wh-what?" Despite the stammer, I sound shockingly pragmatic. At least I hope.

Vylet folds her arms, leans toward her camera, and nods with confidence. "That Cassian Court was going to be the man who changed you."

They both smile. I blush furiously. "Wh-when did you tell her that?"

"From the second he first took your hand, at that reception."

Brooke nods. "That is what she said."

Vy maintains her close-up angle. Studies me with the intensity only possible in her big movie star eyes. "Mishella—"

I get in my turn at hoisting a hand. "No. Do not ask it, Vylet Hester."

"—are you in love with him?"

Yes.

No!

"I—I do not know." I let out a new moan, conking my head back against the wall. "By the Creator. I am a mess..."

"That's all right." Brooke's interjection is as gentle as the rain against the glass. "Who said life is always neat and clean?"

"She did," Vy snorts.

After joining my watery laugh to theirs, I mutter, "Point made...dammit."

"Karma is a nasty bitch sometimes."

"No," Brooke interjects. "That little Prim what's-her-name. She's the bitch."

I shake my head—more violently than I can believe. "It is...bizarre...but I do not believe that. She does have a connection to Cassian—"

"You mean hooks?" Vy charges.

"Perhaps even that." My concession clearly spoils a little of her fun—the woman is always up for a rowdy debate—but I continue, "Though they are not romantic ones." I shrug, trying to sort through my bafflement. It is no use. "Aggghh. There are simply things I do not know." Rough breath in. Painful exhale. "Ghosts...he will not reveal."

Silence. Contemplative but not uncomfortable. Though they

are half a world away, sitting with my thoughts is so much easier with the sis-friend-hood around.

At last, Brooke penetrates the pause. "Well, I understand ghosts," she offers quietly. "Samsyn carries a bunch. A real sucky hazard of the job."

I meet her gaze, which has turned as somber as the thunderheads outside. "But he tells you about them, right?"

"Now he does. But we're married, bean—and had six years of friendship before the rings went on our fingers. Things are very different for us."

"Of course." There is no use disguising my disappointment.

Brooke's lips flatten. I know the look but have never dreaded it as much as this moment. Tough love. "Mishella…the plan right now is that you're there for just six months. So now you have to ask yourself—is that a tolerable time to live with the ghosts?" Her shoulders rise then fall. "I can't answer it for you, and neither can Vy."

I swallow deeply. "I just want him to be happy."

She sighs softly. "Perhaps that's your problem, girlfriend."

"Huh?"

"You already make him happy," she contends. "But maybe…"

"Maybe what?"

"Maybe you want something more than just that."

"Just that?" I openly glower. What is she talking about? Are there "levels" of happiness I do not know about, like they talk about on the cable service ads on the television? Basic, deluxe, premium?

"I'm just saying that maybe you crave…more." Her own face twists, as if a small skirmish is taking place in her head, before a heavy breath rushes out. "A more he's not capable of feeling, or giving. Not right now."

Not to you.

I let the words—hers and mine--descend into taut silence. That is usually what people do when their heart is scooped out of their chest…yes?

"Mishella—"

"Fine." I abhor the terse snap, but cannot help it from spilling. I cannot bear a moment of her getting apologetic about it—or worse yet, pitying. "I—I understand, all right? And I am fine."

"All right, stop." Vy points a finger at her camera. "Do not punish Brooke for this. She is trying to help you see this clearly."

I force my lips into a girl Buddha smile. Do not let the serenity climb anywhere near my eyes. Continue to let them simmer while rejoining, "I see everything just fine, Vylet Hester. Now…I am certain both of you have a busy day ahead. I shall let you get to it."

I click my end of the call short without giving them a chance for farewells. It is a childish move—I am taking my sand toys and going home—but I cannot control the reflex any more than the frustration and fury spawning it. Both take over now, annihilating and untamed, then dump out in an unhindered flood. A long, lonely, ugly cry in a room full of silk, satin, and brocade—finery I would trade in a moment for the true fullness of Cassian Court's heart.

*CASSIAN*

Holy fuck.

I must be dreaming.

"No shit," Scott mutters, confirming I've let the words slip aloud. Not surprising—nor would I be stunned if it happened again, as my Ella from the cinders seems to float down the steps, directing her soft smile toward where I wait by the car.

I'm not there for long—as in bolting to get the jump on Scott, who's done the "courtly" thing by stepping up to "collect" her for me—but I'm screwed for watching any man get near her tonight. Delaying the torture a little longer delivers a solid for all.

Annnd, we can start with the solid any time now…

But fate is already having his fun with me tonight. The fucker takes his sweet time about the kumbaya with my nervous system, letting lightning raze me as she steps closer. The skirt of her gown, made of something that looks like a cloud spun into fabric, swirls and sparkles against the stairs with every step she takes. I pray for a breeze, which would likely flatten the filmy fabric around her thighs…

And just like that, solid arrives.

Between my legs.

Focusing on things above her waist is an only slightly better solution. The gown's strapless bodice is encrusted with gold and silver beads, with a band of the same defining the curve of her waist. While the neckline doesn't plunge that far down, thank God, the beads have been glued to lead one's eye toward the center—and the bit of her breasts that are revealed.

Too damn much for my liking.

Yet I can't stop staring.

Fuck. Fuck.

I had to go and hire the city's best hair and makeup to primp her too, didn't I? Damn that Fabiola, rubbing something into Ella's skin to turn it more enticing than it already is. The cream, or whatever the hell it is, gives her neck, shoulders, and arms some kind of iridescence…flooding me with visions of exploring all those planes with my tongue.

Not. Fucking. Helping.

My mind growls it out—like my body needs help remembering how long it's endured without hers. How many days we've wasted in this balance between the heaven of where we started and the hell we're most afraid of, both of us frozen on the tightrope, unwilling to move past the stupidity of surface niceties anymore. I haven't helped the situation by practically living at the office, but coming home to a place that really is temptation for me now, with her scent and her presence in every molecule of the air, has been a fiasco I made no plans for.

Plans.

You actually started thinking of them in conjunction with this woman…when?

Something will have to happen soon. I admit it now. She's not happy, and the sole plug she's given me back to her joy is not a circuit I can connect—not without frying every inch of my psyche. I know that now too, courtesy of the erotic memories that assault my mind's idle hours. Reliving every moment I've spent touching her, kissing her, fucking her, only clarifies the understanding. If she's capable of consuming that much of me sexually, how much more will she gouge from me emotionally?

There's no halfway with her.

Goddammit, there never will be.

Meaning I have to think about letting her leave.

"Bon aksum, Mr. Court."

Especially if she insists on issuing a lot more greetings like that. Professional cool backlit with sensual music, making me a new fan of the whole boss-and-secretary thing...

"And good evening to you, Miss Santelle."

And especially if I'll keep being required to bend over her hand like this—snapping a certain something beneath the tux like a goddamn ripe cucumber.

"Well." She yanks in a breath, lifting a shaky smile. I'll take it. After ten days of watching the dry cleaners' delivery guy get more friendly words than me, I'll fucking take it. "Here...we are."

Only by filling my lungs with air do I resist kissing away her nervousness. Instead, I go for a friendly smile and an overlay of charm. "It would appear so."

"That tuxedo is on the cutting edge of...something." She gestures with her free hand. "Fabiola told me. Several times."

I press in my lips, working the dimples. No way have I missed what their deployment usually does to her libido—and friendly or not, I'm still not above a few dirty tactics. "I'm sure she did."

She lowers her hand. Flits it at her skirt. "Well, you look very dashing."

"And you look like something I've only ever dreamed."

It wasn't what I'd planned to say—though that isn't astounding anymore; not when Ella's involved. And dammit, I may be ready to think about letting her go, but sure as hell haven't reached acceptance yet. Psychologically speaking, I'm in the "fight for it" phase.

I've fought for things a lot less important—

and won.

"Should we be off?" I murmur, tucking her hand beneath my elbow.

Her flits at the dress turn into full twists. "Sure. Um—I mean—certainly. Of course."

I mold my hand over the back of hers. "It's okay, Ella. I already know you're going to be the most beautiful one at the ball."

It's also what I'm afraid of.

She licks the seam of her lips, looking tempted to fully bite despite the contours of lip rouge representing at least thirty minutes of Fabiola's time. "I suppose I shall do," she finally mutters. "I mean...for the hired help."

I halt where I'm at. Slide my grip to her wrist and twist in—though now, we're close enough to the Jag that I have to let her go. She dives into the backseat like a pony let off its training harness—after a charming greeting and smile for Scott.

I remain rooted in place. Carefully reel back the ire that's just tumbled in with her. Tug hard at my jacket—and with gritted teeth, order my cock to a stand-down too.

Fighting for this shit just got very serious.

Scott bounces on his toes, his normal puppy-bright self. "And good evening to you as well, Mr. Court. To the Public Library, right?"

"Not. Yet."

The puppy freezes. "Sir?"

I don't swerve my glare from its angle into the car—and the lofty posture of the woman inside, thinking she's stilled me on the tightrope yet again. "Take the long way there," I command tightly. "A couple of times. No,"—I stop, one hand on the open door—"just keep driving, until you hear from me."

Scott, not being stupid, raises the driver barrier the second he starts the car.

I'm not a stupid man either. As soon as we roll, I reach and brace Mishella by the hips. Haul her over from the spot beneath the opposite window, until she's in the middle of the bench seat—right next to me.

"What on—"

"Be quiet, Ella." With a violent thwick, I pull a seatbelt out. Snap it into the holster at her hip, securing her arm to her side in the doing.

"Cassian. What the hell are you—"

"I said be quiet." I let her glimpse my eyes, on fire with rage, while pressing her other arm to her side. "You'll have your chance to speak—momentarily."

Thwick.

Since the seat can accommodate three, one of the seatbelts descends the opposite direction.

Clack.

I slam the buckle in, ensuring the straps are crisscrossed over her arms and torso. Now, the belts rise and fall with the frenetic pumps of her lungs. Hell. That neckline isn't as demure as I first thought. The sight of her breasts, creamy and gorgeous and just an inch from spilling full nipple, take my cock to something between throbbing and unbearable. Not that I help matters by leaning over and clamping my hands over her wrists—but dammit, this shit has gone on long enough. If I'm going to be ordering up the plane to take her back to Arcadia tomorrow, she'll fucking hear out my side of all this first.

"I—I object to this!" Her eyes fire at me, bright as sun through blue glass. Her breasts show subtle pink strips from where they push at the straps. Goddamn. Why didn't I think of doing this a week ago?

"Are you in any physical pain?"

Her lips, already open to rage at me more, clamp shut. Pop back open to retort, "I—you're—"

"Hurting you?" I volley. "In any way at all?"

"Well—no. But—"

"Then you'll sit right here—and listen to me." I take in her open astonishment—and actually share some of it. My first sight of her full anger is more potent than I ever expected. She's an extra shot at last call. A hard bite into a jalapeño. A scoop of phaal curry. Intoxicating. Blistering. I want more and hate myself for it.

"Listen to you?" Her eyes narrow. "All I have wanted to do is listen to you, Cassian. I begged you to let me do just that—"

"When you were calling the subject matter." I constrict my grip. "Well, now I'm calling it. And the subject tonight—is you."

Her mouth opens again. Releases nothing but pissed-off little grunts, as her brain clearly struggles for a comeback. "There—there is nothing about me worth—"

"Oh no? Except the fact that you have labeled yourself everything from my fuck friend, my booty call, and now my hired help?"

I push deeper into her personal space, until my hips prod her knees apart and I breathe in her perfect scents. That exotic vanilla of her hair, its up-do layered with products from Fabiola's arsenal.

Equally exclusive perfume—Chanel Grand Extrait, Fab's favorite—jasmine and rose in a lush mix. The creamy luxury of whatever the hell makes her skin shimmer like this...and feel this damn good.

So. Damn. Good.

"Goddammit, Ella," I finally snarl. "You are none of those things. You never have been. How can you think them, let alone speak them?"

We both breathe harder. Our gazes meet and tangle. "Cassian." It's a sob, and I'm glad of it. I rejoice in her conflict. Good. It's been hell for you too. I hope it's been a lot of hell.

"Do you really think you're just a toy to me? A trinket I wanted and went after, like a car or a house or a suit?" I spit the final syllable, hating the raw emotion I swore not to expose—then even more for the surge of satisfaction as she flinches. "Did I experience something different, the moment our hands first touched...the second our eyes first locked?" I drill my stare harder into her. Slip my hands down until our fingers lace. "Was I the only one who thought the whole room had fallen away—hell, the whole damn island—until it was just you and me, standing on a rock in the middle of that ocean, put there by destiny?"

"No." As she rasps it, her fingers curl into mine. Her face lifts, eyes searching into mine. "No. You...were not...the only one."

More feelings hit. They're like waves in the sea I've just evoked: some fast and powerful and violent, some deep and rolling and continent-changing. I grit my teeth, willing them to get the hell over with things and drown me, but they're a storm surge, relentless against the ramparts of my spirit and soul. They tumble in, taking over my dark corners—the places I've vowed no one will get to, ever again. But here my Ella is, not just flooding them. She's changing them. Moving my continents...

"Then why?" I finally grate. "Why do you reduce it all to such ugliness? Why do you brand my heart with nothing but dollar signs—when I would have cut the fucker right out of my body and given it to your father, if that's what he demanded?" Maybe that would've been the better call, anyway. Inside my chest or out, the thing is destined to beat on empty space without her. Maybe that's better, in the end—more bearable than the memories, the helplessness, the pain.

Her lips tremble. Her eyes shimmer. "Is that the key to knowing that heart, then?" A sound chokes from her throat, bitterness that doesn't make it to a laugh. "Because that is all *I* want, Cassian. Can you not see? The same way you have taken my heart, my life, and given them so much more meaning and worth...all I want to do is the same for you. To show you—"

"Show me what?" I release the burst without restraint or balance. Isn't this what you want, Miss Santelle? Glorious, violent honesty? Fan-fucking-tastic. Let's do honest. "You want to show that you can 'get' to me? That you can make me give you the 'ghosts', so you can—what—exorcise them for me? That the power of your adoration is going to 'change' me? Christ."

The last of it scorches my throat—burning past my crumbled resistance, overcoming the flood, eviscerating everything inside with its rage and shame and scorn. With a terrible growl, I let up on her arms. With another one, set her free from the seatbelts. But the fire sweeps in, worse than before. It slams me to my haunches, coiling fists against my gut, fighting its incursion—and losing.

The car takes a corner. It's a gentle roll, but joined with the heat in my psyche, is enough to pitch me forward once more. My head swims, dizzy. My heart lurches, lost.

"C-Cassian?"

I watch my fist, clenched against the limo's gray carpet, vanish beneath the volumes of her skirt. Jerk it back, twisting it against the center of my chest. "Get away, Ella."

"No." Tears crack her voice, and I steel myself against them. Stiffen myself against the perfect warmth of her hands, pulling on the back of my neck, the whole of my scalp. "No. You do not want that." She draws me closer. Tighter into the embrace of her softness, her fragrance...her light.

*It is time to live in the light...*

Denial explodes from my soul. Churns in my chest. Snarls up my throat. "Leave. Me. Alone!"

*Alone is the only place that makes sense.*

*Alone is the only place I won't hurt you.*

*The only place you won't hurt me.*

But she pulls me harder—how the fuck did she get so strong?—and I'm letting her—how the fuck did I get so weak?—

and her fingers dig into my face, forcing it up, commanding me to take in every breathtaking inch of hers. Yes, even the tears streaking it. Even the smudges of her lipstick, from where she's buried her face into my hair. But especially the glory of her eyes, adoring me...ambushing me...

"You are not alone."

Before she forces me closer, and kisses me.

And kisses me.

And kisses me.

I am helpless against the magic of her lips. Consumed by the power of her embrace. Hardened by the nearness of her body.

Suffused by the force of her light.

"Fuck." It's helpless and guttural, as she washes over me...into me. "Fuck."

I lurch up, matching the force of her mouth with mine. Suck her in, feasting on the wet, warm depths that haven't been mine for so long. Too damn long...

Moans escape us. Our mouths reverberate with the sounds, inciting more heat through our limbs. Ella's hands cascade to my shoulders, finding their way beneath my jacket then scratching at my shoulders through my shirt. I go at her with the same ferocity, wrapping one arm around her waist, sliding the opposite hand beneath her bodice.

"Oh!" It sparks off her lips, high-pitched and breathless, as soon as I find her first full nipple. I tease a finger across the tight peak. Then another.

"So hard," I utter against her lips. "So erect. So perfect."

She mewls as I glide my touch to the other. "They have been like this...all week."

"Really?"

She meets my frown with a kittenish smile. "Side effect of the injection. And being without you."

I lean in, kissing her deeply once more. "I've missed you too. Dammit, armeau...like missing my own legs. One day, I even forgot what day of the week it was—in the middle of a huge meeting, at that."

We laugh together. It feels so fucking good that I slide my eyes shut, savoring the emotional orgasm of the moment, praying the blinding blast of it lasts forever.

The glaring light of it...

I bolt from the recognition by losing myself in another kiss—and dragging her into its illicit darkness with me. Plunging the corners of her mouth with open, wicked, searing abandon, rolling our tongues until we both can't breathe, then pulling us both even deeper into the lusting, wild abyss...

Yes.

Yes.

This is what we need. If only for now, this is what we can claim as right between us. This is where I can give her exactly what she wants. I pull back, letting her see exactly that in my gaze, before spinning her around and making her face the seat. I tug at her arms, directing her to spread them out—then press in and down, letting her feel every hard, lusting inch of my body.

I dip in, fitting my mouth against her neck. Snarl again, reveling in the hammer of her pulse under my lips.

"Cassian." She battles to lift up, hitching her shoulders against my chest. Mewls with passionate force as I push her back down, skating my hands down her arms, twining my hands over the backs of hers. "Oh, please..."

"Please what, favori?" I softly bite her shoulder. "You want to keep talking about the light..." Another bite. Harder. "Or do you want a trip into the darkness?"

Her breath expels in a needy rush. "By the powers."

"That's not an answer."

"Take me...down," she finally pleads. "Into the...darkness. With you, Cassian. With all of you..."

As soon as the concession leaves her lips, I start shoving her skirts up. It takes a shorter time than I'd estimated to find her ass, barely sheathed in a thong surely mandated by Fabiola, but right now I'm certain I could locate this woman in another galaxy if forced to.

Appropriate imagery—since I damn near see stars the moment my fingers glide beneath those scant panties, to the wet perfection between her legs. "And all of you too?" I work my fingers beyond her damp curls then between her slick lips, stroking the inlet to her tunnel with the rhythmic touch that drives her crazy. In return, her thighs clench, her whole pussy shivers.

"Yes. Oh dear Creator; yes...with all of me!"

At first, I can only grunt. The heaven of touching her again, along with the hell of controlling my cock's reaction, are a purgatory too intense for words. My brain scrambles, trying to tell my body what to do. Unlatch pants. Pull down zipper. Get yourself out of these fucking briefs.

Another grunt, rapidly turned into a groan, as I lube myself with pre-come. Wildly unnecessary. "So wet," I growl, stating the obvious. "Christ, Ella. Your cunt is dripping."

She whimpers. "Take it. Take me. Into the dark. All the way. Please..."

I shove her panties farther aside. Notch my agonized crown against her tight cushions. "This isn't going to be gentle." It's not an apology.

"Thank the fucking Creator."

I lunge.

She screams.

We shake together, our bodies roaring in gratitude. I'm seated inside her, naked and pulsing, head to balls. Fucking heaven.

My forehead falls to her collarbone. My hands force hers outward, stretching her...until she's crushed against the seat beneath me.

I pull out. Nearly all the way.

Thrust in again, deeper than before.

Again.

Again.

Scott keeps driving. Around us, the city thrums with horns and hawkers, sirens and shouts, rock music and rowdy madness—but in here, in the haven of our darkness, there is only the wet rhythm of our bodies, the climbing force of our passion...the precipice to which we climb, aching to fall over together once again...

"Cassian. Oh...my. Cassian!"

"I know, sweet armeau. I know."

"So...close. I...am...so close."

"Widen your knees. It's going to spread everything for you."

I feel the exact moment she complies. Before she can even cry out, her walls clench in, surrounding me in the heated vise of her body. My dick answers with a swell of pressure, punching me deeper in, pulling me closer to the sublime end of my sanity. To make it better for us both, I add a subtle roll at the end of each thrust. If the seat is grinding her clit as I think it is, the effect on her arousal will be—

"Cassian! Fuck!"

Damn. Damn. That word, on her lips…even my hair follicles sizzle. I sink my teeth into her shoulder, and don't relent one inch on driving hard into her sweet, tight body. "You like that, favori?"

"Uh," she gasps. "Uh-huh…"

"Of course you do. My perfect girl." I run my hands back up, cupping beneath her bodice. Pinch her nipples again, reveling in her throaty cry, before delving my hold back beneath the dress. My hands dive in, bracing her hips. My head fits against her neck. "My perfect girl, in the dark…where it's filthy and hot, and my cock is buried so deep inside you…"

She inhales, shaky and edgy. Exhales between her teeth, as her hands fist around the seat buckles. "Yes," she pants. "Yes. More. Take me there. Take. Me. There."

And…that's it. Her plea snicks open the lock on my remaining restraint. With a punishing pace, I fuck her body back onto mine. I ram forward with the same force, feeding her the dialogue she craves with equally nasty intensity.

"The only place I'm taking you is under me, woman."

"Yes…"

"Taking my cock…bare…hard…deep."

"Yes!"

"Your cunt will keep taking it…and so will your clit." The tiny tremors of her nub, now flicked by my balls, have not escaped my attention.

"Yes, Cassian. Yes."

"Without barriers this time."

"None!"

"Feel me filling you…invading you…making you hotter by the moment, until you think you can't stand it anymore, and—"

Her shriek finally breaks in. "I cannot! Creator help me—Cassian, please—I cannot take it anymore!"

# Chapter Eleven

*MISHELLA*

"What?" His voice is rougher, harder, and more ruthless with lust than I have ever fathomed it could be. It terrifies me. It galvanizes me. "What can't you take anymore, Ella? Tell. Me."

And as he finishes it with a sharp smack to my bottom...it soaks me.

"W-waiting," I finally stammer. "I cannot wait any longer!"

"For what?"

I should be wiser about this by now. Should have known he would get me to this precipice, only to make me beg for the final fall over the cliff.

Because he knows I will adore him for every moment of it.

I shove my mind through sexual smoke. Pull up the words he demands—the words I need—to take us both to the edge...

"I cannot wait..." I frantically lick my lips. "To come. For you. Around you, Cassian."

A sound chugs from his chest, full of sensual approval. I swear I am glowing from it, though instantly he is all animal impatience again, prompting, "And what else?"

"And...for you to come too," I rasp.

The husky approval again. Brighter glow.

"Like this?" he encourages. "With my bare cock in your cunt?"

Oh. My.

This. Man.

How does he do this? How does he know the exact angle for his mental scalpel, dipping it into the exact place in my psyche that holds my naughtiest triggers…my deepest arousals?

And right now, does that answer even matter?

"Yes." I shove my hips back, grinding in time to the raw pace he sets. "Yes, Cassian…with your naked cock inside me."

"Right here? Fucking you in my back seat?"

"Right here, Cassian. Right now. Here, in the back of your car."

"Spilling my hot, thick come inside you…as anyone on this street can hear you screaming because of it?"

I cut into his last word by embodying it. My climax rips straight from my fantasies and rampages my body, tearing a shriek from my throat, and filling my sex with a storm. Within seconds, it spirals into a tempest. With a violent groan of his own, Cassian gives me the flood of his seed, relentless with his thrusts until we are both breathless, limp, and sated.

Slowly, he relents his grip on my hips. Though I melt forward a little, he follows me down. With his body still locked inside mine, he trails kisses down then back up my shoulder. Continues around, to the dip between my shoulder blades. His breaths are long and lingering, turning my perspiration into tiny shivers. When they trickle the length of my body, my walls clench around him once more.

"Christ." He grits it before zigzagging the tip of a finger down my back, causing me to grip him harder. He reprises the word, harsher now.

I cannot help a little laugh. Add a saucy glance over my shoulder. "It is your own fault."

"Yeah? You may just make it my 'fault' again." His face, defined by taut arousal, is still an ideal pairing with his tuxedo. He was probably one of those children who play-acted James Bond for the martinis and the girls, not the bad guy butt kicking. "Holy fuck, woman. I'm half-hard again already." When I tighten all my muscles again, deliberately this time, he delivers a sound slap to the cheek that didn't get it the first time. I yelp. He purrs.

"You are a beast," I tease.

"A beast who has to make an appearance at this goddamn gala. So tell your sweet body to let me go…please."

With as much care as we can give my gown, we slide away

from each other. "At least the ball is at the library," I offer, while he scoops a towel from the limo's bar and helps clean me up. "I can sneak off and read while you hog-nog with your people."

"Hob-nob?" he prompts.

"Hm. That too."

"Well, there's only one 'knob' that concerns me." His face contorts as he wraps a second towel around his sex—which backs up his honesty with its beautiful, half-erect state. "And yes, it misses you already."

"Well, *I* miss him."

He stills, towel still on his groin. "Him?"

Quick shrug. "Well, of course. He is part of you, so…"

"So is it just 'him'?" His lips twist once more, as he tucks himself back in. "Or is there a proper name involved here? How about…Eugene? Or something more basic? Bill? Bob?"

I hold up both hands. Return with a chuckle, "All right, now. There is such a thing as carrying things too far."

"We just fucked like animals from the Upper West Side to SoHo. How far would you consider too far?"

I do not miss the tightened corners of his eyes, nor the tension now twining his tone. Perhaps he already feels the difference in the air between us…how I have stuffed away my heart the same way he has pushed down his penis. Clinical? Yes. But survivable? That is the more important yes. Nothing has proved that more clearly than what has just happened between us—a joining that blazed my heart and soul more thoroughly than his essence seared my sex—making it doubly necessary to re-shield them both.

Before he can take over any more of them…

Before they swell too huge, even for the shields.

I smooth my skirts. Pull some tissues from the built-in dispenser in the ledge behind the seat, dabbing at the lipstick that now must be all over my face. "I simply think that boundaries are a smart idea…in some circumstances."

Cassian stiffens. His gaze turns the shade and texture of jade. "In what circumstances?"

I draw in a breath. You knew this might happen. Remember what you mentally rehearsed.

I re-set my shoulders. Force my stare to align with his. Creator help me. A little of my resolve weakens. His eyes are still jade—but now cut into battle daggers. Comprehension has started to seep in.

"In this circumstance," I state, folding calm hands around the tissues. "Everything you said earlier, Cassian…it is true, of course. We enjoy a good connection. A blend of chemistry that is…very nice, and—"

"Nice?" As his growl slams the air, his brows descend over his glare. "Fuck. Are you really doing this? Nice?"

I toss the tissues aside. Recollect myself. I have vowed to remain clear about this, even if he cannot view the situation accurately. Not if we are both to emerge from this arrangement as sane entities. "We…enjoy each other," I venture again. "In many ways."

He matches my determined inhalation. Wraps one hand around his knee, the other on the back of the seat. A posture of openness—

and challenge.

"Fair statement," he replies. "And in many ways, correct." His stare sobers. The car glides through a small dip and sways gently, becoming the expectant metronome to his follow-up. "But…?"

"But…" I fill my lungs again. "I cannot keep 'enjoying' them as thoroughly as I have been. This is for the best, Cassian. I truly believe it, and need you to do so, as well."

## CASSIAN

I don't know whether to throw a punch through the back window, or just throw up. Neither option is comforting. Both are confusing as fuck.

This isn't the first time I've heard those words from a woman. If I had a dollar, right? It's damn near the borderline of my norm. Cassian meets girl. Cassian screws girl. Cassian tells girl she gets the Court charm, the Cassian cock, and the designer-clad arm at a few parties. Even pillow talk is part of the package…perhaps a few jokes as bonus, if things are going well.

No hearts. No flowers. And goddammit, no life story sharing.

Which brings us, at some point, to here. A here I am just fine with. Perhaps, in many instances, am grateful for.

But this time, the confines of this car—of this fucking life, and the price fate has demanded from me for it—render me nothing but gutted. Same effect, anyhow.

I grit my teeth, pumping air like a bull as bile hollows my belly and self-disgust dices my intestines. I combat both by focusing on the floor near her feet. Minutes ago, my knees were planted there in order to pleasure her. I'm not above dropping there again, if I have to beg her.

But I wonder if even that will make a difference.

Her regal strength, one of the qualities that blew me away when first meeting her, is now my worst enemy. It retaliates from the depths of her eyes, dark and serious as a graveyard before dawn. In short, her resolve looks pretty fucking set.

Dammit.

Dammit.

"All right." Concealing the gravel from it is as hopeless as hiding bird crap on this car. Poetic fit, since my psyche is about the same texture. "I'd ask you to define 'for the best', but it looks like you've got that figured out too."

A heavy gulp moves down her throat. "I—I have to take care of my heart, Cassian." For the first time since our bodies broke apart, her voice shakes. "I have not even been here a month, and I already feel it…"

"You feel what, armeau?"

Her gaze flares into a glare. Armeau. I'm exploiting her hesitation and we both know it.

"Disappearing."

Hell. Her tactic is worse than mine. Honesty—as only she can use it against me. Like a laser wielded by a master surgeon, aimed right at my ugliest tumors…my deepest fear.

A world without connection again.

A world without her again.

"It is disappearing, Cassian…into you." Her hands rise, covering her whole face. The tips of her fingers turn white as she shakes her head, fighting the very words she's just confessed. "But there is nothing there for it," she rasps. "Nothing…except…"

"Walls." I take the responsibility of it from her. Let the word weigh my shoulders instead, praying like hell that somehow it will—

what?

Change anything?

Because it doesn't change a fucking thing.

Her heart is still her heart—a gift too precious for my keeping.

And mine is still mine—a mess too morbid for her to handle. For anyone to handle. So many have tried—Kate, Prim, and the countless others who thought they had "the right key" to me—but the truth is, only one person has even gotten close to that entrance. To breaking me open.

Shattering me whole.

And like an idiot, I reach again for her now.

I thank God—and any other entity who cares to take credit—when she lets me pull her closer, fitting her cheek atop my heart, spreading her warmth over my whole body. And yes, enticing the twitch parade to carry on in my dick—though that need comes a very distant second to getting an answer to the question on my lips now.

"So…what happens now, Ella?"

She shifts, nuzzling closer. Good sign?

"Are you asking if I want to go home?"

Bad sign.

"Yeah." I practically choke on the syllable. "Yeah, I guess that's what I am asking."

I remember something about her taking special courses on Arcadia, about courtly arts and practices. Undoubtedly, the fine skill of torture was in that mix. Her silence is nothing less.

"I do not want to go home, Cassian."

I breathe in, claiming back the year she's just stripped out of me. "Thank you." It needs to be said. Perhaps more than once. Maybe from that position I was contemplating, at her feet.

"But I need to move into one of the guest rooms."

"Sure." It spews too quickly and too eagerly, and I don't give a flying shit. I make a mental note to text Hodge and direct him to clutter up the two guest rooms farthest from the master, forcing her into the third. "Yeah. Okay."

"And we make dates to see each other," she goes on. "Real ones, where we go out in public and I get to meet your friends. What?" She knuckles me curiously in the ribs, responding to my snort. "You do have friends?"

"I suppose." I don't have the heart to tell her my closest "buddy" is Doyle, whose idea of stimulating conversation is four grunts, two beers, and a good Knicks game.

"Well, we can start with Kate. Is she dating anyone?"

"I don't know." Which is usually the case—which, for the first time, comes as truly troubling.

"We can figure it out." The woman in my arms shifts back to central focus. I curl in my fingers, making light circles on her creamy shoulder, enjoying the musical cadence of her voice…rejoicing in the fact that it's not leaving me anytime soon. "The important thing is, we get away from Temptation, so we are not always…well…tempted."

Light chuckle. A gentle kiss into her hair. "Why, Miss Santelle, whatever do you mean?"

"Says the man with a woodshed poking my thigh?"

I laugh harder. Much harder. "You mean some wood?"

"Hm. That too."

# Chapter Twelve

MISHELLA

"Mishella?"

I hear Scott's concerned prompt, backed by the rush of traffic along 5th Avenue behind us, but cannot answer. My jaw has dropped on one of the most stunned gapes of my life.

"Armeau?" Cassian now, his body large and close, one hand curving around my elbow, his cedar scent a perfect blend with the grass, trees, and spring flowers abounding through Bryant Park. I now remember Brooke gushing about this place, once she learned that the Literacy Ball would be held at the big library here. Before her family went into hiding on Arcadia, when she was just a young senator's daughter, she attended something called Fashion Week. The event was a bore, she claimed, but the magnificence of Bryant Park was a win.

Now I understand why.

"Ella."

The urgency in his voice finally causes me to turn. I do not hide my continuing shock—as if that is even possible. "Cassian..."

His mouth hitches up at one end. "What, beautiful?"

"We are in the wrong place." I blurt it despite the small throng of other partygoers, strolling along the wide pathways and majestic steps of the soaring Beaux-Arts building before us.

Scott steps forward, darting a worried look. "This thing is at the Library?" he queries Cassian. "Right?"

"But this is not a library."

"Huh?"

"It is a palace!"

Though Scott relaxes, his posture takes on a shrug. "No better place for books then, yeah?"

I absorb that with a wider smile. "Cassian?"

"Yes, armeau?"

"Give Scott a raise."

The young man breaks into a chuckle. "I think I'm going to like having her around, Mr. Court."

Cassian loops an arm around my waist, tugging me tightly. "Me too, Scott. Me too."

The Schwarzman building is more breathtaking on the inside. We enter Astor Hall by descending wide stone steps flanked by balustrades worthy of a Parisian palace, their fancy scrolls and swirls matching archways down the length of the room, all supporting a soaring, ornate ceiling. Similar carvings adorn the stone bases of multiple candelabra, all at least twenty feet high, lending a romantic glow along with colored lighting, purple and orange and amber, around the room's perimeter. From some hidden location, a string ensemble plays classic pieces.

I pull Cassian to a stop at the top of the stairs. Pull in a long breath, celebrating the very best aspect of the place.

"Books." I close my eyes, letting the glorious scent fill me. His guttural growl brings me back to attention. "What?" I add a perplexed giggle. It turns into a sigh when he lifts a grin, dimples on full display.

"Just ignore me." He leans closer, gaze hooded. "I was pretending the smell of three and a half million books really just hit you like an aphrodisiac."

I slink my regard to his mouth. It's one of the most fascinating parts of him, curving in new ways with all his moods. Aroused is definitely one of my favorites. "Maybe…it did." I slide a finger up his satin lapel. "Add some chocolate and you may get lucky in the library, Cassian Court."

New growl. "I thought we were 'scheduling' dates now."

"Chocolate gets you priority status on the calendar."

His eyes darken to my favorite color—sage smoke—as he dips

in, brushing those captivating lips to mine. "Before we sprint to the dessert buffet, I need to make a mental note."

"About what?"

"About buying a chocolate factory."

My giggle expands to a laugh, opening me for his full plunder. I am secretly—perhaps not-so-secretly—delighted when he does just that. Though we do not give in to a full "mack session," in Vy's terms, it is enough of a tangle to reheat my body's need for him—and rekindle my heart's hope that one day, he will think about trusting me with more than just his playful side.

"Well, Cassian Court! There you are!"

The exclamation, bursting the air like a full flock of geese, breaks us apart with matching effect. I look up, stunned to realize the voice belongs to a woman who appears more like a swan. Her steps are fluid glides, her arms float like a ballerina's, and her eyes are huge and dark against practically translucent skin.

"Carol Idelle." Cassian transforms back into a gallant courtier, stepping forward and bowing low. The woman laughs, a new honk on the air, while tugging him close for air kisses. "Yes. Here I am."

Carol bats her eyes, making her false lashes look like swan wings in flight. The impression cannot be helped, since the lengths are a curious blend of black and white strands—but when the woman notices my gawk, she exaggerates the effect by tossing me a saucy wink.

I believe I like her.

"Well, better late than never—especially in your case, darling. You look a-maz-ing. Who did this for you? Tom Ford?"

"Valentino."

She huffs, accenting with a honk. "Of course. I was just speaking with Yolanda Wood. She guessed you'd pick Valentino. I was hoping for Ford."

Cassian's responding smile is, for a long moment, mesmerizing. I have not seen the expression for two weeks, since becoming obsessed with it from across the room at official Sancti court events. It is one part charm, one part decorum, one hundred percent sexy. From his first night on Arcadia, Vy nicknamed it "The Panty Melter." Watching Carol Idelle react to it now, I send a long-distance fist bump to my friend. Right on the money, Vy.

The reminiscence of my friend brings a shot of confidence at the perfect moment—for the woman decides to ogle me now. "And who is this...exquisite...creature?"

She draws out "exquisite" in a way that makes me doubt her sincerity. Glancing to Cassian for clarification lends no help. The Panty Melter remains across his lips but the warmth is miles from reaching his eyes, even as he curves a hand around my waist again.

"I'm honored to introduce Mishella Santelle, gracing us with her presence from the Court of Arcadia. Ella, this is Dame Carol Idelle, a bastion of the city's library foundation, among other worthy endeavors."

I dip my head, offer my hand, and debate a curtsy. In the end, I simply murmur, "Bon aksam. It is lovely to make your acquaintance, Dame Idelle."

I refrain—barely—from starting when the woman releases her largest honk of all. Since the sound could be anything from a climax to a sneeze, I am not sure about selecting any other reaction.

Finally, she exclaims, "Oh, my word. Cassian, she is a-dor-a-ble. It is lovely to make your acquaintance as well, Mishella."

I open my mouth, preparing a proper return in the form of asking about the building's grand architecture—but the air is sliced by a new interruption.

No. Not sliced.

Butchered.

"Lovely."

The word hacks at us, a mixture of drawl and shout that is so unmistakable, I can think of at least three Vy-isms to fit the mahogany brunette in the Romanesque red sheath, approaching on slinky steps with her clutch in one hand and martini glass in the other.

Tanked.

Shitfaced.

Annihilated.

But none of the labels matter, the moment Cassian gives her just one.

"Amelie."

My heart tumbles into my stomach. Plummets even further, sinking until my knees are weighted with the burden, and I grip

Cassian for purchase. I have no doubts about getting it. Beneath my hold, his arm is a log of tension—a limb extended from the taut tree of his whole body.

Yolanda Wood at the Literacy Guild will need to be called. Clarify my RSVP is for two…my guest's name will definitely not be Amelie Hampton's.

"Well look who's here!" Carol saves us all from a honk—thank the Creator—with a cheerful clap. "Amelie, my dear. Don't you look stunning? Is that Christian Siriano?"

"Valentino." Amelie's button nose quirks with a strange expression, something between a huff and a flare. "I picked it tah match mah date." New nostril twitch. At some point in her life, someone probably told her the expression was cute. It is not cute—but it is also impossible for me to accept it for what it is: a drunk girl's dig at the man she wants to keep her claws embedded into. My heart continues racing through my body. My belly lurches, trying to keep up with the pace.

"Isn't that a coincidence," Carol croons. "Cassian is also—" She stops herself with a comprehending honk. "Oh. Oh, dear."

Cassian, confirming he truly must have been James Bond in another life, dips a nod as if Amelie's glare is made of silk instead of mud. "You always have been the go-getter, Amelie. But it's always best to make sure the parachute's strapped on before you leap from the plane."

"Ha!" Carol claps again. "Isn't that just the way of it? Ohhh Cassian, you're a clever fellow by half."

Amelie sips at what is left of her drink. Bursts with a brittle laugh. "Isn't he just? Carol, ya make the most astute obsahvations." Another laugh gurgles out her nose. "Ya gettit? Asssss-tute. Asssss-tute. Hee hee."

Carol huffs. "It might be time to call a car for you, young lady."

Amelie hurls her a glare. "Ah'm fine." Pulls back her shoulders so hard, her balance is thrown off. She wobbles. Drops her clutch. I hasten to help but am shoved away. "I said ah'm fine! Don't you dare touch my things, bitch!"

"Amelie." Cassian steadies me with both hands, his grip as forceful as his voice. "Enough."

"I am all right." I address the question in his gaze before he even utters it.

"I am all right." Surprisingly, her sing-song echo does not change my stance—perhaps because I know it for the imbecile move that it is. Even so, the poor woman does not know the difference. "'I am all right, Cassian. Jush because you're here now, Cassian. Oh, hold muh now, Cassian. Ah love you, Cassian!"

By the powers. Could she dig her grave any deeper?

"Amelie." Cassian is not a tree anymore. His frame is now a monolith of rancor, pushing the confines of his clothes. His hands tremor against my arms, betraying his battle for composure. "You. Are. Done."

She spurts a high-pitched laugh. "Oh God, Cassian. I've known that for weeks now. But does she?" One whip of motion in my direction, and the woman has surrendered her martini to the center of my chest.

"Saint George on gingerbread," Carol mutters.

Cassian wheels away from me—straight at her. "Are you out of your goddamn mind?"

"No." She plants an action hero stance—stunning, given her gown and condition—and flings up an arm, cocktail glass still in hand. "But it's clear you are."

Before I can blink in comprehension, the glass has left her hand—cracking against Cassian's forehead before smashing to the floor.

"By the Creator!" I rush to him as Carol shouts for security. Amelie struggles against the two officers who arrive, though the stare she swerves toward me, filled with she-cat celebration, is the first thing to truly scare me about the woman since she arrived.

"Gah 'head, sugar plum," she purrs. "He's all yours now. Take gooood care of him, because ya won't get a chance at it for long."

Carol marches forward. Blasts at the guards, "Get her out of here!"

But their persistent prisoner breaks free. "Ya haven't told her yet—have ya Cassian?" She cackles through a laugh as they wrestle her in again. "Ha! Imagine that. Cassian Court, preachin' about a girl bein' readah with the parachute—only he's holdin' the rip cord." Her head lolls to the side. "Or was it Lily who had the cord…in the end?"

I finally fish a tissue out of my purse—but as I raise it to Cassian's face, my hand trembles. The crowd that's gathered…they are surely here to watch the rambling soused girl, not her hapless target…

Then why do I feel the weight of a hundred stares on my back? Squirm against the potent heft of their curiosity and shock?

Feel the probe of Cassian's desperation because of it, even before he looks up, through his own blood, at me?

"Don't listen to her, Ella. Don't. Listen."

I feel my stare narrow—as my heartbeat quickens. "Is there something to listen to?" A boulder careens down my throat when he gives back only thick silence. "Cassian?"

"Ohhhh, wait. Maybuh she's jusss your type, Cas. Sweet. Cute. Clingy. Suicidal. Right?"

"Fuck." Cassian mutters it—as the tissue drops from my limp fingers.

"What'd'ya think, little Arcadian princess? Ya have what it takes to be a real Lily Rianna Court, hmmm?"

Her giggle blends with the crowd's buzz, rising with the pitch only possible with a mix of nerves and scandal—a sound with which I am sadly familiar, thanks to the machinations of the Sancti Court.

As the guards jostle her out the door, Amelie starts to sing, high-pitched and off-key. "Lileee of the vallleee…you are so beeeaut-i-fulll to meee…"

In the strange hush that follows, my lungs fight for air.

The crowd still gawks.

As the whispers begin.

And the walls close in. And the room becomes my prison.

"Ella?"

And his voice, my cruel jailer.

"Ella?"

I take jerking steps back. Hold out my hands at his face, now wavering in the blur of my tears. "I—I need air. I have to get air."

"Ella!"

I do not listen. I do not turn. I cannot.

Somehow, I find my way back outside. It is not the same way

we entered the building. Nothing is as bright here, and I am grateful for the shadowed paths. They…fit. More than I want to comprehend…

The only thing I can think about now.

Ella…it's time to live in the light.

"Bull…shit." It stutters out between sobs. Ends in a rasp, mingling with the streams down my face, that are finally rescued by gravity to fall away…

into the dark.

"Ella."

His voice makes me falter.

Fool. Fool.

I double my pace.

"Ella, for fuck sake!"

I stop, telling myself it is more for me than him—that it has nothing to do with the serration in his voice, or how his breath clutches at the end. I freeze, staring across the dark expanse of the park's main lawn. In the distance, le carrousel glows, alight but empty, only a promise of magic.

Like the man who scrambles to stand in front of me now.

"Ella."

"No." It hurtles out, unthinking and unmitigated, from the same awful place where my tears live. My fears. The dread with which I have wrestled since the day I went to Kate's and learned that the knight who carried me off to his kingdom is not the shining Lancelot I originally painted into my Cassian Court journal…the omen that his "ghosts" were much more than just that, and I would confront those specters too damn late?

After too much of my heart belonged to him.

Like now.

After the point of no return, between it hurting me…and crushing me.

Like now.

"No, Cassian. I—I cannot—"

"Or you will not?"

Again without thought, I whirl. Launch myself at him. "How dare you." Drive fists into his chest with any shred of strength I have left. "How fucking dare you." Pummel him again and again, until the tears build and swell and spill once more. "I will not? I will not what, Cassian? Hear your side now, after I begged you for it at Temptation? Try to make sense of you now? Try to figure out why you have crooned to me about our destiny, our connection, and our light, only to learn—in front of hundreds of people—that you were—that…you have…been…"

It grinds to a halt deep in my belly. Stuck in my soul. Brimming instead in my tears.

He speaks it instead.

With his tears soaking through it.

"Married."

I hate myself for gazing back to him. Hate myself even more for how my heart bursts once more for him, sprouting a million vines that reach for the brilliant sustenance of him…even now, as he falls to the grass in his darkest grief.

No.

Especially now.

Slowly, quietly, I lower next to him. As my skirt floats atop the grass, his hand folds over mine. Grips me with fervent force.

I hold on in return. Just as tight.

Finally, his voice quivers the air between us. "We were together…for a year. Married…for most of the next."

"Until she took her life." When he only nods, I go on. "And you…loved her?"

I pray he is not insulted by the query. It feels important for me to know…for absolute certain. Aside from Brooke and Samsyn, and soon Evrest and Camellia, I do not know a single marriage born from love.

"Yes," he utters. "I loved her."

"But…?" It is as heavy in his tone as the dew across the grass.

"But it was a young love." He lifts his head. The wind loosens his hair, tumbling it into his eyes, which are earnest…and honest. "A boy's, for a girl. Not a man's—for a woman." His fingers twist tighter into mine. "Mishella…"

He pauses, giving me time to swallow. To breathe. To think.

Then to yank free from him.

To bolt to my feet. And turn. And run.

I refuse to let him speak it. I possess no doubt that he means it.

But accepting it now, as some kind of enchanted glue to "fix" tonight—

No.

Not here, in our dark. In our rawness and weakness.

I need time. I am still…

afraid.

"Heyyyy. What is such a pretty lady doing, running around in the darkness like this?"

The voice clutches me to a new stop. My head jerks up and my stare circles around. Lost in my emotions, I have stumbled all the way to the other side of the lawn—to the darker side of the park.

The much darker side.

Into a triangle of men who are definitely not attending the Literacy Ball.

Their faces are unshaven, though their heads are shiny and bald. Piercings turn the three of them into walking jewelry counters. More silver gleams from their fingers—and from the smirk I get from the one now blocking my path.

"I—umm—I apologize, gentlemen. I seem to have gotten a little turned around."

"Ohhhh." Another one sidles in from the left. "Did you hear that, guys? We're gentlemen now."

"Moron." The first one snorts. "We always have been gentlemen." His pierced brows waggle. "We just…got a little turned around too."

The third thug steps in from the right. "Maybe we can all get back on the 'straight and narrow' together."

I may be from an island not much larger than this one—and have not seen any of the world beyond it before two weeks ago.

Some may even call me naïve.

But I am not stupid.

I know when to scream as if my life is depending on it.

Because it is.

The world cartwheels and tilts. I kick and struggle but they are strong and many—and the bushes into which they drag me are thick and twisted. And dark. By the Creator, so dark…

Somehow, I get my teeth into the grimy hand that's been clamped over my mouth. "Dammit! Bitch!"

For a blessed moment, I am able to breathe again. And scream again. "Help! Somebod—"

"Shut her up!"

"And hold her down, dammit!"

A new hand clamps my mouth. More hands pin me down in a pile of leaves and dirt. Still, I never stop struggling, even as they shove my skirts to my waist. I never stop resisting, even as they grab at my thighs, and—

"Get. Your. Fucking. Hands. Off of her."

Like a bullet shot into a flock of birds, the thugs jump up. I scramble backward, ignoring the twigs and thorns scratching me everywhere, unwilling to trust my trembling knees enough to stand. Fear seizes me like ice. Panic battles it, searing and dizzying. Nausea bubbles in my throat. "C-Cassian?" I finally get out in a choke.

"I'm not alone." It is him but not him. Rage is a living thing in his voice, a walking beast in his steps. "NYPD's two blocks away, and they've got a GPS lock on my cell."

"Let's beat it!"

"Come on, dickwad! Now!"

The new Cassian creature snarls again—and right now, it is the most wonderful sound in the world. "Listen to your pals, dickwad."

I blink, battling to focus on him. Wonderful or not, he has confronted these monsters head on. I plead the thug with every exigency in my heart. Please be a good dickwad and go away. Just go away!

Creator's mercy. There is so much movement. So many shadows. It is all happening so fast—

"You know what, fancy ass? Fuck you."

Then entirely too slow.

And with the cruel joke of horror, I can see him again.

As three bursts of light flare in the night.

And three bullets rip into the man I love.

## CASSIAN

*Way to fuck up a night, asshole.*

At least I think it's still night. Police sirens sound different in the city at night. More desperate. And isn't that the moon, over the buildings, floating in the stars? It's right there. So beautiful. So unreachable.

*'Cause you're a sky; 'cause you're a sky full of stars…*

So cold.

Like me. Why the hell am I so cold? It's the end of May in New York City. I'm still in New York, right? At the Literacy Ball…kissing the woman I love.

No.

Chasing the woman I love.

*I'm gonna give you my heart…*

"Ella?"

"Cassian!"

"Ella." Why can't I reach her? Why can't I *move*? "Fuck. Ella."

"Do not move!"

"Okay."

"Help is coming!"

"Help for…what?"

"Sssshh. Save your strength. Be *still*, for Creator's sake!"

"Sssshh." I hurl it back defiantly. Reach up, needing to brush her tears back. Why is she still crying? All I've done tonight is make her cry. "It'll be all right. Everything will be all right."

Her shoulders shake. The cream curves of them are so perfect against the stars. Satin and light…my warmth in the chill. "Ridiculous man." Her watery smile beams into me. *All* of me. The soul I can no longer hide from her… "That is supposed to be my line."

"Why?"

Her head snaps up. The rest of her follows, scattering leaves—*leaves?*—before she's gone and I'm cold again. So fucking cold.

*Go on and tear me apart…*

"Over here!" Her shout is shrill and scared. No. Terrified. "He is over here! Please—hurry!"

Why is she so frightened?

"Ella." It resonates in my head but is just a puff on my lips. *Ella. Come back. Please…*

"Help him. Please help him!"

"We will—but Miss, in order for that to happen, you need to stand back."

"Cassian. I'm still here. I'm right here. Cassian…please hang on!"

I blink, forcing my head to twist, following the call of her voice. Focusing on her. Only on her…even as the cold closes in, gripping more of me than before…

*'Cause you get lighter the more it gets dark…*

# Chapter Thirteen

*MISHELLA*

"Are you out of your fucking mind?"

Answering my brother's snarl with a manic giggle, even from thousands of miles away, does not feel like a good idea. He sounds like a completely different person. A forceful man has taken the place of my sweet little Saynt. How can so much have changed in just two weeks?

All too easily, my heart answers that one.

Two weeks can change everything.

One night can change everything.

I drag my head up. Force myself to gaze at my weary reflection in the window of the hospital's hallway. Beneath the denim jacket Prim offered from her own back after she and Hodge arrived, my gown is torn and dirty. I behold each smudge proudly. I am not the same person who first climbed into this dress.

I am a survivor.

I have earned the full right to laugh in my brother's face.

"I shall accept that as a supreme compliment, brother mine. And the short answer is: yes, I probably am out of my fucking mind. And proud of it."

Saynt huffs more heavily. "Mishella, you were assaulted—"

"Because I wandered somewhere I was not supposed to be, in the middle of the night."

"—by three men—"

"And Brooke was taken captive by twice that many, less than a mile from the Sancti Palais."

"—in a city full of savages!"

"Saynt." My laughter vanishes. "That. Is. Enough."

Moody silence. Then another guttural growl. "I told Court that if anything happened to you…if one hair on your head was hurt—"

"Enough!"

His answering breath is so rough, static invades the line. "Mishella…please," he finally grates. "Come home, where I can protect you."

I sigh, but with conviction to match his. "Do Paipanne and Maimanne know you are asking this?"

"Do you know how unfair that question is?"

I give a mixture of grunt and hum, our sibling shorthand for an apology. He is right. My brief call with our parents, just thirty minutes ago, yielded their subdued concern—mostly about whether Cassian would hold his "misfortune" against me or not—but little else. If the decision is solely theirs, I am definitely staying in New York.

As Vy would say: oh, the glorious irony. For the first time in a long time, I want exactly what Mother and Father do.

"But what you are asking is equally unfair, Saynt Austyn Santelle." I let the rebuke set in before softly going on. "I know it sounds strange, even unbelievable, after what has happened…but please, please try to understand. I…belong here now, Saynt. In New York. With Cassian."

"Because you signed that fucking contract?"

"Because I have fallen in love with him."

And it took nearly losing him to realize it.

Another long silence.

As I have expected.

Saynt emerges from the shock with a few sputters—and I brace myself for the string of questions to come after that—but Cassian's nurse sprints into his room, clawing me with new dread from head to toe. Past the exposed nerves in its wake, I blurt a promise to Saynt that I shall call back, and race in behind her.

"What is it? What is wrong? Is he—"

"Being completely difficult?" The nurse spits it over her shoulder, fighting Cassian for control of his oxygen mask.

"Oh." My fingers press my laughing lips. Surely I have earned a spot on the woman's "shit list" because of it, but holding back my exhilaration is a physical and emotional impossibility.

Ridiculous, tenacious, wonderfully alive man.

My man.

"This is New York Presbyterian, not Court Tower, mister." The nurse forces the plastic dome back over his nose and mouth. "You've just had three bullets pulled out of your body, which means I'm the boss for a while—and the boss says this stays on until your oxygen levels are better."

To my wonder—and, it seems, to hers—Cassian sinks back to the pillow. Gives a terse nod. She returns the action, looking satisfied with his sincerity.

I bite my lip.

I know better.

Sure enough, as soon as her footsteps fade down the hall, he shoves the mask away. His other hand is already full of mine, dragging me as close as his wounds will allow. Not being his immediate family, I have only been given generalities for updates. By the grace of the Creator, the punk in the park was a lousy shot, and none of the bullets hit major organs. The trauma surgery went well—and one look at the magnificence of Cassian Court's body, even encased in a hospital gown, is testament to his outstanding base health.

Still, the intensity of his grip is enough to pop my stare wide. "Cassian." I almost add a maternal cluck, despite the non-maternal thoughts inspired simply by his exposed knees. "Save your strength. The nurse is right. Your levels—"

"Will be fine." His throat sounds coated in twelve layers of rust—though after one second of his gaze, it is clear some are not physically related. "I have my air again."

Oh.

Him.

I lift the union of our hands. Several tubes take up the space on the back of his, so I turn it over, then press a kiss into his palm. "And I have mine."

His beautiful lips push together. He swallows heavily. "My mother—"

"Has been called," I assure. "Hodge handled it. He and Prim

are downstairs, waiting for her." I crunch a little frown. "For some reason, he was listed as your emergency contact."

"Yeah." He nods before closing his eyes for a moment. "He can break things to her better than emergency personnel."

My frown deepens. "Has he had to do this before?"

He lets that fall into a long silence. Keeps his eyes closed the whole time. When he finally looks back up at me, it is with his lagoon-dark eyes—and his not-to-be-brooked intent. "I was awake…for a little while…before you came in. I heard you on the phone…with Saynt."

His allusion rests between us like a wick just catching fire—beautiful but uncertain. At last I whisper back, "Oh you did, did you?"

His hand lifts. Frames my face. "Did you mean it? Have you fallen in love with me, Ella…despite the secrets, the ghosts, the flying martini glasses, the New York City wildlife…"

I lean over…unable to hold back from sealing my mouth to his now. And yes, even here and even now, I am shocked we do not make the building's lights flicker with the flare of our attraction. Before his monitors dance too crazily, I pull away—if only by a few inches.

"Living in the wild is just perfect for me, Mr. Court…as long as I live in it with you."

## CASSIAN

Nurse Ratchet is going to have to deal.
Kissing my woman again isn't negotiable.
Of course…this is more than a kiss.
It's a seal. The signet of my spirit, my soul, my heart…
Everything she has given back to me.
Everything I thought I'd never have again.
Everything that was robbed from me because of pain and loss and fear, instead of hope and belief and light.
And love.
Yeah…that.
I curl fingers into her hair. Pull her down a little more.
"I'm in love with you too." As a smile brims her lips and tears

edge her eyes, I quickly clarify, "But favori, I'm rusty at this shit. Really rusty. I'm…I'm not going to get everything right."

She caresses through the stubble along my jaw. "And that is a news flush?"

"Well. It might be a news flash to some—but if you're patient, I promise…I'm a fast learner. It'll get better."

Fuck. So much better. My little sorceress probably doesn't realize it, but she's just dangled the biggest carrot for recuperating I could ever have. Dammit, I will get my ass out of this bed—then get cracking on making every one of her dreams come true. There's an action item list well underway…

One: make love to her for a week straight.

Two: take her to turret two—and include all the details this time.

Three: make love to her for another week straight.

Four: bid on chocolate factories—preferably near libraries.

Five: take her to the newly purchased factory. Collect on preferred calendar status for date night.

"Cassian." Her sweet, high sigh refocuses me on the here and now—and the temptation of her full lips, now parted in perfect invitation. I lift up…and sweep in. She moans, sighing again. I steal her breath, and give her back my own.

My air…

Our tongues tangle. Taste. Conquer. Surrender.

My love…

But the completion of the moment…is the beating of her heart. Pressed to mine, matching mine…knowing mine so far beyond the flimsy confines of the time we've had physically together. She knows me from the depths of fate—from the forever of the destiny that has completely, absolutely, brought us together. The destiny I'm trusting again now…no matter how fucking terrified I am.

But I refuse to live in that fear.

Once more, despite the fear raiding every cell of my body because of it, I choose love.

I choose her.

I'm opening the gift.

Thank you for reading! I truly hope you enjoyed the beginning of Cassian and Mishella's story, because I loved getting to tell it.

More of Cassian and Mishella's love story is on its way…

Part 2, coming in *Pretty Perfect Toy*:
Available on August 23, 2016.

Part 3 (final), coming in *Bold Beautiful Love*:
Available on September 27, 2016.

Discover the Cimarrons of Arcadia:

Book 1: *Into His Dark* (Evrest and Camellia)
Available Now—PURCHASE HERE

Book 2: *Into His Command* (Samsyn and Brooke)
Available Now—PURCHASE HERE

Book 3: *Into Her Fantasies* (Shiraz and Lucy) – Available November 2016
(Pre-order available soon)

Book 4: *Into His Sin* (Jagger and Jayd) – Available February 2017

# Other Books By Angel Payne

THE SECRETS OF STONE SERIES
(With Victoria Blue)

THE WILD BOYS OF SPECIAL FORCES

# About Angel Payne

*USA Today* bestselling romance author Angel Payne has been reading and writing her entire life, though her love for romances began in junior high, when writing with friends on "swap stories" they'd trade between classes. Needless to say, those stories involved lots of angst, groping, drama, and French kissing.

She began getting a paycheck for her writing in her twenties, writing record reviews for a Beverly Hills-based dance music magazine. Some years, various entertainment industry gigs, and a number of years in the hospitality industry later, Angel returned to the thing she loves the most: creating character-based romantic fiction. Along the way, she also graduated with two degrees from Chapman University in Southern California, taking departmental honors for English, before writing five historical romances for Kensington and Bantam/Doubleday/Dell.

Angel found a true home in writing contemporary-based romances that feature high heat and high concepts, focusing on memorable alpha men and the women who tame them. She has numerous book series to her credit, including the Secrets of Stone series (with Victoria Blue), the Kinky Truth, the WILD Boys of Special Forces, and the popular Cimarron Saga, as well as its spin-off, the Temptation Court series.

Angel still lives in Southern California, where she is married to her soulmate and lives on a street that looks like Brigadoon, with their awesome daughter and Lady Claire, the dog with impeccable manners. When not writing, she enjoys reading, pop culture, alt rock, cute shoes, enjoying the outdoors, and being a gym rat.

*\*\*Receive monthly updates and exclusive content by receiving The Wing, Angel's monthly newsletter. Sign up here: eepurl.com/LoNkz*

You can also contact her at:

www.angelpayne.com
https://www.facebook.com/authorangelpayne/
https://twitter.com/AngelPayneWrtr
https://www.instagram.com/angelpaynewriter/
https://www.pinterest.com/angelwrites/
https://www.goodreads.com/author/show/6452869.Angel_Payne

# The Sentinel
A London Mob Novella
by Michelle St. James

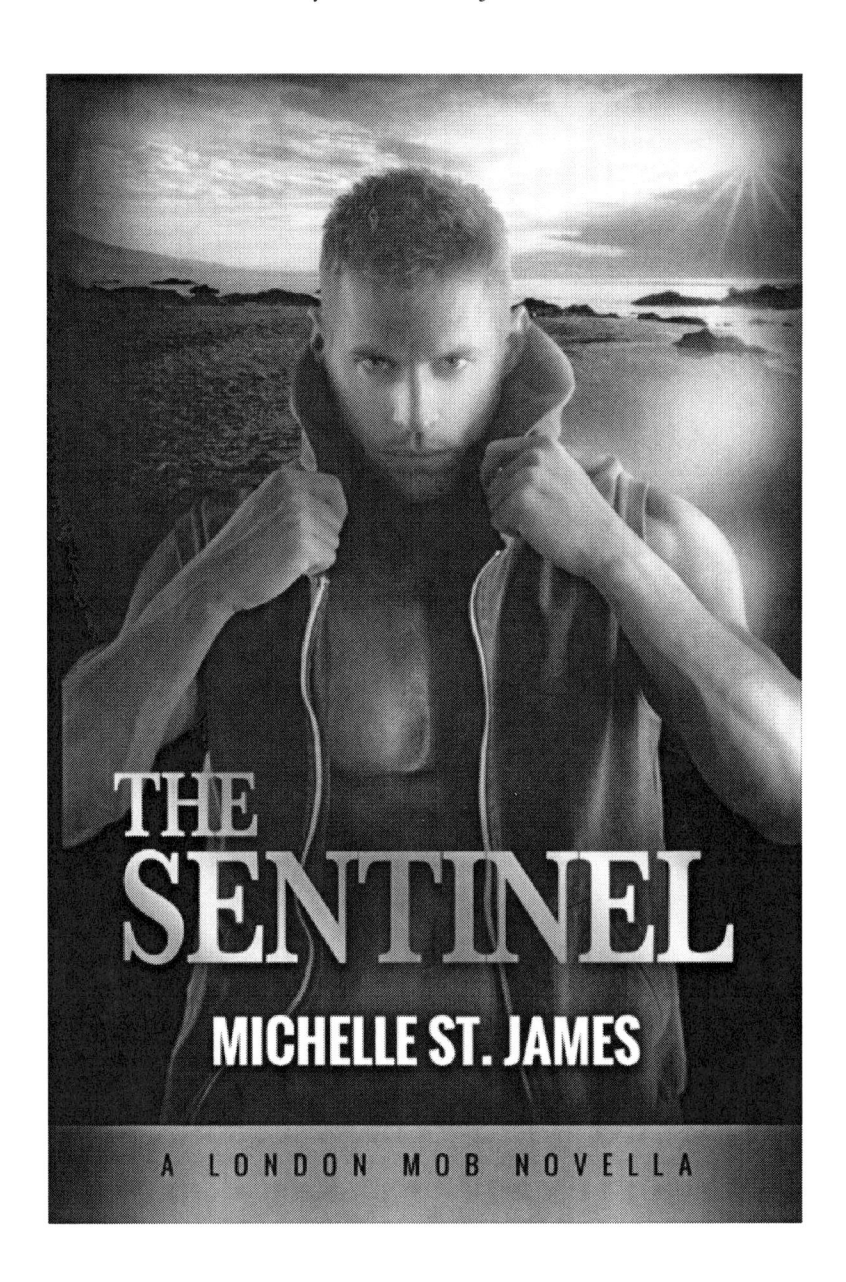

# Chapter One

Diana Barrett forced herself not to glance at the time on her computer. Logic told her not more than five minutes had passed since she'd last checked, but she couldn't seem to help herself. It was worse than she thought.

Three minutes.

She took a deep breath, rolled her shoulders and tried to refocus on the list of wire transfers in front of her. It was always like this when she was meeting Leo, but that didn't make it any less insane. She'd known him most of her life, since year five at St. Ives Primary when he'd helped her up from a game of tag that turned unexpectedly rough. She could still see him in her mind's eye, a tall, gangly boy with soulful brown eyes and unkempt hair that fell over his forehead. On the outside, they couldn't have been more different.

She liked him immediately.

She didn't remember how they'd come to be friends, but one day she realized that it had been a very long time since she hadn't sat with Leo at lunch, since he hadn't been her companion in a game of conkers. Since seeing him hadn't been the highlight of every day.

And then, all at once it seemed, he wasn't lanky, awkward Leo anymore. He was tall and broad, with wide shoulders, a deep voice, and a fierce expression of protection wherever Diana was concerned. They were in their final year of high school when she noticed that he'd become a man, but by then it was too late to change the fact that he was her best friend. She went off to university. Leo took a series of entry level jobs that eventually led him to an executive position at Global Media. They spent summers together when she was home from school, falling back into their old patterns of long days on the beach, chowder on the waterfront when the sun went down, hours spent laying under an inky sky strung with stars.

He was a self made man, unlike Diana, who had every advantage, including worldly, attentive parents on the affluent side of middle class. But he was her Leo, and she thought about him every single day. Now they were adults, both with busy schedules that involved a lot of business travel, but still they managed to coordinate schedules to meet in cities all over the world.

And she got nervous every single time.

She dared a glance at the clock and was relieved to find that she'd spent fifteen minutes lost in her memories of Leo. She logged out of her computer — standard protocol at Abbott, a small but wealthy bank known for its discretion— and grabbed her bag, then rose from her chair and headed to the restroom.

Standing in front of the mirror, she tried to tame her wild curls, then gave up and let them have their way. Leo always said he liked her hair, and anyway, there was no help for it; she'd inherited the unruly mop from her mother's ancestors. She touched up her makeup, grateful for her dark eyelashes and good bone structure. She had her father's DNA and all its classic English features to thank for that one. She finished with a swipe of sheer berry lip stain, closed her bag, and headed back to her desk. She was halfway down the hall when she spotted Maggie's open office door.

"You're alive," Diana said, poking her head into the plush office.

Maggie Kinsley had been Diana's mentor since the day she'd plucked Maggie from an internship program during university. She was one of the smartest women Diana had ever known. Chic and formidable, she'd raised her seventeen-year-old son on her own and was the first woman to become a Vice President at Abbott. Diana didn't know yet if she wanted a career at the bank, but it was nice to know she could have one, and even nicer to know Maggie would be there to guide her along the way, whatever life she chose for herself.

Maggie looked up from her computer with a tired smile. She was as thin as a school girl, with an open face and wide blue eyes. It wasn't at all difficult to imagine her as an ambitious young woman making her way in the male-dominated banking industry of the 1990s.

"I know," she said. "It's ridiculous how busy I've been, isn't it?"

Diana smiled. "That's why they pay you the big bucks."

"I suppose so." She leaned back in her chair, narrowing her eyes as she took in Diana's newly freshened appearance. "I take it you're seeing Leo?"

"I'd ask how you know, but I've already resigned myself to the fact that you know everything."

"Hardly."

Any other day, the word would have been accompanied by laughter, but there was something resigned and tense in the way she said it now. It drew Diana's attention to the dark circles under her friend's eyes, the stern set of her jaw, usually reserved for business rivals.

"You okay, Mags?" Diana was careful about using the nickname at the office. She never wanted to overstep, or to use her friendship with Diana to unfairly further her career. And she definitely didn't want anyone else in the office to become resentful of their relationship. But she couldn't help herself. How long had Maggie looked this tired? Had Diana been so wrapped up in her own life that she hadn't noticed Maggie needed a week on a tropical beach with an umbrella drink in hand?

"You look like you could use a holiday," Diana said.

Something faltered on Maggie's face, and for a split second, Diana thought she might actually confide in her. She didn't do it often — she was a woman who prided herself on independence in all things — but every now and then she would open up to Diana about Evan, her son, her plans for the future, the loneliness that plagued her so rarely that it passed before she ever found the motivation to do anything about it.

It was gone a moment later, Maggie's usual cool facade taking the place of the indecision Diana could have sworn she saw a moment before.

"Nonsense," Maggie said. "There's too much work for a holiday."

"That's what you always say." Diana didn't buy the change of subject, but the time wasn't right for a long conversation about life. She would convince Maggie to go out for drinks soon, come clean about what was bothering her.

"Because it's always true," Maggie said. "And I have a birthday supper to cook for Evan this weekend. You will be there, won't you?"

"With bells on," Diana said. Evan was an unusually wise, witty kid who was currently number three in his class at Newton Prep. "I haven't seen him since Christmas."

"He'll be happy to see you," Maggie said, "although I'm beginning to suspect all this talk about me serves only to avoid talking about Leo."

Diana smiled. "Nothing to say."

Maggie raised an eyebrow. "At least be honest with yourself, my dear. Otherwise you might find thirty years of your life gone by. You might even go home to a cushy flat with no more company than a bottle of wine and a cat."

Diana laughed. "Sounds lovely."

It wasn't entirely true. She wanted more than the bank, didn't she? Someone to share her life? A home? Maybe children one day?

Someone like Leo?

"Liar."

Diana waved, stepping out of the doorway. "See you after lunch."

"We're not done talking about this," Maggie called after her.

Diana smiled as she made her way toward the elevators. She pressed the button, then stepped inside, taking a deep breath.

*It's just Leo. And we're only friends. We'll only ever be friends.*

## Chapter Two

Leo Gage left the club and headed north on foot. The restaurant he'd chosen as a place to meet Diana was a long walk, but he needed the time to clear his head before he saw the woman who was both his best friend and the object of all his private fantasies.

It had been that way as long as he could remember, ever since he'd seen Albert Boone shove her on the playground. Leo's rush toward her had been instinctual even then. She'd been small, with bones as fine and delicate as a bird and an unruly head of black hair that was always escaping from the elastic bands her mother used in a vain attempt to keep it off her daughter's face. He'd held out a hand to help her, and she'd looked up at him, her brown eyes holding an expression of such goodness, such sincerity, that he'd been lost from that moment forward. He'd spent every moment since trying to preserve all the things that made her better than him.

And that meant, first and foremost, shielding her from his influence.

Her parents had made it easy. Clarence and Gwen Barrett had been kind and welcoming, and while he hadn't realized how rare that was when he was a kid, eventually he understood that not everyone would give him the benefit of the doubt like they had.

Leo's mother worked at Charlie's Pub, slinging beer to drunk patrons while she dodged their advances. Leo had never known his father. He spent his time after school wandering the streets, getting into trouble, or sometimes just watching TV at home. While he was throwing rocks at the windows of abandoned buildings, Diana was practicing the piano, developing a lasting affinity for the classical pieces of music she would come to favor. While Leo stole comic books from the corner grocery, Diana learned to paint next to an easel set up next to her mother's on the wide lawn of the Barrett property. Leo ran wild until all hours. Diana was due home promptly after school. Leo ate greasy fish and chips from the stand by the beach, shoving the hot, flakey fish into his mouth while he walked. Diana sat down promptly at six each night to a well rounded meal cooked by her mother.

Still, the Barretts never made him feel self-conscious or embarrassed about their differences, even when he grew from a rough and tumble boy to a young man with two arrests (vandalism and petty theft) and a chip on his shoulder a mile wide. Clarence Barrett had spared Leo no sternness, lecturing him eloquently and frequently on his potential, on his need to develop a path for himself before life took him in a direction from which he could not recover. But he was always kind and fair, and Leo sensed his concern and genuine affection. It was for them as much as Diana that he kept up the charade of his professed career.

And the reason he steered clear of Diana romantically.

The Barretts might welcome him as a wayward foster son, the tough, angry foil to Diana's cultured softness, but he was under no illusion they would continue doing so if he were to profess his love for their daughter.

Besides, Diana deserved better. And so did her parents.

He lifted a hand to his tie as he approached the restaurant. He hated wearing ties. He always felt like he was being lynched by his own clothing. It was one of the many perks of his real job, one that required nothing more than the ability to think on his feet and a willingness to use his fists — and sometimes a weapon.

He ran a hand over his dark hair, pushing back the piece in front that fell over his forehead. He'd been wearing his hair the same way for so long the gesture was like a tic. His hands wouldn't know what to do with themselves without it.

He opened the door to the restaurant and stepped into a sea of suits and dresses, jackets and ties. Everyone looked the same. All of them wearing their cool expressions like armor.

Except her.

She was standing in an alcove against the wall, watching the crowd with an expression of peaceful interest. It was an expression that was quintessentially Diana. Curiosity coupled with a kind of calming serenity. It was one of the many things that drew him to her. Leo was curious, too, but his curiosity was laced with cynicism and a deep-seated belief that whatever he would find in his fellow man wouldn't be good. It was part of why he needed her. She was a dead calm to his stormy sea, Brahms to his classic rock, peaceful slumber to his erratic energy. Just when he thought he couldn't face the ugliness of the world another day, she would call to see if he could meet her for dinner. Maybe it would be London. Maybe Prague or Tokyo. It didn't matter. He came when she called, though he tried to make it seem like he would be in the area anyway. He would meet her in any city across the world, slide into a seat across from her in some crowded restaurant or bar, and his mind would immediately quiet. He would look into her kind eyes, and he would know for sure there was still goodness in the world.

He hesitated before joining her, taking in the elegant neck that begged for his lips, the full mouth he'd dreamt of plundering. Her hair was loose and crazy — just the way he liked it. He'd had more than one fantasy about her naked body under him, her luxurious hair spread out on the pillow under her head.

She was wearing a gray dress that kicked into a flare at the knee, and he had to forcibly banish the desire to cross the room, kneel at her feet, slide his hands up her slender calves to thighs that he knew would be soft and plush.

He was so lost in the fantasy that he hadn't noticed he'd been spotted. Diana was already halfway to him when he emerged from his reverie, and he plastered a smile on his face, trying to quiet the storm in his blood.

"Hey, you!" She stood on tiptoe, touched her lips to his cheek.

"Diana."

She leaned back, looked up at him with the clinical eyes of someone who knew him all too well. "You all right? You look a little pale. Is everything okay at work?"

Work. Right. Diana believed he was an executive at Global Media, a lie he'd been upholding for nearly five years.

"Fine," he said. "I was in Paris for a bit. It's taken me awhile to catch up."

She smiled. "I know how it is," she said. "We travel for work, then do double duty when we come back. Someday we should take a holiday. If we're going to pay for being away, we may as well have some fun."

He had a flash of Diana next to him on the beach, her brown skin glistening in the sun, her fingers intertwined with his own.

Tempting.

And dangerous.

"Someday," he said. It was all he could do to keep his hands off her in a restaurant or on the street. He wasn't foolish enough to overestimate his willpower if they found themselves in some tropical locale, without the trappings of the real world to remind him who they were.

Who he was.

"Shall we?" She gestured to the maitre d' standing behind a podium. "Unfortunately, I can't stay long. I'm swamped at work."

"I understand."

He led them to the uniformed man maintaining the reservation list. A few minutes later, they were seated at a quiet table in the back of the restaurant. They perused the menu, then ordered — seared salmon for Diana and a rib eye for himself. Then he was staring into her eyes, feeling the familiar combination of affection and lust that always battled inside him while in her company.

"How are your parents?" he asked, anxious to keep her talking. To keep the conversation moving. Anything that might distract him from the pillowy softness of her lips, the delicate angle of her collarbone, the hollow at her throat.

She smiled. "You know Mum and Dad. Mum is retired now. She spends all her time in the garden and at the piano."

"There are worse things," he said.

"True, but she's also taken to bothering me about grandchildren." She laughed. "It's become insufferable!"

Leo forced a smile, but the thought of Diana marrying someone else, sleeping beside another man every night, bearing children with her kind eyes and gentle smile with a man who might not fully appreciate her, who might not give her all she deserved — or almost as bad, would give her everything she deserved, everything Leo couldn't give her — was like an ice pick to his heart.

"And what about you?" he asked. "Would you like to have children?"

She turned her water glass in her hand, her expression growing pensive. "Someday. But I'd have to find the right person first. And he seems to be making himself scarce."

Leo nodded, swallowing the lump in his throat. "And your dad? Still teaching?"

Her father was a professor of literature at a small college not far from Cornwall. It wasn't overly prestigious, but it allowed him time to study and read, and he seemed as content a man as Leo had ever known. Leo had grown comfortable with his life, with the uncertainty of it, with the isolation. But thinking about Clarence Barrett always left him with a hint of melancholy. Could Leo be happy with such a life? Did he deserve one?

"He is," she said. "He could retire, but I don't know if he'll ever actually do it."

"He still loves his work," Leo said.

She nodded. "He does."

The waiter appeared at the edge of the table and set down their plates before retreating.

"This looks wonderful," Diana said, picking up her fork. "What about you? How are things at Global?"

Leo cut into his steak, bracing himself for the string of lies he would be forced to tell her. He should have gotten used to it by now, but he didn't think he'd ever get used to lying to Diana, looking into her guileless eyes and adding to the elaborate charade he'd been building for her since they were kids. Back then he'd lie about the fact that he'd had a warm meal, that his mother had read to him before bed, that there was something more than ketchup and pasta and white bread in the cupboard. He never knew for sure if she bought it, but she never called him on it, and that had been good enough for him.

Was it good enough for him now? Was it still more important that she believe he was like her than really know him?

"It's good," he said. "Business is booming. Everyone's looking for the next frontier. You know how it is."

She laughed. "Not really. The business of money hasn't

changed much, I'm afraid."

"Surely more is done digitally now?"

"Well, yes. There's that. But otherwise, it's money in, money out. Numbers never change. And they never lie either."

There was something wistful in her voice, words left unsaid in the breath exhaled at the end of her sentence.

He met her eyes over their food. "Is that what you like about it? That it's always the same?"

"Well, there's something to be said for dependable, isn't there?"

"Is there?"

She smiled a little. "You always did see too much of me, Leo Gage."

The words sent a rush of warmth barreling through his chest. Both because she believed he really saw her, and because he wanted to see even more of her. And he increasingly wanted her to see all of him, too. It would be a mistake, of course. Their friendship had survived so long not in spite of his lies, but because of them. It was as solid as any fortress, but it was built on the foundation of her belief about him. Take that belief away, and everything they had would crumble into the sea.

"That goes double for you, Diana."

He regretted the words as soon as they had escaped his mouth. Did she hear the insinuation in them? Catch the undertone of sex that had crept into them?

He covered it by turning the conversation to safer topics. The weather (typically gray and cold). Football (her team always seemed to be winning, unlike his own). Leo's mother (now retired to a small flat in Cornwall, thanks to Leo's not insubstantial income as Farrell Black's second-in-command). And then, all too soon, they were standing, walking out of the restaurant, Diana's full hips swaying in front of him under the silk of her dress. They stopped on the pavement outside, and a gust of wind blew a strand of hair loose around her face.

He reached up before he could stop himself, tucked it behind her ear. "It's getting cold," he said, to cover the gesture. "Let me get you a taxi."

She shook her head. "The walk will warm me up, and it will do me good after that delicious meal. Besides, it's not that far."

He knew better than to push. To act like a boyfriend instead of a pal. He'd already come too close to crossing the carefully drawn line between them.

"It was nice to see you," he said instead.

"It was nice to see you, too." She stood on tiptoe and kissed his cheek. "Talk soon."

And then she was gone, making her way down the sidewalk amid a throng of others returning to work, their numbers doing nothing to distract him from the gloss of her hair as she moved through the crowd, the strong set of her shoulders.

He watched until she turned the corner, then started off the other way. He was itching for his weapon. It was time to get back to work.

# Chapter Three

Diana leaned back in her chair and stretched her arms over her head. Other than a couple of trips to the employee room for coffee and one run to the restroom, she'd been sitting in the same position ever since she'd come back from lunch. The work wasn't overly challenging — she was auditing a list of deposits and withdrawals for the previous month — but it was enough to keep her mind occupied, and that was of paramount importance after the lunch with Leo.

She'd hoped it would be different this time. She always hoped it would be different.

It never was.

Some deeply buried part of her soul responded to him, reaching for him like a flower to the sun. She kept hoping he would grow bald.

Or fat.

Unfortunately, she'd had no such luck. He was as beautiful as ever. In fact, the bastard seemed to grow even more sexy with age. His boyish face had somehow morphed into perfect cheekbones and a jaw that could cut glass. The eyes that had once been kind and guarded were now tempered with a kind of wisdom she only found more appealing because it spoke to experiences they hadn't shared. To mystery in the lessons he'd learned and the knowledge he'd gained without her.

The knowledge of a man.

Her cheeks flushed at the thought — and its implication — and the cleft between her thighs grew warm. It was almost obscene to think about her childhood friend in such a way. And yet here she was, sitting alone in the office imagining Leo Gage naked, the perfectly formed muscles of his chest tapering to corded abs that would be hard and well formed under her tongue. His cock would be as big as the rest of him, thick and long, big enough to fill every inch of her.

She squirmed in her chair, all too aware of the wetness now coating her knickers. What was she doing? He'd had twenty years to make a move. He hadn't. Which could only mean he didn't want to. He probably had a woman in every city, someone to warm his bed wherever Global Media sent him. She was just the girl next door.

And she had a feeling Leo wanted something entirely different in a woman.

Her mother was right; she needed to find a man. Get married. Have children. Anything to stop the ridiculous fantasy that was a happily ever after with Leo.

A glance at the clock told her it was nearly eleven. She stood and stretched, then walked into the empty hall. The office was dark and hushed, shadows angling ominously away from the dim sconces on the walls. She knew from experience that they stayed lit all night, only turning off in the morning when the office was flooded with sunlight, or more often, when the weak, gray light of London managed to seep in through the cloud cover.

Everyone else had gone, and the cleaning service wouldn't arrive for two more hours. She should go home, take a bath and get some sleep before she had to be up again for work tomorrow. She was about to return to her office for her bag and coat when she had a thought.

She reached into the bottom drawer of her desk and removed a bottle of red wine and two glasses, then headed toward Maggie's office. She wasn't eager to answer her mentor's questions about the lunch with Leo, but Maggie had seemed unusually tired, even worried, earlier in the day. She'd been a good friend to Diana. It was only right that Diana would repay the favor when Maggie needed someone to talk to. Besides, they'd had some of their best conversations over wine after everyone else had gone home.

She slipped her shoes off next to the desk, then continued down the quiet hall, her footsteps muffled on the plush carpet. She was almost to Maggie's office when she stopped in her tracks.

There had been a noise, something she couldn't quite place. She heard it again, and this time she was certain; a wet thwack, the sound of flesh meeting flesh, followed by a low moan.

She stood still in the hall, training her ears to the sound. She'd never known Maggie to have a man in the office, and she was almost positive the sound hadn't been sexual. But there was something unsettling about it, something that chilled her skin under the silk of her dress. A moment later, the sound came again and she understood.

It wasn't the muffled moan of pleasure, but the stifled whimper of pain.

Diana stepped back against the wall, every muscle in her body screaming at her to run while her heart moved her slowly forward, compelled by her worry for Maggie. She was almost to the door of Maggie's office when she heard a man's voice.

"Tell us why; if you don't intend to tell anyone, why were you accessing the files?"

Maggie's voice emerged from the confines of her office. "There were anomalies. It's my job."

There was something defiant in the tone of Maggie's voice, but Diana was still surprised to hear the strike of flesh against flesh, and a moment later, a moan that could only be Maggie in pain.

What the hell was going on here? And who did these men think they were to come in here and terrorize Maggie Kinsley when she was alone and defenseless?

Diana straightened, fully prepared to march into the office and tell the men to leave before she called security. How had they gotten upstairs past the guards in the lobby anyway? She would have to speak to someone about that tomorrow.

She'd just stepped out of the shadows when she heard the telltale cock of a gun. She'd never heard the sound outside of the movies, but it was strangely familiar. There was something elemental about it, something that set off a storm of panic in her body. Her heart hammered in her chest, and she found herself back against the wall, the sheetrock cool against her back.

"Who knows about this?" the man asked, his voice low.

"No one," Maggie said. "Do you really think I would risk

someone else's safety by telling them what you were doing?"

*Thwack.*

Another strike against Maggie.

"Answer my questions only."

Diana heard it then — some kind of accent. Russian? Eastern European?

His statement was followed by another voice, also male. But this one spoke quickly and fluidly in a language Diana couldn't place. There was a rapid exchange between the two men that Diana couldn't understand, and then the first man spoke again in English.

"You understand, I'm sure," he said. "We cannot take the chance."

And then Maggie, begging. "No, please... I have a son. He needs me. I won't tell anyone. Please don't — "

Diana didn't have time to consider her options. She didn't even have time to contemplate the horror of what might be happening inside the office. There was only a series of muffled thumps followed by a slightly different kind of impact that could only be Maggie's body hitting the floor.

Diana stifled a cry. She suddenly couldn't feel her legs, and she was only vaguely aware of the wall against her back as she slid to the floor.

"What was that?" one of the men said from inside Maggie's office.

"I don't know. I'll find out."

Footsteps sounded from inside the office. They were heavy and purposeful on the carpet and got louder as the man approached the door to Maggie's office. The door that would lead them to the hall where Diana was still trying to clear the fog from her brain. Still trying to mobilize herself to do the only left to do.

Run.

# Chapter Four

She heard the command in her mind, but it didn't seem to reach the rest of her body. Paralyzed by a horrific combination of fear and grief, she could only listen as the man's footsteps got closer to the hall. He was almost there when the adrenaline kicked in, suddenly flooding her body with a rush of energy that prompted her to move.

She clambered to her feet and turned away from Maggie's office. Then she ran, ducking behind the first row of cubicles in the open part of the office reserved for general accounting and administrative staff.

The footsteps were in the hall as she hit her knees, crawling along the carpet, careful to stay low as she made her way to the stairs.

"Hello?" the man called out. "Is anyone there?"

She navigated her way through the winding partitions, trying to orient herself to the stairwell while listening for the man's footsteps, trying to make sure she didn't inadvertently work her way to his position.

*Say something,* she thought. She was flying blind without the sound of his voice, scrambling along the floor in what she hoped was the general direction of the stairs while hoping she wasn't playing right into his hands.

He remained quiet, hunting her while she moved at what felt like an excruciatingly slow pace, careful not to knock anything over. Not to bump into anything or make any noise. She'd lost all track of time when she finally saw something she recognized — the pair of potted Ficus trees that flanked the hallway just past the lobby.

She was almost there. She just had to make it through the wide open space of the executive foyer without being seen. Then she'd be in front of the elevators, only steps from the door leading to the stairwell.

Still on her knees, she glanced back. She didn't know where the man had gone, but time was her judge, jury and executioner. He was somewhere in the offices behind her. It was inevitable that he would make his way to the lobby, and that was assuming he wasn't already watching, waiting for her to make a break for the elevator or stairs.

But she didn't have a choice. If she stayed, she was dead. As dead as Maggie...

*Oh, god. Maggie...*

She couldn't think about that right now. She had to get out of the office. Find the guards. Get help. Maybe they could save Maggie. Maybe she was still alive.

She clung to the idea for a moment before putting it out of her mind. She wouldn't do Maggie any good unless she could escape the men who had shot her. She turned her attention on the hall beyond the lobby. The elevators were right there, the stairwell just a few feet past them.

She got off her knees, rose to a crouching position like a runner waiting for the starting shot in a race. Then, before she could change her mind, she bolted, making a run for the elevator lobby. She was free. Out of the office, past the first elevator, then the second. She pulled open the door of the stairwell and rushed headlong down the concrete and metal stairs. The door had just closed behind her when she heard the ping of metal on metal.

He'd spotted her. Had shot at her. But the bullet had hit the stairwell door, and now she had a head start. It wasn't much comfort against the knowledge that Maggie had been mixed up in something, that she'd been shot, that the same men who had shot her were now after Diana.

But it was something.

The stairwell door opened above her. She barely had time to register it before a series of shots rang out in the enclosed space. Muffled by the silencer, the sound was surreal — a soft thud followed by the deafening ping of bullets embedding themselves in the metal staircase.

She moved against the wall, as close as she dared without slowing her pace, trying to shield herself from the view of anyone peering over the railings above her. She looked at the door as she raced past another floor. It was painted with a large "3".

Third floor then. Almost to the bottom and the guards who could protect her.

Another round of gunfire opened up behind her. She kept moving, half expecting to feel the tear of hot metal into her skin. And then she was passing another door.

2...

Cursing above her, something in the language she couldn't identify followed by a word she could have sworn was "bitch." Then more gunfire and the hot sting of something hitting her upper arm, a flash of pain that was gone a moment later.

She launched herself onto the ground floor landing and pulled open the door, spilling out into the bank's main lobby. She was almost to the guard's desk when she realized her error.

His body was sprawled out on the floor, half behind the long desk that was used to check in visitors, half in the open. A small circle marred the center of his forehead, blood caked around the opening. His eyes were open, unseeing.

He was dead.

She didn't have time to feel anything. Her body and mind were singularly focused on survival. On the new reality that she would now have to clear the lobby to get help for Maggie.

She ran as fast as her feet would carry her, only vaguely aware that she was barefoot. Had she taken off her shoes? Had they fallen off? She couldn't remember.

She sprinted for the glass doors, trying to remember if they were left open from the inside or if she needed her key. Her mind was a canvas, blank except for the overwhelming desire to escape, find help for Maggie, make the men who had shot her pay for what they had done.

She didn't have a chance to ponder the consequences of being wrong. She hit the door at full speed as a series of muffled shots hit the floor around her, some of the bullets burying themselves in the tempered glass that surrounded the lobby.

She expected to be met with resistance. To find the door was indeed locked. Instead it seemed to fly open as if by magic.

Easily. Almost like someone had opened it from the other side.

Except she was alone on the darkened street. A car sped past, disappearing into the distance. She hesitated only a split second before turning right, then broke into a sprint, wondering if she would be shot in the back.

She wasn't, and she rounded the corner into an alley and plastered herself against the brick wall of a restaurant, already closed for the night. Everything came into sharp focus as she caught her breath.

The cool night air moving into her lungs, touching her skin with icy fingers.

The pavement, wet and cold under her bare feet.

The distant sound of tires *whooshing* through puddles.

It was foolish to stand still. She knew it in some distant part of her mind, but she couldn't seem to make herself move. She was paralyzed, immobile against the wall, relieved to feel something strong and unmoving at her back.

She didn't know how much time passed before her head began to clear, but slowly, her brain started working again, cataloging everything that had happened. Everything that still might happen. She hadn't seen anyone run past the alley, but that didn't mean they wouldn't be looking for her. She'd left her light on in her office. Her handbag was there, and yes, now she remembered, her shoes. It would be simple to figure out her identity. To realize she'd witnessed Maggie's shooting. Then it was only a matter of looking at her identification. Showing up at her flat.

She couldn't go home. That much was obvious.

She ran through the list of other possibilities in her mind. It didn't take long. It was a short list. She didn't dare contact her parents. Whomever had hurt Maggie — she still refused to believe her friend was dead — would expect her to go there. She would have to call them.

Eventually.

The only other person she would have trusted was lying in one of the executive offices, counting on Diana to get help. She didn't have any more time to be indecisive.

She pushed off the wall and sprinted to the other end of the alley. They might come after her, but she could at least try not to be in their path when they did. She emerged onto Cannon Street and hurried toward the intersection, looking for one of the old phone booths that could still be found downtown.

She found one near Mansion House, the official residence of the Lord Mayor. Shutting herself inside the booth, she looked blankly at the machine in front of her. She'd never made a call from a pay phone. Did it cost money to dial in an emergency?

There was only one way to find out, and she picked up the handset and dialed 9-9-9. She held her breath while it rang, then exhaled in a rush when the dispatcher came on the line. She gave them the bank's address, told them there had been a shooting. Then she hung up before they could ask her name.

She stepped back onto the street a moment later, relieved against all reason to be out of the booth's close quarters. She looked both ways, debating. Then she started running.

# Chapter Five

Leo was half asleep on the sofa when something broke through the blankness of his slumber. He was standing with his weapon in hand before the fog had even lifted from his brain. A moment later, he realized someone was banging on the door.

He moved carefully toward the front of his flat, the TV flickering blue against the walls. He was thankful for his bare feet, although less so for the fact that he'd stripped down to nothing but his jeans before he'd passed out on the sofa. He still had some hope of getting the jump on whoever was on the other side of the door.

Two feet away, he flattened himself against the wall, his weapon raised to his chest as he waited for the knocking to come again. It did, and this time it was accompanied by a voice.

"Leo? It's me, Diana. Are you there?"

He exhaled his relief, then stuffed the gun in the drawer of the console table where he kept his mail and keys. A quick look around the flat only made him more nervous. He wished he'd had time to give it a once over, make sure there were no signs of his real life, but then Diana knocked again, her voice more urgent.

"I need help! Open the door!"

He hurried to the door, unlocked the two massive bolts. He didn't know what he expected. Diana wasn't in the habit of paying him late night visits, or any kind of visit at all in fact. But what he didn't expect was to find her barefoot and disheveled, blood dripping from some kind of wound on her upper arm.

"What the fuck…" It was instinct to pull her inside, bolt the door behind her. Then he was holding her head in his hands. "What happened? Are you all right?"

"There were some men… at the office…. they… oh, my

god..." She choked on a sob. "I think they killed her, Leo."

Leo forced himself to stay calm. Diana was all right. She was alive, right here in front of him. He ran his hands down to her shoulders as if trying to prove her vitality, then carefully turned over her arm. What he saw made him suck in his breath.

She'd been grazed by a bullet.

"Come on," he said, leading her gently to the sofa. "Sit down."

She obeyed his command like a child, and he went to the kitchen and poured whiskey into two glasses. He carried them, along with the bottle, back into the living room. He handed her one of the glasses, watched as she drained it, then poured her another drink before he sat next to her on the sofa with his own.

"We'll have to clean up that arm soon," he said. "But first, tell me what happened."

She took another drink, inhaled deeply, and began to talk. He listened carefully, his mind attuned to the details that would matter when it was time to act.

And he would act.

He would have to. But more than that, he would act because no one could be allowed to scare Diana. To hunt her. To hurt her. There weren't many things in his life worth protecting, but she was at the top of that very short list.

She sipped on her drink as she talked, and he watched as her shoulders began to loosen, the tension slowly leaving her jaw. Her eyes took on a faraway look as the alcohol seeped into her bloodstream. Good. That would help when it came time to clean up her arm, and when it came time for her to sleep, too. When she was done, he paged through everything she'd said for the questions that would help him.

"Had you ever seen the man who chased you? Had he ever come to the office? Visited Maggie there?" Leo asked her.

She shook her head. "I don't think so. He didn't look familiar."

"And what about the man inside Maggie's office?" Leo asked. "Did you get a look at him, even briefly?"

"I was too scared to look." Her shoulders slumped in shame.

He reached out, took her delicate hand in his big one. "You did exactly the right thing by getting out alive. Was there anything about their voices? Anything that would make them easier to identify."

"They had accents," she said. "And... they spoke in a foreign language. I thought it was Russian at first, but now I don't think that's right."

"But they spoke English as well?"

She nodded.

"This is important, Diana; I want you to think back to their conversation with Maggie, to the words they exchanged with each other. Did they say anything that might help us figure out who they are or what they wanted?"

Her eyes glazed over, and her chest rose and fell with shallow breaths. She was remembering, and he left her to it, resisting the urge to pull her into his arms. To tell her not to remember, not to think about it because he didn't want her to relive anything ugly or scary. But that wouldn't help her, and she was going to need his help. That he already knew.

"They... spoke in the other language the one time they exchanged a lot of words," she said. "I couldn't understand them. Before that, they were asking Maggie questions. Asking who else knew, who else she told."

"But they didn't say what they were talking about?" he asked. "What she knew about?"

"Not outright," she said. "They acted like Maggie understood."

"Did she?" Leo asked.

Diana nodded. "I think so. She didn't deny it. She just said no one else knew. She said... She said she was doing her job, that she wouldn't tell anyone."

"Good," Leo said. "Is there anything else you can remember? Tattoos or scars on the man who chased you? Anything at all?"

"I don't... I don't think so."

He nodded. "Stay here."

He stood, and she grabbed his hand with panic in her eyes. "Where are you going?"

He sat next to her again, looked into her eyes. "I'm going to the bathroom to get something to clean up that arm. You don't have to worry, Diana. You're safe here."

*I'll kill anyone who tries to hurt you. Tear them limb from limb.*

He left the words unsaid. He didn't know how long he'd be able to keep up the charade of his real life — especially now — but he would try. For her sake, he would try. Because she didn't deserve what he'd done to her. The lies he'd told.

But neither did she deserve the brutality of the truth on the heels of what had happened tonight.

She nodded, and he rose again, hurrying to the bathroom so he could get back to her as quickly as possible. He returned less than two minutes later with a washcloth, a roll of gauze, some disinfectant, tweezers (in case he was wrong, and pieces of the bullet were still lodged in her skin), and some first aid tape. He set everything down on the coffee table and went to the kitchen where he filled a large bowl with warm water.

When he had everything in place, he poured them both another drink and sat next to her on the sofa.

"Are you sure you should be drinking that before you dig around in my arm?" she asked softly, eying the drink in his hand.

"Would it make you feel better if I didn't?"

She shrugged. "I trust you."

*Trusting me is the last thing you should do*, he thought. *The very last thing.*

He set down the drink. He couldn't tell her the truth: that the idea of hurting her, of touching her warm skin with the cold metal tweezers, of probing her slender arm for remnants of a bullet, made him want to hit something hard. That it made him want to hunt the streets of London for the man who had dared do this to her. That he had hoped the drink would smooth out his rage.

"I don't need it," he lied, submerging the washcloth in the basin of hot water. "You don't have to look if you don't want."

She met his eyes, her gaze unflinching. "I don't mind looking."

He nodded, then squeezed the excess water out of the washcloth before applying it gently to her arm. He held it there for a few seconds, wanting to let the heat loosen some of the dried blood so he wouldn't have to rub too hard. It was strangely intimate. It seemed he'd known Diana forever, but it had been ages since he'd been close to her without the press of his physical attraction, the weight of his feelings. When they'd been kids, they'd had foot wars in the summer, Diana's bare feet pressed to his on her front lawn. They'd eaten ice cream off the same spoon. Had grabbed onto each other in the sea, trying to gain purchase on slippery skin as they tried to dunk each other under the waves.

But that had all changed. Somewhere along the way, she'd become an other. A girl.

And a beautiful one at that.

Even the most innocent physical attraction had felt charged after that. Like the air just before lightening cracked the summer sky. He'd grown used to their distance, but only because he hadn't been forced to endure her closeness.

Now she was right here, her knees bare under the dress, only inches from his denim-clad legs. Her arm was soft in his hands, and he could smell traces of her perfume — vanilla and jasmine — alone with a subtle tang of sweat he found remarkably sensual even as he cleaned the blood off her arm.

True to her word, she didn't look away. She didn't flinch either, and for the first time he had the sense that there were things he didn't know about Diana. Not the stuff he knew he didn't know — the stuff he didn't want to know — like how many men she'd slept with or if she'd even been really in love.

It was the other stuff he was catching a glimpse of: a spine of steel under the graceful exterior, courage in the face of clear and present danger, determination that went beyond her desire to have a successful career or to make her parents proud.

"Let's take a closer look," he said, his voice gruff as he dropped the washcloth into the basin of water. "Make sure there's nothing left of the bullet."

He turned her arm over, exposing the paler underside. The wound was shallow and jagged, like a particularly deep and vicious scrape. He ran his fingers lightly around its edges, feeling for anything sharp or hard under the skin. When he didn't feel anything, he looked into her eyes.

"I don't feel anything, but I'm going to have to look a little more closely to be sure. Would you like to take another drink?"

"I'm good. Just do it, Leo."

He bent his head to her arm and used his fingers to gently spread the wound. A little bit of blood began to flow again, but its quantity suggested the wound was as minor as it appeared, and when he looked more closely, he didn't see anything to make him think there was shrapnel trapped in her skin.

He grabbed the gauze. "I think you're clear. You were lucky."

He wouldn't have wanted to take Diana to the hospital. There would have been questions — a lot of them — and he was almost certain it was better for Diana to lay low until he could figure out what Maggie Kinsley had been involved in. He could have called the doctor Farrell used for these kinds of situations, but then he would have exposed his real life to Diana, and he was still hoping for a way around it.

He covered the wound with a bandage, then began winding the soft gauze around her arm. He finished with first aid tape, then picked up the bowl of bloody water and returned to the bathroom. When he came back, Diana was studying him with interest.

"What?" he asked.

"You don't seem very surprised by all of this," she said.

After working for Farrell Black, nothing much surprised him. Farrell's organization ran the London crime scene. They had their hands in almost everything — drugs, insurance, bookmaking, loansharking, black market sales. They were even dipping their toes in the water of corporate espionage, although Farrell would never be a refined criminal like Nico Vitale before the fall of the Syndicate.

No, Farrell Black made no apologies about the brutality of the business, and Leo was more than happy to work alongside him. It was all he'd ever known. He had no real desire for another kind of life.

But he couldn't tell Diana any of that.

He shrugged, avoiding her eyes like that would somehow diminish the lie he was about to tell. The lies he'd already told. "I'm just taking it all in, thinking about what to do next."

"I think it's obvious what we should do next."

"And what is that?" he asked.

She looked at him like he was insane. "Go to the police, of course."

He stood, packing up the rest of the first aid supplies. "Let's give it until morning," he said. "You need rest."

"I don't need rest," she said firmly. "I need to help the police find the men who…. who shot Maggie."

"That's not a good idea." He headed for the bathroom, glad of the excuse to return the gauze, tape, tweezers, and anti-bacterial spray. He was putting everything back in the cabinet when she spoke from the doorway.

"We can't do nothing," she said. "Maggie has a son."

He closed the cupboard door and faced her, then crossed his arms over his chest. "I assure you that I don't intend to do nothing."

Her eyes flashed. "What else is there but to go to the police?" she asked. "That's what people do when someone's been shot."

"You already called the police," he reminded her.

"But I didn't tell them anything. I was too scared. I need to tell them about the man who chased me. Give them a description so they can look for him."

"I'm not saying no," Leo said carefully. "I'm just saying let's give it until morning."

Her laugh was incredulous, a little bitter even. "You're not saying *no*? What makes you think you can say no? I came to you for help, Leo."

She turned and disappeared into the hall, her words accusatory in the vacuum left by her presence. He followed her into the living room and into the foyer.

"I'm going to help you, Diana, but we don't know anything about these men. And I hate to break it to you, but the police aren't always on the up and up."

She turned to face him. "What's that supposed to mean?"

He sighed, searching his brain for an explanation that would make sense without giving too much away. He wasn't ready to tell her that there were always people in the police department — from the lowliest street cop to the highest ranking officer — who were on the take. He should know — he often delivered their payday.

"Is it fair to say that whoever shot Maggie was probably involved in some kind of financial crime?" he asked.

She hesitated. "I have no idea."

"Yes, but they were talking to Maggie about something at the bank, right? And Abbott is known for being discreet when it comes to their clients?"

"No more discreet than any other bank." A hint of defensiveness had crept into her voice.

"You know what I mean," he said. There had long been rumors that Abbott brokered offshore accounts for influential clients. It wasn't illegal, although Leo suspected the secrecy surrounding the bank's activities had more to do with the power of their clientele than any metric for legality.

"All right, yes," she admitted. "That is our reputation."

"So don't you think it's at least possible that whoever is involved in this is powerful? That they might have resources enough to have someone in the police force on their side?" he asked.

Her throat rippled as she swallowed, and he wondered if she was just this moment realizing how much danger she was in. "I suppose."

"Then let's give it the night," he said. "That's all I'm saying. I have some friends in the department. Let me ask some questions. See if I can get any information. Tomorrow we'll get help."

She met his eyes. "Promise?"

"I promise."

"What about Maggie?"

The pain in her eyes was like a knife in his gut. He wanted to do anything to banish it. Tell her Maggie was almost certainly fine. That people survived gunshots all the time.

But he wouldn't compound his lies where he could help it.

"I don't know," he said. "But you called for an ambulance. She's getting the help she needs. There's nothing else you can do. Whether we go to the police tonight or tomorrow won't change anything."

He didn't say the rest of it. That he had no intention of going to the police. That the information the police would be willing to give them — the information the police were even capable of giving them — was nothing compared to the work Leo could do on his own.

She sighed. "All right."

"Come on," he said. "Let's get you to bed."

*Alone,* he thought. *Because if I lay within an inch of you, it will be impossible not to pull you into my arms.*

And that would ruin everything.

## Chapter Six

She woke up to the smell of coffee and bacon, a strange pair of words running through her mind.

Benny Saff.

The words had seemed to drift to her in the half light between sleep and wakefulness. But it wasn't her voice she heard in her mind.

It was the man from the bank. The one who'd been talking to Maggie.

Benny Saff? The name meant nothing to her, and yet she was almost positive it had been said when the men had exchanged words in the language she couldn't understand. Was it something that would help them identify the language, and therefore the nationality, of the men who had hurt Maggie?

She didn't know, and she lay in bed working the words in her mind, trying to make sense of them before she mentioned them to Leo.

The room was dim, filled with only the weak London light that made it impossible to determine the time of day. She hadn't wanted to take Leo's bed, but he'd insisted. He'd even sat in the chair next to the bed as she fell asleep. She thought she'd be too upset to sleep, her body filled with a strange mixture of adrenaline and shock. But something about Leo's presence had soothed her, and she'd drifted off suddenly and completely.

She looked around, wondering why she'd never been to Leo's

flat in London. She'd offered to meet him here, hadn't she? Or had she been too wrapped up in her own life to suggest it? Maybe she simply hadn't wanted to know what she would find — likely some kind of bachelor pad designed to get women out of their knickers.

Except that's not at all how she would describe the flat. Instead it was small and comfortable, obviously expensive, but not overly lavish. It was clean and homey, an escape from the noise and grit of the city.

But this wasn't some kind of holiday. Maggie had been shot. Diana didn't even know if her friend was still alive. She'd followed Leo's lead. Had taken the night to rest and regroup.

Now it was time to go to the police.

She got out of bed and stretched, then nearly jumped out of her skin when she saw Leo leaning against the door frame. He wore the same pair of well-worn jeans he'd had on the night before. They were a little too big in the waist, hanging low enough on his hips to give her a glimpse of a perfectly chiseled "V" under the thin white shirt that clung to every well defined muscle in his upper body. His hair was deliciously tousled, the rogue lock skimming his forehead even more rakishly than normal. He looked like he'd just rolled out of bed, but somehow he was even sexier than when he was dressed and polished, while she was probably a hot mess.

Damn him.

Was it her imagination that his gaze was predatory? That his eyes combed her body from head to toe like he'd never seen her before that moment?

She looked down, wondering if she'd gone to sleep in her underwear and bra. But no. She was in Leo's sweatpants and one of his old T-shirts, just like she remembered. Hardly tempting to a man who'd known her since they were old enough to run wild together.

"Good morning," she said, suddenly desperate to break the tension between them.

A smile barely touched the corners of his mouth. "Morning, Diana."

*Diana...*

There was something in the way he said her name. Something possessive, even a little subversive. It sent a shiver up her spine, sent little electric shocks to the far recesses of her body.

"Did you sleep well?" he asked.

"Surprisingly, yes," she said.

His nod was slow. He bent down, picked up a shopping bag she only now noticed on the floor, and held it out to her. She took it, careful not to get too close, not to let her fingers brush against his.

"What's this?"

"I thought you might need a few things," he said. "Come have breakfast. There's coffee."

He turned, giving her a clear view of his tight ass before he disappeared into the hall.

*Get a grip, Diana. This is no time to explore your childhood crush.*

She peeked into the bag and caught sight of folded silk and wool, cotton and lace. How on earth had Leo managed to find her new clothes between last night and this morning? Had he chosen them himself? And were those new knickers under the pants and blouse?

Her cheeks burned at the thought of him choosing something so personal for her. She dropped the bag like it was on fire, then turned her attention to Leo's bureau. She was looking for an elastic band when his voice traveled to her from the kitchen.

"This food isn't going to eat itself, Diana."

She sighed, then gave up and made her way to the kitchen. He was leaning against the counter in front of the coffee pot, holding a steaming mug. Coffee and a barefoot, morning-tousled Leo? Who could blame her for being distracted, even under the circumstances?

She approached the counter. "Where are the cups?"

He held out the cup in his hand.

"Thank you." She took a sip of the hot coffee, avoiding his eyes. When she finally dared to meet his gaze, he was looking at the hair springing wildly around her head. She laughed, reached up with one hand to touch it. "Still crazy, right? I looked for an elastic, but I couldn't find one."

He lifted a hand, touched a curl, twisted it around one of his fingers, his eyes on hers. She couldn't breathe. Couldn't take her eyes off his. And now she remembered why she'd never been to Leo's apartment. Why they always met in pubs and restaurants.

They were controllable environments. Places designed to keep Leo at a distance. To keep them separated by a table or a crowd of people.

This... This was dangerous.

"Your hair is beautiful," he said, his voice low. "Like the rest of you."

She was still reeling from the words, still wondering if she'd imagined them, when he turned away, busying himself with something on the counter like it hadn't happened.

"Have a seat," he said. "I hope you like bacon and pancakes."

She lowered herself into one of the chairs around a roughly hewn but well designed dining table. As Leo came toward her bearing two plates heaped with food, she thought the table could have been a metaphor for the man in front of her. She shook her head a moment later to dispel the notion.

She did *not* need to think about Leo being roughly hewn.

Or well designed.

He set the plates down and took the other chair, then turned the mug in his hand before speaking.

"Maggie didn't make it, Diana." He met her eyes. "I'm sorry, love."

She shook her head, swallowed the coffee that threatened to make its way back up her throat. "How do you know?"

"I contacted my friends on the police force. Did some quiet fishing."

She pushed the plate of food away as tears sprang to her eyes. "I can't believe it. Evan..."

"Her son," Leo said softly.

Diana nodded. When she looked at him, his features were drawn tight. "What will happen to him?"

He hesitated. "I don't know. He's seventeen. I imagine he'll live with his father until he goes to university."

"His father is a bastard," Diana said angrily.

"I'm sorry."

He was. She could hear it in his voice. But still she was angry. She wanted to throw something. To scream. To run. Anything but sit at this table in this flat doing nothing at all.

She stood. "I have to get out of here."

She was unlocking the door when Leo spoke behind her. "Diana, wait."

She froze with her hand on the knob. "I don't want to wait. I need... I need to get out of here."

She opened the door and left before he could stop her.

# Chapter Seven

She was halfway down the block when she felt the hand on her arm. She turned to find Leo holding out a pair of sneakers and a beat up leather jacket.

"It's cold," he said. "I didn't know if you had a chance to try on the new stuff."

She looked at the shoes. "I'm guessing we don't wear the same size."

He shrugged, and she realized that while he was holding out his jacket for her, he was in nothing but shirt sleeves. He must have left the flat in a hurry to catch her.

"It'll do for now." She didn't know what that meant. Would they go back to her apartment? Is that what she was supposed to do? Go home. Go back to work like nothing had happened? "Diana," he said. "Please. Take the jacket."

She slipped it on, then shoved her bare feet into the too-large sneakers. Leo immediately dropped to his knees to tie the laces. She looked down at his head and was transported back to grade school. She couldn't count the times Leo had kneeled at her feet.

To inspect a skinned knee.

To pick up a shiny coin that he would inevitably present to her.

To pick tiny wildflowers she would use to weave a crown.

But it was different now. Now when he stood, he towered over her. He was no longer a boy, a playmate. He was a man. And he was still willing to kneel at her feet.

"Thank you."

"You're welcome." He rubbed the whiskers at his jaw. "There's just one thing."

"What's that?"

"I can't let you walk alone."

She sighed. "Leo, I just need — "

He held up a hand. "I understand, Diana. And I'm happy to follow at a discreet distance. But you were witness to a murder last night." She saw the anguish in his eyes, knew that he hated having to say it out loud. "And you left your bag. Your identification. I'm sure I don't have to explain why it's a bad idea for you to be out and about alone."

"You think they'll come after me?"

He hesitated, like he was considering lying, then exhaled. "I don't know. But I'm not willing to take the chance."

She turned away, used her fingers to pull the hair back from her face. "This is mad. Utterly mad." She turned to face him. "It's time to go to the police."

A shadow passed over his eyes. It was gone a moment later. "Okay."

"Okay?"

He nodded.

She eyed him suspiciously. He'd put up such a fight the night before. Had been so worried about whether or not they could trust the police.

"What aren't you telling me, Leo?"

He sighed. "I have one stop to make first. If you want to go to the police after that, I'll drive you there myself."

"Promise?"

"I promise," he said. "But first we're going to have breakfast." She started to object and he held up a hand to stop her. "I know you don't feel like eating, but if you want justice for Maggie, you need to be strong."

She did want justice for Maggie, and she would tell the police everything she could remember to get it, even if it put her at risk.

"All right."

He tucked her arm in his. "Still want to walk?"

She shook her head. "Let's just get it over with."

They were heading back to the flat when she remembered the name that had drifted through her mind on the heels of sleep.

"I think I remember something," she said, looking up at him as they walked. "Something the man said last night."

"The man who chased you? Or the other one."

She appreciated his avoidance of Maggie and what had happened to her. There would be time enough to mourn her friend later. Now was the time to do right by her, and she could only do that by staying focused on the men who had murdered her.

"I'm not sure," she said. "It was when they were in the office. I was in the hall."

Leo held the door open to his building. "What do you remember?"

"It's a name, I think. Benny Saff."

"Benny Saff?" He made sure the door was locked behind them before following her up the stairs.

"I'm pretty sure that's what he said."

"Does it mean anything to you?" he asked.

"No," she said. "And I can't even be sure it's English. It's just something that jumped out at me when they were talking, one of the things that didn't sound like it fit with the other stuff they were saying."

He opened the door to the flat. "Why didn't it fit?"

She thought about it. "I can't explain it. It just… felt like a name."

"I'll look into it," he said. "Why don't you finish breakfast while I take a shower? Then we'll head out."

She wasn't sure she could eat. Maggie's death sat like a lead balloon in her stomach. But Leo was right; she needed to be strong for Maggie — and for Evan. There would be time later for grief.

She headed to the dining room while Leo made his way down the hall. A few minutes later, she heard the water running in the bathroom. She poured herself a fresh cup of coffee and sat down at the dining table. The food was cold, but she forced herself to take bites anyway. Her eyes wandered the flat as she ate, and she tried to imagine Leo watching TV on the overstuffed couch, putting his feet on the rustic coffee table, maybe snuggling with a woman late at night.

She couldn't. The place was nice, but it lacked Leo's presence, the quiet strength and warmth that he brought to every situation, every room. She had been able to feel it even when they were teenagers. She would walk down the staircase and know he was there before she ever reached the bottom. She wouldn't even have to hear his voice. She just knew.

It didn't feel like Leo was here. It didn't feel like he'd ever been here.

Which wasn't that strange. She worked a lot, too. Traveled a lot. Judging from all the times they'd been able to meet on the road, Leo was probably home as little as she was. She wondered if her apartment felt as empty. If it felt cold in spite of the designer furniture and all the care she'd taken decorating it. The truth is, she didn't like being there very much. It was lonely. Silent in a way that would have been hard to explain, even when she listened to music or on the rare occasions when she watched a movie on her perfect ivory sofa.

What were they both running from?

She put her cup and plate in the sink, then went to the bedroom to get dressed. She forced herself not to look at the bathroom door as she passed. Forced herself not to think of Leo, naked and wet in the shower. But then she was closing the door to the bedroom, and her gaze snagged on a sliver of white tile.

He hadn't closed the door. Not all the way.

*Look away, look away, look away...*

Except she couldn't. Her eyes were pulled to the crack in the doorway, past the white tile, the steam rising from the hot water to the blurry figure moving behind the foggy shower door.

He was bent over a little, that much she could tell. He moved his hands over his legs, and for a moment, it was like they were her hands. She could almost feel his big thighs under her palms, feel his muscles tense as she worked her way up to his muscular buttocks. She could feel his skin slip under the soap in her hands, could hear his breath become labored as she moved her hands down the ridges of his stomach, reaching for his —

The water shut off, and she was immediately pulled from her fantasy. What the hell was she doing?

She closed the door to the bedroom before she could catch a glimpse of Leo stepping naked from the shower. That was the last thing she needed.

Obviously.

Leaning her head against the door, she forced herself to breath slowly, to try and calm the too-rapid beating of her heart. This whole situation had thrown her off balance. It was completely understandable. She'd been witness to a murder. Not just any murder — the murder of someone important to her. She'd fled for her life, dodged bullets, raced through the city in the dark of night, half expecting to be killed at any moment.

It was only natural that she would be acting irrationally.

She jumped as a knock sounded at the door.

"Are you decent?" Leo asked from the other side.

She straightened, drew in a deep breath. Thank god she hadn't started to change. "Perfectly decent."

The door opened, and he walked in wearing nothing but a towel. It was hung low on his waist, barely clinging to his hips from what she could see. She knew she was staring, but her eyes seemed to have a will of their own. His hair was damp from the shower and darker than usual, the way it had been when they went swimming as kids. She wanted to slip her hands into it, feel the strands of it in her fingers as she tugged his lips to hers.

His chest was wide, and strong, the muscles perfectly sculpted, the ridges of his pecs narrowing to corded abs which only narrowed further to the trim waist, a perfect showcase for the line of hair that started at his naval and disappeared beneath the towel.

She could step toward him, reach him in three steps. It would only take one tug and the towel would be at their feet. She could wrap her arms around his neck, press her body against his. It would be cool and slightly damp. She could lift her leg, wrap it around his thigh. Would he lift her off the ground, allow her to wrap her legs around his waist, to press her soaking pussy against his cock?

"Diana?"

She forced her gaze upward only to find him staring at her. Was it her imagination that there was a knowing look in his eyes? The shadow of a grin on his mouth? She busied herself looking through the shopping bag he'd given her earlier.

"Hmm-mmm?"

"Are you all right?" he asked behind her.

"I'm fine," she said. "Just a little out of sorts." It wasn't a lie.

"I'll get dressed in the other room," he said. "Give you some privacy."

She didn't turn around. "Thank you."

The door clicked quietly behind him as he disappeared into the hall. She dropped onto the bed, clutching the pile of new clothes in her hands.

She needed to go to the police immediately. For Maggie, first and foremost. But also because she couldn't stay here with Leo. Couldn't rely on him for protection. Not when it was becoming more and more obvious that she was her own worst enemy.

# Chapter Eight

He drove through London and continued outside the city. He was grateful Diana hadn't asked where they were going. He was still debating the merit of telling her the truth: that he was a career criminal. That he worked with people who were both dangerous and violent. That he himself was both dangerous and violent when the situation called for it.

That he was in love with her and had been since he'd first helped her up on that playground all those years ago.

He told himself it wasn't the right time. Wasn't the right circumstance. The last thing Diana needed was another shock. Deep down, he knew it was an excuse. A convenient one, but an excuse nonetheless. The truth is, he feared her reaction. Feared she would no longer trust him, or even worse, that she would no longer want him in her life. If that were to happen, he wouldn't even be able to blame her. And yet he didn't want to think about his life without the bright spot that was Diana Barrett. She was his sun.

Had been for as long as he could remember.

He navigated the car off the highway and wound his way through the streets outside London to a generic looking office building. Pulling into the parking lot made him feel better. It looked like any other company where people pushed paper all day. He would use his cover story. Tell Diana it was a friend's information technology company. He felt like a bastard lying yet again, but this wasn't the time nor the place to spill his guts.

*No, that had been back at the flat, you lying coward.*

He silenced the inner voice. There was enough time to feel like shit later, and he had no doubt he would do so.

"What is this?" Diana asked as they walked toward the nondescript glass doors at the side of the building.

"It's a friend's company," he said, punching numbers into the keypad next to the door. A muffled beep sounded from inside the walls of the building, and he pulled open the door. "I called early this morning. I think they might have some information on the men who were at the bank last night."

She nodded, a shadow crossing her features. His fists tightened at his sides. It was an involuntary reaction: the desire to hurt someone who had hurt Diana. Bloodlust for the pain of someone who had caused her pain. He had felt it when they were kids. Had had to count to ten in an effort to keep himself from pummeling anyone who teased her, and later, any boy who looked at her too long and hard. He knew instinctively that while Diana's patience seemed boundless, she wouldn't like that about him. And he still wanted her to like everything about him.

They stepped into a small hall with an empty, glassed-in reception area. The carpet was somewhere on the color spectrum between blue and gray, something that was probably bought by every company in London looking to save a buck. Farrell wasn't cheap. He spent money where it was necessary. Where it mattered. But the headquarters of their digital operation was meant to be under the radar, and Farrell was good at playing the part.

Any part.

But Leo obviously still had a lot to learn if he was having so much trouble keeping the truth from Diana. He fished out his keys and opened the door to another long hall, then closed it securely behind them.

"You have a key to your friend's company?" Diana asked.

"It's for emergencies." Leo almost winced as he said it. "In case something happens to him."

She nodded, her brow furrowed as she processed all the information.

They moved down the hall, past large rooms lined with computers. Some of the chairs were manned by people staring intently at the screens or typing furiously. Others were empty. There was no noise except for the tapping of keys, no Muzak to give the place ambience. The coders and hackers they had on staff had their own rituals. They came armed with headphones and smart phones, with an array of food — some of it imported from other countries — and wearing everything from hipster flannel and skinny jeans to three piece suits. The people who worked at Digital Operations weren't of the same ilk as the people in the rest of Farrell's operations. They weren't hired to scare people. To hurt them.

They were hired for their skill at coding and hacking, their ability to trace a well-hidden IP address or access systems with multiple firewalls and one-of-a-kind security measures.

They didn't hire themselves out. Didn't take corporate clients the way Nico Vitale had in New York. Farrell was all about Farrell, and now, about Jenna, the woman who'd once left him for New York, and Lily, their daughter. Everything he did, including the Digital Operations Center, was done to increase his power — and his monetary return — over London's organized crime. The DOC allowed them to hack computer systems that gave them firsthand knowledge of police activity, information from associates that allowed them to increase their profit margin, and most importantly, a heads up when someone had turned traitor — or when they were thinking about it.

"Leo! There you are!"

He turned toward the voice, his gaze landing on a tall, slender woman with long blond hair and a wide smile that was more suited to the red carpet than Farrell's hidden DOC.

"Here I am," he said, turning to Diana. "Diana, this is Briony. Briony, Diana Barrett."

He wasn't worried about Briony giving anything away. She'd proven time and again to be as secure as one of the vaults at Abbott Bank. She would answer his questions directly, but she would volunteer nothing.

They were all trained to do exactly the same.

She tucked a piece of hair behind one of her ears and held out a hand. "So nice to meet you, Diana. Welcome to our humble abode."

Diana smiled. "Thank you."

"We have that information all cued up for you in the

conference room," Briony said. She was slightly nervous around him, a product of his position as Farrell's second-in-command. He didn't like the deference — he never had — and he hurried forward, avoiding her eyes.

"Can I get you something?" Briony asked behind him. "Coffee? Tea? Water?"

"Diana?"

"No, thank you," she said.

"Great," Briony said. "Let me grab my laptop. I'll meet you in the conference room."

Leo led Diana to the end of the hall. The room at the end of it was monopolized by a long table of polished wood and three enormous screens mounted to one of the walls.

Leo pulled out a chair. Diana lowered herself into the plush leather, and Leo took the seat next to her. She looked around, her eyes taking in the room. It was more luxurious than the rest of the office, something that wouldn't go unnoticed. Diana always had an eye for the finer things, yet another reason they weren't on the same playing field. He saw the flicker of interest in her eyes as she combed the simple but high-end furnishings, the expensive electronic equipment, the glowing mahogany of the conference table.

"Sorry about that," Briony said, closing the door behind her. She sat at the head of the table and set up her laptop, then looked to Leo for approval. He nodded, and a picture bloomed to life on one of the television screens.

He heard Diana's soft gasp beside him, knew she was shocked by the image of two men striding across the bank's lobby. He reached out, took her hand under the table. He'd wanted to spare her this, but he wouldn't be able to protect her unless she agreed not to go to the police. And she wouldn't agree to that unless he made it clear how much danger she would be in if she did.

"Two men entered the lobby of Abbot Bank of London five hours after closing." Briony spoke in a clipped voice. This wasn't personal for her. It was just another job, another task handed down from on high. "We don't know how they got in, although there was no evidence on the cameras of any kind of force, not during their entry anyway."

"How did you get this?" Diana said next to him.

"We hacked into the security cameras at Abbott," Briony said simply. "It's what we do."

Diana pulled her arm away from Leo's grasp, turned her eyes back to the screen. "Go ahead."

"The men continued despite protestations from the guard, who was promptly shot." Leo watched as the men on the camera raised their weapons, the guns flaring as they fired. Diana flinched next to him as Briony continued. "They went to the elevators, which by all accounts, they took to the fifteenth floor."

"No time gap?" Leo asked.

"Nothing significant," Briony said. "It took them thirty seconds to reach the elevators after shooting the guard, and another fifty-six seconds to emerge in the executive lobby. It checks out."

Leo nodded, and she continued.

"The suspects exited on the thirteenth floor, where they continued through the lobby and open work area to the office of Margaret Kinsley." The image on the screen switched angles. Briony had obviously edited the footage together from multiple cameras to give them a continuous look at the path the men had taken.

"Was anyone else in the office at the time?" Leo asked.

"Only Miss Barrett."

"Continue."

"The men entered Ms. Kinsley's office at approximately 10:59PM."

Maggie's image blossomed on the screen. Leo watched as she looked up from her computer, her mouth opening in shock as the men entered her office. She got up from her desk, stumbled backward toward the window that overlooked the city. The men advanced, and one of them grabbed her, forced her back into her desk chair.

"I don't want to see this," Diana said.

Briony looked at Leo as if for permission. He nodded, and the screen went black.

"Are these the men who chased you?" Leo asked Diana.

"One of them," she said, her head in her hands. "The shorter one."

Leo looked at Briony. "Who are they?"

Two of the television screens came back to life, this time with pictures of the two men and a list of basic statistics.

"We put the images through the facial recognition software and got a hit on both. The one on the left, the shorter one as Miss Barrett said, is Omar Toumi. Spent a lot of time in Algerian prison, rumored ties to organized crime there."

Leo let that sink in. Their business had once had rules. An honor code of sorts. But that had all ended with the fall of the Syndicate over a year ago. Now their business was like the Wild West.

No law. No rules. No honor code.

The name wasn't familiar, but he wanted to ask if Omar Toumi was known to them. If they'd worked with him before. He glanced at Diana and decided against it. There was only so much she could be expected to hear without asking more questions. He would do the homework himself in private.

"And the other one?" Leo asked.

"Antonis Stavros."

Leo looked at her. "Antonis Stavros?" The name was familiar, but he couldn't quite place it.

She nodded. "Ties to the Greek mob, rumored dealings with arms dealers in Russia, the Middle East, Israel... You name it."

Leo rubbed his jaw as he processed the information, trying to formulate the questions he could conceivably ask in Diana's company.

"Any ties to Abbott that we know of?" he asked.

"We're still working on that. They have surprisingly good security. I'll let you know when we crack it, although that's no guarantee. A lot of it's done by account number. Might not find anything even if Stavros did have an account there."

"What do we know about his family? His home?"

The image on the screen changed to one of a map. Leo immediately recognized Morocco, the Alboran sea running between it and Spain. The image teased his mind, and he spent a few seconds trying to put his finger on the knowledge that hid there.

"Hometown is Thessaloniki, Greece. Has a compound there, and a sister."

"Would she help us?" Leo didn't have to be more specific. They needed to find Antonis Stavros. Leo needed to put him down — and anyone else who knew about Diana — before they came after her in earnest.

"Doubt it," Briony said. "She's married to her brother's best friend."

"Why are we even having this conversation?" Diana asked. "It's not our problem. It's up to the police to find these men, although I'm sure they'll be grateful for the legwork you've done."

Leo sat in silence for a minute, debating his next move before finally deciding he didn't have a choice. "Put it up."

Diana looked from him to Briony, clearly confused. A moment later, the center screen filled with a list of names. Leo waited, letting Diana's eyes travel the length of the list as she read. Leo read as well, although he knew the list by heart. It was broken up by districts and divisions, with the names of their informants listed under each one.

Diana stood. "What is this?"

"I think you know," Leo said softly.

"I'd like to hear it from you."

"It's a list of police officers on the take from organized crime." Leo avoided looking at Briony, knowing Diana would pick up on the cue, would see it as a sign that there were more secrets to be revealed.

"How do you know this?" she asked.

"We know," Leo said.

"How?"

Leo slammed his hand down on the table, then forced himself to draw in a calming breath before standing, facing her. "The people who work here are good at finding things out. You're just going to have to trust me. We know."

She stared into his eyes, like she might find the answers to all her questions there. Then she turned away, pacing the room. "This is why you brought me here first," she said. "To keep me from going to the police."

"To protect you from them," Leo corrected her.

"There has to be some way…" she started. "Some way to get their help."

"Everyone talks on the police force," Briony said. "If you go to them, it's almost inevitable that word will get out you're cooperating."

Leo held his breath as she talked, then released it when she avoided the issue of the DOC's status as one of Farrell's criminal enterprises. One that was a crucial part of the business Leo conducted on a daily basis.

"So what am I supposed to do?" Diana's cheeks were flushed as she turned back to Leo, her eyes flashing. "Hide? Change my name?"

"I need some time," Leo said. "Time to find out more about Stavros and Toumi. Time to figure out a way to get them in without alerting the wrong people. Without letting them know where you are."

"They could be getting away right now," Diana said. "They could be anywhere. The longer we wait, the greater the chance they'll have disappeared."

"They aren't going to disappear," he said. "Not right away."

"How do you know?"

Briony answered for him. "Because they have to find you first."

## Chapter Nine

Diana looked out the window, her mind spinning. Seeing the pictures of the men who had shot Maggie had sent a visceral pool of dread seeping like an oil slick through her body.

Fear.

Panic.

Loss.

She was still processing the trauma of what had happened, the reality that Maggie was dead. And then there was the other stuff — the quiet office full of hackers working at computer terminals like it was any other job. Briony, who seemed familiar with Leo.

And Leo, who seemed familiar with it all.

She didn't know what it meant, but she had the sense that she didn't have all the information. It was the same feeling she'd sometimes get doing old jigsaw puzzles with her father as an adolescent. The nagging feeling as they got close to completing the picture that there were missing pieces, her brain doing the calculation and coming up short.

"I'm sorry," Leo said, navigating the car back to the flat.

"It's not your fault London is full of crooked police."

He almost seemed to wince. "There are lots of good ones, too. Keeping you hidden is just a precaution."

She turned her face back to the window. "I know."

They rode the rest of the way in silence, the city passing by on the other side of the glass. She didn't speak again until Leo pulled next to the curb two blocks from his flat.

"Why are we parking so far away?"

"Almost impossible to find parking up front," he said. "I just got lucky last time."

She got out of the car and they started down the sidewalk toward the apartment. "What now?"

He hesitated, like he was choosing his words carefully. "I'm going to call in some favors, see if I can get help flushing these guys out."

She stared up at him. "That's a bad idea, Leo. These men are dangerous."

He'd always been her protector, a sentinel whose sole purpose it seemed was to keep her safe. But this wasn't a playground bully or a high school mean girl. These men were killers, and Leo was a media executive, more familiar with laptops and business class than assassins and arms dealers. She wouldn't be able to survive it if he was hurt because of her. Just the thought of living in the world without Leo sent a sharp jab into the center of her heart, like a cleaver cleanly dividing it in two.

"Don't worry," he said, grabbing her hand. "Everything will be okay."

She wondered how he could sound so sure. It was almost enough to distract her from the feel of her hand in his, the soft scratch of his skin against the softness of her own. He'd held her hand before, but there was something different about it this time. Something intimate and loaded with meaning.

She pushed the thought aside. She was being fanciful, probably just because she'd seen him nearly naked not three hours before.

They were half a block from the flat when Leo suddenly slowed down. She looked up to find his mouth set in a grim line, his jaw clenched.

"What is it?" she asked.

He looked down at her, still walking, but more slowly now. "I need you to do exactly as I say," he said. "You'll have questions. I won't be able to answer them until later, but I will answer them."

"You're scaring me." The alarm bells ringing in her mind made it hard to think straight, but she was sure of this much.

"Don't be scared. I won't let anything happen to you. Just do as I say, okay?"

She didn't have time to answer. A moment later three men

stepped out of a doorway near Leo's flat. They might have been anybody, but instinct told her that wasn't the case.

These were people who meant her — and Leo — harm.

They were big, dressed in black and wearing bulky overcoats. But it wasn't until they reached inside their jackets that she understood how much trouble she and Leo were in. And then the impossible was happening, because Leo was shoving her behind him and reaching into his own jacket, withdrawing his own weapon.

She was struggling to process the image of Leo — her Leo — wielding an evil looking gun with what seemed to be perfect calm. But there was no time to process anything. One minute Leo was withdrawing his gun: the next, a hail of bullets erupted around them. She had to fight the urge to hit the concrete, cover her head. She would be a sitting duck then, and instinct was screaming at her to move.

Leo backed them up into an alley, then flattened himself against the brick of an old building, The gun seemed perfectly at home in his hand. He held it near his chest, and she could tell from the calm intensity on his face that he was calculating. A moment later, he spoke.

"I'm going to hold them off here," he said. "You run for the other end of the alley."

"I'm not leaving you," she said.

"You're not. But I need you to get a head start. Once I stop shooting, they'll come for us, and I want you as close to the street as you can get. Wait for me when you get there. We're going to make a run for the Tube."

"What about the car?" she asked.

"Too easy to get stuck in traffic this time of day," he said. "Easier to get lost underground."

She nodded. "Okay."

"Go," he said.

She sprinted for the other end of the alley as he started firing. He was met with answering fire from the men who had been in front of his building. The bullets fell like a cacophonous symphony, embedding themselves in the surrounding brick, ricocheting off concrete. She'd almost reached the end of the alley when the gunfire fell silent behind her. She glanced back and saw Leo sprinting toward her, his weapon still drawn. He pulled her around the corner of the building and into the street just as another storm of gunfire roared behind them.

He took her hand, pulling her through the streets, expertly dodging pedestrians as they made their way home from work, people walking their dogs, tourists scoping out the city. They flew through them all, and the crowd seemed to part as if by magic, either because Leo knew exactly where to direct them or because people saw them coming.

Diana's lungs were burning by the time she saw the sign for Paddington station. Leo hit the stairs full throttle, letting go of her hand as he took the stairs two at a time with a backward glance to make sure she was with him. He took her hand again when they hit the bottom, then wound his way toward the front of the waiting train, elbowing through the crowd to make sure they got a spot. Then they were on board, smashed against one side as more people piled in.

She drew air into her bursting lungs, trying to calm her ragged breath, the rapid beating of her heart, as Leo pulled her toward the back of the train. The conductor's voice came over the loudspeaker, announcing their destination in a scratchy voice too distorted by the intercom to be understood. And then the bells were sounding, indicating the doors were about to close.

Except it wasn't fast enough. Movement caught Diana's eye through the window, and she saw two of the black-clad men racing for the doors of the train.

"There," she said.

"I know." Leo's voice was grim.

She lost sight of the men in the crowd, had no way of knowing if they'd made it on board before the train started moving. Leo was still pulling her to the back as the train barreled through the tunnels under London, rattling across the tracks at what seemed like warp speed as they raced through the train cars, bumping into people and pushing them aside in their hurry to stay ahead of the men who may or may not have made it on board.

The train was slowing down, Leo and Diana pushing through the doors into the second to last car, when Diana heard a voice shout above the crowd.

"There!"

She glanced back in time to see the two men from the tube platform pushing into the car she and Leo were vacating.

"They're too close," she said.

Leo didn't miss a beat. "Just stay with me."

The train had almost come to a stop.

Almost.

They were entering the last car as the wheels squeaked against the tracks, skidding as the conductor applied the breaks. Leo pulled her through the crowd and headed for the door at the back of the final car.

She glanced behind her and thought she saw the men pushing through the crowd. Then the train was stopped, the doors were opening, and Leo was dragging her out onto the subway platform, racing toward the stairs that would take them back onto the streets of the city.

She was having a hard time breathing, but her body pushed her relentlessly forward, spurred on by its desire for survival. Leo half dragged her up the stairs, breaking out into the weak afternoon light. She thought they would run again. Instead, Leo pulled her into the vestibule of a small boutique. She fought panic, sure they would be caught.

*I won't let anything happen to you. Just do as I say.*

And then, behind them in the reflection of the glass, she saw the men race past, seemingly unaware that she and Leo were right there. She couldn't believe it would work, but a split second after they passed, Leo grabbed her arm and pulled her back onto the sidewalk. They went back the way they came, down the steps to the tube. Then they were on the train again, speeding away from the station.

She drew in a deep breath, hardly daring to believe they'd escaped the people who had been chasing them. People undoubtedly sent by the man who'd killed Maggie.

But they had. She was alive. They both were.

She looked up at Leo, a new realization dawning on her. She was alive because of him. Because he'd been carrying a gun. Because he'd known how to use it.

And that meant he'd been lying to her all along.

# Chapter Ten

She looked around as they stepped onto the boat, half expecting someone to burst out of the crowd with a weapon. But there was nothing in the crowd to give her alarm. Just the usual group of tourists looking to see London's sights from the water of the Thames.

Leo kept hold of her arm and guided her to the stern. He hadn't spoken once since they'd escaped the men who had been chasing them, and she hadn't pressed him. She didn't know where they were going, but now she understood something new about Leo.

He wasn't a marketing executive for Global Media.

Whatever he was, he was someone who knew what he was doing. Who knew how to handle a weapon — and an enemy. Who knew how to run and how to hide. She felt instinctively that she was in capable hands, and she'd let him lead her out of the Tube and through the streets, down to the dock that was the boarding spot for the Thames river tour.

They leaned against the railing as the boat moved away from the dock. She watched the water open up between the boat and the pier, felt the boat shift under her feet. She was in no hurry to hear what Leo had to say, both because it would kill once and for all her belief that she really knew him, and because whatever he told her would be the next step in what was an epic upheaval of her life.

The boat had picked up steam, the tinny voice of the tour guide crackling through the loudspeaker, when Leo finally spoke.

"Ask."

She looked up at him. "Why don't you just tell me?"

He looked out over the water, his jaw tight. Even now, with all the secrets between them, she wanted nothing more than to touch him. To slip her hand around his neck, press her body to his, tell him it was all right.

"I don't work for Global Media," he finally said. "I never have."

She sucked in a breath. She'd known. Of course, she had. But hearing him say it made it seem all the more real. She wasn't sure she was ready for what he would say next, but there was no time for fragility.

"I think I've figured out that part," she said.

He faced her, his eyes hardening. "I'm a criminal, Diana. I've never been anything but that."

She swallowed hard, torn between wanting to hit him and wanting to ease the pain in his eyes. "We can debate that later. Right now I just want to know how you did what you did back there. And I want to know why you have a gun."

He nodded. "Have you ever heard of the Syndicate?"

"Of course," she said. "A bunch of people were arrested last year. It was a mob thing, wasn't it?"

"It was a lot more sophisticated than a mob thing," he said. "But that's the gist of it. The Syndicate controlled organized crime around the world."

"What does that have to do with you?" she asked.

"I worked for them," he said. "Here in London."

She blinked, trying to process his words. She didn't know what she expected. Maybe that he worked for MI6 or Interpol. Maybe even that he was a hired assassin of some kind.

That's what she got for watching too many movies.

But this? The mob? Her Leo — her beautiful, gentle Leo — a member of the mafia?

That, she hadn't expected.

"You were part of the mob?" She felt stupid repeating it, but she needed time to get her head around what he was saying.

He looked at her. "I still am, Diana."

"But... they were put out of business. By the FBI in the States, wasn't it? And Interpol?"

He shook his head. "It's not that simple. You don't shut down that kind of business with the flip of a switch. It's been around for hundreds of years. There were organizations all over the world, each one with a leader and several hundred soldiers. The criminal investigation took out the people at the very top — a few of them anyway. For everyone else it's been more or less business as usual."

The announcer pointed out Buckingham Palace in the distance, and the passengers swung their heads in the direction of the stately building that had been home of the British monarchy for over three hundred years. She gripped the railing, forcing the cold from the metal into her skin as a way to keep herself present. To keep from covering her ears and refusing to listen. When the tour guide was done speaking, she tried to find the words she needed to clarify Leo's statement.

"So the London mob is still in business," she said. "And you work for them."

The wind blew across the water, ruffling Leo's hair until the stray lock fell over his forehead. He pushed it back, then spoke slowly. "A more accurate statement would be that I help run it."

She shook her head, fighting the urge to laugh hysterically. "You run the London mob?"

"No, but I work for the man who does."

Memories of Leo flashed through her mind.

Leo rushing to meet her by the river in Prague, wearing a leather jacket, looking disheveled.

Leo getting a text over late night drinks in Tokyo and rushing to leave, despite the fact that she could tell he didn't want to go.

Leo meeting her for coffee in New York, then expertly steering her away as a fight broke out in the crowd.

She suddenly felt stupid. She'd never gone to visit him at Global. Had never offered to meet him there for drinks after work. She'd been all too happy to let him come to her. To meet him in pubs and restaurants. To have him for the occasional dinner at her parent's house during holidays and weekends when they both happened to be home.

*Because you're in love with him*, a voice whispered in her head. *Because you've always been in love with him. Because you knew if you got too close you would ruin everything by telling him.*

"So you… what?" she asked. "Hurt people? Kill people?"

She saw the pain flash across his face in the moment before he composed his features into a mask of indifference. The expression was intimately familiar to her. It was the same one he'd worn when they were kids and someone made fun of his too-short pants. The same one he wore when he'd asked Abigail Dickenson to the dance and she'd laughed in his face. He'd learned early to buffer himself against the judgement of others. That he was doing it now with her made her feel like someone had cracked open her chest with a crowbar.

"Sometimes," he said. "Yes."

She shook her head. "But… why? You could have gone to university…"

He laughed. "So I could spend four more years with a bunch of prats who think they are better than me?"

"It's different at university…" But the words sounded lame even to her own ears. Nothing was very different anywhere. That's one thing she'd learned being out in the world.

He leveled his eyes at her, a silent challenge.

She sighed. "All right, they aren't always different. But you could have done anything, Leo. Why this?"

He shrugged, and she knew from the defiant set of his shoulders that he was shutting down. She wouldn't get anything more of out him. Not now. Not about this. And they had bigger problems. More immediate problems.

"So what now?" she asked.

He ran a hand through his hair and surveyed the swiftly approaching dock. The tour was all but over, London's famous tourist attractions summarized and photographed by everyone on board.

"We have to get out of the city," he said.

"We could go home," she suggested. "Back to Cornwall."

He shook his head. "That would only put your parents in danger."

She fought panic. "Do you think those men will go after my parents?"

She was glad he seemed to consider the question, that he didn't answer quickly simply to ease her mind. It meant he was telling the truth. "Not if you don't contact them. Something bigger is going on. My guess is they want out of the city as badly as we do."

She crossed her arms over her body. "Not badly enough to leave me alone."

"They were just covering their bases at my place," he said. "Going through a list of close friends — probably from the phone you left in your office — to see if they could find you. I don't think they're going to turn the city upside down to do it. Which doesn't mean we should take the chance."

"I'm not coming up with an answer here," she said as the boat bumped gently against the dock. They stayed at the back of the crowd as the other passengers started disembarking. She watched Leo's face as he scanned the crowd on the pier.

"I am." He took her hand. "Stay close."

# Chapter Eleven

Leo looked around the plush apartment, wondering what Diana was thinking. The place was nice. Too nice for Hyrum Seaver, the twenty-two-year-old uni drop out who owned it. Leo wasn't surprised. The market for authentic looking forgeries was always hot, and never more so than in the twenty-first century when it was nearly impossible to get past chip readers and databases and all the technology that made being off the grid virtually impossible.

But Hyrum knew his shit. Passports, driver's licenses, birth certificates. Hyrum Seaver could reproduce them all.

And from the looks of the high end flat overlooking the river, business was booming.

Leo had thought about going to the club, asking Farrell for help. But Farrell and Jenna had only been back from Paris for a few weeks. They'd been through hell over the past couple of months. They deserved time with their daughter, and Leo knew Farrell was busy getting things under control with the business.

This was his problem. He would take care of it himself.

Still, he'd felt bad calling Farrell, asking for time off, being cagey about his reasons. But it was better than involving his boss — his friend — in yet another mess.

"You'll have to pay extra for the rush."

Leo turned his attention on the guy sitting at the computer in front of him. "It's fine."

Leo didn't love bringing Diana here. In fact, he didn't love anything about this, not the least of which was having to take her with him as he tried to find the men who were hunting her.

But he didn't have a choice. He couldn't leave her in London, even with a friend. Despite what he'd told her, he wasn't at all sure Antonis Stavros wouldn't come after her. Leo had no doubt the man's informants had been deputized at the police station, but a man like that had connections everywhere. He might flee the country, but that didn't mean he wouldn't leave people behind to find Diana.

Which meant she had to come with him, arguably just as dangerous given that he'd finally figured out why the name she remembered the men saying felt so familiar.

"I need a picture," Hyrum said, looking nervously at Diana. Behind his computer monitor, he was perfectly at ease, a king surveying his kingdom. But his nervousness around Diana made him look like the geeky college kid he should have been.

"Diana," Leo said, directing her to the chair on the other side of Hyrum's desk.

She sat down, and Hyrum tapped a few buttons on his keyboard. "I'll need a couple hours. You guys are welcome to hang in the living room while you wait."

"That's okay," Leo said. "I have a few things to do. We'll be back in two hours."

He led Diana out of the flat and onto London's darkened streets. Night had fallen while they'd been inside Hyrum's flat. Leo relaxed a little. He was comfortable in the shadows. Had been living there all his life.

"Where are we going?" Diana asked.

"We're going to need a few things. Come on."

They stopped at a discount store and picked up a change of clothes, toiletries, and two backpacks. They would be suspicious going through customs with no baggage, and Leo was careful to choose things that would help them pass as a young couple on a budget holiday. The thought caused him a pang of regret. He would much rather be traveling with Diana on holiday, preparing to lay next to her on a sandy beach, than fleeing to a part of the world that was as dangerous as it was mysterious.

He wasn't surprised that Diana didn't ask many questions. It was one of the things he'd always loved about her. She seemed to know when he needed time. Seemed perfectly willing to give him all the space he needed before he was ready to talk. And he was under no illusion; she was likely still figuring things out for herself. Figuring out how she felt about the fact that everything she believed about him had been a lie.

*Not everything*, he corrected himself. *Not the way he felt about her. The way he'd always felt about her.*

They left the store with an hour to spare and found a dimly lit pub with a nondescript sign and a blue collar clientele. They were both ravenous, and they passed the time plowing through plates of crispy fried fish washed down with cheap beer. When they were done, they headed back to Hyrum's flat. Leo approached cautiously, wanting to make sure they hadn't been made. It wasn't Hyrum. Leo trusted him as much as he trusted anybody in the business.

But the business bred paranoia. You never knew when someone might trade you for something more valuable. He assumed his connection to Farrell's operation gave him some form of protection, but he wasn't about to risk Diana's life on the bet.

Leo transferred the bags to his left hand so he'd be able to grab his weapon if the situation called for it, but the street outside looked clean, and a few minutes later they were being ushered back into Hyrum's flat.

"Almost done," he said.

His eyes were glassy, and he turned away from them and sat down in front of the computer. Several documents emerged from the printer, and Hyrum spent twenty more minutes carefully applying stamps to the documents, including two that looked like three dimensional holograms. Leo didn't know much about forgeries, but he knew one thing; it was impossible to replicate the holographic stamps that had become standard on identifying documents. The stamps used by Hyrum were the real deal. Farrell didn't even want to know how he'd come into possession of them.

"All set." Hyrum stood and handed the documents to Leo. "The stamps are solid, and the printing technology is about ninety-eight percent there."

Leo raised an eyebrow. "Ninety-eight percent?"

Hyrum shrugged. "It changes fast, mate. We do our best to keep up." He looked over at Diana. "She's not going to have any problem."

Leo knew what Hyrum meant. Diana looked like what she was

— an affluent, educated woman. It wasn't just the expensive clothes Leo had chosen for her or her classic bone structure. It was something about the way she carried herself. About the regal lift of her chin and the way she moved so easily through the world, even now. Like she didn't have a care in the world. As if she could part a crowd like the Red Sea simply by moving through it.

Leo wouldn't have been surprised if she could.

He took the documents from Hyrum and gave them a cursory glance. The name was fake, but the picture was Diana, and everything looked legitimate.

"Thanks." He handed Hyrum a wad of cash, thankful all over again that he'd learned from Farrell's example and stashed a sizable chunk of cash and an alternate set of identification for himself in a safe deposit box in the city. He had gone to the bank after the boat ride on the Thames and withdrawn it all.

Hyrum gripped his hand in the kind of bro handshake Leo despised. "No problem."

"Remember," Leo said. "We were never here."

Hyrum nodded as he walked them to the door. "I know the drill."

Leo and Diana stepped out into the hall. They were almost to the elevator when Hyrum spoke behind them.

"Yo, Leo."

He turned around. "Yeah?"

"Watch your back, mate." He glanced at Diana. "And hers, too."

"You can count on it."

They stepped into the elevator and pushed the button for the ground floor. When they got there, they exited the building, and Leo flagged a cab.

"Heathrow," he told the driver, settling back into the seat.

"Where are we going?" Diana asked.

"Spain." He hesitated, wondering how much he should tell her, then deciding there had been enough secrets between them. "And then Algeria."

## Chapter Twelve

Diana looked out the window of the taxi, trying to adjust to the scenery on the other side of the glass. They'd left London in the dead of night, transferred planes in Tangier, then landed in Almeria, Spain as the sun was just beginning to lighten the sky. She'd slept most of the way, her exhaustion finally overcoming the questions and fears that had been swirling in her head since the night before. She'd woken up to find her head on Leo's shoulder, the crisp cotton of his T-shirt soft under her cheek, his solid strength propping her up, just like always.

She still wasn't sure what Leo planned to do or why they were in Spain, let alone Algeria, which he'd mentioned in passing as they left London. She had questions, and she wasn't some kind of shrinking violet who wouldn't ask them.

But she liked to have her thoughts in order when she looked for answers. It was difficult to get them in the best of situations. Starting with the right questions narrowed the odds significantly. Besides, the drawbridge was still shut tight over Leo's face. He wasn't ready to talk yet. She could wait. She'd been waiting for years.

They wound their way through the seaside town of Almeria as exotic music sounded from the radio in the taxi. She knew they were in Spain, but the proximity to Algeria across the Mediterranean Sea lent a Middle Eastern flavor to the town. The city was a fortress unto itself, built on sloping hills with a castle-like structure perched on a hill at its center. It would have been a difficult one to conquer with the hills at its back and the sea at its front, and she could almost imagine it being attacked by Berber pirates in the 16th century. Now the buildings were pristine and whitewashed, and a series of hotels lined the waterfront where yachts and cruise ships dotted the sapphire water.

They continued toward the water, then passed a string of lush properties, all of them backing up to the white sand beaches of Almeria. They continued past them, gradually leaving behind the more densely packed parts of the city. The land became drier and more scrubby, long stretches of rocky hills punctuated with desert-like shrubs. The sea was a jewel, glittering and stretching into the distance like a blanket of diamonds under the sun.

Finally, the car slowed around a curve, emerging onto a long paved road leading to a large house balanced on the edge of a hill. The taxi came to a stop. Leo helped her out and grabbed the backpacks they'd bought before leaving London. Then they were alone in front of the whitewashed building, watching the taxi disappear around the curve, the waves rolling onto the beach below.

"Come on," Leo said. "You must be tired."

Tired didn't exactly describe the low-level lethargy that had settled into her bones since they boarded the plane in London, but it was close enough. She took in the white stucco structure as she followed him up a pathway to the house. From this side, it looked like a simple home with minimal windows, but when they stepped into the double height foyer, she saw that it had been an illusion.

The house was large and airy, with a wall of glass on the other side that provided an expansive view of the sea. She knew that Morocco and Algiers lay on the other side of it, but there was no sign of land from their perch on the cliff. The water seemed to go on forever. Leo reached for the glass, withdrawing a door she hadn't seen and pulling it back until it disappeared into a pocket in the wall. The sound of the ocean immediately invaded the house, a rhythm of white noise that enveloped her in an immediate calm.

She walked to the window and stepped onto a large balcony, gazed out over the endless blue water. Even the smell of it — dry and salty — made her feel better. She had the sudden sense of being completely alone in the world — no one but Leo, nothing but this place and the glittering sea and the hot sun overhead.

"It's gorgeous," she said. "Is it yours?"

She didn't look at him as she asked the question. He was both her Leo and not her Leo. Someone she knew better than she knew herself, and a complete and utter stranger. Did he have the kind of money that could buy such a place? Was he the kind of person that would buy such a place?

It was only the first of many questions she would have to ask.

"No." He hesitated. "I do own a couple of properties. Nothing this grand. Just little places to escape to when the need arises."

She turned to face him, a new question urgent in her mind. "And do you feel the need to escape often?"

He seemed to think about it. "No. Not often."

She wondered suddenly if he traveled alone. If another woman had stood in this place, looking out over the ocean. If another woman had slept on his shoulder as they flew across the sky. Had slept in his bed when they landed.

The idea caused a violent surge of jealousy to rage through her. She walked back into the house to distract herself. "Who owns this place?"

The living room was modest in size, though obviously well designed and furnished with high end decor. It opened directly onto a dining room, which in turn led to a large kitchen visible from the living room.

"An associate," he said.

She looked at him. "Is that part of your… business? Keeping secrets?"

His eyes darkened. "I'll keep no more secrets from you, Diana. You can ask me anything you like, and I'll tell you the truth. But first you should rest."

"What about Antonis Stavros?" she asked. "Isn't that why we're here?"

"I'm still working on it," he said. "But it's been a long night, and already a long day. I have some things to do before I'll know more. Why don't you shower and rest? We'll have dinner later, and then we'll figure out what to do next."

She felt like she should rebel. She wasn't used to relinquishing control of her everyday life. She lived alone. Went to work and the gym. Made decisions about her present and future. Now she was on the run for her life, and her best friend was dead. It didn't feel like the right time to give up control, even to Leo.

But she was out of her element. She had no idea what to do next. How to find out more information about Antonis Stavros and why he'd killed Maggie.

She nodded. "All right."

He picked up her bag, led her up a set of tile stairs to a second floor hall, and continued into the second room on the left. Like the rest of the house, it was modest in size, grand in design, another wall of windows opening to yet another balcony overlooking the ocean. Was this whole side of the house made up of windows? She resolved to walk down to the beach later and get a look for herself.

"The bathroom's there." He pointed to a half open door, and Diana got a glimpse of more pristine white tile. "There should be towels and everything else you need. If not, just let me know."

"Thank you."

They looked at each other for a long moment, a lifetime of questions weighing heavily between them. He opened his mouth as if to say something, then seemed to change his mind.

"I'll see you in a few hours."

He turned and left the room, leaving Diana to wonder what he might have said. And why he hadn't said it.

# Chapter Thirteen

She woke to the sound of the waves rolling onto the beach below the balcony. She was in a pleasant state of limbo, between the horror of all that had happened and the uncertainty of what would come next. She was in no hurry to re-enter reality, and she stretched her naked body against the crisp, cool sheets and watched as the shadows from the fading sunlight played against the ceiling.

She'd showered right after Leo left her alone in the bedroom, standing under the spray for what had seemed like an hour, letting the water wash off the sweat and grime of travel. When she'd finally shut off the water, she'd dried herself off with one of the thick, white towels and walked naked into the bedroom. The balcony doors let in a wind that was both warm and dry, and she'd crawled between the sheets without a second thought and fallen into a deep and dreamless sleep.

The room had fallen under the spell of dusk when she finally kicked off the sheets, let the ocean breeze lay its fingers on her skin. Her nerve endings came alive, and she thought of Leo, of the way he'd looked when he'd emerged from the shower in London. Of the hard planes of his body and the line of hair that had led under the towel. The way it would feel under her palms, the touch of his lips on hers, the press of his body.

She groaned, squeezing her thighs together to stop the pulsing at her center. What was wrong with her? It was true that she'd found Leo attractive since adolescence when her body had come alive, making her notice boys in a way she'd somehow missed until then. But she'd never wanted them. Never *longed* for them.

Not like this.

Why now when everything had gone to shit? When everything was up in the air with no guarantee she would make it back to her old life alive?

She hit the bed with one fist, then got out of bed. She dug through the discount clothes in the backpack and came away with a painfully short list of options for dinner. Not at all like her expansive closet at home, filled with designer clothes and shoes suitable for every occasion. Sighing, she settled on a maxi dress. It was cheaply made, but when she slipped it over her head, allowing the garment to skim her curves, she was surprised to find that it looked quite good on her. The thin straps highlighted her slender but toned arms, and the white cotton stood in elegant contrast to her dark skin. She turned sideways, pleased with the way it hugged her waist, expanded just enough to showcase the hips of her hourglass figure.

Not bad. Maybe she'd been spending too much money on clothes all this time after all.

She contemplated trying to tame her hair, then gave up and let the springy curls have their way. Finally, she removed a pair of gold sandals from the bag and slipped them on her feet, then touched her lips with gloss. She gave herself one last look in the mirror before slipping into the hall, oddly nervous to see Leo.

Someone was in the kitchen. She could hear the sound of running water, the clank of pots and pans. Did Leo cook? It was something else she didn't know about him in spite of their long friendship. She resolved to correct the oversight immediately. If nothing else, the situation that had thrown them into such close, extended proximity had highlighted her failings as Leo's friend.

Friend being the operative word.

Maybe if she focused on being a good friend to Leo she would stop thinking about him naked.

She stepped into the living room and continued into the kitchen, then stopped in her tracks.

A woman with a long black braid stood with her back to Diana, her hands moving in the water running from the kitchen faucet. Steam rose from a pot on the stove, a cutting board on the counter next to it covered with what looked like parsley and garlic.

A large knife sat on the counter.

Diana looked around, but Leo was nowhere to be seen. She turned her focus back on the woman, still oblivious to Diana's presence, then cleared her throat.

"Hello."

The woman spun, her cheeks flushed. Her smile was shy, and when she smiled, faint wrinkles fanned out from the corners of her eyes.

"Hello. You must be Miss Barrett." Her English was good, with only the faint hint of an accent that didn't sound Spanish.

"Yes," Diana said, moving toward her and holding our her hand.

The woman dried her hands on a towel before taking Diana's hand. "I am Mina."

"It's a pleasure meeting you." Diana looked around the great room and onto the empty balcony beyond. "Do you know where I might find Leo?"

The woman raised an eyebrow. "Leo?"

"Mr. Gage?"

"Oh, yes!" The woman smiled. "Mr. Gage is on the beach."

"Down there?" Diana asked, gesturing to the balcony.

The woman nodded. "He's expecting you."

Diana smiled. "Thank you."

She crossed the living room and stepped onto the balcony. The sunset had turned the sky orange and pink. To the south, the city of Almeria was already lit up for the night, the sea expanding along the coast like an indigo ribbon. It was stunningly beautiful, but it wasn't the scenery that made it hard to breathe.

It was the man on the sand below, walking toward her from farther up the beach.

Leo.

He wore black trousers rolled up at the ankles, his white shirt unbuttoned halfway to his naval. He was looking out to sea as he walked, like the water held the answers to all of his questions. Even from the house she could see that his brow was furrowed, the familiar piece of hair falling over his forehead.

He turned his attention back to the beach, then spotted her. He seemed to hesitate, then raised a hand in greeting. She lifted hers in response, waited for him to make his way down the beach, relishing the opportunity to look at him. To really look at him.

When he neared the house, he called up. "Come down!"

She smiled, then made her way to the stairs that led to the beach. The white dress fluttered deliciously around her bare legs, but when Leo stopped in front of her, she wasn't at all sure the goosebumps on her body were a result of the cool breeze blowing off the water.

He gazed at her for a long moment, his eyes seeming to see everything she'd been thinking all too clearly.

"You look lovely."

Was it her imagination that his voice was gruff?

"Thank you." She averted her eyes, pretended to scan the beach she'd already studied to avoid looking at him. "It's so beautiful."

"It is." She thought he was agreeing with her about the beach, but when she turned to look at him, his eyes were on her.

She swallowed hard. "Who is Mina, the woman in the kitchen?"

"She works for the owner of the property," he said. "I didn't want to leave you to go to the market for supplies, so I asked her to cook for us instead."

So maybe Leo did cook. Interesting.

"That sounds nice. I'm starving." She laughed a little, realizing it was true.

He smiled, looked at her a beat too long.

"What?"

He shook his head a little. "Your laugh. It reminds me of something."

"What does it remind you of?" she asked.

He hesitated, then shook his head again. "I'll let you know when it comes to me."

She had the feeling he was hedging, but she suddenly didn't want to push the issue. Wasn't sure she was ready to handle the truth.

"Shall we?" he asked.

"Shall we…?"

He gestured behind her, and she turned to find a table set up under the balcony, its underside strung with white lights.

She looked up at him. "You did this for me?"

She thought she caught the hint of color in his cheeks before he hurried forward to pull out one of the chairs. "Well, the lights were already here. I just brought down the table and chairs. As long as we're here, we might as well enjoy the view."

She sat down, felt a shiver run up her spine when his fingers brushed against her bare arms. He retreated to the other side of the table and poured wine into her glass. He raised his in a toast.

"To old friends." The words seemed to stick in his throat, and she wondered if he regretted their friendship now. She'd brought him nothing but trouble the last two days.

"To old friends," she said, swallowing around the lump in her throat as she clinked her glass against his.

She heard footsteps on the balcony stairs, and a moment later, Mina appeared with a plate of oysters on a bed of crushed ice. She set it between them on the table before heading back to the kitchen.

"Please," Leo said, gesturing at the platter.

She took one of the oysters, squeezed some lemon on top, tipped her head back and let the slippery morsel slide down her throat. She closed her eyes, savoring the taste, primitive and salty, like eating a bite of the sea. When she opened her eyes, Leo was looking at her, his eyes dark with something she couldn't define.

It was lost a moment later when he reached for one of the oysters. Diana took another long swallow of her wine, sighing as the alcohol reached her bloodstream. She was here, in a place almost too beautiful to describe, with Leo. She would try to enjoy their meal. Try not to overthink everything he said and did.

Try not to wonder if he felt it, too.

"So I found something," Leo said. "Something about Stavros."

She looked up, grateful for the distraction from her thoughts. "What did you find?"

"A shipment," Leo said, "coming in to Beni Saf tomorrow night."

"Beni Saf..." The name was like a punch to the stomach, and she was immediately taken back to the hall outside Maggie's office, the paralyzing fear, the moment Stavros had killed her friend.

"It's the name of a port in Algeria. More specifically, a port rumored to have more than its share of illegal arms shipments," he said. "I didn't put it together right away, but it came to me after those men showed up at the flat in London. I wanted to do some more research before I said anything."

So that's what Stavros and Toumi had been talking about when they'd been interrogating Maggie. Not the name of a person, but the name of a port used to traffic illegal weapons.

"Do you think that's why they came after Maggie?" she asked. "Because she found out about it?"

"Maybe not the shipment itself," he said. "But it's not outside the realm of possibility that she discovered anomalies in wire transfers that made her suspect money was being used to fund some kind of illegal exchange."

She remembered how tired Maggie had looked the last day she'd been alive. She'd been worried, and Diana had postponed talking to her because of her lunch plans with Leo. She wished she could go back, do it all differently, insist Maggie tell her everything.

But there was plenty of time for guilt. Now was the time for justice.

"How can you be sure the shipment you're talking about is connected to Stavros?" she asked.

"Because it's registered to a company registered to a company registered to another company that's in Stavros' name. And because Briony was able to trace said company to other questionable shipments that have come in to Beni Saf in the past."

She sat back in her chair. "What are we going to do about it?"

"I'll know more tomorrow." He lifted his glass again. "Until then, I say we enjoy the food. And the view."

It was a tall order, but somehow they passed the next two hours in pleasant conversation punctuated both by the comfortable silences of old friends and a new kind of tension that was either real or imaginary. They talked about her parents, about her job at Abbott and whether she would be able to return to it once they'd found Antonis Stavros, about their childhood. They laughed over their shared memories, arguing about who had the more accurate recollection of events. The only thing they didn't talk about was the truth Leo had only recently revealed.

And all the while Mina brought plate after plate of amazing

food: fish so flaky it melted in Diana's mouth, tender salad greens served with nothing but fresh lemon and sea salt, smoky lamb, roasted vegetables in a spicy tomato sauce. The food was an explosion of spices — chili and caraway and cumin all coming together to create a symphony of flavor. By the time she cleared the last plate, they'd worked their way through two bottles of wine, and Diana was feeling more than a little relaxed.

"Why didn't you tell me?"

The candles on the table were flickering low in their votive holders when the question tumbled out her mouth.

He turned his glass in his hand. She held her breath, waiting for an answer. Instead, he stood.

"Come on."

"Come where?" she asked.

"Let's put our feet in the water," he said. "Like when we were kids."

She smiled. "We didn't just put our feet in when we were kids. Not usually anyway."

A smile touched his lips. "You're absolutely right."

He grabbed her hand, pulled her up out of her chair, started running for the water.

She laughed, all too happy to let herself be pulled along in Leo's wake, just like always. "What are you doing?"

He stopped at the water line and dropped her hand, then stripped off his shirt. "Going in the water. Like when we were kids."

"Leo..."

He unbuttoned his pants, and she sucked in a breath, half afraid and half hoping there would be nothing underneath. She didn't know whether to be relieved or disappointed to discover he was, in fact, wearing boxer briefs.

Then again, any relief was short lived when he turned for the water, revealing perfect buttocks, hard and well-formed above big, muscular thighs.

"Come on, Diana." His words were snatched by the wind as he rushed for the water. "We've done it a thousand times."

Not like this.

"Oh, bollocks. Fine." She stripped off her dress and ran for the water, glad Leo was diving under a wave so he couldn't see her half naked.

By the time he came up, she was already waist deep in the surf, the waves buoying her upward as they swelled underneath her, dropping her back to the sand as they rolled onto the beach.

She swam a little farther out to meet him, then treaded water to keep herself afloat.

"Still crazy," she said, splashing him.

"You were the one who usually wanted to go swimming," he said.

"Yes, but not at night, and not without our suits."

He grinned. "What's the difference?"

She didn't have an answer. She didn't know the difference. She only knew there was one.

"No difference," she said.

For a long moment, neither of them spoke. The ocean had grown calm, the waves turned to small swells. His wet hair was dark under the shimmer of the moon, drops of water clinging to his lips. She wanted to wrap her arms around his neck, twine her legs around his waist, kiss the droplets of the sea from his mouth.

She was in a dangerous place, a place far from the reality of their lives, a reality that had kept them at a distance in spite of their childhood closeness. Here there was nothing but the moon and the sea, Leo looking at her with liquid eyes over the salty water that separated her from the thing she wanted and the things she knew to be true. It would be so easy. She would wrap her arms around his neck, press her lips to his. Maybe he wouldn't want her the way she wanted him, but at least she'd know.

But then it would be between them. What would it mean for their friendship if he didn't feel the same way? Was she willing to risk losing what they had for the chance to kiss him? To see if all the possibility she sensed bubbling under the surface of their long standing camaraderie was real or fantasy?

No. He meant too much to her. His friendship was part of the bedrock of her life, a foundation comprised of the love of her parents and the knowledge that Leo would always be there to pick her up if she fell.

Decision made, she was willing herself to turn away, willing her legs to propel her body back to shore, when she heard the wave approaching. She knew from the sound of it — a subtle roar she felt in her stomach — that it was bigger than the swells that had been rolling under them until now.

She barely had time to look at Leo before they both ducked, letting it roll overhead the way they had when they were kids. When she was sure it was past, she came up to find that the water had moved her closer to Leo.

Much closer.

He was only inches away now, his lips parted as he looked at her with what she was almost sure was desire.

"Leo…"

It was all she managed to say in the moment before he pulled her toward him. She slid her hands into the hair at the back of his head and wrapped her legs around his waist as his mouth closed on hers. He was taller than her, his feet firmly planted in the sand as the waves crashed around them. She was only dimly aware of their power. It paled in comparison to the need rolling through her body as Leo's tongue swept her mouth, his hands pressing her ass against the hard-on wedged between her thighs.

She opened her mouth, wanting all of him, meeting every thrust of his tongue with her own, fisting his wet hair in her hands. They were in their own universe now. Nothing but them and the empty beach and the almost full moon casting a column of light over the sea. He was mapping her mouth, exploring it with his tongue, then nibbling at her bottom lip before capturing it again.

He pulled away, leaving her gasping — for breath and for him. She wanted more.

So much more.

"Diana…"

She placed a finger over his lips. "I don't want to talk, Leo. We've been talking our whole lives."

"We haven't talked about it. About what I do. About what that would mean for you."

"I don't care, Leo. I don't fucking care, okay? I just want you to make love to me now."

He seemed to hesitate, and for a moment she feared he would turn her away. Then he groaned and pressed his lips to hers, and this time the kiss wasn't an exploration but a possession.

Her hands traveled down, across the broad expanse of his shoulders, down to the biceps that bulged as they held her ass. He kissed his way along her jaw toward her ear, nibbled at the lobe until she gasped, throwing her head back until her hair fanned out in the water around them.

She let her hands travel down the rise of his pecs, past the hard muscles of his abs, into the swim shorts at his hips. Then he was in her hand.

Long. Thick. Hard.

The feel of him in her hand sent an explosion of lust to her core. She was slippery for him, so on fire she could imagine the feel of him inside her. All she would have to do is pull aside her knickers, push herself onto the pulsing shaft in her hands.

"Fuck, Diana…" He held her aloft with one hand, then slid the other one around to the front, sliding it between their bodies, past the mound of her pubis. She moaned as his fingers brushed against her clit on the way to her secret folds, his mouth trailing kisses along her shoulder to her collarbone. Then his fingers were inside her, claiming her as he licked the hollow of her throat on his way to her breasts.

He was throbbing in her hand as she moved her palm over his shaft in long, languid strokes, relishing the feel of him expand as his need for her grew. It took every ounce of willpower she had not to position herself over the thick head, envelop him in her heat. She'd waited her whole life for this moment, and she had no idea what would happen when it was over.

She was going to lose herself in it while she could.

He lowered his lips to one lace-covered breast, closed his mouth over the fabric of the bra. She moaned as her nipple, cold from the water and wind, was enveloped in the heat of his mouth. It was a wicked combination: his cock in her hand, his fingers inside her, his mouth on her breast, the surf pounding around them in perfect rhythm to the longing beating through her body.

He lifted his head, looked into her eyes. "I need to see you. And I need to feel you."

He turned her around in his arms so he was carrying her like a bride over the threshold, then stalked through the surf toward the beach. Her body hurt with the absence of his fingers inside her, the lack of his mouth on her skin. How had she lived without them — without him — all this time? How had she sat across from him, making polite conversation over drinks when his body — his heart — had been made for her.

He didn't take his eyes off her as he made his way toward the beach, the water gradually growing more shallow, falling away from their bodies. She registered the chill in the air with detachment. Nothing mattered but him.

His strong arms around her. His body warming hers. His eyes seeing into her soul.

"We should go inside," he said. "It's cold."

She kissed him. "I don't want to go inside, Leo. I've waited too long already."

His eyes seemed to turn black in the moonlight. "Then let's not wait any longer."

## Chapter Fourteen

He lowered her to the sand, laying her out carefully. It had been ages since they'd been in bathing suits together. She'd been little more than a kid the last time he'd seen her so scantily clad, and he'd been too young to understand the depth of his feelings for her.

Now he saw that her body was more magnificent than he could have imagined, her breasts full and perfectly formed, the dusky brown nipples barely visible through the lace of her bra. He let himself have the luxury of looking at her, allowed his eyes to travel to the tiny waist, the full hips that were made for his big hands. Her panties were wet, plastered to the mound at the top of her thighs. His pulse quickened as he remembered the walls of her pussy clenching around his fingers. Her legs were full at the top, narrowing to slender knees and calves, and he knew the skin on the inside of her thigh would be soft and fleshy when he raked it with his teeth. Her skin shimmered with droplets of water.

She lifted a hand. "Please."

It was so polite, so Diana, to ask nicely when the fire raged in his body. When he thought he would be consumed by it if he didn't bury himself inside her before another moment could pass.

He lowered himself next to her on the sand, pulled her into his arms. "I don't want you to be uncomfortable," he said, thinking of the sand.

She wrapped her hands around his neck, licked the salt from his lips. "The only thing that's making me uncomfortable is the fact that you're not inside me yet."

She kissed him, slipping her tongue inside his mouth as she

hooked a leg around one of his hips, pressing herself against him until he could feel the heat of her pussy against his engorged cock.

He rolled her gently under him, used one of his knees to spread her thighs while he kissed her. He wanted to know every inch of her body, and he started with her mouth, kissing her deeply and thoroughly, letting his mouth explore every corner of it, pulling back to lick her full lips. She bit his bottom lip, hard enough to give him a shock of pleasure-pain that shot right to the tip of his shaft.

"All this time you've been hiding a naughty side," he murmured, moving his lips down her neck, licking his way to her collarbone.

"All this time you thought I was a good girl?" she asked.

He unhooked her bra, tossed it aside. "All this time I've known you were *my* girl." It thrilled him to say it.

His. For now at least, she was his.

He lowered his head to her breast and captured the nipple in his mouth. She gasped as he sucked, working the insistent peak with his tongue while he fingered the other one with his free hand. The little bud rose quickly to a stiff peak, and he tugged at it gently with his teeth before lapping at it with his tongue, soothing it before he sucked and nibbled again.

She grabbed a handful of his hair, almost hard enough to hurt. It only made him bigger. Hotter. He released the nipple from his mouth and kissed his way down her stomach. It was flat but deliciously soft, and he dipped his tongue into the well of her naval, before making his way farther downward.

Kneeling between her legs, he took one slender calf in his hand and kissed his way from her ankle to the tender spot behind her knee. She lifted her head from the sand, watched him spread her open, his mouth moving up her thigh, kissing and nibbling at the delicate flesh inside her legs. The scent of her pussy hit him like a bolt of lightning.

Earthy. Sweet. Musky.

It set his blood boiling, causing another painful rush of need to his already about-to-explode cock. He distracted himself by lowering his head to look at the dewy wetness clinging to her folds, proof that she wanted him as much as he wanted her. He ran a finger through them, upward toward her clit. Her sigh was like a summer breeze, rising up, mingling with the wind blowing in off the water. He wanted to hear that sigh again. Wanted to look in her eyes when she came for him.

When he poured himself into her.

He ran his tongue through the petals of her sex, resisting the urge to bury his face in her pussy. It was too soon for that, and he circled her clit with his tongue, flicking the tiny bundle of nerves until she moaned. Her hips rose off the sand to meet him, and he lay a hand flat on her belly, both to keep her still and because it was a form of possession. A way to make it clear that for now, at least, her body was his.

He slid his fingers inside her while increasing the pressure on her clit with his tongue and was rewarded with an increase in the juices lubricating his fingers. She moaned, moving her hips against him as he lapped at her clit, slid another finger inside her, moving them in and out in time to the rhythm of his tongue.

Her channel was tight, the muscles already clenching down on his fingers. He sucked at the little seed while he hooked his finger inside her, putting pressure on her G-spot.

"Oh, my god… Leo… I can't…"

She was close. He could feel it in the way the walls of her pussy were tightening around him, the increase in wetness around his fingers, her swollen clit, the way she pressed her hips against his mouth.

"Please…" she gasped.

His cock was so hard it hurt, but he wouldn't take her until she came against his mouth.

He wanted to taste her.

He buried his face deeper in her warm sweetness, covering her clit with the heat of his mouth while he plunged his fingers inside her, holding one against the secret spot that was slowly driving her mad.

She was moving against him hard and fast now, her hips fucking his fingers and his mouth, her body determined to take its own pleasure, her mind occupied only with release. He increased the speed of his tongue and fingers, letting the friction carry her to the abyss until she cried out, shuddering against his mouth, the creaminess of her come invading his tongue as he lapped her clean.

When she settled back into the sand, he rose on his knees and reached for his jeans, extracting a condom from the back pocket. She sat up, licked from the base of his shaft to the tip, sucking on his swollen head until he growled. He shoved her gently back onto the sand and rolled the condom on his rigid staff, then nestled the crown against the wetness of her opening.

He paused, looking down at her, at their almost joined bodies.

"What is it?" she asked, breathless.

"Nothing," he said. "I just want to look at you."

"Look at me all you want," she said. "Just do it while you fuck me, please."

He chuckled, his love for her welling inside him like a secret spring. How had he lied to himself — to her — about it for so long? The question didn't linger. A moment later, he thrust inside her in one powerful movement, burying himself balls deep.

She cried out, lifting her hips to meet him. He didn't move right away. Just closed his eyes against the exquisite pleasure of her heat all around him, the pressure of her pussy wrapping him in an intoxicating cocktail of warmth and comfort and safety and something like home.

She opened her legs wider, and he sunk deeper inside her. The subtle shift removed the last vestige of his self-control, and he dragged his cock out of her, then drove into her hard and fast, his head slamming again the top of her cervix as she screamed.

"Okay?" he asked, forcing himself not to repeat the motion until she answered. Forcing himself not to drive into her again and again until he exploded inside her.

She answered by grabbing his ass, pushing him harder and farther inside her. It was all the encouragement he needed, and he thrust inside her again and again, feeling his orgasm build at the center of his body even as her movements became more frantic.

He was desperate to come inside her. But he wasn't ready for it to end.

He rolled her on top of him, his breath catching at the sight of her naked body straddling his in the moonlight. She moved on him without prompting, grinding her hips in a rhythm that was so sensual, the image alone almost sent him over the edge.

He grabbed her gloriously full ass, thrusting upward to meet her as her head fell back. Her breath was coming fast now, a flush spreading across her chest as she moved on him. He reached up, circled her clit with his thumb as he impaled her again and again on his cock.

Gasping, she rested her hands on his chest, leaned back a little so that his cock sank even more deeply inside her. He increased the pressure on her clit and felt her hips quicken, her body taking over as it reached for its promised climax.

"Look at me when you come, Diana."

She opened her eyes, met his gaze. His whole world was in her eyes.

Past. Present. Future.

And then she was convulsing around his cock, the muscles of her pussy clenching hard around him as she came. It was the moment he'd been waiting for, and he let go, falling after her into the void, the orgasm ripping through him like an earthquake. It was like being suspended in space.

Weightless. Empty. Soundless.

He let himself drift. Let himself burn.

When he finally came back to himself, it was with the sweet weight of her body draped over his, her hair every which way, just the way he liked it. He wrapped his arms around her, slipping one hand into her hair, holding her close. She'd been his forever, he just hadn't known it.

He kissed the top of her head, letting a fresh surge of rage flow though him at the thought of someone trying to hurt her. They would have to go through him, and he would do anything to see that she was safe.

Maim. Wound. Kill.

Anything.

## Chapter Fifteen

She felt his absence even before she opened her eyes. She kept them closed for awhile, replaying the events of the night before. It was somehow both a surprise and an inevitability that she had ended up in his bed. That's how it felt now anyway.

His claiming of her on the beach had been every bit as forceful as the tide roaring in from the depths of the Mediterranean, but it had only been the beginning. Afterward, he'd carried her naked to the empty house, continuing up the stairs and into the large master bathroom where he'd tenderly washed the sand from her skin before taking her from behind, her hands and breasts pressed against the glass doors as he drove into her. When they were done, he'd led her to the big bed facing the glass doors. Beyond them, the ocean swept unchanging onto the beach, oblivious to the fact that her whole world had opened up in the three hours since she'd gone down for dinner.

But Leo wasn't done with her, and he spent the next few hours exploring every inch of her, making her come again and again, wringing her out with the intensity of the pleasure he wrought from her body. In between, they lay in silence, her head on his chest, his heart beating out a comforting rhythm against her ear. It felt like a part of her, like she'd heard it since before she was born. They talked about everything — their childhood and their memories and all the secrets they'd kept from each other. And sometimes they talked about nothing at all.

She'd fallen asleep as the first light of dawn began creeping across the ceiling, Leo's arms wrapped securely around her. Now she opened her eyes, looked around the room, flooded with light. He was gone, just as she suspected, but she could hear the sound of water running in the kitchen, could smell melted butter and warm sugar. Was it Leo or Mina?

She bit her lower lip, suddenly nervous. Would things be weird between them now? Would he regret what had happened? She didn't know, but even if they weren't weird, even if he didn't regret it, they weren't in the clear. Antonis Stavros was out there somewhere. It was possible he'd pushed aside his mission to kill her in the name of getting his shipment safely to port, but she couldn't count on that forever. And even if she could, she was not okay with Maggie's killer going free. Not okay with such a vicious man brokering the sale of weapons whose one purpose was to kill.

She sat up, stretched, then reached for Leo's shirt. She held it to her nose, breathing in his scent — salt and wind and denim. She stood, slipping it over her head, then looked at herself in the mirror over the bureau. She only thought about trying to tame her hair for a minute. There was really no point.

The sounds from the kitchen got louder as she made her way down the stairs. She looked at her bare legs, rethinking Leo's shirt. What if Mina was in the kitchen? Diana wasn't exactly dressed for company.

But when she turned the corner into the living room, she saw Leo standing at the stove, flipping a pancake. For a moment, she could hardly breathe. Her fingers itched to touch his shoulders, to trace the perfectly formed muscles she already knew by heart, to touch the line of hair disappearing into the jeans slung low on his hips.

"Good morning."

She looked up, licking her lips involuntarily. "Good morning."

He grinned. "Hungry?"

She didn't look away as she walked toward him. "Starving."

He slid the pancake onto a plate, turned off the stove, and pulled her to him as she rounded the granite island. "We'll have to eat first."

She laughed. "You're no fun."

He squeezed her ass, pressed her into the already-impressive erection growing between his legs. Then he lowered his head until his lips were inches from hers. "Really?"

"No." She was already breathless with her desire for him. "Not really."

"That's what I thought." He captured her mouth in a long, lingering kiss that was as tender as it was all-consuming. "I'm sorry I had to leave you in bed. We have a big day. I wanted to get started."

"I understand," she said, trying to will away the wetness between her legs.

He swatted her bottom. "Let's eat. I think we both need some energy after last night."

They ate on a table out on the balcony, overlooking the beach where Leo had finally made her his. The sun reflected off the water from a clear blue sky, and the air was scented with the brine of the sea and the strong, black coffee Leo had brewed in the french press. She was in heaven, and she swallowed the last bite of pancake on her plate and closed her eyes, trying to memorize every bit of it.

"What are you thinking?"

She opened her eyes to find Leo studying her. "I was thinking this is a perfect morning. A perfect moment. I was thinking I wish it could last."

His expression was serious as he nodded. "I know what you mean."

"But it can't, can it?" she asked.

"I plan to give you thousands of perfect mornings like this one, Diana." His voice was hard, his gaze fierce. "But I have work to do first. And we have things we need to talk about."

She nodded, looking at her hands. "Because you lied."

"Because I lied," he said. "And because the reasons I lied are valid."

"What reasons?" she asked.

"The work that I do is dangerous," he said. "To me and to anyone who's part of my life. But that's not all."

She looked up. "What else is there?"

He flipped over the knife next to his plate, turning it back and forth. She recognized the fidgeting. It was something Leo did when he was nervous, when he was choosing his words.

"I don't want this life for you, Diana."

She looked around, taking in the sea beneath them, the long stretch of pristine sand, the beautiful house. "It doesn't look like a bad life."

He scowled. "It's not all this. It's strange hours and strange countries. It's the kind of instability most people can't imagine. Not the fear of losing your job — fear of losing your life, of being put in prison. And…"

He swallowed hard, and she knew they were finally getting to the crux of his argument. "And?" she prompted.

He shook his head. "You're better than this, Diana. You should be with someone who has read the classics, who knows Brahms from Beethoven, who knows what it means to live right."

Tears stung her eyes, but she blinked them away. The only thing worse than Leo's confession — this confession — would be to think Diana pitied him. And that wasn't why she felt like crying, why it felt like someone was scraping out her insides with a pickaxe.

It was because this was Leo, saying he wasn't good enough, and she knew suddenly that this is what he'd always believed.

All the summer days he'd spent at her parent's house, playing games of IT on the big lawn while Mozart leaked from the windows of the house.

All the times he came across her reading a book that had been written before either of them were born. Before her parents and grandparents were born.

All the times he'd sat at her dinner table while her father asked questions about college and her future.

She'd never once thought to imagine Leo felt inferior, because she'd never once thought of him that way. But now she saw it all, like a long and painful film whose sadness only fully hit you at the end.

His expression was guarded as she rose from her chair, came around to his side of the table, sat unceremoniously in his lap. His arms slid around her hips, and his face was just inches away. She almost couldn't breathe with the need to touch her lips to his.

"What does it mean to you to live right, Leo?"

"You know what it means," he said gruffly.

"I know what it means to me," she said. "I want to know what it means to you."

"It means a stable job with a stable paycheck. The kind of job that can't get you killed or arrested, and dinner at six every night."

"It sounds terribly boring," she said. "And not at all the way I would describe living right."

He looked confused. "How would you describe it?"

She held his face in her palms, looked into his eyes. "As sharing life with the one person in the world I can't live without, building a future with that person, laughing and crying with that person. I'd describe it as working toward something together, no matter what. My parents have been married since they were twenty-two. When I look at them, I don't see the house filled with antiques and art, the money they've worked so hard to save. I see the love in their eyes. That's what I want for myself, Leo. And I want it for you, too. I want it *with* you."

"You might change your mind," he said.

She touched her lips to his. "I've had twenty-eight years to change my mind, Leo Gage. I think you're stuck with me."

"I should be so lucky," he said. A cloud of worry passed over his features.

"What is it?"

"I want you to live in peace. And that means we have to get Stavros."

"How do we do that?" she asked.

An aggressive knock sounded from the front door as he opened his mouth to answer. He gently removed her from his lap and stood.

"That will be your answer."

# Chapter Sixteen

"Diana, Braden Kane," Leo said. "Kane, this is Diana Barrett."

The man was tall and broad-shouldered, his dark hair cut so short she could could almost see his scalp. His face was perfectly symmetrical, the face of a model or leading man. She sensed it was an illusion, that underneath the cover model exterior he was every bit as dangerous as Leo.

They shook hands, and Leo led Kane into the living room. He looked around, taking in the view beyond the glass, the open architecture, the simple but expensive furnishings. "Nice."

"It's not mine."

She wondered if it was her imagination that Leo sounded defensive. She sensed a kind of camaraderie between the men, but a competition, too, and maybe even a wary kind of distrust. It set her on edge. Antonis Stavros wanted her dead. She didn't have time for a pissing contest between two Alpha males.

"Who are you?" she asked. "I mean, I know your name, of course. But who are you?"

"Kane is an FBI liaison to Homeland Security."

"Homeland Security?" That explained the American accent at least. "What does that have to do with… what happened in London?" She had no idea how much Kane knew, and she wasn't about to spill her guts until she had a better handle on who he was and what he was doing there.

"Let's just say the US has as much of an investment in seizing the weapons coming into Algiers as England."

"You said we couldn't trust the police," she said to Leo.

"Kane isn't police."

"It doesn't seem that different to me," she said.

"It is." A hard edge crept into his voice.

"Tell me how," she insisted. She didn't care what Leo did for a living. Her life was on the line, and so was justice for Maggie. She was entitled to answers.

"I've worked with him before. I know him. I trust him." There was a kind of resignation in his voice, like he didn't enjoy admitting it. "We need to take out Stavros. It's the only way to keep you alive, and Kane can help us do that without tipping off someone who might try to kill you first."

She nodded. "All right."

Leo's shoulders relaxed a little, and he turned his attention to Kane. "Where are your men?"

"On site. Ready to go."

"Good. What's the plan?"

"Intercept the shipment, take Stavros into custody," Kane said. "Simple."

Diana had the feeling it would be anything but simple.

"And we go on our way?" Leo asked.

"That's our deal."

Diana looked from one to the other of them, trying to gauge their obviously complicated history. She had no idea how Leo, a career criminal with ties to the London mob, had come to have such a civil relationship with a man who worked for the FBI, but she was beginning to believe she would be glad he did. Braden Kane seemed calm and at ease, completely confident in the upcoming mission.

Leo looked at his phone. "We have less than fourteen hours before the shipment is due to come in."

"Then we better get going," Kane said. "You got a car?"

"Wait... we're driving to Algiers?" Diana asked.

Leo's eyes darkened. "If I had my way, *we* wouldn't be driving anywhere. You would be staying here while we drove to Algiers."

Diana lifted an eyebrow. "But?"

"But... I'm not leaving you alone in Spain while I go to Algiers, not while Stavros and his men are still on the loose." He sighed. "So yes, we're driving to Algiers. Taking a plane is too risky.

This is Stavros' territory. He might have eyes on the airport."

"Right." It was yet another sign that she was in a whole new world. She couldn't just hop on a plane, not right now. She had to think like the men hunting her. Had to be on the offensive.

"Which brings us back to the car," Kane said.

Leo nodded. "Let's pack up."

# Chapter Seventeen

"I can't get away from these fucking SUVs," Kane complained from the back seat. "Suburbans in the States, Rovers in Europe... I was hoping for something... sexier."

"I'm not Nico Vitale," Leo said.

"Doesn't have to be a Ferrari."

"I'm not Farrell Black."

"Doesn't have to be a Lotus either," Kane said.

Leo sighed. He didn't want to be Nico Vitale or Farrell Black. Nico was in Thailand now, living more or less off the grid with the woman who had inadvertently caused the fall of the Syndicate. And Farrell's lifestyle was too stylized for Leo. He didn't want mansions and security detail, blood and bodyguards.

He was more than happy to be the muscle, but for him blood was a necessary part of the job, not an aphrodisiac like it was for Farrell.

"This is the safest way for us to travel," Leo said, navigating the Rover toward the seaport. "We could be anybody — a diplomat, an entrepreneur, the UN. It will help us get through customs on the other side."

He hadn't given voice to his darkest fears about the trip to Algiers. Namely, that they were in a car bound for a notoriously complex political region, one that had become a haven for black market arms and drug dealers, sex traffickers, and terrorists. They'd loaded most of their guns into a hidden compartment in the trunk, but Leo had placed his own weapon under the driver's seat, unwilling to leave Diana's safety to chance if they were intercepted.

Braden Kane was more obvious — strapping his handgun into a holster at his side — a perk of his FBI badge that would quickly turn into a detriment if the wrong people got ahold of it.

None of it made Leo feel any better about the excursion.

He scanned the crowd as they approached the automobile loading dock for the ferry. There was no reason to believe Stavros expected them to try and get into Algiers, but that didn't mean it wasn't possible.

And Stavros wasn't the only thing they had to be worried about. The region was loaded with people who despised Westerners, to say nothing of Kane's affiliation with the FBI, an association that could either do them tremendous good, or tremendous harm. They were traveling with a beautiful woman, obviously British, another mark against them.

He pulled up to the line of cars waiting to pull onto the ferry, then rolled his shoulders, trying to relax. Diana reached over, touched the back of his neck as if she could sense that he was nervous. The gesture sent a flush of warmth through his body. It was nice until it was followed by a surge of fear at the thought of losing her.

They handed over their passports to a ferry employee and were waved onto the boat without incident. It did nothing to ease his mind. Spain wasn't the problem — Algeria was. Security would be considerably tighter there, and considerably less regulated. The wad of cash in his pocket might help them, but like everything else, it could hurt them as well. Would greed trump pride and principle with the Algerian police?

It was anybody's guess, and they had no way of knowing until they tried.

The cargo compartment was cavernous and dark, a floating parking garage that was wall to wall cars, motorbikes, and bicycles. They locked the car and stepped into the underside of the boat as it started to pull away from the dock.

The ferry was like a mini cruise ship, and they found a cafe and bought kebabs and water, which they took to the upper deck to eat while Kane flirted with a tall, slender brunette in a short sundress.

The upper deck was crowded with an assortment of people — tourists and parents with their children and young people kissing at the railing. Above them, the cloudless sky seemed infinite as Almeria became smaller on one side of the boat, the Mediterranean stretching toward Morocco and Algeria, still invisible to the naked eye.

He was happy to have the moment alone with Diana. It was a relief to have Kane and his team from the States on their side, but there was never any guarantee when it came to these kinds of operations. Now that he had Diana, it felt like he had something to lose, and he looked over at her, trying to memorize the way her mouth turned up at the corners as she tipped her head to the sun. Her hair blew around her face, barely tamed by the scarf tied around her head. He had the sudden memory of her riding him the night before, her thighs pressing against his hips as she worked her clit against him, pursuing her own pleasure with a ferocity that had surprised him.

He suddenly wanted to freeze time, and he fought the dread seeping through his stomach. He didn't believe in intuition. This would be a routine operation like so many he'd been part of with Farrell. They would intercept the shipment, Kane would take Antonis Stavros and his men into custody, Leo and Diana would return to London, figure out the logistics of building a life together. Figure out if it was even possible.

He could almost believe it.

When they were done eating, Leo leaned back, stretching his arm across Diana's shoulders. "It's a long trip," he said. "You should try to sleep."

"Impossible with this view." She looked at the bench. "And this seat."

He gestured to his lap. "It's all yours."

She smiled up at him, then lay down, resting her head across his thighs. He smoothed the curls back from her forehead, stroked her cheek as she closed her eyes with a sigh.

They passed the next ten hours in various states of unrest: Diana dozing on his lap while he closed his eyes behind his sunglasses, he and Kane running down the possibilities in Beni Saf and catching up on news of Farrell, Luca, Nico. The sun swept the sky while they cruised across the channel toward Algeria. By the time they drove off the ferry in Ghazaouet, it was after ten pm, the light of day nothing but a memory.

They were stopped almost immediately by a group of uniformed men carrying weapons. Leo handed over their papers, offering Kane's driver's license rather than his FBI ID badge. They would save that for a situation when the reward outweighed the risk. Three of the police — if that's what they were — circled the car, eyeing Diana through the window as the fourth flipped through their passports. He wasn't worried about the authenticity of the documents Hyrum had created for Diana. There were no bar code readers here. No computers.

But this was far more dangerous: a group of armed men with seemingly no oversight, standing between them and the desolate road leading to Beni Saf and the man who wanted to kill the woman he loved.

Leo forced his expression to remain calm even as he calculated how long it would take him to reach the weapon under his seat. Even as he watched every move the men made, prepared to push Diana's head out of the line of fire and lunge for the gun at the first sign of trouble.

Ten minutes later, the man grudgingly handed back their passports. Leo nodded, put the car in gear, and rolled forward. The car was filled with tension as they made their way along the deserted road leading to the seaside town of Beni Saf. Street lights were few and far between, and Leo quickly became accustomed to driving through long stretches of darkness. He wanted to believe the worst was behind them, but he knew that was about as far from the truth as they could get. There was every possibility of more police as they entered Beni Saf, and even the possibility that they'd been let go so the men could alert Antonis Stavros of their arrival. Leo wasn't stupid enough to comforted by Kane's presence. This was an unofficial mission. The Americans owed no loyalty to Leo, and he had no doubt they'd extract their own people and leave he and Diana behind if it was the only way to get out alive.

Which meant he was the only thing really standing between Diana and Stavros.

*Fine*, he thought. *Let him come. Let him try.*

They were nearing town when they spotted the next group of police. They weren't manning a road block but sitting atop cars on the side of the road. They were heavily armed, eyes watchful, bodies ready to pounce as they watched Leo drive past them into the city. He should have been happy they weren't stopped, but he couldn't help wondering if it was because Stavros already knew they were there.

"You okay?" he asked Diana.

She nodded. "Fine."

She was probably lying, but he couldn't really blame her. He would have said the same thing in her position. The situation was what it was, and the only way through it was through it.

He navigated the Rover through the rundown city. It was different from the capital city of Algiers, the buildings old and startlingly white against the blue of the sky and sea, the surrounding brush that was reminiscent of Greece. There you could feel the history, could see it in the domed architecture and even the Church of the Holy Trinity built in the late 1800s.

Beni Saf was a seaport town in the truest sense, a place where people lived hard lives unloading cargo from aging docks, where their skin was etched by the moisture-less air, the salt of the sea, the sun that always seemed too bright. Leo could see why Antonis Stavros would find it an ideal location to bring in illegal cargo. It wasn't a place anyone wanted to go, wasn't a place that drew tourists or travelers.

Finally, they came to a low slung house on the outskirts of town. It was old but not derelict, well maintained but not at all grand.

In other words, the perfect safe house.

The Americans knew how to do something right at least.

He turned off the car, and turned to Diana. "Let's go."

# Chapter Eighteen

Diana knew as soon as they pulled up outside the house what was happening. She should have expected it; Leo would never let her come along as they intercepted the arms shipment coordinated by Stavros.

She took his hand and let him pull her into the house. He was expecting her to argue. She could see it in the set of his shoulders, the rigid line of his mouth. Could tell by the way he avoided her eyes.

Braden Kane followed them into the house, locking the door behind them. The ceilings were low, the rooms small and dark except for a couple of small lamps flanking a low slung sofa. They had just stepped into a narrow, tiled living room when a giant hulk of a man rose from a chair near the wall.

He was at least six-four, with wide shoulders made even wider by the tactical gear covering his back, chest, and arms. His hair was cut so close to his head Diana might have thought he was bald if not for the glimmer of gold hair at his scalp.

"Miller," Kane said as they entered the room.

"They have you dressing like a pussy, too?" The man asked, eyeing Kane's trousers and button down shirt. The question had a hint of humor even as it sounded like a challenge.

"Fuck you." Kane's voice was nonchalant as they moved into the room. "Everything cool?"

"Everything's cool," the man named Miller said.

Kane made the introductions, then turned to Leo. "Ten minutes."

Leo nodded, his face grim, then gestured to a long hallway. "Diana."

Diana followed him into a sparsely furnished bedroom and sat on the bed against one wall. "It's okay."

"What's okay?" he asked.

"You're leaving me here with that guy, Miller."

"It has to be this way." His voice was hard, like he was bracing himself for her argument. "I won't be able to think straight if you're there, and I can't guarantee your safety there either."

She smiled, then stood and wrapped her arms around his waist, leaned her head against his chest. "I understand."

"You do?"

She nodded, relishing the soft feel of his cotton T-shirt under her cheek, the spicy, purely male scent of him. She slid her hands up his chest, lacing them around his neck as she tipped her head back to look up at him.

"I hate to admit it, of course, but I won't be of any use to you there."

He looked down at her. "You're amazing, you know that?"

"Maybe," she said. "But that doesn't mean you need to stop saying it."

He chuckled, and the echo of it spread through her chest. It had been awhile since she'd heard him laugh. She'd forgotten how his face lit up, how he was transformed from a serious man carrying the weight of shame on his shoulders to the playful boy who'd chased her across the lawn.

She touched his face. "Promise me more of that."

"More of what?"

"More of your laughter. More of your love." She swallowed against the tears in her eyes. There would be no place for crying in Leo's life. No place for it in their life together. She would be strong for him instead. She would start now. "Just promise you'll come back."

He bent his head, took possession of her mouth, kissed her until she was breathless. "I'll come back," he said against her lips.

She nodded, then stepped away from him. She had a feeling the impending separation was just as difficult for him. She would make it easier. From now on, that would be her goal. To make things easier for the man who had done it for her through her entire life.

She forced her hands at her side, resisted the urge to touch him again. "I love you, Leo Gage. I've loved you as long as I can remember."

He smiled. "I've loved you longer. And I'll be back."

And then he was gone.

# Chapter Nineteen

"Where the fuck are they? You confirmed the shipment, right?" Leo asked Kane.

"The shipment's in," Kane said. "We're just waiting on Stavros to pick it up."

They were crouched in the shadows of the cargo port in Beni Saf, their weapons at the ready. Somewhere in the darkness, fifteen men like them watched through infrared goggles, waiting for someone to claim the shipment of weapons that had arrived two hours before.

"How do we know Stavros will pick it up himself?" Leo asked.

"Pattern," Kane said, scanning the area through his goggles. "He's a control freak. Doesn't leave the big stuff to his men. We've missed him by minutes in the past. Not this time."

The note of determination in Kane's voice made Leo feel better. Kane knew what he was doing, and he had the skill and knowledge of Homeland Security behind him, not to mention all the other armed men waiting in the shadows of the cargo containers. If Leo had any chance of neutralizing the threat against Diana, this was it.

And he had to neutralize the threat against her. He'd become convinced it was his purpose. The life he'd chosen, everything he'd learned and experienced, had brought him to this place where he was the only thing standing between Diana Barrett and the man who would make it his mission to kill her.

*"Two Rovers entering the gates. Stand by."*

The voice sounded through Leo's earpiece, and a moment

later, the shine of headlights swept a tower of containers.

"Roger that," Kane said softly. "We have eyes."

The port was smaller than most cargo ports, a simple "U" with fishing boats on one side and metal shipping containers on the other. Leo watched as two vehicles eased onto the long stretch of pavement between the stacks of containers and the dock leading to the water.

Kane looked at him, his voice a warning. "Let us lead, Gage."

Leo nodded, holding back the words he wanted to say: that he would let them lead as long as they got Stavros. That the minute is seemed like Stavros might get away, Leo would break protocol and take the guy down. Whatever the cost.

The cars stopped halfway up the row of containers. Leo held his breath as the vehicles idled, wondering if there was any way Stavros had seen the men lying-in wait for him. But then the rear doors opened on the lead vehicle, and two men in black jackets stepped from the back of the car. They looked around and moved to the car behind them, flanking the back doors.

Leo sharpened the focus on his goggles, played with the contrast as he honed in on the figure stepping from the car. His mind compared the man against the images Briony had shown him in London, the photographs Kane's people had shown him in the pre-mission briefing.

Tall and meaty, the man's face was pockmarked with old scars, his hair slicked back and oily even from a distance.

It was him. It was Antonis Stavros. The man who had killed Maggie Kinsley. The man who would kill Diana unless Leo got to him first.

He hadn't told Kane about his plans to kill the man. As far as the Americans knew, this was an intercept operation. Get the guns. Take the man behind their sale into custody. Interrogate him about the network of underground arms dealers that criss-crossed the globe.

Except Leo didn't care about any of that. He cared only about saving Diana. And she wouldn't be safe until Stavros was dead. Kane could interrogate Stavros' men all he wanted, but Stavros was his.

*"Target in motion,"* the voice said in his earpiece.

"Copy," Kane said softly.

Leo watched as Stavros walked to one of the containers, the men on either side of him armed with semi-automatic weapons. Watching Stavros move toward his cargo sent a flood of fresh anger through Leo's body. The other man didn't seem at all concerned. Didn't seem rushed or afraid. This was a man who hurt people to get what he wanted. Who was so sure of his power and control that it never occurred to him that he might one day be stopped. That he might one day go too far.

Stavros gestured absentmindedly at the container, and one of the other men jumped forward, keyed something into the control panel. The man on the other side handed him a crowbar, and the first man used it to pry open the metal door. It shrieked as it creaked open, the sound like a beast howling into the Algerian night.

"Waiting for your go," Kane whispered into the mouthpiece attached to his jacket.

They'd already discussed the necessity of confirming the contents of the shipment before taking Stavros, and Leo tried to see inside the container as Stavros stepped inside with the two men. It was dark, the interior nothing but a smudge on the darker smudge of the night around it. He could only hope one of Kane's men had a better view. Stavros wasn't leaving here alive either way, but Leo wanted to see Kane get his hands on the shipment.

"Still waiting for your go," Kane said again.

*"Stand by."*

Leo held his breath, his finger itchy on the weapon in his hands. And then the voice came again.

*"Cargo confirmed. Move in."*

"Let's go," Kane said.

But Leo was already gone, moving into position according to the plans Kane's men had outlined before they left the old warehouse that had acted as a staging area.

He hustled around the container that had given him and Kane shelter, staying low as he moved toward the murmur of voices coming from inside. Several black-clad figures moved in his periphery, surrounding the container as Leo made a beeline for the entrance.

And then all hell broke loose, the men inside the container crying out in alarm as they realized something was wrong, a flash of gunfire erupting from the interior of the container. Kane's men took up positions behind surrounding cargo holds, firing into the night as Leo made his way toward the still idling vehicles.

Stavros' men would try to get him out alive, and the Rovers were the best way to do it.

The doors had already opened on the lead car, and two more men emerged, firing in the direction of Kane's men. It was a flash of color in the goggles, and Leo wondered if their enemy could even see them or if they were just firing blindly in the night, hoping to give Stavros cover.

He got his answer a few seconds later when two figures darted across the pavement near the end of the dock, doubling back toward the vehicles. One of Stavros' men had gotten him out of the container, moved him toward the front of the dock, away from the gunfire while the others held off Kane and his men.

And now Stavros was coming back for the car, just like Leo had expected.

He dropped to the ground, used the car in back to low crawl to the car in front while bullets tore through the night. When he reached the lead vehicle, he waited, listening for the sound of approaching footsteps in the break between gunfire, hoping he was right and that Stavros would make a run for the car in front.

He did, and Leo positioned himself at the rear of the car, listening as the sound of footsteps crunching on pavement got closer. Then the back door on the other side of the car was being opened, someone shouting urgently in Arabic.

Leo pulled open the door on his side, making sure he had eyes on Stavros before he fired. After that it was a series of flashes, one bleeding into the other.

Stavros' eyes wide with surprise.

The familiar sound of Leo's gun firing, the hot kick of it in his hand.

A man standing in the door near Stavros and firing across the back seat.

The hole, neat and clean, opening up in Stavros's forehead as a lightening bolt drove itself through Leo's chest.

His momentary elation at the knowledge that he'd gotten Stavros. Elation that lasted only as long as it took to realize that he'd been shot, too.

The man on the other side of the car was raising his weapon again. The barrel of it was startlingly clear, a long, dark tunnel leading to eternal slumber.

He braced himself for the impact. It was worth it. He had done what he came to do.

But then the man was crumbling, falling onto the back seat over Stavros' dead body as a bullet hit him from behind.

Leo collapsed onto the ground. He wasn't sure if the gunfire had really stopped or if he was already someplace else, moving far away from his body. From this place. From Diana.

He closed his eyes. It didn't matter.

She would be safe now.

# Chapter Twenty

Diana walked down the long, white hallway, trying to stifle the fear that threatened to overtake her. It had been that way since they first brought her to the hospital, and now her panic at the thought of losing Leo was inexorably tied to the fluorescent lighting and smell of antiseptic.

"Back so soon, Miss Barrett?"

She looked up, her eyes landing on a familiar nurse with blue hair and hot pink scrubs. "What can I say?" Diana asked. "I can't stay away."

The nurse winked. "Can't say that I blame you."

Diana laughed, the sound unfamiliar and strange as it emerged from her throat. It had been awhile since she'd laughed.

Two long weeks to be exact.

She continued past the nurses station, raising a hand in greeting as she made her way to the room halfway down the hall.

She stopped when she got to the door, taking a deep breath and reminding herself that Leo needed her to be strong. He was improving, and while the doctors said he had a long road ahead, he would survive. So why did she still feel the clutch of panic when she entered his room? Why did she still wake up in the middle of the night, alone in Leo's flat, crying?

They were stupid questions. It didn't take a psychologist to know that even thought she hadn't been on the dock in Algiers, almost losing Leo had delivered its own kind of blow to her psyche. She'd known as she waited at the safe house with the big soldier named Miller that she loved Leo.

She just hadn't realized how much.

Not until she had to make the long drive to the military base in Tunisia where Leo was already being loaded onto a medi-flight. Not until she'd held his cold, still hand as they made their way back to London, looked at his pale face, wondering if he would ever laugh or grin or kiss her again.

Then she'd known unequivocally that she didn't want to live without him. She'd spent every moment since — every second he was in surgery, every hour he was unconscious — praying to a god she wasn't sure she believed in to make him well. Because now her life without him had been exposed for what it was: barren, lonely, so very dark.

She took a deep breath as she approached the door, then pushed it open with a smile on her face. And there he was, head turned toward the window, chest rising and falling.

She stepped quietly into the room and made her way around the bed, not wanting to wake him. His face was peaceful in repose, the masculine features she'd become accustomed to somehow morphing into the boyish ones she remembered. She watched him for a moment, her heart overflowing. Then she brushed back the stray lock of hair and kissed his forehead.

His eyes opened with a start. She was glad he didn't have a gun. He undoubtedly would have reached for it.

"Shhhh," she said, touching his cheek. "It's me. I'm sorry to startle you."

He sank back into the pillow. "You were supposed to get some rest."

"I did."

He smiled. "I bet you haven't been gone two hours."

"Almost," she protested.

He laughed, then clutched the bandage on his chest. "Fuck. Will it always hurt to laugh?"

"I hope not," she said. "You'e coming home tomorrow. And I plan to make you laugh plenty, so you better toughen up."

He grinned. "That's my girl."

It had been a learning curve, teaching herself not to hover, not to show pity for him even when his face contorted in pain after the four hour surgery to repair the nick in his heart. She'd had to resist the urge to baby him, to do everything for him, to hiss at anyone who asked too much of him. It wasn't what he wanted, and she'd quickly learned to hide her own fear, her own pain, behind a mask of indifference.

*Of course, everything you'll be fine.*
*Of course, you can do it yourself.*
"Kane was here," he said.

She sat down next to the bed in a chair that had become as familiar to her as the one she used to occupy at Abbott. "Really? What did he say?"

"They've intercepted six arms shipments in the two weeks since Beni Saf, I'm an asshole for taking Stavros out on my own… you know, the usual."

"Yes, well, it takes an asshole to know an asshole," she said.

He laughed, clutching his chest again. "You're going to kill me." He patted the bed. "At least comfort me before you do it."

She eyed him suspiciously. "I don't think Nurse Owens would approve."

"Fuck Nurse Owens," he said. "I want to feel you next to me."

She sighed, then eased onto the bed beside him, laying her head gingerly against his shoulder. "Is this okay?"

He sighed, stroking her hair. "It's more than okay. It's perfect. Totally worth being shot for."

She reached up, gave his face a light slap as she laughed. "Stop!"

He leaned his head against hers. "It's true."

She heard it in his voice. Felt the echo of it in her heart.

She didn't know what the future held. Didn't know how they would blend their disparate lives. Didn't know if Leo would be able to continue working for Farrell Black, if she would ever be able to go back to the bank.

But as she lifted her face to his, she knew one thing was true: all those years, they hadn't been running away from each other at all.

They'd been running toward each other.

And it was exactly where they were meant to be.

# About Michelle St. James

Michelle St. James aka Michelle Zink is the author of seven published books and six novellas. Her first series, Prophecy of the Sisters (YA), was one of Booklist's Top Ten Debut novels. Her work has also been an Indie Next selection and has appeared on prestigious lists such as the Lonestar List, New York Public Library's Stuff for the Teen Age, and Chicago Public Library's Best of the Best. Her books have been published in over thirty countries and translated into over twenty languages. She lives in New York with too many teenagers and too many cats.

# Also From Michelle St. James

Ruthless
Fearless
Lawless
The Muscle
Savage
Primal
Eternal

# Covenant
Paris Mob, Book 1
By Michelle St. James

BOOK ONE IN THE PARIS MOB SERIES FEATURING CHRISTOPHE MARCHAND

Coming September 6, 2016!

Sign up for the 1001 Dark Nights Newsletter
and be entered to win a Tiffany Key necklace.

There's a contest every month!

Go to www.1001DarkNights.com to subscribe.

As a bonus, all subscribers will receive a free
1001 Dark Nights story
The First Night
by Lexi Blake & M.J. Rose

Turn the page for a full list of the
1001 Dark Nights fabulous novellas...

# Discover 1001 Dark Nights Collection One

FOREVER WICKED by Shayla Black
CRIMSON TWILIGHT by Heather Graham
CAPTURED IN SURRENDER by Liliana Hart
SILENT BITE: A SCANGUARDS WEDDING by Tina Folsom
DUNGEON GAMES by Lexi Blake
AZAGOTH by Larissa Ione
NEED YOU NOW by Lisa Renee Jones
SHOW ME, BABY by Cherise Sinclair
ROPED IN by Lorelei James
TEMPTED BY MIDNIGHT by Lara Adrian
THE FLAME by Christopher Rice
CARESS OF DARKNESS by Julie Kenner

Also from 1001 Dark Nights

TAME ME by J. Kenner

*For more information, visit www.1001DarkNights.com.*

# Discover 1001 Dark Nights Collection Two

WICKED WOLF by Carrie Ann Ryan
WHEN IRISH EYES ARE HAUNTING by Heather Graham
EASY WITH YOU by Kristen Proby
MASTER OF FREEDOM by Cherise Sinclair
CARESS OF PLEASURE by Julie Kenner
ADORED by Lexi Blake
HADES by Larissa Ione
RAVAGED by Elisabeth Naughton
DREAM OF YOU by Jennifer L. Armentrout
STRIPPED DOWN by Lorelei James
RAGE/KILLIAN by Alexandra Ivy/Laura Wright
DRAGON KING by Donna Grant
PURE WICKED by Shayla Black
HARD AS STEEL by Laura Kaye
STROKE OF MIDNIGHT by Lara Adrian
ALL HALLOWS EVE by Heather Graham
KISS THE FLAME by Christopher Rice
DARING HER LOVE by Melissa Foster
TEASED by Rebecca Zanetti
THE PROMISE OF SURRENDER by Liliana Hart

Also from 1001 Dark Nights

THE SURRENDER GATE By Christopher Rice
SERVICING THE TARGET By Cherise Sinclair

*For more information, visit www.1001DarkNights.com.*

# Discover 1001 Dark Nights Collection Three

HIDDEN INK by Carrie Ann Ryan
A Montgomery Ink Novella

BLOOD ON THE BAYOU by Heather Graham
A Cafferty & Quinn Novella

SEARCHING FOR MINE by Jennifer Probst
A Searching For Novella

DANCE OF DESIRE by Christopher Rice

ROUGH RHYTHM by Tessa Bailey
A Made In Jersey Novella

DEVOTED by Lexi Blake
A Masters and Mercenaries Novella

Z by Larissa Ione
A Demonica Underworld Novella

FALLING UNDER YOU by Laurelin Paige
A Fixed Trilogy Novella

EASY FOR KEEPS by Kristen Proby
A Boudreaux Novella

UNCHAINED by Elisabeth Naughton
An Eternal Guardians Novella

HARD TO SERVE by Laura Kaye
A Hard Ink Novella

DRAGON FEVER by Donna Grant
A Dark Kings Novella

KAYDEN/SIMON by Alexandra Ivy/Laura Wright
A Bayou Heat Novella

STRUNG UP by Lorelei James
A Blacktop Cowboys® Novella

MIDNIGHT UNTAMED by Lara Adrian
A Midnight Breed Novella

TRICKED by Rebecca Zanetti
A Dark Protectors Novella

DIRTY WICKED by Shayla Black
A Wicked Lovers Novella

A SEDUCTIVE INVITATION by Lauren Blakely
A Seductive Nights New York Novella

SWEET SURRENDER by Liliana Hart
A MacKenzie Family Novella

*For more information, visit www.1001DarkNights.com.*

# On behalf of 1001 Dark Nights,
Liz Berry and M.J. Rose would like to thank ~

Steve Berry
Doug Scofield
Kim Guidroz
Jillian Stein
InkSlinger PR
Dan Slater
Asha Hossain
Chris Graham
Pamela Jamison
Jessica Johns
Dylan Stockton
Richard Blake
BookTrib After Dark
The Dinner Party Show
and Simon Lipskar

CPSIA information can be obtained
at www.ICGtesting.com
Printed in the USA
LVOW12s1605111117
555908LV00002B/447/P